Johann Wolfgang von Goethe, Anna Swanwick, Walter Scott

# Dramatic Works Of Goethe

Johann Wolfgang von Goethe, Anna Swanwick, Walter Scott

**Dramatic Works Of Goethe**

ISBN/EAN: 9783741124419

Manufactured in Europe, USA, Canada, Australia, Japa

Cover: Foto ©Andreas Hilbeck / pixelio.de

Manufactured and distributed by brebook publishing software
(www.brebook.com)

Johann Wolfgang von Goethe, Anna Swanwick, Walter Scott

# Dramatic Works Of Goethe

# DRAMATIC WORKS

OF

# GOETHE

COMPRISING

FAUST, IPHIGENIA IN TAURIS, TORQUATO TASSO,
EGMONT,

TRANSLATED BY ANNA SWANWICK.


AND

## GOETZ VON BERLICHINGEN,

TRANSLATED BY SIR WALTER SCOTT, AND CAREFULLY REVISED
BY HENRY G. BOHN.


LONDON : GEORGE BELL & SONS, YORK STREET,
COVENT GARDEN.
1875.

# CONTENTS.

# TRANSLATOR'S PREFACE.

Notwithstanding the numerous versions of Faust which are already before the public,* and the ability with which fragments of this great poem have been rendered into English verse, it is, I believe, admitted, that no translator has yet succeeded in embodying its entire spirit in a metrical form. How far I have been successful in accomplishing this difficult task, I must leave others to determine; I can only say that, impelled by admiration of the splendid poetry scattered through its pages, I have laboured diligently to render my translation a faithful reflection of the original, and if I have sometimes failed, it must not be attributed to any want of earnest endeavour.

To the merit of Mr. Hayward's prose version, I gladly record my humble testimony; yet, notwithstanding the occasional freedom unavoidable in metrical translations, I cannot agree with those who regard prose as an appropriate medium for the re-production of poetry. In original composition, a natural relation is recognized as existing between thought and verse, inasmuch as the latter is the spontaneous utterance of the poetic mind, when, in moments of inspiration, it teems with

> " Thoughts which voluntary move
> Harmonious numbers."

But the inspiring influence of such thoughts is also felt, when, instead of springing from the depths of the creative spirit, they are derived from a foreign source; and as the seed, if it take root, and spring forth anew, must produce a flower

> " Like to the mother-plant in semblance,"

so the poetic thought can only find adequate expression in tones which harmonize with the music of the original verse.

A poet, in describing the pleasure attending the exercise of the creative faculty, exclaims—

> " Oh! to create within the soul is bliss!"

A faint echo of this emotion accompanies the endeavour to body forth the conceptions of the inspired master, and hence it is that passages of the highest beauty are those which least tax the energies of the translator. Far more laborious is the attempt to

---

* I am credibly informed that there are upwards of twenty complete versions in print, and even a greater number of fragments.

render into verse ideas not essentially poetical; and the reader perchance,

> "Aware of nothing arduous in a task
> He never undertook,"

thinks little of

> "The shifts and turns,
> The expedients and inventions multiform,
> To which the mind resorts in chase of terms,
> Though apt, yet coy, and difficult to win."

The endeavour to render into English verse the finer passages of Faust, has been to me a source of the highest enjoyment; and if others derive any pleasure from the perusal of my translation, I shall feel amply rewarded for the labour attending the less inviting portions of my task.

I shall not attempt any analysis of the poem, but merely allude to what appears to me to be the fundamental idea underlying its varied and complicated elements, and which we find expressed in the prologue, in the words—

> "A good man in the direful grasp of ill,
> His consciousness of right retaineth still."

We have here a recognition of conscience as belonging to the deepest roots of man's inner life. The soul, whose inborn tendency it is

> "To rush aloft, to struggle still towards heaven,"

can never derive permanent satisfaction from low and sensual gratifications; and when, from the misdirection of its energies, or the ascendancy of the passions, the harmony of the spiritual nature is destroyed, the voice of the inward monitor is still heard in the recesses of the heart, and the agonies of remorse attest that its dictates can never be violated with impunity. This deep moral instinct has been characterized as "the handwriting of the creator on the soul," and is the ground of that reverent faith in humanity which ever distinguishes the noblest minds. But while thus recognizing the moral truth embodied in the poem, I deeply regret the blemishes which, in my opinion, disfigure its pages; it contains passages which I would fain have omitted or modified, had I not held it to be the imperative duty of a translator to render faithfully even the defects of the original.

To those who are curious in contemplating the growth of a work of art, and tracing it through its successive stages of development, Faust offers a study of peculiar interest. As early as the year 1774, we find Goethe reading the first scenes of the poem to Klopstock, during the visit of the latter to Frankfort; from that period, it was resumed at intervals till the year 1790, when it

first appeared before the public in the form of " A Fragment."
This fragment Schiller likened to the Torso of Hercules, " mani-
festing a vigour and exuberance which betrayed unmistakeably
the hand of the great master;" it commences with the first
monologue and ends with the scene in the cathedral; the scene
with Valentine, together with some other passages, were introduced at a subsequent period. After the lapse of several years,
Goethe's thoughts again reverted to Faust, and in 1797 he produced the Dedication, the Prologue for the Theatre, and the Prologue in Heaven. The Intermezzo must be referred to the same
year. Goethe was continually urged by Schiller to the completion
of the work, and the correspondence of the two poets at this period
contains several interesting passages relative to its continuation
and further development. It was not, however, till the year 1808
after it had been brooded over in the poet's mind for upwards of
thirty years, that the first part of Faust was published in its present form. In compiling the foregoing brief sketch of the progress
of the poem, I have followed Düntzer's recent work upon Faust.

My translations of Iphigenia and of the first act of Tasso
have already appeared in a volume, entitled " Selections from the
Dramas of Goethe and Schiller." The remainder of the Tasso,
together with my versions of Faust and of Egmont, are published
now for the first time.

In Goethe's " Dichtung and Wahrheit," known in England
as his Autobiography, we have an account of the origin of Goëtz
von Berlichingen, to which an interest attaches from its having
been the first great dramatic work of the author, and also from
its translation being among the earliest literary efforts of Sir
Walter Scott. When he undertook the task his knowledge of
German must have been very imperfect, as his version abounds
with errors; these have been corrected in the present edition,
and omissions of some length supplied. My publisher has assisted
in the alterations, and is responsibl for the greater number of
them.

A. S.

London,
November, 1850.

As without some key this scene is utterly incomprehensible to the English reader, a brief notice of some of the allusions it contains is here subjoined; they are dwelt upon at greater length in Düntzer's work.

It may be regarded as a kind of satirical jeu d'esprit, and consists of a series of epigrams, directed against a variety of false tendencies in art, literature, religion, philosophy, and political life.

The introductory stanzas are founded upon the Midsummer Night's Dream, and Wieland's Oberon. To celebrate the reconciliation of the fairy king and queen a grotesque assemblage of figures appear upon the stage. Common-place musicians, and poetasters, having no conception that every poem must be an organic whole, are satirized as the bagpipe, the embryo spirit, and the little pair. Then follows a series of epigrams, having reference to the plastic arts, and directed against that false pietism and affected purity which would take a narrow and one-sided view of artistical creations. Nicolai, the sworn enemy of ghosts and Jesuits, is introduced as the inquisitive traveller, and Stolberg, who severely criticised Schiller's poem, "The Gods of Greece," is alluded to in the couplet headed "Orthodox."

Hennings, the editor of two literary journals, entitled the Musaget, and the Genius of the Age, had attacked the Xenien, a series of epigrams, published jointly by Goethe and Schiller; Goethe, in retaliation, makes him confess his own unfitness to be a leader of the Muses, and his readiness to assign a place on the German Parnassus to any one who was willing to bow to his authority. Nicolai again appears as the inquisitive traveller, and Lavater is said to be alluded to as the crane. The metaphysical philosophers are next the objects of the poet's satire ; allusion is made to the bitter hostility manifested by the contending schools, the characteristics of which are so well known that it is needless to dwell upon them here. The philosophers are succeeded by the politicians ; "the knowing ones," who, in the midst of political revolutions, manage to keep in with the ruling party, are contrasted with those unfortunate individuals who are unable to accommodate themselves to the new order of things. In revolutionary times also, parvenus are raised to positions of eminence, while worthless notabilities, deprived of their hereditary splendour, are unable to maintain their former dignified position. "The massive ones" typify the men of the revolution, the leaders of the people, who, heedless of intervening obstacles, march straight on to their destined goal. Puck and Ariel, who had introduced the shadowy procession, again make their appearance, and the fairy pageant vanishes into air.

What relation this fantastic assemblage bears to Faust is not immediately obvious, unless, indeed, as Düntzer suggests, the poet meant to shadow forth the various distractions with which Mephistophiles endeavours to dissipate the mind of Faust, who had turned with disgust from the witch-society of the Brocken.

# INTRODUCTION.—IPHIGENIA IN TAURIS.

THE drama of 'IPHIGENIA IN TAURIS' has been considered Goethe's masterpiece; it is conceived in the spirit of Greek ideality, and is characterized throughout by moral beauty and dignified repose. Schlegel * styles it an echo of Greek song, an epithet as appropriate as it is elegant; for, without any servile imitation of classic models, this beautiful drama, through the medium of its polished verse, reproduces in softened characters the graceful and colossal forms of the antique.

The destiny of Agamemnon and his race was a favourite theme of the ancients. It has been dramatized in a variety of forms by the three great masters of antiquity; and from these various sources Goethe has gathered the materials for his drama, enriching it with touches of sublimity and beauty selected indiscriminately from the works of each. The description of the Furies in the third act is worthy of Æschylus, and in the spirit of the same great writer is the exclusion of these terrific powers from the consecrated grove, symbolical of the peace which religion can alone afford to the anguish of a wounded conscience. The prominence given to the idea of destiny, together with the finished beauty of the whole, remind us of Sophocles; while the passages conveying general moral truths, scattered throughout the poem, not unfrequently recall to our recollection those of a similar character in the dramas of Euripides.

Two dramas of Euripides are founded upon the well-known story of Iphigenia. In the 'Iphigenia in Aulis,' we are introduced to the assembled hosts of Greece, detained by contrary winds in consequence of Diana's anger against Agamemnon. An oracle had declared that the Goddess could only be propitiated by the sacrifice of Iphigenia, who is accordingly allured with her mother to the camp. On discovering the fearful doom which awaits her, she is at first overwhelmed with grief. She implores her father to spare her life, endeavours to touch his heart by recalling the fond memories of by-gone times, and holds up her infant brother, Orestes, that he may plead for her with his tears. Learning however that the glory of her country depends upon her death. she rises superior to her fears, subdues her womanly weakness, and devotes herself a willing sacrifice for Greece. She is conducted to the altar, the sacred garlands are bound around her

Dramatic Literature, Bohn's edition, page 518.

head, Calchas lifts the knife to deal the fatal stroke, when Iphigenia suddenly vanishes, and a hind of uncommon beauty lies bleeding at his feet.

In the 'IPHIGENIA IN TAURIS,' our heroine re-appears, in the temple of Diana, situated in the Tauric Chersonese, a savage region washed by the Euxine Sea, where, according to the ancients, all strangers were sacrificed at the altar of Diana. To this wild shore Iphigenia had been conveyed by the pitying goddess, and there, in her character of priestess, she presided over the bloody rites of the barbarians. The incidents in this drama have been adopted by Goethe as the groundwork of his poem, the chief interest in which, as in the drama of Euripides, turns upon the departure of Iphigenia and Orestes from the Taurian shore. A brief outline of the Grecian drama will show in what particulars the modern poet has adhered to his classic model, and where he has deviated from it.

The scene of both is in the vicinity of the temple of Diana. In the opening soliloquy of the Grecian drama, Iphigenia, after lamenting her unhappy destiny, relates her dream of the previous night, from which she infers the death of Orestes. She determines to offer a libation to his memory, and while engaged in performing this pious rite, she is informed that two strangers have been captured on the shore, for whose sacrifice she is commanded to prepare. Orestes and Pylades are shortly after introduced, and, learning from the former that he is a native of Argos, she offers to spare his life provided he will carry a letter for her to Mycene. He refuses to abandon his friend; Pylades is equally disinterested; a generous contest ensues, and the latter, yielding at length to the entreaties of Orestes, consents to accept life on the proposed conditions. The letter addressed to Orestes is produced, and Iphigenia discovers her brother in the intended victim. They anxiously consider how they may escape, and Iphigenia suggests that in her character of priestess she shall lead them, together with the image of Diana, to the sea, there to be purified in the ocean waves, where they may find safety in the attendant bark. With all the wily subtlety of a Greek, she imposes upon the credulity of the barbarian monarch, and induces him not only to sanction her project, but to assist in its execution, which she at length successfully achieves. In this drama, Iphigenia, though exhibiting some noble traits, offends us by her unscrupulous violation of the truth, and by the cunning artifice which Goethe, with admirable art, has attributed to Pylades. We are the more displeased with this portrait, because we are unwilling to recognize in the crafty priestess the innocent victim, who so strongly awakens our sympathy in the beautiful drama of 'Iphigenia in Aulis.' In the Iphigenia of Goethe on the contrary, we discover with pleasure the same filial tenderness, and the same touching mixture of timidity and courage which characterized that interesting heroine.

In the drama of Euripides we are chiefly interested in the generous friendship of Orestes and Pylades: in that of Goethe the character of Iphigenia constitutes the chief charm, and awakens our warmest sympathy. While contemplating her, we feel as if some exquisite statue of Grecian art had become animated by a living soul, and moved and breathed before us: though exhibiting the severe simplicity which characterizes the creations of antiquity, she is far removed from all coldness and austerity; and her character, though cast in a classic mould, is free from that harsh and vindictive spirit which darkened the heroism of those barbarous times when religion lent her sanction to hatred and revenge.

The docility with which, in opposition to her own feelings, she at first consents to the stratagem of Pylades, though apparently inconsistent with her reverence for truth, is in reality a beautiful and touching trait. The conflict in her mind between intense anxiety for her brother's safety, and detestation of the artifice by which alone she thinks it can be secured, amounts almost to agony; in her extremity she calls upon the Gods, and implores them to save their image in her soul. The struggle finally subsides; she remains faithful to her high convictions, reveals the project of escape, and thus saves her soul from treachery. From the commencement of the fifth act she assumes a calm and lofty tone, as if feeling the inspiration of a noble purpose. The dignity and determination with which she opposes the cruel project of the barbarian king, remind us of the similar qualities displayed by the Antigone of Sophocles, who is perhaps the noblest heroine of antiquity. Thus when called upon by the king to reverence the law, Iphigenia appeals to that law written in the heart, more ancient and more sacred than the ordinances of man; and Antigone, when by the interment of her brother Polynices, she has incurred the anger of the tyrant Creon, and become subjected to a cruel death, justifies herself by an appeal to the same sacred authority.

The remaining characters of the drama, though subordinate to the central figure, are in admirable keeping with it, the poet having softened down the harsh features of the barbarians, so as not to form too abrupt a contrast with the more polished Greeks, and thereby interfere with the harmony of the piece. The colossal figures of the Titans appearing in the background, and the dread power of Destiny overarching all, impart a character of solemn grandeur to the whole.

# INTRODUCTION.—TORQUATO TASSO.

The annals of biography offer no page the perusal of which awakens a greater variety of emotions than that which records the fate of Torquato Tasso. This great poet, distinguished alike by his genius and his misfortunes, concentrates in his own person the deepest interests of humanity; while the mystery which broods over his derangement and his love, imparts to his story the air rather of poetic fiction than of sober truth. Goethe's poem, founded upon the residence of Tasso at the court of Ferrara, is justly celebrated for its fine delineations of character and its profound insight into the depths of the human heart. It exhibits a striking picture of the great bard at the most momentous period of his existence, which was signalized by the completion of his immortal work; and though the action of the drama embraces only a few hours, by skilfully availing himself of retrospect and anticipation, Goethe has presented us with a beautiful epitome of the poet's life.

Thus, in the third scene of the drama, Tasso alludes to his early childhood, the sorrows of which he has so pathetically sung; we accompany the youthful bard, in his twenty-second year, to the brilliant court of Ferrara, where he arrived at a period when the nuptials of the Duke with the Emperor's sister were celebrated with unrivalled splendour. At the conclusion of these festivities, he was presented by the Princess Lucretia to her sister, Leonora, who was destined to exert such a powerful influence over his future life; we behold him the honoured and cherished inmate of Belriguardo, a magnificent palace, surrounded by beautiful gardens, where the Dukes of Ferrara were accustomed to retire with their most favoured courtiers, and where, under the inspiring influences of love, beauty, and court favour, he completed his ' Gerusalemme Liberata,' one of the proudest monuments of human genius.

Goethe has with great skill made us acquainted with some of the circumstances which, acting upon the peculiar temperament of the poet, at length induced the mental disorder which cast so dark a shadow over his later years. His hopeless love for Leonora no doubt conspired with other causes to unsettle his fine intellect,—a calamity which in him appears like the bewilderment of a mind suddenly awakened, from the visions of poetry and love passionately cherished for so many years, into the cold realities of actual life, where his too sensitive ear was stunned by the harsh and discordant voices of envy and superstition. We are thus prepared for his distracted flight from Ferrara, and Goethe has introduced prospectively the touching incident related by Manso,—how, in the disguise of a shepherd, he presented himself to his sister Cornelia, to whom he related his story in language so pathetic, that she fainted from the violence of her grief.

His return to Ferrara, his imprisonment in the Hospital of Santa Anna, and his subsequent miserable wanderings from city to city, are not mentioned in the drama; but the allusion of Alphonso to the crown which should adorn him on the Capitol, brings to our remembrance the affecting circumstances of his death.

It appears from his letters, that at one period of his life, he earnestly desired a triumph similar to that which Petrarca had enjoyed; but when at length this honour was accorded him, when a period was assigned for this splendid pageant, a change had come over his spirit.  His long sufferings had weaned his thoughts from earth; he felt that the hand of death was upon him, and hoped—to use his own words—"to go crowned, not as a poet to the Capitol, but with glory as a saint to Heaven."  On the eve of the day appointed for the ceremony, he expired at the monastery of Saint Onofrio, and his remains, habited in a magnificent toga, and adorned with a laurel crown, were carried in procession through the streets of Rome.

Goethe has faithfully portrayed the times in which Tasso lived, and circumstances apparently trivial have an historical significance, and impart an air of reality to the drama.  Thus the fanciful occupation and picturesque attire of the Princess and Countess at the opening of the piece, transport us at once to that graceful court where the pastoral drama was invented and refined, and where, not long before, Tasso's 'Aminta,' which is considered one of the most beautiful specimens of this species of composition, had been performed for the first time with enthusiastic applause.

The crown adorning the bust of Ariosto, together with the enthusiastic admiration expressed for that poet by Antonio, is likewise characteristic of the age.  The 'Orlando Furioso' had been composed at the same court about fifty years before, and had become so universally popular, that, according to Bernardo Tasso, the father of Torquato, "neither learned man nor artisan, no youth, no maid, no old man, could be satisfied with a single perusal;"—" passengers in the streets, sailors in their boats, and virgins in their chambers, sang for their disport the stanzas of Ariosto*."

The project of dethroning this monarch of Parnassus, or, at least, of placing upon his own brow a crown as glorious, appears

* Black's Life of Tasso.

from his own letters early to have awakened the ambition of Tasso.

The subordinate characters of the drama are also historical portraits. Alphonso II. is represented by his biographers as the liberal patron of the arts, and as treating Tasso at this period with marked consideration; nor had he yet manifested that implacable and revengeful spirit which has rendered his memory justly hateful to posterity. In the relation which subsisted between this prince and Tasso, Goethe has exhibited the evils resulting from the false spirit of patronage prevalent at that period throughout Italy, when talent was regarded as the necessary appendage of rank, and works of genius were considered as belonging rather to the patron than to the individual by whom they had been produced.

Antonio Montecatino, the Duke's secretary, is also drawn from life. He is an admirable personification of that spirit of worldly wisdom which looks principally to material results, and contemplates promotion and court favour as the highest objects of ambition. This "earth-born prudence," having little sympathy with poetic genius, affects to treat it with contempt, resents as presumptuous its violation of ordinary rules, holds up its foibles and eccentricities to ridicule, and at the same time envies the homage paid to it by mankind.

At the period of the drama, the court of Ferrara was graced by the presence of Leonora, Countess of Scandiano, in whom Goethe has portrayed a woman eminently graceful and accomplished, but who fails to win our sympathy because her ruling sentiment is vanity. Tasso paid to this young beauty the tribute of public homage, and addressed to her some of his most beautiful sonnets; according to Ginguené, however, his sentiment for her was merely poetical, and could easily ally itself with the more genuine, deep, and constant affection which he entertained for Leonora of Este.

Lucretia and Leonora of Este were the daughters of Renée of France, celebrated for her insatiable thirst for knowledge, and for the variety and depth of her studies. She became zealously attached to the tenets of the Reformers, in consequence of which she was deprived of her children, and closely imprisoned for twelve years.

To the intellectual power, the knowledge, heresy, and consequent misfortunes of her unhappy mother, the Princess Leonora twice alludes in the course of the drama. The daughters of this heroic woman inherited her mental superiority, and Leonora, the younger, is celebrated by various writers for her genius, learning, beauty, and early indifference to the pleasure of the world.

# INTRODUCTION.—EGMONT

In Schiller's critique upon the tragedy of Egmont, Goethe is censured for departing from the truth of history in the delineation of his hero's character, and also for misrepresenting the circumstances of his domestic life. The Egmont of history left behind him a numerous family, anxiety for whose welfare detained him in Brussels when most of his friends sought safety in flight. His withdrawal would have entailed the confiscation of his property, and he shrank from exposing to privation those whose happiness was dearer to him than life ;—a consideration which he repeatedly urged in his conferences with the Prince of Orange, when the latter insisted upon the necessity of escape. We see here, not the victim of a blind and fool-hardy confidence, as portrayed in Goethe's drama, but the husband and father, regardless of his personal safety in anxiety for the interests of his family.

I shall not inquire which conception is best suited for the purposes of art, but merely subjoin a few extracts from the same critique, in which Schiller does ample justice to Goethe's admirable delineation of the age and country in which the drama is cast, and which are peculiarly valuable from the pen of so competent an authority as the historian of the Fall of the Netherlands.

"Egmont's tragical death resulted from the relation in which he stood to the nation and the government ; hence the action of the drama is intimately connected with the political life of the period—an exhibition of which forms its indispensable groundwork. But if we consider what an infinite number of minute circumstances must concur in order to exhibit the spirit of an age, and the political condition of a people, and the art required to combine so many isolated features into an intelligible and organic whole ; and if we contemplate, moreover, the peculiar character of the Netherlands, consisting not of one nation, but of an aggregate of many smaller states, separated from each other by the sharpest contrasts, we shall not cease to wonder at the creative genius, which, triumphing over all these difficulties, conjures up before us, as with an enchanter's wand, the Netherlands of the sixteenth century.

"Not only do we behold these men living and working before us, we dwell among them as their familiar associates; we see on the one hand, the joyous sociability, the hospitality, the loquacity, the somewhat boastful temper of the people, their republican spirits, ready to boil up at the slightest innovation, and often subsiding again as rapidly on the most trivial grounds; and on the other hand, we are made acquainted with the burthens under which they groaned, from the new mitres of the bishops, to the French psalms which they were forbidden to sing;—nothing is omitted, no feature introduced which does not bear the stamp of nature and of truth. Such delineation is not the result of premeditated effort, nor can it be commanded by art; it can only be achieved by the poet whose mind is thoroughly imbued with his subject; from him such traits escape unconsciously, and without design, as they do from the individuals whose characters they serve to portray.

"The few scenes in which the citizens of Brussels are introduced appear to us to be the result of profound study, and it would be difficult to find, in so few words, a more admirable historical monument of the Netherlands of that period.

"Equally graphic is that portion of the picture which portrays the spirit of the government, though it must be confessed that the artist has here somewhat softened down the harsher features of the original. This is especially true in reference to the character of the Duchess of Parma. Before his Duke of Alva we tremble, without however turning from him with aversion; he is a firm, rigid, inaccessible character; 'a brazen tower without gates, the garrison of which must be furnished with wings.' The prudent forecast with which he makes his arrangements for Egmont's arrest, excites our admiration, while it removes him from our sympathy. The remaining characters of the drama are delineated with a few masterly strokes. The subtle, taciturn Orange, with his timid, yet comprehensive and all-combining mind, is depicted in a single scene. Both Alva and Egmont are mirrored in the men by whom they are surrounded. This mode of delineation is admirable. The poet, in order to concentrate the interest upon Egmont, has isolated his hero, and omitted all mention of Count Horn, who shared the same melancholy fate."

The appendix to Schiller's History of the Fall of the Netherlands contains an interesting account of the trial and execution of the Counts Egmont and Horn, which is, however, too long for insertion here.

# DRAMATIS PERSONÆ

---

### Characters in the Prologue for the Theatre

THE MANAGER.
THE DRAMATIC POET.
MERRYMAN.

### Characters in the Prologue in Heaven.

THE LORD.
RAPHAEL ⎫
GABRIEL ⎬ The Heavenly Hosts.
MICHAEL ⎭
MEPHISTOPHELES.

### Characters in the Tragedy.

FAUST.
MEPHISTOPHELES.
WAGNER, a Student.
MARGARET.
MARTHA, Margaret's Neighbour.
VALENTINE, Margaret's Brother.
OLD PEASANT.
A STUDENT.
ELIZABETH, an acquaintance of Margaret's.
FROSCH, ⎫
BRANDER, ⎬ Guests in Auerbach's Wine-Cellar.
SIEBEL, ⎪
ALTMAYER, ⎭

Witches, old and young; Wizards, Will-o'the-Wisp, Witch Pedlar Protophantasmist, Servibilis, Monkeys, Spirits, Journeymen, Country-Folk, Citizens, Beggar, Old Fortune-Teller, Shepherd, Soldier Students, &c.

### In the Intermezzo.

| | |
|---|---|
| OBERON. | ARIEL. |
| TITANIA. | PUCK, &c., &c. |

# DEDICATION.

Dim forms, ye hover near, a shadowy train,
As erst upon my troubl'd sight ye stole.
Shall I yet strive to hold you once again?
Still for the fond illusion yearns my soul?
Ye press around!   Come then, resume your reign,
As upwards from the vapoury mist ye roll,
Within my breast youth's throbbing pulses bound,
Fann'd by the magic air that breathes around.

Shades fondly-loved appear, your train attending,
And visions fair of many a blissful day;
First-love and friendship their fond accents blending,
Like to some dim, traditionary lay;
Sorrow revives, her wail of anguish sending
Back o'er life's chequer'd labyrinthine way,
Recalling cherish'd friends, in life's fair morn,
From my embrace, by cruel fortune torn.

Alas! my closing song they hear no more,
The friends, for whom my earlier strains I sang;
Dispers'd the throng who greeted me of yore,
And mute the voices that responsive rang;
My tuneful grief 'mong strangers now I pour,
E'en their applauding tones inflict a pang,
And those to whom my music once seem'd sweet
If yet on earth, are scatter'd ne'er to meet.

A strange, unwonted longing doth upraise
To yon calm spirit-realm my yearning soul!
In soften'd cadence, as when Zephyr plays
With Æol's harp, my tuneful numbers roll;
My pulses thrill, the tear unbidden strays,
My stedfast heart resigns its self-control;
As from afar the present meets my view,
While what hath pass'd away alone seems true.

# PROLOGUE FOR THE THEATRE

MANAGER, DRAMATIC POET, MERRYMAN.

MANAGER.

Ye twain, whom I so oft have found
True friends in trouble and distress,
Say, in our scheme on German ground,
What prospect have we of success?
Fain would I please the public, win their thanks;
They live and let live, that I call fair play;
The posts are ready fix'd, and laid the planks,
And all anticipate a treat to-day.
They've ta'en their places, and with eyebrows rais'd,
Sit patiently, and fain would be amaz'd.
I know the art to hit the public taste,
Yet so perplex'd I ne'er have been before;
'Tis true, they're not accustom'd to the best,
But then they read immensely, that's the bore.
How make our entertainment striking, new,
And yet significant and pleasing too?
For to be plain, I love to see the throng,
As to our booth the living tide progresses;
As wave on wave successive rolls along,
And through the narrow gate in tumult presses.
Still in broad day, ere yet the clock strikes four,
Their way to the receiver's box they take;
And, as in famine at the baker's door,
For tickets are content their necks to break.
Such various minds the bard alone can sway,
My friend, oh work this miracle to-day!

POET.

Oh speak not of the motley multitude,
Whose aspect puts each gentler thought to flight;
Shut out the noisy crowd, whose vortex rude
Draws down the spirit with resistless might.
Lead me to some still nook, where none intrude
'Where only for the bard blooms pure delight,

Where love and friendship, fair angelic powers,
Crown with the heart's best joys the circling hours.

What in the spirit's depths was there conceiv'd,
What there the timid lip shap'd forth in sound,
Imperfect now, now adequate believ'd,
In the wild tumult of the hour is drown'd;
The perfect work, through years of toil achiev'd,
Appears, at length, with finish'd beauty crown'd;
What dazzles satisfies the present hour,
The genuine lives, of coming years the dower.

MERRYMAN.

This cant about posterity I hate;
About posterity were I to prate,
Who then the living would amuse, for they
Require diversion, ay, and 'tis their due.
A sprightly fellow's presence at your play,
Methinks should always go for something too;
Whose ready wit a genial vein inspires,
He'll ne'er be wounded by the captious throng;
A wider circle doubtless he desires,
Where sympathy exalts the power of song.
To work, then! Prove a master in your art!
Fancy invoke, with all her choral train—
Let reason, passion, feeling, bear their part,
But mark! let folly mingle in the strain.

MANAGER.

And chief, let incidents enough arise!
A show they want, they come to feast their eyes
When stirring scenes before them are display'd
At which the wond'ring multitude may gaze,
Your reputation is already made,
And popular applause your toil repays.
A mass alone will with the mass succeed,
Then each at length selects what he requires
Who bringeth much, of many suits the need,
And each contented from the house retires.
What though your drama should like patchwork show,
No matter—the ragout will take, I know;
As easy 'tis to serve as to invent.

A finish'd whole what boots it to present,
'Twill be in pieces by the public rent.

POET.

How mean such handicraft you cannot feel!
How it degrades the genuine artist's mind!
The bungling work in which these coxcombs deal,
Is an establish'd maxim here, I find.

MANAGER.

Such a reproof disturbs me not a whit!
Who on efficient working is intent,
Must choose the most appropriate instrument.
Consider! 'tis soft wood you have to split,
Remember too for whom you write, I pray!
One comes perchance to while an hour away;
One from the festive board, a sated guest;
Others, whom more I dread than all the rest,
From journal-reading hurry to the play.
With absent minds, as to a masque they press,
By curiosity alone drawn here;
Ladies display their persons and their dress,
And without pay in character appear.
What dreams beguile you on your poet's height?
What puts a full house in a merry mood?
More closely view your patrons of the night,
Half are unfeeling, half uncultur'd, rude.
One hopes the night in wanton joy to spend,
Another's thinking of a game of cards;
Why, ye poor fools, for such a paltry end,
Plague the coy muse, and court her fair regards?
Only give more and more, 'tis all I ask;
Thus you will ne'er stray widely from the goal;
Your audience seek to mystify, cajole;—
To satisfy them—that's a harder task.
Ah! what comes o'er you? rapture or vexation?

POET.

Depart! elsewhere another servant choose!
What! shall the bard his godlike power abuse?
Man's loftiest right, kind nature's high bequest,
For your mean purpose basely sport away?
Whence comes his mast'ry o'er the human breast?
What bends the elements beneath his sway?

Oh, is it not his own poetic soul,
Whose gushing harmony, with strong controi,
Draws back into his heart the wondrous whole?
When round her spindle, with unceasing drone,
Nature still whirls th' unending thread of life;
When Being's jarring crowds, together thrown,
Mingle in harsh inextricable strife;
Whose spirit quickens the unvarying round,
And bids it flow to music's measur'd tone?
Who calls the individual to resound,
With nature's chords in noble unison?
Who hears the voice of passion in the storm?
Who sees the flush of thought in evening's glow?
Who lingers fondly round the lov'd one's form,
Spring's fairest blossoms in her path to strow?
Who from unmeaning leaves a wreath doth twine
For glory, gather'd in whatever field?
Who raises mortals to the realms divine?—
Man's lofty spirit in the bard reveal'd.

MERRYMAN.

Come then, employ your lofty inspiration,
And carry on the poet's avocation,
Just as we carry on a love-affair.
Fortune together brings a youthful pair;
They're touch'd, their spirits rise with fond elation,
Insensibly they're link'd, they scarce know how;
Fortune seems now propitious, adverse now,
Then come alternate rapture and despair;
And 'tis a true romance ere one's aware.
Just such a drama let us now compose!
Plunge boldly into life—its depths disclose!
Each lives it, not to many is it known,
'Twill interest wheresoever seiz'd and shown;
Bright pictures, but obscure their meaning,
A ray of truth through error gleaming,
This is the best elixir you can brew,
To charm mankind, and edify them too.
Then youth's fair blossoms crowd to view your play,
And wait as on an oracle; while they,
The tender souls, who love the melting mood,
Suck from your work their melancholy food;

With wonder and delight they witness there,
The secret working of their hearts laid bare;
Their tears, their laughter you command with ease;
The dazzling, the illusive still they love,
Still doth each lofty thought their reverence move,
Your finish'd gentlemen you ne'er can please,
A growing mind alone will grateful prove.

POET.

Then give me back youth's golden prime,
When my own spirit too was growing,
When from my heart th' unbidden rhyme
Gush'd forth, a fount for ever flowing,
Then shadowy mist the world conceal'd,
Through vales, with odorous blooms inlaid,
Culling a thousand flowers I stray'd,
And every bud sweet promise made,
Of wonders still to be reveal'd.
Nought had I, yet a rich profusion;
The thirst for truth, joy in each fond illusion.
Give me unquell'd those impulses to prove;—
Rapture so deep, its ecstasy was pain,
The power of hate, the energy of love,
Give me, oh give me back, my youth again!

MERRYMAN.

Youth, my good friend, you certainly require
When foes in battle round you press,
When a fair maid, her heart on fire,
Hangs on your neck with fond caress;
When from afar, the victor's crown,
Allures you in the race to run;
Or when in revelry you drown
Your sense, the whirling dance being done
But the familiar chords among
Boldly to sweep, with graceful cunning,
While to its goal, the verse along
Its winding path is sweetly running;
With you, old gentlemen, this duty lies;
Nor are you thence less rev'rend in our eyes;
That age doth make us childish, some maintain—
No, it but finds us children once again.

### MANAGER.

A truce to words, mere empty sound,
Let deeds at length appear, my friends,
While idle compliments you round,
You might achieve some useful ends.
Why talk of the poetic vein?
Who hesitates will never know it;
If bards ye are, as ye maintain,
Now let your inspiration show it.
To you our present need is known,
Strong draughts will suit our taste alone,
Come, brew me such without delay!
That which to-day is not begun,
Is on the morrow still undone!
In dallying never lose a day!
Resolve should grasp, as if inspir'd,
The Possible, with courage bold,
Then she will ne'er resign her hold,
But labour on with zeal untir'd.

On German boards, you're well aware,
The taste of each may have full sway;
Therefore in bringing out your play,
Nor scenes nor mechanism spare.
The lights of heaven, both great and small, produce;
Squander away the stars, expend
Fire, rocks, and water, without end;
And birds and beasts of all kinds introduce.
Thus the whole circle of creation bring
Within the girdle of our wooden shell,
And with considerate speed, on fancy's wing,
Journey from heaven, thence through the earth, to hell.

# PROLOGUE IN HEAVEN.

The Lord. The Heavenly Hosts. *Afterwards*
Mephistopheles.

*The three Archangels come forward.*

### RAPHAEL.
Still quiring as in ancient time
With brother spheres in rival song,
The sun with thunder-march sublime
Moves his predestin'd course along.
Angels are strengthen'd by his sight,
Though fathom him no angel may;
Resplendent are the orbs of light,
As on creation's primal day.

### GABRIEL.
And lightly spins earth's gorgeous sphere,
Swifter than thought its rapid flight;
Alternates Eden-brightness clear,
With solemn, dread-inspiring night;
The foaming waves, with murmurs hoarse,
Against the rocks' deep base are hurl'd;
And in the sphere's eternal course,
Are rocks and ocean swiftly whirl'd.

### MICHAEL.
And rival tempests rush amain
From sea to land, from land to sea,
And raging form a wondrous chain
Of deep mysterious agency.
Full in the thunder's fierce career,
Flaming the swift destructions play;
But, Lord, thy messengers revere
The mild procession of thy day.

### THE THREE.
Angels are strengthen'd by the sight,
Though fathom thee no angel may;
Thy works still shine with splendour bright
As on creation's primal day.

MEPHISTOPHELES.

Since, Lord, thy levee thou again dost hold,
To learn how all things are progressing here,
Since thou hast kindly welcom'd me of old,
Thou see'st me now among thy suite appear.
Excuse me, fine harangues I cannot make,
Though all the circle look on me with scorn ;
My pathos soon thy laughter would awake,
Had'st thou the laughing mood not long forsworn,
Concerning suns and worlds I've nought to say,
I but consider man's self-torturing lot,
As wondrous now as on creation's day,
His stamp the little world-god changeth not.
A somewhat better life he'd lead, poor wight,
But for thy gift, a gleam of heavenly light;
Reason he calls it, and doth use it so,
That e'en than brutes more brutish he doth grow.
With all due deference he appears to me
Much like your long-legged grasshopper to be,
Which flits about, and flying bounds along,
Then in the grass sings his familiar song;
Would he but always in the grass repose!
In every dirty place he thrusts his nose.

THE LORD.

Hast thou nought else to say?   Is thy sole aim
In coming here, as ever, but to blame?
Does nothing on the earth to thee seem right?

MEPHISTOPHELES.

No, Lord!   Things there are in a wretched plight.
Men's sorrow from my heart I so deplore,
E'en I would not torment the poor things more.

THE LORD.

Say, is to thee my servant, Faustus, known?

MEPHISTOPHELES.

The doctor?

THE LORD.

Him I mean.

MEPHISTOPHELES.

Well, we must own,

His service in a curious way is shown.

Poor fool!   He liveth not on earthly food.
An inward impulse hurries him afar,
Himself half conscious of his frenzied mood;
From heaven he claims its brightest star,
From earth demands its highest good,
Nor can their gather'd treasures soothe to rest,
The cravings of his agitated breast.

### THE LORD.

Though now he serve me with imperfect sight,
I will ere long conduct him to the light.
The gard'ner knoweth, when the green appears,
That flowers and fruit will crown the coming years.

### MEPHISTOPHELES.

What wilt thou wager?   Mine he yet shall be,
Let me, with thy permission, be but free,
Him my own way with quiet lure to guide!

### THE LORD.

So long as on the earth he doth abide,
So long it shall not be forbidden thee!
Man, while he striveth, still is prone to err.

### MEPHISTOPHELES.

I'm much oblig'd, the dead delight not me!
The plump fresh cheek of youth I much prefer.
I'm not at home to corpses; 'tis my way,
Like cats with captive mice to toy and play.

### THE LORD.

Enough! it is permitted thee!   Divert
This mortal spirit from his source divine,
And, can'st thou seize on him, thy power exert
To draw him downward, and to make him thine.
Then stand abash'd, when baffl'd thou shalt own,
A good man, in the direful grasp of ill,
His consciousness of right retaineth still.

### MEPHISTOPHELES.

Well, well,—the wager will be quickly won.
For my success no fears I entertain;
And if my end I finally should gain,
Excuse my triumphing with all my soul.
Dust he shall eat, ay, and with relish take,
As did of yore, my cousin, the old snake.

THE LORD.

Here too thou'rt free to act without control.
Towards such as thou, I entertain no hate.
Among the spirits of denial, thee,
The scoffer, I esteem least reprobate.
Prone to relax is man's activity;
In indolent repose he fain would live;
Hence this companion purposely I give,
Who stirs, excites, and must, as devil, work.
But ye, the genuine sons of heaven, rejoice:
In the full living beauty still rejoice!
Let the creative power your spirits bound
With love's eternal and benign control,
And Being's changeful forms that hover round,
Arrest in thoughts, enduring as the soul.

*(Heaven closes, the Archangels disperse.)*

MEPHISTOPHELES (*alone*).

The ancient one I like sometimes to see,
And not to break with him am always civil;
'Tis courteous in a lord so great as he,
To speak so kindly even to the devil.

*Night.*

## A high vaulted narrow Gothic chamber

**FAUST** *restless seated at his desk.*

FAUST.

I've now alas! Philosophy,
Med'cine and Jurisprudence too,
And to my cost Theology,
With ardent labour studied through.
And here I stand, with all my lore,
Poor fool, no wiser than before.
Master, ay doctor styl'd, indeed,
Already these ten years I lead,
Up, down, across, and to and fro,
My pupils by the nose, and learn,
That we in truth can nothing know!
This in my heart like fire doth burn.
True, I've more wit than all your solemn fools;
Priests, doctors, scribes, magisters of the schools;
Nor doubts, nor scruples torture now my breast;
No dread of hell or devil mars my rest;
Hence is my heart of every joy bereft;
No faith in knowledge to my soul is left:
No longer doth the hope delude my mind,
By truth to better and convert mankind.
Then I have neither goods, nor treasure,
No worldly honour, rank, or pleasure;
No dog would longer such a life desire!
Hence I've applied to magic, to inquire
Whether the spirit's voice and power to me
May not unveil full many a mystery;
That I no more, the sweat upon my brow,
Need speak of things, of which I nothing know;
That I may recognise the hidden ties
That bind creation's inmost energies;

Her vital powers, her embryo seeds survey,
And fling the trade in empty words away.

Thou full-orb'd moon! Would thou wert gazing now,
For the last time upon my troubl'd brow!
Beside this desk, at midnight, seated here,
Oft have I watch'd to hail thy soothing beam;
Then, pensive friend, thou cam'st, my soul to cheer;
Shedding o'er books and scrolls thy silv'ry gleam.
Oh that I could, in thy beloved light,
Now wander freely on some Alpine height;
Could I round mountain caves with spirits ride,
In thy mild radiance o'er the meadows glide,
And purg'd from knowledge-fumes, my strength renew,
Bathing my spirit in thy healing dew.

Woe's me! still prison'd in the gloom
Of this abhorr'd and musty room,
Where heaven's dear light itself doth pass
But dimly through the painted glass!
Girt round with volumes thick with dust,
A prey to worms and mould'ring rust,
And to the high vault's topmost bound,
With smoky paper compass'd round;
Boxes in strange confusion hurl'd,
Glasses and antique lumber, blent
With many a curious instrument—
This is thy world! a precious world!

And dost thou ask why heaves thy heart,
With tighten'd pressure in thy breast?
Why the dull ache will not depart,
By which thy life-pulse is oppress'd?
Instead of nature's living sphere,
Created for mankind of old,
Brute skeletons surround thee here,
And dead men's bones in smoke and mould

Up!  Forth into the distant land!
Is not this book of mystery
By Nostradam's prophetic hand,
An all-sufficient guide?  Thou'lt see

The planetary orbs unroll'd;
When nature doth her thoughts unfold
To thee, thy soul shall rise, and seek
Communion high with her to hold,
As spirit doth with spirit speak!
Vain by dull poring to divine
The meaning of each hallow'd sign.
Spirits!   I feel you hov'ring near;
Make answer, if my voice ye hear!

   (*He opens the book and perceives the sign of Macro-*
    *cosmos.*)

Ah! at this spectacle through every sense,
What sudden ecstasy of joy is flowing!
I feel new rapture, hallow'd and intense,
Through every nerve and vein with ardour glowing.
Was it a god who character'd this scroll,,
Which stills my inward tumult; to my heart,
Wither'd and sick, new rapture doth impart;
And by a mystic impulse, to my soul,
Unveils the working of the wondrous whole.
Am I a God?   What light intense!
In these pure symbols I distinctly see,
Nature exert her vital energy.
Now of the wise man's words I learn the sense:
  " Unlock'd the realm of spirits lies;—
  Thy sense is shut, thy heart is dead!
  Scholar, with quenchless ardour, rise,
  And bathe thy breast in the morning red!"

     (*He contemplates the sign,*)

How all things live and work, and ever blending,
Weave one vast whole from Being's ample range!
How powers celestial, rising and descending,
Their golden buckets ceaseless interchange!
Their flight on rapture-breathing pinions winging,
From heaven to earth their genial influence bringing,
Through the wide whole their chimes melodious ringing.

A wondrous show! but ah! a show alone!
Where shall I grasp thee, infinite nature, where?
Ye breasts, ye fountains of all life, whereon

Hang heaven and earth, from which the blighted soul
Yearn.eth to draw sweet solace, still ye roll
Your sweet and fost'ring tides—where are ye—where!
Ye gush, and must I languish in despair?
> (*He turns over the leaves of the book impatiently, and
> perceives the sign of the Earth-spirit.*)

How differently this sign affects me!   Thou,
Spirit of earth, to me art nigher,
My energies are rising higher,
As from new wine I feel a quick'ning glow;
Courage I feel to stem the tide of life,
To suffer weal and woe, man's earthly lot,
When warring tempests rage to share their strife,
And 'midst the crashing wreck to tremble not.
Clouds gather over me—
The moon conceals her light—
The lamp is quench'd!
Vapours are rising!   Quiv'ring round my head
Flash the red beams.   Down from the vaulted roof
A shuddering horror floats,
And seizes me!
I feel it, spirit, prayer-compell'd, 'tis thou
Art hov'ring near.
Unveil thyself!
Ha!   How my heart is riven now!
Each sense, with eager palpitation,
Is strain'd to catch some new sensation.
I feel my heart surrender'd unto thee!
Thou must!   Thou must!   Though life should be the fee!
> (*He seizes the book, and pronounces mysteriously the sign of
> the spirit.   A ruddy flame flashes up; the spirit appears
> in the flame.*)

SPIRIT.

Who calls on me?

FAUST.            (Turning aside.)

     Appalling shape!

SPIRIT.

With might,

Thou hast compell'd me from my sphere,
Long hast thou striv'n to draw me here,
And now—

FAUST.

Torture! I cannot bear thy sight.

SPIRIT.

To know me thou did'st breathe a fervent prayer,
To hear my voice, to gaze upon my brow,
Me doth thine earnest adjuration bow—
Lo! I am here!—What pitiful despair
Grasps thee, the demigod?   Where's now the soul's deep cry?
Where is the breast, which in its depths a world conceiv'd,
And bore and cherish'd; which, with ecstasy,
To rank itself with us, the spirits, heav'd?
Where art thou, Faust? whose voice I heard resound,
Who towards me press'd with energy profound?
Art thou he?   Thou,—whom thus my breath can blight,
Whose inmost being trembles with affright,
A crush'd and writhing worm!

FAUST.

Shall I yield, thing of flame, to thee?
Faust, and thine equal, I am he!

SPIRIT.

In the currents of life, in action's storm,
I float and I wave
With billowy motion!
Birth and the grave,
A limitless ocean,
A constant weaving
With change still ri
A restless heaving,
A glowing life,
Thus time's whizzing loom unceasing I ply,
And weave the life-garment of deity.

FAUST.

Spirit, whose restless energy doth sweep
The ample world, how near I feel to thee!

SPIRIT.

Thou'rt like the spirit whom thou can'st conceive;
Not me!                                    (*Vanishes*.)

FAUST (*deeply moved*).

Not thee?
Whom then?
I, God's own image!

 FAUST.

And not rank with thee! (*a knock.*)
Oh death! I know it—'tis my famulus—
My fairest fortune now escapes!
That all these visionary shapes
A soulless groveller should banish thus!
  (WAGNER *in his dressing-gown and night-cap, a lamp*
    *in his hand.* FAUST *turns round reluctantly.*)
      WAGNER.
Your pardon, Sir! I heard you here declaim;
A Grecian tragedy you doubtless read.
Improvement in this art is now my aim,
For now-a-days it much avails. Indeed
An actor, oft I've heard it said at least,
May give instruction even to a priest.
      FAUST.
Ay, if your priest should be an actor too,
As not improbably may come to pass.
      WAGNER.
When in his study pent the whole year through,
Man views the world, as through an optic glass,
On a chance holiday, and scarcely then,
How by persuasion can he govern men?
      FAUST.
If feeling prompt not, if it doth not flow
Fresh from the spirit's depths, with strong control
Swaying to rapture every list'ner's soul,
Idle your toil; the chase you may forego!
Brood o'er your task! Stray thoughts together glue,
Cook from another's feast your own ragout,
Still prosecute your miserable game,
And fan your paltry ash-heaps into flame!
Thus children's wonder you'll perchance excite
And apes' applause, if such your appetite:
But that which issues from the heart, alone
Will bend the hearts of others to your own.
      WAGNER.
But in deliv'ry will the speaker find
Success alone; I still am far behind.
      FAUST.
A worthy object still pursue!
Be not a hollow tinkling fool!

Good sense, sound reason, judgment true,
Find utterance without art or rule;
And when with genuine earnestness you speak,
Then is it needful cunning words to seek?
Your fine harangues, so polish'd in their kind,
Wherein the shreds of human thought ye twist,
Are unrefreshing as the empty wind,
Whistling through wither'd leaves and autumn mist.

WAGNER.

Oh Heavens! art is long and life is short!
Still as I prosecute with earnest zeal
The critic's toil, I'm haunted by this thought,
And vague misgivings o'er my spirit steal.
The very means how hardly are they won,
By which we students to the fountains rise!
And then, perchance, ere half his labour's done,
Check'd in his progress, the poor devil dies.

FAUST.

Is parchment then the consecrated spring
From which, he thirsteth not, who once hath quaffed?
Oh, if it gush not from the depths within,
Thou hast not won the soul-reviving draught.

WAGNER.

Yet surely 'tis delightful to transport
Oneself into the spirit of the past,
To see before us how a wise man thought,
And what a glorious height we've reach'd at last.

FAUST.

Ay truly! even to the loftiest star!
A seal'd-up volume, seven-fold sealèd are
To us, my friend, the ages that are pass'd;
And what the spirit of the times men call,
Is merely their own spirit after all,
Wherein, distorted oft, the times are glass'd.
Then truly 'tis a sight to grieve the soul!
At the first glance we fly it in dismay;
A very lumber-room, a rubbish-hole!
At best a sort of mock-heroic play,
With saws pragmatical, and maxims sage,
To suit the puppets and their mimic stage.

WAGNER.

But then the world and man, his heart and brain!
Touching these things all men would something know

FAUST.

Ay! what 'mong men as knowledge doth obtain!
Who on the child its true name dares bestow?
The few who somewhat of these things have known,
Who their full hearts unguardedly reveal'd,
Nor thoughts, nor feelings, from the mob conceal'd,
Have died on crosses, or in flames been thrown.
Excuse me, 'tis the deep of night, my friend,
We must break off, and for the present end.

WAGNER.

I fain would keep awake the whole night through,
Thus to converse so learnedly with you.
To-morrow, being Easter-day, I hope
A few more questions you will let me bring.
With zeal I've aim'd at learning's amplest scope;
True, I know much, but would know everything.　　　(*Exit.*)

FAUST (*alone*).

How he alone is ne'er bereft of hope,
Who clings to tasteless trash with zeal untir'd,
Who doth, with greedy hand, for treasure grope,
And finding earthworms, is with joy inspir'd!

And dare a voice of merely human birth,
E'en here, where shapes immortal throng'd, intrude?
Yet ah! thou poorest of the sons of earth,
For once, I e'en to thee feel gratitude.
Despair the power of sense did well-nigh blast,
And thou didst save me ere I sank dismay'd;
So giant-like the vision seem'd, so vast,
I felt myself shrink dwarf'd as I survey'd.

I, God's own image, who already hail'd
The mirror of eternal truth unveil'd,
Who, freed already from this toil of clay,
In splendour revell'd and celestial day:—
I, more than cherub, whose unfetter'd soul
With penetrative glance aspir'd to flow
Through nature's veins, and, still creating, know
The life of gods,—how am I punish'd now!
One thunder-word hath hurl'd me from the goal!

Spirit! I dare not lift me to thy sphere.
What though my power compell'd thee to appear,
My art was powerless to detain thee here.
In that great moment, rapture fraught,
I felt myself so small, so great;
You thrust me fiercely from the realm of thought,
Back on humanity's uncertain fate.
Who'll teach me now?   What ought I to forego?
Shall I that impulse of the soul obey?
Alas! our very actions as our woe,
Alike impede the tenor of our way!

E'en to the noblest by the soul conceiv'd,
Some feelings cling of baser quality;
And when the goods of this world are achiev'd,
Each nobler aim is term'd a cheat, a lie.
Our aspirations, our soul's genuine life,
Grow torpid in the din of worldly strife.

Though youthful phantasy, while hope inspires,
Stretch o'er the infinite her wing sublime,
A narrow compass limits her desires,
When wreck'd our fortunes in the gulph of time.
In the deep heart of man, care builds her nest,
O'er sorrows undefin'd she broodeth there,
And, rocking ceaseless, scareth joy and rest;
Still is she wont some new disguise to wear,
As house, land, wife, or child, or kindred blood,
As sword or poison'd cup, as fire or flood;
We tremble before ills that ne'er assail,
And what we ne'er shall lose we still bewail.

I rank not with the gods!   I feel with dread,
That the mean earth-worm I resemble more,
Which still is crush'd beneath the wanderer's tread,
As in its native dust it loves to bore.

And may not all as worthless dust be priz'd,
That in these hundred shelves confines me round?
Rubbish, in many a specious form disguis'd,
That in this moth-world doth my being bound?
Here shall I satisfy my craving soul?
Here must I read in many a pond'rous scroll,

That here and there one mortal hath been blest,
Self-torture still the portion of the rest?—
Thou hollow skull, what means that grin of thine?
But that thy brain, bewilder'd once, like mine,
Sought, yearning for the truth, the light of day,
And in the twilight wander'd far astray?
Ye instruments, forsooth, ye mock at me,—
With wheel, and cog, and ring, and cylinder,
To nature's portals ye should be the key;
Your wards are intricate, yet fail to stir
Her bolts.   Inscrutable in broadest light,
To be unveil'd by force she doth refuse.
What she reveals not to thy mental sight,
Thou wilt not wrest from her with bars and screws.
Old useless furnitures!   Ye still are here,
Because my sires ye serv'd in times long past!
Old scroll!   The smoke of years thou yet dost wear,
As when yon lamp its sickly ray first cast.
Better have squander'd at an earlier day
My paltry means, than 'neath its weight to groan!
Would'st thou possess thy heritage, essay
By active use to render it thine own.
What we employ not, but impedes our way;
What it brings forth the hour can use alone.

But why doth yonder spot attract my sight?
Is yonder flask a magnet to my gaze?
Whence this mild radiance, as when Cynthia's light,
Amid the forest-gloom, around us plays?

Hail, precious phial!   Thee, with rev'rent awe,
Down from thine old receptacle I draw;
Science in thee I hail and human art;
Essence of deadliest powers, refin'd and sure,
Of soothing anodynes abstraction pure,
Now in thy master's need thy grace impart!
I gaze on thee, my pain is lull'd to rest;
I grasp thee, calm'd the tumult in my breast;
The flood-tide of my spirit ebbs away;
Onward I'm summon'd o'er a boundless main,
Calm at my feet expands the glassy plain,
To shores unknown allures a brighter day.

Lo, where a car of fire, on airy pinion,
Comes floating towards me!   I'm prepar'd to fly
By a new track through ether's wide dominion,
To distant spheres of pure activity.
This life intense!   This godlike ecstasy?
Worm that thou art, such rapture can'st thou earn?
Only resolve with courage stern and high,
Thy visage from the radiant sun to turn!
Dare with determin'd will to burst the portals
Past which in terror others fain would steal;
Now is the time to testify that mortals
The calm sublimity of gods can feel.
To shudder not at yonder dark abyss,
Throng'd with self-torturing fancy's grisly brood;
Right onward to the yawning gulph to press,
Round whose dark entrance rolls hell's fiery flood;
With glad resolve to take the fatal leap,
E'en though thy soul should sink to endless sleep!

Pure crystal goblet, forth I draw thee now,
From out thine antiquated case, where thou
Forgotten hast repos'd for many a year.
Oft at my father's revels thou didst shine,
Gladd'ning the earnest guests with gen'rous wine
As each the other pledg'd with sober cheer.

The gorgeous brede of figures, quaintly wrought,
Which he who quaff'd must first in rhyme expound,
Then drain the goblet at one draught profound,
Hath nights of boyhood to fond memory brought;
I to my neighbour shall not reach thee now,
Nor on thy rich device my cunning show;
Here is a juice makes drunk without delay;
Its dark brown flood thy crystal round doth fill;
Let this last draught, the product of my skill,
My own free choice, be quaff'd with resolute will,
A solemn greeting to the coming day!

(He places the goblet to his mouth.)<br>(The ringing of bells, and choral voices.)

*Chorus of* ANGELS.
Christ is arisen!
Mortal, all hail to thee,
Thou whom mortality,
Earth's sad reality,
Held as in prison.

FAUST.
What hum melodious, what clear, silv'ry chime,
Thus draws the goblet from my lips away?
Ye deep-ton'd bells, do ye with voice sublime,
Announce the solemn dawn of Easter-day?
Sweet choir! are ye the hymn of comfort singing,
Which once around the darkness of the grave,
From seraph-voices, in glad triumph ringing,
Of a new covenant assurance gave?

CHORUS OF WOMEN.
Embalm'd with spices rare,
In sorrow and in gloom,
His faithful followers bare
His body to the tomb.
For their sepulchral rest,
We swath'd the reliques dear;
Ah! vain is now our quest,
Christ is no longer here!

CHORUS OF ANGELS.
Christ is arisen!
Perfect through earthly ruth,
Radiant with love and truth,
Girt with eternal youth,
He soars from earth's prison.

FAUST.
Wherefore, ye tones celestial, sweet and strong,
Come ye a dweller in the dust to seek?
Ring out your chimes believing crowds among,
I hear the message, but my faith is weak;
From faith her darling, miracle, hath sprung.
I dare not soar aloft to yonder spheres
Whence sound the joyful tidings; yet this strain,
Familiar even from my boyhood's years,
Binds me to earth, as with a mystic chain.

Then would celestial love, with holy kiss,
Come o'er me in the Sabbath's stilly hour,
While, fraught with solemn and mysterious power,
Chim'd the deep-sounding bell, and prayer was bliss;
A yearning impulse, undefin'd yet dear,
Drove me to wander on through wood and field;
With heaving breast and many a burning tear,
I felt with holy joy a world reveal'd.
This Easter hymn announc'd, with joyous pealing,
Gay sports and festive hours in times of old,
And early memories, fraught with child-like feeling,
From death's dark threshold now my steps withhold.
O still sound on, thou sweet celestial strain,
Tears now are gushing,—Earth, I'm thine again!

CHORUS OF DISCIPLES.

O'er death itself victorious,
Whom we interr'd in love,
Exalted now and glorious
Is rais'd to realms above.
Near the creative spirit
Joys aye-increasing flow.
Ah! we on earth inherit
Disquietude and woe.
He left us here in anguish,
His glory we bemoan,
For ah, our spirits languish,
We're comfortless, alone.

CHORUS OF ANGELS.

Christ is arisen,
Redeem'd from decay;
The bonds which imprison
Your souls, rend away!
Praising the Lord with zeal,
By deeds that love reveal,
Like brethren true and leal
Sharing the daily meal,
To all that sorrow feel
Whisp'ring of heaven's weal,
Still is the master near,
Still is he with you here!

BEFORE THE GATE.

*Promenaders of all sorts pass out.*

MECHANICS.

Why choose ye that direction, pray?

OTHERS.

To the Jager-house we're on our way.

THE FIRST.

We towards the mill are strolling on.

A MECHANIC.

A walk to Wasserhof were best.

A SECOND.

The road is not a pleasant one.

THE OTHERS.

What will you do?

A THIRD.

I'll join the rest.

A FOURTH.

Let's up to Burghof, there you'll find good cheer,
The prettiest maidens and the stoutest beer,
And brawls of a prime sort.

A FIFTH.

You scapegrace! How;
Your skin still itching for a row?
I will not go, I loathe the place.

SERVANT GIRL.

No, no! To town I will my steps retrace

ANOTHER.

Near yonder poplars he is sure to be.

THE FIRST.

And if he is, what matters it to me!
With you he'll walk, he'll dance with none but you,
And with your pleasures what have I to do?

THE SECOND.

To-day he will not be alone, he said
His friend would be with him, the curly head.

STUDENT.

Why how those buxom girls step on!
Brother, we'll follow them anon.
Strong beer, a damsel smartly dress'd,
Stinging tobacco,—these I love the best.

CITIZEN'S DAUGHTER.

Look at those handsome fellows there!
'Tis really shameful, I declare,
The best society they shun,
After those servant-girls forsooth, to run.

SECOND STUDENT (*to the first*).

Not quite so fast! for in our rear,
Two girls, well-dress'd, are drawing near;
Not far from us the one doth dwell,
And sooth to say, I like her well.
They walk demurely, yet you'll see,
They'll let us join them presently.

THE FIRST.

Not I! restraints of all kinds I detest.
Quick! let us catch the game before it flies,
The hand on Saturday the mop that plies,
Will on the Sunday fondle you the best.

CITIZEN.

This Burgomaster likes me not; each hour
He grows more insolent now he's in power,
And for the town, what doth he do for it?
Is it not growing worse from day to day?
To more restrictions we must still submit;
Ay, and more taxes now than ever pay.

BEGGAR *sings*.

Kind gentlemen and ladies fair,
So rosy-cheek'd and trimly dress'd,
Be pleas'd to listen to my prayer,
Relieve and pity the distress'd.
Let me not vainly sing my lay!
His heart's most glad whose hand is free.
Now when all men keep holiday,
Should be a harvest-day to me.

### ANOTHER CITIZEN.

I know nought better of a holiday,
Than chatting about war and war's alarms,
When folk in Turkey are all up in arms,
Fighting their deadly battles far away,
Within the window we our glasses drain,
Watch down the stream the painted vessels glide,
Then, blessing peace and peaceful times, again
Homeward we turn our steps at eventide.

### THIRD CITIZEN.

Ay, neighbour!   So let matters stand for me!
There they may scatter one another's brains,
And hurly-burly innovations see—
So here at home all undisturb'd remains.

### OLD WOMAN (*to the* CITIZENS' DAUGHTERS).

Heyday!   How smart!   The fresh young blood!
Who would not fall in love with you ?
Not quite so proud'   'Tis well and good !
And what you wish, that I could help you to.

### CITIZEN'S DAUGHTER.

Come, Agatha!   I care not to be seen
Walking in public with these witches.   True,
My future lover, last St. Andrew's E'en,
In flesh and blood she brought before my view.

### ANOTHER.

And mine she show'd me also in the glass,
A soldier's figure, with companions bold ;
I look around, I seek him as I pass,
In vain, his form I nowhere can behold.

### SOLDIERS.

Towns with walls
Encompass'd round,
Maids with lofty
Beauty crown'd.
On ! regardless
Of the toil !
Bold the venture,
Rich the spoil !

And the trumpet's
Martial breath,
Calls to pleasure,
Calls to death.
Mid the tumult
There is rapture;
Maids and fortress,
Both we capture.
Bold the venture,
Rich the prize!
Onward then
The soldier hies.

FAUST *and* WAGNER.
FAUST.

Loos'd from their icy fetters, streams and rills
In spring's effusive, quick'ning, mildness flow;
Hope's budding promise every valley fills,
And winter, spent with age, and powerless now,
Draws off his forces to the savage hills.
Thence he discharges nought in his retreat,
Save, ever and anon, a drizzling shower,
Striping the verdant fields with snow and sleet;
But white the sun endures not,—vital power,
Productive energy, abroad are rife,
Investing all things with the hues of life;
And joyous crowds, in suits of varied dye,
The absent charm of blooming flowers supply.
Now hither turn, and from this height
Back to the town direct your sight.
Forth from the arch'd and gloomy gate,
The multitudes, in bright array,
Stream forth, and seek the sun's warm ray.
Their risen Lord they celebrate,
For they themselves have also risen to-day!
From the mean tenement, the sordid room,
From manual craft, from toil's imperious sway,
From roofs' and gables' overhanging gloom,
From the close pressure of the narrow street,
And from the churches' venerable night,
They've issued now from darkness into light;
Look, only look, how borne on nimble feet,

Through fields and gardens roam the scatter'd throng ;
How o'er yon peaceful water's ample sheet,
Gay wherries, pleasure-laden, glide along ;
And see, deep sinking in the yielding tide,
The last now leaves the shore ; e'en from yon height,
The winding paths along, which mark its side,
Gay-colour'd dresses flash upon the sight.
And hark ! the sounds of village mirth arise ;
This is the people's genuine paradise.
Both great and small send up a joyous cheer ;
Yes ! I am still a man,—I feel it here.

WAGNER.

Sir doctor, in a walk with you
There's honour and instruction too ;
Alone I would not here resort,
Coarseness I hate of every sort.
This fiddling, shouting, bawling, I detest ;
I hate the tumult of the vulgar throng ;
They roar as by the evil one possess'd,
And call the discord pleasure, call it song.

PEASANTS (under the linden-tree).<br>Dance and song.

The shepherd for the dance was dress'd,
With ribbon, wreath, and coloured vest,
He made a gallant show.
And round about the linden-tree,
They footed it right merrily.
    Juchhe ! Juchhe !
    Juchheisa ! Heisa ! He !
So went the fiddle-bow.

Our swain amidst the circle press'd,
He push'd a maiden trimly dress'd,
And jogg'd her with his elbow ;
The buxom damsel turn'd her head,
" Now that's a stupid trick !" she said.
    Juchhe ! Juchhe !
    Juchheisa ! Heisa ! He !
Don't be so rude, good fellow !

Swiftly they foot it in the ring,
Abroad the ample kirtles swing,

Now right, now left they go.
And they grow red, and they grow warm,
And now rest, panting, arm in arm,
    Juchhe!  Juchhe!
    Juchheisa!  Heisa!  He!
Upon their hip their elbow!

Stand off!  Don't plague me! many a maid
Has been betroth'd and then betray'd:
No man shall me befool so!
Yet still he flatter'd her aside,
And from the linden, far and wide
    Juchhe!  Juchhe!
    Juchheisa!  Heisa!  He!
Ring shout and fiddle-bow.

### OLD PEASANT.

Doctor, 'tis really kind of you,
To condescend to come this way,
And deeply learned as you are,
To join our mirthful throng to-day.
Our fairest cup I offer you,
Which we with sparkling drink have crown'd,
And pledging you, I pray aloud,
That every drop within its round,
While it your present thirst allays,
May swell the number of your days.

### FAUST.

I take the cup you kindly reach,
Health and prosperity to each!
        (*The crowd gather round in a circle.*)

### OLD PEASANT.

Ay, truly! 'tis well done, that you
Our festive meetings thus attend;
You, who in evil days of yore,
So often shew'd yourself our friend
Full many a one stands living here,
Who from the fever's deadly blast,
Your father rescu'd, when his skill
The fatal sickness stay'd at last.
A young man then, each house you sought,

Where reign'd the mortal pestilence.
Corpse after corpse was carried forth,
But still unscath'd you issued thence.
Sore then your trials and severe;
The Helper yonder aids the helper here.

ALL.

Heaven bless the trusty friend, and long
To help the poor his life prolong!

FAUST.

To him above in grateful homage bend,
Who prompts the helper and the help doth send.

(*He proceeds with* WAGNER.)

WAGNER.

With what emotions must your heart o'erflow,
Receiving thus the rev'rence of the crowd!
Great man! How happy, who like you doth know
Rightly to use the gifts by heaven bestow'd!
You to the son the father shows;
They press around, inquire, advance,
Hush'd is the music, check'd the dance,
Still where you pass they stand in rows,
The caps fly upwards, and almost,
To you they bow, as to the host.

FAUST.

A few steps further, up to yonder stone;
Here rest we from our walk. In times long pas:
Absorb'd in thought, here oft I sat alone,
And disciplin'd myself with prayer and fast.
Then rich in hope, possess'd with faith sincere,
With sighs, and groans, and hands in anguish press'd,
The end of that sore plague, with many a tear,
From the dread Lord of heaven I sought to wrest.
These praises have to me a scornful tone.
Oh, could'st thou in my inner being read,
And learn how little either sire or son,
Of thanks deserve the honourable meed!
My sire, of good repute and sombre mood,
O'er nature's powers and every mystic zone.
With honest zeal, but methods of his own,
Still lov'd, with toil fantastical to brood.

Secluded in his dark, alchemic cell.
His time with brother adepts he would spend,
And after numberless receipts, compel
Opposing elements to fuse and blend.
A ruddy lion there, a suitor bold,
In tepid bath was with the lily wed,
Thence both, while open flames around them roll'd,
Were tortur'd to another bridal bed.
Did then the youthful queen at length arise
In our alembic, bright with varied dyes,
Our med'cine this, who took it soon expir'd,
" Who were by it recover'd?" none inquir'd.
With our infernal mixture, thus, ere long,
These hills and peaceful vales among,
We rag'd more fiercely than the pest;
Myself to thousands did the poison give,
They pin'd away, I yet must live,
To hear the reckless murderers blest.

WAGNER.

Why let this thought your spirit overcast?
Can man do more than with nice skill,
With firm and conscientious will,
Practise the art transmitted from the past?
If duly you revere your sire in youth,
His lore, with docile mind, you will receive;
In manhood, if you spread the bounds of truth,
Then may your son a higher goal achieve.

FAUST.

How blest is he whom still the hope inspires,
To lift himself from error's turbid flood!
The knowledge which he hath not man requires,
With what he hath, he nought achieves of good.
But let not moody thoughts their shadow throw
O'er the calm beauty of this hour serene !
In the rich sunset see how brightly glow
Yon cottage homes, girt round with verdant green.
Slow sinks the orb, the day is now no more;
Yonder he hastens to diffuse new life.
Oh for a pinion from the earth to soar,
And after, ever after him to strive !
Then should I see the world outspread below,

D

Illumin'd by the deathless evening-beams,
The vales reposing, every height a-glow,
The silver brooklets meeting golden streams.
The savage mountain, with its cavern'd side,
Bars not my godlike progress.   Lo, the ocean,
Its warm bays heaving with a tranquil motion,
To my rapt vision opes its ample tide!
But now at length the god appears to sink;
A gushing impulse wings anew my flight,
Onward I press his quenchless light to drink,
The day before me, and behind the night,
The waves below, above the vaulted skies.
Fair dream, it vanish'd with the parting day.
Alas! that when on spirit-wing we rise,
No wing material lifts our mortal clay.
But 'tis our inborn impulse, deep and strong,
To rush aloft, to struggle still towards heaven,
When far above us, pours its thrilling song
The sky-lark, lost amid the purple even;
When on extended pinion sweeps amain
The lordly eagle o'er the pine-crown'd height;
And when, still striving towards its home, the crane
O'er moor and ocean wings its onward flight.

WAGNER.

To strange conceits myself at times must own.
But impulse such as this I ne'er have known ;
Nor woods, nor fields, can long our thoughts engage,
Their wings I envy not the feather'd kind;
Far otherwise the pleasures of the mind,
Bear us from book to book, from page to page!
Then winter nights grow cheerful; keen delight
Warms every limb; and ah! when we unroll
Some old and precious parchment, at the sight
All heaven itself descends upon the soul.

FAUST.

Your heart by one sole impulse is possess'd;
Unconscious of the other still remain!
Two souls, alas! are lodg'd within my breast,
Which struggle there for undivided reign
One to the world, with obstinate desire,
And closely-cleaving organs, still adheres

Above the mist, the other doth aspire,
With sacred vehemence, to purer spheres.
Spirits, if ye indeed are hov'ring near,
Wielding 'twixt heaven and earth potential sway,
Stoop hither from your golden atmosphere,
And bear me to more varied life away!
A magic mantle did I but possess,
Abroad to waft me as on viewless wings,
I'd prize it far beyond the costliest dress,
Nor would I change it for the robe of kings.

WAGNER.

Call not the spirits who on mischief wait!
Their troop familiar, streaming through the air,
From every quarter threaten man's estate,
And danger in a thousand forms prepare.
They drive impetuous from the frozen north,
With fangs sharp-piercing, and keen arrowy tongues
From the ungenial east they issue forth,
And prey, with parching breath, upon your lungs;
If, wafted on the desert's flaming wing,
They from the south heap fire upon the brain,
Refreshing moisture from the west they bring,
Then with huge torrents deluge field and plain.
In wait for mischief, they are prompt to hear;
With guileful purpose our behests obey;
Like ministers of grace they oft appear,
And with an angel's voice our trust betray.
But let us hence!   Grey eve doth all things blend,
The air grows chilly, and the mists descend!
'Tis in the evening first our home we prize—
Why stand you thus, and gaze with wond'ring eyes?
What in the gloom thus moves you?

FAUST.

Yon black hound,

See'st thou, through corn and stubble scamp'ring round

WAGNER.

I've mark'd him long, but nothing strange I see!

FAUST.

Note him.   What should you take the brute to be?

D 2

WAGNER.

Merely a poodle, whom his instinct serves
His master's missing track to find once more.

FAUST.

Dost mark how round us, with wide spiral curves,
He wheels, each circle closer than before?
And, if I err not, he appears to me
A fiery whirlpool in his track to leave.

WAGNER.

Nought but a poodle doth he seem to be;
'Tis some delusion doth your sight deceive.

FAUST.

Methinks a magic coil our feet around,
He for a future snare doth lightly spread.

WAGNER.

Round us in doubt I see him shyly bound,
Two strangers seeing in his master's stead.

FAUST.

The circle narrows, he's already near!

WAGNER.

A dog you see, no spectre have we here;
He growls, he hesitates, he crouches too—
And wags his tail—as dogs are wont to do.

FAUST.

Come hither, Sirrah! join our company!

WAGNER.

A very poodle, he appears to be!
But speak to him, and on you he will spring;
To sit on his hind legs, he knows the trick;
Aught you may chance to lose, again he'll bring,
And plunge into the water for your stick.

FAUST.

You're right indeed; no traces now I see
Whatever of a spirit's agency.
'Tis training—nothing more.

WAGNER.

     A dog well taught
E'en by the wisest of us may be sought.
Ay, to your favour he's entitled too,
Apt scholar of the students, 'tis his due!

(They enter the gate of the town.)

## Study.

FAUST, *entering with the poodle.*
Behind me now lie field and plain,
As night her veil doth o'er them draw,
Our better soul resumes her reign
With feelings of foreboding awe.
Lull'd is each stormy deed to rest,
And tranquilliz'd each wild desire:
Pure charity doth warm the breast,
And love to God the soul inspire.

Poodle, be still!   Cease up and down to rove!
What on the threshold are you snuffing there?
Here's my best cushion, lie behind the stove.
As you amus'd me in the mountain air,
With freak and gambol, like a quiet guest
Receive my kindness now, and take your rest

Ah! when within our narrow room,
The friendly lamp again doth glow;
An inward light dispels the gloom
In hearts that strive themselves to know.
Reason begins again to speak,
Again the bloom of hope returns,
The streams of life we fain would seek,
Yea, for life's source our spirit yearns.

Cease, poodle, cease to growl!   This brutish sound
Accords not with the pure and hallow'd tone
Whose influence o'er my soul now reigns alone.
Among mankind, indeed, they oft are found,
Who, what they do not understand, despise,
And what is good and beautiful, contemn,
Because beyond their sympathies it lies.—
And will the poodle snarl at it like them?

But ah! I feel, howe'er I yearn for rest,
Content flows now no longer from my breast.
Yet wherefore must the stream so soon be dry,
And we again all parch'd and thirsting lie?
This sad experience I've so oft approv'd;
But still the want admits of compensation,
We learn to treasure what's from sense remov'd,
With yearning hearts, we long for revelation.

And nowhere is the heavenly radiance sent
So pure and bright as in the Testament.
Towards the ancient text an impulse strong
Moves me the volume to explore,
And render faithfully its sacred lore,
In the lov'd accents of the German tongue.
    (*He opens a volume and applies himself to it.*)

'Tis writ, " In the beginning was the Word!"
I pause, perplex'd! Who now will help afford?
I cannot the mere word so highly prize;
If by the spirit guided as I read,
I must translate the passage otherwise.
 ' In the beginning was the Sense!" Take heed,
The import of this primal sentence weigh,
Lest your too hasty pen be led astray!
Doth sense work all things, and control the hour?
'Tis writ " In the beginning was the Power!"
Thus should it stand: yet while the words I trace,
I'm warn'd again the passage to efface.
The spirit aids: from anxious scruples freed,
I write, " In the beginning was the Deed!"

   If I'm with you my room to share,
   Cease barking, poodle, and forbear
   My quiet thus to start!
   I cannot suffer in my cell
   Inmate so troublesome to dwell,
   Or you or I depart.
   I'm loath the guest-rite to withhold;
   The door's ajar, the passage clear;
   But what must now mine eyes behold!
   Are nature's laws suspended here?
   Is 't real, or a phantom show?
   In length and breadth how doth my poodle grow!
   Aloft he lifts himself with threat'ning mien,
   In likeness of a dog no longer seen!
   What spectre have I harbour'd thus!
   Huge as a hippopotamus,
   With fiery eye, terrific jaw!
   Ah! thou art subject to my law!
   For such a base, half-hellish brood,
   The key of Solomon is good.

SPIRITS (*without*).
Captur'd there within is one!
Stay without and follow none.
Like a fox in iron snare,
Hell's old lynx is quaking there,
  But take heed!
Hover round, above, below,
  To and fro,
Then from durance is he freed.
Can ye aid him, spirits all,
  Leave him not in mortal thrall!
Many a time, and oft hath he
Serv'd us, when at liberty.

FAUST.
The monster to confront, at first,
The spell of four must be rehears'd
  Salamander shall kindle,
  Writhe nymph of the wave,
  In air sylph shall dwindle,
  And Kobold shall slave.

The elements who doth not know,
Nor can their powers and uses show,
He were no master to compel
Spirits, with charm and magic spell.

    Vanish in the fiery glow,
    Salamander!
    Rushingly together flow,
    Undine!
    Shimmer in the meteor's gleam,
    Sylphide!
    Hither bring thine homely aid,
    Incubus!   Incubus!
    Step forth!   I do adjure thee thus

None of the elemental four
Doth within the creature dwell;
He lies, untroubl'd as before,
He grins at me, and mocks my spe
By more potent magic still,
I must compel him to my will.

    A fugitive from hell's confine
    Art hither come?   Then see this sign.

> At whose dread power the grisly troop
> Of hellish fiends in terror stoop!

With bristling hair now doth the creature swell

> Canst thou read him, reprobate?
> The infinite, the increate,
> Bright essence, unpronounceable,
> Diffus'd through the celestial sphere,
> Vilely transpierc'd, who suffer'd here?

O'er-master'd by the potent spell,
Behind the stove, the fiend of hell
Huge as an elephant doth swell;
Wide as the room expands the shape
In mist he'll vanish and escape.
Rise not the vaulted roof to meet
Now lay thee at the master's feet
Thou see'st that mine's no idle threat.
With holy fire I'll scorch thee yet!
Come forth, thou progeny of night,
Nor wait the torture of thrice-glowing light!
Await not of mine art the utmost measure!

MEPHISTOPHELES

*(As the mist sinks, comes forward from behind the
stove, in the dress of a travelling scholar.)*

Why all this uproar? What's the master's pleasure?

FAUST.

So this is then the kernel of the brute!
A travelling scholar? Why I needs must smile

MEPHISTOPHELES.

Your learned rev'rence humbly I salute!
You've made me swelter in a pretty style.

FAUST.

Your name?

MEPHISTOPHELES.

The question trifling seems from one,
Who it appears the Word doth rate so low;
Who, undeluded by mere outward show,
To Being's depths would penetrate alone.

FAUST.

With gentlemen like you we're wont indeed
The inward essence from the name to read,

As it doth all too obviously appear,
When we, Destroyer, Liar, Fly-god, hear.
Who then are you?

MEPHISTOPHELES.
Part of that power which still
Produceth good, while it deviseth ill.

FAUST.
What hidden mystery in this riddle lies?

MEPHISTOPHELES.
The spirit I, which evermore denies!
And justly too; for whatsoe'er hath birth
Deserves again to be reduc'd to nought;
Better were nothing into being brought.
Thus every essence which you sons of earth
Destruction, sin, or briefly, Evil, name,
As my peculiar element I claim.

FAUST.
You call yourself a part, yet, as it seems,
Stand there a whole?

MEPHISTOPHELES.
I speak the modest truth.
Though folly's microcosm, man, forsooth,
Himself to be a perfect whole esteems,
Part of the part am I that once was all.
A part of darkness, which gave birth to light.
Proud light, who now his mother would enthrall,
Contesting rank and space with ancient night.
Yet he succeeds not, struggle as he will;
To forms material he adhereth still;
From them he streameth, them he maketh fair,
And still the progress of his beams they check;
And so, I trust, when comes the final wreck,
Light will, ere long, the doom of matter share.

FAUST.
Your worthy avocation now I guess!
Wholesale annihilation won't prevail,
So you're beginning on a smaller scale.

MEPHISTOPHELES.
And, to say truth, as yet with small success.
Oppos'd to nothingness, the world,
This clumsy mass, subsisteth still;
Not yet is it to ruin hurl'd.

Despite the efforts of my will.
Tempests and earthquakes, fire and flood, I've tried;
Yet land and ocean still unchang'd abide!
And then of beasts and men, the accursed brood,—
Neither o'er them can I extend my sway.
What countless myriads have I swept away!
Yet ever circulates the fresh young blood.
It is enough to drive me to despair!
As in the earth, in water, and in air,
In moisture and in drought, in heat and cold.
Thousands of germs their energies unfold!
If fire I had not for myself retain'd,
No sphere whatever had for me remain'd.

FAUST.

So then with your cold devil's fist,
Still clench'd in malice impotent,
You the creative power resist,
The active, the beneficent!
Chaos' strange son! elsewhere I pray
Your mischief-working power essay!

MEPHISTOPHELES.

It should, in truth, be thought upon;
We'll talk about it more anon!
But have I now permission to retire?

FAUST.

I see not why you should inquire.
Since we're acquainted now, you're free,
As often as you list, to call on me.
There is the door, the window here,
Or there's the chimney.

MEPHISTOPHELES.

Sooth to say,
There to my exit doth appear
A trifling hindrance in the way;
The Druid-foot upon your threshold—

FAUST.

How!
You're by the pentagram embarrass'd now?
If that have power to hold you, son of hell,
Say, how you came to enter in my cell?
What could a spirit such as you deceive?

**MEPHISTOPHELES.**

The drawing is rot perfect; by your leave,
The outward angle is not fairly clos'd.

**FAUST.**

Chance hath the matter happily dispos'd!
So you're my prisoner then?   You're nicely caught!

**MEPHISTOPHELES.**

In sprang the dog, indeed, observing nought;
The matter now assumes another shape,
The devil's in the house and can't escape.

**FAUST.**

But why not through the window?

**MEPHISTOPHELES.**

'Tis a law,
Binding on ghosts and devils, to withdraw
The way they first stole in.   We enter free,
But, as regards our exit, slaves are we.

**FAUST.**

E'en hell hath its peculiar laws, I see!
I'm glad of that, a binding compact, then,
May be establish'd with you gentlemen?

**MEPHISTOPHELES.**

Ay!   And the promis'd good therein express'd,
Shall to a tittle be by you possess'd.
But such arrangements time require;
We'll speak of them when next we meet;
Most earnestly I now entreat,
This once permission to retire.

**FAUST.**

Another moment prithee linger here,
And give some fair prediction to mine ear.

**MEPHISTOPHELES.**

Now let me go! ere long I'll come again,
And you may question at your leisure then.

**FAUST.**

To capture you I laid no snare.
The net you enter'd of your own free will.
Let him who holds the devil hold him still!
A second time he will not catch him there.

**MEPHISTOPHELES.**

If it so please you, I'm at your command;
Only on this condition, understand;

That worthily your leisure to beguile,
I here may exercise my arts awhile.

FAUST.

You're free to do so!   Gladly I'll attend;
But be your art a pleasant one!

MEPHISTOPHELES.

My friend,

This hour enjoyment more intense,
Shall captivate each ravish'd sense,
Than thou could'st compass in the bound
Of the whole year's unvarying round;
And what the dainty spirits sing,
The lovely images they bring,
Are no fantastic sorcery.
Rich odours shall regale your smell,
On choicest sweets your palate dwell,
Your feelings thrill with ecstasy.
No preparation we require,
Now warble on my viewless quire!

SPIRITS.

Hence overshadowing gloom
Vanish from sight!
O'er us thine azure dome,
Bend, beauteous light!
Dark clouds that o'er us spread,
Melt in thin air!
Stars, your soft radiance shed,
Tender and fair.
Girt with celestial might,
Winging their airy flight,
Spirits are thronging.
Follows their forms of ligh
Infinite longing!
Flutter their vestures bright
O'er field and grove!
Where in their leafy bower
Lovers the livelong hour
Vow deathless love.
Soft bloometh bud and bower
Bloometh the grove!

Grapes from the spreading vine
Crown the full measure;
Fountains of foaming wine
Gush from the pressure.
Still where the currents wind,
Gems brightly gleam.
Leaving the hills behind
On rolls the stream;
Now into ample seas,
Spreadeth the flood;
Laving the sunny leas,
Mantled with wood.
Rapture the feather'd throng,
Gaily careering,
Sip as they float along;
Sunward they're steering;
On towards the isles of light
Winging their way,
That on the waters bright
Dancingly play.
Hark to the choral strain,
Joyfully ringing!
While on the grassy plain
Dancers are springing;
Climbing the steep hill's side,
Skimming the glassy tide,
Wander they there;
Others on pinions wide
Wing the blue air;
On towards the living stream,
Towards yonder stars that gleam,
Far, far away;
Seeking their tender beam
Wing they their way.

MEPHISTOPHELES.

Well done my dainty spirits! now he slumbers!
Ye have entranc'd him fairly with your numbers!
This minstrelsy of yours I must repay.
Thou'rt not the man to hold the devil it seems!
Now play around him with illusive dreams
Until with ravishment his sense you take;
But tooth of rat I now require, to break

This wizard spell; brief conjuring will suffice.
One rustles towards me, and will soon appear.

> The master of the rats and mice,
> Of flies and frogs, of bugs and lice,
> Commands thy presence; without fear
> Come forth and gnaw the threshold here,
> Where he with oil has smear'd it.—Thou
> Com'st hopping forth already!   Now
> To work!   The point that holds me bound
> Is in the outer angle found.
> Another bite—so—now 'tis done—
> Faust, till we meet again, dream on.

FAUST   (*awaking*).

Am I once more deluded? must I deem
This troop of thronging spirits all ideal?
The devil's presence, was it nothing real?
The poodle's disappearance but a dream?


*Study.*

FAUST.   MEPHISTOPHELES.

FAUST.

A knock?   Come in!   Who now would break my rest?

MEPHISTOPHELES.

'Tis I!

FAUST.

Come in!

MEPHISTOPHELES.

Thrice be the words express'd.

FAUST.

Then I repeat, Come in!

MEPHISTOPHELES.

'Tis well.

I hope that we shall soon agree!
For now, your fancies to expel,
Here as a youth of high degree
I'm come, in gold-lac'd scarlet vest,
And stiff-silk mantle richly dress'd,
A cock's gay feather for a plume,
A long and pointed rapier, too;

And briefly I would counsel you
To don at once the same costume,
And, free from trammels, speed away,
That what life is you may essay.

FAUST.

In every garb I needs must feel oppress'd,
My heart to earth's low torturing cares a prey.
Too old I am the trifler's part to play,
Too young, to live by no desire possess'd.
What can the world afford to ease my pain?
Renounce! renounce!   This the eternal song
Which in our ears still rings, our whole life long;
Each hour, in murmurs hoarse, repeats the strain.
But to new horror I awake each morn,
And I could weep hot tears, to see the sun
Dawn on another day, whose round forlorn
Accomplishes no wish of mine—not one.
Which still, with froward captiousness, impairs
E'en the presentiment of every joy,
While low realities and paltry cares
The spirit's fond imaginings destroy.
And then when falls again the veil of night,
Stretch'd on my couch I languish in despair;
Appalling dreams my troubl'd soul affright;
No soothing rest vouchsaf'd me even there.
The god, who thron'd within my breast reside
Deep in my inmost soul can stir the springs;
With sovereign sway my energies he guides,
But hath no power to move external things;
And thus my very being I deplore,
Death ardently desire, and life abhor.

MEPHISTOPHELES.

And yet, methinks, by most 'twill be confess'd
That death is never quite a welcome guest.

FAUST.

Happy the man around whose brow he binds
The bloodstain'd wreath in conquest's dazzling hour;
Or whom, excited by the dance, he finds
Dissolv'd in bliss, in love's delicious bower;
Oh that before that lofty spirit's might,
My soul, entranc'd, had sunk to endless night!

MEPHISTOPHELES.
Yet did a certain man, one night, refrain
Of its brown juice the crystal bowl to drain.
. FAUST.
To play the spy diverts you, then?
MEPHISTOPHELES.
I own,
Though not omniscient, much to me is known.
FAUST.
If o'er my soul the tone familiar, stealing,
Drew me from harrowing thought's bewild'ring maze,
Touching the ling'ring chords of childlike feeling,
With the sweet harmonies of happier days;
So now I breathe my curse on all that windeth
Its coil of magic influence round the soul,
And with delusive flatt'ry fondly bindeth
The wretched spirit to this dismal hole!
And before all, curs'd be the high opinion
Wherewith the spirit girds itself around!
Of shows delusive curs'd be the dominion,
Within whose mocking sphere our sense is bound!
Accurs'd of lying dreams the treacherous wiles,
The cheat of glory, fame's exalted rage!
Accurs'd as property what each beguiles,
As wife and child, as slave and heritage!
Accurs'd be mammon, when with treasure
He doth to daring deeds incite;
Or when to steep the soul in pleasure,
He spreads the couch of soft delight.
Curs'd be the grape's balsamic juice!
Accurs'd love's dream, of joys the first!
Accurs'd be hope! accurs'd be faith!
And more than all, be patience curs'd!
CHORUS OF SPIRITS (invisible).
Woe! woe!
Thou hast destroy'd
The beautiful world
With violent blow;
'Tis shiver'd! 'tis shatter'd!
The fragments abroad by a demigod scatter'd.
Now we sweep

The wrecks into nothingness!
Fondly we weep
The beauty that's gone!
Thou, 'mongst the sons of earth,
Lofty and mighty one,
Build it once more!
In thine own bosom the lost world restore!
Now with unclouded sense
Enter a new career;
Songs shall salute thine ear,
Ne'er heard before!

MEPHISTOPHELES
My little ones these spirits be.
Hark! with shrewd intelligence,
How they recommend to thee
Action, and the joys of sense!
In the busy world to dwell,
Fain they would allure thee hence;
Stagnate in this lonely cell,
Sap of life, and powers of sense.


Forbear to trifle longer with your grief,
Which, vulture-like, consumes you in this den.
The worst society is some relief,
You'll feel yourself a man with fellow-men.
Not that I'd thrust you 'mid the vulgar throng;
Nor do I to the upper ranks belong;
But if through life I may your steps attend,
I will at once engage to be your friend.
I am your comrade; should it suit your need,
Your servant I, your very slave indeed!

FAUST.
And how must I requite your service, pray?

MEPHISTOPHELES.
There's time enough to think of that!

FAUST.
Nay! Nay!
The devil is an egotist I know;
And never for God's sake doth kindness show.
Let the condition plainly be exprest;
Such a domestic is a dangerous guest.

#### MEPHISTOPHELES.

I'll pledge myse.f to be your servant *here*,
Ne'er at your call to slumber or be still.;
But when together *yonder* we appear,
You shall submissively obey my will.

#### FAUST.

But small concern I feel for yonder world,
Hast thou this system into ruin hurl'd,
Another may arise the void to fill.
This earth the fountain whence my pleasures flow,
This sun doth daily shine upon my woe,
And can I but from these divorce my lot,
Then come what may,—to me it matters not.
Henceforward to this theme I close mine ears,
Whether hereafter we shall hate and love,
And whether, also, in those distant spheres,
There is a depth below or height above.

#### MEPHISTOPHELES.

In this mood you may venture it.   But make
The compact, and at once I'll undertake
To charm you with mine arts.   I'll give you more
Than mortal eye hath e'er beheld before.

#### FAUST.

And what, poor devil, hast thou to bestow?
Was mortal spirit, in its high endeavour,
E'er fathom'd by a being such as thou?
Yet food thou hast which satisfieth never,
Red gold indeed thou hast, that swiftly flies,
Gliding like restless quicksilver away,
A game, at which none ever win who play,
A damsel, who, while on my breast she lies,
To lure a neighbour fondly doth essay;
Thine, too, ambition's bright and godlike dream,
Baseless and transient as the meteor's gleam;
Show me the fruits that, ere they're pluck'd, decay,
And trees whose verdure buddeth every day.

#### MEPHISTOPHELES.

Such a demand affrights me not;  with ease
I can provide you treasures such as these,
But in due course a season will come round,
When on what's good we may regale in peace.

FAUST.

If e'er in indolent repose I'm found,
Then let my life upon the instant cease!
Can'st thou thy flatt'ring spells around me cast,
And cheat me into self-complacent pride,
Or sweet enjoyment,—Be that hour my last!
Be this our wager!

MEPHISTOPHELES.

Done!

FAUST.

   "Tis ratified!
If ever to the passing hour I say
" So beautiful thou art! thy flight delay!"
Then round my soul thy fetters throw,
Then to perdition let me go!
Then may the solemn death-bell sound,
Then from thy service thou art free,
The index-hand may cease its round,
And time be never more for me!

MEPHISTOPHELES.

We shall remember, pause, ere 'tis too late.

FAUST.

You're authoriz'd to do so if you choose,
My strength I do not rashly overrate.
Since here to be a slave I'm doom'd by fate,
It matters little whether thine or whose.

MEPHISTOPHELES.

At your inaugural feast this very day,
I will attend, my duties to commence.
But one thing!—Accidents may happen, hence
A line or two in writing grant I pray.

FAUST.

A writing, pedant, dost demand from me?
Is man, and is man's word to thee unknown?
Is't not enough that by my word alone
I pledge my interest in eternity?
Raves not the world in all its streams along,
And must a promise my career impede?
Yet in our hearts the prejudice is strong,
And who from the delusion would be freed?
How blest within whose bosom truth reigns pure,

E 2

No sacrifice will he repent when made!
A formal deed, with seal and signature,
A spectre this from which all shrink afraid.
The word resigns its essence in the pen,
Leather and wax usurp the mast'ry then.—
Spirit of evil! what dost thou require?
Brass, marble, parchment, paper?   Shall I use
Style, pen, or graver?   Name which you desire.
Tc me it matters not, you've but to choose!

MEPHISTOPHELES.

With passion why so hotly burn,
And thus your eloquence inflame?
The merest scrap will serve our turn,
And with a drop of blood you'll sign your name.

FAUST.

If this will satisfy you, well and good!
I'll gratify your whim, howe'er absurd!

MEPHISTOPHELES.

A quite peculiar sort of juice is blood!

FAUST.

Be not afraid that I shall break my word.
The present scope of all my energy,
Is in exact accordance with my vow.
With vain presumption I've aspir'd too high;
I'm on a level but with such as thou;
I am rejected by the great First Cause,
Nature herself doth veil from me her laws;
Rent is the web of thought, my mind
Doth knowledge loathe of every kind.
In depths of sensual pleasure drown'd,
Let us our fiery passions still!
Enwrapp'd in magic's veil profound,
Let wondrous charms our senses thrill!
Plunge we in time's tempestuous flow,
Stem we the rolling surge of chance!
There may alternate weal and woe,
Success and failure, as they can,
Mingle and shift in changeful dance,
Excitement is the sphere for man.

MEPHISTOPHELES.

Nor goal, nor measure is prescrib'd to you.

If you desire to taste of every thing,
To snatch at pleasure while upon the wing,
May your career amuse and profit too.
Only fall to and don't be over coy!

FAUST.

Hearken!   The end I aim at is not joy.
I crave excitement, agonizing bliss,
Enamour'd hatred, quickening vexation.
Purg'd from the love of knowledge, my vocation,
The scope of all my powers henceforth be this,
To bare my breast to every pang,—to know
In my heart's core all human weal and woe,
To grasp in thought the lofty and the deep,
Men's various fortunes on my breast to heap,
To their's dilate my individual mind,
And share at length the shipwreck of mankind.

MEPHISTOPHELES.

Oh, credit me, who still as ages roll,
Have chew'd this bitter fare from year to year,
No mortal, from the cradle to the bier,
Digests the ancient leaven.   Know, this Whole
Doth for the Deity alone subsist!
He in eternal brightness doth exist,
Us unto darkness he hath brought, and here
Where day and night alternate, is your sphere.

FAUST.

But 'tis my will!

MEPHISTOPHELES.
                  Well spoken, I admit!
There is but one thing puzzles me, my friend;
Time's short, art long; methinks 't were only fit,
That you to friendly counsel should attend.
A poet choose as your ally,
Let him thought's wide dominion sweep,
Each good and noble quality,
Upon your honour'd brow to heap;
The lion's magnanimity,
The fleetness of the hind,
The fiery blood of Italy,
The Northern's firm enduring mind.

Let him for you the mystery solve, and show
How to combine high aims with cunning low,
And how, while young desires the heart inflame,
To fall in love according to a plan.
Myself would gladly meet with such a man.
And him I would Sir Microcosm name.

FAUST.

What then am I, if I may never hope
The crown of our humanity to gain,
Of all our energies the final scope?

MEPHISTOPHELES.

Your own poor self you are, and must remain.
Put on your head a wig with countless locks,
Raise to a cubit's height your learned socks,
To more than now you are you'll ne'er attain.

FAUST.

I feel it, I have heap'd upon my brain
The gather'd treasure of man's thought in vain,
And when at length from studious toil I rest,
No power, new-born, springs up within my breas?
A hair's breadth is not added to my height,
I am no nearer to the infinite.

MEPHISTOPHELES.

These matters, sir, you view, indeed,
Just as by other men they're view'd;
We must more cleverly proceed,
Before life's joys our grasp elude.
The devil! thou hast hands and feet,
And head and heart are also thine;
What I enjoy with relish sweet,
Is it on that account less mine?
If for six horses I can pay,
Do I not own their strength and speed?
A proper man I dash away,
As their two dozen legs were mine indeed
Up then, from idle pond'ring free,
And forth into the world with me!
I tell you what;—a speculating wretch,
Is like a brute, on bare, uncultur'd ground,
Driv'n by an evil spirit round and round,
While all beyond rich pastures smiling stretch.

FAUST.

But how commence?
MEPHISTOPHELES.
Why we with speed
Must leave this place of torture; you
A precious life of it must lead,
Tiring yourself and pupils too!
Leave it to neighbour Paunch;—withdraw,
Why plague yourself with thrashing straw?
The very best of what you know
You dare not to the youngsters show.
One in the passage waits to-day.
FAUST.
I'm in no mood to see him now.
MEPHISTOPHELES.
Poor lad!   He must be tir'd, I trow;
Hopeless he must not go away.
Hand me your cap and gown, I pray;
Now leave it to my wit;—the mask
Will suit me famously,—

(He changes his dress.)

I ask
But quarter of an hour; meanwhile equip,
And make all ready for our pleasant trip!

(Exit FAUST.)

MEPHISTOPHELES (in FAUST'S long gown).
Reason and Knowledge only thus contemn,
Despise the loftiest attributes of men,
Still let the Prince of lies, without control,
With shows, and mocking charms, delude thy soul,
I have thee unconditionally then—
Fate hath endow'd him with an ardent mind,
Which unrestrain'd still presses on for ever,
And whose precipitate and mad endeavour
O'erleaps itself, and leaves earth's joys behind.
Him will I drag along through life's wild waste,
Through scenes of vapid dulness, where at last
Bewilder'd, he shall falter, and stick fast;
And, as in mock'ry of his greedy haste,
Viands shall hang his craving lips beyond,—
Vainly he'll seek refreshment, anguish-tost,

And were he not the devil's by his bond,
Yet must his soul infallibly be lost!
*A* Student *enters.*
STUDENT.

But recently I've quitted home,
Full of devotion am I come,
Attracted hither by the fame
Of one whom all with rev'rence name.
MEPHISTOPHELES

Your courtesy much flatters me!
A man like other men you see;
Pray have you yet applied elsewhere?
STUDENT.

I would entreat your friendly care!
I've youthful blood and courage high;
Of gold I bring a fair supply;
My mother scarce would let me go;
But wisdom here I longed to know.
MEPHISTOPHELES.

You've hit upon the very place.
STUDENT.

And yet my steps I'd fain retrace.
These walls, this melancholy room,
O'erpower me with a sense of gloom.
The space is narrow, nothing green,
No friendly tree is to be seen;
And in these halls, the powers of sense
Forsake me, and intelligence.
MEPHISTOPHELES.

It all depends on habit.   Thus at first
The infant takes not kindly to the breas
But soon delighted slakes its eager thirst,
To the maternal bosom fondly prest.
Thus at the breasts of wisdom day by day
With keener relish you'll your thirst allay.
STUDENT.

Enraptur'd I upon her neck will fall;
How to attain it, Sir, be pleas'd to show.
MEPHISTOPHELES.

Ere further you proceed, just let me know,
What faculty you choose, and what your call

### STUDENT.

Profoundly learned I should wish to grow,
What heaven contains I'd comprehend.
O'er earth's wide realm my gaze extend,
Nature and science I desire to know.

### MEPHISTOPHELES.

You are upon the proper track I find;
Take heed that nothing dissipates your mind.

### STUDENT.

My heart and soul are in the chase;
Though to be sure I fain would seize
On pleasant summer holidays,
A little liberty and careless ease.

### MEPHISTOPHELES.

Waste not your time, so fast it flies;
Method will teach you time to win;
Hence, my young friend, I would advise,
With college logic to begin.
Then will your mind be so well brac'd,
In Spanish boots so tightly lac'd,
That on 'twill circumspectly creep,
Thought's beaten track securely keep,
Nor will it, ignis-fatuus like,
Into the path of error strike.
Then many a day they'll teach you how
The mind's spontaneous acts, till now
As eating and as drinking free,
Require a process;—one, two, three!
In truth the subtle web of thought
Is like the weaver's fabric wrought,
One treadle moves a thousand lines,
Swift dart the shuttles to and fro.
Unseen the threads unnumber'd flow,
A thousand knots one stroke combines.
Then forward steps your sage to show,
And prove to you it must be so;
The first being so, and so the second,
The third and fourth deduc'd we see;
And if there were no first and second,
Nor third nor fourth would ever be.

This, scholars of all countries prize,
Yet 'mong themselves no weavers rise,
Who would describe and study aught alive
Seeks first the living spirit thence to drive,
Then are the lifeless fragments in his hand,
There only fails, alas! the spirit-band.
This process, chemists name, in learned thesis
Mocking themselves, *Naturæ encheiresis.*

STUDENT.

Your words I cannot fully comprehend.

MEPHISTOPHELES.

In a short time you will improve, my friend,
If of scholastic forms you learn the use;
And how by method all things to reduce.

STUDENT.

I feel, so doth all this my brain confound,
As if a mill-wheel there were turning round.

MEPHISTOPHELES.

And next to this, before aught else you learn,
You must with zeal to metaphysics turn!
There see that you profoundly comprehend,
What doth the limit of man's brain transcend;
For that which is or is not in the head
A sounding phrase will serve you in good stead:
But before all strive this half year
From one fix'd order ne'er to swerve.
Five lectures daily you must hear;
The hour still punctually observe!
Yourself with studious zeal prepare,
And every paragraph o'erlook,
That you may then be quite aware
He never deviates from the book;
Yet write away without cessation,
As at the Holy Ghost's dictation!

STUDENT.

This, Sir, a second time you need not say!
Your prudent counsel I appreciate quite;
For, what we've written down in black and white
We can in peace and comfort bear away.

MEPHISTOPHELES.
But a profession I entreat you name.
STUDENT.
For jurisprudence I've no taste, I own.
MEPHISTOPHELES.
To me this branch of science is well known,
And hence I cannot your repugnance blame.
Laws are a fatal heritage,—
Like a disease, an heir-loom dread;
Their curse they trail from age to age,
And furtively abroad they spread.
Reason doth nonsense, good doth evil grow;
That thou'rt a grandson is thy woe!
But of the law on man impress'd
By nature's hand, there's ne'er a thought.

STUDENT.
You deepen my dislike; how blest
The pupil who by you is taught!
To try theology I'm half inclin'd.

MEPHISTOPHELES.
I would not lead you willingly astray,
But as regards this science you will find,
'Tis difficult to shun the erring way,
It offers so much poison in disguise,
Which scarce from med'cine you can recognize.
Here too, 'tis best to listen but to one,
And by the master's words to swear alone.
To sum up all—To words hold fast!
Then the safe gate securely pass'd,
You'll reach the fane of certainty at la

STUDENT.
But then some meaning must the words convey.
MEPHISTOPHELES.
Right!  But o'er-anxious thought's of no avail;
For there precisely where ideas fail,
A word comes opportunely into play.
Most admirable weapons words are found,
On words a system we securely ground,
In words we can conveniently believe,
Nor can we of one jot a word bereave.

       STUDENT.

Your pardon for my importunity;
With but one more request I'll trouble you
Ere I retire, I'll thank you to supply
A pregnant utt'rance touching med'cine too .
Three years! how brief the appointed tide!
The field, heaven knows, is all too wide!
If but a friendly hint be thrown,
'Tis easier then to feel one's way.

      MEPHISTOPHELES (*aside*).

I'm weary of this dry pedantic tone,
And must again the genuine devil play.

       (*Aloud.*)

Of med'cine you the spirit catch with ease;
The great and little world you study thro',
Then in conclusion, just as heaven may please,
You let things quietly their course pursue;
In vain you range through science' ample space
Each man learns only that which learn he can;
Who knows the passing moment to embrace,
He is your proper man.
In person you are tolerably made,
Nor in assurance will you be deficient,
Self-confidence acquire, be not afraid,
The world will then esteem you a proficien
Learn how to treat the sex, of that be sure;
Their thousand ahs and ohs
The sapient doctor knows,
He from a single point alone can cure.
Assume a decent tone of courteous ease,
You have them then to humour as you please.
First a diploma must belief infuse,
That you in your profession take the lead;
You then at once those easy freedoms use,
For which another many a year must plead;
Learn how to feel with nice address
The dainty wrist;—and how to press,
With furtive glance, the slender waist,
To feel how tightly it is lac'd.

       STUDENT.

'There's sense in that ! one sees the how and why.

**MEPHISTOPHELES.**

Grey is, young friend, all theory;
And green of life the golden tree.

**STUDENT.**

I swear it seemeth like a dream to me.
May I some future time repeat my visit,
To hear on what your rev'rence grounds your views?

**MEPHISTOPHELES.**

Command my humble service when you choose

**STUDENT.**

Ere I retire, one boon I must solicit:
Here is my album, do not, Sir, deny
This token of your favour.

**MEPHISTOPHELES.**

    Willingly.
        (*He writes and returns the book.*)

**STUDENT** (*reads*).

ERITIS SICUT DEUS, SCIENTES BONUM ET MALUM.

    (*He reverently closes the book and retires* )

**MEPHISTOPHELES.**

Let but this ancient proverb be your rule,
My cousin follow still, the wily snake,
And with your likeness to the gods, poor fool,
Ere long be sure your poor sick heart will quake!

**FAUST** (*enters*).

Whither away?

**MEPHISTOPHELES.**

    'Tis your's our course to steer.
The world, both great and small, we'll view;
With what delight and profit too,
You'll revel through your gay career !

**FAUST.**

But with my length of beard I also need
The easy manners that insure success;
Th' attempt I'm certain never can succeed;
To mingle in the world I want address;
I still have an embarrass'd air, and then
I feel myself so small with other men.

**MEPHISTOPHELES.**

Time, my good friend, will all that's needful give;
Gain self-reliance, and you've learn'd to live.

**FAUST.**

But how do you propose to start, I pray?
Your horses, servants, carriage, where are they?

**MEPHISTOPHELES.**

We've but to spread our mantles wide,
They'll serve whereon through air to ride.
No heavy baggage need you take,
When we our bold excursion make.
A little gas which I'll prepare
Lifts us from earth; aloft through air
Light laden, we shall swiftly steer ;—
I wish you joy of your new life-career.


*Auerbach's Cellar in Leipzig.*

(A DRINKING PARTY.)

FROSCH.

No drinking?   Nought a laugh to raise?
None of your gloomy looks, I pray!
You, who so bright were wont to blaze,
Are dull as wetted straw to-day.

BRANDER.

'Tis all your fault; no part you bear,
No beastliness, no folly.

FROSCH

*(pours a glass of wine over his head).*
         There,

You have them both !

BRANDER.

         You double beast !

FROSCH.

'Tis what you ask'd me for, at least !

SIEBEL.

Whoever quarrels, turn him out !
With open throat drink, roar, and shout.
Hollo !  Hollo !  Ho !

ALTMAYER.

Zounds, fellow, cease your deaf'ning cheer:
Bring cotton here !   He splits my ears.

SIEBEL.

'Tis when the roof rings back the tone,
The full power of the bass is known.

FROSCH.

Right ! out with him who takes offence !
A tara lara la !

ALTMAYER.

A tara lara la !

FROSCH.

Our throats are tun'd.   Come let's commence.
(*Sings.*)
The holy Roman empire now,
How holds it still together ?

BRANDER.

An ugly song !   Psha ! a political song !
A song offensive !   Thank God, every morn
That you to rule the empire were not born !
I always bless my stars that mine is not
Either a kaiser's or a chancellor's lot.
Yet 'mong ourselves one still should rule the rest :
That we elect a pope I now suggest.
What qualifies a man for consecration
Ye know, and what ensures his elevation.

FROSCH (*sings*).
Bear, lady nightingale above,
Ten thousand greetings to my love
SIEBEL.

No amorous trash !   No greetings shall there be !
FROSCH.

Greetings and kisses too !   Who'll hinder me ?
(*Sings.*)
Undo the bolt, in stilly night,
Undo the bolt, thy love's awake !
Shut to the bolt with morning light !

SIEBEL.

Ay, sing away, her praises celebrate !
My turn for laughing will come round some day.

She jilted me, you the same trick she'll play.
To have a goblin-lover be her fate,
To toy with her upon some lone cross-way!
Or fresh from Blocksberg, may an old he-goat
Send her a greeting from his hairy throat!
A proper lad of genuine flesh and blood,
Is for the saucy damsel far too good;
I'll in her honour hear of no love-strains,
Unless it be to smash her window-panes!

BRANDER (striking on the table).

Silence! Attend! to me give ear!
That I know, life you must admit;
Some love-sick folk are sitting here;
Hence, ere we part, it is but fit,
To sing them a good night their hearts to cheer,
Hark! of the newest fashion is my song!
Strike boldly in the chorus, clear and strong!

(He sings.)

  Once in a cellar lived a rat,
  He feasted there on butter,
  Until his paunch became as fat
  As that of Dr. Luther.
  The cook laid poison for the guest,
  Then was his heart with pangs oppress'd,
  As if his frame love wasted.

CHORUS (shouting).

  As if his frame love wasted.

BRANDER.

  He ran around, he ran abroad,
  Of every puddle drinking,
  The house with rage he scratch'd and gnaw'd,
  In vain,—he fast was sinking;
  Full many an anguish'd bound he gave,
  Nothing the hapless brute could save,
  As if his frame love wasted.

CHORUS.

  As if his frame love wasted.

BRANDER.

  By torture driven, in open day,
  The kitchen he invaded,
  Convuls'd upon the hearth he lay

With anguish sorely jaded;
The poisoner laugh'd, Ha! ha! quoth she,
His life is ebbing fast, I see,
As if his frame love wasted.

CHORUS.

As if his frame love wasted.

SIEBEL.

How the dull boors exulting shout!
A fine exploit it is no doubt,
Poison for the poor rats to strew!

BRANDER.

They, as it seems, stand well with you!

ALTMAYER.

Old bald-pate! with the paunch profound!
The rat's mishap hath tam'd his nature;
For he his counterpart hath found
Depicted in the swoll'n creature.

FAUST AND MEPHISTOPHELES.

MEPHISTOPHELES.

I now must introduce to you
Before aught else, this jovial crew,
To show how lightly life may glide away;
With them each day's a holiday.
With little wit and much content,
Each on his own small round intent,
Like sportive kitten with its tail,
While no sick-headache they bewail,
And while their host will credit give,
Joyous and free from care they live.

BRANDER.

They're off a journey, that is clear,—
They look so strange; they've scarce been here
An hour.

FROSCH.

You're right! Leipzig's the place for me.
'Tis quite a little Paris; people there
Acquire a certain, easy, finish'd air.

SIEBEL.

What take you now these travellers to be?

FROSCH.

Let me alone!  O'er a full glass you'll see,
As easily I'll worm their secret out,
As draw an infant's tooth.  I've not a doubt
That my two gentlemen are nobly born,
They look dissatisfied, and full of scorn.

BRANDER.

They are but mountebanks, I'll lay a bet!

ALTMAYER.

Most like.

FROSCH.

Mark me, I'll screw it from them yet!

MEPHISTOPHELES (*to* FAUST).

These fellows would not scent the devil out,
E'en though he had them by the very throat.

FAUST.

Your humble servant, gentlemen!

SIEBEL.

Thanks, we return your fair salute.

(*Aside, glancing at* MEPHISTOPHELES.)

How! goes the fellow on a halting foot?

MEPHISTOPHELES.

Are we allow'd to sit among you?  Then,
Though no good liquor is forthcoming here,
Good company at least our hearts will cheer.

ALTMAYER.

You're a fastidious gentleman, 'tis clear.

FROSCH.

You're doubtless recently from Rippach?  Pray,
Did you with Mr. Hans there chance to sup?

MEPHISTOPHELES.

To-day we pass'd him, but we did not stop!
When last we spoke with him he'd much to say
Touching his cousins, and to each he sent
Full many a greeting and kind compliment.

(*With an inclination towards* FROSCH).

ALTMAYER     (*aside to* FROSCH).

You have it there!

SIEBEL.

Faith! he's a knowing one!

FROSCH.
Have patience!   I will show him up anon!
MEPHISTOPHELES.
Unless I err, as we drew near
We heard some practis'd voices pealing.
A song must admirably here
Re-echo from this vaulted ceiling!
FROSCH.
That you're an amateur one plainly sees!
MEPHISTOPHELES.
Oh no, though strong the love, I lack the skill.
ALTMAYER.
Give us a song!
MEPHISTOPHELES.
As many as you will.
SIEBEL.
But let it be a new one, if you please!

MEPHISTOPHELES.
But just return'd from beauteous Spain are we,
The pleasant land of wine and minstrelsy.

(*Sings.*)
Once on a time a monarch
Possess'd a splendid flea.

FROSCH.
Hark! did you catch the words? a flea,—
An odd sort of a guest he needs must be.
MEPHISTOPHELES (*sings*).
Once on a time a monarch
Possess'd a splendid flea,
The which he fondly cherish'd,
As his own son were he!
His tailor then he summon'd,
The tailor to him goes:
Now measure me the youngster
For breeches and for hose!
BRANDER.
Let him the tailor strictly charge,
The nicest measurement to take,
And as he loves his head, to make
The breeches smooth and not too large!

MEPHISTOPHELES.

In satin and in velvet,
Behold the younker dress'd;
Bedizen'd o'er with ribbons,
A cross upon his breast.
Prime minister they made him,
He wore a star of state;
And all his poor relations
Were courtiers, rich and great.

The gentlemen and ladies
At court were sore distress'd;
The queen and all her maidens
Were bitten by the pest,
And yet they dar'd not scratch them,
Or chase the fleas away.
If we are bit, we catch them
And crush without delay.

CHORUS                    *(shouting)*.

If we are bit, &c.

FROSCH.

Bravo!   That's the song for me!

SIEBEL.

Such be the fate of every flea!

BRANDER.

With clever finger catch and kill!

ALTMAYER.

Hurrah for wine and freedom still!

MEPHISTOPHELES.

Were but your wine a trifle better, friend,
A glass to liberty I'd gladly drain.

SIEBEL.

You'd better not repeat those words again!

MEPHISTOPHELES.

I am afraid the landlord to offend;
Else freely would I treat each worthy guest
From our own cellar to the very best.

SIEBEL.

Out with it then!   Lay all the blame on me.

FROSCH.

Give a good glass, and loud our praise shall be;
But hark'ye, to the brim our glasses crown,

For if a judgment is requir'd from me,
An ample mouthful I must swallow down.

ALTMAYER (*aside*).

I guess, they're from the Rhenish land.

MEPHISTOPHELES.

Fetch me a gimlet!

BRANDER.

What therewith to bore?
You cannot have the wine-casks at the door?

ALTMAYER.

A tool-chest of our host doth yonder stand.

MEPHISTOPHELES (*takes the gimlet*)

(*To* FROSCH.)

Now say! what liquor will you take?

FROSCH.

How mean you? have you every sort?

MEPHISTOPHELES.

Each may his own selection make.

ALTMAYER (*to* FROSCH).

You lick your lips already at the thought.

FROSCH.

If I've my choice, the Rhenish I propose;
The fairest gifts the fatherland bestows.

MEPHISTOPHELES

(*boring a hole in the edge of the table opposite to where*
FROSCH *is sitting*).

Now get some wax—and make some stoppers—quick!

ALTMAYER.

Why this is nothing but a juggler's trick.

MEPHISTOPHELES (*to* BRANDER).

And you?

BRANDER.

Champagne's the wine for me;
Right brisk, and sparkling let it be!

(MEPHISTOPHELES *bores, one of the party has in the
meantime prepared the wax-stoppers and stopped
the holes.*)

BRANDER.

Your foreign things one always can't decline,

What's good is often scatter'd far apart.
A German hates the French with all his heart.
Yet still he has a relish for their wine.

SIEBEL
(as MEPHISTOPHELES approaches him)

I like not acid wine, I must allow,
Give me a glass of genuine sweet!

MEPHISTOPHELES      (bores).
Tokay

Shall, if you wish it, flow without delay.

ALTMAYER.

Come! look me in the face! no fooling now!
You are but making fun of us, I trow.

MEPHISTOPHELES.

Ah! ah! that would indeed be making free
With such distinguished guests.   Come, no delay;
What liquor can I serve you with, I pray?

ALTMAYER.

Only be quick, it matters not to me.
(After the holes are all bored and stopped)

MEPHISTOPHELES      (with strange gestures).

Grapes the vine-stock bears!<br>
Horns the buck-goat wears,<br>
Wine is sap, the vine is wood,<br>
The table yieldeth wine as good.<br>
With a deeper glance and true<br>
The mysteries of nature view!<br>
Have faith and here's a miracle!<br>

Your stoppers draw and drink your fill!

ALL
(as they draw the stoppers and the wine chosen by each<br>
runs into his glass).

Oh beauteous spring, which flows so fair!

MEPHISTOPHELES.

Spill not a single drop, beware!      (They drink repeatedly.)

ALL      (sing).

Happy as cannibals are we,<br>
Or as five hundred swine.

MEPHISTOPHELES.

They're in their glory, mark their elevation!

FAUST.

Let's hence, nor here our stay prolong.

MEPHISTOPHELES.

Attend, of brutishness ere long
You'll see a glorious revelation.

SIEBEL

*(drinks carelessly; the wine is spilt upon the ground, and
turns to flame).*

Help! fire, help!   Hell is burning here!

MEPHISTOPHELES

*(addressing the flames).*

Peace, friendly element!   Be still, I say!
*(To the Company.)*
A drop of purgatory! never fear!

SIEBEL.

What means the knave!   For this you'll dearly pay;
With whom you're dealing, Sir, you do not know.

FROSCH.

Such tricks a second time he'd better show!

ALTMAYER.

'Twere well we pack'd him quietly away.

SIEBEL.

What, sir! with us your hocus-pocus play!

MEPHISTOPHELES.

Silence, old wine-cask!

SIEBEL.

How! add insult, too!

Vile broomstick!

BRANDER.

Hold! or blows shall rain on you!

ALTMAYER

*(Draws a stopper out of the table; fire springs out
against him).*

I burn! I burn!

SIEBEL.

'Tis sorcery, I vow!
Strike home!   The fellow is fair game, I trow!

*(They draw their knives and attack* MEPHISTOPHELES.)
MEPHISTOPHELES *(with solemn gestures).*

Visionary scenes appear!
Words delusive cheat the ear!
Be ye there, and be ye here!

*(They stand amazed and gaze on each other.)*
ALTMAYER.
Where am I?  What a beauteous land?
FROSCH.
Vineyards! unless my sight deceives?
SIEBEL.
And clust'ring grapes too, close at hand!
BRANDER.
And underneath the spreading leaves,
What stems there be!
What grapes I see!

*(He seizes* SIEBEL *by the nose.   The others reciprocally
do the same, and raise their knives.)*

MEPHISTOPHELES   *(as above).*
Delusion, from their eyes the bandage take!
Note how the devil loves a jest to break!
*(He disappears with* FAUST; *the fellows draw back from
one another.)*
SIEBEL.
What was it?

ALTMAYER.
How?

FROSCH.
Was that your nose?
BRANDER *(to* SIEBEL).
And look, my hand doth thine enclose!
ALTMAYER.
I felt the shock through every limb!
A chair! I'm fainting!   All things swim!
FROSCH.
Say what has happen'd, what's it all about
SIEBEL.
Where is the fellow?   Could I scent him out,
His body from his soul I'd soon divide!

ALTMAYER.

With my own eyes, upon a cask astride,
Forth through the cellar-door I saw him ride——
Like lumps of lead my feet are growing.
(*Turning to the table.*)

I wonder, is the wine still flowing?

SIEBEL.

'Twas all a cheat, our senses to deceive.

FROSCH.

Yet I made sure that I was drinking wine

BRANDER.

How was it with the grapes and with the vine?

ALTMAYER.

Who miracles henceforth will disbelieve?


## WITCHES' KITCHEN.

*A large caldron hangs over the fire on a low hearth; various figures appear in the flames rising from it. A* FEMALE MONKEY *sits beside the caldron to skim it, and watch that it does not boil over. The* MALE MONKEY *with the young ones is seated near, warming himself. The walls and ceiling are adorned with the strangest articles of witch-furniture.*


## FAUST, MEPHISTOPHELES.

FAUST.

This senseless, juggling witchcraft I detest;
Dost promise me, forsooth, that in this nest
Of loathsome madness, I shall be restor'd?
Must I seek counsel from an ancient dame?
And can she cancel, by these rites abhorr'd
Full thirty winters, and renew my frame?
Woe's me, if thou nought better can'st suggest!
Hope has already vanish'd from my breast;
Has neither nature nor a noble mind
A balsam yet devis'd of any kind?

MEPHISTOPHELES.

My friend, you now speak sensibly. In tru'h,

There is one method of renewing youth;
But in another book the lesson's writ;—
It forms a curious chapter I admit.

FAUST.

I'd know it.

MEPHISTOPHELES.

Good! A natural means to try
Without physician, gold, or sorcery:
Away forthwith, and to the fields repair,
Begin to delve, to cultivate the ground,
Confine your senses to one narrow round,
Support yourself upon the simplest fare.
Live like a very brute the brutes among,
Esteem it neither robbery nor wrong,
The harvest, which you reap, yourself to dung.
This method, friend, believe me, will avail,
At eighty to continue young and hale!

FAUST.

I am not used to it, nor can degrade
So far my nature as to ply the spade.
For this mean life, my spirit soars too high.

MEPHISTOPHELES.

Then to the witch, we must perforce apply.

FAUST.

Will none but just this ancient beldame do?
Can'st not thyself the magic bev'rage brew?

MEPHISTOPHELES.

A pretty play our leisure to beguile!
A thousand bridges I could build meanwhile;
Not science only and consummate art,
Patience must in the process bear her part.
A quiet spirit worketh whole years long;
Time only makes the subtle ferment strong.
And all things that belong thereto,
Are wondrous and exceeding rare!
The devil taught her, it is true;
But yet the draught the devil can't prepare,

(*Perceiving the beasts.*)

Look yonder, what a pretty race!
Both lass and lad; in both what grace!

(*To the beasts.*)

It seems your dame is not at home?

THE MONKEYS.

Gone to carouse,
Out of the house,
Thro' the chimney and away !

MEPHISTOPHELES.

How long is it her wont to roam ?

THE MONKEYS.

While we can warm our paws she'll stay.

MEPHISTOPHELES  (*To* FAUST).

What think you of the charming creatures ?

FAUST.

I loathe alike their form and features !

MEPHISTOPHELES.

Nay. a discourse so exquisite,
Is that in which I most delight !

(*To* THE MONKEYS.)

Tell me, ye whelps, accursed crew !
What stir ye in the broth about ?

MONKEYS.

Coarse beggar's gruel here we stew.

MEPHISTOPHELES.

Of customers you'll have a rout.

THE HE-MONKEY
(*approaching and fawning on* MEPHISTOPHELES).

Quick ! quick ! throw the dice,
Make me rich in a trice,
Oh give me the prize !
Alas, for myself !
Had I plenty of pelf,
I then should be wise.

MEPHISTOPHELES.

How happy would the monkey be,
Could he put in the lottery !

(*In the meantime the young* MONKEYS *have been playing
with a large globe, which they roll forwards.)*

THE HE-MONKEY.

The world here behold ;
Unceasingly roll'd.
It riseth and falleth ever ;

It ringeth like glass!
How brittle, alas!
'Tis hollow, and resteth never
How bright the sphere,
Still brighter here!
Alive am I?
Dear son, beware!
Ne'er venture there!
Thou too must die!
It is of clay;
'Twill crumble away;
There fragments lie.

MEPHISTOPHELES.

Of what use is the sieve?

THE HE-MONKEY (*taking it down*).

The sieve would show,
If thou wert a thief or no?

(*He runs to the* SHE-MONKEY, *and makes her look
through it.*)

Look through the sieve!
Dost know him the thief,
And dar'st thou not call him so?

MEPHISTOPHELES (*approaching the fire*)

And then this pot?

THE MONKEYS.

The half-witted sot!
He knows not the pot!
He knows not the kettle!

MEPHISTOPHELES.

Unmannerly beast!
Be civil at least!

THE HE-MONKEY

Take the whisk and sit down in the settle:

(*He makes* MEPHISTOPHELES *sit down.*)

FAUST.

(*Who all this time has been standing before a looking-glass.
now approaching, and now retiring from it.*)
What do I see? what form, whose charms transcend
The loveliness of earth, is mirror'd here!
O Love, to waft me to her blissful sphere,
The swiftest of thy downy pinions lend!

If I remain not rooted to this place,
If to approach more near I'm fondly lur'd,
Her image fades, in veiling mist obscur'd.
Model of beauty both in form and face!
Is't possible?  Hath woman charms so rare?
Is that recumbent form, supremely fair,
The very essence of all heavenly grace?
Can aught so exquisite on earth be found?

MEPHISTOPHELES.

The six days' labour of a god, my friend,
Who doth himself cry bravo, at the end,
By something clever doubtless should be crown'd.
For this time gaze your fill, and when you please
Just such a prize for you I can provide;
How blest to whom propitious fate decrees,
To carry to his home the lovely bride!

(FAUST *continues to gaze into the mirror.* MEPHISTOPHELES
*stretching himself on the settle and playing with the whisk,*
*continues to speak.*)

Here I sit, like a monarch on his throne:
My sceptre this;—the crown I want alone.

THE MONKEYS

(*Who have hitherto been making all sorts of strange gestures,*
*bring* MEPHISTOPHELES *a crown, with loud cries*).

Oh,  e so good,
With sweat and with blood
The crown to lime!

(*They handle the crown awkwardly and break it in two pieces,*
*with which they skip about.*)

'Twas fate's decree!
We speak and see!
We hear and rhyme.

FAUST   (*before the mirror*).

Woe's me! well-nigh distraught I feel!

MEPHISTOPHELES
(*pointing to the beasts*).

And e'en my head begins to reel.

THE MONKEYS.

If good luck attend,
If fitly things blend

Our jargon with thought
And with reason is fraught!

FAUST   (*as above*).

Fire is kindl'd in my breast!
Let us begone! nor linger here!

MEPHISTOPHELES

(*in the same position*).

It now at least must be confess'd,
That poets sometimes are sincere.

  (*The caldron which the* SHE-MONKEY *has neglected,
   begins to boil over; a great flame arises, which
   streams up the chimney. The* WITCH *comes down
   the chimney with horrible cries.*)

THE WITCH.

Ough! ough! ough! ough!
Accursed brute! accursed sow!
Thou dost neglect the pot, for shame!
Accursed brute to scorch the dame!

  (*Perceiving* FAUST *and* MEPHISTOPHELES.)
  Whom have we here?
  Who's sneaking here?
  Whence are ye come?
  With what desire?
  The plague of fire
  Your bones consume!

  (*She dips the skimming-ladle into the caldron and
   throws flames at* FAUST, MEPHISTOPHELES, *and
   the* MONKEYS. *The* MONKEYS *whine.*)

MEPHISTOPHELES

  (*twirling the whisk which he holds in his hand, and
   striking among the glasses and pots*).

    Dash! Smash!
    Glasses crash!
    There lies the slime!
    'Tis but a jest,
    I but keep time
    Thou hellish pest
    To thine own chime.

(*While the* WITCH *steps back in rage and astonishment.*)
You skeleton! you scarecrow!   How!
Know you your lord and master now?
What should prevent my dashing you
To atoms, with your monkey-crew!
Have you for my red vest no more respect?
Does my cock's feather no allegiance claim?
Have I conceal'd my visage? recollect!
My rank must I be forc'd myself to name?
THE WITCH.
Master, forgive this rude salute!
But I perceive no cloven foot.
And your two ravens, where are they?
MEPHISTOPHELES.
This once I must admit your plea;—
For truly I must own that we
Have liv'd apart for many a day.
The culture, too, that shapes the world, at last
Hath e'en the devil in its sphere embrac'd;
The northern phantom from the scene hath pass'd,
Tail, talons, horns, are nowhere to be trac'd!
As for the foot, with which I can't dispense,
'Twould injure me in company, and hence,
Like some young gallants through the world who steer
False calves I now have worn for many a year.
THE WITCH (dancing).
I am beside myself with joy,
To see the gallant Satan here!
MEPHISTOPHELES.
Woman, no more that name employ!
THE WITCH.
But why? what mischief hath it done?
MEPHISTOPHELES.
To fable it too long hath appertain'd;
But people from the change have nothing won.
Rid of the evil one, the evil has remain'd.
Call me Lord Baron, so the matter's good;
Of other cavaliers the mien I wear.
You make no question of my gentle blood;
Mark well, this is the scutcheon that I bear!
(He makes an unseemly gesture.)

THE WITCH

*(laughing immoderately).*

Just like yourself!   You're still, I see,
The same mad wag you us'd to be!

MEPHISTOPHELES        (*to* FAUST).

My friend, learn this to understand, I pray!
To deal with witches this is still the way.

THE WITCH.

Now tell me, gentlemen, what you desire?

MEPHISTOPHELES.

Of your known juice a goblet we require.
But for the very oldest let me ask!
With years its virtue doubles, as you know.

THE WITCH.

Most willingly!   And here I have a flask,
From which I've sipp'd a drop myself ere now;
What's more, it doth no longer stink.
To you a glass I joyfully will give.

(*Aside.*)

If unprepar'd, however, this man drink,
He hath not, as you know, an hour to live.

MEPHISTOPHELES.

He's my good friend, with whom 'twill prosper well;
I grudge him not the choicest of your store.
Now draw your circle, speak your spell,
And straight a bumper for him pour!

> (*The* WITCH, *with extraordinary gestures, describes a
> circle, and places strange things within it.   The
> glasses meanwhile begin to ring, the caldron to
> sound, and to make music.   Lastly, she brings a
> great book; places the* MONKEYS *in the circle to
> serve her as a desk, and to hold the torches.   She
> beckons* FAUST *to approach.*)

FAUST        (*to* MEPHISTOPHELES).

Tell me, to what doth all this tend?
Where will these frantic gestures end?
This loathsome cheat, this senseless stuff
I've known and hated long enough.

**MEPHISTOPHELES.**

Mere mummery, a laugh to raise!
Pray don't be so fastidious!   She
But as a leech, her hocus-pocus plays,
That well with you her potion may agree.

*(He compels* FAUST *to enter the circle.)*

*(The* WITCH, *with a strange emphasis, begins to declaim from the book.)*

Be't known to men!
From one make ten,
And pass two o'er,
And lose the four,
Even make three—
So art thou rich.
Thus saith the witch,
To five affix
The number six,
Then you have straight
Made seven and eight,
And nine is one,
And ten is none,
This is the witch's one-time-one!

**FAUST.**

Like feverish raving sounds the witch's spell.

**MEPHISTOPHELES.**

There's yet much more to come, I know it well,
So the whole volume rings ; both time and pains
I've thrown away, in puzzling o'er its pages,
For downright contradiction still remains
Alike mysterious both to fools and sages.
Ancient the art and modern too, my friend.
'Tis still the fashion as it used to be,
Error instead of truth abroad to send
By means of three and one, and one and three.
'Tis ever taught and babbl'd in the schools.
Who'd take the trouble to dispute with fools ?
When words men hear, they usually believe,
That there must needs be something to conceive

**THE WITCH** *(continues).*

The lofty power
Of wisdom's dower,
From all the world conceal'd!                    G

Who thinketh not,
To him I wot,
Unsought it is reveal'd.

FAUST.

What nonsense doth the hag propound?
My brain it doth well-nigh confound.
A hundred thousand fools or more,
Her words in chorus seem to roar.

MEPHISTOPHELES.

Incomparable Sibyl cease, I pray!
Hand us your liquor without more delay.
And hark ye, to the brim the goblet crown
My friend he is, and need not be afraid;
Besides, he is a man of many a grade,
Who hath drunk deep already.

(*The* WITCH, *with many ceremonies, pours the liquor into
a cup; as* FAUST *lifts it to his mouth, a light
flame arises.*)

MEPHISTOPHELES.

Gulp it down
No hesitation!   It will prove
A cordial, and your heart inspire!
What! with the devil hand and glove,
And yet shrink back afraid of fire?

(*The* WITCH *dissolves the circle.* FAUST *steps out.*)

MEPHISTOPHELES.

Now forth at once! you must not rest.

WITCH.

And much, sir, may the liquor profit you!

MEPHISTOPHELES   (*to the* WITCH).

And if to pleasure you I aught can do;
Pray on Walpurgis mention your request.

WITCH.

Here is a song, sung o'er sometimes, you'll see
That 'twill a singular effect produce.

MEPHISTOPHELES   (*to* FAUST).

Come, quick, and let yourself be led by me;
You must perspire, in order that the juice
May penetrate your frame through every part
Your noble indolence you'll learn to prize,
And soon with ecstasy you'll recognize
How Cupid stirs and gambols in your heart.

FAUST.

Let me but gaze one moment in the glass!
Too lovely was that female form!

MEPHISTOPHELES.

Nay! nay.

A model which all women shall surpass,
In flesh and blood ere long you will survey.

(*Aside.*)

As works the draught, you presently shall greet
A Helen in each female form you meet.

## A Street.

FAUST.    (MARGARET *passing by.*)

FAUST.

Without offence, fair lady, may I dare
To offer you my arm and escort, pray?

MARGARET.

I am no lady and I am not fair,
Without an escort I can find my way.

(*She disengages herself and exit.*)

FAUST.

By heaven!  This girl is fair indeed!
No form like her's can I recall.
Virtue she hath, and modest heed,
Is piquant too, and sharp withal.
Her cheek's soft light, her rosy lips,
No length of time will e'er eclipse!
Her downward glance in passing by,
Deep in my heart is stamp'd for aye;
Her very anger charm'd me too,—
My ravish'd heart to rapture grew!

MEPHISTOPHELES    (*enters*).

FAUST.

This girl you must procure for me.

MEPHISTOPHELES.

Which?

FAUST.

She who but now pass'd.

MEPHISTOPHELES.

What!  She?

Straight from her priest she cometh here,
From every sin absolv'd and clear;
I crept near the confessor's chair,
All innocence her virgin soul,
For next to nothing went she there;
O'er such as she I've no control!

FAUST.

She's just fourteen.

MEPHISTOPHELES.
You really talk

Like any gay Lothario,
Who'd pluck each floweret from its stalk,
And deems nor honour, grace, or truth,
Secure against his arts, forsooth.
But this you'll find wont always do.

FAUST.

Sir Moralizer, prithee, pause;
Nor plague me with your tiresome laws.
To cut the matter short, my friend,
She must this very night be mine,—
And if to help me you decline,
Midnight shall see our compact end.

MEPHISTOPHELES.

What may occur just bear in mind!
A fortnight's space, at least, I need,
A fit occasion but to find.

FAUST.

With but seven hours I could succeed;
Nor should I want the devil's wile,
So young a creature to beguile.

MEPHISTOPHELES.

Like any Frenchman now you speak,
But do not fret, I pray; why seek
To hurry to enjoyment straight?
The pleasure is not half so great,
As when the interest to prolong
You trifle with your love, until
You mould the puppet to your will
As pictur'd in Italian song.

FAUST.

No such incentives do I need.

MEPHISTOPHELES.

But now, without offence or jest;
You cannot quickly, I protest,
In winning this sweet child succeed.
By storm we cannot take the fort,
To stratagem we must resort.

FAUST.

Conduct me to her place of rest!
Some token of the angel bring!
A 'kerchief from her snowy breast,
A garter bring me,—any thing!

MEPHISTOPHELES.

That I my anxious zeal may prove,
Your pangs to sooth and aid your love,
I will proceed without delay,
And bear you to her room away.

FAUST.

And shall I see her?—call her mine?

MEPHISTOPHELES.

No! at a friend's she'll be to-day;
But in her absence, I opine,
You in her atmosphere alone,
The tedious hours may well employ
In blissful dreams of future joy.

FAUST.

Can we go now?

MEPHISTOPHELES.

      'Tis yet too soon.

FAUST.

Some present for my love procure.      (*Exit.*)

MEPHISTOPHELES.

Presents so soon! 'tis well! success is sure.
I know full many a secret store
Of treasure, buried long before,
I must a little look them o'er.      (*Exit.*)

### *Evening.   A neat little Room.*

MARGARET
*(braiding and binding up her hair)*

I would give something now to know,
Who yonder gentleman could be!
He had a gallant air, I trow,
And doubtless was of high degree!
That from his noble brow I told,
Nor would he else have been so bold.          (*Exit.*)

MEPHISTOPHELES.
Come in! tread softly! be discreet!

FAUST   (*after a pause*).
Begone and leave me, I entreat!

MEPHISTOPHELES   (*looking round*).
Not every maiden is so neat.                   (*Exit.*)

FAUST   (*gazing round*).
Welcome sweet twilight-gloom which reigns,
Through this dim place of hallow'd rest!
Fond yearning love, inspire my breast,
Feeding on hope's sweet dew thy blissful pains.
What stillness here environs me!
Content and order brood around.
What fulness in this poverty!
In this small cell what bliss profound!

(*He throws himself on the leather arm-chair beside the bed.*)

Receive me! thou, who hast in thine embrace,
Welcom'd in joy and grief, the ages flown!
How oft the children of a by-gone race,
Have cluster'd round this patriarchal throne!
Haply, she, too, as closed each circling year,
For Christmas gift, with grateful joy possess'd
Hath with the full round cheek of childhood, here,
Her grandsire's wither'd hand devoutly press'd.
Maiden! I feel thy spirit haunt the place,
Breathing of order and abounding grace.
As with a mother's voice it prompteth thee,
Daily the cover o'er the board to spread,
To strew the crisping sand beneath thy tread.
Dear hand! so godlike in its ministry!
The hut becomes a paradise through thee!

And here!                    (*He raises the bed-curtain.*)
How thrills my pulse with strange delight!
Here I could linger hours untold;
Thou Nature! didst in vision bright,
The embryo angel here unfold.
Here lay the child, her bosom warm
With life, while steep'd in slumber's dew,
To perfect grace, her godlike form,
With pure and hallow'd weavings grew!

And thou! ah here, what seekest thou?
How is thine inmost being troubl'd now!
What would'st thou here? what makes thy heart so sore?
Unhappy Faust! I know thee now no more.

Do I a magic atmosphere inhale?
Erewhile, my passion would not brook delay!
Now in a pure love-dream I melt away.
Are we the sport of every passing gale?

Should she return and enter now,
How would'st thou rue thy guilty flame!
Proud vaunter! thou would'st hide thy brow,
And at her feet sink down with shame.

MEPHISTOPHELES.

Quick! quick! below I see her there!

FAUST.

Away! I will return no more!

MEPHISTOPHELES.

Here is a casket, with a store
Of jewels, which I got elsewhere.
Quick! place it here, her press within,
I swear to you 'twill turn her brain;
Another I had thought to win,
With the rich gems it doth contain,
But child is child, and play is play.

FAUST.

I know not—shall I?

MEPHISTOPHELES.

Do you ask?
Perchance you would retain the treasure?
If such your wish, why then, I say,
Henceforth absolve me from my task,
Nor longer waste your hours of leisure.

I trust you're not by avarice led!
I rub my hands, I scratch my head,—

   (*he places the casket in the press and closes the lock*)

But now away, without delay!—
The sweet young creature to your will to bend;
Yet here you are, as cold, my friend,
As to the class-room you would wend,
And metaphysics' form were there,
And physic too, with hoary hair!
Away!—         (*Exeunt.*)

  MARGARET (*with a lamp*).

Here 'tis so close, so sultry now,

    (*she opens the window.*)

Yet out of doors 'tis not so warm.
I feel so strange, I know not how—
I wish my mother would come home.
Through me there runs a shuddering—
I'm but a foolish timid thing!

   (*While undressing herself she begins to sing.*)

  There was a king in Thule,
  True even to the grave ·
  To whom his dying mistress
  A golden beaker gave.

  Beyond aught else he priz'd it,
  And drain'd its purple draught,
  His tears came gushing freely
  As often as he quaff'd.

  When death he felt approaching,
  His cities o'er he told;
  And grudg'd his heir no treasure
  Except his cup of gold.

  Girt round with knightly vassals
  At a royal feast sat he,
  In yon proud hall ancestral,
  In his castle o'er the sea.

  Up stood the jovial monarch,
  And quaff'd his last life's glow,
  Then hurl'd the hallow'd goblet
  In the ocean depths below.

He saw it splashing, drinking,
And plunging in the sea;
His eyes meanwhile were sinking,
And never more drank he.

*(She opens the press to put away her clothes, and
perceives the casket.)*

How came this casket here? I cannot guess!
'Tis very strange! I'm sure I lock'd the press.
What can be in it? perh'ps some pledge or other,
Left here for money borrow'd from my mother.
Here by a ribbon hangs a little key;
I have a mind to open it and see!
Heavens! only look! what have we here,
Ne'er saw I such a splendid sight!
Jewels a noble dame might wear,
For some high pageant richly dight.
I wonder how the chain would look on me,
And whose the brilliant ornaments may be?

*(She puts them on and steps before the glass.)*

Were but the ear-rings only mine!
Thus one has quite another air.
What boots it to be young and fair?
It doubtless may be very fine;
But then, alas, none come to woo,
And praise sounds half like pity too.

Gold all doth lure,
Gold doth secure
All things. Alas, the poor!

### *Promenade.*

*(*FAUST *walking thoughtfully up and down. To him*
MEPHISTOPHELES.*)*

MEPHISTOPHELES.

By love despis'd! By Hell's fierce fires I curse,
Would I could make my imprecation worse!

FAUST.

What ails you, pray? what chafes you now so sore?
A face like that I never saw before!

MEPHISTOPHELES.

I'd yield me to the devil instantly,
Did it not happen that myself am he!

FAUST.

There must be some disorder in your wit!
To rave thus like a madman, is it fit?

MEPHISTOPHELES.

Just think!   The gems for Margaret brought
A burly priest hath made his own!—
A glimpse of them the mother caught,
And 'gan with secret fear to groan.
The woman's scent is keen enough;
Still in the prayer book she doth snuff;
Smells everything to ascertain
Whether 'tis holy or profane,
And scented in the jewels rare,
That there was not much blessing there.
My child, she cries, ill-gotten good
Ensnares the soul, consumes the blood.
With them we'll deck our Lady's shrine,
She'll cheer our soul with bread divine!
At this poor Gretchen 'gan to pout,
'Tis a gift-horse, at least, she thought
And sure, he godless cannot be,
Who placed them there so cleverly.
A priest the mother then address'd,
Who when he understood the jest,
Survey'd the treasure with a smile.
Quoth he: " This shows a pious mind,
Who conquers, wins.   The Church we find
Hath a good stomach, she, erewhile,
Hath lands and kingdoms swallow'd down,
And never yet a surfeit known.
Daughters, the Church alone, with zest,
Can such ill-gotten wealth digest."

FAUST.

It is a general custom, too,
Practis'd alike by King and Jew.

MEPHISTOPHELES,

With that, clasp, chain, and ring, he swept
As they were mushrooms; and the casket,
Without one word of thanks he kept,
As if of nuts it were a basket.
Reward in heaven he promis'd fair;——
And greatly edified they were.

FAUST.

And Gretchen?

MEPHISTOPHELES.

In unquiet mood
Knows neither what she would nor should ;
The trinkets night and day thinks o'er,
On him who brought them dwells still more.

FAUST.

Her sorrow grieves me, I must say.
Another set of jewels bring!
The first, methinks, was no great thing.

MEPHISTOPHELES.

All's to my gentleman child's play !

FAUST.

Plan all things to achieve my end ;
Engage the attention of her friend.
To work !   A thorough devil be,
And bring fresh jewels instantly !

MEPHISTOPHELES.

Ay, sir!   Most gladly I'll obey.

(FAUST exit.)

MEPHISTOPHELES.

Your doting love-sick fool, with ease,
Merely his lady-love to please,
Sun, moon, and stars would puff away.                (Exit )


*The Neighbour's House.*

MARTHA   (alone).

God pardon my dear husband, he
Doth not in truth act well tow'rds me !
Forth in the world abroad to roam,
And leave me widow'd here at home.
And yet his will I ne'er did thwart,
God knows I lov'd him from my heart.

(She weeps.)

Perchance he's dead!—oh wretched state !—
Had I but a certificate !

MARGARET (comes).

MARGARET.

Dame Martha !

MARTHA.
Gretchen?
                    MARGARET.
                              Only think!
My knees beneath me well-nigh sink!
Within my press I've found to-day,
Another case of ebony.
And splendid jewels too there are,
More costly than the former, far.
                    MARTHA.
You must not name it to your mother;
It would to shrift, just like the other.
                    MARGARET.
Nay look at them! now  only see!
                    MARTHA          (dresses her up)
You happy creature!
                    MARGARET.
                              Woe is me!
I can't in them at church appear,
Nor in the street, nor any where.
                    MARTHA.
Come often over here to me,
And put them on quite privately.
Walk past the glass an hour or so,
Thus we shall have our pleasure too.
Then suitable occasions we must seize,
As at a feast, to show them by degrees.
A chain at first, then ear-drops,—and your mother
Won't see them, or we'll coin some tale or other.
                    MARGARET.
But who, I wonder, could the caskets bring?
I fear there's something wrong about the thing!      (a knock.)
Good heavens! can that my mother be?
                    MARTHA (peering through the blind).
No!   'Tis a stranger gentleman, I see.
Come in.
               MEPHISTOPHELES (enters).
               MEPHISTOPHELES.
      I've ventur'd to intrude to-day.
Ladies, excuse the liberty, I pray.
               (He steps back respectfully before MARGARET.)

For Mrs. Martha Schwerdtlein, I inquire!

MARTHA.

I'm she, pray what have you to say to me?

MEPHISTOPHELES (*aside to her*)

I know you now,—and therefore will retire;
At present you've distinguished company.
Pardon the freedom, Madam, with your leave,
I will make free to call again at eve.

MARTHA. (*aloud.*)

Why, child, of all strange things I ever knew!
The stranger for a lady taketh you.

MARGARET.

I am in truth of humble blood;
The gentleman is far too good;
Nor gems nor trinkets are my own.

MEPHISTOPHELES.

Oh 'tis not the mere ornaments alone;
Her glance and mien far more betray.
I am rejoic'd that I may stay.

MARTHA.

Your business, Sir? I long to know—

MEPHISTOPHELES.

Would I could happier tidings show!
But let me not my errand rue;
Your husband's dead, and greeteth you.

MARTHA.

Is dead? True heart! Oh misery!
My husband dead! Oh I shall die!

MARGARET.

Alas! good Martha! don't despair!

MEPHISTOPHELES.

Now listen to the sad affair!

MARGARET.

I for this cause should fear to love.
The loss my certain death would prove.

MEPHISTOPHELES.

Joy still must sorrow, sorrow joy attend.

MARTHA.

Proceed, and tell the story of his end?

MEPHISTOPHELES.

At Padua, in St. Anthony's,
In holy ground his body lies;
Quiet and cool his place of rest,
With pious ceremonials blest.

MARTHA.

And had you nought besides to bring?

MEPHISTOPHELES.

Oh yes! one grave and solemn prayer;
Let them for him three hundred masses sing!
But in my pockets, ma'am, I've nothing there.

MARTHA.

What! not a coin! no token from the dead!
Such as the meanest artisan will hoard,
Safe in his pouch, as a remembrance stor'd,
And not to part with, starves or begs his bread

MEPHISTOPHELES.

Madam, in truth, it grieves me much; but he
His money hath not squander'd lavishly.
Besides, his failings he repented sore,
Ay! and his evil plight bewail'd still more.

MARGARET.

That men should be so luckless!   Every day
I for his soul will many a requiem pray.

MEPHISTOPHELES.

Forthwith, to find a husband you deserve!
A child so lovely and in youth's fair prime.

MARGARET.

Oh no; to think of that there's ample time.

MEPHISTOPHELES.

A lover then, meanwhile, at least might serve.
Of heaven's best gifts, there's none more dear,
Than one so lovely to embrace.

MARGARET.

But that is not the custom here.

MEPHISTOPHELES.

Custom or not, such things take place.

MARTHA.

Proceed!

MEPHISTOPHELES.

I stood by his bedside.

'Twas rotten straw, something less foul than dung;
But at the last a Christian man he died.
And sorely hath remorse his conscience wrung.
" Wretch that I was," quoth he, with parting breath,
" So to forsake my business and my wife!
Ah! the remembrance of it is my death.
Could I but have her pardon in this life!"—

MARTHA      (weeping).

Dear soul! I've long forgiven him, indeed!

MEPHISTOPHELES.

" Though she, God knows, was more to blame than I."

MARTHA.

What, on the brink of death assert a lie!

MEPHISTOPHELES.

If I am skill'd the countenance to read,
He doubtless fabled as he parted hence.
" To gape for pleasure, I'd no time," he said,
" First to get children, and then get them bread ;
And bread, too, in the very widest sense;
In peace I could not even eat my share."

MARTHA.

What all my truth and love forgotten quite?
My weary drudgery by day and night!

MEPHISTOPHELES.

Not so!  He thought of you with tender care.
Quoth he: " Heaven knows how fervently I prayed,
For wife and children when from Malta bound;—
The prayer propitious heaven with favour crown'd;
We took a Turkish vessel which conveyed
Rich store of treasure for the Sultan's court;
It's own reward our gallant action brought.
The captur'd prize was shar'd among the crew,
And of the treasure I receiv'd my due."

MARTHA.

How?  Where? The treasure hath he buried, pray?

MEPHISTOPHELES.

Where the four winds have blown it, who can say?
In Naples as he stroll'd, a stranger there,—
A comely maid took pity on my friend;
And gave such tokens of her love and care,
That he retain'd them to his blessed end.

MARTHA.

Scoundrel! to rob his children of their bread!
And all this misery, this bitter need,
Could not his course of recklessness impede!

MEPHISTOPHELES.

Well, he hath paid the forfeit, and is dead.
Now were I in your place, my counsel hear;
My widow's weeds I'd wear for one chaste year,
And for another lover seek meantime.

MARTHA.

Alas, I might in vain search every clime,
Nor find another husband like my first!
There could not be a fonder fool at home,
Only he lik'd too well abroad to roam;
Lik'd women, too, and had for wine a thirst,
Besides his passion for those dice accurs'd.

MEPHISTOPHELES.

Well! well! all doubtless had gone swimmingly,
Had he but given you as wide a range.
And upon such condition, I declare,
Myself with you would gladly rings exchange!

MARTHA.

The gentleman is surely pleas'd to jest!

MEPHISTOPHELES       (*aside*).

Now to be off in time, methinks, were best!
She'd make the very devil marry her
                (*To* MARGARET.)
How fares it with your heart?

MARGARET.
              How mean you, Sir?

MEPHISTOPHELES       (*aside*).
The sweet young innocent!
                (*aloud.*)
                Ladies, farewell!

MARGARET.

Farewell!

MARTHA.
        But ere you leave us, quickly tell!
I much should like to have it certified,
Where, how, and when my buried husband died.
To forms I've always been attach'd indeed,
His death I fain would in the journals read.

MEPHISTOPHELES.

Ay, madam, when two witnesses appear
The truth is everywhere made manifest;
A gallant friend I have, not far from here,
Who will before the judge his death attest.
I'll bring him hither.

MARTHA.

Oh, I pray you do!

MEPHISTOPHELES.

And this young lady, we shall find her too?
A noble youth!—has travell'd far and wide,
And is most courteous to the sex beside.

MARGARET.

I in his presence needs must blush for shame.

MEPHISTOPHELES.

Not in the presence of a crownèd king!

MARTHA.

The garden, then, behind my house, we'll name,
There we'll await you both this evening.


*A Street.*

FAUST.    MEPHISTOPHELES.

FAUST.

How is it now? How speeds it? Is't in train?

MEPHISTOPHELES.

Bravo! I find you all on fire again?
Gretchen will soon be your's, I promise you;—
This very eve to meet her I've agreed
At neighbour Martha's, who seems fram'd indeed
The gipsy's trade expressly to pursue.

FAUST.

Good!

MEPHISTOPHELES.

But from us she something would request.

FAUST.

A favour claims return as this world goes.

MEPHISTOPHELES.

We have an oath but duly to attest,
That her dead husband's limbs, outstretch'd, repose
In holy ground at Padua.

FAUST.
Sage indeed!
So I suppose we straight must journey there '
MEPHISTOPHELES.
*Sancta simplicitas!* For that no need!
Without much knowledge we have but to swear
FAUST.
If you have nothing better to suggest,
Against your plan I must at once protest.

MEPHISTOPHELES.
Oh, holy man! methinks I have you there!
Is this the first time you false witness bear?
Have you not often definitions vain,
Of God, the world, and all it doth contain,
Man, and the working of his heart and brain,
In pompous language, forcibly express'd,
With front unblushing, and a dauntless breast?
Yet, if into the depth of things you go,
Touching these matters it must be confess'd
As much as of Herr Schwerdtlein's death you know
FAUST.
Liar and sophist, still thou wert and art.
MEPHISTOPHELES.
Perchance my view is somewhat more profound!
Now you yourself to-morrow, I'll be bound,
Will, in all honour, fool poor Margaret's heart,
And plead your soul's deep love, in lover's fashion.
FAUST.
And truly from my heart.
MEPHISTOPHELES.
All good and fair!
Then deathless constancy you'll doubtless swear;
Speak of one mast'ring, all-absorbing passion.—
Will that too issue from your heart?
FAUST.
Forbear!
When passion sways me, and I seek to frame
Fit utt'rance for my feeling, deep, intense,
And for my frenzy finding no fit name,
Sweep round the ample world with every sense,
Grasp at the loftiest words to speak my flame,

And call the fiery glow, wherewith I burn
Quenchless, undying,—yea, eterne, eterne,—
Is that of sophistry a devilish play?
                    MEPHISTOPHELES.
Yet am I right!

                    FAUST.
              Friend, spare my lungs, I pray;—
Mark this, who his opinion will maintain,
If he have but a tongue, his point will gain.
But come, of gossip I am weary quite,
Because I've no resource, you're in the right.


## Garden.

MARGARET *on* FAUST's *arm,* MARTHA *with* MEPHISTOPHELES
*walking up and down.*


                    MARGARET.
I feel it, you but spare my ignorance,
To put me to the blush you stoop thus low.
Travellers are ever wont from complaisance,
To make the best of things where'er they go
My humble prattle, surely never can
Have power to entertain so wise a man.
                    FAUST.
One glance, one word of thine doth charm me more,
Than the world's wisdom or the sage's lore.
                    (*He kisses her hand.*)

                    MARGARET.
Nay! trouble not yourself! how can you kiss
A hand so very coarse and hard as this!
What work am I not still oblig'd to do!
And then my mother's so exacting too.

                    (*They pass on.*)
                    MARTHA.
Thus are you ever wont to travel, pray?
                    MEPHISTOPHELES.
Duty and business urge us on our way;
Full many a place indeed we leave with pain,
At which we're not permitted to remain!

                              II 2

MARTHA.

In youth's wild years, with lusty vigour crown'd,
'Tis not amiss thus through the world to sweep;
But ah, the evil days at length come round,
And to the grave a bachelor to creep,
No one as yet hath good or pleasant found

MEPHISTOPHELES.

The distant prospect fills me with dismay.

MARTHA.

Therefore, in time, dear sir, reflect, I pray.

*(They pass on.)*

MARGARET.

Still are the absent out of mind, 'tis true!
Politeness is familiar, sir, to you,
But many friends you have, who doubtless are
More sensible than I, and wiser far.

FAUST.

My angel, often what doth pass for sense
Is self-conceit and narrowness.

MARGARET.

How so?

FAUST.

Simplicity and holy innocence,—
When will ye learn your hallow'd worth to know?
Ah, when will meekness and humility,
Kind and all-bounteous nature's loftiest dower—

MARGARET.

Only one little moment think of me,
To think of you I shall have many an hour.

FAUST.

You're doubtless much alone?

MARGARET.

Why yes, for though
Our household's small, yet I must see to it.
We keep no maid, and I must sew, and knit,
And cook and sweep, and hurry to and fro;
And then my mother is so accurate!
Not that for thrift there is such pressing need
Than others we might make more show indeed:
My father left behind a small estate,
A house and garden just outside the town.

Quiet enough my life has been of late.
My only brother for a soldier's gone;
My little sister's dead; the babe to rear
Occasion'd me some care and fond annoy;
But I would go through all again with joy,
The little darling was to me so dear.

FAUST.

An angel, sweet, if it resembled you!

MARGARET.

I reared it up, and soon my face it knew.
Dearly the little creature lov'd me too.
After my father's death it saw the day;
We gave my mother up for lost, she lay
In such a wretched plight, and then at length
So very slowly she regain'd her strength.
Weak as she was, 'twas vain for her to try
Herself to suckle the poor babe, so I
Rear'd it on bread and water all alone,
And thus the child became as 'twere my own.
Within my arms it stretch'd itself and grew,
And smiling, nestl'd in my bosom too.

FAUST.

Doubtless the purest happiness was your's.

MARGARET.

Oh yes—but also many weary hours.
Beside my bed at night its cradle stood,
If it but stirr'd, I was at once awake,
One while I was oblig'd to give it food,
Or with me into bed the darling take,
Then, if it would not hush, I had to rise,
And strive with fond caress to still its cries,
Pacing the little chamber to and fro;
And then at dawn to washing I must go,
See to the house affairs, and market too,
And so, from day to day, the whole year through.
Ah, sir, thus living, it must be confess'd
One's spirits are not always of the best;
But toil gives food and sleep a double zest.   (*They pass on.*)

MARTHA.

Poor women! we are badly off, I own:
A bachelor's conversion's hard, indeed!

MEPHISTOPHELES.

Madam, with one like you it rests alone,
To tutor me a better course to lead.

MARTHA.

But tell me! no one have you ever met?
Has your heart ne'er attach'd itself as yet?

MEPHISTOPHELES.

One's own fire-side, and a good wife, we're told
By the old proverb, are worth pearls and gold.

MARTHA.

I mean has passion  never fir'd your breast?

MEPHISTOPHELES.

I've everywhere been well receiv'd, I own.

MARTHA.

Yet hath your heart no earnest pref'rence known?

MEPHISTOPHELES.

With ladies one should ne'er presume to jest.

MARTHA.

Ah! you mistake!

MEPHISTOPHELES.

     I'm sorry I'm so blind!
But this I know—that you are very kind.

                  *(They pass on.)*

FAUST.

So, little angel, in the garden when
I enter'd first, you knew me once again?

MARGARET.

Did you not see it?  I cast down my eyes.

FAUST.

And you forgive my boldness, and the guise
Of freedom towards you, as you left the dome,
The day I offer'd to escort you home?

MARGARET.

I was confus'd, never until that day
Could any one of me aught evil say.
Alas, thought I, he doubtless in your mien,
Something unmaidenly or bold hath seen?
It seemed as if it struck him suddenly,
" Here's just a girl with whom one may make free."
Yet I must own that then I scarcely knew
What in your favour here began to plead;

Yet I was angry with myself indeed,
That I more angry could not feel with you.

FAUST.

Sweet love!

MARGARET.

Just wait!
(*She gathers a star-flower and plucks off the leaves one
after another.*)

FAUST.

A nosegay may that be?

MARGARET.

No! 'Tis a game.

FAUST

How?

MARGARET

Go! you'll laugh at me.
(*She plucks off the leaves and murmurs to herself.*)

FAUST.

What murmur you?

MARGARET  (*half aloud*).

He loves me,—loves me not.

FAUST.

Sweet angel, with thy face of heav'nly bliss!

MARGARET  (*continues*).

He loves me,—loves me not—
(*plucking off the last leaf with fond joy.*)
He loves me!

FAUST.

Yes!
And this flower-language, darling, let it be,
E'en as a heav'nly oracle to thee!
Know'st thou the meaning of, " He loveth me?"
(*He seizes both her hands.*)

MARGARET.

I tremble so!

FAUST.

Nay! do not tremble, love!
Oh, let this pressure, let this glance reveal
Feelings, all power of utt'rance far above;
To give oneself up wholly and to feel
A rapturous joy that must eternal prove!

Eternal!—Yes, it's end would be despair.
No end!—It cannot end!
>          (MARGARET *presses his hand; extricates herself, and
>                 runs away.  He stands a moment in thought, and
>                 then follows her.*)

MARTHA          (*approaching*).
Night's closing.

MEPHISTOPHELES.
Yes, we'll presently away.

MARTHA.
I would entreat you longer yet to stay,
But 'tis a wicked place, just here about.
'Tis as the folks had nought to do,
And nothing else to think of too,
But watch their neighbours, who goes in and out;
And scandal's busy still, do what one may.
And our young couple?

MEPHISTOPHELES.
They have flown up there,
Gay butterflies!

MARTHA.
He seems to take to her.

MEPHISTOPHELES.
And she to him.   'Tis of the world the way.

*A Summer-House.*

>          (MARGARET *runs in, hides behind the door, holds the tip
>                 of her finger to her lip, and peeps through the crevice.*)

MARGARET.
He comes!

FAUST.
Ah, little rogue, so thou
Think'st to provoke me!   I have caught thee now!
>                              (*He kisses her.*)

MARGARET
(*embracing him, and returning the kiss*).
Dearest of men   I love thee from my heart!

MEPHISTOPHELES          (*knocks*).

FAUST          (*stamping*).
Who's there?

MEPHISTOPHELES.

**A** friend!

FAUST.

A brute!

MEPHISTOPHELES.

'Tis time to part.

MARTHA         (*comes*).

Yes, sir, 'tis late.

FAUST.

Mayn't I attend you, sweet?

MARGARET.

Oh no—my mother would—adieu, adieu!

FAUST.

And must I really then take leave of you?
Farewell!

MARTHA.

Good-bye!

MARGARET.

Ere long again to meet!

(*Exeunt* FAUST *and* MEPHISTOPHELES.)

MARGARET.

Good heavens! how all things far and near
Must fill his mind,—a man like this !
Abash'd before him I appear,
And say to all things only, yes.
Poor simple child, I cannot see,
What 'tis that he can find in me.         (*Exit.*)

*Forest and Cavern.*

FAUST         (*alone*).

Spirit sublime!   Thou gav'st me, gav'st me all
For which I prayed.   Not vainly hast thou turn'd
To me thy countenance in flaming fire.
Thou gav'st me glorious nature for my realm,
And also power to feel her and enjoy.
Not merely with a cold and wond'ring glance,
Thou dost permit me in her depths profound,
As in the bosom of a friend to gaze.

Before me thou dost lead her living tribes,
And dost in silent grove, in air and stream
Teach me to know my kindred.   And when roars
The howling storm-blast through the groaning wood,
Wrenching the giant pine, which in it's fall
Sweeps, crushing down, its neighbour trunks and boughs,
While with the hollow noise the hill resounds,
Then thou dost lead me to some shelter'd cave,
Dost there reveal me to myself, and show
Of my own bosom the mysterious depths.
And when with soothing beam, the moon's pale orb
Full in my view climbs up the pathless sky,
From crag and vap'rous grove, the silv'ry forms
Of by-gone ages hover, and assuage
The too severe delight of earnest thought.
Oh, that nought perfect is assign'd to man,
I feel, alas! With this exalted joy,
Which lifts me near and nearer to the gods,
Thou gav'st me this companion, unto whom
I needs must cling, though cold and insolent,
He still degrades me to myself, and turns
Thy glorious gifts to nothing, with a breath.
He in my bosom with malicious zeal
For that fair image fans a raging fire;
From craving to enjoyment thus I reel,
And in enjoyment languish for desire.

(MEPHISTOPHELES enters.)

MEPHISTOPHELES.

Of this lone life have you not had your fill?
How for so long can it have charms for you?
'Tis well enough to try it if you will;
But then away again to something new!

FAUST.

Would you could better occupy your leisure,
Than in disturbing thus my hours of joy.

MEPHISTOPHELES.

Well! Well! I'll leave you to yourself with pleasure,
A serious tone you hardly dare employ;
To part from one so crazy, harsh, and cross,
I should not find methinks a grievous loss.
The live-long day, for you I toil and fret.

Ne'er from your worship's face a hint I get,
What pleases you, or what to let alone.

FAUST.

Ay truly! that is just the proper tone!
Tires me, forsooth, and would with thanks be paid!

MEPHISTOPHELES.

Poor child of clay, without my aid,
How would thy weary days have flown?
Thee of thy foolish whims I've cur'd,
Thy vain imaginations banish'd,
And but for me, be well assur'd,
Thou from this sphere must soon have vanish'd.
In rocky cleft and cavern drear
Why like an owl sit moping here?
And wherefore suck, like any toad,
From dripping rocks and moss thy food?
A pleasant pastime!   Verily,
The doctor cleaveth still to thee.

FAUST.

Couldst thou divine what bliss without alloy
From this wild wand'ring in the desert springs,—
Couldst thou but guess the new life-power it brings,
Thou still wert fiend enough to grudge my joy.

MEPHISTOPHELES.

What super-earthly ecstasy! at night,
To lie in darkness on the dewy height,
Embracing heaven and earth in rapture high,
The soul dilating to a deity,
With prescient yearnings pierce the core of earth,
Feel in your labouring breast the six-days' birth,
Enjoy, in proud delight what no one knows,
While your love-rapture o'er creation flows,—
The earthly lost in beatific vision,
And then the lofty intuition—

(with a gesture.)

I need not tell you how—to close.

FAUST.

Fie on you!

MEPHISTOPHELES.

This displeases you?   " For shame!"
You are forsooth entitl'd to exclaim

We to chaste ears it seems must not impart,
Thoughts that may dwell unquestion'd in the heart.
Well, to be brief, as fit occasions rise,
I grudge you not the joy of specious lies.
But soon 'tis past, the self-deluding vein ;
Back to your former course you're driven again,
And, should it longer hold, your anguish'd breast
By frenzied horror soon would be possess'd.
Enough of this !  Your true love dwells apart,
And every thing to her seems flat and tame.
Alone your cherish'd image fills her heart,
She loves you with an all-devouring flame.
First came your passion with o'erpowering rush,
Like mountain torrent, fed by melted snow,
Full in her heart you pour'd the sudden gush,
And now again your stream has ceas'd to flow.
Instead of sitting thron'd midst forests wild,
Methinks it would become so great a lord,
Fondly to comfort the enamour'd child,
And the young monkey for her love reward.
To her the hours seem miserably long ;
She from the window sees the clouds float by
As o'er the ancient city-walls they fly.
" Were I a bird," so runs her song,
Half through the night and all the day.
One while, indeed, she seemeth gay,
And then with grief her heart is sore;
Fairly outwept seem now her tears,
Anon she tranquil is, or so appears,
And love-sick evermore.

FAUST.

Snake ! Serpent vile!

MEPHISTOPHELES  (aside).

Good !  If I catch thee with my guile !

FAUST.

Vile reprobate! go get thee hence ;
Forbear the lovely girl to name !
Nor in my half-distracted sense,
Kindle anew the smould'ring flame !

MEPHISTOPHELES.

How now !   She thinks you've taken flight:
It seems, she's partly in the right.

FAUST.

I'm near her still—and should I distant rove,
I'd ne'er forget her, ne'er resign her love;
And all things touch'd by those sweet lips of hers,
Even the very host, my envy stirs.

MEPHISTOPHELES.

'Tis well !   I oft have envied you indeed,
The twin-pair, that among the roses feed.

FAUST.

Pander, avaunt !

MEPHISTOPHELES.

        My friend, the while
You rail, excuse me if I smile;
The power which fashion'd youth and maid,
Well understood the noble trade,
Of making also time and place.
But hence !—In truth a doleful case !
Your mistress' chamber doth invite,
Not the cold grave's o'ershadowing night.

FAUST.

What in her arms the joys of heaven to me ?
Oh let me kindle on her gentle breast !
Do I not ever feel her misery ?
Wretch that I am, whose spirit knows no rest,
Inhuman monster, homeless and unblest,
Who, like the greedy surge, from rock to rock,
Sweeps down the dread abyss with desp'rate shock
While she, within her lowly cot, which grac'd
The Alpine slope, beside the waters wild,
Her homely cares in that small world embrac'd,
Secluded lived, a simple artless child.
Was't not enough, in thy delirious whirl
To blast the steadfast rocks,—her quiet cell,
Her too, her peace, to ruin must I hurl!
Dost claim this holocaust, remorseless Hell!
Fiend, help me to cut short the hours of dread!
Let what must happen, happen speedily !

Her direful doom fall crushing on my head.
And into ruin let her plunge with me.

MEPHISTOPHELES.

Why how again it seethes and glows !
Away, thou fool !   Her torment ease !
When such a head no issue sees,
It pictures straight the final close.
Long life to him who boldly dares !
A devil's pluck you're wont to show ;
As for a devil who despairs,
There's nought so mawkish here below

MARGARET'S *Room.*

MARGARET (*alone at her spinning wheel*).

My heart's oppress'd,
  My peace is o'er ;
I know no rest,
  No, nevermore.

The world's a grave
  Where he is not;
And grief is now
  My bitter lot.

My wilder'd brain
  Is overwrought ;
My feeble senses
  Are distraught.

My heart's oppress'd,
  My peace is o'er ;
I know no rest,
  No, nevermore.

For him I watch
  The live-long day,
For him alone
  Abroad I stray.

His lofty step,
  His bearing high,
The smile of his lip,
  The power of his eye

His witching words,
   Their tones of bliss,
His hand's fond pressure,
   And then, his kiss!

My heart's oppress'd
   My peace is o'er,
I know no rest,
   No, nevermore.

   My bosom aches
To feel him near.
   Ah, could I clasp
And fold him here!

In love's fond blisses
   Entranc'd I'd lie,
And die on his kisses,
   In ecstasy!


## MARTHA'S *Garden.*

### MARGARET *and* FAUST.

#### MARGARET.

Promise me, Henry!

#### FAUST.
What I can!

#### MARGARET.

How is it with religion in your mind?
You are 'tis true a good, kind-hearted man,
But I'm afraid not piously inclin'd.

#### FAUST.

Forbear!  I love you darling, you alone!
For those I love, my life I would lay down,
And none would of their faith or church bereave.

#### MARGARET.

That's not enough, we must ourselves believe.

#### FAUST.

Must we?

#### MARGARET.

   Ah, could I but your soul inspire!
You honour not the sacraments, alas!

#### FAUST.

I honour them.

#### MARGARET.

But yet without desire
'Tis long since you have been to shrift or mass
Do you believe in God?

#### FAUST.

My love, forbear!
Who dares acknowledge, I in God believe?
Ask priest or sage, the answer you receive,
Seems but a mockery of the questioner.

#### MARGARET.

Then you do not believe?

#### FAUST.

Sweet one! my meaning do not misconceive!
Him who dare name
And yet proclaim,
Yes, I believe?
Who that can feel,
His heart can steel,
To say: I disbelieve?
The All-embracer,
All-sustainer,
Doth He not embrace, sustain
Thee, me, himself?
Lifts not the Heaven its dome above?
Doth not the firm-set earth beneath us lie?
And beaming tenderly with looks of love,
Climb not the everlasting stars on high?
Are we not gazing in each other's eyes?
Nature's impenetrable agencies,
Are they not thronging on thy heart and brain,
Viewless, or visible to mortal ken,
Around thee weaving their mysterious reign?
Fill thence thy heart, how large soe'er it be,
And in the feeling when thou'rt wholly blest,
Then call it what thou wilt,—Bliss! Heart! Love! God!
I have no name for it—'tis feeling all.
Name is but sound and smoke
Shrouding the glow of heaven.

MARGARET.
All this is doubtless beautiful and true;
The priest doth also much the same declare,
Only in somewhat diff'rent language too.
FAUST.
Beneath Heaven's genial sunshine, everywhere,
This is the utt'rance of the human heart;
Each in his language doth the like impart;
Then why not I in mine?
MARGARET.
                    What thus I hear
Sounds plausible, yet I'm not reconcil'd;
There's something wrong about it; much I fear
That thou art not a Christian.
FAUST.
                         My sweet child!
MARGARET.
Alas! it long hath sorely troubl'd me,
To see thee in such odious company.
FAUST.
How so?
MARGARET.
            The man who comes with thee, I hate,
Yea, in my spirit's inmost depths abhor;
As his loath'd visage, in my life before,
Nought to my heart e'er gave a pang so great.
FAUST.
Fear not, sweet love!
MARGARET.
                His presence chills my blood.
Towards all beside I have a kindly mood;
Yet, though I yearn to gaze on thee, I feel
At sight of him strange horror o'er me steal;
That he's a villain my conviction's strong,
May Heaven forgive me if I do him wrong!
FAUST.
Yet such strange fellows in the world must be!
MARGARET.
I would not live with such an one as he
If for a moment he but enter here,
He looks around him with a mocking sneer,
And malice ill-conceal'd.

I

That he can feel no sympathy is clear,
Upon his brow 'tis legibly reveal'd,
That to his heart no living soul is dear.
So blest I feel, abandon'd in thine arms,
So warm and happy,—free from all alarms,
And still my heart doth close when he comes near.

FAUST.

Foreboding angel!  prithee check thy fear!

MARGARET.

The feeling so o'erpowers my mind, that when,
Or wheresoe'r, I chance his step to hear,
Methinks almost I cease to love thee then.
Besides, when he is near I ne'er could pray,
And this it is that eats my heart away;
Thou also, Henry, surely feel'st it so.

FAUST.

This is  antipathy!

MARGARET.

I now must go.

FAUST.

And may I never then in quiet rest,
For one brief hour, upon thy gentle breast.

MARGARET.

Ah if I slept alone!   The door, to-night
I'd leave unbarr'd;  but mother's sleep is light;
And if she should by any chance awake,
Upon the floor I should at once fall dead.

FAUST.

Sweet angel!  there's no cause for dread,
Here is a little phial,—if she take
But three drops mingl'd in her drink, 'twill steep
Her nature in a deep and soothing sleep.

MARGARET.

What is there I'd not do for thy dear sake :
To her 'twill surely do no injury?

FAUST.

Else, my own love, should I thus counsel thee

MARGARET.

Gazing on thee, belov'd, I cannot tell,
What doth my spirit to thy will compel;

So much I have already done for thee,
That more to do there scarce remains for me.

(Exit.)

MEPHISTOPHELES (enters).

MEPHISTOPHELES.

The monkey!  Has she left you then?

FAUST.

Have you been spying here again?

MEPHISTOPHELES.

Of all that pass'd I'm well appriz'd,
I heard the doctor catechis'd,
And trust he'll profit by the rede.
The girls show always much concern,
Touching their lover's faith, to learn
Whether it tallies with the creed.
If men are pliant there, think they,
Us too, they'll follow and obey.

FAUST.

Thou monster!  thou canst not perceive
How a true loving soul, like this,
Full of the faith she doth believe
To be the pledge of endless bliss,
Must mourn, her soul with anguish tost,
Thinking the man she loves for ever lost.

MEPHISTOPHELES.

Most sensual supersensualist!  a flirt,
A gipsy, leads thee by the nose!

FAUST.

Abortion vile of fire and dirt!

MEPHISTOPHELES.

In physiognomy strange skill she shows;
She in my presence feels she knows not how
My mask it seems some hidden sense reveal
That I'm a genius she must needs allow.
That I'm the very devil perhaps she feels.
So then to-night?—

FAUST.

What's that to you?

MEPHISTOPHELES.

I've my amusement in it too!

I 2

*At the Well.*

Margaret *and* Bessy, *with pitchers*

BESSY.
And have you then of Barbara nothing heard?
MARGARET.
I rarely go from home,—no, not a word.
BESSY.
'Tis true :  Sybilla told me so to-day!
She's play'd the fool at last, I promise you;
That comes of pride.

MARGARET.
How  so?

BESSY.
                    Why people say
That when she eats and drinks she feedeth two.
MARGARET.

BESSY.
          She's rightly served, in sooth.
How long she hung upon the youth!
What promenades, what jaunts there were,
To dancing booth and village fair,
The first she everywhere must shine,
He treating her to cakes and wine.
Of her good looks she was so vain,
And e'en his presents would retain.
Sweet words and kisses came anon,
And then the virgin flower was gone!

MARGARET.
Poor thing!
BESSY.
          And do you pity her?
Why of a night, when at our wheels we sat,
Abroad our mothers ne'er would let us stir.
Then with her lover she forsooth must chat,

Or near the bench, or in the dusky walk,
Thinking the hours too brief for their sweet talk;
Beshrew me! her proud head she'll have to bow.
And in white sheet do penance now!

MARGARET.

But he will surely marry her?

BESSY.

Not he!
He won't be such a fool! a gallant lad
Like him, can roam o'er land and sea,
Besides, he's off.

MARGARET.

That is not fair!

BESSY.

If she should get him, 'twere almost as bad;
Her myrtle wreath the boys would tear;
And then we girls would plague her too,
Chopp'd straw before her door we'd strew!

(*Exit.*)

MARGARET (*walking towards home*).

How stoutly once I could inveigh,
If a poor maiden went astray!
Not words enough my tongue could find,
'Gainst others' sin to speak my mind'
How black soe'er their fault before,
I strove to blacken it still more,
And did myself securely bless.
Now are the sin, the scandal, mine!
Yet ah!—what urg'd me to transgress,
Heaven knows, was good! ah, so divine!


ZWINGER

(*In the niche of the wall a devotional image of the
Mater dolorosa, with flower-pots before it.*)

MARGARET (*putting fresh flowers in the pots*).

Ah, rich in sorrow, thou,
Stoop thy maternal brow,
And mark with pitying eye my misery'

The sword in thy pierc'd heart,
Thou dost with bitter smart,
Gaze upwards on thy Son's death agony.

To the dear God on high,
Ascends thy piteous sigh,
Pleading for his and thy mute misery.

Ah, who can know
The torturing woe
That harrows me, and racks me to the bone
How my poor heart, without relief,
Trembles and throbs, its yearning grief
Thou knowest, thou alone!

Ah, wheresoe'er I go,
With woe, with woe, with woe,
My anguish'd breast is aching!
Wretched, alone I keep,
I weep, I weep, I weep,
Alas! my heart is breaking!

The flower-pots at my window
Were wet with tears of mine,
The while I pluck'd these blossoms
At dawn to deck thy shrine!

When early in my chamber
Shone bright the rising morn,
I sat there on my pallet,
My heart with anguish torn.

Help! death and shame are near!
Mother of sorrows, now
Stoop thy maternal brow,
And to thy suppliant turn a gracious ear.


*Night.   Street before Margaret's door.*

VALENTINE (*soldier,* MARGARET's *brother*).

When seated 'mong the jovial crowd
Where merry comrades boasting loud,
Each nam'd with pride his favourite lass,
And in her honour drain'd his glass;

Upon my elbows I would lean,
With easy quiet view the scene,
Nor give my tongue the rein, until
Each swagg'ring blade had talk'd his fill.
Then with a smile my beard I'd stroke,
The while, with brimming glass, I spoke;
" Each to his taste:—but to my mind,
Where in the country will you find,
A maiden, be she ne'er so fair,
Who with my Gretchen can compare?'
Cling! Clang! so rang the jovial sound !
Shouts of assent went circling round;
Pride of her sex is she!—cried some;
Then were the noisy boasters dumb.

And now!—I could uproot my hair,
Or dash my brains out in despair!
Me every scurvy knave may twit,
With stinging jest and taunting sneer!
Like skulking debtor I must sit,
And sweat each casual word to hear!
And though I smash'd them one and all,
Yet them I could not liars call.

Who comes this way? who's sneaking here?
If I mistake not, two draw near.
If he be one, have at him;—well I wot
Alive he shall not leave this spot!

Faust, Mephistopheles.

FAUST.

How from yon sacristy, athwart the night,
Its beams the ever-burning taper throws,
While ever waning, fades the glimm'ring light,
As gath'ring darkness doth around it close!
So night-like gloom doth in my bosom reign.

MEPHISTOPHELES.

I'm like a tom-cat in a thievish vein,
That round the walls doth slyly creep;
And up fire-ladders tall, and steep,
Virtuous withal I feel, with, I confess,
A touch of thievish joy and wantonness.

Thus through my limbs already there doth bound
The glorious advent of Walpurgis night;
After to-morrow it again comes round,
What one doth wake for then one knows aright.

FAUST.

Meanwhile, the flame which I see glimm'ring there,
Is it the treasure rising in the air?

MEPHISTOPHELES.

Ere long, I make no doubt, but you
To raise the chest will feel inclin'd;
Erewhile I peep'd within it too,
With lion-dollars 'tis well lin'd.

FAUST.

And not a trinket? not a ring?
Wherewith my lovely girl to deck?

MEPHISTOPHELES.

I saw among them some such thing,
A string of pearls to grace her neck.

FAUST.

'Tis well! I'm always loath to go,
Without some gift my love to show.

MEPHISTOPHELES.

Some pleasures gratis to enjoy,
Should surely cause you no annoy.
While bright with stars the heavens appear,
I'll sing a masterpiece of art.
A moral song shall charm her ear,
More surely to beguile her heart.

(Sings to the guitar.)

Fair Catherine say,
Why ling'ring stay
At dawn of day
Before your lover's door?
You enter there,
A maid, beware.
Lest forth you fare,
A maiden never more.

Maiden take heed!
Reck well my rede!

Is't done, the deed?
Good night, you poor, poor thing!
The spoiler's lies,
His arts despise,
Nor yield your prize,
Without the marriage ring.
VALENTINE (*steps forward*).
Whom are you luring here?   I'll give it you!
Accursed rat-catchers, your strains I'll end!
First, to the devil the guitar I'll send!
Then to the devil with the singer too!
MEPHISTOPHELES
The poor guitar!   'Tis done for now.
VALENTINE.
Your skull shall follow next, I trow!
MEPHISTOPHELES (*to* FAUST)
Doctor, stand fast! your strength collect!
Be prompt, and do as I direct.
Out with your whisk! keep close, I pray.
I'll parry! do you thrust away!
VALENTINE.
Then parry that!
MEPHISTOPHELES.
Why not?
VALENTINE.
That too!
MEPHISTOPHELES.
With ease!

VALENTINE.
The devil fights for you!
Why how is this? my hand's already lam'd!
MEPHISTOPHELES (*to* FAUST).
Thrust home!
VALENTINE (*falls*).
Alas!
MEPHISTOPHELES.
There!   Now the bully's tam'd.
But quick, away!   We must at once take wing.
A cry of murder strikes upon the ear.
With the police I know my course to steer,
But with the blood-ban 'tis another thing.

MARTHA (*at the window*).
Without! without!

MARGARET (*at the window*).
Quick, bring a light!

MARTHA (*as above*).
They rail and scuffle, scream and fight!

PEOPLE.
One lieth here already dead!

MARTHA (*coming out*).
Where are the murderers? are they fled?

MARGARET (*coming out*).
Who lieth here?

PEOPLE.
Thy mother's son.

MARGARET.
Almighty Father! I'm undone!

VALENTINE.
I'm dying!   'Tis a soon-told tale!
And sooner done the deed!
Why, women, do ye weep and wail?
To my last words give heed.        (*All gather round him.*)
Gretchen, thou'rt still of tender age,
And, well I wot, not over sage,
Thou dost thy matters ill.
Let this in confidence be said:
She who the path of shame doth tread,
Should tread it with good will.

MARGARET.
My God! what can this mean?

VALENTINE.
Abstain,
Nor dare God's holy name profane.
What's done, alas, is done and past!
Matters will take their course at last!
By stealth thou dost begin with one,
And more will follow him anon;
When to a dozen swells the train,
A common outcast, thou'lt remain.

When first the monster shame is born,
Clandestinely she's brought to light,

And the mysterious veil of night
Around her head is drawn.
The loathsome birth men fain would slay!
But soon, full grown, she waxes bold,
And though not fairer to behold,
With brazen front insults the day.
The more abhorr'd her visage grows,
The more her hideousness she shows!

The time already I discern,
When thee all honest men will spurn,
And shun thy hated form to meet,
As when a corpse infects the street.
Thy heart will sink in blank despair,
When they shall look thee in the face!
A golden chain no more thou'lt wear!
Nor near the altar take thy place!
In fair lace collar simply dight
Thou'lt dance no more with spirits light!
In darksome corners thou wilt bide,
Where beggars vile and cripples hide;
And e'en though God thy crime forgive
On earth, a thing accurs'd, thou'lt live.

MARTHA.
Your parting soul to God commend;
Nor your last breath in slander spend.

VALENTINE.
Could I but reach thy wither'd frame,
Thou wretched beldame, void of shame!
Full measure I might hope to win
Of pardon then for every sin.

MARGARET.
Brother! what agonizing pain!

VALENTINE.
I tell thee! from vain tears abstain!
'Twas thy dishonour pierc'd my heart;
Thy fall the fatal death-stab gave.
Through the death-sleep I now depart
To God, a soldier true and brave.        (dies.)

## *Cathedral.*

### *Service, Organ, and Anthem.*

MARGARET (*amongst a number of people*)

EVIL-SPIRIT (*behind* MARGARET).

#### EVIL-SPIRIT.

How diff'rent, Gretchen, was it once with thee,
When thou, still full of innocence,
Cam'st to the altar here,
And from the small and well-conn'd book
Did'st lisp thy prayer,
Half childish sport,
Half God in thy young heart!
Gretchen!
What thoughts are thine?
What deed of shame
Lurks in thy sinful heart?
Is thy prayer utter'd for thy mother's soul,
Who into long, long torment slept through thee?
Whose blood is on thy threshold?
—And stirs there not already 'neath thy heart
Another quick'ning pulse, that even now
Tortures itself and thee
With its foreboding presence?

#### MARGARET.

Woe! Woe!
Oh could I free me from the harrowing thoughts
That 'gainst my will,
Throng my disorder'd brain!

#### CHORUS.
*Dies iræ, dies illa,*
*Solvet sæclum in favilla.*
          (*The organ sounds*

#### EVIL-SPIRIT.

Grim horror seizes thee!
The trumpet sounds
The graves are shaken!
And thy sinful heart,
From its cold ashy rest

For torturing flames
Anew created,
Trembles into life!

MARGARET.

Would I were hence!
It is as if the organ
Chok'd my breath,
As if the choir
Melted my inmost heart.

CHORUS.

*Judex ergo cum sedebit,*
*Quidquid latet adparebit,*
*Nil inultum remanebit.*

MARGARET.

I feel oppress'd!
The pillars of the wall
Are closing round me!
And the vaulted roof
Weighs down upon me!—air!

EVIL-SPIRIT.

Wouldst hide thee? sin and shame
Remain not hidden.
Air! light!
Woe's thee!

CHORUS.

*Quid sum miser tunc dicturus*
*Quem patronum rogaturus!*
*Cum vix justus sit securus.*

EVIL-SPIRIT.

The glorified their faces turn
    Away from thee!
Shudder the pure to reach
    Their hands to thee!
Woe!

CHORUS.

*Quid sum miser tunc dicturus*

MARGARET.

Neighbour! your smelling bottle!

(*She swoons away.*)

# WALPURGIS-NIGHT.

## *The Hartz Mountains.*

### *District of Schirke and Elend.*

FAUST *and* MEPHISTOPHELES.

MEPHISTOPHELES.

A broomstick do you not at least desire?
The roughest he-goat fain would I bestride,
By this road from our goal we're still far wide

FAUST.

Except this knotty staff I nought require,
I still am fresh upon my legs.   Beside,
What boots it to abridge a pleasant way
Along the labyrinth of these vales to creep,
Then scale these rocks, whence, in eternal spray,
Adown the cliffs the silv'ry torrents leap,
Such is the joy that seasons paths like these;
Spring weaves already in the birchen trees;
E'en the late pine-grove feels her quick'ning power,
Should she not stimulate these limbs of ours?

MEPHISTOPHELES.

Nought of this genial influence do I know!
Within me all is wintry.   Frost and snow
I should prefer my dismal path to bound;
How sadly, yonder, with belated glow,
Rises the ruddy moon's imperfect round,
Shedding so faint a light, at every tread
One's sure to stumble 'gainst a rock or tree!
An Ignis Fatuus I must call instead.
Yonder one burning merrily, I see.
Holla! my friend, I must request your light!
Why should you flare away so uselessly?
Be kind enough to show us up the height!

IGNIS FATUUS.

I hope from rev'rence to subdue
The lightness of my nature; true,
Our course is but a zigzag one.

MEPHISTOPHELES.
Ho! ho!
So man, forsooth, he thinks to imitate!
Now, in the devil's name, for once go straight,
Or out at once your flick'ring life I'll blow!
IGNIS FATUUS.
That you are master here is obvious quite;
To do your will, I'll cordially essay;
But think! The hill is magic-mad to-night;
And if as guide you choose a meteor's light,
You must not wonder should we go astray.

FAUST, MEPHISTOPHELES, IGNIS FATUUS
(*in alternate song*).

Through this dream and magic-sphere,
Lead us on, thou flick'ring guide.
Pilot well our bold career!
That we may with rapid stride
Gain yon regions waste and wide.

Trees on trees, how swift they flow!
How the steadfast granite blocks
Make obeisance as they go!
Hark! the grim, long-snouted rocks,
How they snort and how they blow!

Through the turf and through the stones
Brook and brooklet speed along.
Hark, the rustling! Hark, the song!
Hearken too love's plaintive tones!
Voices of those heavenly days,
When around us and above,
Like enchantment's mystic lays,
Breath'd the notes of hope and love!
Like the song of olden time,
Echo's voice repeats the chime.

To-whit! To whoo! upon the ear
The mingl'd discord sounds more near,
The owl, the pewit, and the jay,
Wakeful and in voice are they?
Salamanders in the brake,
Busy too, and wide awake!
Stout of paunch and long of limb
Sporting in the twilight dim?

While from every rock and slope
Snakelike, coil the roots of trees.
Flinging many a mystic rope,
Us to frighten, us to seize;
From rude knots, with life embued,
Polyp-fangs abroad they spread,
To snare the wand'rer.  'Neath our tread,
Mice, in myriads, thousand-hued,
Through the heath and through the moss.
Frisk, a gamesome multitude ;
Glow-worms flit our path across ;
Swiftly, the bewild'ring throng,
A dazzling escort, whirls along.

FAUST.

Tell me, stand we motionless,
Or still forward do we press ?
All things round us whirl and fly ;
Rocks and trees make strange grimaces,
Dazzling meteors change their places.
How they puff and multiply !

MEPHISTOPHELES.

Now grasp my doublet—we at last
Have reach'd a central precipice,
Whence we a wond'ring glance may cast,
Where Mammon lights the dark abyss.

FAUST.

How through the chasms strangely gleams,
A lurid light, like dawn's red glow !
Pervading with its quiv'ring beams,
The gorges of the gulph below.
There vapours rise, there clouds float by,
And here through mist the splendour shines:
Now, like a fount, it bursts on high,
Now glideth on in slender lines.
Far-reaching, with a hundred veins,
Through the far valley see it glide,
Here, where the gorge the flood restrains,
At once it scatters far and wide.
And near us sparks of sputt'ring light,
Like golden sand-showers, rise and fall
While see, in all its tow'ring height,
How fiercely glows yon rocky wall!

MEPHISTOPHELES.

Doth not his hall Sir Mammon light,
With splendour for this festive night?
To see it was a lucky chance,
E'en now the boist'rous guests advance

FAUST.

How the fierce tempest sweeps around!
My neck it strikes with sudden shock!

MEPHISTOPHELES.

Cling to these ribs of granite rock,
Or it will hurl you in yon gulf profound.
A murky vapour thickens night.
Hark! through the forest what a crash!
The scar'd owls flit in wild affright.
The shiver'd branches creak and clash!
The deaf'ning clang the ear appals,
Prostrate the leafy palace falls,
Rent are the pillars, grey with eld,
That the aye-verdant roof upheld.
The giant trunks, with mighty groan,
By the fierce blast are overthrown!
The roots, upriven, creak and moan!
In fearful and entangl'd fall,
One crashing ruin whelms them all,
While through the desolate abyss,
Sweeping the wreck-strown precipice,
The raging storm-blasts howl and hiss.

  Hear'st thou voices sounding clear,
  Distant now and now more near?
  Hark! the mountain ridge along,
  Streams the witches' magic-song!

WITCHES  (*in chorus*).

Now to the Brocken the witches hie,
The stubble is yellow, the corn is green;
Thither the gath'ring legions fly,
And sitting aloft is Sir Urian seen,
O'er stick and o'er stone they go whirling along,
Witches and he-goats a motley throng.

VOICES.

Alone old Baubo's coming now;
She rides upon a farrow sow.

K

CHORUS.
Honour to who merits honour!
Baubo forwards! 'Tis her due!
A goodly sow, and dame upon her,
Follows then the whole witch crew.

VOICE.
Which way didst come?

VOICE.
O'er Ilsenstein!
There I peep'd in an owlet's nest.
With her broad eye she gaz'd in mine!

VOICE.
Drive to the devil, thou hellish pest!
Why ride so hard?

VOICE.
She has graz'd my side,
Look at the wounds, how deep and how wide!

WITCHES   (in chorus).
The way is broad, the way is long;
Scratches the besom and sticks the prong.
What mad pursuit!   What tumult wild!
Crush'd is the mother and stifl'd the child.

WIZARDS   (half chorus).
Like house-encumber'd snail we creep,
While far ahead the women keep.
For, when to the devil's house we speed,
By a thousand steps they take the lead.

THE OTHER HALF.
Not so, precisely do we view it;—
They with a thousand steps may do it.
But let them hasten as they can,
With one long bound 'tis clear'd by man.

VOICES   (above).
Come with us, come with us from Felsensee.

VOICES   (from below).
Aloft to you we would mount with glee!
We wash, and free from all stain are we,
Yet are doom'd to endless sterility.

BOTH CHORUSES.
The wind is hush'd, the stars grow pale,
The pensive moon her light doth veil,

And whirling on, the magic quire,
Sputter forth sparks of drizzling fire.

VOICE (from below).

Stay! stay!

VOICE (from above).
What voice of woe

Calls from the cavern'd depths below?

VOICE (from below).

Stay, stay, stay for me!
Three centuries I climb in vain,
And yet can ne'er the summit gain!
Fain would I with my kindred be!

BOTH CHORUSES.

Broom and pitch-fork, goat and prong,
Serve whereon to whirl along;
Who vainly strives to climb to-night,
Is lost for ever, luckless wight!

DEMI-WITCH (below).

I've totter'd after now so long;
How far before me are the throng!
No peace at home can I obtain,
Here too my efforts are in vain.

CHORUS OF WITCHES

Salve gives the witches strength to rise;
A rag for a sail does well enough;
A goodly ship is in every trough;
To-night who flies not, never flies.

BOTH CHORUSES.

And when the topmost peak we round,
Then alight we on the ground;
The heath's wide regions cover ye
With your mad swarms of witchery.

(They let themselves down

MEPHISTOPHELES.

They crowd and jostle, whirl and flutter!
They whisper, babble, twirl, and splutter!
They glimmer, burn, they stink and stutter!
All noisomely together blent,
A genuine witch's element!
Stick close, or you'll be borne away.
Where art thou?

K 2

                              FAUST       (*in the distance*).
              Here!

MEPHISTOPHELES.

Already whirl'd so far!
The master then indeed I needs must play.
Make way!  Squire Voland comes!  Sweet folk, make way!
Here, doctor, grasp me! From this ceaseless jar
With one long bound a quick retreat we'll make.
Even for me too mad these people are.
Hard by shines something with peculiar glare,
I feel myself allur'd towards yonder brake.
Come, come along with me! we'll slip in there.

FAUST.

Spirit of contradiction!  Lead the way!
Go on, and I will follow after straight.
'Twas wisely done, however, I must say,
On May-night to the Brocken to repair,
And then by choice ourselves to isolate.

MEPHISTOPHELES.

Look at those colour'd flames which yonder flare
A merry club is met together there.
In a small circle one is not alone.

FAUST.

I'd rather be above, though, I must own!
Already fire and eddying smoke I view.
The impetuous millions to the devil ride;
Full many a riddle will be there untied.

MEPHISTOPHELES.

Ay! and full many a one be tied anew.
But let the great world rave and riot,
While here we house ourselves in quie
 Tis an old practice to create
Our lesser worlds within the great.
Young naked witches there I spy,
And old ones, veil'd more prudently.
For my sake courteous be to all,
The pastime's great, the trouble small.
Of instruments I hear the cursed din!
One must get used to it.  Come in! come in
There's now no help for it.  I'll step before,

And introducing you as my good friend,
Confer on you one obligation more.
How say you now?   'Tis no such paltry room.
Why only look, you scarce can see the end;
A hundred fires in rows disperse the gloom;
They dance, they talk, they cook, make love, and drink,
Where could we find aught better, do you think?

FAUST.

To introduce us, do you purpose here
As devil or as wizard to appear?

MEPHISTOPHELES.

Though wont indeed to strict incognito,
On gala-days one must one's orders show.
No garter have I to distinguish me.
But here the cloven foot gives dignity.
Dost mark yon crawling snail?   This way she hies·
She with her searching feelers, hath no doubt,
Already with quick instinct. found me out.
Here, if I would, for me there's no disguise.
From fire to fire, we'll saunter at our leisure,
The gallant you, I'll cater for your pleasure.

(*To a party seated round some expiring embers.*)

Old gentlemen, why are ye moping here?
You should be in the midst of all the riot,
Girt round with revelry and youthful cheer;
At home one surely has enough of quiet.

GENERAL.

Who is there can rely upon the nation,
How great soe'er hath been its obligation?
'Tis with the people as with women, they
To rising stars alone their homage pay.

MINISTER.

Too far astray they wander now-a-days;
I, for my part, extol the good old ways;
For truly when ourselves were all the rage,
Then was indeed the genuine golden age.

PARVENU.

We were among the knowing ones, I own,
And often did what best were let alone.
Yet now when we would gladly keep our ground,
With hurly-burly every thing spins round.

AUTHOR.

Who, speaking generally, now cares indeed,
A work of even moderate depth to read!
As for our youth, there ne'er has risen yet
So shallow and so malapert a set.

MEPHISTOPHELES

(suddenly appearing very old).

Since I the last time now the Brocken scale,
That all are ripe for doom one plainly sees;
And just because my cask begins to fail,
So the whole world is also on the lees.

HUCKSTER-WITCH.

Stop, gentlemen, nor pass me by!
Lose not this opportunity!
Of wares I have a choice collection,
Pray honour them with your inspection.
No fellow to my booth you'll find
On earth, for 'mong my store there's nought,
Which to the world, and to mankind,
Hath not some direful mischief wrought.
No dagger here, which hath not flow'd with blood,
No bowl, which hath not in some healthy frame
Infus'd the poison's life-consuming flood,
No trinket, but hath wrought some woman's shame,
No weapon but hath cut some sacred tie,
Or stabb'd behind the back an enemy.

MEPHISTOPHELES.

Gossip! but ill the times you understand;
What's done is done!   The past's beyond recall!
For your antiquities there's no demand!
With novelties pray furnish forth your stall.

FAUST.

May this wild scene my senses spare!
This, with a vengeance, is a fair!

MEPHISTOPHELES.

Upward the eddying concourse throng,
Thinking to push, thyself art push'd along.

FAUST.

Who's that, pray?

MEPHISTOPHELES.

Mark her well!   That's Lilith.

#### FAUST.

Who?

#### MEPHISTOPHELES.

Adam's first wife. Of her rich locks beware!
That charm in which she's parallel'd by few!
When in its toils a youth she doth ensnare,
He will not soon escape, I promise you.

#### FAUST.

There sit a pair, the old one with the young;
Already they have bravely danc'd and sprung!

#### MEPHISTOPHELES.

To-night there's no cessation; come along!
Another dance begins; we'll join the throng.

#### FAUST
*(dancing with the young one).*

Once there appear'd in vision bright,
   An apple-tree to glad mine eyes.
Two apples with their rosy light
   Allur'd me, and I sought the prize.

#### THE FAIR ONE.

Apples still fondly ye desire,
   From paradise it hath been so.
Feelings of joy my breast inspire
   That such too in my garden grow.

#### MEPHISTOPHELES   *(with the old one).*

Once a wild vision troubl'd me.
In it I saw a rifted tree.
It had a ——————;
But as it was it pleas'd me too.

#### THE OLD ONE.

I beg most humbly to saute
The gallant with the cloven foot;
Let him a —————— have ready here,
If he a —————— does not fear.

#### PROCTOPHANTASMIST.

Accursed mob! How dare ye thus to meet?
Have I not shown and demonstrated too,
That ghosts stand not on ordinary feet?
Yet here ye dance as other mortals do!

#### THE FAIR ONE   *(dancing).*

Then at our ball, what doth he here?

FAUST (*dancing*).

Ha! He in all must interfere.
When others dance, with him it lies
Their dancing still to criticise.
Each step he counts as never made,
On which his skill is not display'd.
He's most annoy'd if we advance;
If in one narrow round you'd dance,
As he in his old mill doth move,
Your dancing doubtless he'd approve.
And still more pleas'd he'd be **if you**
Would him salute with rev'rence due.

PROCTOPHANTASMIST.

Still here! what arrogance! unheard of quite!
Vanish! we now have fill'd the world with light!
Laws are unheeded by the devil's host;
Wise as we are, yet Tegel hath its ghost.
How long at this delusion, day and night,
Have I not vainly swept? 'Tis monstrous quite!

THE FAIR ONE.

Cease here to teaze us any more, I pray.

PROCTOPHANTASMIST.

Phantoms, I plainly to your face declare,
Since my own spirit can exert no sway,
No spiritual control myself will bear.

(*The dancing continues.*)

To-night I see I shall in nought succeed;
But I'm prepar'd my travels to pursue,
And hope before my final step indeed,
To triumph over bards and devils too.

MEPHISTOPHELES.

Now in some puddle will he take his station,
Such is his mode of seeking consolation;
Where leeches, feasting on his blood, will drain
Spirit and spirits from his haunted brain.

(*To* FAUST, *who has left the dance.*)

But why the charming damsel leave, I pray,
Who to you in the dance so sweetly sang?

FAUST.

Ah! in the very middle of her lay,
Out of her mouth a small red mouse there sprang.

MEPHISTOPHELES.

Suppose there did!   One must not be too nice:
'Twas well it was not grey, let that suffice.
Who 'mid his pleasures for a trifle cares?

FAUST.

Then saw I——

MEPHISTOPHELES.

What?

FAUST.

Mephisto, seest thou there
Standing far off, a lone child, pale and fair?
Slow from the spot her drooping form she tears,
And seems with shackl'd feet to move along.
I own within me the delusion's strong
That she the likeness of my Gretchen wears.

MEPHISTOPHELES.

Gaze not upon her!   'Tis not good!   Forbear!
'Tis lifeless, magical, a shape of air,
An idol!   Such to meet with, bodes no good ;
That rigid look of her's doth freeze man's blood,
And well-nigh petrifies his heart to stone,—
The story of Medusa thou hast known.

FAUST.

Ay, verily! a corpse's eyes are those,
Which there was no fond loving hand to close.
That is the bosom I so fondly press'd,
That my sweet Gretchen's form, so oft caress'd.

MEPHISTOPHELES.

Deluded fool!   'Tis magic, I declare !
To each she doth his lov'd one's image wear.

FAUST.

What bliss ! what torture ! vainly I essay
To turn me from that piteous look away.
How strangely doth a single crimson line
Around that lovely neck its coil entwine,
It shows no broader than a knife's blunt edge.

MEPHISTOPHELES.

Quite right !   I see it also, and allege
That she beneath her arm her head can bear,
Since Perseus cut it off.—But you I swear

Your fondness for delusion cherish still !
Come now, my friend, and let's ascend the hill !
As on the Prater all is bright and gay.
And truly if my senses are not gone,
I see a theatre,—what's going on ?

SERVIBILIS.

They are about to recommence ;—the play
Will be the last of seven, and spick-span new.
'Tis usual here that number to present.
A dilettante did the piece invent,
And dilettanti will enact it too.
Excuse me, gentlemen ; to me's assign'd
As dilettante to uplift the curtain.

MEPHISTOPHELES.

You on the Blocksberg I'm rejoic'd to find.
That 'tis your most appropriate sphere is certain

# WALPURGIS-NIGHT'S DREAM;

## OR,

## OBERON AND TITANIA'S

## GOLDEN WEDDING-FEAST.

### INTERMEZZO.

### *Theatre.*

#### MANAGER.
Vales, where mists still shift and play,
    To ancient hill succeeding,—
These our scenes ;—so we, to-day,
    May rest, brave sons of Mieding.

#### HERALD.
That the marriage golden be,
    Must fifty years be ended.
More dear this feast of gold to me,
    Contention now suspended.

#### OBERON.
Spirits, are ye hov'ring near,
    On downy pinions sailing?
Before your king and queen appear,
    Their reconcilement hailing.

#### PUCK.
Puck draws near and wheels about
    In mazy circles dancing!
Hundreds swell his joyous shout,
    Behind him still advancing.

#### ARIEL.

Ariel wakes his dainty air,
  His lyre celestial stringing.—
Fools he lureth, and the fair,
  With his celestial singing.

#### OBERON.

Wedded ones, would ye agree,
  We court your imitation;
Would ye fondly love as we,
  We counsel separation.

#### TITANIA.

If husband scold and wife retort,
  Then bear them far asunder;
Her to the burning south transport,
  And him the North Pole under.

#### THE WHOLE ORCHESTRA.   (*Fortissimo.*)

Flies and midges all unite
  With frog and chirping cricket,
Our orchestra throughout the night,
  Resounding in the thicket!

#### *Solo.*

Yonder doth the bagpipe come!
  Its sack an airy bubble.
Schnick, schnick, schnack, with nasal hum,
  Its notes it doth redouble.

#### EMBRYO SPIRIT.

Spider's foot and midge's wing,
  A toad in form and feature;
Together verses it can string,
  Though scarce a living creature

#### A LITTLE PAIR.

Tiny step and lofty bound,
  Through dew and exhalation;
Ye trip it deftly on the ground,
  But gain no elevation.

#### INQUISITIVE TRAVELLER.

Can I indeed believe my eyes?
  Is't not mere masquerading?
What! Oberon in beauteous guise,
  Among the groups parading!

ORTHODOX.

No claws, no tail to whisk about,
  To fright us at our revel;—
Yet like the gods of Greece, no doubt,
  He too's a genuine devil.

NORTHERN ARTIST.

These that I'm hitting off to-day
  Are sketches unpretending;
Towards Italy without delay,
  My steps I think of bending.

PURIST.

Alas! ill-fortune leads me here,
  Where riot still grows louder;
And 'mong the witches gather'd here,
  But two alone wear powder.

YOUNG WITCH.

Your powder and your petticoat,
  Suit hags, there's no gainsaying;
Hence I sit fearless on my goat,
  My naked charms displaying.

MATRON.

We're too well-bred to squabble here,
  Or insult back to render;
But may you wither soon, my dear,
  Although so young and tender.

LEADER OF THE BAND.

Nose of fly and gnat's proboscis,
  Throng not the naked beauty!
Frogs and crickets in the mosses,
  Keep time and do your duty!

WEATHERCOCK (*towards one side*).

What charming company I view
  Together here collected!
Gay bachelors, a hopeful crew,
  And brides so unaffected.

WEATHERCOCK (*towards the other side*).

Unless indeed the yawning ground
  Should open to receive them,
From this vile crew, with sudden bound
  To Hell I'd jump and leave them.

### XENIEN.

With small sharp shears, in insect guise,
  Behold us at your revel!
That we may tender, filial-wise,
  Our homage to the devil.

### HENNINGS.

Look now at yonder eager crew,
  How naïvely they're jesting;
That they have tender hearts and true
  They stoutly keep protesting.

### MUSAGET.

Oneself amid this witchery
  How pleasantly one loses;
For witches easier are to me
  To govern than the Muses!

### CI-DEVANT GENIUS OF THE AGE

With proper folks when we appear,
  No one can then surpass us!
Keep close, wide is the Blocksberg here
  As Germany's Parnassus.

### INQUISITIVE TRAVELLER.

How name ye that stiff formal man,
  Who strides with lofty paces?
He tracks the game wh're'er he can,
  He scents the Jesuits' traces.

### CRANE.

Where waters troubl'd are or clear,
  To fish I am delighted;
Your pious gentlemen appear
  With devils here united.

### WORLDLING.

By pious people it is true,
  No medium is rejected;
Conventicles, and not a few,
  On Blocksberg are erected.

### DANCER.

Another choir is drawing nigh,
  Far off the drums are beating.
Be still! 'tis but the bittern's cry,
  Its changeless note repeating.

DANCING MASTER.

Each twirls about and never stops.
  And as he can advances.
The crooked leaps!　The clumsy hops
  Nor careth how he dances.

FIDDLER.

To take each other's life, I trow,
  Would cordially delight them!
As Orpheus' lyre the beasts, so now
  The bagpipe doth unite them.

DOGMATIST.

My views, in spite of doubt and sneer
  I hold with stout persistance,
Inferring from the devils here,
  The evil one's existence.

IDEALIST.

My every sense rules Phantasy
  With sway quite too potential.
Sure I'm demented if the *I*
  Alone is the essential.

REALIST.

This entity's a dreadful bore
  And cannot choose but vex me;
The ground beneath me ne'er before
  Thus totter'd to perplex me.

SUPERNATURALIST.

Well pleas'd assembl'd here I view
  Of spirits this profusion;
From devils, touching angels too,
  I gather some conclusion.

SCEPTIC.

The ignis fatuus they track out,
  And think they're near the treasure.
Devil alliterates with doubt,
  Here I abide with pleasure.

LEADER OF THE BAND.

Frog and cricket in the mosses, —
  Confound your gasconading!
Nose of fly and gnat's proboscis;—
  Most tuneful serenading!

#### THE KNOWING ONES.

As sans-souci this host we greet,
　Their jovial humour showing,
There's now no walking on our feet,
　So on our heads we're going.

#### THE AWKWARD ONES.

In seasons past we snatch'd, tis true,
　Some tit-bits by our cunning;
Our shoes, alas, are now danced through
　On our bare soles we're running.

#### WILL-O'-THE-WISPS.

From marshy bogs we sprang to light,
　Yet here behold us dancing;
The gayest gallants of the night,
　In glitt'ring rows advancing.

#### SHOOTING STAR.

With rapid motion from on high,
　I shot in starry splendour;
Now prostrate on the grass I lie;—
　Who aid will kindly render?

#### THE MASSIVE ONES.

Room there! wheel round! They're coming! lo!
　Down sink the bending grasses.
Though spirits, yet their limbs we know,
　Are hugh substantial masses.

#### PUCK.

Don't stamp so heavily, I pray,
　Like elephants you're treading;
And 'mong the elves be Puck to-day
　The stoutest at the wedding.

#### ARIEL.

If nature boon, or subtle sprite,
　Endow your soul with pinions;—
Then follow to yon rosy height,
　Through ether's calm dominions.

#### ORCHESTRA     (*pianissimo*).

Drifting cloud and misty wreathes
　Are fill'd with light elysian.
O'er reed and leaf the zephyr breathes,
　So fades the fairy vision!

## *A gloomy Day    A Plain.*

### FAUST *and* MEPHISTOPHELES

#### FAUST.

In misery! despairing! long wandering pitifully on the face ot the earth and now imprison'd! This gentle hapless creature, immur'd in the dungeon as a malefactor and reserved for horrid tortures! That it should come to this! To this!—Perfidious, worthless spirit, and this thou hast concealed from me!—Stand! ay, stand! roll in malicious rage thy fiendish eyes! Stand and brave me with thine insupportable presence! Imprison'd! In hopeless misery! delivered over to the power of evil spirits and the judgment of unpitying humanity! And me, the while, thou wert lulling with tasteless dissipations!—concealing from me her growing anguish, and leaving her to perish without help!

#### MEPHISTOPHELES.

She is not the first.

#### FAUST.

Hound! Execrable monster! Back with him, oh thou infinite spirit! back with the reptile into his dog's shape, in which it was his wont to scamper before me at eventide, to roll before the feet of the harmless wanderer, and to fasten on his shoulders when he fell. Change him again into his favourite shape, that he may crouch on his belly before me in the dust, whilst I spurn him with my foot, the reprobate!—Not the first!—Woe! Woe! By no human soul is it conceivable that more than one human creature has ever sunk into a depth of wretchedness like this, or that the first, in her writhing death-agony, should not have atoned in the sight of all-pardoning Heaven, for the guilt of all the rest! The misery of this one pierces me to the very marrow, and harrows up my soul; thou art grinning calmly over the doom of thousands!

#### MEPHISTOPHELES.

Now we are once again at our wit's end, just where the o'erstrained reason of you mortals snaps. Why dost thou seek our fellowship, if thou canst not go through with it? Would'st fly, and art not proof against dizziness? Do we force ourselves on thee, or thou on us?

#### FAUST.

Cease thus to gnash thy ravenous fangs at me! I loathe thee!—Great and glorious spirit, thou who didst vouchsafe to reveal thyself unto me, thou who dost know my very heart and soul, why hast thou linked me with this base associate, who feeds on mischief and revels in destruction?

#### MEPHISTOPHELES.

Hast done?

#### FAUST.

Save her! or woe to thee! The direst of curses on thee for thousands of years!

#### MEPHISTOPHELES.

I cannot loose the bands of the avenger, nor withdraw his bolts.—Save her!—Who was it plunged her into perdition? 1 or thou?

#### Faust

(*looks wildly around*).

#### MEPHISTOPHELES.

Would'st grasp the thunder? Well for you, poor mortals, that 'tis not yours to wield! To smite to atoms, the being however innocent, who obstructs his path, such is the tyrant's fashion of relieving himself in difficulties.

#### FAUST.

Convey me thither! She shall be free!

#### MEPHISTOPHELES.

And the danger to which thou dost expose thyself? Know, the guilt of blood, shed by thy hand, lies yet upon the town. Over the place where fell the murdered one, avenging spirits hover and watch for the returning murderer.

#### FAUST.

This too from thee? The death and downfall of a world be on thee, monster! Conduct me thither, I say, and set her free!

#### MEPHISTOPHELES.

I will conduct thee, and what I can do,—hear! Have I all power in heaven and upon earth? I'll cloud the senses of the warder,—do thou possess thyself of the keys and lead her forth with human hand. I will keep watch! The magic steeds are waiting, I bear thee off. Thus much is in my power.

#### FAUST.

Up and away!"

*Night.   An open Plain.*

FAUST, MEPHISTOPHELES.

*(Rushing along on black horses.)*

FAUST.
What weave they round the Ravenstone?

MEPHISTOPHELES.
I know not what they shape and brew.

FAUST.
They're soaring, swooping, bending, stooping.

MEPHISTOPHELES.
A witches' pack.

FAUST.
They charm, they strew.

MEPHISTOPHELES.
On! On!

*Dungeon.*

FAUST (*with a bunch of keys and a lamp before a small iron
door*).
A fear unwonted o'er my spirit falls;
Man's concentrated woe o'erwhelms me here;
She dwells immur'd within these dripping walls;
Her only trespass a delusion dear!
And thou dost linger at the fatal door!
Thou dread'st to look upon her face once more!
On! While thou dalliest, draws her death-hour near.

*(He seizes the lock.   Singing within.)*

My mother, the harlot,
She took me and slew!
My father, the scoundrel,
Hath eaten me too!
My sweet little sister
Hath all my bones laid,
Where soft winds are playing
All in the green shade;

'Then became I a wood-bird, and sang on the spray,
Fly away! little bird, fly away! fly away!
                    (FAUST—*opening the lock.*)
Ah! she forebodes not that her lover's near,
The clanking chains, the rustling straw to hear.
                    *He enters.*
          MARGARET (*hiding her face in the bed of straw*).
Woe! woe! they come! oh bitter 'tis to die!
                    FAUST (*softly*).
Hush! hush! be still! I come to set thee free?
              MARGARET (*throwing herself at his feet*).
If thou art human, feel my misery.
                    FAUST.
Thou wilt awake the jailor with thy cry!
              (*He grasps the chains to unlock them.*)
                    MARGARET (*on her knees*).
Who, executioner, to thee could give
O'er me this cruel power?
To bear me off at midnight's solemn hour!
Be merciful, and spare me! let me live!
Is dawn not time enough?

                    (*she stands up.*)
              I'm still so young!
So very young, and must so early die!
Fair was I once, thence hath my ruin sprung.
My love is now afar, he then was nigh;
Torn lies the garland, the fair blossoms strew'd.
Oh do not seize me with a hand so rude!
Spare me!   What harm have I e'er done to thee?
For mercy let me not in vain implore,
I ne'er have seen thee in my life before!
                    FAUST.
Can I endure this bitter agony?
                    MARGARET.
I'm wholly in thy power.   Ah suffer me
But once again to give my babe the breast.
Through the long night I sooth'd it and caress'd;
They took it from me but to give me pain,
And now, they say that I my child have slain.
Ah, ne'er shall I be happy, ne'er again.
Then they sing songs about me! How wicked of the throng,

A ballad of the olden time ends so,
How came they to apply the song?

FAUST

(*throwing himself on the ground*).

See, at thy feet a lover bendeth low,
To loose the bonds of wretchedness and woe.

MARGARET

(*throws herself beside him*).

Oh, let us kneel and move the saints by prayer!
Look! look! yon stairs below
Under the threshold there,
Hell's flames are all aglow!
Beneath the floor
With hideous noise.
The devils roar!

FAUST (*aloud*).

Gretchen! Gretchen!

MARGARET (*listening*).

That was my lov'd one's voice!

(*she springs up, the chains fall off.*)

Where is he? I have heard him call, I'm free!
I will away, there's none shall hinder me.
I to his neck will fly,
Upon his bosom lie!
Gretchen, he call'd! on yonder threshold stood.
Through all the howling of Hell's fiery flood,
The fiends' dark sneers, their devilish scorn above,
I knew the sweet, the blissful tones of love.

FAUST.

'Tis I! .

MARGARET.

'Tis thou! O say so once again!

(*embracing him.*)

'Tis he! 'Tis he! where's now the torturing pain?
Where are the fetters? where the dungeon's gloom?
'Tis thou! 'Tis thou! To save me thou art come!
And I am sav'd!—
Already now the very street I see
Where the first time I caught a glimpse of thee.

And there too is the pleasant garden shade,
'Where I and Martha for thy coming staid.

FAUST

(endeavouring to lead her away).

Come! come away!

MARGARET.

Oh still delay!
I love to linger where thou stay'st.

(caressing him.)

FAUST.

Oh come! for if thou dost not haste,
Our ling'ring we shall both deplore.

MARGARET.

What dearest? can'st thou kiss me now no more!
So short a time away from me, and yet,
Love's fond embrace thou could'st so soon forget!
Why on thy neck so anxious do I feel?
When formerly a perfect heaven of bliss,
From thy dear looks and words would o'er me steal.
Ah! with what tenderness thou then did'st kiss!
Kiss me!
Or I'll kiss thee!

(she embraces him.)

Woe! woe! Thy lips are cold,—are dumb.
Thy love where hast thou left?
Who hath me of thy love bereft?

(she turns away from him.)

FAUST.

Only take courage! dearest! prithee, come!
Thee to my heart with tenderness I'll hold,
And cherish thee with ardour thousand-fold;
I but entreat thee now to follow me!

MARGARET

(turning towards him).

And art thou he? and art thou really he?

FAUST.

'Tis I! Oh come!

MARGARET.

Thou wilt strike off my chain,

And thou wilt take me to thine arms again.

How comes it that thou dost not shrink from me?—
And dost thou know, love, whom thou would'st set free?

FAUST.

Come! come! already night begins to wane.

MARGARET.

I sent my mother to her grave,
I drown'd my child beneath the wave.
Was it not given to thee and me—thee too?
'Tis thou thyself! I scarce believe it yet.
Give me thy hand! It is no dream! 'Tis true!
Thine own dear hand!—But how is this?   'Tis wet!
Quick, wipe it off!   It seems like blood—Ah me!
Whose blood? what hast thou done? put up thy sword;
I pray thee, do!

FAUST.

Death is in every word.
Oh, dearest, let the past forgotten be.

MARGARET.

Yet must thou linger here in sorrow.
The graves I will describe to thee,
And thou must see to them to-morrow.
Reserve the best place for my mother,
Close at her side inter my brother,
Me at some little distance lay,
But, I entreat thee, not too far away!
And place my little babe on my right breast.
The little one alone will lie near me!—
Ah 'twas a sweet, a precious joy, of yore
To nestle at thy side so lovingly!
It will be mine no more, ah never more!
I feel as if I forc'd my love on thee,
As if thou still wert thrusting me away;
Yet 'tis thyself, thy fond, kind looks I see.

FAUST.

If thou dost feel 'tis I, then come, I pray.

MARGARET.

What, there? without?

FAUST.

Yes, forth in the free air.

MARGARET.

Ay, if the grave's without,—If death lurk there!
Hence to the everlasting resting-place,
And not one step beyond!—Thou'rt leaving me?
Oh Henry! would that I could go with thee!

FAUST.

Thou can'st! But will it! open stands the door.

MARGARET.

I dare not go! I've nought to hope for more.
What boots it to escape? They lurk for me.
'Tis wretched still to beg from day to day,
And burthen'd with an evil conscience too!
'Tis wretched in a foreign land to stray,
And they will catch me whatsoe'er I do!

FAUST.

But I will ever bear thee company.

MARGARET.

Quick! Quick!
Save thy poor child
Keep to the path
The brook along,
Over the bridge
To the wood beyond,
To the left, where the plank is,
In the pond.
Seize it at once!
It tries to rise,
It struggles yet!
Save it. Oh save!

FAUST.

Collect thy thoughts, one step and thou art free!

MARGARET.

Were we but only past the hill!
There sits my mother on a stone.
Over my brain there falls a chill!
There sits my mother on a stone;
Slowly her head moves to and fro
She winks not, nods not, her head droops low.
She slumber'd so long, nor wak'd again.
That we might be happy she slumber'd then.
Ah! those were pleasant times!

FAUST.

Alas! since here
Nor argument avails, nor prayer, nor tear,
I'll venture forcibly to bear thee hence!

MARGARET.

Loose me!   I will not suffer violence!
Withdraw thy murd'rous hand, hold not so fast!
I have done all to please thee in the past.

FAUST.

Day dawns! My love! My love!

MARGARET.

Yes! day draws near
The day of judgment, too, will soon appear.
It should have been my bridal!   No one tell,
That thy poor Margaret thou hast known too well.
Woe to my garland! Its bloom is o'er!
Though not at the dance, we shall meet once more.
The crowd doth gather, in silence it rolls.
The squares, the streets, scarce hold the throng.
The staff is broken,—the death-bell tolls,—
They bind and seize me; I'm hurried along,
To the seat of blood already I'm bound;
Quivers each neck as the naked steel
Quivers on mine the blow to deal.
The silence of the grave now broods around!

FAUST.

Would I had ne'er been born!

MEPHISTOPHELES (*appears without*).

Up! or you're lost.
Vain hesitation!   Babbling, quaking!
My steeds are shiv'ring.   Morn is breaking.

MARGARET.

What from the floor ascendeth like a ghost?
'Tis he!   'Tis he!   Him from my presence chase!
What is his purpose in this holy place?
It is for me he cometh!

FAUST.

Thou shalt live!

MARGARET.

Judgment of God!   To thee my soul I give!

MEPHISTOPHELES (*to* FAUST).
Come! come!   I'll leave thee else to share her doom.

MARGARET.
Father, I'm thine!   Save me!   To thee I come
Angelic hosts! your downy pinions wave,
Encamp around me to protect and save!
Henry.   I shudder now to look on thee.

MEPHISTOPHELES.
She now is judg'd!

VOICES (*from above*).
Is saved!

MEPHISTOPHELES (*to* FAUST.)
Come thou with me!
(*Vanishes with* FAUST.)

VOICE (*from within, dying away*).
Henry! Henry!

# IPHIGENIA IN TAURIS.

## PERSONS OF THE DRAMA.

IPHIGENIA.     THOAS, *King of the Taurians*
ORESTES.     PYLADES.     ARKAS.

## ACT THE FIRST.

### SCENE I.

*A Grove before the Temple of Diana.*

#### IPHIGENIA.

BENEATH your leafy gloom, ye waving boughs
Of this old, shady, consecrated grove,
As in the goddess' silent sanctuary,
With the same shudd'ring feeling forth I step,
As when I trod it first, nor ever here
Doth my unquiet spirit feel at home.
Long as the mighty will, to which I bow,
Hath kept me here conceal'd, still, as at first,
I feel myself a stranger.   For the sea
Doth sever me, alas! from those I love,
And day by day upon the shore I stand,
My soul still seeking for the land of Greece.
But to my sighs, the hollow-sounding waves
Bring, save their own hoarse murmurs, no reply
Alas for him! who friendless and alone,
Remote from parents and from brethren dwells;
From him grief snatches every coming joy
Ere it doth reach his lip.   His restless thoughts
Revert for ever to his father's halls,
Where first to him the radiant sun unclos'd
The gates of heav'n; where closer, day by day,
Brothers and sisters, leagu'd in pastime sweet,
Around each other twin'd the bonds of love.
I will not judge the counsel of the gods;

Yet, truly, woman's lot doth merit pity.
Man rules alike at home and in the field,
Nor is in foreign climes without resource;
Possession gladdens him, him conquest crowns,
And him an honourable death awaits.
How circumscrib'd is woman's destiny!
Obedience to a harsh, imperious lord,
Her duty, and her comfort; sad her fate,
Whom hostile fortune drives to lands remote:
Thus I, by noble Thoas, am detain'd,
Bound with a heavy, though a sacred chain.
Oh! with what shame, Diana, I confess
That with repugnance I perform these rites
For thee, divine protectress! unto whom
I would in freedom dedicate my life.
In thee, Diana, I have always hop'd,
And still I hope in thee, who didst infold
Within the holy shelter of thine arm
The outcast daughter of the mighty king.
Daughter of Jove! hast thou from ruin'd Troy
Led back in triumph to his native land
The mighty man, whom thou didst sore afflict,
His daughter's life in sacrifice demanding,—
Hast thou for him, the godlike Agamemnon,
Who to thine altar led his darling child,
Preserv'd his wife, Electra, and his son,
His dearest treasures?—then at length restore
Thy suppliant also to her friends and home,
And save her, as thou once from death didst save,
So now, from living here, a second death.


## SCENE II.

IPHIGENIA.        ARKAS.

### ARKAS.

The king hath sent me hither, and commands
To hail Diana's priestess. This the day,
On which for new and wonderful success,
Tauris her goddess thanks. The king and host
Draw near,—I come to herald their approach.

### IPHIGENIA.

We are prepar'd to give them worthy greeting;
Our goddess doth behold with gracious eye
The welcome sacrifice from Thoas' hand.

### ARKAS.

Oh, priestess, that thine eye more mildly beam'd,- -
Thou much-rever'd one,—that I found thy glance,
O consecrated maid, more calm, more bright,
To all a happy omen!   Still doth grief,
With gloom mysterious, shroud thy inner mind;
Still, still, through many a year we wait in vain
For one confiding utt'rance from thy breast.
Long as I've known thee in this holy place,
That look of thine hath ever made me shudder;
And, as with iron bands, thy soul remains
Lock'd in the deep recesses of thy breast.

### IPHIGENIA.

As doth become the exile and the orphan.

### ARKAS.

Dost thou then here seem exil'd and an orphan?

### IPHIGENIA.

Can foreign scenes our fatherland replace?

### ARKAS.

Thy fatherland is foreign now to thee.

### IPHIGENIA.

Hence is it that my bleeding heart ne'er heals.
In early youth, when first my soul, in love,
Held father, mother, brethren fondly twin'd,
A group of tender germs, in union sweet,
We sprang in beauty from the parent stem,
And heavenward grew.   An unrelenting curse
Then seiz'd and sever'd me from those I lov'd,
And wrench'd with iron grasp the beauteous bands.
It vanish'd then, the fairest charm of youth,
The simple gladness of life's early dawn;
Though sav'd, I was a shadow of myself,
And life's fresh joyance bloom'd in me no more.

### ARKAS.

If thus thou ever dost lament thy fate,
I must accuse thee of ingratitude.

IPHIGENIA.
Thanks have you ever.

ARKAS.
Not the honest thanks
Which prompt the heart to offices of love;
The joyous glance, revealing to the host
A grateful spirit, with its lot content.
When thee a deep mysterious destiny
Brought to this sacred fane, long years ago,
To greet thee, as a treasure sent from heaven,
With reverence and affection, Thoas came.
Benign and friendly was this shore to thee,
Which had before each stranger's heart appall'd,
For, till thy coming, none e'er trod our realm
But fell, according to an ancient rite,
A bloody victim at Diana's shrine.

IPHIGENIA.
Freely to breathe alone is not to live.
Say, is it life, within this holy fane,
Like a poor ghost around its sepulchre
To linger out my days?   Or call you that
A life of conscious happiness and joy,
When every hour, dream'd listlessly away,
Leads to those dark and melancholy days,
Which the sad troop of the departed spend
In self-forgetfulness on Lethe's shore?
A useless life is but an early death;
This, woman's lot, is eminently mine.

ARKAS.
I can forgive, though I must needs deplore,
The noble pride which underrates itself.
It robs thee of the happiness of life.
And hast thou, since thy coming here, done nought?
Who cheer'd the gloomy temper of the king?
Who hath with gentle eloquence annull'd,
From year to year, the usage of our sires,
By which, a victim at Diana's shrine,
Each stranger perish'd, thus from certain death
Sending so oft the rescued captive home?
Hath not Diana, harbouring no revenge
For this suspension of her bloody rites,

In richest measure heard thy gentle prayer?
On joyous pinions o'er the advancing host,
Doth not triumphant conquest proudly soar
And feels not every one a happier lot,
Since Thoas, who so long hath guided us
With wisdom and with valour, sway'd by thee,
The joy of mild benignity approves,
Which leads him to relax the rigid claims
Of mute submission?   Call thyself useless! Thou,
Thou, from whose being o'er a thousand hearts,
A healing balsam flows? when to a race,
To whom a god consign'd thee, thou dost prove
A fountain of perpetual happiness,
And from this dire inhospitable shore
Dost to the stranger grant a safe return?

IPHIGENIA.

The little done doth vanish to the mind,
Which forward sees how much remains to do.

ARKAS.

Him dost thou praise, who underrates his deeds?

IPHIGENIA.

Who estimates his deeds is justly blam'd.

ARKAS.

We blame alike, who proudly disregard
Their genuine merit, and who vainly prize
Their spurious worth too highly.   Trust me, priestess,
And hearken.to the counsel of a man
With honest zeal devoted to thy service:
When Thoas comes to-day to speak with thee
Lend to his purpos'd words a gracious ear.

IPHIGENIA.

The well-intention'd counsel troubles me:
His offer studiously I've sought to shun.

ARKAS.

Thy duty and thy interest calmly weigh.
Since the king lost his son, he trusts but few,
Nor those as formerly.   Each noble's son
He views with jealous eye as his successor;
He dreads a solitary, helpless age,
Or rash rebellion, or untimely death.
A Scythian studies not the rules of speech,

And least of all the king.   He who is used
To act and to command, knows not the art,
From far, with subtle tact, to guide discourse
Through many windings to its destin'd goal.
Do not embarrass him with shy reserve
And studied misconception : graciously,
And with submission, meet the royal wish.

IPHIGENIA.

Shall I then speed the doom that threatens me?

ARKAS.

His gracious offer canst thou call a threat?

IPHIGENIA.

'Tis the most terrible of all to me.

ARKAS.

For his affection grant him confidence.

IPHIGENIA.

If he will first redeem my soul from fear.

ARKAS.

Why dost thou hide from him thy origin?

IPHIGENIA.

A priestess secrecy doth well become.

ARKAS.

Nought to our monarch should a secret be ;
And, though he doth not seek to fathom thine,
His noble nature feels, ay, deeply feels,
That studiously thou hid'st thyself from him.

IPHIGENIA.

Displeasure doth he harbour 'gainst me, then ?

ARKAS.

Almost it seems so.   True, he speaks not of thee,
But casual words have taught me that the wish
To call thee his hath firmly seiz'd his soul ;
Oh, do not leave the monarch to himself!
Lest his displeasure, rip'ning in his breast,
Should work thee woe, so with repentance thou
Too late my faithful counsel shalt recall.

IPHIGENIA.

How ! doth the monarch purpose what no man
Of noble mind, who loves his honest name,
Whose bosom reverence for the gods restrains,
Would ever think of?   Will he force employ

To tear me from this consecrated fane?
Then will I call the gods, and chiefly thee,
Diana, goddess resolute, to aid me;
Thyself a virgin, thou'lt a virgin shield,
And succour to thy priestess gladly yield.

ARKAS.

Be tranquil!   Passion, and youth's fiery blood
Impel not Thoas rashly to commit
A deed so lawless.   In his present mood,
I fear from him another harsh resolve,
Which (for his soul is steadfast and unmov'd,)
He then will execute without delay.
Therefore I pray thee, canst thou grant no more,
At least be grateful—give thy confidence.

IPHIGENIA.

Oh tell me what is further known to thee.

ARKAS.

Learn it from him.   I see the king approach;
Thou honour'st him, and thy own heart will prompt thee
To meet him kindly and with confidence.
A noble man by woman's gentle word
May oft be led.

IPHIGENIA, *alone.*
             I see not how I can
Follow the counsel of my faithful friend.
But willingly the duty I perform
Of giving thanks for benefits receiv'd,
And much I wish that to the king my lips
With truth could utter what would please his ear.

## SCENE III.

IPHIGENIA.        THOAS.

IPHIGENIA.

Her royal gifts the goddess shower on thee
Imparting conquest, wealth, and high renown.
Dominion, and the welfare of thy house,
With the fulfilment of each pious wish,
That thou, who over numbers rul'st supreme,
Thyself may'st be supreme in happiness!

M

THOAS.

Contented were I with my people's praise;
My conquests others more than I enjoy.
Oh! be he king or subject, he's most blest,
Who in his home finds happiness and peace.
Thou shar'dst my sorrow, when a hostile sword
Tore from my side my last, my dearest son;
Long as fierce vengeance occupied my heart,
I did not feel my dwelling's dreary void;
But now, returning home, my rage appeas'd,
My foes defeated, and my son aveng'd,
I find there nothing left to comfort me.
The glad obedience, which I used to see
Kindling in every eye, is smother'd now
In discontent and gloom; each, pond'ring, weighs
The changes which a future day may bring,
And serves the childless king, because compell'd.
To-day I come within this sacred fane,
Which I have often enter'd to implore
And thank the gods for conquest. In my breast
I bear an old and fondly-cherish'd wish,
To which methinks thou canst not be a stranger;
Thee, maid, a blessing to myself and realm,
I hope, as bride, to carry to my home.

IPHIGENIA.

Too great thine offer, king, to one unknown;
Abash'd the fugitive before thee stands,
Who on this shore sought only what thou gav'st,
Safety and peace.

THOAS.

　　　　　　Thus still to shroud thyself
From me, as from the lowest, in the veil
Of mystery which wrapp'd thy coming here,
Would in no country be deem'd just or right.
Strangers this shore appall'd; 'twas so ordain'd
Alike by law and stern necessity.
From thee alone—a kindly welcom'd guest,
Who hast enjoy'd each hallow'd privilege,
And spent thy days in freedom unrestrain'd—
From thee I hop'd that confidence to gain
Which every faithful host may justly claim.

IPHIGENIA.

If I conceal'd, O king, my name, my race,
'Twas fear that prompted me, and not mistrust.
For didst thou know who stands before thee now,
And what accursed head thy arm protects,
A shudd'ring horror would possess thy heart;
And, far from wishing me to share thy throne,
Thou, ere the time appointed, from thy realm
Wouldst banish me perchance, and thrust me forth
Before a glad reunion with my friends
And period to my wand'rings is ordain'd,
To meet that sorrow, which in every clime,
With cold, inhospitable, fearful hand,
Awaits the outcast, exil'd from his home.

THOAS.

Whate'er respecting thee the gods decree,
Whate'er their doom for thee and for thy house,
Since thou hast dwelt amongst us, and enjoy'd
The privilege the pious stranger claims,
To me hath fail'd no blessing sent from Heaven;
And to persuade me, that protecting thee
I shield a guilty head, were hard indeed.

IPHIGENIA.

Thy bounty, not the guest, draws blessings down.

THOAS.

The kindness shown the wicked is not blest.
End then thy silence, priestess; not unjust
Is he who doth demand it.   In my hands
The goddess plac'd thee; thou hast been to me
As sacred as to her, and her behest
Shall for the future also be my law.
If thou canst hope in safety to return
Back to thy kindred, I renounce my claims:
But is thy homeward path for ever clos'd—
Or doth thy race in hopeless exile rove,
Or lie extinguish'd by some mighty woe—
Then may I claim thee by more laws than one.
Speak openly, thou know'st I keep my word.

IPHIGENIA.

Its ancient bands reluctantly my tongue
Doth loose, a long-hid secret to divulge;

M 2

For once imparted, it resumes no more
The safe asylum of the inmost heart,
But thenceforth, as the powers above decree,
Doth work its ministry of weal or woe.
Attend!   I issue from the Titan's race.

THOAS.

A word momentous calmly hast thou spoken.
Him nam'st thou ancestor whom all the world
Knows as a sometime favourite of the gods ?
Is it that Tantalus, whom Jove himself
Drew to his council and his social board ?
On whose experienc'd words, with wisdom fraught,
As on the language of an oracle,
E'en gods delighted hung ?

IPHIGENIA.

'Tis even he;
But gods should not hold intercourse with men
As with themselves.   Too weak the human race,
Not to grow dizzy on unwonted heights.
Ignoble was he not, and no betrayer;
To be the Thunderer's slave, he was too great;
To be his friend and comrade,—but a man.
His crime was human, and their doom severe;
For poets sing, that treachery and pride
Did from Jove's table hurl him headlong down.
To grovel in the depths of Tartarus.
Alas, and his whole race their hate pursues.

THOAS.

Bear they their own guilt, or their ancestors' ?

IPHIGENIA.

The Titan's mighty breast and nervous frame
Was his descendant's certain heritage;
But round their brow Jove forg'd a band of brass.
Wisdom and patience, prudence and restraint,
He from their gloomy, fearful eye conceal'd;
In them each passion grew to savage rage,
And headlong rush'd uncheck'd.   The Titan's son,
The strong-will'd Pelops, won his beauteous bride,
Hippodamia, child of Œnomaus,
Through treachery and murder; she ere long
Bore him two children, Atreus and Thyestes;

With envy they beheld the growing love
Their father cherish'd for a first-born son
Sprung from another union.   Bound by hate,
In secret they contrive their brother's death.
The sire, the crime imputing to his wife,
With savage fury claim'd from her his child,
And she in terror did destroy herself—

THOAS.

Thou'rt silent?   Pause not in thy narrative:
Do not repent thy confidence—say on!

IPHIGENIA.

How blest is he who his progenitors
With pride remembers, to the list'ner tells
The story of their greatness, of their deeds,
And, silently rejoicing, sees himself
Link'd to this goodly chain!   For the same stock
Bears not the monster and the demigod:
A line, or good or evil, ushers in
The glory or the terror of the world.—
After the death of Pelops, his two sons
Rul'd o'er the city with divided sway.
But such an union could not long endure.
His brother's honour first Thyestes wounds.
In vengeance Atreus drove him from the realm.
Thyestes, planning horrors, long before
Had stealthily procur'd his brother's son,
Whom he in secret nurtur'd as his own.
Revenge and fury in his breast he pour'd,
Then to the royal city sent him forth,
That in his uncle he might slay his sire,
The meditated murder was disclos'd,
And by the king most cruelly aveng'd,
Who slaughter'd, as he thought, his brother's son.
Too late he learn'd whose dying tortures met
His drunken gaze; and seeking to assuage
The insatiate vengeance that possess'd his soul,
He plann'd a deed unheard of.   He assum'd
A friendly tone, seem'd reconcil'd, appeas'd,
And lur'd his brother, with his children twain,
Back to his kingdom; these he seiz'd and slew;
Then plac'd the loathsome and abhorrent food

At his first meal before the unconscious sire.
And when Thyestes had his hunger still'd
With his own flesh, a sadness seiz'd his soul;
He for his children ask'd,—their steps, their voice
Fancied he heard already at the door;
And Atreus, grinning with malicious joy,
Threw in the members of the slaughter'd boys.—
Shudd'ring, O king, thou dost avert thy face:
So did the sun his radiant visage hide,
And swerve his chariot from the eternal path.
These, monarch, are thy priestess' ancestors,
And many a dreadful fate of mortal doom,
And many a deed of the bewilder'd brain,
Dark night doth cover with her sable wing,
Or shroud in gloomy twilight.

THOAS.
Hidden there
Let them abide.　A truce to horror now,
And tell me by what miracle thou sprang'st
From race so savage.

IPHIGENIA.
Atreus' eldest son
Was Agamemnon; he, O king, my sire:
But I may say with truth, that, from a child,
In him the model of a perfect man
I witness'd ever.　Clytemnestra bore
To him, myself, the firstling of their love,
Electra then.　Peaceful the monarch rul'd,
And to the house of Tantalus was given
A long-withheld repose.　A son alone
Was wanting to complete my parent's bliss;
Scarce was this wish fulfill'd, and young Orestes,
The household's darling, with his sisters grew,
When new misfortunes vex'd our ancient house.
To you hath come the rumour of the war,
Which, to avenge the fairest woman's wrongs,
The force united of the Grecian kings
Round Ilion's walls encamp'd.　Whether the town
Was humbl'd, and achiev'd their great revenge,
I have not heard.　My father led the host.
In Aulis vainly for a favouring gale

They waited; for, enrag'd against their chief,
Diana stay'd their progress, and requir'd,
Through Chalcas' voice, the monarch's eldest daughter.
They lur'd me with my mother to the camp,
And at Diana's altar doom'd this head.—
She was appeas'd, she did not wish my blood,
And wrapt me in a soft protecting cloud;
Within this temple from the dream of death
I waken'd first.   Yes, I myself am she;
Iphigenia,—I who speak to thee
Am Atreus' grandchild, Agamemnon's child,
And great Diana's consecrated priestess.

THOAS.

I yield no higher honour or regard
To the king's daughter than the maid unknown;
Once more my first proposal I repeat;
Come, follow me, and share what I possess.

IPHIGENIA.

How dare I venture such a step, O king?
Hath not the goddess who protected me
Alone a right to my devoted head?
'Twas she who chose for me this sanctuary,
Where she perchance reserves me for my sire,
By my apparent death enough chastis'd,
To be the joy and solace of his age.
Perchance my glad return is near; and ho
If I, unmindful of her purposes,
Had here attach'd myself against her will?
I ask'd a signal, did she wish my stay.

THOAS.

The signal is that still thou tarriest here.
Seek not evasively such vain pretexts.
Not many words are needed to refuse,
By the refus'd the *no* alone is heard.

IPHIGENIA.

Mine are not words meant only to deceive;
I have to thee my inmost heart reveal'd.
And doth no inward voice suggest to thee,
How I with yearning soul must pine to see
My father, mother, and my long-lost home?

Oh let thy vessels bear me thither, king?
That in the ancient halls, where sorrow still
In accents low doth fondly breathe my name,
Joy, as in welcome of a new-born child,
May round the columns twine the fairest wreath.
Thou wouldst to me and mine new life impart.

THOAS.

Then go! the promptings of thy heart obey;
Despise the voice of reason and good counsel.
Be quite the woman, sway'd by each desire,
That bridleless impels her to and fro.
When passion rages fiercely in her breast,
No sacred tie withholds her from the wretch
Who would allure her to forsake for him
A husband's or a father's guardian arms;
Extinct within her heart its fiery glow,
The golden tongue of eloquence in vain
With words of truth and power assails her ear.

IPHIGENIA.

Remember now, O king, thy noble words!
My trust and candour wilt thou thus repay?
Thou seem'dst, methought, prepar'd to hear the truth.

THOAS.

For this unlook'd-for answer not prepar'd.
Yet 'twas to be expected; knew I not
That 'twas with woman I had now to deal?

IPHIGENIA.

Upbraid not thus, O king, our feeble sex!
Though not in dignity to match with yours,
The weapons woman wields are not ignoble.
And trust me, Thoas, in thy happiness
I have a deeper insight than thyself.
Thou thinkest, ignorant alike of both,
A closer union would augment our bliss;
Inspir'd with confidence and honest zeal
Thou strongly urgest me to yield consent;
And here I thank the gods, who give me strength
To shun a doom unratified by them.

THOAS.

'Tis not a god, 'tis thine own heart that speaks.

IPHIGENIA.
'Tis through the heart alone they speak to us.
THOAS.
To hear them have I not an equal right?
IPHIGENIA.
The raging tempest drowns the still, small voice.
THOAS.
This voice no doubt the priestess hears alone.
IPHIGENIA.
Before all others should the prince attend it.
THOAS.
Thy sacred office, and ancestral right
To Jove's own table, place thee with the gods
In closer union than an earth-born savage.
IPHIGENIA.
Thus must I now the confidence atone
Thyself extorted from me!
THOAS.
I'm a man,
And better 'tis we end this conference.
Hear then my last resolve.   Be priestess still
Of the great goddess who selected thee;
And may she pardon me, that I from her,
Unjustly and with secret self-reproach,
Her ancient sacrifice so long withheld.
From olden times no stranger near'd our shore
But fell a victim at her sacred shrine.
But thou, with kind affection (which at times
Seem'd like a gentle daughter's tender love,
At times assum'd to my enraptur'd heart
The modest inclination of a bride),
Didst so inthral me, as with magic bonds,
That I forgot my duty.   Thou didst rock
My senses in a dream: I did not hear
My people's murmurs: now they cry aloud,
Ascribing my poor son's untimely death
To this my guilt.   No longer for thy sake
Will I oppose the wishes of the crowd,
Who urgently demand the sacrifice.
IPHIGENIA.
For mine own sake I ne'er desired it from thee.

Who to the gods ascribe a thirst for blood
Do misconceive their nature, and impute
To them their own inhuman dark desires.
Did not Diana snatch me from the priest,
Preferring my poor service to my death?

THOAS.

'Tis not for us, on reason's shifting grounds,
Lightly to guide and construe rites divine.
Perform thy duty; I'll accomplish mine.
Two strangers, whom in caverns of the shore
We found conceal'd, and whose arrival here
Bodes to my realm no good, are in my power.
With them thy goddess may once more resume
Her ancient, pious, long-suspended rites!
I send them here,--thy duty not unknown.        [*Exit.*

IPHIGENIA, *alone.*

Gracious protectress! thou hast clouds
To shelter innocence distress'd,
And genial gales from Fate's rude grasp,
Safely to waft her o'er the sea,
O'er the wide earth's remotest realms,
Where'er it seemeth good to thee.
Wise art thou,--thine all-seeing eye
The future and the past surveys,
And doth on all thy children rest,
E'en as thy pure and guardian light
Keeps o'er the earth its silent watch
The beauty and the life of night.
O Goddess! keep my hands from blood!
Blessing it never brings, nor peace;
And still in evil hours the form
Of the chance-murder'd man appears
To fill the unwilling murderer's soul
With horrible and gloomy fears.
For fondly the Immortals view
Man's widely-scatter'd, simple race;
And the poor mortal's transient life
Gladly prolong, that he may raise
Awhile to their eternal heavens
His sympathetic joyous gaze.

# ACT THE SECOND.

## SCENE I.

### ORESTES.        PYLADES.

### ORESTES.

It is the path of death that now we tread:
At every step my soul grows more serene.
When I implor'd Apollo to remove
The grisly band of Furies from my side,
He seem'd, with hope-inspiring, godlike words,
To promise aid and safety in the fane
Of his lov'd sister, who o'er Tauris rules.
Thus the prophetic word fulfils itself,
That with my life shall terminate my woe.
How easy 'tis for me, whose heart is crush'd,
Whose sense is deaden'd by a hand divine,
Thus to renounce the beauteous light of day!
And must the son of Atreus not entwine
The wreath of conquest round his dying brow—
Must I, as my forefathers, as my sire,
Bleed like a victim,—an ignoble death—
So be it!   Better at the altar here,
Than in a nook obscure, where kindred hands
Have spread assassination's wily net.
Yield me this brief repose, infernal Powers!
Ye, who, like loosen'd hounds, still scent the blood,
Which, trickling from my feet, betrays my path.
Leave me! ere long I come to you below.
Nor you, nor I, should view the light of day.
The soft green carpet of the beauteous earth
Is no arena for unhallow'd fiends.
Below I seek you, where an equal fate
Binds all in murky, never-ending night.
Thee only, thee, my Pylades, my friend,
The guiltless partner of my crime and curse,
Thee am I loath, before thy time, to take
To yonder cheerless shore!   Thy life or death
Alone awakens in me hope or fear.

**PYLADES.**

Like thee, Orestes, I am not prepar'd
Downwards to wander to yon realm of shade.
I purpose still, through the entangl'd paths,
Which seem as they would lead to blackest night,
Again to guide our upward way to life.
Of death I think not; I observe and mark
Whether the gods may not perchance present
Means and fit moment for a joyful flight.
Dreaded or not, the stroke of death must come;
And though the priestess stood with hand uprais'd,
Prepar'd to cut our consecrated locks,
Our safety still should be my only thought:
Uplift thy soul above this weak despair;
Desponding doubts but hasten on our peril.
Apollo pledg'd to us his sacred word,
That in his sister's holy fane for thee
Were comfort, aid, and glad return prepar'd.
The words of Heaven are not equivocal,
As in despair the poor oppress'd one thinks.

**ORESTES.**

The mystic web of life my mother spread
Around my infant head, and so I grew,
An image of my sire; and my mute look
Was aye a bitter and a keen reproof
To her and base Egisthus.   Oh, how oft,
When silently within our gloomy hall
Electra sat, and mus'd beside the fire,
Have I with anguish'd spirit climb'd her knee,
And watch'd her bitter tears with sad amaze!
Then would she tell me of our noble sire:
How much I long'd to see him—be with him!
Myself at Troy one moment fondly wish'd,
My sire's return, the next.   The day arrived—

**PYLADES.**

Oh, of that awful hour let fiends of hell
Hold nightly converse!   Of a time more fair
May the remembrance animate our hearts
To fresh heroic deeds.   The gods require
On this wide earth the service of the good,

To work their pleasure.   Still they count on thee;
For in thy father's train they sent thee not,
When he to Orcus went unwilling down.

ORESTES.

Would I had seiz'd the border of his robe,
And follow'd him!

PYLADES.

They kindly car'd for me
Who here detain'd thee; for if thou hadst died
I know not what had then become of me;
Since I with thee, and for thy sake alone,
Have from my childhood liv'd, and wish to live.

ORESTES.

Do not remind me of those tranquil days,
When me thy home a safe asylum gave;
With fond solicitude thy noble sire
The half-nipp'd, tender flow'ret gently rear'd;
While thou, a friend and playmate always gay,
Like to a light and brilliant butterfly
Around a dusky flower, didst around me
Still with new life thy merry gambols play,
And breathe thy joyous spirit in my soul,
Until, my cares forgetting, I with thee
Was lur'd to snatch the eager joys of youth.

PYLADES.

My very life began when thee I lov'd.

ORESTES.

Say, then thy woes began, and thou speak'st truly
This is the sharpest sorrow of my lot,
That, like a plague-infected wretch, I bear
Death and destruction hid within my breast;
That, where I tread, e'en on the healthiest spot,
Ere long the blooming faces round betray
The writhing features of a ling'ring death.

PYLADES.

Were thy breath venom, I had been the first
To die that death, Orestes.   Am I not,
As ever, full of courage and of joy?
And love and courage are the spirit's wings
Wafting to noble actions.

ORESTES.

                  Noble actions?
Time was, when fancy painted such before us!
When oft, the game pursuing, on we roam'd
O'er hill and valley; hoping that ere long
With club and weapon arm'd, we so might track
The robber to his den, or monster huge.
And then at twilight, by the glassy sea,
We peaceful sat, reclin'd against each other
The waves came dancing to our very feet,
And all before us lay the wide, wide world.
Then on a sudden one would seize his sword,
And future deeds shone round us like the stars,
Which gemm'd in countless throngs the vault of night.

PYLADES.

Endless, my friend, the projects which the soul
Burns to accomplish.   We would every deed
At once perform as grandly as it shows
After long ages, when from land to land
The poet's swelling song hath roll'd it on.
It sounds so lovely what our fathers did,
When, in the silent evening shade reclin'd,
We drink it in with music's melting tones;
And what we do is, as their deeds to them,
Toilsome and incomplete!
Thus we pursue what always flies before;
We disregard the path in which we tread,
Scarce see around the footsteps of our sires,
Or heed the trace of their career on earth.
We ever hasten on to chase their shades,
Which godlike, at a distance far remote,
On golden clouds reclin'd, the mountains crown.
The man I prize not who esteems himself
Just as the people's breath may chance to raise him.
But thou, Orestes, to the gods give thanks,
That they have done so much through thee already.

ORESTES.

When they ordain a man to noble deeds,
To shield from dire calamity his friends,
Extend his empire, or protect its bounds,
Or put to flight its ancient enemies,

Let him be grateful!   For to him a god
Imparts the first, the sweetest joy of life.
Me have they doom'd to be a slaughterer,
To be an honour'd mother's murderer,
And shamefully a deed of shame avenging,
Me throrgh their own decree they have o'erwhe.m'd.
Trust me, the race of Tantalus is doom'd;
Nor may his last descendant leave the earth,
Or crown'd with honour or unstain'd by crime.

**PYLADES.**

The gods avenge not on the son the deeds
Done by the father.   Each, or good or bad,
Of his own actions reaps the due reward.
The parents' blessing, not their curse, descends.

**ORESTES.**

Methinks their blessing did not lead us here.

**PYLADES.**

It was at least the mighty gods' decree.

**ORESTES.**

Then is it their decree which doth destroy us.

**PYLADES.**

Perform what they command, and wait the event.
Do thou Apollo's sister bear from hence,
That they at Delphi may united dwell,
Rever'd and honour'd by a noble race:
Thee, for this deed, the heav'nly pair will view
With gracious eye, and from the hateful grasp
Of the infernal Powers will rescue thee.
E'en now none dares intrude within this grove.

**ORESTES.**

So shall I die at least a peaceful death.

**PYLADES.**

Far other are my thoughts, and not unskill'd
Have I the future and the past combin'd
In quiet meditation.   Long, perchance,
Hath ripen'd in the counsel of the gods
The great event.   Diana wish'd to leave
This savage region foul with human blood:
We were selected for the high emprize;
To us it is assign'd, and strangely thus
We are conducted to the threshold here.

ORESTES.

My friend, with wondrous skill thou link'st thy wish
With the predestin'd purpose of the gods.

PYLADES.

Of what avail is prudence, if it fail
Heedful to mark the purposes of Heaven?
A noble man, who much hath sinn'd, some god
Doth summon to a dangerous enterprize,
Which to achieve appears impossible.
The hero conquers, and atoning serves
Mortals and gods, who thenceforth honour him.

ORESTES.

Am I foredoom'd to action and to life,
Would that a god from my distemper'd brain
Might chase this dizzy fever, which impels
My restless steps along a slipp'ry path,
Stain'd with a mother's blood, to direful death;
And pitying, dry the fountain, whence the blood,
For ever spouting from a mother's wounds,
Eternally defiles me!

PYLADES.

     Wait in peace!
Thou dost increase the evil, and dost take
The office of the Furies on thyself.
Let me contrive,—be still! And when at length
The time for action claims our powers combin'd,
Then will I summon thee, and on we'll stride,
With cautious boldness to achieve the event.

ORESTES.

I hear Ulysses speak!

PYLADES.

     Nay, mock me not.
Each must select the hero after whom
To climb the steep and difficult ascent
Of high Olympus. And to me it seems
That him nor stratagem nor art defile
Who consecrates himself to noble deeds.

ORESTES.

I most esteem the brave and upright man.

#### PYLADES.

And therefore have I not desir'd thy counsel.
One step is ta'en already: from our guards
I have extorted this intelligence.
A strange and godlike woman now restrains
The execution of that bloody law:
Incense, and prayer, and an unsullied heart,
These are the gifts she offers to the gods.
Her fame is widely spread, and it is thought
That from the race of Amazon she springs,
And hither fled some great calamity.

#### ORESTES.

Her gentle sway, it seems, lost all its power
At the approach of one so criminal,
Whom the dire curse enshrouds in gloomy night.
Our doom to seal, the pious thirst for blood
Again unchains the ancient cruel rite:
The monarch's savage will decrees our death;
A woman cannot save when he condemns.

#### PYLADES.

That 'tis a woman is a ground for hope!
A man, the very best, with cruelty
At length may so familiarize his mind,
His character through custom so transform,
That he shall come to make himself a law
Of what at first his very soul abhorr'd.
But woman doth retain the stamp of mind
She first assum'd.   On her we may depend
In good or evil with more certainty.
She comes; leave us alone.   I dare not tell
At once our names, nor unreserv'd confide
Our fortunes to her.   Now retire awhile,
And ere she speaks with thee we'll meet again.

## SCENE II.

IPHIGENIA.          PYLADES.

IPHIGENIA.

Whence art thou?   Stranger, speak!   To me thy bearing
Stamps thee of Grecian, not of Scythian race.

(*She unbinds his chains.*)

The freedom that I give is dangerous:
The gods avert the doom that threatens you!

PYLADES.

Delicious music! dearly welcome tones
Of our own language in a foreign land!
With joy my captive eye once more beholds
The azure mountains of my native coast.
Oh, let this joy that I too am a Greek
Convince thee, priestess!   How I need thine aid,
A moment I forget, my spirit wrapt
In contemplation of so fair a vision.
If fate's dread mandate doth not seal thy lips,
From which of our illustrious races, say,
Dost thou thy godlike origin derive?

IPHIGENIA.

A priestess, by the Goddess' self ordain'd
And consecrated too, doth speak with thee.
Let that suffice : but tell me, who art thou,
And what unbless'd o'erruling destiny
Hath hither led thee with thy friend?

PYLADES.

The woe,
Whose hateful presence ever dogs our steps,
I can with ease relate.   Oh, would that thou
Couldst with like ease, divine one, shed on us
One ray of cheering hope!   We are from Crete,
Adrastus' sons, and I, the youngest born,
Named Cephalus; my eldest brother, he,
Laodamus.   Between us two a youth
Of savage temper grew, who oft disturb'd
The joy and concord of our youthful sports.
Long as our father led his powers at Troy,

Passive our mother's mandate we obey'd;
But when, enrich'd with booty, he return'd,
And shortly after died, a contest fierce
For the succession and their father's wealth.
Parted the brothers.   I the eldest joined;
He slew the second; and the Furies hence
For kindred murder dog his restless steps.
But to this savage shore the Delphian god
Hath sent us, cheer'd by hope, commanding us
Within his sister's temple to await
The blessed hand of aid.   We have been ta'en,
Brought hither, and now stand for sacrifice.
My tale is told.

IPHIGENIA.
            Tell me, is Troy o'erthrown?
Assure me of its fall.

PYLADES.
            It lies in ruins.
But oh, ensure deliverance to us!
Hasten, I pray, the promis'd aid of heav'n.
Pity my brother, say a kindly word;
But I implore thee, spare him when thou speakest.
Too easily his inner mind is torn
By joy, or grief, or cruel memory.
A feverish madness oft doth seize on him,
Yielding his spirit, beautiful and free,
A prey to furies.

IPHIGENIA.
            Great as is thy woe,
Forget it, I conjure thee, for a while,
Till I am satisfied.

PYLADES.
            The stately town,
Which ten long years withstood the Grecian host,
Now lies in ruins, ne'er to rise again;
Yet many a hero's grave will oft recall
Our sad remembrance to that barbarous shore;
There lies Achilles and his noble friend.

IPHIGENIA.
And are ye, godlike forms, reduc'd to dust!

PYLADES.

Nor Palamede, nor Ajax, ere again
The daylight of their native land behold.

IPHIGENIA.

He speaks not of my father, doth not name
Him with the fallen.   He may yet survive!
I may behold him! still hope on, my heart!

PYLADES.

Yet happy are the thousands who receiv'd
Their bitter death-blow from a hostile hand!
For terror wild, and end most tragical,
Some hostile, angry, deity prepar'd,
Instead of triumph, for the home-returning.
Do human voices never reach this shore?
Far as their sound extends, they bear the fame
Of deeds unparallel'd.   And is the woe
Which fills Mycene's halls with ceaseless sighs
To thee a secret still?—And know'st thou not
That Clytemnestra, with Ægisthus' aid,
Her royal consort artfully ensnar'd,
And murder'd on the day of his return?—
The monarch's house thou honourest!   I perceive
Thy heaving bosom vainly doth contend
With tidings fraught with such unlook'd-for woe.
Art thou the daughter of a friend? or born
Within the circuit of Mycene's walls?
Do not conceal it, nor avenge on me
That here the horrid crime I first announc'd.

IPHIGENIA.

Proceed, and tell me how the deed was done.

PYLADES.

The day of his return, as from the bath
Arose the monarch, tranquil and refresh'd,
His robe demanding from his consort's hand,
A tangl'd garment, complicate with folds,
She o'er his shoulders flung and noble head;
And when, as from a net, he vainly strove
To extricate himself, the traitor, base
Ægisthus, smote him, and envelop'd thus
Great Agamemnon sought the shades below,

IPHIGENIA.

And what reward receiv'd the base accomplice?

PYLADES.

A queen and kingdom he possess'd already.

IPHIGENIA.

Base passion prompted, then, the deed of shame?

PYLADES.

And feelings, cherish'd long, of deep revenge.

IPHIGENIA.

How had the monarch injured Clytemnestra?

PYLADES.

By such a dreadful deed, that if on earth
Aught could exculpate murder, it were this.
To Aulis he allur'd her, when the fleet
With unpropitious winds the goddess stay'd;
And there, a victim at Diana's shrine,
The monarch, for the welfare of the Greeks,
Her eldest daughter doom'd.   And this, 'tis said,
Planted such deep abhorrence in her heart,
That to Ægisthus she resign'd herself,
And round her husband flung the web of death.

IPHIGENIA (*veiling herself*).

It is enough!   Thou wilt again behold me.

PYLADES, *alone*.

The fortune of this royal house, it seems,
Doth move her deeply.   Whosoe'er she be,
She must herself have known the monarch well;—
For our good fortune, from a noble house.
She hath been sold to bondage.   Peace, my heart!
And let us steer our course with prudent zeal
Toward the star of hope which gleams upon us.

## ACT THE THIRD.

### SCENE I.

IPHIGENIA.        ORESTES.

IPHIGENIA.

Unhappy man, I only loose thy bonds
In token of a still severer doom.
The freedom which the sanctuary imparts,

Like the last life-gleam o'er the dying face,
But heralds death.   I cannot, dare not say
Your doom is hopeless; for, with murd'rous hand,
Could I inflict the fatal blow myself?
And while I here am priestess of Diana,
None, be he who he may, dare touch your heads.
But the incensed king, should I refuse
Compliance with the rites himself enjoin'd,
Will choose another virgin from my train
As my successor.   Then, alas! with nought,
Save ardent wishes, can I succour you,
Much honour'd countryman!   The humblest slave,
Who had but near'd our sacred household hearth,
Is dearly welcome in a foreign land;
How with proportion'd joy and blessing, then,
Shall I receive the man who doth recall
The image of the heroes, whom I learn'd
To honour from my parents, and who cheers
My inmost heart with flatt'ring gleams of hope!

ORESTES.

Does prudent forethought prompt thee to conceal
Thy name and race? or may I hope to know
Who, like a heavenly vision, meets me thus?

IPHIGENIA.

Yes, thou shalt know me.   Now conclude the tale
Of which thy brother only told me half :          .
Relate their end, who coming home from Troy,
On their own threshold met a doom severe
And most unlook'd for. ˙ I, though but a child
When first conducted hither, well recall
The timid glance of wonder which I cast
On those heroic forms.   When they went forth,
It seem'd as though Olympus from her womb
Had cast the heroes of a by-gone world,
To frighten Ilion; and, above them all,
Great Agamemnon tower'd pre-eminent!
Oh tell me!   Fell the hero in his home,
Through Clytemnestra's and Ægisthus' wiles?

ORESTES.

He fell!

IPHIGENIA.

Unblest Mycene!   Thus the sons
Of Tantalus, with barbarous hands, have sown
Curse upon curse; and, as the shaken weed
Scatters around a thousand poison-seeds,
So they assassins ceaseless generate,
Their children's children ruthless to destroy.---
Now tell the remnant of thy brother's tale,
Which horror darkly hid from me before.
How did the last descendant of the race,—
The gentle child, to whom the Gods assign'd
The office of avenger,—how did he
Escape that day of blood?   Did equal fate
Around Orestes throw Avernus' net?
Say, was he saved? and is he still alive?
And lives Electra, too?

ORESTES.
They both survive.

IPHIGENIA.
Golden Apollo, lend thy choicest beams!
Lay them an offering at the throne of Jove!
For I am poor and dumb.

ORESTES.
If social bonds
Or ties more close connect thee with this house,
As this thy joy evinces, rein thy heart;
For insupportable the sudden plunge
From happiness to sorrow's gloomy depth.
As yet thou only know'st the hero's death.

IPHIGENIA.
And is not this intelligence enough?

ORESTES.
Half of the horror yet remains untold.

IPHIGENIA.
Electra and Orestes both survive,
What have I then to fear?

ORESTES.
And fear'st thou nought
For Clytemnestra?

IPHIGENIA.
Her, nor hope nor fear
Have power to save.

ORESTES.
She to the land of hope
Hath bid farewell.

IPHIGENIA.
Did her repentant hand
'Shed her own blood?

ORESTES.
Not so; yet her own blood
Inflicted death.

IPHIGENIA.
Speak less ambiguously.
Uncertainty around my anxious head
Her dusky, thousand-folded, pinion waves.

ORESTES.
Have then the powers above selected me
To be the herald of a dreadful deed,
Which, in the arear and soundless realms of night,
I fain would hide for ever?   'Gainst my will
Thy gentle voice constrains me; it demands,
And shall receive, a tale of direst woe.
Electra, on the day when fell her sire,
Her brother from impending doom conceal'd;
Him Strophius, his father's relative,
With kindest care receiv'd, and rear'd the child
With his own son, named Pylades, who soon
Around the stranger twin'd the bonds of love.
And as they grew, within their inmost souls
There sprang the burning longing to revenge
The monarch's death.   Unlook'd for, and disguis'd,
They reach Mycene, feigning to have brought
The mournful tidings of Orestes' death,
Together with his ashes.   Them the queen
Gladly receives.   Within the house they enter;
Orestes to Electra shows himself:
She fans the fires of vengeance into flame,
Which in the sacred presence of a mother
Had burn'd more dimly.   Silently she leads
Her brother to the spot where fell their sire;

Where lurid blood-marks, on the oft-wash'd floor,
With pallid streaks, anticipate revenge.
With fiery eloquence she pictures forth
Each circumstance of that atrocious deed,—
Her own oppress'd and miserable life,
The prosperous traitor's insolent demeanour,
The perils threat'ning Agamemnon's race
From her who had become their stepmother;
Then in his hand the ancient dagger thrusts,
Which often in the house of Tantalus
With savage fury rag'd,—and by her son
Is Clytemnestra slain.

IPHIGENIA.
     Immortal powers!
Whose pure and blest existence glides away
'Mid ever shifting clouds, me have ye kept
So many years secluded from the world,
Retain'd me near yourselves, consign'd to me
The childlike task to feed the sacred fire,
And taught my spirit, like the hallow'd flame,
With never-clouded brightness to aspire
To your pure mansions,—but at length to feel
With keener woe the misery of my house?
Oh tell me of the poor unfortunate!
Speak of Orestes!

ORESTES.
     Would that he were dead!
Forth from his mother's blood her ghost arose,
And to the ancient daughters of the night
Cries,—" Let him not escape,—the matricide!
Pursue the victim, dedicate to you!"
They hear, and glare around with hollow eyes,
Like greedy eagles. In their murky dens
They stir themselves, and from the corners creep
Their comrades, dire Remorse and pallid Fear;
Before them fumes a mist of Acheron;
Perplexingly around the murderer's brow
The eternal contemplation of the past
Rolls in its cloudy circles. Once again
The grisly band, commission'd to destroy,
Pollute earth's beautiful and heaven-sown fields,

From which an ancient curse had banish'd them.
Their rapid feet the fugitive pursue;
They only pause to start a wilder fear.

IPHIGENIA.

Unhappy one: thy lot resembles his,
Thou feel'st what he, poor fugitive, must suffer.

ORESTES.

What say'st thou? why presume my fate like his?

IPHIGENIA.

A brother's murder weighs upon thy soul;
Thy younger brother told the mournful tale.

ORESTES.

I cannot suffer that thy noble soul
Should be deceiv'd by error.   Rich in guile,
And practis'd in deceit, a stranger may
A web of falsehood cunningly devise
To snare a stranger;—between us be truth.
I am Orestes! and this guilty head
Is stooping to the tomb, and covets death;
It will be welcome now in any shape.
Whoe'er thou art, for thee and for my friend
I wish deliverance;—I desire it not.
Thou seem'st to linger here against thy will;
Contrive some means of flight, and leave me here:
My lifeless corpse hurl'd headlong from the rock,
My blood shall mingle with the dashing waves,
And bring a curse upon this barbarous shore!
Return together home to lovely Greece,
With joy a new existence to commence.

[ORESTES *retires.*

IPHIGENIA.

At length Fulfilment, fairest child of Jove,
Thou dost descend upon me from on high!
How vast thine image! scarce my straining eye
Can reach thy hands, which, fill'd with golden fruit
And wreaths of blessing, from Olympus' height
Shower treasures down.   As by his bounteous gifts
We recognize the monarch (for what seems
To thousands opulence is nought to him),
So you, ye heavenly Powers, are also known
By bounty long withheld, and wisely plann'd.

Ye only know what things are good for us;
Ye view the future's wide-extended realm;
While from our eye a dim or starry veil
The prospect shrouds.   Calmly ye hear our prayers,
When we like children sue for greater speed.
Not immature ye pluck heaven's golden fruit;
And woe to him, who with impatient hand,
His date of joy forestalling, gathers death.
Let not this long-awaited happiness,
Which yet my heart hath scarcely realiz'd,
Like to the shadow of departed friends,
Glide vainly by with triple sorrow fraught!

ORESTES, returning.

Dost thou for Pylades and for thyself
Implore the gods, blend not my name with yours;
Thou wilt not save the wretch whom thou wouldst join,
But wilt participate his curse and woe.

IPHIGENIA.

My destiny is firmly bound to thine.

ORESTES.

No, say not so; alone and unattended
Let me descend to Hades.   Though thou shouldst
In thine own veil enwrap the guilty one,
Thou couldst not shroud him from his wakeful foes;
And e'en thy sacred presence, heavenly maid,
Drives them aside, but scares them not away.
With brazen impious feet they dare not tread
Within the precincts of this sacred grove:
Yet in the distance, ever and anon,
I hear their horrid laughter, like the howl
Of famish'd wolves, beneath the tree wherein
The traveller hides.   Without, encamp'd they lie,
And should I quit this consecrated grove,
Shaking their serpent locks, they would arise,
And, raising clouds of dust on every side,
Ceaseless pursue their miserable prey.

IPHIGENIA.

Orestes, canst thou hear a friendly word?

ORESTES.

Reserve it for one favour'd by the gods.

IPHIGENIA.
To thee they give anew the light of hope.
ORESTES.
Through clouds and smoke I see the feeble gleam
Of the death-stream which lights me down to hell.
IPHIGENIA.
Hast thou one sister only, thy Electra?
ORESTES.
I knew but one : yet her kind destiny,
Which seem'd to us so terrible, betimes
Removed an elder sister from the woe
That dogs the race of Pelops.   Cease, oh cease
Thy questions, maiden, nor thus league thyself
With the Eumenides, who blow away,
With fiendish joy, the ashes from my soul,
Lest the last spark of horror's fiery brand
Should be extinguish'd there.   Must then the fire,
Deliberately kindl'd and supplied
With hellish sulphur, never cease to sear
My tortur'd bosom?

IPHIGENIA.
                In the flame I throw
Sweet incense.   Let the gentle breath of love,
Low murmuring, cool thy bosom's fiery glow.
Orestes, fondly lov'd,—canst thou not hear me ?
Hath the terrific Furies' grisly band
Completely dried the lifeblood in thy veins?
Creeps there, as from the Gorgon's direful head,
A petrifying charm through all thy limbs ?
If hollow voices, from a mother's blood,
Call thee to hell, may not a sister's word
With benediction pure ascend to heaven,
And summon thence some gracious power to aid thee !
ORESTES.
She calls ! she calls !—Thou too desirs't my death ?
Is there a fury shrouded in thy form ?
Who art thou, that thy voice thus horribly
Can harrow up my bosom's inmost depths ?
IPHIGENIA.
Thine inmost heart reveals it.   I am she,—
Iphigenia,—look on me, Orestes !

ORESTES.

Thou!

IPHIGENIA.

My own brother!

ORESTES.

Hence, away, begone!
Touch not these locks, I counsel thee; from me,
As from Creusa's bridal robe, proceeds
An unextinguishable fire. Depart!
Like Hercules, an ignominious death,
Unworthy wretch, lock'd in myself, I'll die.

IPHIGENIA.

Thou shalt not perish! Would that I might hear
One quiet word from thee! dispel my doubts,
Make sure the bliss I have implor'd so long.
A wheel of joy and sorrow in my heart
Ceaseless revolves. With shy reserve I turn
From one unknown; but unto thee, my brother,
My inmost heart resistlessly impels me.

ORESTES.

Is this Lyæus' temple? Doth the glow
Of holy rage unbridl'd thus possess
The sacred priestess?

IPHIGENIA.

Hear me, oh, look up!
See how my heart, which hath been clos'd so long
Doth open to the bliss of seeing thee,
The dearest treasure that the world contains,—
Of falling on thy neck, and folding thee
Within my longing arms, which have till now
Met the embraces of the empty wind.
Do not repulse me,—the eternal spring,
Whose crystal waters from Parnassus flow,
Bounds not more gaily on from rock to rock.
Down to the golden vale, than from my heart
The waters of affection freely gush,
And round me form a circling sea of bliss.
Orestes! Oh, my brother!

ORESTES.

Lovely nymph!
Nor thy caresses, nor thyself I trust;

Diana claims attendants more severe,
And doth avenge her desecrated fane.
Remove thy circling arm! and if thou wilt
Safety and love upon a youth bestow,
Unto my friend, more worthy than myself,
Impart thy gifts; among yon rocks he roves;
Go seek him, guide him hence, and heed not me.

IPHIGENIA.

Brother, command thyself, and better know
Thy new-found sister, nor misconstrue thus
Her pure and heav'nly joy.   Ye Gods, remove
From his fix'd eye delusion, lest this hour
Of highest bliss should make us trebly wretched!
Oh she is here, thine own, thy long-lost sister,
Whom great Diana from the altar snatch'd,
And safely plac'd here in her sacred fane.
A captive thou, prepar'd for sacrifice,
And findest here a sister in the priestess.

ORESTES.

Accursed race!   Now may the sun behold
Your final doom.   Is not Electra here?
That she with us may perish, nor her life
For heavier doom and deeper woe reserve.
'Tis well,—I follow, priestess!   Fratricide
Is an old custom of our ancient house;
And you, ye Gods, I thank, that ye resolve
Childless to root me hence.   Thee let me counsel,
To view too fondly neither sun nor stars.
Come follow to the gloomy realms below!
As dragons, gender'd in the sulphur pool,
Swallow each other with voracious rage,
So our accurs'd race destroys itself.
Childless and guiltless come below with me!
There's pity in thy look! oh, gaze not so,—
'Twas with such looks that Clytemnestra sought
An entrance to her son Orestes' heart,
And yet his uprais'd arm her bosom pierc'd.
His mother fell!—Appear, indignant shade!
Within the circle step, ye fiends of hell,
Be present at the welcome spectacle,
The last, most horrible, that ye prepare!

Nor hate, nor vengeance, whets the poignard now,
A sister is constrain'd to deal the blow.
Weep not!  Thy guiltless soul is free from crime.
From earliest infancy I nought have lov'd,
As thee I could have lov'd, my sister.   Come,
The weapon raise, spare not, this bosom rend,
And make an outlet for its boiling streams!

(He sinks exhausted.)

IPHIGENIA.

Alone I cannot bear this bliss and woe.
Where art thou, Pylades?   Thine aid I need.

(Iphigenia retires.)

## SCENE II.

ORESTES.

Recovering from his swoon and standing up.

Give yet another! reach from Lethe's stream
The last reviving draught of cool refreshment.
Soon shall its waters in my bosom still
Life's fitful fever; and my spirit then
Adown oblivion's stream shall glide to you,
Ye spirits, shrouded in eternal mist.
With tranquil pleasure in your deep repose
A weary son of earth may lave his soul!—
What whisp'ring sounds pervade the dreary grove?
What hollow murmurs haunt its twilight gloom?—
They gather round to view the stranger guest!
Who are yon troop in high communion met,
Like an assembl'd family of princes?
They mingle peacefully, of every age,
And either sex, yet are their godlike forms
Cast in a kindred mould.   'Tis they, 'tis they,
The fathers of my race!   With Atreus,
In friendly converse glides Thyestes' shade,
And children playfully around them sport.
Is there no enmity among you now?
And is revenge extinguish'd with the sun?
I then am welcome, and may hope to join
Your solemn company.   My fathers, hail!
Orestes, last descendant of your race,
Salutes you.   What ye sow'd, that hath he reap'd.

Laden with curses he descends to you.
But burdens here are lighter far to bear.
Receive him, oh, receive him in your circle!
Thee, Atreus, I revere, and thee, Thyestes:
Here all are free from enmity and hate.—
Show me my father, whom I only once
In life beheld.—Art thou my father, thou,
My mother leading thus familiarly?
Dares Clytemnestra reach her hand to thee;
Then may Orestes also draw near her,
And say, behold thy son!—My ancestors,
Behold your son, and bid him welcome here.
Among the sons of ancient Tantalus,
A kind salute on earth was murder's watchword,
And all their joys commence beyond the grave.
Ye welcome me! Ye bid me join your circle!
Oh, lead me to my honour'd ancestor!
Where is the aged hero? that I may
Behold the dear, the venerable head,
Of him, who with the gods in council sat.
You seem to shudder and to turn away?
What may this mean?   Suffers the godlike man
Alas! the mighty gods, with ruthless hate,
To his heroic breast, with brazen chains,
Have cruel pangs indissolubly bound.

## SCENE III.

ORESTES.          IPHIGENIA.          PYLADES.

ORESTES.

How! are ye come already?   Sister, welcome.
Electra still is missing; some kind god
With gentle arrow send her quickly hither.
Thee, my poor friend, I must compassionate!
Come with me, come to Pluto's gloomy throne,
There to salute our hosts like stranger guests.

IPHIGENIA.

Celestial pair, who from the realms above
By night and day shed down the beauteous light
To cheer mankind, but who may not illume
Departed spirits, save a mortal pair!

A brother's and a sister's anguish pity!
For thou, Diana, lov'st thy gentle brother
Beyond what earth and heaven can offer thee;
And dost, with quiet yearning, ever turn
Thy virgin face to his eternal light.
Let not my only brother, found so late,
Rave in the darkness of insanity!
And is thy will, when thou didst here conceal me,
At length fulfill'd,—would'st thou to me through him,
To him through me, thy gracious aid extend,—
Oh, free him from the fetters of this curse,
Lest vainly pass the precious hours of safety.

PYLADES.

Dost thou not know us, and this sacred grove,
And this blest light, which shines not on the dead?
Dost thou not feel thy sister and thy friend,
Who hold thee living in their firm embrace?
Grasp us! we are not shadows.   Mark my words!
Collect thyself,—each moment now is precious,
And our return hangs on a slender thread,
Which, as it seems, some gracious fate doth spin.

ORESTES to IPHIGENIA.

My sister, let me for the first time taste,
With open heart, pure joy within thine arms!
Ye gods, who charge the heavy clouds with dread,
And sternly gracious send the long-sought rain
With thunder and the rush of mighty winds,
A horrid deluge on the trembling earth;
Yet dissipate at length man's dread suspense,
Exchanging timid wonder's anxious gaze
For grateful looks and joyous songs of praise,
When in each sparkling drop which gems the leaves,
Apollo, thousand-fold, reflects his beam,
And Iris colours with a magic hand
The dusky texture of the parting clouds;
Oh, let me also in my sister's arms,
And on the bosom of my friend, enjoy
With grateful thanks the bliss ye now bestow
My heart assures me that your curses cease.
The dread Eumenides at length retire,
The brazen gates of Tartarus I hear

O

Behind them closing with a thund'ring clang.
A quick'ning odour from the earth ascends,
Inviting me to chase, upon its plains,
The joys of life and deeds of high emprise.

PYLADES.

Lose not the moments which are limited!
The favouring gale, which swells our parting sail,
Must to Olympus waft our perfect joy.
Quick counsel and resolve the time demands.

# ACT THE FOURTH.

## SCENE I.

IPHIGENIA.

When the Powers on high decree
For a feeble child of earth
Dire perplexity and woe,
And his spirit doom to pass
With tumult wild from joy to grief,
And back again from grief to joy,
In fearful alternation;
They in mercy then provide,
In the precincts of his home,
Or upon the distant shore,
That to him may never fail
Ready help in hours of need,
A tranquil, faithful friend.
Oh, bless, ye heavenly powers, our Pylades,
And every project that his mind may form!
In combat his the vigorous arm of youth,
And in the counsel his the eye of age.
His soul is tranquil; in his inner mind
He guards a sacred, undisturb'd repose,
And from its silent depths a rich supply
Of aid and counsel draws for the distress'd.
He tore me from my brother, upon whom,
With fond amaze, I gaz'd and gaz'd again,
I could not realize my happiness,
Nor loose him from my arms, and heeded not
The danger's near approach that threatens us.
To execute their project of escape,

They hasten to the sea, where in a bay
Their comrades in the vessel lie conceal'd
And wait a signal.  Me they have supplied
With artful answers, should the monarch send
To urge the sacrifice.  Alas! I see
I must consent to follow like a child.
I have not learn'd deception, nor the art
To gain with crafty wiles my purposes.
Detested falsehood! it doth not relieve
The breast like words of truth: it comforts not,
But is a torment in the forger's heart,
And, like an arrow which a god directs,
Flies back and wounds the archer.  Through my hear
One fear doth chase another; perhaps with rage,
Again on the unconsecrated shore,
The Furies' grisly band my brother seize.
Perchance they are surpris'd?  Methinks I hear
The tread of armed men.  A messenger
Is coming from the king, with hasty steps.
How throbs my heart, how troubl'd is my soul,
Now that I see the countenance of one,
Whom with a word untrue I must encounter!

## SCENE II.

IPHIGENIA.      ARKAS.

ARKAS.

Priestess, with speed conclude the sacrifice!
Impatiently the king and people wait.

IPHIGENIA.

I had perform'd my duty and thy will,
Had not an unforeseen impediment
The execution of my purpose thwarted.

ARKAS.

What is it that obstructs the king's commands?

IPHIGENIA.

Chance, which from mortals will not brook control

ARKAS.

Possess me with the reason, that with speed
I may inform the king, who hath decreed
The death of both.

IPHIGENIA.

The gods have not decreed it.
The elder of these men doth bear the guilt
Of kindred murder; on his steps attend
The dread Eumenides.   They seiz'd their prey
Within the inner fane, polluting thus
The holy sanctuary.   I hasten now,
Together with my virgin-train, to bathe
Diana's image in the sea, and there
With solemn rites its purity restore.
Let none presume our silent march to follow!

ARKAS.

This hindrance to the monarch I'll announce:
Do not commence the rite till he permit.

IPHIGENIA.

The priestess interferes alone in this.

ARKAS.

An incident so strange the king should know.

IPHIGENIA.

Here, nor his counsel nor command avails.

ARKAS.

Oft are the great consulted out of form.

IPHIGENIA.

Do not insist on what I must refuse.

ARKAS.

A needful and a just demand refuse not.

IPHIGENIA.

I yield, if thou delay not.

ARKAS.

I with speed
Will bear these tidings to the camp, and soon
Acquaint thee, priestess, with the king's reply.
There is a message I would gladly bear him;
'Twould quickly banish all perplexity:
Thou didst not heed thy faithful friend's advice.

IPHIGENIA.

I willingly have done whate'er I could.

ARKAS.

E'en now 'tis not too late to change thy mind.

IPHIGENIA.

To do so is, alas, beyond our power

ARKAS.

What thou wouldst shun, thou deem'st impossible.

IPHIGENIA.

Thy wish doth make thee deem it possible.

ARKAS.

Wilt thou so calmly venture everything?

IPHIGENIA.

My fate I have committed to the gods.

ARKAS.

The gods are wont to save by human means.

IPHIGENIA.

By their appointment everything is done.

ARKAS.

Believe me, all doth now depend on thee.
The irritated temper of the king
Alone condemns these men to bitter death.
The soldiers from the cruel sacrifice
And bloody service long have been disused;
Nay, many, whom their adverse fortunes cast
In foreign regions, there themselves have felt
How godlike to the exil'd wanderer
The friendly countenance of man appears.
Do not deprive us of thy gentle aid!
With ease thou canst thy sacred task fulfil:
For nowhere doth benignity, which comes
In human form from heaven, so quickly gain
An empire o'er the heart, as where a race.
Gloomy and savage, full of life and power,
Without external guidance, and oppress'd
With vague forebodings, bear life's heavy load.

IPHIGENIA.

Shake not my spirit, which thou canst not bend
According to thy will.

ARKAS.

   While there is time,
Nor labour nor persuasion shall be spar'd.

IPHIGENIA.

Thy labour but occasions pain to me;
Both are in vain; therefore, I pray, depart.

ARKAS.

I summon pain to aid me, 'tis a friend.
Who counsels wisely.

IPHIGENIA.

        Though it shakes my soul
It doth not banish thence my strong repugnance.

ARKAS.

Can then a gentle soul repugnance feel
For benefits bestow'd by one so noble?

IPHIGENIA.

Yes, when the donor, for those benefits,
Instead of gratitude, demands myself.

ARKAS.

Who no affection feels doth never want
Excuses.   To the king I'll now relate
All that has happen'd.   Oh, that in thy soul
Thou wouldst revolve his noble conduct, priestess,
Since thy arrival to the present day!


## SCENE III.

IPHIGENIA, alone.

These words at an unseasonable hour
Produce a strong revulsion in my breast;
I am alarm'd!—For as the rushing tide
In rapid currents eddies o'er the rocks
Which lie among the sand upon the shore;
E'en so a stream of joy o'erwhelm'd my soul.
I grasp'd what had appear'd impossible.
It was as though another gentle cloud
Around me lay, to raise me from the earth,
And rock my spirit in the same sweet sleep
Which the kind goddess shed around my brow,
What time her circling arm from danger snatch'd me.
My brother forcibly engross'd my heart;
I listen'd only to his friend's advice;
My soul rush'd eagerly to rescue them,
And as the mariner with joy surveys
The less'ning breakers of a desert isle,
So Tauris lay behind me.   But the voice
Of faithful Arkas wakes me from my dream,

Reminding me that those whom I forsake
Are also men.   Deceit doth now become
Doubly detested.   O my soul, be still!
Beginn'st thou now to tremble and to doubt?
Thy lonely shelter on the firm-set earth
Must thou abandon? and, embark'd once more,
At random drift upon tumultuous waves,
A stranger to thyself and to the world?


## SCENE IV.

### IPHIGENIA.       PYLADES.

#### PYLADES.

Where is she? that my words with speed may tell
The joyful tidings of our near escape!

#### IPHIGENIA.

Oppress'd with gloomy care, I much require
The certain comfort thou dost promise me.

#### PYLADES.

Thy brother is restor'd!  The rocky paths
Of this unconsecrated shore we trod
In friendly converse, while behind us lay,
Unmark'd by us, the consecrated grove;
And ever with increasing glory shone
The fire of youth around his noble brow.
Courage and hope his glowing eye inspir'd;
And his free heart exulted with the joy
Of saving thee, his sister, and his friend.

#### IPHIGENIA.

The gods shower blessings on thee, Pylades!
And from those lips which breathe such welcome news,
Be the sad note of anguish never heard!

#### PYLADES.

I bring yet more,—for Fortune, like a prince,
Comes not alone, but well accompanied.
Our friends and comrades we have also found.
Within a bay they had conceal'd the ship,
And mournful sat expectant.  They beheld
Thy brother, and a joyous shout uprais'd,
Imploring him to haste the parting hour.
Each hand impatient long'd to grasp the oar,

While from the shore a gently murmuring breeze,
Perceiv'd by all, unfurl'd its wing auspicious.
Let us then hasten; guide me to the fane,
That I may tread the sanctuary, and seize
With sacred awe the object of our hopes.
I can unaided on my shoulder bear
Diana's image: how I long to feel
The precious burden!
      [*While speaking the last words, he approaches the Temple,*
         *without perceiving that he is not followed by Iphi-*
         *genia: at length he turns round.*]
                Why thus ling'ring stand?
Why art thou silent? wherefore thus confus'd?
Doth some new obstacle oppose our bliss?
Inform me, hast thou to the king announc'd
The prudent message we agreed upon?
IPHIGENIA.

I have, dear Pylades; yet wilt thou chide.
Thy very aspect is a mute reproach.
The royal messenger arriv'd, and I,
According to thy counsel, fram'd my speech.
He seem'd surpris'd, and urgently besought,
That to the monarch I should first announce
The rite unusual, and attend his will.
I now await the messenger's return.
PYLADES.

Danger again doth hover o'er our heads!
O priestess, why neglect to shroud thyself
Within the veil of sacerdotal rites?
IPHIGENIA.

I never have employ'd them as a veil.
PYLADES.

Pure soul! thy scruples will destroy alike
Thyself and us.   Why did I not foresee
Such an emergency, and tutor thee
This counsel also wisely to elude?
IPHIGENIA.

Chide only me, for mine alone the blame.
Yet other answer could I not return
To him, who strongly and with reason urg'd
What my own heart acknowledg'd to be right.

PYLADES.

The danger thickens; but let us be firm,
Nor with incautious haste betray ourselves:
Calmly await the messenger's return,
And then stand fast, whatever his reply:
For the appointment of such sacred rites
Doth to the priestess, not the king belong.
Should he demand the stranger to behold,
Who is by madness heavily oppress'd,
Evasively pretend, that in the fane,
Securely guarded, thou retain'st us both.
Thus you secure us time to fly with speed,
Bearing the sacred treasure from this race,
Unworthy its possession.   Phœbus sends
Auspicious omens, and fulfils his word,
Ere we the first conditions have perform'd.
Free is Orestes, from the curse absolv'd!
Oh, with the freed one, to the rocky isle
Where dwells the god, waft us, propitious gales.
Thence to Mycene, that she may revive;
That from the ashes of the extinguish'd hearth,
The household gods may joyously arise,
And beauteous fire illumine their abode!
Thy hand from golden censers first shall strew
The fragrant incense.   O'er that threshold thou
Shalt life and blessing once again dispense,
The curse atone, and all thy kindred grace
With the fresh bloom of renovated life.

IPHIGENIA.

As doth the flower revolve to meet the sun,
Once more my spirit to sweet comfort turns,
Struck by thy words' invigorating ray.
How dear the counsel of a present friend,
Lacking whose godlike power, the lonely one
In silence droops! for, lock'd within his breast,
Slowly are ripen'd purpose and resolve,
Which friendship's genial warmth had soon matur'd.

PYLADES.

Farewell! I haste to re-assure our friends,
Who anxiously await us: then with speed
I will return, and, hid within the brake,

Attend thy signal.—Wherefore, all at once,
Doth anxious thought o'ercloud thy brow serene?
                    IPHIGENIA.
Forgive me!   As light clouds athwart the sun,
So cares and fears float darkling o'er my soul.
                    PYLADES.
Oh, banish fear! With danger it hath form'd
A close alliance,—they are constant friends.
                    IPHIGENIA.
It is an honest scruple, which forbids
That I should cunningly deceive the king,
And plunder him who was my second sire.
                    PYLADES.
Him thou dost fly, who would have slain thy brother.
                    IPHIGENIA.
To me, at least, he hath been ever kind.
                    PYLADES.
What Fate commands is not ingratitude.
                    IPHIGENIA.
Alas! it still remains ingratitude;
Necessity alone can justify it.
                    PYLADES.
Thee, before gods and men it justifies.
                    IPHIGENIA.
But my own heart is still unsatisfied.
                    PYLADES.
Scruples too rigid are a cloak for pride.
                    IPHIGENIA.
I cannot argue, 1 can only feel.
                    PYLADES.
Conscious of right, thou shouldst respect thyself
                    IPHIGENIA.
Then only doth the heart know perfect ease,
When not a stain pollutes it.
                    PYLADES.
                              In this fane
Pure hast thou kept thy heart.   Life teaches us
To be less strict with others and ourselves;
Thou'lt learn the lesson too.   So wonderful
Is human nature, and its varied ties
Are so involv'd and complicate, that none

May hope to keep his inmost spirit pure,
And walk without perplexity through life.
Nor are we call'd upon to judge ourselves;
With circumspection to pursue his path,
Is the immediate duty of a man.
For seldom can he rightly estimate,
Or his past conduct or his present deeds.

IPHIGENIA.

Almost thou dost persuade me to consent.

PYLADES.

Needs there persuasion when no choice is granted?
To save thyself, thy brother, and a friend,
One path presents itself, and canst thou ask
If we shall follow it?

IPHIGENIA.

      Still let me pause,
For such injustice thou couldst not thyself
Calmly return for benefits receiv'd.

PYLADES.

If we should perish, bitter self-reproach,
Forerunner of despair, will be thy portion.
It seems thou art not used to suffer much,
When, to escape so great calamity,
Thou canst refuse to utter one false word.

IPHIGENIA.

Oh, that I bore within a manly heart!
Which, when it hath conceiv'd a bold resolve,
'Gainst every other voice doth close itself.

PYLADES.

In vain thou dost refuse; with iron hand
Necessity commands; her stern decree
Is law supreme, to which the gods themselves
Must yield submission.   In dread silence rules
The uncounsell'd sister of eternal fate.
What she appoints thee to endure,—endure;
What to perform,—perform.   The rest thou know'st.
Ere long I will return, and then receive
The seal of safety from thy sacred hand.

## SCENE V.

IPHIGENIA, *alone.*

I must obey him, for I see my friends
Beset with peril.   Yet my own sad fate
Doth with increasing anguish move my heart.
May I no longer feed the silent hope
Which in my solitude I fondly cherish'd?
Shall the dire curse eternally endure?
And shall our fated race ne'er rise again
With blessings crown'd?—All mortal things decay!
The noblest powers, the purest joys of life
At length subside: then wherefore not the curse?
And have I vainly hop'd that, guarded here,
Secluded from the fortunes of my race,
I, with pure heart and hands, some future day
Might cleanse the deep defilement of our house?
Scarce was my brother in my circling arms
From raging madness suddenly restor'd,
Scarce had the ship, long pray'd for, near'd the strand,
Once more to waft me to my native shores,
When unrelenting fate, with iron hand,
A double crime enjoins; commanding me
To steal the image, sacred and rever'd,
Confided to my care, and him deceive
To whom I owe my life and destiny.
Let not abhorrence spring within my heart!
Nor the old Titan's hate, toward you, ye gods
Infix its vulture talons in my breast!
Save me, and save your image in my soul!
An ancient song comes back upon mine ear—
I had forgotten it, and willingly—
The Parcæ's song, which horribly they sang,
What time, hurl'd headlong from his golden seat,
Fell Tantalus.   They with their noble friend
Keen anguish suffer'd; savage was their breast
And horrible their song.   In days gone by,
When we were children, oft our ancient nurse
Would sing it to us, and I mark'd it well.

Oh, fear the immortals,
Ye children of men !
Eternal dominion
They hold in their hands,
And o'er their wide empire
Wield absolute sway.

Whom they have exalted
Let him fear them most !
Around golden tables,
On cliffs and clouds resting
The seats are prepar'd.

If contest ariseth ;
The guests are hurl'd headlong,
Disgrac'd and dishonour'd,
And fetter'd in darkness,
Await with vain longing,
A juster decree.

But in feasts everlasting,
Around the gold tables
Still dwell the immortals.
From mountain to mountain
They stride ; while ascending
From fathomless chasms,
The breath of the Titans,
Half stifl'd with anguish,
Like volumes of incense
Fumes up to the skies.

From races ill-fated,
Their aspect joy-bringing,
Oft turn the celestials,
And shun in the children
To gaze on the features
Once lov'd and still speaking
Of their mighty sire.

Thus sternly the Fates sang :
Immur'd in his dungeon,
The banish'd one listens,
The song of the Parcæ,
His children's doom ponders,
And boweth his head.

# ACT THE FIFTH.

## SCENE I.

### THOAS.     ARKAS.

#### ARKAS.

I own I am perplex'd, and scarcely know
'Gainst whom to point the shaft of my suspicion,
Whether the priestess aids the captives' flight,
Or they themselves clandestinely contrive it.
'Tis rumour'd that the ship which brought them here
Is lurking somewhere in a bay conceal'd.
This stranger's madness, these new lustral rites,
The specious pretext for delay, excite
Mistrust, and call aloud for vigilance.

#### THOAS.

Summon the priestess to attend me here!
Then go with speed, and strictly search the shore,
From yon projecting land to Dian's grove:
Forbear to violate its sacred depths;
A watchful ambush set, attack and seize,
According to your wont, whome'er ye find.

[Arkas retires.

## SCENE II.

### THOAS, alone.

Fierce anger rages in my riven breast,
First against her, whom I esteem'd so pure;
Then 'gainst myself, whose foolish lenity
Hath fashion'd her for treason.   Man is soon
Inur'd to slavery, and quickly learns
Submission, when of freedom quite depriv'd.
If she had fallen in the savage hands
Of my rude sires, and had their holy rage
Forborne to slay her, grateful for her life,
She would have recogniz'd her destiny,
Have shed before the shrine the stranger's blood,
And duty nam'd what was necessity.
Now my forbearance in her breast allures
Audacious wishes   Vainly I had hop'd

To bind her to me; rather she contrives
To shape an independent destiny.
She won my heart through flattery; and now
That I oppose her, seeks to gain her ends
By fraud and cunning, and my kindness deems
A worthless and prescriptive property.

## SCENE III.

#### IPHIGENIA.        THOAS.

#### IPHIGENIA.

Me hast thou summon'd? wherefore art thou here?

#### THOAS.

Wherefore delay the sacrifice? inform me.

#### IPHIGENIA.

I have acquainted Arkas with the reasons.

#### THOAS.

From thee I wish to hear them more at large.

#### IPHIGENIA.

The goddess for reflection grants thee time.

#### THOAS.

To thee this time seems also opportune.

#### IPHIGENIA.

If to this cruel deed thy heart is steel'd,
Thou shouldst not come!   A king who meditates
A deed inhuman. may find slaves enow,
Willing for hire to bear one half the curse.
And leave the monarch's presence undefil'd.
Enwrapt in gloomy clouds he forges death,
Whose flaming arrow on his victim's head
His hirelings hurl; while he above the storm
Remains untroubl'd, an impassive god.

#### THOAS.

A wild song, priestess, issued from thy lips.

#### IPHIGENIA.

No priestess, king! but Agamemnon's daughter;
While yet unknown, thou didst respect my words:
A princess now,—and think'st thou to command me?
From youth I have been tutor'd to obey,
My parents first and then the deity;

And thus obeying, ever hath my soul
Known sweetest freedom.   But nor then nor now
Have I been taught compliance with the voice
And savage mandates of a man.

THOAS.

Not I,
An ancient law doth claim obedience from thee

IPHIGENIA.

Our passions eagerly catch hold of laws
Which they can wield as weapons.   But to me
Another law, one far more ancient, speaks,
And doth command me to withstand thee, king!
That law declaring sacred every stranger.

THOAS.

These men, methinks, lie very near thy heart,
When sympathy with them can lead thee thus
To violate discretion's primal law,
That those in power should never be provok'd.

IPHIGENIA.

Speaking or silent, thou canst always know
What is, and ever must be, in my heart.
Doth not remembrance of a common doom,
To soft compassion melt the hardest heart?
How much more mine! in them I see myself.
I trembling kneel'd before the altar once,
And solemnly the shade of early death
Environ'd me.   Aloft the knife was rais'd
To pierce my bosom, throbbing with warm life;
A dizzy horror overwhelm'd my soul;
My eyes grew dim;—I found myself in safety.
Are we not bound to render the distress'd
The gracious kindness from the gods receiv'd?
Thou know'st we are, and yet wilt thou compel me!

THOAS.

Obey thine office, priestess, not the king.

IPHIGENIA.

Cease! nor thus seek to cloak the savage force
Which triumphs o'er a woman's feebleness.
Though woman, I am born as free as man.
Did Agamemnon's son before thee stand,
And thou requiredst what became him not,

His arm and trusty weapon would defend
His bosom's freedom.   I have only words;
But it becomes a noble-minded man
To treat with due respect the words of woman.

THOAS.

I more respect them than a brother's sword.

IPHIGENIA.

Uncertain ever is the chance of arms,
No prudent warrior doth despise his foe;
Nor yet defenceless 'gainst severity
Hath nature left the weak; she gives him craft
And wily cunning; artful he delays,
Evades, eludes, and finally escapes.
Such arms are justified by violence.

THOAS.

But circumspection countervails deceit.

IPHIGENIA.

Which a pure spirit doth abhor to use.

THOAS.

Do not incautiously condemn thyself.

IPHIGENIA.

Oh, couldst thou see the struggle of my soul,
Courageously to ward the first attack
Of an unhappy doom, which threatens me!
Do I then stand before thee weaponless?
Prayer, lovely prayer, fair branch in woman's hand,
More potent far than instruments of war,
Thou dost thrust back.   What now remains for me
Wherewith my inborn freedom to defend?
Must I implore a miracle from heaven?
Is there no power within my spirit's depths?

THOAS.

Extravagant thy interest in the fate
Of these two strangers.   Tell me who they are
For whom thy heart is thus so deeply mov'd.

IPHIGENIA.

They are—they seem at least—I think them Greeks.

THOAS.

Thy countrymen; no doubt they have renew'd
The pleasing picture of return.

P

IPHIGENIA, *after a pause.*
                        Doth man
Lay undisputed claim to noble deeds?
Doth he alone to his heroic breast
Clasp the impossible?    What call we great?
What deeds, though oft narrated, still uplift
With shudd'ring horror the narrator's soul,
But those which, with improbable success,
The valiant have attempted?    Shall the man
Who all alone steals on his foes by night,
And raging like an unexpected fire,
Destroys the slumbering host, and press'd at length
By rous'd opponents or his foemen's steeds,
Retreats with booty—be alone extoll'd?
Or he who, scorning safety, boldly roams
Through woods and dreary wilds, to scour the land
Of thieves and robbers?    Is nought left for us?
Must gentle woman quite forego her nature,
Force against force employ,—like Amazons,
Usurp the sword from man, and bloodily
Revenge oppression?    In my heart I feel
The stirrings of a noble enterprize;
But if I fail—severe reproach, alas!
And bitter misery will be my doom.
Thus on my knees I supplicate the gods.
Oh, are ye truthful, as men say ye are,
Now prove it by your countenance and aid;
Honour the truth in me!    Attend, O king!
A secret plot is laid; 'tis vain to ask
Touching the captives; they are gone, and seek
Their comrades who await them on the shore.
The eldest,—he whom madness lately seiz'd,
And who is now recover'd,—is Orestes,
My brother, and the other Pylades,
His early friend and faithful confidant.
From Delphi, Phœbus sent them to this shore
With a divine command to steal away
The image of Diana, and to him
Bear back the sister, promising for this
Redemption to the blood-stain'd matricide.
I have deliver'd now into thy hands

The remnants of the house of Tantalus.
Destroy us—if thou canst.

THOAS.

And dost thou think
The savage Scythian will attend the voice
Of truth and of humanity, unheard
By the Greek Atreus?

IPHIGENIA.

'Tis heard by all,
Whate'er may be their clime, within whose breast
Flows pure and free the gushing stream of life.—
What silent purpose broods within thy soul?
Is it destruction?   Let me perish first!
For now, deliv'rance hopeless, I perceive
The dreadful peril into which I have
With rash precipitancy plung'd my friends.
Alas! I soon shall see them bound before me!
How to my brother shall I say farewell?
I, the unhappy author of his death.
Ne'er can I gaze again in his dear eyes!

THOAS.

The traitors have contriv'd a cunning web,
And cast it round thee, who, secluded long,
Giv'st willing credence to thine own desires.

IPHIGENIA.

No, no!   I'd pledge my life these men are true.
And shouldst thou find them otherwise, O king,
Then let them perish both, and cast me forth,
That on some rock-girt island's dreary shore
I may atone my folly.   Are they true,
And is this man indeed my dear Orestes,
My brother, long implor'd,—release us both,
And o'er us stretch the kind protecting arm,
Which long hath shelter'd me.   My noble sire
Fell through his consort's guilt,—she by her son;
On him alone the hope of Atreus' race
Doth now repose.   Oh, with pure heart and hands
Let me depart to expiate our house.
Yes, thou wilt keep thy promise; thou didst swear,
That were a safe return provided me,
I should be free to go.   The hour is come.

A king doth never grant like common men,
Merely to gain a respite from petition ;
Nor promise what he hopes will ne'er be claim'd.
Then first he feels his dignity complete
When he can make the long-expecting happy.

THOAS.

As fire opposes water, and doth seek
With hissing rage to overcome its foe,
So doth my anger strive against thy words.

IPHIGENIA.

Let mercy, like the consecrated flame
Of silent sacrifice, encircl'd round
With songs of gratitude, and joy, and praise,
Above the tumult gently rise to heaven.

THOAS.

How often hath this voice assuag'd my soul

IPHIGENIA.

Extend thy hand to me in sign of peace.

THOAS.

Large thy demand within so short a time.

IPHIGENIA.

Beneficence doth no reflection need.

THOAS.

'Tis needed oft, for evil springs from good.

IPHIGENIA.

'Tis doubt which good doth oft to evil turn.
Consider not: act as thy feelings prompt thee.

## SCENE IV.

ORESTES (*armed*).      IPHIGENIA.      THOAS.

ORESTES, *addressing his followers.*

Redouble your exertions! hold them back!
Few moments will suffice; retain your ground,
And keep a passage open to the ship
For me and for my sister.

*To* IPHIGENIA, *without perceiving* THOAS.

Come with speed!
We are betray'd,—brief time remains for flight.

THOAS.

None in my presence with impunity
His naked weapon wears.

#### IPHIGENIA.

Do not profane
Diana's sanctuary with rage and blood.
Command your people to forbear awhile,
And listen to the priestess, to the sister.

#### ORESTES.

Say, who is he that threatens us?

#### IPHIGENIA.

In him
Revere the king, who was my second father.
Forgive me, brother, that my childlike heart
Hath plac'd our fate thus wholly in his hands.
I have betray'd your meditated flight,
And thus from treachery redeem'd my soul.

#### ORESTES.

Will he permit our peaceable return?

#### IPHIGENIA.

Thy gleaming sword forbids me to reply.

ORESTES, *sheathing his sword.*

Then speak! thou seest I listen to thy words.

## SCENE V.

ORESTES.      IPHIGENIA.      THOAS.

*Enter* PYLADES, *soon after him* ARKAS, *both with
drawn swords.*

#### PYLADES.

Do not delay! our friends are putting forth
Their final strength, and yielding step by step,
Are slowly driven backward to the sea.—
A conference of princes find I here?
Is this the sacred person of the king?

#### ARKAS.

Calmly, as doth become thee, thou dost stand,
O king, surrounded by thine enemies.
Soon their temerity shall be chastis'd;
Their yielding followers fly,—their ship is ours.
Speak but the word and it is wrapt in flames.

THOAS.

Go, and command my people to forbear!
Let none annoy the foe while we confer.     (*Arkas retires.*)

ORESTES.

I willingly consent.   Go, Pylades!
Collect the remnant of our friends, and wait
The appointed issue of our enterprize.

(*Pylades retires.*)

## SCENE VI.

IPHIGENIA.          THOAS.          ORESTES.

IPHIGENIA.

Relieve my cares ere ye begin to speak.
I fear contention, if thou wilt not hear
The voice of equity, O king,—if thou
Wilt not, my brother, curb thy headstrong youth.

THOAS.

I, as becomes the elder, check my rage.
Now answer me: how dost thou prove thyself
The priestess' brother, Agamemnon's son?

ORESTES.

Behold the sword with which the hero slew
The valiant Trojans.   From his murderer
I took the weapon, and implor'd the Gods
To grant me Agamemnon's mighty arm,
Success, and valour, with a death more noble
Select one of the leaders of thy host,
And place the best as my opponent here.
Where'er on earth the sons of heroes dwell,
This boon is to the stranger ne'er refus'd.

THOAS.

This privilege hath ancient custom here
To strangers ne'er accorded.

ORESTES.
                    Then from us
Commence the novel custom! A whole race
In imitation soon will consecrate
Its monarch's noble action into law.
Nor let me only for our liberty,—
Let me, a stranger, for all strangers fight.

If I should fall, my doom be also theirs;
But if kind fortune crown me with success,
Let none e'er tread this shore, and fail to meet
The beaming eye of sympathy and love,
Or unconsol'd depart!

### THOAS.

    Thou dost not seem
Unworthy of thy boasted ancestry.
Great is the number of the valiant men
Who wait upon me; but I will myself,
Although advanc'd in years, oppose the foe,
And am prepar'd to try the chance of arms.

### IPHIGENIA.

No, no! such bloody proofs are not requir'd.
Unhand thy weapon, king! my lot consider;
Rash combat oft immortalizes man;
If he should fall, he is renown'd in song;
But after ages reckon not the tears
Which ceaseless the forsaken woman sheds;
And poets tell not of the thousand nights
Consum'd in weeping, and the dreary days,
Wherein her anguish'd soul, a prey to grief,
Doth vainly yearn to call her lov'd one back.
Fear warn'd me to beware lest robber's wiles
Might lure me from this sanctuary, and then
Betray me into bondage.   Anxiously
I question'd them, each circumstance explor'd,
Demanded signs, and now my heart 's assur'd.
See here, the mark as of three stars impress'd
On his right hand, which on his natal day
Were by the priest declar'd to indicate
Some dreadful deed by him to be perform'd.
And then this scar, which doth his eyebrow cleave
Redoubles my conviction.   When a child,
Electra, rash and inconsiderate,
Such was her nature, loos'd him from her arms.
He fell against a tripos.   Oh, 'tis he!—
Shall I adduce the likeness to his sire,
Or the deep rapture of my inmost heart,
In further token of assurance, king?

THOAS.

E'en though thy words had banish'd every doubt,
And I had curb'd the anger in my breast,
Still must our arms decide.   I see no peace.
Their purpose, as thou didst thyself confess,
Was to deprive me of Diana's image.
And think ye that I'll look contented on?
The Greeks are wont to cast a longing eye
Upon the treasures of barbarians,
A golden fleece, good steeds, or daughters fair;
But force and guile not always have avail'd
To lead them, with their booty, safely home.

ORESTES.

The image shall not be a cause of strife!
We now perceive the error which the God,
Our journey here commanding, like a veil,
Threw o'er our minds.   His counsel I implor'd,
To free me from the Furies' grisly band.
He answer'd, "Back to Greece the sister bring,
Who in the sanctuary on Tauris' shore
Unwillingly abides; so ends the curse!"
To Phœbus' sister we applied the words,
And he referr'd to thee!   The bonds severe,
Which held thee from us, holy one, are rent,
And thou art ours once more.   At thy blest touch,
I felt myself restor'd.   Within thine arms,
Madness once more around me coil'd its folds,
Crushing the marrow in my frame, and then
For ever, like a serpent, fled to hell.
Through thee, the daylight gladdens me anew.
The counsel of the Goddess now shines forth
In all its beauty and beneficence.
Like to a sacred image, unto which
An oracle immutably hath bound
A city's welfare, thee Diana took,
Protectress of our house, and guarded here
Within this holy stillness, to become
A blessing to thy brother and thy race.
Now when each passage to escape seems clos'd,
And safety hopeless, thou dost give us all.

O king, incline thine heart to thoughts of peace!
Let her fulfil her mission, and complete
The consecration of our father's house,
Me to their purified abode restore,
And place upon my brow the ancient crown!
Requite the blessing which her presence brought thee,
And let me now my nearer right enjoy!
Cunning and force, the proudest boast of man,
Fade in the lustre of her perfect truth;
Nor unrequited will a noble mind
Leave confidence, so childlike and so pure.

IPHIGENIA.

Think on thy promise; let thy heart be mov'd
By what a true and honest tongue hath spoken!
Look on us, king! an opportunity
For such a noble deed not oft occurs.
Refuse thou canst not,—give thy quick consent.

THOAS.

Then go!

IPHIGENIA.

   Not so, my king! I cannot part
Without thy blessing, or in anger from thee.
Banish us not! the sacred right of guests
Still let us claim: so not eternally
Shall we be sever'd.  Honour'd and belov'd
As mine own father was, art thou by me:
And this impression in my soul remains.
Should e'en the meanest peasant of thy land
Bring to my ear the tones I heard from thee
Or should I on the humblest see thy garb,
I will with joy receive him as a god,
Prepare his couch myself, beside our hearth
Invite him to a seat, and only ask
Touching thy fate and thee.  Oh, may the gods
To thee the merited reward impart
Of all thy kindness and benignity!
Farewell! Oh, do not turn away, but give
One kindly word of parting in return!
So shall the wind more gently swell our sails,

And from our eyes with soften'd anguish flow
The tears of separation.   Fare thee well!
And graciously extend to me thy hand,
In pledge of ancient friendship.

      THOAS, *extending his hand.*
         Fare thee well!

# TORQUATO TASSO.

## PERSONS OF THE DRAMA.

ALPHONSO II., *Duke of Ferrara.*
LEONORA D'ESTE, *Sister to the Duke.*
LEONORA SANVITALE, *Countess of Scandiano.*
TORQUATO TASSO.
ANTONIO MONTECATINO, *Secretary of State.*

## ACT THE FIRST.

### SCENE I

*A Garden adorned with busts of the Epic Poets.   To the right,
a bust of Virgil; to the left, one of Ariosto.*

PRINCESS *and* LEONORA, *habited as shepherdesses.*

**PRINCESS.**
Smiling thou dost survey me, Leonora,
Then with a smile thou dost survey thyself.
What is it?   Let a friend partake thy thought!
Thou seemest pensive, yet thou seemest pleased.
**LEONORA.**
Yes, princess, I am pleas'd to see us both
In rural garb thus tastefully attir'd.
Two happy shepherd maidens we appear,
And our employment speaks our happiness;
Garlands we wreath.   This one, so gay with flowers,
Beneath my hand in varied beauty grows;
Whilst thou, with loftier taste and larger heart,
Hast of the pliant laurel made thy choice.
**PRINCESS.**
The laurel wreath, which aimlessly I twin'd,
Hath found at once a not unworthy head;
I place it gratefully on Virgil's brow.
*She crowns the bust of Virgil.*)

LEONORA.

With my full joyous wreath I crown the brow
Of Ludovico, of the tuneful lyre—

      (*She crowns the bust of Ariosto.*)

Let him whose sportive sallies never fade,
Receive his tribute from the early spring.

PRINCESS.

My brother is most kind, to bring us here
In this sweet season to our rural haunts;
Here, by the hour, in freedom unrestrain'd,
We may dream back the poet's golden age.
I love this Belriguardo; in my youth
Full many a joyous day I linger'd here,
And this bright sunshine, and this verdant green,
Bring back the feeling of that by-gone time.

LEONORA.

Yes, a new world surrounds us!   Grateful now
The cooling shelter of these evergreens.
The tuneful murmur of this gurgling spring
Once more revives us.   In the morning wind
The tender branches waver to and fro.
The flowers look upwards from their lowly beds,
And smile upon us with their childlike eyes.
The gard'ner, fearless grown, removes the roof
That screened his citron and his orange-trees;
The azure dome of heaven above us rests;
And, in the far horizon, from the hills
The snow in balmy vapour melts away.

PRINCESS.

Most dearly welcome were the spring to me,
Did it not rob me of my much lov'd friend.

LEONORA.

My princess, in these sweet and tranquil hours,
Remind me not how soon I must depart.

PRINCESS.

Yon mighty city will restore to thee,
In double measure, what thou leavest here.

LEONORA.

Duty and love both call me to my lord,
Forsaken long.   I bring to him his son,
Whose mind and form have rapidly matur'd

Since last they met,—I share his father's joy.
Florence is great and noble, but the worth
Of all her treasur'd riches doth not reach
The prouder jewels that Ferrara boasts.
That city to her people owes her power;
Ferrara grew to greatness through her princes.

PRINCESS.

More through the noble men whom chance led here,
And who, in sweet communion, here remain'd.

LEONORA.

Chance doth again disperse what chance collects;
A noble nature can alone attract
The noble, and retain them, as ye do.
Around thy brother, and around thyself,
Assemble spirits worthy of you both,
And ye are worthy of your noble sires.
Here the fair light of science and free thought
Was kindled first, while o'er the darken'd world
Still hung barbarian gloom.   E'en when a child
The names resounded loudly in mine ear,
Of Hercules and Hypolite of Este.
My father oft with Florence and with Rome
Extoll'd Ferrara!   Oft in youthful dream
Hither I fondly turn'd, and now am here.
Here was Petrarca kindly entertain'd,
And Ariosto found his models here.
Italia boasts no great, no mighty name,
This princely mansion hath not call'd its guest.
In fost'ring genius we enrich ourselves;
Dost thou present her with a friendly gift,
One far more beautiful she leaves with thee.
The ground is hallow'd where the good man treads;
When centuries have roll'd, his sons shall hear
The deathless echo of his words and deeds.

PRINCESS.

Yes, if those sons have feelings quick as thine.
This happiness full oft I envy thee.

LEONORA.

Which purely and serenely thou, my friend.
As few beside thee, dost thyself enjoy.
When my full heart impels me to express

Promptly and freely what I keenly feel,
Thou feel'st the while more deeply, and—art silent.
Delusive splendour doth not dazzle thee,
Nor wit beguile; and flatt'ry strives in vain
With fawning artifice to win thine ear;
Firm is thy temper, and correct thy taste,
Thy judgment just, and, truly great thyself,
With greatness thou dost ever sympathize.

PRINCESS.

Thou shouldst not to this high wrought flatt'ry lend
Confiding friendship's consecrated garb.

LEONORA.

Friendship is just; she only estimates
The full extent and measure of thy worth.
And though we give to fortune and to chance
Their portion in thy culture,—still 'tis thine,
And all extol thy sister and thyself
Before the noblest women of the age.

PRINCESS.

That can but little move me, Leonora,
When I reflect how poor at best we are,
To others more indebted than ourselves.
My knowledge of the ancient languages,
And of the treasures by the past bequeath'd,
I owe my mother, who, in varied lore
And mental power, her daughters far excell'd.
Might either claim comparison with her,
'Tis undeniably Lucretia's right.
Besides, what nature and what chance bestow'd
As property or rank I ne'er esteem'd.
'Tis pleasure to me when the wise converse,
That I their scope and meaning comprehend;
Whether they judge a man of by-gone times
And weigh his actions, or of science treat,
Which, when extended and applied to life,
At once exalts and benefits mankind.
Where'er the converse of such men may lead,
I follow gladly, for with ease I follow.
Well pleas'd the strife of argument I hear,
When, round the powers that sway the human breast,
Waking alternately delight and fear,

With grace the lip of eloquence doth play;
And listen gladly when the princely thirst
Of fame, of wide dominion, forms the theme,
When of an able man, the thought profound,
Develop'd skilfully with subtle tact,
Doth not perplex and dazzle, but instruct.

LEONORA.

And then, this grave and serious converse o'er,
Our ear and inner mind with tranquil joy
Upon the poet's tuneful verse repose,
Who through the medium of harmonious sounds
Infuses sweet emotions in the soul.
Thy lofty spirit grasps a wide domain;
Content am I to linger in the isle
Of poesy, her laurel groves among.

PRINCESS.

In this fair land, I'm told, the myrtle blooms
In richer beauty than all other trees;
Here, too, the muses wander, yet we seek
A friend and playmate 'mong their tuneful choir
Less often than we seek to meet the bard,
Who seems to shun us, nay, appears to flee,
In quest of something that we know not of,
And which perchance is to himself unknown.
How charming were it, if in happy hour
Encountering us, he should with ecstasy
In our fair selves the treasure recognize,
Which in the world he long had sought in vain!

LEONORA.

To your light raillery I must submit,
So light its touch it passeth harmless by.
I honour all men after their desert,
And am in truth toward Tasso only just.
His eye scarce lingers on this earthly scene,
To nature's harmony his ear is tuned.
What hist'ry offers, and what life presents,
His bosom promptly and with joy receives.
The widely scatter'd is by him combined,
And his quick feeling animates the dead.
Oft he ennobles what we count for nought;
What others treasure is by him despis'd.

Thus moving in his own enchanted sphere,
The wondrous man doth still allure us on
To wander with him and partake his joy;
Though seeming to approach us, he remains
Remote as ever, and perchance his eye,
Resting on us, sees spirits in our place.

PRINCESS.

Thou hast with taste and truth portray'd the bard.
Who hovers in the shadowy realm of dreams.
And yet reality, it seems to me,
Hath also power to lure him and enchain.
In the sweet sonnets, scatter'd here and there,
With which we sometimes find our trees adorn'd,
Creating like the golden fruit of old
A new Hesperia, perceiv'st thou not
The gentle tokens of a genuine love?

LEONORA.

In these fair leaves I also take delight.
With all his rich diversity of thought
He glorifies one form in all his strains.
Now he exalts her to the starry heavens
In radiant glory, and before that form
Bows down, like angels in the realms above.
Then stealing after her through silent fields,
He garlands in his wreath each beauteous flower;
And should the form he worships disappear,
Hallows the path her gentle foot hath trod.
Thus like the nightingale, conceal'd in shade,
From his love-laden breast he fills the air
And neighbouring thickets with melodious plaint;
His blissful sadness and his tuneful grief
Charm every ear, enrapture every heart.

PRINCESS.

And Leonora is the favour'd name
Selected for the object of his strains.

LEONORA.

Thy name it is, my princess, as 'tis mine.
It would displease me were it otherwise.
Now I rejoice that under this disguise
He can conceal his sentiments for thee,
And am no less contented with the thought

This sweet harmonious name should picture me.
Here is no question of an ardent love,
Seeking possession, and with jealous care
Screening its object from another's gaze.
While he enraptur'd contemplates thy worth
He in my lighter nature may rejoice.
He loves not us,—forgive me what I say,—
His lov'd ideal from the spheres he brings,
And doth invest it with the name we bear;
His feeling we participate; we seem
To love the man, yet only love in him
The highest object that can claim our love.

PRINCESS.

In this deep science thou art deeply vers'd,
My Leonora, and thy words in truth
Play on my ear, yet scarcely reach my soul.

LEONORA.

Thou, Plato's pupil! and not comprehend
What a mere novice dares to prattle to **thee?**
It must be then that I have widely err'd;
Yet well I know I do not wholly err.
For love doth in this graceful school appear
No longer as the spoilt and wayward child;
He is the youth whom Psyche hath espous'd:
Who sits in council with the assembl'd Gods.
He hath relinquish'd passion's fickle sway,
He clings no longer with delusion sweet
To outward form and beauty, to atone
For brief excitement by disgust and hate.

PRINCESS.

Here comes my brother! let us not betray
Whither our converse hath conducted us;
Else we shall have his raillery to bear
As in our dress he found a theme for jest.

SCENE II.

PRINCESS.      LEONORA.      ALPHONSO

ALPHONSO.

Tasso I seek, but nowhere can I find him;
And even here, with you, I meet him not.
Can you inform me where he hides himself?

Q

PRINCESS.

I have scarce seen him for the last two days.

ALPHONSO.

'Tis his habitual failing that he seeks
Seclusion rather than society.
I can forgive him when the motley crowd
He shuns thus studiously, and loves to hold
Free converse with himself in solitude;
But I cannot approve, that thus he flies
The circle of his more immediate friends.

LEONORA.

If I mistake not, thou wilt soon, O Prince,
Convert this censure into joyful praise.
To-day I saw him from afar; he held
A book and scroll, in which at times he wrote,
And then resum'd his walk, then wrote again.
A passing word, which yesterday he spoke,
Seem'd to announce to me his work complete;
His sole anxiety is now to add
A finish'd beauty to minuter parts,
That to your grace, to whom he owes so much,
A not unworthy offering he may bring.

ALPHONSO.

A welcome, when he brings it, shall be his,
And long immunity from all restraint.
Great, in proportion to the lively joy
And interest which his noble work inspires,
Is my impatience at its long delay.
After each slow advance he leaves his task;
He ever changeth, and can ne'er conclude,
Till baffled hope is weary; for we see
Reluctantly postpon'd to times remote
A pleasure we had fondly deem'd so near.

PRINCESS.

I rather praise the modesty, the care
With which thus, step by step, he nears the goal.
His aim is not to string amusing tales,
Or weave harmonious numbers, which at length,
Like words delusive, die upon the ear.
His numerous rhymes he labours to combine
Into one beautiful, poetic, whole;

And he whose soul this lofty aim inspires,
Must pay devoted homage to the muse.
Disturb him not, my brother, time alone
Is not the measure of a noble work;
And, is the coming age to share our joy,
We of the present must forget ourselves.

ALPHONSO.

Let us, dear sister, work together here,
As for our mutual good we oft have done.
Am I too eager—thou must then restrain;
Art thou too gentle—I will urge him on.
Then we perchance shall see him at the goal,
Where to behold him we have wish'd in vain.
His father-land, the world, shall then admire
And view with wonder his completed work.
I shall receive my portion of the fame,
And Tasso will be usher'd into life.
In a contracted sphere, a noble man
Cannot develope all his mental powers.
On him his country and the world must work.
He must endure both censure and applause,
Must be compell'd to estimate aright
Himself and others.   Solitude no more
Lulls him delusively with flatt'ring dreams.
Opponents will not, friendship dare not, spare,
Then in the strife the youth puts forth his powers
Knows what he is, and feels himself a man.

LEONORA.

Thus, Prince, will he owe everything to thee,
Who hast already done so much for him.
Talents are nurtured best in solitude,—
But character on life's tempestuous sea.
Oh that according to thy rules he would
Model his temper as he forms his taste,
Cease to avoid mankind, nor in his breast
Nurture suspicion into fear and hate!

ALPHONSO.

He only fears mankind who knows them not,
And he will soon misjudge them who avoids.
This is the case with him, till gradually,
His noble mind is trammell'd and perplex'd.

Thus to secure my favour he betrays,
At times, unseemly ardour; against some
Who, I am well assur'd, are not his foes,
He cherishes suspicion; if by chance
A letter go astray, a hireling leave
His service, or a paper be mislaid,
He sees deception, treachery, and fraud
Working insidiously to sap his peace.

PRINCESS.

Let us, beloved brother, not forget
That his own nature none can lay aside.
But should a lov'd companion wound his foot,
We would relax our speed, and lend our hand
Gently to aid the sufferer on his way.

ALPHONSO.

Better it were to remedy his pain,
With the physician's aid attempt a cure,
Then with our heal'd and renovated friend
A new career of life with joy pursue.
And yet, dear friends, I hope that I may ne'er
Incur the censure of the cruel leech.
I do my utmost to impress his mind
With feelings of security and trust.
Oft purposely in presence of the crowd,
With marks of favour I distinguish him.
Should he complain of aught, I sift it well,
As lately when his chamber he suppos'd
Had been invaded; then, should nought appear
I calmly show him how I view the affair.
And, as we ought to practise every grace—
With Tasso, seeing he deserves it well,
I practise patience; you I'm sure will aid.
I now have brought you to your rural haunts,
And must myself at eve return to town.
For a few moments you will see Antonio;
He calls here for me on his way from Rome.
We have important business to discuss,
Resolves to frame, and letters to indite,
All which compels me to return to town.

PRINCESS.

Wilt thou permit that we return with thee?

ALPHONSO.

Nay, rather linger here in Belriguardo,
Or go together to Consandoli ;
Enjoy these lovely days as fancy prompts.

PRINCESS.

Thou canst not stay with us ?   Not here arrange
All these affairs as well as in the town ?

LEONORA.

So soon, thou takest hence Antonio, too,
Who has so much to tell us about Rome.

ALPHONSO.

It must be so, but we will soon return ;
Then he shall tell you all you wish to hear,
And you shall aid me to reward the man
Who, in my cause, hath labour'd with such zeal.
And having talk'd our fill, the crowd may come,
That mirth and joy may revel in our groves,
And that some beauteous form, as is but meet,
May, should I thither turn, frequent the shade.

LEONORA.

And we meanwhile will kindly shut our eyes.

ALPHONSO.

Such kindness you know well I too can show.

PRINCESS, (*turned towards the scene*).

I long have notic'd Tasso from afar.
This way he slowly doth direct his steps ;
At times he pauses suddenly ; anon.
As if irresolute, retires in haste,
And then again stands still.

ALPHONSO.

Disturb him not,
Nor when the poet dreams and versifies
Intrude upon his musings,—let him roam.

LEONORA.

No, he has seen us, and he comes this way.

## SCENE III.

PRINCESS.      LEONORA.      ALPHONSO.

TASSO, *with a volume bound in parchment.*

TASSO.

Slowly I come to bring my work to thee,

And yet I linger ere presenting it.
Although apparently it seem complete,
Too well I know it is unfinish'd still.
But, if I cherish'd once an anxious fear
Lest I should bring thee an imperfect work,
A new solicitude constrains me now.
I would not seem ungrateful, nor appear
Unduly anxious; and, as to his friends,
A man can say but simply, "Here I am,"
That they, with kind forbearance, may rejoice.
So I can only say,—Receive my work!

                                [*He presents the volume.*

ALPHONSO.

Thou hast surpris'd me, Tasso, with thy gift,
And made this lovely day a festival.
I hold it then at length within my hands,
And in a certain sense can call it mine.
Long have I wish'd that thou couldst thus resolve,
And say at length "'Tis finish'd! here it is."

TASSO.

Are you contented? then it is complete;
For it belongs to you in every sense.
Were I to contemplate the pains bestow'd
Or dwell upon the written character,
I might, perchance, exclaim,—This work is mine.
But when I mark what 'tis that to my song,
Its inner worth and dignity imparts,
I humbly feel I owe it all to you.
If nature from her liberal stores on me
The genial gift of poesy bestow'd,
Capricious fortune, with malignant power
Had thrust me from her; though this beauteous world
With all its varied splendour lur'd the boy,
Too early was his youthful eye bedimm'd
By his lov'd parents' undeserved distress.
Forth from my lips when I essay'd to sing,
There ever flow'd a melancholy song,
And I accompanied, with plaintive tones,
My father's sorrow and my mother's grief.
'Twas thou alone, who from this narrow sphere
Rais'd me to glorious liberty, reliev'd

From each depressing care my youthful mind,
And gave me freedom, in whose genial air
My spirit could unfold in harmony.
Then whatsoe'er the merit of the work,
Thine be the praise, for it belongs to thee.
ALPHONSO.
A second time thou dost deserve applause,
And honour'st modestly thyself and us.
TASSO.
Fain would I say how sensibly I feel
That what I bring is all derived from thee!
The inexperienc'd youth—could he produce
The poem from his own unfurnish'd mind?
Could he invent the conduct of the war?
The gallant bearing and the martial skill
Which every hero on the field display'd,
The leader's prudence, and his followers' zeal,
How vigilance the arts of cunning foil'd,—
Hast thou not, valiant Prince, infus'd it all,
As if my guardian genius thou hadst been,
Through a mere mortal, deigning to reveal
His nature high and inaccessible?
PRINCESS.
Enjoy the work in which we all rejoice!
ALPHONSO.
Enjoy the approbation of the good!
LEONORA.
Rejoice too in thy universal fame!
TASSO.
This single moment is enough for me.
Of you alone I thought while I compos'd:
Your pleasure was my first, my dearest wish,
And your approval was my highest aim.
Who does not in his friends behold the world,
Deserves not that the world should hear of him,
Here is my fatherland, and here the sphere
In which my spirit fondly loves to dwell:
Here I attend and value every hint;
Here speak experience, knowledge, and true taste;
Here stand the present and the future age.
With shy reserve the poet shuns the crowd,—

Its judgment but perplexes.   Those alone
With minds like yours can understand and feel,
And such alone should censure and reward.

ALPHONSO.

If thus the present and the future age
We represent, it is not meet that we
Receive the poet's song unrecompens'd.
The laurel-wreath, fit chaplet for the bard,
Which e'en the hero, who requires his verse,
Sees without envy round his temples twin'd,
Adorns, thou seest, thy predecessor's brow.

[Pointing to the bust of Virgil

Hath chance, hath some kind genius twin'd the wreath,
And brought it hither?   Not in vain it thus
Presents itself: Virgil I hear exclaim,
" Wherefore confer this honour on the dead?
They in their lifetime had reward and joy;
Do ye indeed revere the bards of old?
Then to the living bard accord his due.
My marble statue has been amply crown'd,
And the green laurel branch belongs to life."

[Alphonso makes a sign to his sister; she takes the<br>
crown from the bust of Virgil, and approaches<br>
Tasso: he steps back.

LEONORA.

Thou dost refuse?   Seest thou what hand the wreath,
The fair, the never-fading wreath, presents!

TASSO.

Oh let me pause; I scarce can comprehend
How I can live after an hour like this.

ALPHONSO.

Live in enjoyment of the high reward,
From which thy inexperience shrinks with fear.

PRINCESS, raising the crown.

Thou dost afford me, Tasso, the rare joy
Of giving silent utt'rance to my thought.

TASSO.

The beauteous burden from thy honour'd hands,
On my weak head, thus kneeling, I receive.

[He kneels down; the Princess places the<br>
crown upon his head.

LEONORA, *applauding.*
Long live the poet, for the first time crown'd!
How well the crown adorns the modest man!

[ *Tasso rises*

ALPHONSO.
It is an emblem only of that crown
Which shall adorn thee on the Capitol.
PRINCESS.
There louder voices will salute thine ear;
Friendship with lower tones rewards thee here.
TASSO.
Take it, oh take it quickly, from my brow!
Pray thee remove it!  It doth scorch my locks;
And like a sunbeam, that with fervid heat
Falls on my forehead, burns up in my brain
The power of thought; while fever's fiery glow
Impels my blood.  Forgive! it is too much.
LEONORA.
This garland rather doth protect the head
Of him who treads the burning realm of fame,
And with its grateful shelter cools his brow.
TASSO.
I am not worthy to receive its shade,
Which only round the hero's brow should wave.
Ye gods, exalt it high among the clouds,
To float in glory inaccessible,
That, through eternity, my life may be
An endless striving to attain this goal!
ALPHONSO.
He who in youth acquires life's noblest gifts,
Learns early to esteem their priceless worth;
He who in youth enjoys, resigneth not
Without reluctance what he once possess'd;
And he who would possess, must still be arm'd.
TASSO.
And he who would be always arm'd, must feel
Within his breast a power that ne'er forsakes.
Ah, it forsakes me now!  In happiness
The inborn pow'r subsides, which prompted me
To meet injustice with becoming pride,
And steadfastly to face adversity.

Hath the delight, the rapture of this hour,
Dissolv'd the strength and marrow of my limbs?
My knees sink feebly, and, a second time,
Thou seest me, Princess, here before thee bow'd;
Grant my petition, and remove the crown,
That, as awaken'd from a blissful dream,
A new and fresh existence I may feel.

PRINCESS.

If thou with quiet modesty canst wear
The glorious talent from the gods receiv'd,
Learn also now the laurel wreath to wear,
The fairest gift that friendship can bestow
The brow it once hath worthily adorn'd,
It shall encircle through eternity.

TASSO.

Oh let me then asham'd from hence retire!
Let me in deepest shades my joy conceal,
As there my sorrow I was wont to shroud.
There will I range alone; no eye will there
Remind me of a bliss, so undeserv'd;
And if perchance I should behold a youth
In the clear mirror of a crystal spring,
Who, in the imag'd heaven, 'midst rocks and trees,
Absorb'd in thought appears, his brow adorn'd
With glory's garland, it shall seem to me
As 'twere Elysium mirror'd in the flood.
I pause and calmly ask, Who may this be?
What youth of by-gone times, so fairly crown'd?
Whence can I learn his name, and his desert?
I linger long, and musing fondly think:
Oh might there come another, and yet more
To join with him in friendly intercourse!
Oh could I see assembl'd round this spring
The heroes and the bards of ancient times!
Could I behold them still united here
As they in life were ever firmly bound!
As with mysterious power the magnet binds
Iron with iron, so do kindred aims
Unite the souls of heroes and of bards.
Himself forgetting, Homer spent his life
In contemplation of two mighty men;

And Alexander in the Elysian fields
Doth Homer and Achilles haste to seek.
Oh would that I were present to behold
Those mighty spirits in communion met.
LEONORA.
Awake, awake! let us not feel that thou
Dost quite forget the present in the past.
TASSO.
The present 'tis that elevates my mind;
I only seem oblivious, I'm entranc'd.
PRINCESS.
When thou dost speak with spirits, I rejoice
The voice is human, and I gladly hear.
[A Page steps to the Prince.
ALPHONSO.
He is arriv'd! and in a happy hour;
Antonio!   Bring him hither;—here he comes!

SCENE IV.

PRINCESS.   LEONORA.   ALPHONSO.   TASSO.   ANTONIO
ALPHONSO.
Thou'rt doubly welcome! thou who bring'st at once
Thyself and welcome tidings.
PRINCESS.
Welcome here!
ANTONIO.
Scarce dare I venture to express the joy
Which in your presence quickens me anew.
In your society I find restor'd
What I have miss'd so long.   You seem content
With what I've done, with what I have accomplish'd
And thus I'm recompens'd for every care,
For many days impatiently endur'd,
And many others wasted purposely.
At length our wish is gain'd,—the strife is o'er.
LEONORA.
I also greet thee, though I'm half displeased;
Thou dost arrive when I must hence depart.
ANTONIO.
As if to mar my perfect happiness,
Thou tak'st away one lovely part of it.

TASSO.
My greetings too!   I also shall rejoice
In converse with the much-experienc'd man.
ANTONIO.
Thou'lt find me true, whenever thou wilt deign
To glance awhile from thy world into mine.
ALPHONSO.
Though thou by letter hast announc'd to me
The progress and the issue of our cause,
Full many questions I have yet to ask
Touching the course thou hast pursued therein.
In that strange region a well-measur'd step
Alone conducts us to our destin'd goal.
Who doth his sovereign's interest pure'y seek,
In Rome a hard position must maintain ;
For Rome gives nothing, while she grasps at all.
Let him who thither goes some boon to claim,
Go well provided, and esteem himself
Most happy if e'en then he gaineth aught.
ANTONIO.
'Tis neither my demeanour nor my art
By which thy will has been accomplish'd, Prince.
For where the skill which at the Vatican
Would not be over-master'd ?   Much conspir'd
Which I could use in furth'rance of our cause.
Pope Gregory salutes and blesses thee.
That aged man, that sovereign most august,
Who on his brow the load of empire bears,
Recalls the time when he embrac'd thee last
With pleasure.   He who can distinguish men
Knows and extols thee highly.   For thy sake
He hath done much.
ALPHONSO.
So far as 'tis sincere,
His good opinion cannot but rejoice me.
But well thou know'st, that from the Vatican
The pope sees empires dwindl'd at his feet ;
Princes and men must needs seem small indeed.
Own what it was that most assisted thee.
ANTONIO.
It was, in truth, the Pope's exalted mind.

To him the small seems small, the great seems great.
That he may wield the empire of the world,
He wisely yieldeth to surrounding powers.
The value of the land which he resigns,
As of your friendship, Prince, he knows full well.
The peace of Italy must be secur'd,
And friends alone encircle his domain,
That all the might of Christendom, which he
With hand so powerful directs and guides,
May smite at once the Heretic and Turk.

PRINCESS.

And is it known what men he most esteems,
And who approach him confidentially?

ANTONIO.

The experienc'd man alone can win his ear,
The active man his favour and esteem.
He, who from early youth has serv'd the state,
Commands it now, ruling those very courts
Which, in his office of ambassador,
He had observ'd and guided years before.
The world lies spread before his searching gaze,
Clear as the interests of his own domain.
In action we must yield him our applause,
And mark with joy, when time unfolds the plans
Which his deep forethought fashion'd long before.
There is no fairer prospect in the world
Than to behold a prince who wisely rules,
A realm where every one obeys with pride,
And each imagines that he serves himself,
Because 'tis justice only that commands.

LEONORA.

How ardently I long to view that realm!

ALPHONSO.

Doubtless that thou may'st play thy part therein;
For Leonora never could remain
A mere spectator: meet it were, fair friend,
If now and then we let your gentle hands
Join in the lofty game.   Say, is't not so?

LEONORA *to* ALPHONSO.

Thou wouldst provoke me,—thou shalt not succeed.

ALPHONSO.

I am already deeply in thy debt.

LEONORA.

Good; then to-day I will remain in thine!
Forgive, and do not interrupt me now.

[*To* ANTONIO.

Say, has he done much for his relatives?

ANTONIO.

Nor more nor less than equity allows.
The potentate, who doth neglect his friends,
Is even by the people justly blam'd.
With wise discretion Gregory employs
His friends as trusty servants of the state,
And thus fulfils at once two kindred claims.

TASSO.

Do science and the liberal arts enjoy
His fost'ring care, and does he emulate
The glorious princes of the olden time?

ANTONIO.

He honours science when it is of use,—
Teaching to govern states and know mankind;
He prizes art when it embellishes,—
When it exalts and beautifies his Rome,
Erecting palaces and temples there,
Which rank among the prodigies of earth.
Within his sphere of influence he admits
Nought inefficient, and alone esteems
The active cause and instrument of good.

ALPHONSO.

Thou thinkest, then, that we may soon conclude
The whole affair? that no impediments
Will finally be scatter'd in our way?

ANTONIO.

Unless I greatly err, 'twill but require
A few brief letters and thy signature
To bring this contest to a final close.

ALPHONSO.

This day with justice then I may proclaim
A season of prosperity and joy.
My frontiers are enlarg'd and made secure;
Thou hast accomplish'd all without the sword,

And hence deservest well a civic crown.
Our ladies on some beauteous morn shall twine
A wreath of oak to bind around thy brow.
Meanwhile our poet hath enrich'd us too;
He, by his conquest of Jerusalem,
Hath put our modern Christendom to shame.
With joyous spirit and unwearied zeal,
A high and distant goal he hath attain'd;
For his achievement thou behold'st him crown'd.

ANTONIO.

Thou solv'st a riddle.   On arriving here
These two crown'd heads excited my surprise.

TASSO.

Oh, would that, while thou dost behold my joy
Thou with the self-same glance couldst view my heart
And witness there my deep humility!

ANTONIO.

How lavishly Alphonso can reward
I long have known; thou only provest now
What all enjoy who come within his sphere.

PRINCESS.

When thou shalt see the work he hath perform'd,
Thou wilt esteem us moderate and just.
We're but the first, the silent, witnesses
Of praises, which the world and future years
In tenfold measure will accord to him.

ANTONIO.

Through you his fame is certain.   Who so bold
To entertain a doubt when you commend?
But tell me, who on Ariosto's brow
Hath placed this wreath?

LEONORA.
This hand.

ANTONIO.
It hath done well.

It more becomes him than a laurel crown
As o'er her fruitful bosom Nature throws
Her variegated robe of beauteous green,
So he enshrouds in Fable's flow'ry garb,
Whatever can conspire to render man
Worthy of love and honour.   Power and taste,

Experience, understanding, and content,
And a pure feeling for the good and true,
Pervade the spirit of his every song,
And there appear in person, to repose
'Neath blossoming trees, besprinkled by the snow
Of lightly-falling flowers, their heads entwin'd
With rosy garlands, while the sportive Loves
With frolic humour weave their spells around.
A copious fountain, gurgling near, displays
Strange variegated fish, and all the air
Is vocal with the song of wondrous birds;
Strange cattle pasture in the bowers and glades;
Half hid in verdure, Folly slily lurks;
At times, resounding from a golden cloud,
The voice of Wisdom utters lofty truth,
While Madness, from a wild harmonious lute,
Scatters forth bursts of fitful harmony,
Yet all the while the justest measure holds.
He who aspires to emulate this man,
E'en for his boldness well deserves a crown.
Forgive me if I feel myself inspir'd,
Like one entranc'd forget both time and place,
And fail to weigh my words; for all these crowns,
These poets, and the festival attire
Of these fair ladies, have transported me
Out of myself into a foreign land.

PRINCESS.

Who thus can prize one species of desert,
Will not misjudge another; thou to us
Some future day, shalt show in Tasso's song
What we can feel, and thou canst comprehend.

ALPHONSO.

Come now, Antonio! many things remain
Whereof I am desirous to inquire.
Then till the setting of the sun thou shalt
Attend the ladies.   Follow me,—Farewell!

*[Antonio follows the Prince, Tasso the Ladies.*

# ACT THE SECOND.

## SCENE I.

### *A Room.*

PRINCESS.        TASSO.

TASSO.

My doubtful footsteps follow thee, O Princess ;
Tumultuous feelings vex my troubl'd soul,
And solitude appears to beckon me
And courteously to whisper, " Hither come,
I will allay the tumult in thy breast."
Yet if I only catch a glimpse of thee,
If from thy lip a word salute mine ear,
At once the fetters vanish from my soul,
And all around me shines a brighter day.
To thee I freely will confess, the man
Who unexpectedly appear'd among us
Hath rudely wak'd me from a golden dream ;
So strangely have his nature and his words
Affected me, that more than ever now
A want of inward harmony I feel,
And a distracting conflict with myself.

PRINCESS.

'Tis not to be expected that a friend
Who long hath sojourn'd in a foreign land,
Should in the moment of his first return,
The tone of former times at once resume ;
He in his inner mind is still unchang'd,
And a few days of intercourse will tune
The jarring strings, until they blend once more
In perfect harmony.   When he shall know
The greatness of the work thou hast achiev'd,
Believe me, he will place thee by the bard
Whom as a giant now he sets before thee.

TASSO.

My Princess, Ariosto's praise from him
Has more delighted than offended me.
Consoling 'tis, to know the man renown'd,
Whom as our model we have plac'd before us ;

An inward voice then whispers to the heart;
" Canst thou obtain a portion of his worth,
A portion of his fame is also thine."
No, that which hath most deeply mov'd my heart,
Which even now completely fills my soul,
Was the majestic picture of that world,
Which, with its living, restless, mighty, forms
Around one great and prudent man revolves,
And runs with measur'd steps the destin'd course
Prescrib'd beforehand by the demigod.
I listen'd eagerly, and heard with joy
The wise discourse of the experienc'd man ;
But ah ! the more I heard, the more I felt
Mine own unworthiness, and fear'd that I
Like empty sound, might dissipate in air,
Or vanish like an echo or a dream.

PRINCESS.

And yet erewhile thou didst so truly feel
How bards and heroes for each other live,
How bards and heroes to each other tend,
And toward each other know no envious thought
Noble in truth are deeds deserving fame,
But it is also noble to transmit
The lofty grandeur of heroic deeds,
Through worthy song, to our posterity.
Be satisfied to contemplate in peace,
From a small, shelt'ring state, as from the shore
The wild and stormy current of the world.

TASSO.

Was it not here, amaz'd, I first beheld
The high reward on valiant deeds bestow'd ?
An inexperienc'd youth I here arriv'd,
When festival on festival conspir'd
To render this the centre of renown.
Oh what a scene Ferrara then display'd !
The wide arena, where in all its pomp
Accomplish'd valour should its skill display,
Was bounded by a circle, whose high worth
The sun might seek to parallel in vain.
The fairest women sat assembled there,
And men the most distinguish'd of the age.

Amaz'd the eye ran o'er the noble throng;
Proudly I cried, " And 'tis our Fatherland,
That small, sea-girded land, hath sent them here.
They constitute the noblest court that e'er
On honour, worth, or virtue, judgment pass'd.
Survey them singly, and thou'lt not find one
Of whom his neighbour needs to feel asham'd!"—
And then the lists were open'd, chargers pranc'd,
Esquires press'd forward, helmets brightly gleam'd,
The trumpet sounded, shiv'ring lances split,
The din of clanging helm and shield was heard,
And for a moment eddying dust conceal'd
The victor's honour and the vanquish'd's shame.
Oh let me draw a curtain o'er the scene,
The all too brilliant festival conceal,
That in this tranquil hour I may not feel
Too painfully mine own unworthiness!

PRINCESS.

If that bright circle and those noble deeds
Arous'd thee then to enterprize and toil,
I could the while, young friend, have tutor'd thee
In the still lesson of calm sufferance.
The brilliant festival thou dost extol,
Which then and since a hundred voices prais'd,
I did not witness.   In a lonely spot,
So tranquil that unbroken on the ear
Joy's lightest echo faintly died away,
A prey to pain and melancholy thoughts,
I was compell'd to pass the tedious hours.
Before me hover'd, on extended wing,
Death's awful form, concealing from my view
The prospect of this ever-changing world;
Slowly it disappear'd, and I beheld,
As through a veil, the varied hues of life,
Pleasing but indistinct; while living forms
Began once more to flicker through the gloom
Still feeble, and supported by my women,
For the first time my silent room I left,
When hither, full of happiness and life,
Thee leading by the hand, Lucretia came.
A stranger then, thou, Tasso, wast the first

To welcome me on my return to life;
Much then I hop'd for both of us, and hope
Hath not, methinks, deceiv'd us hitherto.
TASSO.
Stunn'd by the tumult, dazzl'd by the glare
Impetuous passions stirring in my breast,
I by thy sister's side pursued my way
In silence through the stately corridors,
Then in the chamber enter'd, where ere long
Thou didst appear supported by thy women.
Oh, what a moment!   Princess, pardon me!
As in the presence of a deity
The victim of enchantment feels with joy
His frenzied spirit from delusion freed;
So was my soul from every phantasy,
From every passion, every false desire
Restor'd at once by one calm glance of thine;
And if, before, my inexperienc'd mind
Had lost itself in infinite desires,
I then, with shame, first turn'd my gaze within,
And recogniz'd the truly valuable.
Thus on the wide sea-shore we seek in vain
The pearl, reposing in its silent shell.
PRINCESS.
'Twas the commencement of a happy time,
And had Urbino's Duke not ta'en away
My sister from us, years would then have pass'd
In calm unclouded happiness.   But now,
We miss too much her buoyancy and life,
And the rich wit of the accomplish'd woman.
TASSO.
Too well I know since she departed hence,
None hath been able to supply to thee
The pure enjoyment which her presence gave.
Alas, how often hath it grieved my soul!
How often have I in the silent grove
Pour'd forth my lamentation!   How! I cried,
Is it her sister's sole prerogative
To be a treasure to the dear one's heart?
Does then no other soul respond to hers,
No other heart her confidence deserve?

Are soul and wit extinguish'd? and should one,
How great soe'er her worth, engross her love?
Forgive me, Princess!   Often I have wish'd
I could be something to thee,—little, perhaps,
But something; not with words alone, with deeds
I wish'd to be so, and in life to prove
How I had worshipp'd thee in solitude.
But I could ne'er succeed, and but too oft
In error wounded thee, offending one
By thee protected, or perplexing more
What thou didst wish to solve, and thus, alas!
E'en in the moment when I fondly strove
To draw more near thee, felt more distant still.

PRINCESS.

Thy wish I never have misconstrued, Tasso;
How thou dost prejudice thyself I know;
Unlike my sister, who possess'd the art
Of living happily with every one,
After so many years, thou scarce canst find
A single friend.

TASSO.

      Blame me! but show me, princess,
The man or woman to whom, as to thee,
I can unbosom freely ev'ry thought.

PRINCESS.

My brother well deserves thy confidence.

TASSO.

He is my Prince!—Yet do not hence suppose
That freedom's lawless impulse swells my breast.
Man is not born for freedom, and to serve
A prince deserving honour and esteem
Is a pure pleasure to a noble mind.
Still he's my sovereign, and of that great word
I deeply feel the full significance.
I must be silent when he speaks, and learn
To do what he commands me, though perchance
My heart and understanding both rebel.

PRINCESS.

That never with my brother can occur.
And in Antonio, who is now return'd,
Thou wilt possess another prudent friend.

TASSO.

I hop'd it once, now almost I despair.
His converse how instructive, and his words
How useful in a thousand instances!
For he possesses, I may truly say,
All that in me is wanting.   But, alas!
When round his cradle all the Gods assembled
To bring their gifts, the Graces were not there,
And he who lacks what these fair Powers impart,
May much possess, and much communicate,
But on his bosom we can ne'er repose.

PRINCESS.

But we can trust in him, and that is much.
Thou shouldst not, Tasso, in one man expect
All qualities combined; Antonio
Will keep his promises.   If he have once
Declared himself thy friend, he'll care for thee
When thou neglect'st thyself.   You must be friends
Ere long I hope I shall obtain my wish,
Only oppose me not, as is thy wont.
Then, Leonora long hath sojourn'd here,
Who is at once refined and elegant;
Her easy manners banish all restraint,
Yet thou hast ne'er approach'd her as she wish'd.

TASSO.

To thee I hearken'd, or believe me, Princess,
I should have rather shunn'd her than approach'd.
Though she appear so kind, I know not why,
But I can rarely feel at ease with her;
E'en when she seeks to benefit her friends
They feel the purpose, and are thence constrain'd.

PRINCESS.

Treading this path we ne'er shall meet with friends;
It only leads through solitary groves
And lonely valleys, where the friendless soul
Fondly endeavours to restore within
The golden age, which in the outward world
Exists no longer,—the attempt how vain!

TASSO.

Oh what a word, my Princess, hast thou spoken!
The golden age, ah whither is it flown,

For which in secret every heart repines?
When o'er the yet unsubjugated earth,
Men roam'd, like herds, in joyous liberty;
When on the flow'ry lawn an ancient tree
Lent to the shepherd and the shepherdess
Its grateful shadow, and the leafy grove
Its tender branches lovingly entwin'd
Around confiding love; when still and clear,
O'er sands for ever pure, the pearly stream
The nymph's fair form encircled; when the snake
Glided innoxious through the verdant grass,
And the bold youth pursued the daring faun:
When every bird winging the limpid air,
And every living thing o'er hill and dale
Proclaim'd to man,—What pleases, that is right.

PRINCESS.

My friend, the golden age hath pass'd away;
Only the good have power to bring it back.
Shall I confess to thee my secret thought?
The golden age, wherewith the bard is wont
Our spirits to beguile, that lovely prime,
Existed in the past no more than now;
And did it e'er exist, believe me, Tasso,
As then it was, it now may be restored.
Still meet congenial spirits, and enhance
Each other's pleasure in this beauteous world;
But in the motto change one single word,
And say, my friend,—What's fitting, that is right.

TASSO.

Would that of good and noble men were form'd
A great tribunal, to decide for all
What is befitting! then no more would each
Esteem that right which benefits himself.
The man of power acts ever as he lists,
And whatsoe'er he does is fitting deem'd.

PRINCESS.

Wouldst thou define exactly what is fitting,
Thou shouldst apply, methinks, to noble women;
For them it most behoveth that in life
Nought should be done unseemly or unfit;
Propriety encircles with a wall

The tender, weak, and vulnerable sex.
Where moral order reigneth, women reign,
They only are despis'd where rudeness triumphs;
And wouldst thou touching either sex inquire,
'Tis order woman seeketh, freedom man.

TASSO.

Thou thinkest us unfeeling, wild, and rude?

PRINCESS.

Not so! but ye with violence pursue
A multitude of objects far remote.
Ye venture for eternity to act,
While we, with views more narrow, on this earth
Seek only one possession, well content
If that with constancy remain our own.
For we, alas! are of no heart secure,
Whate'er the ardour of its first devotion.
Beauty is transient, which alone ye seem
To hold in honour; what beside remains
No longer charms,—what doth not charm is dead.
If among men there were who knew to prize
The heart of woman, who could recognize
What treasures of fidelity and love
Are garner'd safely in a woman's breast;
If the remembrance of bright single hours
Could vividly abide within your souls;
If your so searching glance could pierce the veil
Which age and wasting sickness o'er us fling;
If the possession which should satisfy
Waken'd no restless cravings in your hearts;
Then were our happy days indeed arriv'd,
We then should celebrate our golden age.

TASSO.

Thy words, my Princess, in my breast awake
An old anxiety half lull'd to sleep.

PRINCESS.

What mean'st thou, Tasso?   Freely speak with me.

TASSO.

I oft before have heard, and recently
Again it hath been rumour'd,—had I not
Been told, I might have known it,—princes strive
To win thy hand.   What we must needs expect

We view with dread. nay, almost with despair.
Thou wilt forsake us,—it is natural :
How we shall bear thy loss, I do not know.

PRINCESS.

Be for the present moment unconcern'd !
Almost, I might say, unconcern'd for ever.
I am contented still to tarry here,
Nor know I any tie to lure me hence.
And if thou wouldst indeed detain me, Tasso,
Live peaceably with all, so shalt thou lead
A happy life thyself, and I through thee.

TASSO.

Teach me to do whate'er is possible !
My life itself is consecrate to thee.
When to extol thee and to give thee thanks
My heart unfolded, I experienc'd first
The purest happiness that man can feel.
My soul's ideal I first found in thee.
As destiny supreme is rais'd above
The will and counsel of the wisest men,
So tower the gods of earth o'er common mortals.
The rolling surge which we behold with dread.
Doth all unheeded murmur at their feet
Like gentle billows : they hear not the storm
Which blusters round us, scarcely heed our prayers.
And treat us as we helpless children treat,
Letting us fill the air with sighs and plaints.
Thou hast, divine one ! often borne with me,
And like the radiant sun, thy pitying glance
Hath from mine eyelid dried the dew of sorrow.

PRINCESS.

'Tis only just that women cordially
Should meet the poet, whose heroic song
In strains so varied glorifies the sex.
Tender or valiant, thou hast ever known
To represent them amiable and noble ;
And if Armida is deserving hate,
Her love and beauty reconcile us to her.

TASSO.

Whatever in my song doth reach the heart
And find an echo there, I owe to one,

And one alone!   No image undefin'd
Hover'd before my soul, approaching now
In radiant glory, to retire again.
I have myself, with mine own eyes, beheld
The type of every virtue, every grace;
What I have copied thence will aye endure;
The heroic love of Tancred to Clorinda,
Erminia's silent and unnotic'd truth,
Sophronia's greatness and Olinda's woe;
These are not shadows by illusion bred;
I know they are eternal, for they are.
And what is more deserving to survive,
And silently to work for centuries,
Than the confession of a noble love
Confided modestly to gentle song?

PRINCESS.

And shall I name to thee another charm
Which, all unconsciously, this song may claim?
It doth allure us still to listen to it:
We listen, and we think we understand;
We understand, and yet we censure not,
So with thy song, thou winnest us at last.

TASSO.

Oh what a heaven thou dost open to me,
My Princess! if this radiance blinds me not,
I see unhop'd-for and eternal bliss
Descending gloriously on golden beams.

PRINCESS.

No further, Tasso! many things there are
That we may hope to win with violence;
While others only can become our own
Through moderation and wise self-restraint.
Such, it is said, is virtue, such is love,
Which is allied to her.   Think well of this.

## SCENE II.

TASSO.

And art thou then allow'd to raise thine eyes?
Around thee dar'st thou gaze?   Thou art alone!
O'erheard these pillars what the princess spake?
And hast thou even these mute witnesses

Of thine exalted happiness to fear?
The sun arises of a new life-day,
Whose splendour dims the light of former days.
The goddess, downward stooping, swiftly bears
Aloft the mortal.   What a wide expanse
Is to mine eye discover'd, what a realm!
How richly recompens'd my burning wish!
In dreams the highest happiness seem'd near,
This happiness surpasses all my dreams.
The man born blind conceiveth as he may
Of light and colour; when upon his eye
The daylight pours, he hails a new-born sense.
Full of vague hope and courage, drunk with joy,
Reeling I tread this path.   Thou giv'st me much;
Thou givest lavishly, as earth and heaven,
With bounteous hand, dispense their costly gifts,
Demanding in return what such a boon
Alone empowers thee to demand from me.
I must be moderate, I must forbear,
And thus deserve thy cherish'd confidence.
What have I ever done that she should choose me
What can I do to merit her regard?
Her very confidence doth prove thy worth.
Yes, princess, to thine ev'ry word and look,
Be my whole soul for ever consecrate!
Ask what thou wilt, for I am wholly thine!
To distant regions let her send me forth
In quest of toil, and danger, and renown;
Or in the grove, present the golden lyre,
Devoting me to quiet and her praise.
I'm her's; possessing, she shall fashion me!
For her my heart hath garner'd ev'ry treasure.
Oh! had some heavenly power bestow'd on me
An organ thousandfold, I scarcely then
Could utter forth my speechless reverence.
The painter's pencil, and the poet's lip,
The sweetest that e'er sipp'd the vernal honey,
I covet now.   No! Tasso shall henceforth
Wander no more forlorn, 'mong trees and men,
Lonely and weak, oppress'd with gloomy care'
He is no more alone, he is with thee.

Oh would that visibly the noblest deed
Were present here before me, circled round
With grisly danger!   Onward I would rush,
And with a joyous spirit risk the life
Now from her hand receiv'd.   The choicest men
As comrades I would hail, a noble band,
To execute her will and high behest,
And consummate what seem'd impossible.
Rash mortal! wherefore did thy lips not hide
What thou didst feel, till thou couldst lay thyself
Worthy, and ever worthier, at her feet?
Such was thy purpose, such thy prudent wish!
Yet be it so!   'Tis sweeter to receive,
Free, and unmerited, so fair a boon,
Than, with self-flatt'ry, dream one might perchance
Successfully have claim'd it.   Gaze with joy!
So vast, so boundless, all before thee lies!
And youth, with hope inspir'd, allures thee on
Towards the future's unknown, sunny realms!
My bosom, heave! propitious seasons smile
Once more with genial influence on this plant!
It springeth heavenward, and shooteth out
A thousand branches that unfold in bloom;
Oh may it bring forth fruit,—ambrosial fruit!
And may a hand belov'd the golden spoil
Cull, from its verdant and luxuriant boughs.

### SCENE III.

TASSO.        ANTONIO.

TASSO.

A cordial welcome, Sir!   It seems indeed
As though I saw thee for the first time now!
Nor was arrival e'er more gladly hail'd!
I know thee now, and all thy varied worth,
Promptly I offer thee my heart and hand,
And trust that thou wilt not despise my love.

ANTONIO.

Freely thou offerest a precious gift;
Its worth I duly estimate, and hence
Would pause awhile before accepting it.
I know not yet if I can render thee

A full equivalent.   Not willingly
Would I o'erhasty er unthankful seem ;
Let then my sober caution serve for both.

TASSO.

What man would censure caution ?   Every step
Of life doth prove that 'tis most requisite ;
Yet nobler is it, when the soul reveals,
Where we, with prudent foresight, may dispense.

ANTONIO.

The heart of each be here his oracle,
Since each his error must himself atone.

TASSO.

So let it be !   My duty I've perform'd,
It is the princess' wish we should be friends,
Her words I honour'd and thy friendship sought.
I wish'd not to hold back, Antonio,
But I will never be importunate.
Time and more near acquaintance may induce thee,
To give a warmer welcome to the gift,
Which now thou dost reject, almost with scorn.

ANTONIO.

Oft is the mod'rate man nam'd cold by those
Who think themselves more warm than other men,
Because a transient glow comes over them.

TASSO.

Thou blamest what I blame,—what I avoid
Young as I am I ever must prefer
Unshaken constancy to vehemence.

ANTONIO.

Most wisely said !   Keep ever in this mind.

TASSO.

Thou'rt authoriz'd to counsel and to warn,
For, like a faithful, time-approved, friend,
Experience holds her station at thy side.
But trust me, Sir, the meditative heart
Attends the warning of each day and hour,
And practises in secret ev'ry virtue,
Which in thy rigour thou wouldst teach anew.

ANTONIO.

'Twere well to be thus occupied with self,
If it were only profitable too.

His inmost nature no man learns to know
By introspection ; still he rates himself,
Sometimes too low, but oft, alas ! too high.
Self-knowledge comes from knowing other men ;
'Tis life reveals to each his genuine worth.

TASSO.

I listen with assent and reverence.

ANTONIO.

Yet to my words I know thou dost attach
A meaning wholly foreign to my thought.

TASSO.

Proceeding thus, we ne'er shall draw more near
It is not prudent, 'tis not well, to meet
With purpos'd misconception any man,
Let him be who he may !   The Princess' word
I scarcely needed ;—I have read thy soul.
Good thou dost purpose and accomplish too.
Thine own immediate fate concerns thee not ;
Thou think'st of others, others thou dost aid.
And on life's sea, vexed by each passing gale,
Thou hold'st a heart unmov'd.   I view thee thus ;
What then were I, did I not draw tow'rds thee ?
Did I not even keenly seek a share
Of the lock'd treasure which thy bosom guards ?
Open thine heart to me, thou'lt not repent ;
Know me, and I am sure thou'lt be my friend ;
Of such a friend I long have felt the need.
My inexperience, my ungovern'd youth
Cause me no shame ; for still around my brow
The future's golden clouds in brightness rest.
Oh ! to thy bosom take me, noble man ;
Into the wise, the temperate use of life
Initiate my rash and unfledg'd youth.

ANTONIO.

Thou in a single moment would'st demand
What time and circumspection only yield.

TASSO.

In one brief moment love has power to give
What anxious toil wins not in lengthen'd years,
I do not ask it from thee, I demand.
I summon thee in Virtue's sacred name,

For she is zealous to unite the good;
And shall I name to thee another name?
The Princess, she doth wish it.—Leonora.
Me she would lead to thee, and thee to me.
Oh, let us meet her wish with kindred hearts!
United let us to the goddess haste,
To offer her our service, our whole souls
Leagued to achieve for her the noblest aims.
Yet once again!—Here is my hand!   Give thine!
I do entreat, hold thyself back no longer!
And grudge me not the good man's fairest joy
Freely to yield himself to nobler men!

ANTONIO.

Thou goest on full sail!   It would appear
Thou'rt wont to conquer, everywhere to find
The pathways spacious and the portals wide.
I grudge thee not or merit or success,—
But we yet stand I see too far apart.

TASSO.

It may be so in years and time-tried worth;—
In courage and goodwill I yield to none.

ANTONIO.

Goodwill doth oft prove deedless; courage still
Pictures the goal less distant than it is.
His brow alone is crown'd who reaches it,
And oft the worthiest must forego the crown.
Yet wreaths there are of very different fashion;
Light, worthless wreaths, which, idly strolling on,
The loiterer oft without the toil obtains.

TASSO.

Yet what a God doth freely grant to one,
And from another sternly doth withhold,
Is not obtain'd by each man as he lists.

ANTONIO.

If to a God,—ascribe it then to Fortune.
I'll hear thee gladly, for her choice is blind.

TASSO.

Impartial Justice also wears a band
And shuts her eyes to ev'ry bright illusion.

ANTONIO.

Fortune 'tis for the fortunate to praise!

Let him ascribe to her a hundred eyes
To scan desert,—stern judgment, and wise choice.
Call her Minerva, call her what he will,
He holds as just reward her golden gifts,
Chance ornament as symbol of desert.

TASSO.

Thou need'st not speak more plainly.   'Tis enough
Deeply I see into thine inmost heart,
And know thee now for life.   Oh would that so
My princess knew thee also!   Lavish not
The arrows of thine eyes and of thy tongue!
In vain thou aimest at the fadeless wreath
Entwin'd around my brow.   First be so great
As not to envy me the wreath of fame,
And then perchance thou may'st dispute the prize.
I deem it sacred, yea, the highest good;
Yet only show me him who hath attain'd
That after which I strive; show me the hero,
Of whom on hist'ry's ample page I read;
The poet place before me, who himself
With Homer or with Virgil may compare;
Ay, what is more, let me behold the man
Who hath deserv'd threefold this recompense,
And yet can wear the laurel round his brow,
With modesty thrice greater than my own,—
Then at the feet of the divinity
Who thus endow'd me, thou should'st see me kneel.
Nor would I stand erect, till from my brow,
She had transferr'd the ornament to his.

ANTONIO.

Till then thou'rt doubtless worthy of the crown.

TASSO.

Let me be justly weigh'd;  I shun it not;
But your contempt I never have deserv'd.
The wreath consider'd by my prince my due,
Which for my brow my princess' hand entwin'd,
None shall dispute with me, and none asperse!

ANTONIO.

This haughty tone, methinks, becomes thee not,
Nor this rash glow, unseemly in this place.

TASSO.

The tone thou here assum'st beseems me too.
Say, from these precincts is the truth exil'd?
Within the palace is free thought imprison'd?
Here must the noble spirit be oppress'd?
This is nobility's appropriate seat,
The soul's nobility! and may she not
In presence of earth's mighty ones, rejoice?
She may and shall.   Nobles draw near the prince
In virtue of the rank their sires bequeath'd;
Why should not genius then, which partial nature
Grants, like a glorious ancestry, to few?
Here littleness alone should feel confus'd,
And envy shun to manifest its shame,
As no insidious spider should attach
Its noisome fabric to these marble walls.

ANTONIO.

Thyself dost show that my contempt is just
The impetuous youth, forsooth, would seize by force
The confidence and friendship of the man!
Rude as thou art, dost think thyself of worth?

TASSO.

I'd rather be what thou esteemest rude,
Than what I must myself esteem ignoble.

ANTONIO.

Thou'rt still so young that wholesome chastisement
May tutor thee to hold a better course.

TASSO.

Not young enough to bow to idols down,
Yet old enough to conquer scorn with scorn.

ANTONIO.

From contests of the lips and of the lyre
A conquering hero, thou may'st issue forth.

TASSO.

It were presumptuous to extol my arm;
As yet 'tis deedless; still I'll trust to it.

ANTONIO.

Thou trustest to forbearance, which too long
Hath spoil'd thee in thine insolent career.

S

TASSO.

That I am grown to manhood, now I feel:
It would have been the farthest from my wish
To try with thee the doubtful game of arms.
But thou dost stir tne inward fire; my blood,
My inmost marrow boils; the fierce desire
Of vengeance seeths and foams within my breast.
Art thou the man thou boast'st thyself,—then stand

ANTONIO.

Thou know'st as little who, as where thou art.

TASSO.

No fane so sacred as to shield contempt.
Thou dost blaspheme, thou dost profane this spot,
Not I, who fairest offerings,—confidence,
Respect, and love, for thine acceptance brought.
Thy spirit desecrates this paradise;
And thy injurious words this sacred hall;
Not the indignant heaving of my breast,
Which boils to wipe away the slightest stain.

ANTONIO.

What a great spirit in a narrow breast!

TASSO.

Here there is space to vent the bosom's rage.

ANTONIO.

The rabble also vent their rage in words.

TASSO.

Art thou of noble blood as I am, draw.

ANTONIO.

I am, but I remember where I stand.

TASSO.

Come then below, where weapons may avail.

ANTONIO.

Thou should'st not challenge, therefore I'll not follow.

TASSO.

To cowards welcome such impediments.

ANTONIO.

The coward only threats where he's secure.

TASSO.

With joy would I relinquish this defence.

ANTONIO.

Demean tJ yself; degrade the place thou can'st not.

TASSO.

The place forgive me that I suffer'd it!

[*He draws his sword.*

Or draw or follow, if, as now I hate,
I'm not to scorn thee to eternity!

## SCENE IV.

TASSO.        ANTONIO.        ALPHONSO.

ALPHONSO.

In what unlook'd for strife I find you both?

ANTONIO.

Calm and unmov'd, oh Prince, thou finds't me here,
Before a man whom passion's rage hath seized.

TASSO.

As a divinity I worship thee
That thus thou tam'st me with one warning look.

ALPHONSO.

Relate, Antonio, Tasso, tell me straight;—
Say, why doth discord thus invade my house?
How hath it seized you both, and hurried you
Confus'd and reeling, from the beaten track
Of decency and law?   I stand amazed.

TASSO.

I feel it, thou dost know nor him, nor me.
This man, reputed temperate and wise,
Hath tow'rds me, like a rude, ill-manner'd churl,
Behav'd himself with spiteful insolence.
I sought him trustfully, he thrust me back;
With constancy I press'd myself on him,
And still, with growing bitterness imbued,
He rested not till he had turn'd to gall
My blood's pure current.   Pardon!   Thou, my Prince,
Hast found me here, possess'd with furious rage.
If guilty, to this man the guilt is due;
With violence he fann'd the fiery glow
Which, seizing me, hath injur'd both of us.

ANTONIO.

Poetic phrenzy hurried him away!
Thou hast, oh Prince, address'd thyself to me,
Me thou hast question'd: may I be allow'd
After this rapid orator to speak?

TASSO.

Oh, yes, repeat again each several word!
And if thou can'st recall before this judge
Each syllable, each look,—then dare to do so!
Disgrace thyself a second time, and bear
Witness against thyself!   I'll not disown
A single pulse-throb, nor a single breath.

ANTONIO.

If thou hast somewhat more to say, proceed;
If not, forbear, and interrupt me not.
Whether at first this fiery youth or I
Began this quarrel, whether he or I
Must bear the blame, is a wide question, Prince,
Which stands apart, and need not be discuss'd.

TASSO.

How so?   The primal question seems to me,
Which of the two is right and which is wrong.

ANTONIO.

Not so precisely, as th' ungovern'd mind
Might first suppose.

ALPHONSO.
            Antonio!

ANTONIO.
                Gracious Prince!
Thy hint I honour; but let him forbear:
When I have spoken, he may then proceed;
Thy voice must then decide.   I've but to say,
I can no longer with this man contend;
Can nor accuse him, nor defend myself,
Nor give the satisfaction he desires;
For as he stands, he is no longer free.
There hangeth over him a heavy law,
Which, at the most, thy favour can relax.
Here he hath dar'd to threaten me, to challenge,
Scarce in thy presence sheath'd his naked sword;
And if between us, Prince, thou had'st not stepp'd,
Obnoxious to reproof I now had stood,
Before thy sight, the partner of his fault.

ALPHONSO *to* TASSO.

Thou hast not acted well.

TASSO.
              Mine own heart, Prince,
And surely thine, doth speak me wholly free.
Yes, true it is, I threaten'd, challeng'd, drew;—
But how maliciously his guileful tongue,
With words well chosen, pierc'd me to the quick;
How sharply and how quick his biting tooth
The subtle venom in my blood infus'd;
How more and more the fever he inflam'd,
Thou thinkest not! cold and unmov'd himself,
He to the highest pitch excited me.
Thou know'st him not, and thou wilt never know him!
Warmly I tender'd him the truest love;
Down at my feet he flung the proffer'd gift;
And had my spirit not with anger glow'd,
Of thy fair service and thy princely grace
I were for aye unworthy.   If the law
I have forgotten, and this place,—forgive!
The spot exists not where I dare be base,
Nor yet where I debasement dare endure.
But if this heart in any place be false,
Or to itself or thee,—condemn, reject,—
And let me ne'er again behold thy face.
                    ANTONIO.
How easily the youth bears heavy loads,
And shaketh misdemeanours off like dust!
It were indeed a marvel, knew I not
Of magic poesy the wondrous power,
Which loveth still with the impossible
In frolic mood to sport.   I almost doubt
Whether to thee, and to thy ministers,
This deed will seem so insignificant.
For royalty extends its shield o'er all
Who seek the shelter of its sacred fane,
And bow before it as a deity.
As at the altar's consecrated foot,
So on the regal threshold rage subsides;
No sword there gleams, no threat'ning word resounds,
E'en injur'd innocence seeks no revenge.
The common earth affords an ample scope
For bitter hate, and rage implacable.

There will no coward threat, no true man flee;
Thy ancestors, on sure foundations bas'd
These walls, fit shelter for their dignity;
And, with wise forecast, hedg'd the palace round
With fearful penalties.   Of all transgressors,
Exile, confinement, death, the certain doom.
Respect of persons was not, nor did mercy
The arm of justice venture to restrain.
The boldest culprit felt himself o'erawed.
And now, after a lengthen'd reign of peace,
We must behold unlicens'd rage invade
The realm of sacred order.   Judge, oh Prince,
And punish! for unguarded by the law,
Unshielded by his Sov'reign, who will dare
To keep the narrow path that duty bounds.

ALPHONSO.

More than your words, or aught that ye could say,
My own impartial feelings let me heed.
If that your duty ye had both fulfill'd,
I should not have this judgment to pronounce;
For here the right and wrong are near allied.
If that Antonio has offended thee
Due satisfaction he must doubtless give,
In such a sort as thou shalt choose to ask.
I gladly would be chosen arbiter.

[*To* TASSO.

Meanwhile thy misdemeanour subjects thee
To brief confinement, Tasso.   I forgive thee,
And therefore, for thy sake, relax the law.
Now leave us, and within thy chamber bide,
Thyself thy sole companion, thy sole guard.

TASSO.

Is this, then, thy judicial sentence, Prince?

ANTONIO.

Discern'st thou not a father's lenity?

TASSO *to* ANTONIO.

With thee, henceforth, I have no more to say.

[*To* ALPHONSO.

Thine earnest word, oh Prince, delivers me,
A freeman, to captivity.   So be it!
Thou deem'st it right.   Thy sacred word I hear

And counsel silence to mine inmost heart.
It seems so strange, so strange,—myself and thee,
This sacred spot, I scarce can recognize.
Yet him I know full well.—Oh, there is much
I might and ought to say, yet I submit.
My lips are mute.   Was it indeed a crime?
At least, they treat me as a criminal.
Howe'er my heart rebel, I'm captive now.

ALPHONSO.

Thou tak'st it, Tasso, more to heart than I.

TASSO.

To me it still is inconceivable;
And yet not so, I am no child.   Methinks
I should be able to unravel it.
A sudden light breaks in upon my soul;—
As suddenly it leaves me in the dark;—
I only hear my sentence and submit.
These are, indeed, superfluous, idle words.
Henceforth inure thy spirit to obey.
Weak mortal!   To forget where thou didst stand!
Thou didst forget how high the abode of gods,
And now art stagger'd by the sudden fall.
Promptly obey, for it becomes a man
Each painful duty to perform with joy.
Take back the sword which I receiv'd from thee,
When in the card'nal's suit I went to France;
Though not with glory, not with shame I wore it,—
No, not to-day.   The bright auspicious gift,
With heart sore troubled, I relinquish now.

ALPHONSO.

Thou know'st not, Tasso, how I feel tow'rds thee.

TASSO.

My lot is to obey, and not to think!
And destiny alas! demands from me
Renunciation of this precious gift.
Ill doth a crown become a captive's brow.
I from my head myself remove the wreath
Which seem'd accorded for eternity.
Too early was the dearest bliss bestow'd,
And is, alas, as if I had been boastful,
Too early ta'en away.

Thou takest back what none beside could take,
And what no·God a second time accords.
We mortals are most wonderfully tried;
We could not bear it, were we not endow'd,
By Nature, with a kindly levity.
Capricious fortune teaches us to play
With priceless gifts, with lavish unconcern.
Our hands we open of our own free will,
And the good flies that we can ne'er recall.
A tear doth mingle with this parting kiss,
Devoting thee to mutability!
This tender sign of weakness may be pardon'd!
Who would not weep when what was deem'd immortal
Yields to destruction's power!   Now to this sword
(Alas, it won thee not,) ally thyself,
And round it twin'd, as on a hero's bier,
Reposing, mark the grave where buried lie
My short-liv'd happiness, my wither'd hopes.
Here at thy feet, oh Prince, I lay them down;
For who is justly arm'd if thou art wrath?
Who justly crown'd, on whom thy brow is bent?
I go a captive, and await my doom.

(Exit.)

*[ On a sign from the Prince, a Page raises the sword
and wreath and bears them away.*

## SCENE V.

**ALPHONSO.　　　ANTONIO.**

**ANTONIO.**

Whither doth phrenzied fancy lead the boy?
And in what colours doth he picture forth
His high desert and glorious destiny?
Rash, inexperienc'd, youth esteems itself
A chosen instrument, and arrogates
Unbounded license.   He has been chastis'd,
And chastisement is profit to the boy,
For which the man will render cordial thanks.

**ALPHONSO.**

He is indeed chastis'd, too much I fear.

ANTONIO.

Art thou dispos'd to practice lenity,
Restore again his liberty, my Prince,
And then the sword may arbitrate our strife.

ALPHONSO.

So be it, if the public voice demands.
But tell me, how didst thou provoke his ire?

ANTONIO.

In sooth, I scarce can say how it befel.
As man, I may perchance have wounded him,
As nobleman, I gave him no offence.
And in the very tempest of his rage,
No word unseemly hath escap'd this lip.

ALPHONSO.

Of such a sort your quarrel seem'd to me;
And your own word confirms me in my thought.
When men dispute we justly may esteem
The wiser the offender.   Thou with Tasso
Should'st not contend, but rather guide his steps.
It would become thee more.   'Tis not too late.
The sword's decision is not call'd for here.
So long as I am bless'd with peace abroad,
So long would I enjoy it in my house.
Restore tranquillity, thou can'st with ease.
Leonora Sanvitale may at first
Attempt to sooth him with her honied lip.
Then go thou to him; in my name restore
His liberty; with true and noble words
Endeavour to obtain his confidence.
Accomplish this with all the speed thou can'st.
As a kind friend and father speak with him.
Peace I would know restor'd ere I depart;
All if thou wilt—is possible to thee.
We gladly will remain another hour,
Then leave it to the ladies' gentle tact
To consummate the work commenc'd by thee.
So when we come again, the last faint trace
Of this rash quarrel will be quite effac'd.
It seems thy talents will not rust, Antonio!
Scarcely hast thou concluded one affair
And on thy first return thou seek'st another.
In this new mission may success be thine!

ANTONIO.

I am asham'd; my error in thy words
As in the clearest mirror, I discern.
How easy to obey a noble prince
Who doth convince us while he doth command.

## ACT THE THIRD.

### SCENE I.

PRINCESS, (*alone.*)

Where tarries Leonora?   Anxious fear,
Augmenting every moment, agitates
My inmost heart.   Scarce know I what took place;
Which party is to blame I scarcely know.
Oh, that she would return!   I would not yet
Speak with my brother or Antonio
Till I am more compos'd, till I have heard
How matters stand, and what may be the issue.

### SCENE II.

PRINCESS.      LEONORA.

PRINCESS.

What tidings, Leonora?   Tell me all:
How stands it with our friends?   Say, what occurr'd.

LEONORA.

More than I knew before I have not learn'd.
Contention rose between them; Tasso drew;
Thy brother parted them: yet it would seem
That it was Tasso who began the fray.
Antonio is at large, and with his Prince
Converses freely.   Tasso, in his chamber,
Abides meanwhile, a captive and alone.

PRINCESS.

Doubtless Antonio irritated him,
And met with cold disdain the high-ton'd youth.

LEONORA.

I do believe it, when he join'd us first
A cloud already brooded o'er his brow.

PRINCESS.

Alas, that we're so prone to disregard
The still and holy warnings of the heart!
A God doth whisper softly in our breast,
Softly yet audibly, doth counsel us,
Both what we ought to seek and what to shun.
This morn Antonio hath appear'd to me
E'en more abrupt than ever,—more reserv'd.
When at his side I saw our youthful bard,
My spirit warn'd me.   Only mark of each
The outward aspect;—countenance and tone
Look, gesture, bearing!   Everything oppos'd ,
Affection they can never interchange.
And yet I listen'd to delusive Hope;
They both are sensible, she fondly urg'd,
Both noble, gently nurtur'd, and thy friends.
What bond more sure than that which links the good?
I urg'd the youth; with what devoted zeal,
How ardently he gave himself to me!
Would I had spoken to Antonio then!
But I delay'd:   So recent his return,
That I felt shy, at once and urgently,
To recommend the youth to his regard;
On custom I relied and courtesy,
And on the common usage of the world,
Which e'en twixt foes so smoothly intervenes.
I dreaded not from the experienc'd man,
The rash impetuosity of youth.
The ill seem'd distant, now, alas, 'tis here.
Oh give me counsel!   What is to be done?

LEONORA.

Thy words, my Princess, show that thou dost feel
How hard it is to counsel.   'Tis not here
A misconception twixt congenial minds;
This words, if needful the appeal to arms,
Might easily set right.   Two men they are,
I've felt it long, who therefore are oppos'd,
Because their minds are cast in different moulds,
And were they to consult their common weal,
They'd form a league of closest amity;
Then as one man they'd act, and onward move

With power, and joy, and happiness through life.
I hop'd it once, I now perceive in vain.
To-day's contention, whatsoe'er the cause,
Might be appeas'd, but this assures us not,
Or for the morrow, or for future time.
Methinks 'twere best, that Tasso for awhile
Should journey hence ; he might repair to Rome,
Or visit Florence, I should meet him there
And as a friend could work upon his mind.
While thou, meanwhile, could'st bring Antonio,
Who has become almost a stranger to us,
Once more within the circle of thy friends.
And thus benignant time, that grants so much,
Might grant, perchance, what seems impossible.

PRINCESS.

A happiness will thus, my friend, be thine,
Which I must needs forego ; say, is that right ?

LEONORA.

Thou only would'st forego what thou thyself
As things at present stand, could'st not enjoy.

PRINCESS.

So calmly shall I banish hence a friend ?

LEONORA.

Rather retain, whom thou dost seem to banish

PRINCESS.

The duke will ne'er consent to part with him.

LEONORA.

When he shall see as we do, he will yield.

PRINCESS.

'Tis painful in one's friend to doom oneself.

LEONORA.

Yet with thy friend, thou'lt also save thyself.

PRINCESS.

I cannot give my voice that this shall be.

LEONORA.

An evil still more grievous then expect.

PRINCESS.

Thou giv'st me pain,—uncertain thy success.

LEONORA.

Ere long we shall discover which is right.

PRINCESS.
Well, if it needs must be so, say no more.
LEONORA.
He conquers grief, who firmly can resolve.
PRINCESS.
Resolv'd I'm not; but even let it be,
If he does not absent himself too long.
And let us, Leonora, care for him,
That he may never be oppress'd by want,
But that the duke, e'en in a distant land,
May graciously assign him maintenance.
Speak to Antonio; with my brother he
Can much accomplish, and will not remember
The recent strife against our friend or us.
LEONORA.
Princess, a word from thee would have more power
PRINCESS.
I cannot, well thou knowest, Leonora,
Solicit favours for myself and friends,
As my dear sister of Urbino can.
A calm, secluded life I'm fain to lead,
And from my brother gratefully accept,
Whate'er his princely bounty freely grants
For this reluctance once I blam'd myself;
I've conquer'd now, and blame myself no more.
My friends too would oft censure me and say,
Unselfishness is doubtless beautiful,
But thou art so disinterested, that even
Thy friends' necessities thou can'st not feel.
I let it pass, and suffer'd the reproach.
I am the more rejoic'd that I can now
Be of substantial service to our friend;
My mother's heritage descends to me,
And to his need I'll gladly minister.
LEONORA.
Princess, I too can show myself his friend.
In truth he is no thrifty manager;
My skilful aid shall help him where he fails.
PRINCESS.
Well take him then,—if I must part with him:
'Fore all, I would resign him unto thee:

I now perceive, it will be better so.
This sorrow also must my spirit hail
As good and wholesome?   Such my doom from youth;
I am inur'd to it.   But half we feel
Renunciation of a precious joy,
When we have deem'd its tenure insecure.

LEONORA.

Happy according to thy high desert
I hope to see thee.

PRINCESS.

Leonora!   Happy?
Who then is happy?—So indeed I migi
Esteem my brother, for his constant mir
Still with unswerving temper meets his fate;
Yet even he ne'er reap'd as he deserv'd.
My sister of Urbino, is she happy?
With beauty gifted and a noble heart!
Childless she's doom'd to live; her younger lord
Values her highly and upbraids her not;
But happiness is stranger to their home.
Of what avail our mother's prudent skill,
Her varied knowledge and her ample mind?
Could they protect from foreign heresy?
We were ta'en from her: now she is no more
And dying, left us not the soothing thought,
That reconcil'd with God, her spirit pass'd.

LEONORA.

Oh mark not only that which fails to each;
Consider rather what to each remains!
And Princess, what doth not remain to thee?

PRINCESS.

What doth remain to me, Leonora?   Patience!
Which I have learn'd to practise from my youth.
When friends and kindred, knit in social love,
In joyous pastime wil'd the hours away,
Sickness held me a captive in my chamber;
And in the sad companionship of pain,
I early learn'd the lesson;—to endure!
One pleasure cheer'd me in my solitude,
The joy of song.   I commun'd with myself,
And lull'd with soothing tones, the sense of pain.

The restless longing, the unquiet wish ;—
Till sorrow oft would grow to ravishment,
And sadness self to harmony divine.
Not long, alas! this confort was allow'd;
The leech's stern monition silenc'd me;
I was condemned to live and to endure
E'en of this sole remaining joy bereft.

LEONORA.

Yet many friends attach'd themselves to thee,
And now thou art in health, and joyous too.

PRINCESS.

I am in health, that is, I am not sick ;
And many friends I have, whose constancy
Doth cheer my heart ; and ah, I had a friend—

LEONORA.

Thou hast him still.

PRINCESS.

   But soon must part with him.
That moment was of deep significance
When first I saw him.   Scarce was I restor'd
From many sorrows ; sickness and dull pain
Were scarce subdued, with shy and timid glance
I gaz'd once more on life, once more rejoic'd
In the glad sunshine, and my kindred's love,
And hope's delicious balm inhal'd anew ;
Forwards I ventur'd into life to gaze,
And friendly forms saluted me from far :
Then was it, Leonora, that my sister
First introduc'd to me the youthful bard,
She led him hither, and, shall I confess ?—
My heart embrac'd him, and will hold for aye.

LEONORA.

My Princess !   Let it not repent thee now !
To apprehend the noble is a gain
Of which the soul can never be bereft.

PRINCESS.

E'en what is excellent we needs must fear ;
'Tis like a flame, which nobly serveth us
So long as on our household hearth it burns,
Or sheds its lustre from the friendly torch.
How lovely then !   Who can dispense with it ?
But if unwatch'd, it spreads destruction round.

What anguish it occasions ! Leave me now
I babble, and 'twere better to conceal
Even from thee, how weak I am and sick.

LEONORA.

The sickness of the heart doth soonest yield
To tender plaints, and soothing confidence.

PRINCESS.

If in confiding love a cure be found,
I'm whole, so strong my confidence in thee.
Alas ! my friend, I am indeed resolv'd ;
Let him depart ! But ah ! I feel already
The long protracted anguish of the day
When I must all forego that glads me now.
His beauteous form, transfigur'd in my dream,
The morning sun will dissipate no more ;
No more the blissful hope of seeing him,
With joyous longing, fill my waking sense ;
Nor to discover him, my timid glance
Search wistfully our garden's dewy shade.
How sweetly was the tender hope fulfill'd
To spend each eve in intercourse with him !
How, while conversing, the desire increas'd,
To know each other ever more and more ;
And still our souls, in sweet communion join'd
Were daily tun'd to purer harmonies.
What twilight-gloom now falls around my path '
The gorgeous sun, the genial light of day,
Of this fair world the splendours manifold,
Shorn of their lustre, are envelop'd all,
In the dark mist, which now environs me.
In by-gone times, each day compris'd a life ;
Hush'd was each care, mute each foreboding voice,
And happily embark'd, we drifted on
Without a rudder, o'er life's lucid wave.
Now, in the darkness of the present hour,
Futurity's vague terrors seize my soul.

LEONORA.

The future will restore to thee thy friend ;
And thou wilt find new happiness, new joy.

PRINCESS.

What I possess, that would I gladly hold ;
Change may divert the mind, but profits not.

With youthful longings I have never join d
The motley throng who strive from fortune's urn
To snatch an object for their craving hearts.
I nonour'd him, and could not choose but love him,
For that with him my life was life indeed,
Filled with a joy I never knew before.
At first I whisper'd to my heart, beware !
Shrinking I shunn'd, yet ever drew more near.
So gently lur'd, so cruelly chastis'd !
A pure substantial blessing glides away,
And for the joy that filled my yearning heart,
Some demon substitutes a kindred pain

LEONORA.

If friendship's soothing words console thee not
This beauteous world's, calm power, and healing time,
Will imperceptibly restore thy heart.

PRINCESS.

Ay, beauteous is the world, and many a joy
Floats through its wide dominion.   But, alas,
When we would seize the winged good, it flies,
And, step by step, along the path of life
Allures our yearning spirits to the grave.
To mortal man so seldom is it given
To find what seem'd his heav'n-appointed bliss ;
Alas, so seldom he retains the good
Which, in auspicious hour, his hand had grasp'd ;
The treasure to our heart that came unsought
Doth tear itself away, and we ourselves
Yield that which once with eagerness we seiz'd.
There is a bliss, but 'tis to us unknown—
'Tis known indeed, but yet we prize it not.


## SCENE III.

LEONORA, (*alone.*)

The good and noble heart my pity moves ;
How sad a lot attends her lofty rank !
Alas she loses,—thinkest thou to win ?
Is his departure hence so requisite ?
Or dost thou urge it for thyself alone,—
To make the heart and lofty genius thine,
Which now thou sharest,—and unequally ?

T

Is't honest so to act?   What lack'st thou yet?
Art thou not rich enough?   Husband and son,
Possessions, beauty, rank—all these thou hast,
And him would'st have beside?   What!   Lov'st thou him?
How comes it else that thou can'st not endure
To live without him?   This thou dar'st confess!
How charming is it in his mind's clear depths
Oneself to mirror.   Doth not ev'ry joy
Seem doubly great and noble, when his song
Wafts us aloft as on the clouds of heav'n?
Then first thy lot is worthy to be envied!
Not only hast thou what the many crave,
But each one knoweth what thou art and hast!
Thy fatherland doth proudly speak thy name;
This is the pinnacle of earthly bliss.
Is Laura's then the only favour'd name
That aye from gentle lips shall sweetly flow?
Is it Petrarca's privilege alone,
To deify an unknown beauty's charms?
Who is there that with Tasso can compare?
As now the world exalts him, future time
With honour due shall magnify his name.
What rapture, in the golden prime of life
To feel his presence, and with him to near,
With airy tread, the future's hidden realm!
Thus should old age and time their influence lose,
And powerless be the voice of rumour bold,
Whose breath controls the billows of applause.
All that is transient in his song survives;
Still art thou young, still happy, when the round
Of changeful time shall long have borne thee on.
Him thou shalt have, and yet take nought from her.
For her affection to the gifted man
Doth take the hue her other passions wear;
Pale as the tranquil moon, whose feeble rays
Dimly illumine the night-wanderer's path,
They gleam, but warm not, and diffuse around
No blissful rapture, no keen sense of joy.
If she but know him happy, though afar,
She will rejoice as when she saw him daily.
And then, tis not my purpose from this court,

And her, to banish both myself and friend.
I will return, will bring him here again.
So let it be !--My rugged friend draws near ;
We soon shall see if we have power to tame him.

## SCENE IV.

LEONORA.          ANTONIO.

LEONORA.

War and not peace thou bringest.   'Twould appear
As though thou camest from the tented field,
Where violence bears sway, and force decides,
And not from Rome, where solemn policy
Uplifts the hand to bless a prostrate world
Which she beholds obedient at her feet.

ANTONIO.

I must admit the censure, my fair friend,
But my apology lies close at hand ;
'Tis dangerous to be compell'd so long
To wear the show of prudence and restraint.
Still at our side an evil genius lurks
And with stern voice, demands from time to time
A sacrifice, which I alas to day
Have offer'd, to the peril of my friends.

LEONORA.

So long hast thou with strangers been concern'd,
And to their humours hast conform'd thine own,
That when with friends thou dost mistake their aims,
And dost contend with them as they were strangers?

ANTONIO.

Herein, beloved friend, the danger lies !
With strangers we are ever on our guard,
Still are we aiming with observance due,
To win their favour, which may profit us ;
But with our friends, we throw off all restraint ;
Reposing in their love, we give the rein
To peevish humour ; passion uncontroll'd
Doth break its bounds ; and those we hold most dear
Are thus amongst the first whom we offend.

LEONORA.

In this calm utt'rance of a thoughtful mind
I gladly recognize my friend again.

ANTONIO.

Yes, it has much annoy'd me, I confess,
That I so far forgot myself to day.
But yet admit, that when some man of toil,
From irksome labour comes, with heated brow,
Thinking to rest himself for further toil,
Beneath the long'd-for shade, in the cool evening,
And finds it, in its length and breadth, possess'd
Already, by some idler, he may well,
Feel something human stirring in his breast?

LEONORA.

If he is truly human, then, methinks,
He gladly will partake the shade with one
Who lightens toil, and cheers the hour of rest,
With sweet discourse and soothing melodies.
Ample, my friend, for both, the spreading shade,
Nor either needs the other dispossess.

ANTONIO.

We will not bandy similes, fair friend.
The world containeth many things that we
To others freely yield and with them share;
But there exists one treasure we resign
With willing hearts to high desert alone;
Another too, that without secret grudge,
We share not even with the highest worth.
And would'st thou touching these two treasures ask,
They are the laurel, and fair woman's smile.

LEONORA.

How!   Hath yon chaplet round our stripling's brow
Giv'n umbrage to the grave, experienc'd, man?
Say, for his toil divine, his lofty verse,
Could'st thou thyself a juster meed select?
A ministration in itself divine,
That floateth in the air in tuneful tones,
Evoking airy forms to charm our souls—
Such ministration, in expressive form,
Or graceful symbol, finds its fit reward.
As doth the bard scarce deign to touch the earth,
So doth the laurel lightly touch his brow.
His worshippers, with barren homage, bring
As tribute meet, a fruitless branch, that thus

With ease they may acquit them of their debt.
Thou dost not grudge the martyr's effigy,
The golden radiance round the naked head ;
And, certes, where it rests, the laurel crown
Is more a sign of sorrow than of joy.

ANTONIO.

How, Leonora !   Would thy lovely lips
Teach me to scorn the world's poor vanities?

LEONORA.

There is no need, my friend, to tutor thee
To prize each good according to its worth.
Yet it would seem, that e'en like common men,
The sage philsopher, from time to time,
Needs that the treasures he is blest withal,
In their true light before him be display'd.
Thou, noble man, wilt not assert thy claim
To a mere empty phantom of renown.
The service that doth bind thy prince to thee,
By means of which thou dost attach thy friends,
Is true, is living service, hence the meed
Which doth reward it, must be living too.
Thy laurel is thy sovereign's confidence,
Which, like a cherish'd burden, gracefully,
Reposes on thy shoulders,—thy renown,
Thy crown of glory, is the general trust.

ANTONIO.

Thou speakest not of woman's smile, that, surely,
Thou wilt not tell us is superfluous.

LEONORA.

As people take it.   Thou dost lack it not ;
And were ye both depriv'd of it, methinks,
Thou would'st less miss it, than our youthful friend.
For, should a woman undertake to task
Her skill in thy behalf, to care for thee
In her own fashion, think'st thou she'd succeed?
With thee security and order dwell ;
And as for others, for thyself thou carest ;
Thou dost possess what friendship fain would give;
Whilst in our province he requires our aid.
A thousand things he needs, which to supply,
Is to a woman no unweicome task.

The fine-spun linen, the embroider'd vest
He weareth gladly, and endureth not,
Upon his person, aught of texture rude,
Such as befits the menial.   For with him
All must be rich and noble, fair and good;
And yet all this to win, he lacks the skill;
Nor even when possess'd, can he retain;
Improvident, he's still in want of gold;
Nor from a journey e'er returneth home,
But a third portion of his goods is lost.
His valet plunders him, and thus, Antonio,
The whole year round one has to care for him.

ANTONIO.

And these same cares endear him more and more.
Much favour'd youth, to whom his very faults
As virtues count, to whom it is allow'd
As man to play the boy, and who forsooth
May proudly boast his charming weaknesses!
Thou must forgive me, my fair friend, if here
Some little touch of bitterness I feel.
Thou say'st not all, say'st not how he presumes,
And proves himself far shrewder than he seems.
He boasts two tender flames!   The knots of love,
As fancy prompts him, he doth bind and loose,
And wins with such devices two such hearts!
Is't  credible?

LEONORA.

Well!   Well!   This only proves
That 'tis but friendship that inspires our hearts.
And e'en if we return'd him love for love,
Should we not well reward his noble heart,
Who, self-oblivious, dreams his life away
In lovely visions to enchant his friends?

ANTONIO.

Go on!   Go on!   Spoil him yet more and more
Account his selfish vanity for love;
Offend all other friends, with honest zeal
Devoted to your service; rend apart
The golden links of social confidence!

LEONORA.

We are not quite so partial as thou think'st;

In many cases we exhort our friend.
We wish to mould his mind, that he may know
More happiness himself, and be a source
Of purer joy to others.   What in him
Doth merit blame, is not conceal'd from us.

ANTONIO.

Yet much that's blamable in him ye praise.
I've known him long, so easy 'tis to know him,
For he's too proud to wear the least disguise.
We see him now retire into himself,
As if the world were rounded in his breast ;
Lost in the working of that inner world,
The outward universe he casts aside,
And his rapt spirit, self-included, rests.
Anon, as when a spark doth fire a mine,
Upon a touch of sorrow or of joy,
Anger or whim, he breaks impetuous forth.
Now he must compass all things, all retain,
All his caprices must be realiz'd ;
What should have ripen'd slowly through long years,
Must, in a moment, reach maturity ;
And obstacles, which years of patient toil
Could scarce remove, be levell'd in a trice.
He from himself th' impossible demands,
That ne from others may demand it too ;
Th' extremest limits of existing things
His soul would hold in contiguity.
This one man in a million scarce achieves,
And he is not that man ; at length he falls
No whit the better, back into himself.

LEONORA.

Himself alone he injures, others not.

ANTONIO.

Yet others he doth outrage grievously.
Can'st thou deny that in his passion's height,
Which o'er his spirit oft usurps control,
He hurls abuse at random, and doth load
The Prince and e'en the Princess, with reviling ?
True, for a moment only it endures ;
But then the moment quickly comes again.
His tongue, as little as his breast, he rules.

LEONORA.

To me, indeed, it seems advisable,
That he should leave Ferrara for awhile;—
T'would benefit himself and others too.

ANTONIO.

Perchance,—perchance too not.   But now, my friend
It is not to be thought of.   For myself,
I will not on my shoulders bear the blame.
It might appear as if I drove him hence.
I drive him not.   As far as I'm concern'd,
He at the court may tarry undisturb'd;
And if he will be reconcil'd with us,
And school himself to follow my advice,
We may live peaceably enough together.

LEONORA.

Now thou dost hope to work upon a mind
Which lately thou didst look upon as lost.

ANTONIO.

We always hope, and still in ev'ry case,
'Tis better far to hope than to despair ;
For who can calculate the possible ?
Our Prince esteems him; re must stay with us;
And if we strive to fashion him in vain
He's not the only one we must endure.

LEONORA.

So free from passion and from prejudice
I had not thought thee ;—thy conversion's sudden

ANTONIO.

Age must, my friend, this one advantage claim,
That, though from error it be not exempt,
Its balance it recovers speedily.
Thou didst at first essay to heal the breach
Between thy friend and me.   I urge it now.
Do what thou can'st to bring him to himself,
And to restore things to their wonted calm.
Myself will visit him, when I shall know,
From thee, that he is tranquil, when thou think'st.
My presence will not aggravate the ill.
But what thou dost, that do within the hour;
Alphonso will return to town ere night.
I must attend him there.   Meanwhile, farewell.

## SCENE V.

LEONORA, (*alone.*)

For once, dear friend, we are not of one mind
Our separate interests go not hand in hand.
I'll use the time to compass my design,
And will endeavour to win Tasso.   Quick!

# ACT THE FOURTH.

## SCENE I.

*A Chamber.*

TASSO, (*alone.*)

Art thou awaken'd from a dream, and is
The fair delusion suddenly dissolv'd?
In the fruition of the highest joy
Has sleep o'ermaster'd thee, and does it yet
Torture and bind thy soul with heavy chains?
Ay, thou'rt awake and dream'st.   Where now the hours
That round thy brow with flow'ry garlands play'd?
The days when unrestrain'd thy yearning soul
Freely explor'd the heaven's o'erarching blue?
Thou'rt living still, art sensible to touch,
Feelest, yet know'st not if thou livest still.
Say, for mine own, or for another's fault,
Am I, as criminal, thus captive here?
Have I been guilty that I suffer thus?
Is not my fancied crime a merit rather?
With kindly feeling I encounter'd him,
Persuaded, by the heart's delusive hope,
He must be man who bears a mortal form;
With open arms I sped to his embrace,
And felt no human breast, but bolts and bars.
Oh, had I but with prudent forecast weigh'd,
How I most fitly could receive the man,
Who from the first inspir'd me with mistrust!
Let me, however, whatsoe'er betide,
For ever to this one assurance cling :—
'Twas she herself!   She stood before my view!
She spoke to me! I hearken'd to her voice!
Her look, her tone, her words' sweet import, these,

These are for ever mine; nor time nor fate,
Nor ruthless chance can plunder me of these!
And if my spirit hath too swiftly soar'd,
If all too promptly in my breast I gave
Vent to the flame which now consumes my heart,
So let it be,—I never can repent,
E'en though my fortune were for ever wreck'd.
To her devoted, I obey'd with joy
The hand that beckon'd me to ruin's brink.
So let it be!   Thus have I prov'd myself
Deserving of the precious confidence
That cheers my soul,—ay, cheers it in this hour,
When cruel fate unlocks the sable gates
Of long-protracted woe.—Yes, now tis done!
For me the radiant sun of fortune sets,
Never to rise again; his glance benign
The Prince withdraws, and leaves me standing here,
Abandon'd on this narrow, gloomy path.
The hateful and ill-boding feather'd throng,
Obscene attendants upon ancient night,
Swarm forth and whirl round my devoted head.
Whither, oh whither, shall I bend my steps,
To shun the loathsome brood that round me flit,
And 'scape the dread abyss that yawns before?

SCENE II.

LEONORA.      TASSO.

LEONORA.

Dear Tasso, what hath chanc'd?   Hath passion's glow,
Hath thy suspicious temper urged thee thus?
How has it happen'd?   We are all amaz'd.
Where now thy gentleness, thy suavity,
Thy rapid insight, thy discernment just,
Which doth award to every man his due;
Thine even mind, which beareth, what to bear
The wise are prompt, the vain are slow, to learn;
The prudent mast'ry over lip and tongue?
I scarcely recognize thee now, dear friend.

TASSO.

And what if all were gone, for ever gone!
If as a beggar thou should'st meet the friend

Whom just before thou had'st deem'd opulent.
Thou speakest truth, I am no more myself,
Yet am I now as much so as I was.
It seems a riddle, yet it is not one.
The tranquil moon, that cheers thee through the night,
Whose gentle radiance, with resistless power,
Allures thine eye, thy soul, doth float by day
An insignificant and pallid cloud.
In the bright glare of daylight I am lost.
Ye know me not, I scarcely know myself.

LEONORA.

Such words, dear friend, as thou hast utter'd them,
I cannot comprehend.   Explain thyself.
Say, hath that rugged man's offensive speech
So deeply wounded thee, that now thou dost
Misjudge thyself and us?   Confide in me.

TASSO.

I'm not the one offended.   Me thou seest
Thus punish'd here because I gave offence.
The knot of many words the sword would loose
With promptitude and ease, but I'm not free.
Thou'rt scarce aware,—nay, start not, gentle friend,—
'Tis in a prison thou dost meet me here.
Me, as a schoolboy, doth the Prince chastise.—
His right I neither can, nor will dispute.

LEONORA.

Thou seemest mov'd beyond what reason warrants.

TASSO.

Dost deem me then so weak, so much a child,
That this occurrence could o'erwhelm me thus?
Not what has happen'd wounds me to the quick,
'Tis what it doth portend, that troubles me.
Now let my foes conspire!   The field is clear.

LEONORA.

Many thou holdest falsely in suspect;
Of this, dear friend, I have convinc'd myself.
Even Antonio bears thee no ill-will
As thou presum'st.   The quarrel of to-day—

TASSO.

Let that be set aside; I only view
Antonio as he was and yet remains.

Still hath his formal wisdom fretted me,
His proud assumption of the master's tone.
Careless to learn whether the list'ner's mind
Does not itself the better track pursue,
He tutors thee in much which thou thyself
More truly, deeply feelest; gives no heed
To what thou sayest, and perverts thy words.
Misconstrued thus by a proud man, forsooth,
Who smiles superior from his fancied height
I am not yet or old or wise enough
To answer meekly with a patient smile.
It could not hold, we must at last have broken;
The evil greater had it been postpon'd.
One lord I recognize, who fosters me,
Him I obey, but own no master else.
In poesy and thought I will be free,
In act the world doth limit us enough.

LEONORA.

Yet often with respect he speaks of thee.

TASSO.

Thou meanest with forbearance, prudent, subtle.
'Tis that annoys me ; for he knows to use
Language so smooth and so conditional,
That seeming praise from him is actual blame,
And there is nothing so offends my soul,
As words of commendation from his lips.

LEONORA.

Thou should'st have heard but lately how he spoke
Of thee and of the gift which bounteous nature
So largely hath conferr'd on thee.   He feels
Thy genius, Tasso, and esteems thy worth.

TASSO.

Trust me, no selfish spirit can escape
The torment of base envy.   Such a man
Pardons in others honour, rank, and wealth ;
For thus he argues, these thou hast thyself,
Or thou can'st have them, if thou persevere,
Or if propitious fortune smile on thee.
But that which Nature can alone bestow,
Which aye remaineth inaccessible
To toil and patient effort, which nor gold,

Nor yet the sword, nor stern persistency
Hath power to wrest,—that he will ne'er forgive.
Not envy me?   The pedant who aspires
To seize by force the favour of the muse?
Who, when he strings the thoughts of other bards,
Fondly presumes he is a bard himself?
The Prince's favour he would rather yield,
Though that he would fain limit to himself,
Than the rare gift which the celestial powers
Have granted to the poor, the orphan youth.

LEONORA.

Oh, that thy vision were as clear as mine!
Thou read'st him wrongly, thou'rt deceiv'd in him.

TASSO.

And if I err, I err with right good will!
I count him for my most inveterate foe,
And should be inconsolable, were I
Compell'd to think of him more leniently.
'Tis foolish in all cases to be just;
It is to wrong oneself.   Are other men
Toward us so equitable?   No, oh no!
Man's nature, in its narrow scope, demands
The twofold sentiment of love and hate.
Requires he not the grateful interchange
Of day and night, of wakefulness and sleep?
No, from henceforward I do hold this man
The object of my direst enmity;
And nought can snatch from me the cherish'd joy
Of thinking ever worse and worse of him.

LEONORA.

Dear friend, I see not if this feeling last,
How thou can'st longer tarry at the court.
Thou know'st the just esteem in which he's held.

TASSO.

I'm fully sensible, fair friend, how long
I have already been superfluous here.

LEONORA.

That thou art not, that thou can'st never be!
Thou rather knowest how both Prince and Princess
Rejoice to have thee in their company.
The sister of Urbino, comes she not,

As much for thine as for her kindred's sake?
They all esteem thee, recognize thy worth,
And each confides in thee without reserve.

TASSO.

Oh, Leonora!   Call that confidence!
Of state affairs has he one single word,
One earnest word, vouchsaf'd to speak with me?
In special cases, when he has advis'd
Both with the Princess, and with others too,
To me, though present, no appeal was made.
The cry was ever then, Antonio comes!
Consult Antonio!   To Antonio write!

LEONORA.

Thanks here, methinks, were juster than complaint
Thus in unchalleng'd freedom leaving thee,
He to thy genius fitting homage pays.

TASSO.

He lets me rest, because he deems me useless.

LEONORA.

Thou art not useless, e'en though thou dost rest.
Care and vexation, like a child beloved,
Thou still dost cherish, Tasso, in thy breast.
It oft has struck me, and the more I think
The more convinc'd I feel; on this fair soil,
Where fate auspicious seem'd to plant thy lot,
Thou dost not flourish.—May I speak, my friend?
May I advise thee?—Thou should'st hence depart.

TASSO.

Spare not thy patient, gentle leech!   Extend
The draught medicinal, nor think thereon
If it is bitter.—This consider well,
Kind, prudent friend, if he can yet be cur'd!
I see it all myself, 'tis over now!
Him I indeed could pardon, he not me;
He's needful to them, I, alas! am not.
And he has prudence, I, alas! have none.
He worketh to my injury, and I
Cannot and will not counterwork.   My friends
Leave things to chance, they see things differently,
They scarcely struggle, who should stoutly fight.
Thou think'st I should depart, I think so too;—

Then farewell, friends!—This, too, I must endure.
You're parted from me.—Oh, to me be given
The courage and the strength to part from you!

LEONORA.

Seen from a distance things show less confus'd,
That in the present serve but to perplex.
Perchance, when absent, thou wilt recognize
The love which here environs thee, wilt learn
The worth of friends, and feel how the wide world
Cannot replace those dearest to the heart.

TASSO.

I shall experience this! Alas, I've known
The world from early youth, how, pressing on,
She lightly leaves us, helpless and forlorn,
Like sun and moon and other deities.

LEONORA.

Dear friend, if thou wilt lend an ear to me,
This sad experience thou wilt not repeat.
If I may counsel thee, thou wilt at first
Repair to Florence,—there thou'lt find a friend
Will cherish thee most kindly—'tis myself!
Thither I travel soon to meet my lord,
And there is nothing would afford us, Tasso,
A richer pleasure than thy company.
I need not tell thee, for thyself dost know,
How noble is the Prince who ruleth there;
What men, what women too, our favour'd town
Doth cherish in her bosom.   Thou art silent!
Consider well my counsel, and resolve!

TASSO.

Full of sweet promise are thy words, dear friend
And in accordance with my secret wish.
But 'tis too sudden; let me pause awhile,—
Let me consider!   I will soon resolve!

LEONORA.

I leave thee now, and with the fairest hopes
For thee, for us, and also for this house.
Only reflect, and weigh the matter well,
Scarcely wilt thou devise a better plan.

TASSO.

Yet one thing more, tell me, beloved friend,
How is the Princess minded towards me?   Speak!
Was she displeas'd with me?   Give me her words.--
Hath she severely blam'd me?   Tell me all!

LEONORA.

She knows thee well, and therefore has excus'd thee

TASSO.

Say, have I lost her friendship?   Flatter not.

LEONORA.

A woman's friendship's not so lightly lost.

TASSO.

And will she let me go without reluctance

LEONORA.

If 'twill promote thy welfare, certainly.

TASSO.

Shall I not lose the favour of the Prince?

LEONORA.

His nature's noble, thou may'st trust in him.

TASSO.

And shall we leave the Princess all alone?
Thou leavest her; and though perhaps not much,
I know full well that I was something to her.

LEONORA.

An absent friend is sweet society,
When of his happiness we're well assur'd.
My plan succeeds, I see thee happy now;
Thou wilt not depart hence unsatisfied.
The Prince commands;—Antonio seeks thee, Tasso.
He censures in himself the bitterness
With which he wounded thee.   I do entreat,
Receive him with forbearance when he comes.

TASSO.

I have no cause to shun the interview.

LEONORA.

And oh! dear friend, that Heaven would grant me this,
To make it clear to thee ere thou departest,
That in thy Fatherland there is not one
Pursues thee, hates, or covertly molests.
Thou art deceiv'd, and as for others' pleasure
Thou'rt wont to practise thine inventive art,

So in this case thou weav'st a cunning web
To blind thyself, the which to rend asunder
I'll do mine utmost, that with vision clear
Thou may'st pursue life's glad career untrammell'd.
Farewell!   I hope for happy words ere long.

## SCENE III.

TASSO, (*alone.*)

I must believe, forsooth, that no one hates me,—
That no one persecutes, that all the guile,
The subtle malice that environs me,
Is but the coinage of my own sick brain
I must acknowledge that myself am wrong!
And that tow'rds many who deserve it not
I've been unjust!   What!   This confess e'en now,
When clearly in the open face of day,
Appear their malice and my rectitude!
I ought to feel most deeply how the Prince
With gen'rous breast his sov'reign grace imparts,
And in rich measure loads me with his gifts,
Though at the very time he has the weakness
To let his eyes be blinded by my foes,
Yea, doubtless, and his arms be fetter'd too!

His own delusion he cannot perceive,
That they're deluders I may not reveal;
And that he may uncheck'd delude himself.
And they delude him whensoe'er they please,
I still must hold my peace,—must yield forsooth!

And who thus counsels me?   With prudent zeal,
And thoughtful kindness, who doth urge me thus?
Leonora's self, Leonora Sanvitale,
Considerate friend!   Ha, ha, I know thee now!
Oh, wherefore did I ever trust her words?
She was not honest, when she utter'd forth
With honied lip, her grace and tenderness!
No, she has always had a crafty heart,        .
With prudent step she turns where fortune smiles

How often have I willingly deceiv'd
Myself in her!   And yet it was in truth

But mine own vanity deluded me!
I knew her, but self-flatter'd, argued thus ·—
True, she is so towards others, but towards thee
Her heart is honest, her intention pure.
Mine eyes are open now,—alas, too late!
I was in favour—on the favourite
How tenderly she fawn'd!   I'm fallen now,
And she, like fortune, turns her back on me.

Yes, now she comes, the agent of my foe,
She glides along, the little artful snake,
Hissing, with slipp'ry tongue, her magic tones.
How fair, more fair than ever she appear'd!
How soothingly her honied accents flow'd!
Yet could the flatt'ry not conceal from me
The false intention; on her brow appear'd
Too legibly inscrib'd the opposite
Of all she utter'd.   Quick am I to feel
Whene'er the entrance to my heart is sought
With a dishonest purpose.   I should hence!
Should hie to Florence, with convenient speed.

And why to Florence?   Ah, I see it all.
There reigns the rising house of Medici;
True, with Ferrara not in open feud,
But secret rivalry, with chilling hand,
Doth hold asunder e'en the noblest hearts.
If from those noble princes I should reap
Distinguish'd marks of favour, as indeed
I've reason to expect, the courtiers here
Would soon impugn my gratitude and truth;
And would, with easy wile, achieve their purpose.

Yes, I will go, but not as ye desire:
I will away, and farther than ye think.

Why should I linger?   Who detains me here?
Too well I understood each several word
That I drew forth from Leonora's lips!
With anxious heed each syllable I caught;
And now I fully know the Princess' mind—

That too is certain ; let me not despair !
" Without reluctance she will let me go,
If 'twill promote my welfare."   Would her heart
Were master'd by a passion that would whelm
Me and my welfare !   Oh, more welcome far
The grasp of death than of the frigid hand
That passively resigns me !—Yes, I go !—
Now be upon thy guard, and let no show
Of love or friendship blind thee !   None hath power
Now to deceive thee, if not self-deceiv'd.

## SCENE IV.

ANTONIO.        TASSO.

ANTONIO.

Tasso, I come to say a word to thee,
If thou'rt dispos'd to hear me tranquilly.

TASSO.

I am denied, thou know'st, the power to act ;
It well becomes me to attend and listen.

ANTONIO.

Tranquil I find thee, as I hop'd to find,
And speak to thee in all sincerity.
But in the Prince's name I first dissolve
The slender band that seem'd to fetter thee.

TASSO.

Caprice dissolves it, as caprice impos'd ;
I yield, and no judicial sentence claim.

ANTONIO.

Next, Tasso, on my own behalf I speak.
I have, it seems, more deeply wounded thee,
Than I,—myself by divers passions mov'd,—
Was conscious of.   But no insulting word
Hath from my lip incautiously escap'd.
Thy honour, as a noble, is untouch'd,
And, as a man, thou'lt not refuse thy pardou.

TASSO.

Whether contempt or insult galls the most
I will not now determine.   That doth pierce
The inmost marrow, this but frets the skin.
The shaft of insult back returns to him
Who wing'd the missile, and the practis'd sword

Soon reconciles the opinion of the world—
A wounded heart is difficult to cure.

ANTONIO.

'Tis now my turn to press thee urgently;
Oh, step not back, yield to mine earnest wish,
The Prince's wish, who sends me unto thee.

TASSO.

I know the claims of duty, and submit.
Be it, as far as possible, forgiv'n!
The poets tell us of a magic spear,
Which could, by friendly contact, heal the wound
Itself had giv'n.   The tongue hath such a power;
I will not peevishly resist it now.

ANTONIO.

I thank thee, and desire that thou at once
Would'st put my wish to serve thee to the proof.
Then say if I in aught can pleasure thee;—
Most gladly will I do so;  therefore speak.

TASSO.

Thine offer tallies with my secret wish.
But now thou hast restor'd my liberty,
Procure for me, I pray, the use of it.

ANTONIO.

What meanest thou? more plainly state thy wish.

TASSO.

My poem, as thou knowest, I have ended;
Yet much it wants to render it complete.
To-day I gave it to the Prince, and hop'd
At the same time to proffer my request.
Full many of my friends I now should find
In Rome assembled; they have written me
Their judgments touching various passages;
Many of their suggestions I could use,
Others require reflection, and some lines
I should be loath to alter, till at least
My judgment has been better satisfied.
All this by letter cannot be arrang'd,
While intercourse would soon untie the knots.
I thought myself to ask the Prince to-day,

But miss'd th' occasion ; now, I dare not venture,
And must for this permission trust to thee.

ANTONIO.

It seems imprudent to absent thyself
Just now, when thy completed work commends thee
Both to the Prince and Princess.   When the sun
Of fortune smiles, 'tis like a harvest-day ;—
We should be busy when the corn is ripe.
Nought wilt thou win if thou departest hence,
Perchance thou'lt lose what thou hast won already;
Presence is still a powerful deity,—
Learn to respect her influence,—tarry here.

TASSO.

I've nought to fear ; Alphonso's soul is noble,
Such hath he always prov'd himself tow'rds me ;—
To his heart only will I owe the boon
Which now I crave.   By no mean, servile arts
Will I obtain his favour.   Nought will I receive
Which it can e'er repent him to have given.

ANTONIO.

Then do not now solicit leave to go ;
He will not willingly accord thy suit,
And much I fear he will reject it, Tasso.

TASSO.

Duly entreated, he will grant my prayer :
Thou hast the power to move him if thou wilt.

ANTONIO.

But what sufficient reason shall I urge?

TASSO.

Let every stanza of my poem speak !
The scope was lofty that I aim'd to reach,
Though to my genius inaccessible.
Labour and strenuous effort have not fail'd ;
The cheerful stroll of many a lovely day,
The silent watch of many a solemn night,
Have to this pious lay been consecrate
With modest daring I aspir'd to near
The mighty masters of the olden time .
With lofty courage plann'd to rouse the age
From lengthen'd sleep, to deeds of high emprize ;
Then with a christian host I hop'd to share

The toil and glory of a holy war.
And that my song may rouse the noblest men
It must be worthy of its lofty aim.
What worth it hath is to Alphonso due ;
For its completion I would owe him thanks.

ANTONIO.

The Prince himself is here, with other men
Able as those of Rome to be thy guides ;
Here is thy station, here complete thy work :
Then haste to Rome to carry out thy plan.

TASSO.

Alphonso first inspir'd my muse, and he
Will be the last to counsel me.　Thy judgment,
The judgment also of the learned men
Assembled at our court, I highly value ;
Ye shall determine when my friends at Rome
Fail to produce conviction in my mind.
But them I must consult.　Gonzaga there
Has summon'd a tribunal before which
I must present myself.　I scarce can wait.
Flaminio dé Nobili, Angelio
Da Barga, Antoniano, and Speron Speroni!
They're surely known to thee.—What names they are.
They in my soul, which bows in reverence,
Inspire at once both confidence and fear.

ANTONIO.

Self-occupied, thou think'st not of the Prince.
I tell thee that he will not let thee go ;
And if he does 'twill be against his wish.
Thou wilt not urge what he is loath to grant ;
And shall I mediate when 1 can't approve ?

TASSO.

Dost thou refuse me then my first request
When I would put thy friendship to the proof ?

ANTONIO.

Timely denial is the surest test
Of genuine friendship ; love doth oft confer
A baneful good, when it consults the wish,
And not the happiness of him who sues.
Thou in this moment dost appear to me
To overprize the object of thy wish,

Which, on the instant, thou would'st have fulfil'd.
The erring man would oft by vehemence
Compensate what he lacks in truth and power;
Duty enjoins me now, with all my  might,
To check the rashness that would lead thee wrong.

                    TASSO.
I long have known this tyranny of friendship,
Which of all tyrannies appears to me
The least endurable.   Because forsooth
Our judgments differ, thine must needs be right;
I gladly own that thou dost wish my welfare,
Require me not to seek it in thy way.

                    ANTONIO.
And would'st thou have me, Tasso, in cold blood,
With full and clear conviction injure thee?

                    TASSO.
I will at once absolve thee from this care!
Thou hast no power to hold me with thy words.
Thou hast declar'd me free; these doors which lead
Straight to the  Prince, stand open to me now.
The  choice I leave to thee.   Or thou or I!
The Prince goes forth, no time is to be lost;
Determine promptly!   Dost thou still refuse,
I go myself, let come of it what will.

                    ANTONIO.
A little respite grant me;—not to-day;
Wait I beseech thee till the Prince returns!

                    TASSO.
If it were possible, this very hour!
My soles are scorch'd upon this marble floor,
Nor can my spirit rest until the dust
Of the free highway shrouds the fugitive.
I do entreat thee!  How unfit I am
Now to appear before the Prince thou seest,
And thou must see, how can I hide from thee,
That I'm no longer master of myself?
No power on earth can sway my energies,
Fetters alone can hold me in control.
No tyrant is the Prince, he spoke me free.
Once to his words how gladly I gave ear!
To-day to hearken is impossible.

O let me have my freedom but to-day,
That my vex'd spirit may regain its peace.
Back to my duty I will soon return.

ANTONIO.

Thou mak'st me dubious.　How shall I resolve
That error is contagious, I perceive.

TASSO.

If thy professions I'm to count sincere,
Perform what I desire, as well thou can'st.
Then will the Prince release me; and I lose
Neither his favour nor his gracious aid.
For that I'll thank thee, ay, with cordial thanks.
But if thy bosom bear an ancient grudge,
Would'st thou for ever banish me this court,
For ever would'st thou mar my destiny,
And drive me friendless forth into the world,
Then hold thy purpose and resist my prayer!

ANTONIO.

Oh, Tasso,—for I'm doom'd to injure thee,
I choose the way which thou thyself dost choose;
The issue will determine which is wrong!
Thou wilt away; I warn thee ere thou goest:
Scarce shalt thou turn thy back upon this house,
Ere thou shalt yearn in spirit to return,
While wilful humour still shall urge thee on.
Sorrow, distraction, and desponding gloom
In Rome await thee.　There as well as here
Thou'lt miss thy aim.　But this I do not say
To counsel thee; alas!　I but predict
What soon will happen, and invite thee, Tasso.
In the worst exigence to trust to me.
I now will seek the Prince at thy desire.

## SCENE V.

TASSO, (*alone.*)

Ay, go, and in the fond assurance go,
That thou hast power to bend me to thy will.
I learn dissimulation, for thou art
An able master, and I prompt to learn.
Thus life compels us to appear, yea,—be,
Like those whom in our hearts we proudly scorn.

How obvious now the web of court intrigue!
Antonio desires to drive me hence,
Yet would not seem to drive me.   He doth play
The kind, considerate friend, that I may seem
Incapable and weak; installs himself
My guardian too, degrading to a child,
Him whom he could not bend to be a slave.
With clouds of error thus he darkens truth,
And blinds alike the Princess and the Prince

They should indeed retain me, so he counsels,
For with fair talents Nature has endow'd me;
Although, alas, she has accompanied
Her lofty gifts with many weaknesses,
With a foreboding spirit, boundless pride,
And sensibility too exquisite.
It cannot now be otherwise, since Fate,
In her caprice, has fashion'd such a man,
We must consent to take him as he is,
Be patient, bear with him, and then, perchance,
On days auspicious, as an unsought good,
Find pleasure in his joy-diffusing gift,
While for the rest, why e'en as he was born.
He must have license both to live and die.

Where now Alphonso's firm and constant mind?
In him who treats me thus can I discover
The man who braves his foe, who shields his friend
Now I discern the measure of my woe!
This is my destiny,—towards me alone
All change their nature,—ay, the very men,
Who are with others stedfast, firm, and true,
In one brief moment, for an idle breath,
Swerve lightly from their constant quality.

Has not this man's arrival here, alone,
And in a single hour, my fortune marr'd?
Has he not, even to its very base,
Laid low the structure of my happiness?
This, too, must I endure,—even to-day!
Yea, as before all press'd around me, now
I am by all abandon'd; as before

Each strove to seize, to win me for himself,
All thrust me from them, and avoid me now.
And wherefore?　My desert and all the love,
Wherewith I was so bounteously endow'd,
Does he alone in equal balance weigh?

Yes! all forsake me now.　Thou too!　Thou too
Beloved Princess, thou too leavest me!
Hath she, to cheer me in this dismal hour,
A single token of her favour sent?
Have I deserved this from her?—Thou, poor heart
Whose very nature 'twas to honour her!
How, when her gentle accents touch'd mine ear,
Feelings unutterable thrill'd my breast!
When she appeared, a more ethereal light
Outshone the light of day.　Her eyes, her lips
Drew me resistlessly.　My very knees
Trembled beneath me, and my spirits' strength
Was all requir'd to hold myself erect,
And curb the strong desire to throw myself
Prostrate before her.　Scarely could I quell
The giddy rapture.—Be thou firm, my heart!
No cloud obscure thee, thou clear mind!　She, too
Dare I pronounce what yet I scarce believe?
I must believe, yet dread to utter it.
She too!　She too!　Think not the slightest blame
Only conceal it not.　She too!　She too!
Alas!　This word, whose truth I ought to doubt,
Long as a breath of faith surviv'd in me ;
This word, like fate's decree, doth now at last,
Engrave itself upon the brazen rim
That rounds the full-scroll'd tablet of my woe.
Now first, mine enemies are strong indeed;
For ever now I am bereft of strength.
How shall I combat when she stands opposed
Amidst the hostile army?　How endure
If she no more reach forth her hand to me.
If her kind glance the suppliant meet no more?
Ay, thou hast dar'd to think, to utter it,
And ere thou could'st have fear'd.—behold 'tis true !

And now, ere yet despair, with brazen talons,
Doth rend asunder thy bewilder'd brain,
Lament thy bitter doom, and utter forth
The unavailing cry—She too!   She too!


## ACT THE FIFTH.

### SCENE 1.

*A Garden.*

ALPHONSO.        ANTONIO.

ANTONIO.

Obedient to thy wish, I went to Tasso
A second time. I come from him but now.
I sought to move him, yea, I strongly urged;
But from his fix'd resolve he swerveth not;
He earnestly entreats that for a time
Thou would'st permit him to repair to Rome.

ALPHONSO.

His purpose much annoys me, I confess;—
I rather tell thee my vexation now,
Than let it strengthen, smother'd in my breast
He fain would travel, good!   I hold him not.
He will depart, he will to Rome; so be it!
I would not that the crafty Medici
Detain him though, nor Scipio Gonzaga!
'Tis this hath made our Italy so great,
That rival neighbours zealously contend
To foster and employ the ablest men.
Like chief without an army, shows a prince
Who round him gathers not superior minds;
And who the voice of poesy disdains
Is a barbarian, be he who he may.
Tasso I found, I chose him for myself,
I number him with pride among my train,
And having done so much for him already,
I should be loath to lose him without cause.

ANTONIO.

I feel embarrass'd. Prince, for in thy sight
I bear the blame of what occurr'd to-day;

That I was in the wrong, I frankly own,
And look for pardon to thy clemency.
But I were inconsolable could'st thou,
E'en for a moment, doubt the honest zeal
With which I've sought t'appease him.   Speak to me
With gracious look, that so I may regain
My self-reliance and my wonted calm.

ALPHONSO.

Feel no disquietude, Antonio;—
In no wise do I count the blame as thine;
Too well I know the temper of the man,
What I have done for him, how much I've spar'd him,
How often overlook'd my rightful claims.
O'er many things we gain the mastery,
But stern necessity and lengthen'd time
Scarce give a man dominion o'er himself.

ANTONIO.

When other men toil in behalf of one;
'Tis fit this one with diligence inquire
How he may profit others in return.
He who hath fashion'd his own mind so well,
Who hath aspir'd to make each several science.
And the whole range of human lore, his own,
Is surely doubly bound to rule himself;—
Yet doth he ever give it e'en a thought?

ALPHONSO.

Continued rest is not ordain'd for man!
Still, when we purpose to enjoy ourselves,
To try our valour fortune sends a foe,
To try our equanimity a friend.

ANTONIO.

Does Tasso e'en fulfil man's primal duty,
To regulate his appetite, in which
He is not, like the brute, restrain'd by nature?
Does he not rather, like a child, indulge
In all that charms and gratifies his taste?
When has he mingled water with his wine?
Comfits and condiments, and potent drinks,
One with another still he swallows down,
And then complains of his bewilder'd brain,
His hasty temper, and his fever'd blood,

Railing at nature and at destiny.
How oft I've heard him in a bitter style
With childish folly argue with his leech.
'Twould raise a laugh, if aught were laughable
Which teases others and torments oneself.
" Oh, this is torture !" anxiously he cries,
Then in splenetic mood, " Why boast your art?
Prescribe a cure !"   " Good !" then exclaims the leech.
" Abstain from this or that."   " That can I not."
" Then take this potion."   " No, it nauseates me,
The taste is horrid, nature doth rebel."
" Well then, drink water."   " Water ! never more !
Like hydrophobia is my dread of it."
" Then your disease is hopeless."   " Why, I pray ?"
" One evil symptom will succeed another,
And though your malady should not prove fatal,
'Twill daily more torment you."   " Fine, indeed,
Then wherefore play the leech?   You know my ease.
You should devise a remedy, and one
That's palatable too, that I may not
First suffer pain before reliev'd from it."
I see thee smile, my Prince, 'tis but the truth;
Doubtless thyself hast heard it from his lips.

ALPHONSO.

Often I've heard, as often I've excus'd.

ANTONIO.

It is most certain, an intemperate life,
As it engenders wild, distemper'd dreams,
At length doth make us dream in open day.
What's his suspicion but a troubled dream ?
He thinks himself environ'd still by foes.
None can discern his gift who envy not,
And all who envy, hate and persecute.
Oft with complaints he has molested thee :
Notes intercepted, violated locks,
Poison, the dagger !   All before him float !
Thou dost investigate his grievance,—well,
Doth aught appear ?   Why, scarcely a pretext.
No sovereign's shelter gives him confidence.
The bosom of no friend can comfort him.

Would'st promise happiness to such a man,
Or look to him for joy unto thyself?

ALPHONSO.

Thou would'st be right, Antonio, if from him
I sought my own immediate benefit.
But I have learn'd no longer to expect
Service direct and unconditional.
All do not serve us in the selfsame way;
Who needeth much and would be ably serv'd,
Must employ each according to his gift;
This lesson from the Medici we've learn'd,
'Tis practis'd even by the Popes themselves.
With what forbearance, magnanimity,
And princely patience, have they not endur'd
Full many a genius, who requir'd their aid,
Though it appear'd not that they needed it!

ANTONIO.

Who knows not this, my Prince?   The toil of life
Alone can tutor us life's gifts to prize.
The smiles of fortune have too soon been his,
For him to relish aught in quietness.
Oh, that he were compell'd to earn the blessings
Which now with liberal hand are thrust upon him!
Then would he brace his nerves with manly courage
And at each onward step feel new content.
The needy noble has attain'd the height
Of his ambition, if his gracious prince
Raise him, with hand benign, from poverty,
And choose him as an inmate of the court.
And should he honour him with confidence,
Consulting him in war, or state affairs,
Why then, methinks, the modest man may bless,
With silent gratitude, his lucky fate.
And with all this, Tasso enjoys besides
Youth's purest happiness:—his fatherland
Esteems him highly. looks to him with hope.
Trust me for this,—his peevish discontent
On the broad pillow of his fortune rests.
He comes, dismiss him kindly, give him time
In Rome, in Naples, wheresoe'er he will,

To scarch in vain for what he misses here,
Yet here alone can ever hope to find.

ALPHONSO.

Back to Ferrara will he first return?

ANTONIO.

He rather would remain in Belriguardo.
And, for his journey, what he may require,
He will request a friend to forward to him.

ALPHONSO.

I am content.   My sister, with her friend,
Return immediately to town, and I,
Riding with speed, hope to reach home before them.
Thou'lt follow straight when thou hast car'd for him;
Give orders to the castellan, that here
Tasso may stay as long as he desires;
Till he receives his luggage, till the letters,
Which we shall give him to our friends at Rome,
Have been transmitted.   Here he comes.   Farewell!

## SCENE II.

ALPHONSO.        TASSO.

TASSO, (*with embarrassment.*)
The favour thou so oft hast shown me, Prince,
Is manifest, in clearest light, to-day.
The deed which, in the precincts of thy palace,
I lawlessly committed, thou hast pardon'd.
Thou hast appeas'd and reconcil'd my foe.
Thou dost permit me for a time to leave
The shelter of thy side, and rich in bounty,
Wilt not withdraw from me thy gen'rous aid.
Inspir'd with confidence, I now depart,
And trust that this brief absence will dispel
The heavy gloom that now oppresses me.
My renovated soul shall plume her wing,
And pressing forward on the bright career,
Which, glad and bold, encourag'd by thy glance,
I enter'd first, deserve thy grace anew.

ALPHONSO.

Prosperity attend thee on thy way!
With joyous spirit, and to health restor'd,

Return again amongst us.   Thus thou shalt
A rich requital bring for every hour
Thou now depriv'st us of.—I'll give thee letters
Both to my friends at Rome and to my kinsmen
To them attach thyself;—for this remember,
Though absent, I shall still regard thee mine.

TASSO.

Thou dost o'erwhelm with favours one, oh Prince,
Who feels himself unworthy, who e'en wants
Ability to render fitting thanks.
Instead of thanks I proffer a request!
My poem now lies nearest to my heart.
My labours have been strenuous, yet I feel
That I am far from having reach'd my aim.
Fain would I there resort, where hovers yet
The inspiring genius of the mighty dead,
Still raining influence; there would I become
Once more a learner, then my song indeed
More worthily might merit thine applause.
Oh, give me back the manuscript, which now
I feel asham'd to think is in thy hand.

ALPHONSO.

Thou wilt not surely take from me to-day
What but to-day thou hast consign'd to me.
Between thy poem, Tasso, and thyself
Let me now stand as arbiter.   Beware—
Nor, through assiduous diligence, impair
The genial nature that pervades thy rhymes:
And give not ear to every critic's word!
With nicest tact the poet reconciles
The judgments thousandfold of different men,
In thoughts and life at variance with each other;
And fears not even numbers to displease,
That he may charm the more still greater numbers:
And yet I say not but that here and there
Thou may'st, with modest care, employ the file.
I promise thee at once, that in brief space,
Thou shalt receive a copy of thy poem.
Meanwhile I will retain it in my hands,
That I may first enjoy it with my sisters.
Then, if thou bring'st it back more perfect still,

Our joy will be enhanc'd, and here and there,
We'll hint corrections, only as thy friends.

TASSO.

I can but modestly repeat my prayer;
Let me receive the copy with all speed.
My spirit resteth solely on this work,
Its full completion it must now attain.

ALPHONSO.

I praise the araour that inspires thee, Tasso!
Yet, were it possible, thou for awhile
Should'st rest thy mind, seek pleasure in the world,
And find some means to cool thy heated blood.
Then would thy mental powers restor'd to health,
Through their sweet harmony, spontaneous yield,
What now, with anxious toil, thou seek'st in vain.

TASSO.

So it would seem, my Prince, but I'm in health
When I can yield myself to strenuous toil,
And this my toil again restores my health;
Long hast thou known me, thou must long have seen,
I thrive not in luxurious indolence;
Rest brings no rest to me.   Alas, I feel it;
My mind, by nature, never was ordain'd,
Borne on the yielding billows of the hour,
To float in pleasure o'er time's ample sea.

ALPHONSO.

Thine aims, thy dreams, all whelm thee in thyself.
Around us there doth yawn full many a gulph,
Scoop'd by the hand of destiny; but here,
In our own bosoms, lies the deepest;—ay!
And tempting 'tis to hurl oneself therein!
I charge thee, Tasso, snatch thee from thyself!
The man will profit, though the bard may lose.

TASSO.

To quell the impulse I should vainly strive,
Which ceaseless in my bosom, day and night
Alternates ever.   Life were life no more
Were I to cease to poetize, to dream.
Would'st thou forbid the cunning worm to spin,
For that he spins himself still nearer death?
From his own being, he unfoldeth still

The costly texture, nor suspends his toil,.
Till in his shroud he hath immur'd himself.
Oh, to us mortals may some gracious power
Accord the insect's enviable doom,
In some new sunny vale, with sudden joy,
To spread our eager pinions!

ALPHONSO.

List to me!
Thou givest still to others to enjoy
Life with a twofold relish.   Learn thyself
To know the worth of life, whose richest boon
In tenfold measure is bestow'd on thee.
Now fare thee well!   The sooner thou return'st
All the more cordial will thy welcome be.


## SCENE III.

TASSO, (*alone.*)
Hold fast, my heart, thy work has been well done!
The task was arduous, for ne'er before,
Did'st thou or wish or venture to dissemble.
Ay, thou did'st hear it, that was not his mind,
Nor his the words; to me it still appeared,
As if I heard again Antonio's voice.
Only give heed!   Henceforth on ev'ry side
Thou'lt hear that voice.   Be firm, my heart, be firm
'Tis only for a moment.   He who learns
The trick of simulation late in life,
Doth outwardly the natural semblance wear
Of honest faith; practise, and thou'lt succeed.

[*After a pause*.

Too soon thou triumphest, for lo! she comes!
The gentle Princess!   How the feeling thrills!
She enters now, suspicion in my breast,
And angry sullenness dissolve in grief.


## SCENE IV.

PRINCESS.        TASSO.
(*Towards the end of the Scene the others.*)

PRINCESS.

Thou think'st to leave us then, or rather, Tasso,
To tarry for awhile in Belriguardo,

And then withdraw thyself from us?   I trust
Thine absence will not be for long.   Thou think'st
To visit Rome?

TASSO.

                    Thither I hasten first,
And if, as I have reason to expect,
I receive there kind welcome from my friends,
With care and patient toil I may, at length,
Impart its highest finish to my poem.
There are assembled men who well may claim
In ev'ry sev'ral art the name of master.
Ay, and in that first city of the world,
Hath not each site, yea, every stone a tongue?
How many thousand silent monitors,
With earnest mien, majestic, beckon us!
There if I fail to make my work complete,
I never shall complete it.   Oh, I feel it—
Success doth wait on no attempt of mine!
For ever altr'ing, I shall ne'er succeed!
I feel, yea, deeply feel, the noble art
That quickens others, and does strength infuse
Into the healthy soul, will drive me forth,
And bring me to destruction.   Now I go,
And first to Naples.

PRINCESS.

                    Dar'st thou venture there?
The rigid sentence is not yet repeal'd
Which banish'd thee, together with thy father.

TASSO.

I know the danger, and have ponder'd it.
I go disguis'd, in tatter'd garb, perchance
Of shepherd, or of pilgrim, meanly clad.
Unseen I wander through the city, where
The movements of the many shroud the one.
Then to the shore I hasten, find a bark,
With people of Sorrento, peasant folk,
Returning home from market, for I too
Must hasten to Sorrento, where resides
My sister, ever to my parent's heart,
Together with myself, a mournful joy.
I speak not in the bark, silent I step

x 2

Ashore, then climb the upward path,
And for Cornelia at the gate inquire:
Where may she dwell, Cornelia Sersale?.
With friendly mien, a woman at her wheel
Shows me the street, the house; I hasten on·
The children run beside me, and survey
The gloomy stranger, with the shaggy locks.
Thus I approach the threshold.   Open stands
The cottage door; I step into the house—

PRINCESS.

Oh, Tasso! if 'tis possible, look up,
And see the danger that environs thee!
I spare thy feelings, else I well might ask.
Is't noble, so to speak, as now thou speakest?
Is't noble of thyself alone to think,
As if thou did'st not wound the heart of friends?
My brother's sentiments, are they conceal'd?
And how we sisters prize and honour thee?
Hast thou not known and felt it?   Can it be,
That a few moments should have alter'd all?
Oh, Tasso, if thou wilt indeed depart,
Yet do not leave behind thee grief and care.

[ Tasso turns away.

How soothing to the sorrowing heart to give,
To the dear friend who leaves us for a season,
Some trifling present, though 'twere nothing more
Than a bright weapon, or a mantle new!
There's nought, alas, that we can offer thee,
For thou ungraciously dost fling aside
E'en what thou hast.   Thou choosest for thyself
The pilgrim's scollop shell, his sombre weeds,
His staff to lean on, and departing thus,
In willing poverty, depriv'st us of
The only pleasure we could share with thee.

TASSO.

Then thou wilt not reject me utterly?
Oh precious words!   O comfort dear and sweet!
Do thou defend me!   Shield me with thy care!—
Oh send me to Consandoli, or here,
Keep me in Belriguardo, where thou wilt!
The Prince is lord of many a pleasant seat,

Many a trim garden, which the whole year round
Is duly kept, whose flow'ry paths ye tread not
E'en for a day or hour, the live-long year.
Then, choose among them all the most remote
Which through long years ye've left unvisited,
And which perchance e'en now untended lies.
Oh send me thither!  There let me be yours!
And I will tend thy trees, construct the shed
That shields thy citrons from autumnal blasts,
Fencing them round with interwoven reeds!
Flowers of the fairest hues shall strike their roots,
And ev'ry path be trimm'd with nicest care!
And of the palace should'st thou give me charge,
The windows at convenient times I'll open,
That no injurious vapours mar the works
Of ancient art.—The walls, choice stucco-work,
With the light brush, I'll duly free from dust;
There shall the polish'd pavement brightly shine,
No stone, no tile, miss its right place, and there
No truant weed peep from the crevices.

PRINCESS.

I find no counsel in my troubled mind,
No comfort in my breast for thee or us.
I look around to see if some kind god
Will haply grant us succour, and reveal
Some healing plant, or potion, to restore
Peace to thy wilder'd senses, peace to us?
The truest word that floweth from the lip,
The surest remedy hath lost its power;
Leave thee I must,—yet doth my heart refuse
To part from thee.

TASSO.

       Ye gods!  And is it she?
She who thus pities, thus communes with thee?
And could'st thou e'er mistake that noble heart?
And was it possible despondency
Could, in her presence, overmaster thee?
'Tis thou!  'Tis thou!  I am myself again!
Yet speak once more!  Sweet comfort let me hear
Again from thy dear lips!  Speak, nor withdraw
Thy counsel from me.—Say, what must I do.

That I may win the pardon of the Prince,
That thou thyself may'st freely pardon me,
That ye may both with pleasure take me back
Into your princely service?   Speak to me.
PRINCESS.
It is but little we require from thee,
And yet that little seemeth all too much.
Freely should'st thou resign thyself to us.
We wish not from thee aught but what thou art,
If only with thyself thou wert at peace.
When thou art happy, Tasso, we are happy,
When thou dost seem to shun thy bliss, we grieve;
And if sometimes we are impatient with thee,
'Tis only that we fain would succour thee,
And feel, alas, our succour all in vain,
If thou wilt still refuse the proffer'd hand,
Which fails to reach thee, though stretch'd longing y
TASSO.
'Tis thou thyself, a holy angel still,
As when at first thou didst appear to me!
The mortal's darken'd vision, oh, forgive.
If while he gazed, he for a moment err'd;
Now he again discerns thee, and his soul
Aspires to honour thee eternally.
A flood of tenderness o'erwhelms my heart—
She stands before me!   She!   What feeling this?
Is it distraction draws me unto thee?
Or is it madness? or a sense sublime
Which apprehends the purest, loftiest truth?
Yes, 'tis the only feeling that on earth
Hath power to make and keep me truly blest,
Or that could overwhelm me with despair,
What time I wrestled with it, and resolved
To banish it for ever from my heart.
This fiery passion I had thought to quell,
Still with mine inmost being strove and strove,
And in the strife my very self destroyed,
Which is to thee indissolubly bound.
PRINCESS.
If thou would'st have me, Tasso, listen to thee,
Restrain this fervid glow, which frightens me.

#### TASSO.

Restrains the goblet's rim the bubbling wine
That sparkling foams, and overflows its bounds?
Thine ev'ry word doth elevate my bliss,
With ev'ry word more brightly gleams thine eye,
Over my spirit's depths there comes a change;
Reliev'd from dark perplexity, I feel,
Free as a god, and all I owe to thee!
A charm unspeakable, which masters me,
Flows from thy lips.   Thou makest me all thine.
Of mine own being nought belongs to me.
Mine eye grows dim in the excess of light,
My senses fail me; I can scarcely stand.
Thou draw'st me to thee with resistless might,
And my heart rushes self-impell'd to thee.
Thou'st won me now for all eternity,
Then take my whole of being to thyself.
> [*He throws himself into her arms, and clasps her to his bosom.*]

#### PRINCESS.
> (*Throwing him from her and retiring in haste.*)

Away!

#### LEONORA.
> (*Who has for some time appeared in the back ground, hastening forward.*)

What then has happen'd?   Tasso!   Tasso!
> [*She follows the Princess.*

TASSO, (*about to follow her.*)

Oh God!

#### ALPHONSO.
> (*Who has for some time been approaching with Antonio.*)

He is distracted, hold him fast.

> (*Exit.*)

## SCENE V.

#### TASSO.      ANTONIO.

#### ANTONIO.

If that a foeman,—as thou deem'st thyself
Environ'd by a multitude of foes—
Beside thee stood, how would he triumph now?
Unhappy man!   I am not yet myself!

When something quite unparallel'd occurs,
When something monstrous first arrests our sight,
The stagger'd spirit stands a moment still,
For we know nothing to compare it with.

TASSO, (after a long pause

Fulfil thine office, I perceive 'tis thou!
Ay, thou deserv'st the Prince's confidence.
Fulfil thine office, since my doom is seal'd.
With ling'ring tortures, torture me to death!
Draw! draw the shaft, that I may feel the barb,
That lacerates, with cruel pangs, my heart!
The tyrant's precious instrument art thou;
Ay, be his gaoler,—executioner,—
For these are offices become thee well!

[Towards the scene.

Yes, tyrant, go!   Thou could'st not to the last
Thy wonted mask retain; in triumph go!
Thy slave thou hast well pinion'd, and reserv'd
For predetermin'd and protracted pangs.
Yes, go!   I hate thee.   In my heart I feel
The horror which despotic power excites,
When it is grasping, cruel, and unjust.

[After a pause.

Thus, then, at last I see myself exil'd,
Turn'd off, and thrust forth, like a mendicant!
Thus they with garlands wreath'd me, but to lead
The victim to the shrine of sacrifice!
Thus, at the very last, with cunning words,
They drew from me my only property,
My poem,—ay, and they'll retain it too!
Now is my one possession in their hands,
My bright credential wheresoe'er I went;
My sole resource 'gainst biting poverty!
Ay, now I see why I must take mine ease.
'Tis a conspiracy, and thou the head.
Thus that my song may not be perfected,
That my renown may ne'er be spread abroad,
That envy still may find a thousand faults,
And my unhonour'd name forgotten die,
I must consent forsooth to idleness,
Husband my faculties and spare myself.

Oh precious friendship!   Kind solicitude!
Odious appear'd the dark conspiracy
Which ceaseless round me wove its viewless web
But still more odious does it now appear!

And, thou too, Siren! who so tenderly
Did'st lead me on with thy celestial mien,
Thee now I know!   Wherefore, oh God, so late!

But we so willingly deceive ourselves,
Still hon'ring reprobates that honour us.
True men are never to each other known ;
Such knowledge is reserv'd for galley-slaves
Chain'd to a narrow plank, who gasp for breath,
Where none hath aught to ask, nor aught to lose,
But for a rascal each avows himself,
And holds his neighbour for a rascal too,—
Such men as these perchance may know each other.
But for the rest, we courteously misjudge them,
In hopes that they'll misjudge us in return.

How long thine hallow'd image from my gaze
Veil'd the coquette, working, with paltry arts!
The mask has fallen!—Now I see Armida
Denuded of her charms,—yes, thou art she,
Of whom my bodeful verse prophetic sang!

And then the little, cunning go-between!
With what profound contempt I view her now!
   hear the rustling of her stealthy step,
As round me still she spreads her artful toils.
Ay, now I know you!   And let that suffice!
And misery, though it beggar me of all,
I'll honour still,—for it hath taught me trutl

ANTONIO.

I hear thee with amazement, though I know
How thy rash humour, Tasso, urges thee
To rush in haste to opposite extremes.
Collect thy spirit and command thy rage!
Thou speakest slander, dost indulge in words

Which to thine anguish though they be forgiven,
Thou never can'st forgive unto thyself.

                         TASSO.

Oh, speak not to me with a gentle lip,
Let me not hear one prudent word from thee!
Leave me my sullen happiness, that I
May not regain my senses, but to lose them.
My very bones are crush'd, yet do I live;—
Ay! live to feel the agonizing pain.
Despair enfolds me in its ruthless grasp,
And, in the hell-pang that annihilates,
These sland'rous words are but the feeble cry,
Wrung from the depth of my sore agony.
I will away!   If honest, point the path,
And suffer me at once to fly from hence.

                         ANTONIO.

In thine extremity I will not leave thee;
And should'st thou wholly lose thy self-control,
My patience shall not fail.

                         TASSO.
                    And must I then
Yield myself up a prisoner to thee?
Resign'd I yield myself, and it is done.
I cease to struggle, and 'tis well with me.
Now let mine anguish'd heart recall how fair
What, as in sport, I've madly flung aside.
They go from hence.—Oh God! I there behold
The dust, ascending from their chariot wheels.
The riders in advance—ay, there they go
E'en to the very place from whence I came!
And now they're gone—estrang'd from me they're gone.
Oh that I once again had kiss'd his hand!
That I had still to take a last farewell!
That I could only falter out—"forgive!"
That I could hear him say,—"go, thou'rt forgiven!"
Alas! I hear it not;—I ne'er shall hear it—
Yes, I will go!   Let me but say farewell,
Only farewell!   Give me, oh give me back
Their long'd for presence for a single moment!
Perchance I might recover!   Never more!
I am rejected, doom'd to banishment!

Alas! I am self-banish'd, never more
To hear that gentle voice, that tender glance
To meet no more—

ANTONIO.

Yet hear the voice of one,
Who, not without emotion, stands beside thee!
Thou'rt not so wretched, Tasso, as thou thinkest.
Collect thyself! Too much thou art unmann'd.

TASSO.

And am I then as wretched as I seem?
Am I as weak as I do show myself?
Say, is all lost? Has sorrow's direful stroke.
As with an earthquake's sudden shock, transform'd
The stately pile into a ruin'd heap?
Is all the genius flown that did erewhile
So richly charm, and so exalt my soul?
Is all the power extinguish'd which of yore
Stirr'd in my bosom's depths? Am I become
A nothing? A mere nothing? No, all's here!
I have it still, and yet myself am nothing!
I from myself am sever'd, she from me!

ANTONIO.

Though to thyself thou seemest so forlorn,,
Be calm, and bear in mind what still thou art!

TASSO.

Ay, in due season thou remindest me!
Hath history no example for mine aid?
Before me doth there rise no man of worth
Who hath borne more than I, that with his fate
Mine own comparing, I may gather strength.
No, all is gone! But one thing still remains;
Tears, balmy tears, kind nature has bestow'd.
The cry of anguish, when the man at length
Can bear no more—yea, and to me beside,
She leaveth melody and speech, that I
May utter forth the fulness of my woe.
Though in their mortal anguish men are dumb,
To me a God hath given to tell my grief.

[Antonio approaches him and takes his hand.

### TASSO.

Oh, noble friend, thou standest firm and calm,
While I am like the tempest-driven wave.
But be not boastful of thy strength.   Reflect!
Nature, whose mighty power hath fix'd the rock,
Gives to the wave its instability.
She sends her storm, the passive wave is driven,
And rolls, and swells, and falls in billowy foam.
Yet in this very wave the glorious sun
Mirrors his splendour, and the quiet stars
Upon its heaving bosom gently rest.
Dimm'd is the splendour, vanish'd is the calm!—
In danger's hour I know myself no longer
Nor am I now asham'd of the confession.
The helm is broken, and on ev'ry side
The reeling vessel splits.   The riven planks,
Bursting asunder, yawn beneath my feet!
Thus with my outstretch'd arms I cling to thee !
So doth the shipwreck'd mariner at last,
Cling to the rock whereon his  vessel struck.

# EGMONT.

## DRAMATIS PERSONÆ.

MARGARET OF PARMA, Daughter of Charles V, and Regent of
  the Netherlands.
COUNT EGMONT, Prince of Gaure.
WILLIAM OF ORANGE.
THE DUKE OF ALVA.
FERDINAND, his natural Son.
MECHIAVEL, in the service of the Regent.
RICHARD, Egmont's private Secretary.
SILVA, } in the service of Alva.
GOMEZ, }
CLARA, the Beloved of Egmont.
HER MOTHER.
BRACKENBURG, a Citizen's Son.
SOEST, a Shopkeeper, }
JETTER, a Tailor, }
A CARPENTER, } Citizens of Brussels.
A SOAPBOILER, }
BUYCK, a Hollander, a Soldier under Egmont.
RUYSUM, a Frieslander, an invalid Soldier, and deaf.
VANSEN, a Clerk.

People, Attendants, Guards, &c.


The Scene is laid in Brussels.

# ACT THE FIRST.

SOLDIERS *and* CITIZENS (*with cross-bows*).
JETTER (*steps forward, and bends his cross-bow*).
SOEST.    BUYCK.    RUYSUM.

SOEST.  Come, shoot away, and have done with it!  You won't beat me!  Three black rings, you never made such a shot in all your life.  And so I'm master for this year.

JETTER.  Master and king to-boot; who envies you? You'll have to pay double reckoning; 'tis only fair you should pay for your dexterity.

BUYCK.  Jetter, I'll buy your shot, share the prize, and treat the company.  I have already been here so long, and am a debtor for so many civilities.  If I miss, then it shall be as if you had shot.

SOEST.  I ought to have a voice, for in fact I am the loser.  No matter!  Come, Buyck, shoot away.

BUYCK (*shoots*).  Now, corporal, look out!—One!  Two! Three!  Four!

SOEST.  Four rings!  So be it!

ALL.  Hurrah!  Long live the King!  Hurrah!  Hurrah!

BUYCK.  Thanks, sirs, master even were too much! Thanks for the honor.

JETTER.  You have no one to thank but yourself.

RUYSUM.  Let me tell you!—

SOEST.  How now, gray beard?

RUYSUM.  Let me tell you!—He shoots like his master, he shoots like Egmont.

BUYCK.  Compared with him, I am only a bungler.  He aims with the rifle as no one else does.  Not only when he's lucky or in the vein; no! he levels, and the bull's eye is pierced.  I have learned from him.  He were indeed a blockhead, who could serve under him and learn nothing!—But, sirs, let us not forget! A king maintains his followers; and so, wine here, at the king's charge!

JETTER. We have agreed among ourselves that each—

BUYCK. I am a foreigner and a king, and care not a jot for your laws and customs.

JETTER. Why you are worse than the Spaniard, who has not yet ventured to meddle with them.

RUYSUM. What does he say?

SOEST (*loud to* RUYSUM). He wants to treat us; he will not hear of our clubbing together, the king paying only a double share.

RUYSUM. Let him! under protest, however! 'Tis his master's fashion. too, to be munificent, and to let the money flow in a good cause. [*Wine is brought.*

ALL. Here's to his majesty! Hurrah!

JETTER (*to* BUYCK). That means your majesty, of course.

BUYCK. My hearty thanks, if it be so.

SOEST. Assuredly! A Netherlander does not find it easy to drink the health of his Spanish majesty from his heart.

RUYSUM. Who?

SOEST (*aloud*). Philip the Second, King of Spain.

RUYSUM. Our most gracious king and master! Long life to him

SOEST. Did you not like his father, Charles the Fifth, better?

RUYSUM. God bless him! He was a king indeed! His hand reached over the whole earth, and he was all in all. Yet, when he met you, he'd greet you just as one neighbour greets another,—and if you were frightened, he knew so well how to put you at your ease,—ay, you understand me,—he walked out, rode out, just as it came into his head, with very few followers. We all wept when he resigned the government here to his son. You understand me,—he is another sort of man, he's more majestic.

JETTER. When he was here, he never appeared in public, except in pomp and royal state. He speaks little, they say.

SOEST. He is no king for us Netherlanders. Our princes must be joyous and free like ourselves, must live, and let live. We will neither be despised nor oppressed, good-natured fools though we be.

JETTER. The king, methinks, were a gracious sovereign enough, if he had only better counsellors.

SOEST. No, no! He has no affection for us Netherlanders; he has no heart for the people; he loves us not; how then can we love him? Why is everybody so fond of Count Egmont? Why are we all so devoted to him? Why, because one can read in his face that he loves us; because joyousness, open-heartedness, and good-nature, speak in his eyes; because he possesses nothing that he does not share with him who needs it, ay, and with him who needs it not. Long live Count Egmont! Buyck, it is for you to give the first toast! give us your master's health.

BUYCK. With all my heart; here's to Count Egmont! Hurrah!

RUYSUM. Conqueror of St. Quintin.

BUYCK. The hero of Gravelines.

ALL. Hurrah!

RUYSUM. St. Quintin was my last battle. I was hardly able to crawl along, and could with difficulty carry my heavy rifle. I managed, notwithstanding, to singe the skin of the French once more, and, as a parting gift, received a grazing shot in my right leg.

BUYCK. Gravelines! Ha, my friends, we had sharp work of it there! The victory was all our own. Did not those French dogs carry fire and desolation into the very heart of Flanders? We gave it them, however! The old hard-fisted veterans held out bravely for awhile, but we pushed on, fired away, and laid about us. till they made wry faces, and their lines gave way. Then Egmont's horse was shot under him; and for a long time we fought pell-mell, man to man, horse to horse, troop to troop, on the broad, flat, sea-sand. Suddenly, as if from heaven, down came the cannon shot from the mouth of the river, bang, bang, right into the midst of the French. These were English, who, under Admiral Malin, happened to be sailing past from Dunkirk. They did not help us much, 'tis true; they could only approach with their smallest vessels, and that not near enough; —besides, their shot fell sometimes among our troops. It did some good, however! It broke the French lines, and raised our courage. Away it went. Helter, skelter! topsy, turvy! all struck dead, or forced into the river; the fellows were drowned the moment they tasted the water, while we Hollanders dashed in after them. Being amphibious, we were as much in our element as frogs, and hacked away at the enemy, and shot them down as if they had been ducks. The few who struggled through, were struck dead in their flight by the peasant women, armed with hoes and pitchforks. His Gallic majesty was compelled at once to humble himself, and make peace; and that peace you owe to us, to the great Egmont.

ALL. Hurrah, for the great Egmont! Hurrah! Hurrah!

JETTER. Had they but appointed him Regent, instead of Margaret of Parma!

SOEST. Not so! Truth is truth! I'll not hear Margaret abused. Now it is my turn. Long live our gracious lady!

ALL. Long life to her!

SOEST. Truly, there are excellent women in that family. Long live the Regent!

JETTER. She is prudent and moderate in all she does; if she would only not hold so fast to the priests. It is partly her fault, too, that we have the fourteen new mitres in the land. Of what use are they, I should like to know? Why, that foreigners may be shoved into the good benefices, where formerly abbots were chosen out of the chapters! And we're to believe it's for the sake of religion. We know better. Three bishops were enough for us; things went on decently and reputably. Now each must busy himself as if he were needed; and this gives rise every moment to dissensions and ill-will. And the more you agitate the matter, the worse it grows. [*They drink.*

SOEST. But it was the will of the king; she cannot alter it, one way or another.

JETTER. Then we may not even sing the new psalms; but ribald songs, as many as we please. And why? There is heresy in them, they say, and heaven knows what. I have sung some of them, however; they are new to be sure, but I see no harm in them.

BUYCK. Ask their leave, forsooth! In our province we sing just what we please. That's because Count Egmont is our stadtholder, who does not trouble himself about such matters.

In Ghent, Yprès, and throughout the whole of Flanders, any body sings them that chooses. (*Aloud to* RUYSUM.) There is nothing more harmless than a spiritual song. Is there father?

RUYSUM. What, indeed! It is a godly work, and truly edifying.

JETTER. They say, however, that they are not of the right sort, not of their sort, and, since it is dangerous, we had better leave them alone. The officers of the Inquisition are always lurking and spying about, and many an honest fellow has already fallen into their clutches. They had not gone so far as to meddle with conscience, that was yet wanting. If they will not allow me to do what I like, they might at least let me think and sing as I please.

SOEST. The Inquisition won't do here. We are not made like the Spaniards, to let our consciences be tyrannized over. The nobles must look to it, and clip its wings betimes.

JETTER. It is a great bore. Whenever it comes into their worships' heads to break into my house, and I am sitting there at my work, humming a French psalm, thinking nothing about it, neither good nor bad; singing it just because it is in my throat; forthwith I'm a heretic, and am clapped into prison. Or if I am passing through the country, and stand near a crowd listening to a new preacher, one of those who have come from Germany; instantly I'm called a rebel, and am in danger of losing my head! Have you ever heard one of these preachers?

SOEST. Brave fellows! Not long ago, I heard one of them preach in a field, before thousands and thousands of people. A different sort of dish he gave us from that of our humdrum preachers, who, from the pulpit, choke their hearers with scraps of Latin. He spoke from his heart; told us how we had, till now, been led by the nose, how we had been kept in darkness, and how we might procure more light;—ay, and he proved it all out of the Bible.

JETTER. There may be something in it. I always said as much, and have often pondered the matter over. It has long been running in my head.

BUYCK. All the people run after them.

SOEST. No wonder, since they hear both what is good and what is new.

JETTER. And what is it all about? Surely they might let every one preach after his own fashion.

BUYCK. Come, sirs! While you are talking, you forget the wine and the prince of Orange.

JETTER. We must not forget him. He's a very wall of defence. In thinking of him, one fancies, that if one could only hide behind him, the devil himself could not get at one. Here's to William of Orange! Hurrah!

ALL. Hurrah! Hurrah!

SOEST. Now, gray beard, let's have your toast.

RUYSUM. Here's to old soldiers! To all soldiers! War for ever!

BUYCK. Bravo, old fellow! Here's to all soldiers! War for ever!

JETTER. War! War! Do ye know what ye are shouting about? That it should slip glibly from your tongue is natural enough; but what wretched work it is for us, I have not words to tell you. To be stunned the whole year round by the beating of the drum; to hear of nothing except how one troop marched here, and another there; how they came over this height, and halted near that mill; how many were left dead on this field, and how many on that; how they press forward, and how one wins, and another loses, without being able to comprehend what they are fighting about; how a town is taken, how the citizens are put to the sword, and how it fares with the poor women and innocent children. This is grievous work, and then one thinks every moment. "Here they come! It will be our turn next."

SOEST. Therefore every citizen must be practised in the use of arms.

JETTER. Fine talking, indeed, for him who has a wife and children. And yet I would rather hear of soldiers than see them.

BUYCK. I might take offence at that.

JETTER. It was not intended for you, countryman. When we got rid of the Spanish garrison, we breathed freely again.

SOEST. Faith! They pressed on you heavy enough.

JETTER. Mind your own business.

SOEST. They came to sharp quarters with you.

JETTER. Hold your tongue.

SOEST.   They drove him out of kitchen, cellar, chamber—
and bed.                                        [*They laugh.*

JETTER.   You are a blockhead.

BUYCK.   Peace, sirs!  Must the soldier cry peace?  Since
you will not hear anything about us, let us have a toast of
your own—a citizen's toast.

JETTER.   We're all ready for that!  Safety and peace!

SOEST.   Freedom and order!

BUYCK.   Bravo!  That will content us all.

> [*They ring their glasses together, and joyously repeat the
> words, but in such a manner that each utters a
> different sound, and it becomes a kind of chaunt.
> The old man listens, and at length joins in.*]

A        Safety and peace!   Freedom and order!


*Palace of the Regent.*

MARGARET OF PARMA, (*in a hunting dress.*)

COURTIERS, PAGES, SERVANTS.

REGENT.   Put off the hunt, I shall not ride to-day.  Bid
Mechiavel attend me.               [*Exeunt all but the* REGENT.

The thought of these terrible events leaves me no repose!
Nothing can amuse, nothing divert my mind.  These images,
these cares, are always before me.  The king will now say
that these are the natural fruits of my kindness, of my
clemency; yet my conscience assures me that I have adopted
the wisest, the most prudent course.  Ought I sooner to have
kindled, and spread abroad these flames with the breath of
wrath?  My hope was to keep them in, to let them smoulder
in their own ashes.  Yes, my inward conviction, and my
knowledge of the circumstances, justify my conduct in my
own eyes, but in what light will it appear to my brother!
For, can it be denied that the insolence of these foreign
teachers waxes daily more audacious?  They have desecrated
our sanctuaries, unsettled the dull minds of the people, and
conjured up amongst them a spirit of delusion.  Impure
spirits have mingled among the insurgents, deeds horrible to
think of have been perpetrated, and of these a circumstantial
account must be transmitted instantly to court.  Prompt and
minute must be my communication, lest rumour outrun my

messenger, and the king suspect that some particulars have been purposely withheld. I can see no means, severe or mild, by which to stem the evil. Oh, what are we great ones on the billows of life? We think to control them, and are ourselves driven to and fro, hither and thither.

*Enter* MECHIAVEL.

REGENT. Are the despatches to the king prepared?

MECHIAVEL. In an hour they will be ready for your signature.

REGENT. Have you made the report sufficiently circumstantial?

MECHIAVEL. Full and circumstantial, as the king loves to have it. I relate how the rage of the iconoclasts first broke out at St. Omer. How a furious multitude, with stones, hatchets, hammers, ladders, and cords, accompanied by a few armed men, first assailed the chapels, churches, and convents, drove out the worshippers, forced the barred gates, threw everything into confusion, tore down the altars, destroyed the statues of the saints, defaced the pictures, and dashed to atoms, and trampled under foot, whatever came in their way that was consecrated and holy. How the crowd increased as it advanced, and how the inhabitants of Yprès opened their gates at its approach. How, with incredible rapidity, they demolished the cathedral. and burned the library of the bishop. How a vast multitude, possessed by the like frenzy, dispersed themselves through Menin, Comines, Verviers, Lille, nowhere encountered opposition; and how, through almost the whole of Flanders, in a single moment, the monstrous conspiracy broke forth, and accomplished its object.

REGENT. Alas! Your recital rends my heart anew; and the fear that the evil will increase, adds to my grief. Tell me your thoughts, Mechiavel!

MECHIAVEL. Pardon me, your Highness, my thoughts will appear to you but as idle fancies; and though you always seem well satisfied with my services, you have seldom felt inclined to follow my advice, How often have you said in jest: " You see too far, Mechiavel! You should be an historian; he who acts, must provide for the exigence of the hour." And yet, have I not predicted this terrible history? Have I not foreseen it all?

REGENT. I too can foresee many things, without being able to avert them.

MECHIAVEL. In one word, then :—you will not be able to suppress the new faith. Let it be recognized, separate its votaries from the true believers, give them churches of their own, include them within the pale of social order, subject them to the restraints of law,—do this, and you will at once tranquillize the insurgents. All other measures will prove abortive, and you will depopulate the country.

REGENT. Have you forgotten with what aversion the mere suggestion of toleration was rejected by my brother? Know you not, how in every letter he urgently recommends to me the maintenance of the true faith? That he will not hear of tranquillity and order being restored at the expense of religion? Even in the provinces, does he not maintain spies, unknown to us, in order to ascertain who inclines to the new doctrines? Has he not, to our astonishment, named to us this or that individual residing in our very neighbour- hood, who, without its being known, was obnoxious to the charge of heresy? Does he not enjoin harshness and seve- rity? and am I to be lenient? Am I to recommend for his adoption measures of indulgence and toleration? Should I not thus lose all credit with him, and at once forfeit his con- fidence?

MECHIAVEL. I know it. The king commands and puts you in full possession of his intentions. You are to restore tranquillity and peace by measures which cannot fail still more to embitter men's minds, and which must inevitably kindle the flames of war from one extremity of the country to the other. Consider well what you are doing. The prin- cipal merchants are infected—nobles, citizens, soldiers. What avails persisting in our opinion, when everything is changing around us? Oh, that some good genius would suggest to Philip that it better becomes a monarch to govern subjects of two different creeds, than to exite them to mutual destruction!

REGENT. Never let me hear such words again. Full well I know that the policy of statesmen rarely maintains truth and fidelity; that it excludes from the heart, candour, charity, toleration. In secular affairs, this is, alas! only too true ; but shall we trifle with God as we do with each other? Shall we be indifferent to our established faith, for the sake of which so many have sacrificed their lives? Shall we abandon it to these far-fetched, uncertain, and self-contradicting heresies?

MECHIAVEL. Think not the worse of me for what I have uttered.

REGENT. I know you and your fidelity. I know too that a man may be both honest and sagacious, and yet miss the best and nearest way to the salvation of his soul. There are others, Mechiavel, men whom I esteem, yet whom I needs must blame.

MECHIAVEL. To whom do you refer?

REGENT. I must confess that Egmont caused me to-day deep and heart-felt annoyance.

MECHIAVEL. How so?

REGENT. By his accustomed demeanour, his usual indifference and levity. I received the fatal tidings as I was leaving church, attended by him and several others. I did not restrain my anguish, I broke forth into lamentations, loud and deep, and turning to him, exclaimed, " See what is going on in your province! Do you suffer it, count, you, in whom the king confided so implicitly?"

MECHIAVEL. And what was his reply?

REGENT. As if it were a mere trifle, an affair of no moment, he answered: " Were the Netherlanders but satisfied as to their constitution, the rest would soon follow."

MECHIAVEL. There was, perhaps, more truth than discretion or piety in his words. How can we hope to acquire and to maintain the confidence of the Netherlander, when he sees that we are more interested in appropriating his possessions, than in promoting his welfare, temporal or spiritual? Does the number of souls saved by the new bishops exceed that of the fat benefices they have swallowed? And are they not for the most part foreigners? As yet, the office of stadtholder has been held by Netherlanders; but do not the Spaniards betray their great and irresistible desire to possess themselves of these places? Will not people prefer being governed by their own countrymen, and according to their ancient customs, rather than by foreigners, who, from their first entrance into the land, endeavour to enrich themselves at the general expense, who measure everything by a foreign standard, and who exercise their authority without cordiality or sympathy?

REGENT. You take part with our opponents?

MECHIAVEL. Assuredly not in my heart. Would that with my understanding I could be wholly on our side!

REGENT. If such your disposition, it were better I should resign the regency to them; for both Egmont and Orange entertained great hopes of occupying this position. Then they were adversaries, now they are leagued against me, and have become friends,—inseparable friends.

MECHIAVEL. A dangerous pair.

REGENT. To speak candidly, I fear Orange.—I fear for Egmont.—Orange meditates some dangerous scheme, his thoughts are far-reaching, he is reserved, appears to accede to everything, never contradicts, and while maintaining the show of reverence, with clear foresight accomplishes his own designs.

MECHIAVEL. Egmont, on the contrary, advances with a bold step, as if the world were all his own.

REGENT. He bears his head as proudly, as if the hand of majesty were not suspended over him.

MECHIAVEL. The eyes of all the people are fixed upon him, and he is the idol of their hearts.

REGENT. He has never assumed the least disguise, and carries himself as if no one had a right to call him to account. He still bears the name of Egmont. Count Egmont is the title by which he loves to hear himself addressed, as though he would fain be reminded that his ancestors were masters of Guelderland. Why does he not assume his proper title,— Prince of Gaure? What object has he in view? Would he again revive extinguished claims?

MECHIAVEL. I hold him for a faithful servant of the king.

REGENT. Were he so inclined, what important service could he not render to the government; whereas now, without benefiting himself, he has caused us unspeakable vexation. His banquets and entertainments have done more to unite the nobles and to knit them together, than the most dangerous secret associations. With his toasts, his guests have drunk in a permanent intoxication, a giddy frenzy, that never subsides. How often have his facetious jests stirred up the minds of the populace? and what an excitement was produced among the mob, by the new liveries, and the extravagant devices of his followers!

MECHIAVEL.   I am convinced he had no design.

REGENT.   Be that as it may, it is bad enough.   As I said before, he injures us without benefiting himself.   He treats as a jest matters of serious import; and not to appear negligent and remiss, we are forced to treat seriously what he intended as a jest.   Thus one urges on the other; and what we are endeavouring to avert is actually brought to pass.   He is more dangerous than the acknowledged head of a conspiracy; and I am much mistaken if it is not all remembered against him at court.   I cannot deny that scarcely a day passes in which he does not wound me, deeply wound me.

MECHIAVEL.   He appears to me to act on all occasions according to the dictates of his conscience.

REGENT.   His conscience has a convenient mirror.   His demeanour is often offensive.   He carries himself as if he felt he were the master here, and were withheld by courtesy alone from making us feel his supremacy; as if he would not exactly drive us out of the country; there'll be no need for that.

MECHIAVEL.   I entreat you, put not too harsh a construction upon his frank and joyous temper, which treats lightly matters of serious moment.   You but injure yourself and him.

REGENT.   I interpret nothing.   I speak only of inevitable consequences, and I know him.   His patent of nobility, and the golden fleece upon his breast, strengthen his confidence, his audacity.   Both can protect him against any sudden outbreak of royal displeasure.   Consider the matter closely, and he is alone responsible for the disorders that have broken out in Flanders.   From the first, he connived at the proceedings of the foreign teachers, avoided stringent measures, and perhaps rejoiced in secret, that they gave us so much to do.   Let me alone; on this occasion, I will give utterance to that which weighs upon my heart; I will not shoot my arrow in vain.   I know where he is vulnerable.   For he is vulnerable

MECHIAVEL.   Have you summoned the council?   Will Orange attend?

REGENT.   I have sent for him to Antwerp.   I will lay upon their shoulders the burden of responsibility; they shall either strenuously co-operate with me in quelling the evil, or at once declare themselves rebels.   Let the letters be completed without delay, and bring them for my signature. Then hasten to dispatch the trusty Vasca to Madrid; he is faithful and indefatigable; let him use all diligence, that ho may not be anticipated by common report, that my brother may receive the intelligence first through him.  I will myself speak with him ere he departs.

MECHIAVEL.  Your orders shall be promptly and punctually obeyed.

### *Citizen's house.*

CLARA.  HER MOTHER.  BRACKENBURG.

CLARA.  Will you not hold the yarn for me, Brackenburg?

BRACKENBURG.  I entreat you, excuse me, Clara.

CLARA.  What ails you?  Why refuse me this trifling service?

BRACKENBURG.  When I hold the yarn, I stand as it were spell-bound before you, and cannot escape your eyes.

CLARA.  Nonsense!  Come and hold!

MOTHER (*knitting in her arm-chair*).  Give us a song! Brackenburg sings so good a second.  You used to be merry once, and I had always something to laugh at.

BRACKENBURG.  Once!

CLARA.  Well, let us sing.

BRACKENBURG.  As you please.

CLARA.  Merrily, then, and sing away!  'Tis a soldier's song, my favourite.

[*She winds yarn, and sings with Brackenburg.*

The drum is resounding,
And shrill the fife plays,
My love for the battle.
His brave troop arrays,
He lifts his lance high
And the people he sways.
My blood it is boiling!
My heart throbs pit-pat!
Oh, had I a jacket,
With hose and with hat!

How boldly I'd follow,
And march through the gate;
Through all the wide province
I'd follow him straight.
The foe yield, we capture
Or shoot them!  Ah, me!
What heart-thrilling rapture
A soldier to be!

*During the song, Brackenburg has frequently looked at Clara,
at length his voice falters, his eyes fill with tears, he lets
the skein fall, and goes to the window. Clara finishes
the song alone, her mother motions to her, half displeased,
she rises, advances a few steps towards him, turns back,
as if irresolute, and again sits down.*

MOTHER. What is going on in the street, Brackenburg?
I hear soldiers marching.

BRACKENBURG. It is the Regent's body-guard.

CLARA. At this hour? What can it mean? [*She rises
and joins* BRACKENBURG *at the window.*] That is not the
daily guard; it is more numerous! almost all the troops!
Oh, Brackenburg, do go! Learn what it means. It must
be something unusual. Go, good Brackenburg, do me this
favour.

BRACKENBURG. I am going! I will return immediately.
[*He offers his hand to* CLARA, *and she gives him hers.*
[*Exit* BRACKENBURG.

MOTHER. Do you send him away so soon!

CLARA. I long to know what is going on; and, besides,—
do not be angry, mother,—his presence pains me. I never
know how I ought to behave towards him. I have done him
a wrong, and it goes to my very heart, to see how deeply he
feels it. Well,—it can't be helped now!

MOTHER. He is such a true-hearted fellow!

CLARA. I cannot help it, I must treat him kindly. Often,
without a thought, I return the gentle loving pressure of his
hand. I reproach myself that I am deceiving him, that I am
nourishing in his heart a vain hope. I am in a sad plight.
God knows, I do not willingly deceive him. I do not wish
him to hope, yet I cannot let him despair!

MOTHER. That is not as it should be.

CLARA. I liked him once, and in my soul I like him still.
I could have married him; yet I believe I was never really
in love with him.

MOTHER. You would have been always happy with him.

CLARA. I should have been provided for, and have led a
quiet life.

MOTHER. And it has all been trifled away through your
own folly.

CLARA. I am in a strange position. When I think how

it has come to pass, I know it, indeed, and I know it not. But I have only to look upon Egmont, and I understand it all; ay, and stranger things would seem natural then. Oh, what a man he is  All the provinces worship him. And in his arms, shall I not be the happiest creature in the world?

MOTHER. And how will it be in the future?

CLARA. I only ask, does he love me?—does he love me? —as if there were any doubt about it.

MOTHER. One has nothing but anxiety of heart with one's children. Always care and sorrow, whatever may be the end of it! It cannot come to good! Alas, you have made yourself wretched! You have made your mother wretched too.

CLARA (*quietly*). Yet, you allowed it in the beginning.

MOTHER. Alas, I was too indulgent, I am always too indulgent. ·

CLARA. When Egmont rode by, and I ran to the window, did you chide me then? Did you not come to the window yourself? When he looked up, smiled, nodded, and greeted me; was it displeasing to you? Did you not feel honoured in your daughter?

MOTHER. Go on with your reproaches.

CLARA (*with emotion*). Then, when he passed more frequently, and we felt sure that it was on my account that he came this way, did you not remark it, yourself, with secret joy? Did you call me away, when I stood at the closed window waiting for him?

MOTHER. Could I imagine that it would go so far?

CLARA (*with faltering voice, and repressed tears*). And then, one evening, when, enveloped in his mantle, he surprised us as we sat at our lamp, who busied herself in receiving him, while I remained, lost in astonishment, as if fastened to my chair?

MOTHER. Could I imagine that the prudent Clara would so soon be carried away by this unhappy love? I must now endure that my daughter—

CLARA (*bursting into tears*). Mother! How can you? You take pleasure in tormenting me.

MOTHER (*weeping*). Ay, weep away! Make me yet more wretched by your grief. Is it not misery enough that my only daughter is a cast-a-way?

CLARA (*rising, and speaking coldly*). A cast-away! The beloved of Egmont, a cast-away?—What princess but would envy the poor Clara her place in his heart? Oh, mother,— my own mother, you were not wont to speak thus! Dear mother, be kind!—Let the people think, let the neighbours whisper what they like,—this chamber, this lowly house is a paradise, since Egmont's love dwelt here.

MOTHER. One cannot help liking him! that is true. He is always so kind, frank, and open-hearted.

CLARA. There is not a drop of false blood in his veins. And then, mother, he is indeed the great Egmont; yet, when he comes to me, how tender he is, how kind! How he tries to conceal from me his rank, his bravery! How anxious he is about me! so entirely the man, the friend, the lover.

MOTHER. Do you expect him to-day?

CLARA. Have you not noticed how often I go to the window? How I listen to every noise at the door? Though I know that he will not come before night, yet, from the time when I rise in the morning, I keep expecting him every moment. Were I but a boy, to follow him always, to the court and everywhere! Could I but carry his colours in the field!

MOTHER. You were always such a lively, restless creature; even as a little child, now wild, now thoughtful. Will you not dress yourself a little better?

CLARA. Perhaps I may, if I want something to do.— Yesterday, some of his people went by, singing songs in his honour. At least his name was in the songs! I could not understand the rest. My heart leaped up into my throat,— I would fain have called them back if I had not felt ashamed.

MOTHER. Take care! Your impetuous nature will ruin all. You will betray yourself before the people; as, not long ago, at your cousin's, when you found the wood-cut with the description, and exclaimed, with a cry: "Count Egmont!"— I grew as red as fire.

CLARA. Could I help crying out? It was the battle of Gravelines, and I found in the picture, the letter C, and then looked for it in the description below. There it stood, "Count Egmont, with his horse shot under him." I shuddered, and afterwards I could not help laughing at the wood-cut figure of Egmont, as tall as the neighbouring tower of Gravelines,

and the English ships at the side.—When I remember how I
used to conceive of a battle, and what an idea I had, as a
girl, of Count Egmont, when I listened to descriptions of him,
and of all the other earls and princes;—and think how it
is with me now !

*Enter* BRACKENBURG.

CLARA.   Well, what is going on?

BRACKENBURG.   Nothing certain is known.   It is rumoured that an insurrection has lately broken out in Flanders; the Regent is afraid of its spreading here.   The castle
is strongly garrisoned, the citizens are crowding to the gates,
and the streets are thronged with people.   I will hasten at
once to my old father.                     [*as if about to go.*

CLARA.   Shall we see you to-morrow?   I must change my
dress a little.   I am expecting my cousin, and I look too
untidy.   Come, mother, help me a moment.   Take the book,
Brackenburg, and bring me such another story.

MOTHER.   Farewell.

BRACKENBURG (*extending his hand*).   Your hand!

CLARA (*refusing hers*).   When you come next.

                [*Exeunt* MOTHER *and* DAUGHTER.

BRACKENBURG (*alone*).   I had resolved to go away again
at once, and yet, when she takes me at my word, and lets me
leave her, I feel as if I could go mad.—Wretched man!   Does
the fate of thy fatherland. does the growing disturbance fail
to move thee?—Are countryman and Spaniard the same to
thee? and carest thou not who rules, and who is in the right?
—I was a different sort of fellow as a schoolboy!—Then,
when an exercise in oratory was given; " Brutus' speech
for liberty," for instance, Fritz was ever the first, and the
rector would say: " If it were only spoken more deliberately, the words not all huddled together."—Then my blood
boiled, and I longed for action;—Now I drag along, bound
by the eyes of a maiden.   I cannot leave her! yet she, alas,
cannot love me!—ah—no—she—she cannot have entirely
rejected me—not entirely—yet half love is no love!—I will
endure it no longer!—Can it be true, what a friend lately
whispered in my ear, that she secretly admits a man into the
house by night, when she always sends me away modestly
before evening?   No, it cannot be true!   It is a lie!   A base,
slanderous, lie!   Clara is as innocent as I am wretched.—

She has rejected me, has thrust me from her heart—and shall
I live on thus? I cannot, I will not endure it. Already my
native land is convulsed by internal strife, and do I perish
abjectly amid the tumult? I will not endure it! When the
trumpet sounds, when a shot falls, it thrills through my bone
and marrow! But, alas, it does not rouse me! It does not
summon me to join the onslaught, to rescue, to dare.—
Wretched, degrading position! Better end it at once! Not
long ago, I threw myself into the water; I sank—but nature
in her agony was too strong for me; I felt that I could swim,
and saved myself against my will. Could I but forget the
time when she loved me, seemed to love me!—Why has this
happiness penetrated my very bone and marrow? Why have
these hopes, while disclosing to me a distant paradise, consumed all the enjoyment of life?—And that first, that only
kiss!—Here (*laying his hand upon the table*), here we were
alone,—she had always been kind and friendly towards
me.—then she seemed to soften,—she looked at me,—my
brain reeled,—I felt her lips on mine,—and—and now?—
Die, wretch! Why dost thou hesitate? (*He draws a phial
from his pocket.*) Thou healing poison, it shall not have
been in vain that I stole thee from my brother's medicine
chest! From this anxious fear, this dizziness, this death-
agony, thou shalt deliver me at once.

## ACT THE SECOND.

*Square in Brussels.*

JETTER *and a* MASTER CARPENTER (*meeting*).

CARPENTER. Did I not tell you beforehand? Eight
days ago, at the guild, I said there would be serious disturbances.

JETTER. Is it then true that they have plundered the
churches in Flanders?

CARPENTER. They have utterly destroyed both churches
and chapels. They have left nothing standing but the four
bare walls. The lowest rabble! And this it is that damages
our good cause. We ought rather to have laid our claims
before the Regent, formally and decidedly, and then have

stood by them. If we now speak, if we now assemble, it will be said that we are joining the rebels.

JETTER. Ay, so every one thinks at first. Why should you thrust your nose into the mess? The neck is closely connected with it.

CARPENTER. I am always uneasy when tumults arise among the mob, among people who have nothing to lose. They use as a pretext that to which we also must appeal, and plunge the country in misery.

*Enter* SOEST.

SOEST. Good day, sirs! What news? Is it true that the insurgents are coming straight in this direction?

CARPENTER. Here they shall touch nothing, at any rate.

SOEST. A soldier came into my shop just now to buy tobacco; I questioned him about the matter. The Regent, though so brave and prudent a lady, has for once lost her presence of mind. Things must be bad indeed when she thus takes refuge behind her guards. The castle is strongly garrisoned. It is even rumoured that she means to fly from the town.

CARPENTER. Forth she shall not go! Her presence protects us, and we will ensure her safety better than her mustachioed gentry. If she only maintains our rights and privileges, we will stand faithfully by her.

*Enter a* SOAPBOILER.

SOAPBOILER. An ugly business this! a bad business! Troubles are beginning; all things are going wrong! Mind you keep quiet, or they'll take you also for rioters.

SOEST. Here come the seven wise men of Greece.

SOAPBOILER. I know there are many who in secret hold with the Calvinists, abuse the bishops, and care not for the king. But a loyal subject, a sincere Catholic!—

*[By degrees others join the speakers and listen.*
*Enter* VANSEN.

VANSEN. God save you. sirs! What news?

CARPENTER. Have nothing to do with him, he's a dangerous fellow.

JETTER. Is he not secretary to Dr. Wiets?

CARPENTER. He has already had several masters. First he was a clerk, and as one patron after another turned him off, on account of his roguish tricks. he now dabbles in the business of notary and advocate, and is a brandy-drinker to boot. 		[*More people gather round and stand in groups.*

VANSEN. So here you are, putting your heads together. Well, it is worth talking about.

SOEST. I think so too.

VANSEN. Now if only one of you had heart and another head enough for the work, we might break the Spanish fetters at once.

SOEST. Sirs! you must not talk thus. We have taken our oath to the king.

VANSEN. And the king to us. Mark that!

JETTER. There's sense in that! Tell us your opinion.

OTHERS. Hearken to him; he's a clever fellow. He's sharp enough.

VANSEN. I had an old master once, who possessed a collection of parchments, among which were charters of ancient constitutions, contracts, and privileges. He set great store, too, by the rarest books. One of these contained our whole constitution; how, at first, we Netherlanders had princes of our own, who governed according to hereditary laws, rights, and usages; how our ancestors paid due honour to their sovereign so long as he governed them equitably; and how they were immediately on their guard the moment he was for overstepping his bounds. The states were down upon him at once; for every province, however small, had its own chamber and representatives.

CARPENTER. Hold your tongue! We knew that long ago! Every honest citizen learns as much about the constitution as he needs.

JETTER. Let him speak; one may always learn something.

SOEST. He is quite right.

*Several* CITIZENS. Go on! Go on! One does not hear this every day.

VANSEN. You citizens, forsooth! You live only in the present; and as you tamely follow the trade inherited from your fathers, so you let the government do with you just as it pleases. You make no inquiry into the origin, the history, or the rights of a Regent; and in consequence of this negligence, the Spaniard has drawn the net over your ears.

SOEST. Who cares for that, if one has only daily bread?

JETTER. The devil! Why did not some one come forward and tell us this in time?

VANSEN. I tell it you now. The King of Spain, whose good fortune it is to bear sway over these provinces, has no right to govern them otherwise than the petty princes who formerly possessed them separately. Do you understand that?

JETTER. Explain it to us.

VANSEN. Why, it is as clear as the sun. Must you not be governed according to your provincial laws? How comes that?

A CITIZEN. Certainly!

VANSEN. Are not the laws of Brussels different from those of Antwerp? The laws of Antwerp different from those of Ghent? How comes that?

*Another* CITIZEN. By heaven!

VANSEN. But if you let matters run on thus, they will soon tell you a different story. Fye on you! Philip, through a woman, now ventures to do what neither Charles the Bold, Frederick the Warrior, nor Charles the Fifth could accomplish.

SOEST. Yes, yes! The old princes tried it also.

VANSEN. Ay! But our ancestors kept a sharp look-out If they thought themselves aggrieved by their sovereign, they would perhaps get his son and heir into their hands, detain him as a hostage, and surrender him only on the most favourable conditions. Our fathers were men! They knew their own interests! They knew how to lay hold on what they wanted, and to get it established! They were men of the right sort; and hence it is that our privileges are so clearly defined, our liberties so well secured.

SOEST. What are you saying about our liberties?

ALL. Our liberties! our privileges! Tell us about our privileges.

VANSEN. All the provinces have their peculiar advantages, but we of Brabant are the most splendidly provided for. I have read it all.

SOEST. Say on.

JETTER. Let us hear.

A CITIZEN. Pray do.

VANSEN. First, it stands written:—The Duke of Brabant shall be to us a good and faithful sovereign.

SOEST.   Good!   Stands it so?

JETTER.   Faithful?   Is that true?

VANSEN.   As I tell you.   He is bound to us as we are to him.   Secondly;—in the exercise of his authority he shall neither exert arbitrary power, nor exhibit caprice, himself, nor shall he, either directly or indirectly, sanction them in others.

JETTER.   Bravo! Bravo!   Not exert arbitrary power.

SOEST.   Not exhibit caprice.

ANOTHER.   And not sanction them in others!   That is the main point.   Not sanction them, either directly or indirectly.

VANSEN.   In express words.

JETTER.   Get us the book.

A CITIZEN.   Yes, we must have it.

OTHERS.   The book!   The book!

ANOTHER.   We will to the Regent with the book.

ANOTHER.   Sir doctor, you shall be spokesman.

SOAPBOILER.   Oh, the dolts!

OTHERS.   Something more out of the book!

SOAPBOILER.   I'll knock his teeth down his throat if he says another word.

PEOPLE.   We'll see who dares to lay hands upon him. Tell us about our privileges!   Have we any more privileges?

VANSEN.   Many, very good and very wholesome ones too. Thus it stands: The sovereign shall neither benefit the clergy, nor increase their number, without the consent of the nobles and of the states.   Mark that!   Nor shall he alter the constitution of the country.

SOEST.   Stands it so?

VANSEN.   I'll show it you, as it was written down two or three centuries ago.

A CITIZEN.   And we tolerate the new bishops?   The nobles must protect us, we will make a row else!

OTHERS.   And we suffer ourselves to be intimidated by the Inquisition?

VANSEN.   It is your own fault.

PEOPLE.   We have Egmont!   We have Orange!   They will protect our interests.

VANSEN.   Your brothers in Flanders are beginning the good work.

SOAPBOILER. Dog! [*Strikes him.*

OTHERS *oppose the* SOAPBOILER *and exclaim,* Are you also a Spaniard?

ANOTHER. What! This honourable man?

ANOTHER. This learned man?

[*They attack the* SOAPBOILER.

CARPENTER. For heaven's sake, peace!

[*Others mingle in the fray.*

CARPENTER. Citizens, what means this?

[*Boys whistle, throw stones, set on dogs; citizens stand and gape, people come running up, others walk quietly to and fro, others play all sorts of pranks, shout and huzza.*

OTHERS. Freedom and privilege! Privilege and freedom!

*Enter* EGMONT, *with followers.*

EGMONT. Peace! Peace! good people. What is the matter? Peace, I say! Separate them.

CARPENTER. My good lord, you come like an angel from heaven. Hush! See you nothing? Count Egmont! Greet Count Egmont.

EGMONT. Here, too! What are you about? Citizen against citizen! Does not even the neighbourhood of our royal mistress oppose a barrier to this frenzy? Disperse yourselves, and go about your business. 'Tis a bad sign when you thus keep holiday on working days. How did the disturbance begin.

[*The tumult gradually subsides, and the people gather around* EGMONT.

CARPENTER. They are fighting about their privileges.

EGMONT. Which they will forfeit through their own folly—and who are you? You seem honest people.

CARPENTER. 'Tis our wish to be so.

EGMONT. Your calling?

CARPENTER. A carpenter, and master of the guild.

EGMONT. And you?

SOEST. A shopkeeper.

EGMONT. And you?

JETTER. A tailor.

EGMONT. I remember, you were employed upon the liveries of my people. Your name is Jetter.

JETTER. To think of your grace remembering it!

EGMONT. I do not easily forget any one whom I have seen or conversed with. Do what you can, good people, to keep the peace; you stand in bad repute enough already. Provoke not the king still farther. The power, after all is in his hands. An honest citizen, who maintains himself, industriously, has everywhere as much freedom as he wants.

CARPENTER. That now is just our misfortune! With all due deference, your grace, 'tis the idle portion of the community, your drunkards and vagabonds, who quarrel for want of something to do, and clamour about privilege because they are hungry; they impose upon the curious and the credulous, and in order to obtain a pot of beer, excite disturbances that will bring misery upon thousands. That is just what they want. We keep our houses and chests too well guarded; they would fain drive us away from them with fire-brands.

EGMONT. You shall have all needful assistance; measures have been taken to stem the evil by force. Make a firm stand against the new doctrines, and do not imagine that privileges are secured by sedition. Remain at home, suffer no crowds to assemble in the streets. Sensible people can accomplish much.

[*In the meantime the crowd has for the most part dispersed.*

CARPENTER. Thanks, your excellency—thanks for your good opinion. We will do what in us lies. (*Exit* EGMONT.) A gracious lord! A true Netherlander! Nothing of the Spaniard about him.

JETTER. If we had only him for a regent! 'Tis a pleasure to follow him.

SOEST. The king won't hear of that. He takes care to appoint his own people to the place.

JETTER. Did you notice his dress? It was of the newest fashion—after the Spanish cut.

CARPENTER. A handsome gentleman.

JETTER. His head now were a dainty morsel for a headsman.

SOEST. Are you mad? What are you thinking about?

JETTER. It is stupid enough that such an idea should come into one's head! But so it is. Whenever I see a fine long neck, I cannot help thinking how well it would suit the block. These cursed executions! One cannot get them out of one's head. When the lads are swimming, and I chance

to see a naked back, I think forthwith of the dozens I have
seen beaten with rods.  If I meet a portly gentleman, I fancy
I already see him roasting at the stake.  At night, in my
dreams, I am tortured in every limb; one cannot have a
single hour's enjoyment; all merriment and fun have long
been forgotten.  These terrible images seem burnt in upon
my brain.

*Egmont's residence.*

*His* SECRETARY (*at a desk with papers. He rises impatiently*).

Still he comes not!  And I have been waiting already full
two hours, pen in hand, the papers before me; and just to-
day I was anxious to be out so early.  The floor burns under
my feet.  I can with difficulty restrain my impatience.  "Be
punctual to the hour."  Such was his parting injunction;
now he comes not.  There is so much business to get
through, I shall not have finished before midnight.  He
overlooks one's faults, it is true; methinks it would be
better though, were he more strict, so he dismissed one at the
appointed time.  One could then arrange one's plans.  It is
now full two hours since he left the Regent; who knows
whom he may have chanced to meet by the way?

*Enter* EGMONT.

EGMONT.   Well, how do matters look?

SECRETARY.   I am ready, and three couriers are waiting.

EGMONT.   I have detained you too long; you look somewhat out of humour.

SECRETARY.   In obedience to your command I have already been in attendance for some time.  Here are the
papers!

EGMONT.   Donna Elvira will be angry with me, when she
learns that I have detained you.

SECRETARY.   You are pleased to jest.

EGMONT.   Nay, be not ashamed.  I admire your taste.
She is pretty, and I have no objection that you should have
a friend at court.  What say the letters?

SECRETARY.   Much, my lord, but withal little that is
satisfactory.

EGMONT.   'Tis well that we have pleasures at home, we
have the less occasion to seek them from abroad.  Is there
much that requires attention?

SECRETARY. Enough, my lord; three couriers are in attendance.

EGMONT. Proceed! The most important.

SECRETARY. All is important.

EGMONT. One after the other; only be prompt.

SECRETARY. Captain Breda sends an account of the oc·curences that have further taken place in Ghent and the surrounding districts. The tumult is for the most part allayed.

EGMONT. He doubtless reports individual acts of folly and temerity?

SECRETARY. He does, my lord.

EGMONT. Spare me the recital.

SECRETARY. Six of the mob who tore down the image of the Virgin at Verviers, have been arrested. He inquires whether they are to be hanged like the others?

EGMONT. I am weary of hanging; let them be flogged and discharged.

SECRETARY. There are two women among them; are they to be flogged also?

EGMONT. He may admonish them and let them go.

SECRETARY. Brink, of Breda's company, wants to marry; the captain hopes you will not allow it. There are so many women among the troops, he writes, that when on the march, they resemble a gang of gipsies rather than regular soldiers.

EGMONT. We must overlook it in his case. He is a fine young fellow, and moreover entreated me so earnestly before I came away. This must be the last time, however; though it grieves me to refuse the poor fellows their best pastime; they have enough without that to torment them.

SECRETARY. Two of your people, Seter and Hart, have ill-treated a damsel, the daughter of an inn-keeper. They got her alone and she could not escape from them.

EGMONT. If she be an honest maiden and they used violence, let them be flogged three days in succession; and if they have any property, let him retain as much of it as will portion the girl.

SECRETARY. One of the foreign preachers has been discovered passing secretly through Comines. He swore that he was on the point of leaving for France. According to law, he ought to be beheaded.

EGMONT. Let him be conducted quietly to the frontier, and there admonished, that, the next time, he will not escape so easily.

SECRETARY. A letter from your steward. He writes that money comes in slowly, he can with difficulty send you the required sum within the week; the late disturbances have thrown everything into the greatest confusion.

EGMONT. Money must be had! It is for him to look to the means.

SECRETARY. He says he will do his utmost, and at length proposes to sue and imprison Raymond, who has been so long in your debt.

EGMONT. But he has promised to pay!

SECRETARY. The last time he fixed a fortnight himself.

EGMONT. Well, grant him another fortnight; after that he may proceed against him.

SECRETARY. You do well. His non-payment of the money proceeds not from inability, but from want of inclination. He will trifle no longer when he sees that you are in earnest. The steward further proposes to withhold, for half a month, the pensions which you allow to the old soldiers, widows, and others. In the meantime some expedient may be devised; they must make their arrangements accordingly.

EGMONT. But what arrangements can be made here? These poor people want the money more than I do. He must not think of it.

SECRETARY. How then, my lord, is he to raise the required sum?

EGMONT. It is his business to think of that. He was told so in a former letter.

SECRETARY. And therefore he makes these proposals.

EGMONT. They will never do;—he must think of something else. Let him suggest expedients that are admissible, and, before all, let him procure the money.

SECRETARY. I have again before me the letter from Count Oliva. Pardon my recalling it to your remembrance. Before all others, the aged count deserves a detailed reply. You proposed writing to him with your own hand. Doubtless, he loves you as a father.

EGMONT. I cannot command the time;—and of all detestable things, writing is to me the most detestable. You imi-

tate my hand so admirably, do you write in my name. I am
expecting Orange. I cannot do it;—I wish, however, that
something soothing should be written, to allay his fears.

SECRETARY. Just give me a notion of what you wish to
communicate; I will at once draw up the answer, and lay it
before you. It shall be so written that it might pass for your
hand in a court of justice.

EGMONT. Give me the letter. (*After glancing over it.*) Dear,
excellent, old man! Wert thou then so cautious in thy
youth? Did'st thou never mount a breach? Did'st thou
remain in the rear of battle at the suggestion of prudence?—
What affectionate solicitude! He has indeed my safety and
happiness at heart, but considers not, that he who lives but
to save his life, is already dead.—Charge him not to be anxious on my account; I act as circumstances require, and shall
be upon my guard. Let him use his influence at court in my
favour, and be assured of my warmest thanks.

SECRETARY. Is that all? He expects still more.

EGMONT. What more can I say? If you choose to write
more fully, do so. The matter turns upon a single point; he
would have me live as I cannot live. That I am joyous, live
fast, take matters easily, is my good fortune; nor would I
exchange it for his tomb-like safety. My blood rebels against
the Spanish mode of life, nor have I the least inclination to
regulate my movements by the new and cautious measures of
the court. Do I live only to think of life? Am I to forego
the enjoyment of the present moment in order to secure the
next? And must that in its turn be consumed in anxieties and
idle fears?

SECRETARY. I entreat you, my lord, be not so harsh
towards the venerable man. You are wont to be friendly
towards every one. Say a kindly word to allay the anxiety of
your noble friend. See how considerate he is, with what
delicacy he warns you.

EGMONT. Yet he harps continually on the same string.
He knows of old how I detest these admonitions. They serve
only to perplex and are of no avail. What if I were a som-
nambulist, and trod the giddy summit of a lofty house,—were
it the part of friendship to call me by my name, to warn me
of my danger, to waken, to kill me? Let each choose his
own path, and provide for his own safety.

SECRETARY. It may become you, my lord, to be without a fear, but those who know and love you——

EGMONT (*looking over the letter*). Then he recalls the old story of our sayings and doings, one evening, in the wantonness of conviviality and wine; and what conclusions and inferences were thence drawn and circulated throughout the whole kingdom! Well, we had a cap and bells embroidered on the sleeves of our servants' liveries, and afterwards exchanged this senseless device for a bundle of arrows;—a still more dangerous symbol for those who are bent upon discovering a meaning where nothing is meant. These and similar follies were conceived and brought forth in a moment of merriment. It was at our suggestion, that a noble troop, with beggars' wallets, and a self-chosen nickname, with mock humility recalled the king's duty to his remembrance. It was at our suggestion too—well what does it signify? Is a carnival jest to be construed into high treason? Are we to be grudged the scanty, variegated rags, wherewith a youthful spirit and heated imagination would adorn the poor nakedness of life? Take life too seriously, and what is it worth? If the morning wake us to no new joys, if in the evening we have no pleasures to hope for, is it worth the trouble of dressing and undressing? Does the sun shine on me to-day, that I may reflect on what happened yesterday? That I may endeavour to foresee and control, what can neither be foreseen nor controlled,—the destiny of the morrow? Spare me these reflections, we will leave them to scholars and courtiers. Let them ponder and contrive, creep hither and thither, and surreptitiously achieve their ends.—If you can make use of these suggestions, without swelling your letter into a volume, it is well. Everything appears of exaggerated importance to the good old man. 'Tis thus the friend, who has long held our hand, grasps it more warmly ere he quits his hold.

SECRETARY. Pardon me, the pedestrian grows dizzy when he beholds the charioteer drive past with whirling speed.

EGMONT. Child! Child! Forbear! As if goaded by invisible spirits, the sun-steeds of time bear onward the light car of our destiny; and nothing remains for us but, with calm self-possession, firmly to grasp the reins, and now right, now left, to steer the wheels. here from the precipice and there from the rock. Whither he is hasting, who knows? Does any one consider whence he came?

SECRETARY. My lord! my lord!

EGMONT. I stand high, but I can and must rise yet higher. Courage, stength, and hope possess my soul. Not yet have I attained the height of my ambition; that once achieved, I will stand firmly and without fear. Should I fall, should a thunder-clap, a storm-blast, ay, a false step of my own, precipitate me into the abyss, so be it! I shall lie there with thousands of others. I have never disdained, even for a trifling stake, to throw the bloody die with my gallant comrades; and shall I hesitate now, when all that is most precious in life is set upon the cast?

SECRETARY. Oh, my lord! you know not what you say! May heaven protect you!

EGMONT. Collect your papers. Orange is coming. Dispatch what is most urgent, that the couriers may set forth before the gates are closed. The rest may wait. Leave the Count's letter till to-morrow. Fail not to visit Elvira, and greet her from me. Inform yourself concerning the Regent's health. She cannot be well, though she would fain conceal it.

[*Exit* SECRETARY.

*Enter* ORANGE.

EGMONT. Welcome, Orange; you appear somewhat disturbed.

ORANGE. What say you to our conference with the Regent?

EGMONT. I found nothing extraordinary in her manner of receiving us. I have often seen her thus before. She appeared to me to be somewhat indisposed.

ORANGE. Marked you not that she was more reserved than usual? She began by cautiously approving our conduct during the late insurrection; glanced at the false light in which, nevertheless, it might be viewed; and finally turned the discourse to her favourite topic—that her gracious demeanour, her friendship for us Netherlanders, had never been sufficiently recognized, never appreciated as it deserved; that nothing came to a prosperous issue; that for her part she was beginning to grow weary of it; that the king must at last resolve upon other measures. Did you hear that?

EGMONT. Not all; I was thinking at the time of something else. She is a woman, good Orange, and all women

expect that every one shall submit passively to their gentle
yoke; that every Hercules shall lay aside his lion's skin,
assume the distaff, and swell their train; and, because they
are themselves peaceably inclined, imagine, forsooth, that the
ferment which seizes a nation, the storm which powerful
rivals excite against one another, may be allayed by one
soothing word, and the most discordant elements be brought
to unite in tranquil harmony at their feet. 'Tis thus with
her; and since she cannot accomplish her object, why she has
no resource left but to lose her temper, to menace us with
direful prospects for the future, and to threaten to take her
departure.

ORANGE. Think you not that this time she will fulfil her
threat?

EGMONT. Never! How often have I seen her actually
prepared for the journey! Whither should she go? Being
here a stadtholder, a queen, think you that she could endure to
spend her days in insignificance at her brother's court? Or
to repair to Italy, and there drag on her existence among her
old family connexions.

ORANGE. She is held incapable of this determination,
because you have already seen her hesitate and draw back;
nevertheless, it is in her to take this step; new circumstances
may impel her to the long delayed resolve. What if she
were to depart, and the king to send another?

EGMONT. Why he would come, and he also would have
business enough upon his hands. He would arrive with vast
projects and schemes, to reduce all things to order, to subjugate, and combine; and to-day he would be occupied with
this trifle, to-morrow with that, and the day following have
to deal with some unexpected hindrance. He would spend
one month in forming plans, another in mortification at their
failure, and half a year would be consumed in cares for a
single province. With him also time would pass, his head
grow dizzy, and things hold on their ordinary course, till
instead of sailing into the open sea, according to the plan
which he had previously marked out, he might thank God,
if, amid the tempest, he were able to keep his vessel off the
rocks.

ORANGE. What if the king were advised to try an experiment?

EGMONT.   Which should be—?

ORANGE.   To try how the body would get on without the head.

EGMONT.   How?

ORANGE.   Egmont, our interests have for years weighed upon my heart; I ever stand as over a chess-board, and regard no move of my adversary as insignificant; and as men of science carefully investigate the secrets of nature, so I hold it to be the duty, ay, the very vocation of a prince, to acquaint himself with the dispositions and intentions of all parties.   I have reason to fear an outbreak.   The king has long acted according to certain principles; he finds that they do not lead to a prosperous issue; what more probable than that he should seek it some other way?

EGMONT.   I do not believe it.   When a man grows old, has attempted much, and finds that the world cannot be made to move according to his will, he must needs grow weary of it at last.

ORANGE.   One thing he has not yet attempted.

EGMONT.   What?

ORANGE.   To spare the people, and put an end to the princes.

EGMONT.   How many have long been haunted by this dread!   There is no cause for such anxiety.

ORANGE.   Once I felt anxious; gradually I became suspicious; suspicion has at length grown into certainty.

EGMONT.   Has the king more faithful servants than ourselves?

ORANGE.   We serve him after our own fashion; and between ourselves, it must be confessed, that we understand pretty well how to make the interests of the king square with our own.

EGMONT.   And who does not?   He has our duty and submission, in so far as they are his due.

ORANGE.   But what if he should arrogate still more, and regard as disloyalty what we esteem the maintenance of our just rights?

EGMONT.   We shall know in that case how to defend ourselves.   Let him assemble the knights of the Golden Fleece; we will submit ourselves to their decision.

ORANGE.   What if the sentence were to precede the trial? punishment, the sentence?

Egmont. It were an injustice of which Philip is incapable; a folly, which I cannot impute either to him or his counsellors.

Orange. And how if they were both foolish and unjust?

Egmont. No, Orange, it is impossible. Who would venture to lay hands on us? The attempt to capture us were a fruitless enterprize. No, they dare not raise the standard of tyranny so high. The breeze that should waft these tidings over the land would kindle a mighty conflagration. And what object would they have in view? The king alone has no power either to judge or to condemn us; and would they attempt our lives by assassination? They cannot intend it. A terrible league would unite the entire people. Direful hate, and eternal separation from the crown of Spain would, on the instant, be forcibly declared.

Orange. The flames would then rage over our grave, and the blood of our enemies flow, a vain oblation. Let us consider, Egmont.

Egmont. But how could they effect this purpose?

Orange. Alva is on the way.

Egmont. I do not believe it.

Orange. I know it.

Egmont. The Regent appeared to know nothing of it.

Orange. And, therefore, the stronger is my conviction. The Regent will give place to him. I know his blood-thirsty disposition, and he brings an army with him.

Egmont. To harass the provinces anew? The people will be exasperated to the last degree.

Orange. Their leaders will be secured.

Egmont. No! No!

Orange. Let us retire, each to his province. There we can strengthen ourselves; the duke will not begin with open violence.

Egmont. Must we not greet him when he comes?

Orange. We will delay.

Egmont. What if, on his arrival, he should summon us in the king's name.

Orange. We will answer evasively.

Egmont. And if he is urgent?

Orange. We will excuse ourselves.

Egmont. And if he insist?

Orange. We shall be the less disposed to come.

Egmont. Then war is declared; and we are rebels. Do

not suffer prudence to mislead you, Orange. I know it is not fear that makes you yield. Consider this step.

ORANGE. I have considered it.

EGMONT. Consider for what you are answerable if you are wrong. For the most fatal war that ever yet desolated a country. Your refusal is the signal that at once summons the provinces to arms, that justifies every cruelty for which Spain has hitherto so anxiously sought a pretext. With a single nod, you will excite to the direst confusion what, with patient effort, we have so long kept in abeyance. Think of the towns, the nobles, the people; think of commerce, agriculture, trade! Realize the murder, the desolation! Calmly the soldier beholds his comrade fall beside him in the battle-field. But towards you, carried downwards by the stream, shall float the corpses of citizens, of children, of maidens, till, aghast with horror, you shall no longer know whose cause you are defending, since you shall see those, for whose liberty you drew the sword, perishing around you. And what will be your emotions when conscience whispers, " It was for my own safety that I drew it."

ORANGE. We are not ordinary men, Egmont. If it becomes us to sacrifice ourselves for thousands, it becomes us no less to spare ourselves for thousands.

EGMONT. He who spares himself becomes an object of suspicion ever to himself.

ORANGE. He who is sure of his own motives can, with confidence, advance or retreat.

EGMONT. Your own act will render certain the evil that you dread.

ORANGE. Wisdom and courage alike prompt us to meet an inevitable evil.

EGMONT. When the danger is imminent the faintest hope should be taken into account.

ORANGE. We have not the smallest footing left; we are on the very brink of the precipice.

EGMONT. Is the king's favour ground so narrow?

ORANGE. Not narrow, perhaps, but slippery.

EGMONT. By heavens! he is belied. I cannot endure that he should be so meanly thought of! He is Charles's son and incapable of meanness.

ORANGE. Kings of course do nothing mean.

EGMONT.   He should be better known.

ORANGE.   Our knowledge counsels us not to await the result of a dangerous experiment.

EGMONT.   No experiment is dangerous, the result of which we have the courage to meet.

ORANGE.   You are irritated, Egmont.

EGMONT.   I must see with my own eyes.

ORANGE.   Oh that for once you saw with mine! My friend, because your eyes are open, you imagine that you see. I go! Await Alva's arrival, and God be with you! My refusal to do so may perhaps save you. The dragon may deem the prey not worth seizing, if he cannot swallow us both. Perhaps he may delay, in order more surely to execute his purpose; in the meantime you may see matters in their true light. But then, be prompt! Lose not a moment! Save,— oh, save yourself! Farewell!—Let nothing escape your vigilance:—how many troops he brings with him; how he garrisons the town; what force the Regent retains; how your friends are prepared. Send me tidings—Egmont——

EGMONT.   What would you?

ORANGE.   (*grasping his hand.*) Be persuaded! Go with me!

EGMONT.   How! Tears, Orange!

ORANGE.   To weep for a lost friend is not unmanly.

EGMONT.   You deem me lost?

ORANGE.   You are lost. Consider! Only a brief respite is left you. Farewell.                                   [*Exit.*

EGMONT. (*alone.*) Strange that the thoughts of other men should exert such an influence over us. These fears would never have entered my mind; and this man infects me with his solicitude. Away! 'Tis a foreign drop in my blood! Kind nature, cast it forth! And to erase the furrowed lines from my brow there yet remains indeed a friendly means.

## ACT THE THIRD.
*Palace of the Regent.*

### MARGARET *of* PARMA.

REGENT. I might have expected it. Ha! when we live immersed in anxiety and toil, we imagine that we achieve the utmost that is possible; while he, who, from a distance, looks on and commands, believes that he requires only the possible. O ye kings! I had not thought it could have galled me thus. It is so sweet to reign!—and to abdicate? I know not how my father could do so; but I will also.

[MECHIAVEL *appears in the back-ground.*]

REGENT. Approach, Mechiavel. I am thinking over this letter from my brother.

MECHIAVEL. May I know what it contains?

REGENT. As much tender consideration for me, as anxiety for his states. He extols the firmness, the industry, the fidelity, with which I have hitherto watched over the interests of his majesty in these provinces. He condoles with me that the unbridled people occasion me so much trouble. He is so thoroughly convinced of the depth of my views, so extraordinarily satisfied with the prudence of my conduct, that I must almost say the letter is too politely written for a king—certainly for a brother.

MECHIAVEL. It is not the first time that he has testified to you his just satisfaction.

REGENT. But the first time that it is a mere rhetorical figure.

MECHIAVEL. I do not understand you.

REGENT. You soon will.—For after this preamble, he is of opinion, that without soldiers, without a small army indeed,—I shall always cut a sorry figure here! He intimates that we did wrong to withdraw our troops from the provinces at the remonstrance of the inhabitants; and thinks that a garrison which shall press upon the neck of the citizen, will prevent him, by its weight, from making any lofty spring.

MECHIAVEL. It would irritate the public mind to the last degree.

REGENT. The king thinks however,—attend to this.—he thinks that a clever general, one who never listens to reason, will be able to deal promptly with all parties;—people and nobles, citizens and peasants; he therefore sends, with a powerful army, the duke of Alva.

MECHIAVEL. Alva?

REGENT. You are surprised.

MECHIAVEL. You say, he sends, he asks doubtless whether he should send.

REGENT. The king asks not, he sends.

MECHIAVEL. You will then have an experienced warrior in your service.

REGENT. In my service? Speak out Mechiavel.

MECHIAVEL. I would not anticipate you.

REGENT. And I would I could dissimulate. It wounds me—wounds me to the quick. I had rather my brother would speak his mind, than attach his signature to formal epistles, drawn up by a secretary of State.

MECHIAVEL. Can they not comprehend——

REGENT. I know them thoroughly. They would fain make a clean sweep; and since they cannot set about it themselves, they give their confidence to any one who comes with a besom in his hand. Oh, it seems to me as if I saw the king and his council worked upon this tapestry.

MECHIAVEL. So distinctly!

REGENT. No feature is wanting. There are good men among them. The honest Roderigo, so experienced and so moderate, who does not aim too high, yet lets nothing sink too low; the upright Alonzo, the diligent Frencda, the steadfast Las Vargas, and others who join them when the good party are in power. But there sits the hollow-eyed Toledan, with brazen front and deep fire-glance, muttering between his teeth about womanish softness, ill-timed concession, and that women can ride trained steeds well enough, but are themselves bad horse-breakers, and the like pleasantries, which, in former times, I have been compelled to hear from political gentlemen.

MECHIAVEL. You have chosen good colours for your picture.

REGENT. Confess, Mechiavel, among the tints from which I might select, there is no hue so livid, so jaundice-

like, as Alva's complexion, and the colour he is wont to paint
with. He regards every one as a blasphemer or traitor; for
under this head they can be racked, impaled, quartered, and
burnt at pleasure. The good I have accomplished here,
appears as nothing seen from a distance, just because it is
good. Then he dwells on every outbreak that is past, recalls
every disturbance that is quieted, and brings before the king
such a picture of mutiny, sedition, and audacity, that we
appear to him to be actually devouring one another, when
with us the transient explosion of a rude people has long
been forgotten. Thus he conceives a cordial hatred for the
poor people; he views them with horror, as beasts and
monsters; looks around for fire and sword, and imagines that
by such means human beings are subdued.

MECHIAVEL. You appear to me too vehement; you take
the matter too seriously. Do you not remain regent?

REGENT. I am aware of that. He will bring his instructions. I am old enough in state affairs to understand how
people can be supplanted, without being actually deprived of
office. First, he will produce a commission, couched in terms
somewhat obscure and equivocal; he will stretch his authority, for the power is in his hands; if I complain, he will
hint at secret instructions; if I desire to see them, he will
answer evasively; if I insist, he will produce a paper of
totally different import; and if this fail to satisfy me, he will
go on precisely as if I had never interfered. Meanwhile he
will have accomplished what I dread, and have frustrated my
most cherished schemes.

MECHIAVEL. I wish I could contradict you.

REGENT. His harshness and cruelty will again arouse the
turbulent spirit, which, with unspeakable patience, I have
succeeded in quelling; I shall see my work destroyed before
my eyes, and have besides to bear the blame of his wrong-
doing.

MECHIAVEL. Await it, your highness.

REGENT. I have sufficient self-command to remain quiet.
Let him come; I will make way for him with the best grace
ere he pushes me aside.

MECHIAVEL. So important a step thus suddenly?

REGENT. 'Tis harder than you imagine. He who is
accustomed to rule, to hold daily in his hand the destiny of

thousands, descends from the throne as into the grave.
Better thus, however, than linger a spectre among the living,
and with hollow aspect endeavour to maintain a place which
another has inherited, and already possesses and enjoys.

*Clara's dwelling.*

CLARA *and her* MOTHER.

MOTHER.   Such a love as Brackenburg's I have never
seen; I thought it was to be found only in romance books.
CLARA.   (*walking up and down the room, humming a song.*)

> With love's thrilling rapture
> What joy can compare!

MOTHER.   He suspects your attachment to Egmont; and
yet, if you would but treat him a little kindly, I do believe
he would marry you still, if you would have him.
CLARA.   (*sings.*)

> Blissful
> And tearful,
> With thought-teeming brain;
> Hoping
> And fearing
> In passionate pain;
> Now shouting in triumph,
> Now sunk in despair;—
> With love's thrilling rapture
> What joy can compare!

MOTHER.   Have done with your baby-nonsense.
CLARA.   Nay, do not abuse it; 'tis a song of marvellous
virtue.   Many a time I have lulled a grown child to sleep
with it.
MOTHER.   Ay!   You can think of nothing but your love.
If it only did not put everything else out of your head.   You
should have more regard for Brackenburg, I tell you.   He
may make you happy yet some day.
CLARA.   He?
MOTHER.   Oh, yes!   A time will come!   You children
live only in the present, and give no ear to our experience.   Youth and happy love, all has an end; and there

comes a time when one thanks God if one has any corner to creep into.

CLARA. (*shudders, and after a pause stands up.*) Mother, let that time come—like death. To think of it beforehand is horrible! And if it come! If we must—then—we will bear ourselves as we may. Live without thee, Egmont! (*weeping.*) No! It is impossible.

*Enter* EGMONT. (*Enveloped in a horseman's cloak, his hat drawn over his face.*)

EGMONT. Clara!

CLARA. (*utters a cry and starts back*). Egmont! (*she hastens towards him.*) Egmont! (*she embraces and leans upon him.*) O you good, kind, sweet Egmont! Are you come? Is it you indeed?

EGMONT. Good evening, mother!

MOTHER. God save you, noble sir! My daughter has well nigh pined to death, because you have stayed away so long; she talks and sings about you the live-long day.

EGMONT. You will give me some supper?

MOTHER. You do us too much honour. If we only had anything—

CLARA. Certainly! Be quiet, mother; I have provided everything; there is something prepared. Do not betray me, mother.

MOTHER. There's little enough.

CLARA. Never mind! When he is with me I am never hungry; so he cannot, I should think, have any great appetite when I am with him.

EGMONT. Do you think so?

CLARA. (*stamps with her foot and turns pettishly away.*)

EGMONT. What ails you?

CLARA. How cold you are to-day! You have not yet offered me a kiss. Why do you keep your arms enveloped in your mantle, like a new-born babe. It becomes neither a soldier nor a lover to keep his arms muffled up.

EGMONT. Sometimes, dearest, sometimes. When the soldier stands in ambush and would delude the foe, he collects his thoughts, gathers his mantle around him, and matures his plan; and a lover——

MOTHER. Will you not take a seat, and make yourself

comfortable? I must to the kitchen, Clara thinks of nothing when you are here. You must put up with what we have.

EGMONT. Your good-will is the best seasoning.

*[Exit* MOTHER.

CLARA. And what then is my love?

EGMONT. Just what you please.

CLARA. Liken it to anything, if you have the heart.

EGMONT. But first. *[He flings aside his mantle, and appears arrayed in a magnificent dress.*

CLARA. Oh heavens!

EGMONT. Now my arms are free! *[Embraces her.*

CLARA. Don't! You will spoil your dress. *(she steps back.)* How magnificent! I dare not touch you.

EGMONT. Are you satisfied? I promised to come once arrayed in Spanish fashion.

CLARA. I had ceased to remind you of it; I thought you did not like it—ah, and the Golden Fleece!

EGMONT. You see it now.

CLARA. And did the emperor really hang it round your neck?

EGMONT. He did, my child! And this chain and Order invest the wearer with the noblest privileges. On earth I acknowledge no judge over my actions, except the grand master of the Order, with the assembled chapter of knights.

CLARA. Oh, you might let the whole world sit in judgment over you. The velvet is too splendid! and the braiding! and the embroidery! One knows not where to begin.

EGMONT. There, look your fill.

CLARA. And the Golden Fleece! You told me its history, how it is the symbol of everything great and precious, of everything that can be merited and won by diligence and toil. It is very precious—I may liken it to your love;—even so I wear it next my heart;—and then——

EGMONT. Well—what then?

CLARA. And then again it is not like.

EGMONT. How so?

CLARA. I have not won it by diligence and toil, I have not deserved it.

EGMONT. It is otherwise in love. You deserve it because you have not sought it—and, for the most part, those only obtain love who seek it not.

CLARA. Is it from your own experience that you have learned this? Did you make that proud remark in reference to yourself? you, whom all the people love?

EGMONT. Would that I had done something for them! That I could do anything for them! It is their own good pleasure to love me.

CLARA. You have doubtless been with the Regent to-day?

EGMONT. I have.

CLARA. Are you upon good terms with her?

EGMONT. So it would appear. We are kind and service-able to each other.

CLARA. And in your heart?

EGMONT. I like her. True, we have each our own views; but that is nothing to the purpose. She is an excel-lent woman, knows with whom she has to deal, and would be penetrating enough were she not quite so suspicious. I give her plenty of employment, because she is always sus-pecting some secret motive in my conduct when, in fact, I have none.

CLARA. Really none?

EGMONT. Well, with one little exception, perhaps. All wine deposits lees in the cask in the course of time. Orange furnishes her still better entertainment, and is a perpetual riddle. He has got the credit of harbouring some secret design; and she studies his brow to discover his thoughts, and his steps, to learn in what direction they are bent.

CLARA. Does she dissemble?

EGMONT. She is regent—and do you ask?

CLARA. Pardon me; I meant to say, is she false?

EGMONT. Neither more nor less than everyone who has his own objects to attain.

CLARA. I should never feel at home in the world. But she has a masculine spirit, and is another sort of woman from us housewives and sempstresses. She is great, steadfast, resolute.

EGMONT. Yes, when matters are not too much involved. For once, however, she is a little disconcerted.

CLARA. How so?

EGMONT. She has a moustache, too, on her upper lip, and occasionally an attack of the gout. A regular Amazon.

Clara. A majestic woman! I should dread to appear before her.

Egmont. Yet you are not wont to be timid! It would not be fear, only maidenly bashfulness.

[Clara *casts down her eyes, takes his hand, and leans upon him.*

Egmont. I understand you, dearest! You may raise your eyes. [*He kisses her eyes.*

Clara. Let me be silent! Let me embrace thee! Let me look into thine eyes, and find there everything—hope and comfort, joy and sorrow! (*she embraces and gazes on him.*) Tell me! Oh, tell me! It seems so strange—art thou indeed Egmont! Count Egmont! The great Egmont, who makes so much noise in the world, who figures in the newspapers, who is the support and stay of the provinces?

Egmont. No, Clara, I am not he.

Clara. How?

Egmont. Seest thou, Clara? Let me sit down! (*He seats himself, she kneels on a footstool before him, rests her arms on his knees, and looks up in his face.*) That Egmont is a morose, cold, unbending Egmont, obliged to be upon his guard, to assume now this appearance and now that; harassed, misapprehended and perplexed, when the crowd esteem him light-hearted and gay; beloved by a people who do not know their own minds; honoured and extolled by the intractable multitude; surrounded by friends in whom he dares not confide; observed by men who are on the watch to supplant him; toiling and striving, often without an object, generally without a reward. O let me conceal how it fares with him, let me not speak of his feelings! But this Egmont, Clara, is calm, unreserved, happy, beloved and known by the best of hearts, which is also thoroughly known to him, and which he presses to his own with unbounded confidence and love. (*He embraces her.*) This is thy Egmont.

Clara. So let me die! The world has no joy after this'

## ACT THE FOURTH.
### *A Street.*

JETTER. CARPENTER.

JETTER. Hist! neighbour,—a word!

CARPENTER. Go your way and be quiet.

JETTER. Only one word. Is there nothing new?

CARPENTER. Nothing, except that we are anew forbidden to speak.

JETTER. How?

CARPENTER. Step here, close to this house. Take heed! Immediately on his arrival, the Duke of Alva published a decree, by which two or three, found conversing together in the streets, are, without trial, declared guilty of high treason.

JETTER. Alas!

CARPENTER. To speak of state affairs is prohibited on pain of perpetual imprisonment.

JETTER. Alas for our liberty!

CARPENTER. And no one, on pain of death, shall censure the measures of government.

JETTER. Alas, for our heads!

CARPENTER. And fathers, mothers, children, kindred, friends, and servants, are invited, by the promise of large rewards, to disclose what passes in the privacy of our homes, before an expressly appointed tribunal.

JETTER. Let us go home.

CARPENTER. And the obedient are promised that they shall suffer no injury, either in person or estate.

JETTER. How gracious!—I felt ill at ease the moment the duke entered the town. Since then, it has seemed to me, as though the heavens were covered with black crape, which hangs so low, that one must stoop down to avoid knocking one's head against it.

CARPENTER. And how do you like his soldiers? They are a different sort of crabs from those we have been used to.

JETTER. Faugh! It gives one the cramp at one's heart to see such a troop march down the street, as straight as tapers, with fixed look, only one step, however many there may be; and when they stand sentinel, and you pass one of them, it seems as though he would look you through and through; and he looks so stiff and morose, that you fancy you see a task-master at every corner. They offend my sight. Our militia were merry fellows; they took liberties, stood their legs astride, their hats over their ears, they lived and let live; these fellows are like machines with a devil inside them.

CARPENTER. Were such an one to cry, "Halt!" and to level his musket, think you, one would stand?

JETTER. I should fall dead upon the spot.

CARPENTER. Let us go home!

JETTER. No good can come of it. Farewell.

*Enter* SOEST.

SOEST. Friends! Neighbours!

CARPENTER. Hush! Let us go.

SOEST. Have you heard?

JETTER. Only too much!

SOEST. The Regent is gone.

JETTER. Then heaven help us.

CARPENTER. She was some stay to us.

SOEST. Her departure was sudden and secret. She could not agree with the duke; she has sent word to the nobles that she intends to return. No one believes it, however.

CARPENTER. God pardon the nobles for letting this new yoke be laid upon our necks. They might have prevented it. Our privileges are gone.

JETTER. For heaven's sake not a word about privileges. I already scent an execution; the sun will not come forth; the fogs are rank.

SOEST. Orange, too, is gone.

CARPENTER. Then are we quite deserted!

SOEST. Count Egmont is still here.

JETTER. God be thanked! Strengthen him all ye saints to do his utmost; he is the only one who can help us.

*Enter* VANSEN.

VANSEN. Have I at length found a few brave citizens who have not crept out of sight?

JETTER. Do us the favour to pass on.

VANSEN. You are not civil.

JETTER. This is no time for compliments. Does your back itch again? are your wounds already healed?

VANSEN. Ask a soldier about his wounds! Had I cared for blows, nothing good would have come of me.

JETTER. Matters may grow more serious.

VANSEN. You feel from the gathering storm, a pitiful weakness in your limbs, it seems.

CARPENTER. Your limbs will soon be in motion elsewhere, if you do not keep quiet.

VANSEN. Poor mice! The master of the house procures a new cat, and ye are straight in despair! The difference is very trifling; we shall get on as we did before, only be quiet.

CARPENTER. You are an insolent knave.

VANSEN. Gossip! Let the duke alone. The old cat looks as though he had swallowed devils, instead of mice, and could not now digest them. Let him alone I say; he must eat, drink, and sleep, like other men. I am not afraid if we only watch our opportunity. At first he makes quick work of it; by and by, however, he too will find that it is pleasanter to live in the larder, among flitches of bacon, and to rest by night, than to entrap a few solitary mice in the granary. Go to! I know the stadtholders.

CARPENTER. What such a fellow can say with impunity! Had I said such a thing, I should not hold myself safe a moment.

VANSEN. Do not make yourselves uneasy! God in heaven does not trouble himself about you, poor worms, much less the Regent.

JETTER. Slanderer!

VANSEN. I know some for whom it would be better, if instead of their own high spirits, they had a little tailor's blood in their veins.

CARPENTER. What mean you by that?

VANSEN. Hum! I mean the count.

JETTER. Egmont! What has he to fear?

VANSEN. I'm a poor devil, and could live a whole year round on what he loses in a single night; yet he would do well to give me his revenue for a twelvemonth, to have my head upon his shoulders for one quarter of an hour.

JETTER. You think yourself very clever; yet there is more sense in the hairs of Egmont's head, than in your brains.

VANSEN. Perhaps so! Not more shrewdness, however These gentry are the most apt to deceive themselves. He should be more chary of his confidence.

JETTER. How his tongue wags! Such a gentleman!

VANSEN. Just because he is not a tailor.

JETTER. You audacious scoundrel!

VANSEN. I only wish he had your courage in his limbs for an hour to make him uneasy, and plague and torment him, till he were compelled to leave the town.

JETTER. What nonsense you talk; why he's as safe as a star in heaven.

VANSEN. Have you ever seen one snuff itself out? Off it went!

CARPENTER. Who would dare to meddle with him, I should like to know?

VANSEN. Will you interfere to prevent it? Will you stir up an insurrection if he is arrested?

JETTER. Ah!

VANSEN. Will you risk your ribs for his sake?

SOEST. Eh!

VANSEN. (*Mimicking them.*) Eh! Oh! Ah! Run through the alphabet in your wonderment. So it is, and so it will remain. Heaven help him!

JETTER. Confound your impudence. Can such a noble, upright man, have anything to fear?

VANSEN. In this world the rogue has everywhere the advantage. At the bar, he makes a fool of the judge; on the bench, he takes pleasure in convicting the accused. I have had to copy out a protocol, where the commissary was handsomely rewarded by the court, both with praise and money, because through his cross-examination, an honest devil, against whom they had a grudge, was made out to be a rogue.

CARPENTER. Why that again is a downright lie. What can they want to get out of a man if **he** is innocent?

VANSEN. Oh you blockhead! When nothing can be worked out of a man by cross-examination, they work it into him. Honesty is rash and withal somewhat presumptuous; at first they question quietly enough, and the prisoner, proud of his innocence, as they call it, comes out with much that a sensible man would keep back; then, from these answers the inquisitor proceeds to put new questions, and is on the watch for the slightest contradiction; there he fastens his line; and let the poor devil lose his self-possession, say too much here, or too little there, or, heaven knows from what whim or other, let him withhold some trifling circumstance, or at any moment give way to fear,—then we're on the right track, and, I assure you, no beggar-woman seeks for rags among the rubbish with more care, than such a fabricator of rogues, from trifling, crooked, disjointed, misplaced, misprinted, and concealed facts and information, acknowledged or denied, endeavours at length to patch up a scarecrow, by means of which he may at least hang his victim in effigy; and the poor devil may thank heaven, if he is in a condition to see himself hanged.

JETTER. He has a ready tongue of his own.

CARPENTER. This may serve well enough with flies. Wasps laugh at your cunning well.

VANSEN. According to the kind of spider. The tall duke now, has just the look of your garden spider; not the large-bellied kind, they are less dangerous; but your long-footed, meagre-bodied gentleman, that does not fatten on his diet, and whose threads are slender indeed, but not the less tenacious.

JETTER. Egmont is knight of the Golden Fleece, who dare lay hands on him? He can be tried only by his peers, by the assembled knights of his order. Your own foul tongue and evil conscience betray you into this nonsense.

VANSEN. Think you that I wish him ill? I would you were in the right. He is an excellent gentleman. He once let off, with a sound drubbing, some good friends of mine, who would else have been hanged. Now take yourselves off! be gone, I advise you! yonder I see the patrol again commencing their round. They do not look as if they would be willing to fraternize with us over a glass. We must wait, and bide our time. I have a couple of nieces and a gossip of a tapster; if after enjoying themselves in their company, they are not tamed, they are regular wolves.

### The Palace of Eulenberg.
### Residence of the Duke of Alva

SILVA *and* GOMEZ (*meeting*).

SILVA. Have you executed the duke's commands?

GOMEZ. Punctually. All the day patrols have received orders to assemble at the appointed time, at the various points that I have indicated. Meanwhile, they march as usual through the town to maintain order. Each is ignorant respecting the movements of the rest, and imagines the command to have reference to himself alone; thus in a moment the cordon can be formed, and all the avenues to the palace occupied. Know you the reason of this command?

SILVA. I am accustomed blindly to obey; and to whom can one more easily render obedience than to the duke, since the event always proves the wisdom of his commands.

GOMEZ. Well! Well! I am not surprised that you are become as reserved and monosyllabic as the duke, since you are obliged to be always about his person; to me, however, who am accustomed to the lighter service of Italy, it seems strange enough. In loyalty and obedience I am the same old soldier as ever; but I am wont to indulge in gossip and discussion; here, you are all silent, and seem as though you knew not how to enjoy yourselves. The duke, methinks, is like a brazen tower without gates, the garrison of which must be furnished with wings. Not long ago I heard him say at the table of a gay, jovial fellow, that he was like a bad spirit-shop, with a brandy sign displayed to allure idlers, vagabonds. and thieves

SILVA. And has he not brought us hither in silence?

GOMEZ. Nothing can be said against that. Of a truth, we, who witnessed the address with which he led the troops hither out of Italy, have seen something. How he advanced warily through friends and foes; through the French, both royalists and heretics; through the Swiss and their confederates; maintained the strictest discipline, and accomplished with ease, and without the slightest hindrance, a march that was esteemed so perilous!—We have seen and learned something.

SILVA. Here too! Is not everything as still and quiet as though there had been no disturbance?

GOMEZ. Why, as for that, it was tolerably quiet when we arrived.

SILVA. The provinces have become much more tranquil; if there is any movement now, it is only among those who wish to escape; and to them, methinks, the duke will speedily close every outlet.

GOMEZ. This service cannot fail to win for him the favour of the king.

SILVA. And nothing is more expedient for us than to retain his. Should the king come hither, the duke doubtless and all whom he recommends will not go without their reward.

GOMEZ. Do you really believe then that the king will come?

SILVA. So many preparations are being made, that the report appears highly probable.

GOMEZ. I am not convinced, however.

SILVA. Keep your thoughts to yourself, then. For if it should not be the king's intention to come, it is at least certain that he wishes the rumour to be believed.

Enter FERDINAND.

FERDINAND. Is my father not yet abroad?

SILVA. We are waiting to receive his commands.

FERDINAND. The princes will soon be here.

GOMEZ. Are they expected to-day?

FERDINAND. Orange and Egmont.

GOMEZ. (*aside to* SILVA.) A light breaks in upon me.

SILVA. Well, then, say nothing about it.

Enter the DUKE OF ALVA (*as he advances the rest draw back*).

ALVA. Gomez.

GOMEZ (*steps forward*). My lord.

ALVA. You have distributed the guards and given them their instructions?

GOMEZ. Most accurately. The day patrols——

ALVA. Enough. Attend in the gallery. Silva will announce to you the moment when you are to draw them together, and to occupy the avenues leading to the palace. The rest you know.

GOMEZ. I do, my lord. [*Exit.*

ALVA. Silva.

SILVA. Here, my lord.

ALVA. I shall require you to manifest to-day all the qualities which I have hitherto prized in you: courage, resolve, unswerving execution.

Silva.  I thank you for affording me an opportunity of showing that your old servant is unchanged.

Alva.  The moment the princes enter my cabinet, hasten to arrest Egmont's private secretary.  You have made all needful preparations for securing the others who are specified?

Silva.  Rely upon us.  Their doom, like a well-calculated eclipse, will overtake them with terrible certainty.

Alva.  Have you had them all narrowly watched?

Silva  All.  Egmont especially.  He is the only one whose demeanour, since your arrival, remains unchanged. The live-long day he is now on one horse and now on another; he invites guests as usual, is merry and entertaining at table, plays at dice, shoots, and at night steals to his mistress.  The others, on the contrary, have made a manifest pause in their mode of life; they remain at home, and, from the outward aspect of their houses, you would imagine that there was a sick man within.

Alva.  To work then, ere they recover in spite of us.

Silva.  I shall bring them without fail.  In obedience to your commands we load them with officious honours; they are alarmed; cautiously, yet anxiously, they tender us their thanks, feel that flight would be the most prudent course, yet none venture to adopt it; they hesitate, are unable to work together, while the bond which unites them prevents their acting boldly as individuals.  They are anxious to withdraw themselves from suspicion, and thus only render themselves more obnoxious to it.  I already contemplate with joy the successful realization of your scheme.

Alva.  I rejoice only over what is accomplished, and not lightly over that; for there ever remains ground for serious and anxious thought.  Fortune is capricious; the common, the worthless, she oft-times ennobles, while she dishonours with a contemptible issue the most maturely-considered schemes.  Await the arrival of the princes, then order Gonrez to occupy the streets, and hasten yourself to arrest Egmont's secretary, and the others who are specified.  This done, return, and announce to my son that he may bring me the tidings in the council.

Silva.  I trust this evening I shall dare to appear in your presence.  (Alva *approaches his son, who has hitherto been standing in the gallery.*)  I dare not whisper it even to myself;

but my mind misgives me. The event will, I fear, be different from what he anticipates. I see before me spirits, who,
still and thoughtful, weigh in ebon scales the doom of princes
and of many thousands. Slowly the beam moves up and
down; deeply the judges appear to ponder; at length one
scale sinks, the other rises, breathed on by the caprice of destiny, and all is decided. [*Exit.*

ALVA (*advancing with his son*). How did you find the
town?

FERDINAND. All is again quiet. I rode as for pastime,
from street to street. Your well-distributed patrols hold fear
so tightly yoked, that she does not venture even to whisper.
The town resembles a plain when the lightning's glare
announces the impending storm: no bird, no beast is to be
seen, that is not stealing to a place of shelter.

ALVA. Has nothing further occurred?

FERDINAND. Egmont, with a few companions, rode into
the market-place; we exchanged greetings; he was mounted
on an unbroken charger, which excited my admiration. "Let
us hasten to break in our steeds," he exclaimed; " we shall
need them ere long!" He said that he should see me again
to-day; he is coming here, at your desire, to deliberate with
you.

ALVA. He will see you again.

FERDINAND. Among all the knights whom I know here,
he pleases me the best. I think we shall be friends.

ALVA. You are always rash and inconsiderate. I recognize in you the levity of your mother, which threw her
unconditionally into my arms. Appearances have already
allured you precipitately into many dangerous connexions.

FERDINAND. You will find me ever submissive.

ALVA. I pardon this inconsiderate kindness, this heedless
gaiety, in consideration of your youthful blood. Only forget
not on what mission I am sent, and what part in it I would
assign to you.

FERDINAND. Admonish me, and spare me not, when you
deem it needful.

ALVA. (*after a pause.*) My son!

FERDINAND. My father!

ALVA. The princes will be here anon; Orange and
Egmont. It is not mistrust that has withheld me till now,

from disclosing to you what is about to take place. They will not depart hence.

FERDINAND. What do you purpose?

ALVA. It has been resolved to arrest them.—You are astonished! Learn what you have to do; the reasons you shall know when all is accomplished. Time fails now to unfold them. With you alone I wish to deliberate on the weightiest, the most secret matters; a powerful bond holds us linked together; you are dear and precious to me; on you I would bestow everything. Not the habit of obedience alone would I impress upon you; I desire also to implant within your mind the power to realize, to execute, to command; to you I would bequeath a vast inheritance, to the king a most useful servant; I would endow you with the noblest of my possessions, that you may not be ashamed to appear among your brethren.

FERDINAND. How deeply am I indebted to you for this love, which you manifest for me alone, while a whole kingdom trembles before you.

ALVA. Now hear what is to be done. As soon as the princes have entered, every avenue to the palace will be guarded. This duty is confided to Gomez. Silva will hasten to arrest Egmont's secretary, together with those whom we hold most in suspicion. You, meanwhile, will take the command of the guards stationed at the gates and in the courts. Before all, take care to occupy the adjoining apartment with the trustiest soldiers. Wait in the gallery till Silva returns, then bring me any unimportant paper, as a signal that his commission is executed. Remain in the ante-chamber till Orange retires, follow him; I will detain Egmont here as though I had some further communication to make to him. At the end of the gallery demand Orange's sword, summon the guards, secure promptly the most dangerous man; I meanwhile will seize Egmont here.

FERDINAND. I obey, my father—for the first time with a heavy and an anxious heart.

ALVA. I pardon you; this is the first great day of your life.

*Enter* SILVA.

SILVA. A courier from Antwerp. Here is Orange's letter. He does not come.

ALVA.   Says the messenger so?

SILVA.   No, my own heart tells me.

ALVA.   In thee speaks my evil genius. (*after reading the letter, he makes a sign to the two, and they retire to the gallery.* ALVA *remains alone in front of the stage.*) He comes not! Till the last moment he delays declaring himself. He ventures not to come! So then, the cautious man, contrary to all expectation, is for once sagacious enough to lay aside his wonted caution. The hour moves on! Let the finger travel but a short space over the dial, and a great work is done or lost—irrevocably lost; for the opportunity can never be retrieved, nor can our intention remain concealed. Long had I maturely weighed everything, foreseen even this contingency, and firmly resolved in my own mind what, in that case, was to be done; and now, when I am called upon to act, I can with difficulty guard my mind from being again distracted by conflicting doubts. Is it expedient to seize the others if he escape me? · Shall I delay, and suffer Egmont to elude my grasp, together with his friends, and so many others who now, and perhaps for to-day only, are in my hands? How! Does destiny control even thee—the uncontrolable? How long matured! How well prepared! How great, how admirable the plan! How nearly had hope attained the goal! And now, at the decisive moment, thou art placed between two evils; as in a lottery, thou dost grasp in the dark future; what thou hast drawn remains still unrolled, to thee unknown whether it is a prize or a blank! (*He becomes attentive, like one who hears a noise, and steps to the window.*) 'Tis he! Egmont! Did thy steed bear thee hither so lightly, and started not at the scent of blood, at the spirit with the naked sword who received thee at the gate? Dismount! Lo, now thou hast one foot in the grave! And now both! Ay, caress him, and for the last time stroke his neck for the gallant service he has rendered thee. And for me no choice is left. The delusion, in which Egmont ventures here to-day, cannot a second time deliver him into my hands! Hark! (FERDINAND *and* SILVA *enter hastily.*) Obey my orders! I swerve not from my purpose. I shall detain Egmont here as best I may, till you bring me tidings from Silva. Then remain at hand. Thee, too, fate has robbed of the proud honour of arresting with thine own hand the king's greatest enemy. (*to* SILVA.) Be prompt! (*to* FERDINAND.) Advance to meet him.

> [ALVA *remains some moments alone, pacing the chamber in silence.*

*Enter* EGMONT.

EGMONT. I come to learn the king's commands; to hear what service he demands from our loyalty, which remains eternally devoted to him.

ALVA. He desires, before all, to hear your counsel.

EGMONT. Upon what subject? Does Orange come also? I thought to find him here.

ALVA. I regret that he fails us at this important crisis. The king desires your counsel, your opinion as to the best means of tranquillizing these states. He trusts indeed that you will zealously co-operate with him in quelling these disturbances, and in securing to these provinces the benefit of complete and permanent order.

EGMONT. You, my lord, should know better than I, that tranquillity is already sufficiently restored, and was still more so, till the appearance of fresh troops again agitated the public mind, and filled it anew with anxiety and alarm.

ALVA. You seem to intimate that it would have been more advisable if the king had not placed me in a position to interrogate you.

EGMONT. Pardon me! It is not for me to determine whether the king acted advisedly in sending the army hither, whether the might of his royal presence alone would not have operated more powerfully. The army is here, the king is not. But we should be most ungrateful were we to forget what we owe to the Regent. Let it be acknowledged! By her prudence and valour, by her judicious use of authority and force, of persuasion and finesse, she pacified the insurgents, and, to the astonishment of the world, succeeded, in the course of a few months, in bringing a rebellious people back to their duty.

ALVA. I deny it not. The insurrection is quelled; and the people appear to be already forced back within the bounds of obedience. But does it not depend upon their caprice alone to overstep these bounds? Who shall prevent them from again breaking loose? Where is the power capable of restraining them? Who will be answerable to us for their future loyalty and submission? Their own good will is the sole pledge we have.

Egmont. And is not the good-will of a people the surest, the noblest pledge? By heaven! when can a monarch hold himself more secure, ay, both against foreign and domestic foes, than when all can stand for one, and one for all?

Alva. You would not have us believe, however, that such is the case here at present?

Egmont. Let the king proclaim a general pardon; he will thus tranquillize the public mind; and it will be seen how speedily loyalty and affection will return, when confidence is restored.

Alva. How! And suffer those who have insulted the majesty of the king, who have violated the sanctuaries of our religion, to go abroad unchallenged! living witnesses that enormous crimes may be perpetrated with impunity!

Egmont. And ought not a crime of frenzy, of intoxication, to be excused, rather than horribly chastised? Especially when there is the sure hope, nay, more, where there is positive certainty, that the evil will never again recur? Would not sovereigns thus be more secure? Are not those monarchs most extolled by the world and by posterity, who can pardon, pity, despise an offence against their dignity? Are they not on that account likened to God himself, who is far too exalted to be assailed by every idle blasphemy?

Alva. And therefore, should the king maintain the honour of God and of religion, we the authority of the king. What the supreme power disdains to avert, it is our duty to avenge. Were I to counsel, no guilty person should live to rejoice in his impunity.

Egmont. Think you that you will be able to reach them all? Do we not daily hear that fear is driving them to and fro, and forcing them out of the land. The more wealthy will escape to other countries, with their property, their children, and their friends; while the poor will carry their industrious hands to our neighbours.

Alva. They will, if they cannot be prevented. It is on this account that the king desires counsel and aid from every prince, zealous co-operation from every stadtholder; not merely a description of the present posture of affairs, or conjectures as to what might take place were events suffered to hold on their course without interruption. To contemplate a mighty evil, to flatter oneself with hope, to trust to time, to strike a blow, like the clown in a play, so as to make a noise, and appear to do something, when in fact one would fain do nothing; is not such conduct calculated to awaken a suspicion that those who act thus contemplate with satisfaction a rebellion, which they would not indeed excite, but which they are by no means unwilling to encourage?

EGMONT. (*about to break forth, restrains himself, and after a brief pause, speaks with composure.*) Every design is not immediately obvious, and a man's intentions are often misconstrued. It is widely rumoured, however, that the object which the king has in view is not so much to govern the provinces according to uniform and clearly defined laws, to maintain the majesty of religion, and to give his people universal peace, as unconditionally to subjugate them, to rob them of their ancient rights, to appropriate their possessions, to curtail the fair privileges of the nobles, for whose sake alone they are ready to serve him with life and limb. Religion, it is said, is merely a splendid device, behind which every dangerous design may be contrived with the greater ease; the prostrate crowds adore the sacred symbols pictured there, while behind lurks the fowler ready to ensnare them.

ALVA. Must I hear this from you?

EGMONT. I speak not my own sentiments! I but repeat what is loudly rumoured, and uttered here and there by rich and poor, by wise men and fools. The Netherlanders fear a double yoke, and who will be surety to them for their liberty?

ALVA. Liberty! A fair word when rightly understood. What liberty would they have? What is the freedom of the most free? To do right! And in that the monarch will not hinder them. No! No! They imagine themselves enslaved, when they have not the power to injure themselves and others. Would it not be better to abdicate at once, rather than rule such a people? When the country is threatened by foreign invaders, the citizens, occupied only with their immediate interests, bestow no thought upon the advancing foe, and when the king requires their aid, they quarrel among themselves, and thus, as it were, conspire with the enemy. Far better is it to circumscribe their power, to control and guide them for their good, as children are controlled and guided. Trust me, a people grows neither old nor wise, a people remains always in its infancy.

EGMONT. How rarely does a king attain wisdom! And is it not fit that the many should confide their interests to the many rather than to the one? And not even to the one, but to the few servants of the one, men who have grown old under the eyes of their master. To grow wise, it seems, is the exclusive privilege of these favoured individuals.

ALVA. Perhaps for the very reason that they are not left to themselves.

EGMONT. And therefore they would fain leave no one else to his own guidance. Let them do what they like, however; I have replied to your questions, and I repeat, the measures you propose will never do! They cannot succeed! I know my countrymen. They are men worthy to tread God's earth; each complete in himself, a little king, steadfast, active, capable, loyal, attached to ancient customs. It may be difficult to win their confidence, but it is easy to retain it. Firm and unbending! They may be crushed, but not subdued.

ALVA. (*who during this speech has looked round several times.*) Would you venture to repeat what you have uttered, in the king's presence?

EGMONT. It were the worse, if in his presence I were restrained by fear! The better for him, and for his people, if he inspired me with confidence, if he encouraged me to give yet freer utterance to my thoughts.

ALVA. What is profitable, I can listen to as well as he.

EGMONT. I would say to him—'Tis easy for the shepherd to drive before him a flock of sheep; the ox draws the plough without opposition; but if you would ride the noble steed, you must study his thoughts, you must require nothing unreasonable, nor unreasonably, from him. The citizen desires to retain his ancient constitution; to be governed by his own countrymen; and why? Because he knows in that case how he shall be ruled, because he can rely upon their disinterestedness, upon their sympathy with his fate.

ALVA. And ought not the Regent to be empowered to alter these ancient usages? Should not this constitute his fairest privilege? What is permanent in this world? And

shall the constitution of a state alone remain unchanged?
Must not every relation alter in the course of time? And an
ancient constitution become the source of a thousand evils,
because not adapted to the present condition of the people?
These ancient rights afford, doubtless, convenient loopholes,
through which the crafty and the powerful may creep, and
wherein they may lie concealed, to the injury of the people
and of the entire community; and it is on this account, I fear,
that they are held in such high esteem.

EGMONT. And these arbitrary changes, these unlimited
encroachments of the supreme power, are they not indications
that one will permit himself to do what is forbidden to
thousands? The monarch would alone be free, that he may
have it in his power to gratify his every wish, to realize his
every thought. And though we should confide in him as a
good and virtuous sovereign, will he be answerable to us for
his successors? That none who come after him shall rule
without consideration, without forbearance! And who would
deliver us from absolute caprice, should he send hither his
servants, his minions, who, without knowledge of the country
and its requirements, should govern according to their own
good pleasure, meet with no opposition, and know themselves
exempt from all responsibility?

ALVA (*who has meanwhile again looked round*). There
is nothing more natural than that a king should choose to
retain the power in his own hands, and that he should select
as the instruments of his authority, those who best understand him, who desire to understand him, and who will
unconditionally execute his will.

EGMONT. And just as natural is it, that the citizen should
prefer being governed by one born and reared in the same
land, whose notions of right and wrong are in harmony with
his own, and whom he can regard as his brother.

ALVA. And yet the noble, methinks, has shared rather
unequally with these brethren of his.

EGMONT. That took place centuries ago, and is now sub-
mitted to without envy. But should new men, whose presence is not needed in the country, be sent, to enrich themselves a second time, at the cost of the nation; should the
people see themselves exposed to their bold unscrupulous rapa-
city, it would excite a ferment that would not soon be quelled?

ALVA. You utter words to which I ought not to listen ;—I too am a foreigner.

EGMONT. That they are spoken in your presence is a sufficient proof that they have no reference to you.

ALVA. Be that as it may, I would rather not hear them from you. The king sent me here in the hope that I should obtain the support of the nobles. The king wills, and will have his will obeyed. After profound deliberation, he at length discerns what course will best promote the welfare of the people ; matters cannot be permitted to go on as heretofore ; it is his intention to limit their power for their own good ; if necessary, to force upon them their salvation ; to sacrifice the more dangerous citizens, that the rest may find repose, and enjoy in peace the blessing of a wise government. This is his resolve ; this I am commissioned to announce to the nobles ; and in his name I require from them advice, not as to the course to be pursued,—on that he is resolved,—but as to the best means of carrying his purpose into effect.

EGMONT. Your words, alas, justify the fears of the people, the fears of all ! The king has then resolved as no sovereign ought to resolve. In order to govern his subjects more easily, he would crush, subvert, nay, ruthlessly destroy, their strength, their spirit, and their self-respect ! He would violate the core of their individuality, doubtless with the view of promoting their happiness. He would annihilate them, that they may assume a new, a different shape. Oh ! if his purpose be good, he is fatally misguided ! It is not the king whom we resist ;—we but place ourselves in the way of the monarch, who, unhappily, is about to take the first rash step in a wrong direction.

ALVA. Such being your sentiments, it were a vain attempt for us to endeavour to agree. You must indeed think poorly of the king, and contemptibly of his counsellors, if you imagine that everything has not already been thought of and maturely weighed. I have no commission a second time to balance conflicting arguments. From the people I demand submission ;—and from you, their leaders and princes, I demand counsel and support, as pledges of this unconditional duty.

EGMONT. Demand our heads and your object is attained ; to a noble soul it must be indifferent whether he stoop his neck to such a yoke, or lay it upon the block. I have spoken much to little purpose. I have agitated the air, but accomplished nothing.

*Enter* FERDINAND.

FERDINAND. Pardon my intrusion. Here is a letter, the bearer of which urgently demands an answer.

ALVA. Allow me to peruse its contents. (*Steps aside.*)

FERDINAND (*to* EGMONT). 'Tis a noble steed that your people have brought for you.

EGMONT. I have seen worse. I have had him some time; I think of parting with him. If he pleases you we shall probably soon agree as to the price.

FERDINAND. We will think about it.

ALVA (*motions to his son, who retires to the back-ground*).

EGMONT. Farewell! Allow me to retire; for by heaven I know not what more I can say.

ALVA. Fortunately for you, chance prevents you from making a fuller disclosure of your sentiments. You incautiously lay bare the recesses of your heart, and your own lips furnish evidence against you, more fatal than could be produced by your bitterest adversary.

EGMONT. This reproach disturbs me not. I know my own heart; I know with what honest zeal I am devoted to the king; I know that my allegiance is more true than that of many who, in his service, seek only to serve themselves. I regret that our discussion should terminate so unsatisfactorily, and trust that in spite of our opposing views, the service of the king, our master, and the welfare of our country, may speedily unite us; another conference, the presence of the princes who to-day are absent, may, perchance, in a more propitious moment, accomplish what at present appears impossible. In this hope I take my leave.

ALVA (*who at the same time makes a sign to* FERDINAND). Hold, Egmont!—Your sword!—(*The centre door opens and discloses the gallery, which is occupied with guards, who remain motionless.*)

EGMONT (*after a pause of astonishment*). Was this then your intention? Was it for this purpose that I was summoned here? (*Grasping his sword as if to defend himself.*) Am I then weaponless?

ALVA. The king commands. You are my prisoner. (*At the same time guards enter from both sides.*)

Egmont (*after a pause*). The king?—Orange! Orange! (*after a pause, resigning his sword.*) Take it! It has been employed far oftener in defending the cause of my king, than in protecting this breast.
(*He retires by the centre door, followed by the guard and* Alva's *son.* Alva *remains standing while the curtain falls.*)

## ACT THE FIFTH.

*A street. Twilight.*

Clara. Brackenburg. Citizens.

Brackenburg. Dearest, for heaven's sake, what would'st thou do!

Clara. Come with me, Brackenburg! You cannot know the people, we are certain to rescue him; for what can equal their love for him? I could swear it, the breast of every citizen burns with the desire to deliver him, to avert danger from a life so precious, and to restore freedom to the most free. Come, a voice only is wanting to call them together. In their souls the memory is still fresh of all they owe him, and well they know that his mighty arm alone shields them from destruction. For his sake, for their own sake, they must peril everything. And what do we peril? At most, our lives, which, if he perish, are not worth preserving.

Brackenburg. Unhappy girl! Thou seest not the power that holds us fettered as with bands of iron.

Clara. To me it does not appear invincible. Let us not lose time in idle words. Here come some of our old, honest, valiant citizens! Hark ye, friends! Neighbours! Hark!—Say, how fares it with Egmont?

Carpenter. What does the girl want? Tell her to hold her peace.

Clara. Step nearer, that we may speak low, till we are united and more strong. Not a moment is to be lost! Audacious tyranny, that dared to fetter him, already lifts the dagger against his life. Oh, my friends! With the advancing twilight my anxiety grows more intense. I dread this night. Come! Let us disperse; let us hasten from quarter to quarter, and call out the citizens. Let every one grasp his

,ancient weapons.    In the market-place we meet again, and every one will be carried onward by our gathering stream. The enemy will see themselves surrounded, overwhelmed, and be compelled to yield.    How can a handful of slaves resist us ?    And he will return among us, he will see himself rescued, and can for once thank us, us, who are already so deeply in his debt.    He will behold, perchance, ay doubtless, he will again behold the morn's red dawn in the free heavens.

CARPENTER.    What ails thee, maiden ?

CLARA.    Can ye misunderstand me ?    I speak of the Count ! I speak of Egmont.

JETTER.    Speak not the name, 'tis deadly.

CLARA.    Not speak his name ?    Not Egmont's name ?    Is it not on every tongue ?    Does it not appear everywhere legibly inscribed ?    I read it emblazoned in golden letters among the stars.    Not utter it ?    What mean ye ?    Friends !    Good, kind neighbours ;  ye are dreaming ;  collect yourselves.    Gaze not upon me with those fixed and anxious looks !    Cast not such timid glances on every side !    I but give utterance to the wish of all.    Is not my voice the voice of your own hearts ?    Who, in this fearful night, ere he seeks his restless couch, but on bended knee, will in earnest prayer seek to wrest his life as a cherished boon from heaven ?    Ask each other !    Let each ask his own heart !    And who but exclaims with me,—" Egmont's liberty, or death ! "

JETTER.    God help us !    This is a sad business.

CLARA.    Stay !    Stay !    Shrink not away at the sound of his name, to meet whom ye were wont to press forward so joyously !—When rumour announced his approach, when the cry arose, " Egmont comes !    He comes from Ghent ! "—then happy indeed were those citizens who dwelt in the streets through which he was to pass.    And when the neighing of his steed was heard, did not every one throw aside his work, while a ray of hope and joy, like a sunbeam from his countenance, stole over the toilworn faces that peered from every window.    Then, as ye stood in the doorways, ye would lift up your children in your arms, and pointing to him, exclaim : " See, that is Egmont, he who towers above the rest !    'Tis from him that ye must look for better times than those your poor fathers have known."    Let not your children inquire at

some future day, " Where is he? Where are the better times
ye promised us?"—Thus we waste the time in idle words!
do nothing,—betray him.

SOEST.   Shame on thee, Brackenburg! Let her not run on
thus; prevent the mischief.

BRACKENBURG.   Dear Clara! Let us go! What will your
mother say? Perchance—

CLARA.   Think you I am a child, a lunatic? What avails
perchance?—With no vain hope can you hide from me this
dreadful certainty.

Ye shall hear me and ye will: for I see it, ye are overwhelmed, ye cannot hearken to the voice of your own hearts.
Through the present peril cast but one glance into the past,
—the recent past. Send your thoughts forward into the
future. Could ye live, would ye live, were he to perish?
With him expires the last breath of freedom. What was he
not to you? For whose sake did he expose himself to the
direst perils? His blood flowed, his wounds were healed for
you alone. A dungeon now confines that mighty spirit that
upheld you all, while around him hover the terrors of secret
assassination. Perhaps, he thinks of you,—perhaps he hopes
in you,— he who has been accustomed only to grant favours
to others and to fulfil their prayers.

CARPENTER.   Come, gossip.

CLARA.   I have neither the arms, nor the strength of a
man; but I have that which ye all lack—courage and contempt of danger. Oh that my breath could kindle your
souls! That, pressing you to this bosom, I could arouse and
animate you! Come! I will march in your midst!—As a
waving banner, though weaponless, leads on a gallant army
of warriors, so shall my spirit hover, like a flame, over your
ranks, while love and courage shall unite the dispersed and
wavering multitude into a terrible host.

JETTER.   Take her away, I pity her, poor thing.

*[Exeunt Citizens.*

BRACKENBURG.   Clara! See you not where we are?

CLARA.   Where? Under the dome of heaven, which has
so often seemed to arch itself more gloriously as the noble
Egmont passed beneath it. From these windows I have seen
them look forth, four or five heads one above the other; at
these doors the cowards have stood, bowing and scraping, if the

hero but chanced to look down upon them! Oh how dear they were to me, when they honoured him. Had he been a tyrant they might have turned with indifference from his fall; but they loved him! O ye hands, so prompt to wave caps in his honour, can ye not grasp a sword? And yet, Brackenburg, it is for us to chide them? These arms that have so often embraced him, what do they for him now? Stratagem has accomplished so much in the world. You know the ancient castle, every passage, every secret way.—Nothing is impossible,—suggest some plan.—

BRACKENBURG. If you would but come home.

CLARA. Well.

BRACKENBURG. There at the corner I see Alva's guard; let the voice of reason penetrate to your heart! Do you deem me a coward? Do you doubt that for your sake I would peril my life? Here we are both mad, I as well as you. Do you not perceive that your scheme is impracticable? Oh be calm! You are beside yourself.

CLARA. Beside myself! Horrible. You Brackenburg are beside yourself. When you hailed the hero with loud acclaim, called him your friend, your hope, your refuge, shouted vivats as he passed;—then I stood in my corner, half opened the window, concealed myself while I listened, and my heart beat higher than yours who greeted him so loudly. Now it again beats higher! In the hour of peril you conceal yourselves, deny him, and feel not, that if he perish, you are lost.

BRACKENBURG. Come home.

CLARA. Home?

BRACKENBURG. Recollect yourself! Look around! These are the streets in which you were wont to appear only on the sabbath day, when you walked modestly to church; where, over-decorous perhaps, you were displeased if I but joined you with a kindly greeting. And now you stand, speak, and act before the eyes of the whole world. Recollect yourself, love! How can this avail us?

CLARA. Home! Yes, I remember. Come, Brackenburg, let us go home! Know you where my home lies?

[*Exeunt.*

### A Prison.

*Lighted by a lamp, a couch in the back-ground.*

EGMONT. (*alone.*)

Old friend ! Ever faithful sleep, dost thou too forsake me, like my other friends?  How wert thou wont of yore to descend unsought upon my free brow, cooling my temples as with a myrtle wreath of love !  Amidst the din of battle, on the waves of life, I rested in thine arms, breathing lightly as a growing boy.  When tempests whistled through the leaves and boughs, when the summits of the lofty trees swung creaking in the blast, the inmost core of my heart remained unmoved.  What agitates thee now ?  What shakes thy firm and steadfast mind ?  I feel it, 'tis the sound of the murderous axe, gnawing at thy root.  Yet I stand erect, but an inward shudder runs through my frame.  Yes, it prevails, this treacherous power ; it undermines the firm, the lofty stem, and ere the bark withers, thy verdant crown falls crashing to the earth.

Yet wherefore now, thou who hast so often chased the weightiest cares like bubbles from thy brow, wherefore can'st thou not dissipate this dire foreboding which incessantly haunts thee in a thousand different shapes.  Since when hast thou trembled at the approach of death, amid whose varying forms, thou wert wont calmly to dwell, as with the other shapes of this familiar earth.  But 'tis not he, the sudden foe, to encounter whom the sound bosom emulously pants ;—'tis the dungeon, dread emblem of the grove, revolting alike to the hero, and the coward.  How intolerable I used to feel it, in the stately hall, girt round by gloomy walls, when, seated on my cushioned chair, in the solemn assembly of the princes, questions, which scarcely required deliberation, were overlaid with endless discussions, while the rafters of the ceiling seemed to stifle and oppress me.  Then I would hurry forth as soon as possible, fling myself upon my horse with deep-drawn breath, and away to the wide champaigne, man's natural element, where, exhaling from the earth, nature's richest treasures are poured forth around us, while, from the wide heavens, the stars shed down their blessings through the still air ; where, like earthborn giants, we spring aloft, invigorated by our mother's touch ; where the energies of our

being throb in every vein; where the soul of the young
hunter glows with the desire to overtake, to conquer, to capture, to possess; where the warrior, with rapid stride,
assumes his inborn right to dominion over the world; and,
with terrible liberty, sweeps like a desolating hailstorm over
field and grove, knowing no boundaries, traced by the hand
of man.

Thou art but a shadow, a dream of the happiness I so long
possessed; where has treacherous fate conducted thee? Did
she deny thee, to meet the rapid stroke of never-shunned
death, in the open face of day, only to prepare for thee a foretaste of the grave, in the midst of their loathsome corruption?
How revoltingly its rank odour exhales from these damp
stones! Life stagnates, and my foot shrinks from the couch
as from the grave.

Oh care, care! Thou who dost begin prematurely the
work of murder,—forbear!—Since when has Egmont been
alone, so utterly alone in the world? 'Tis doubt renders thee
insensible, not happiness. The justice of the king, in which,
through life thou hast confided, the friendship of the Regent,
which, thou may'st confess it, was akin to love,—have these
suddenly vanished, like a meteor of the night, and left thee
alone upon thy gloomy path? Will not Orange, at the head
of thy friends, contrive some daring scheme? Will not the
people assemble, and with gathering might, attempt the
rescue of their faithful friend?

Ye walls, which thus gird me round, separate me not from
the well intentioned zeal of so many kindly souls. And may
the courage with which my glance was wont to inspire them,
now return again from their hearts to mine. Yes! they
assemble in thousands! they come! they stand beside me!
their prayers rise to heaven, and implore a miracle; and if
no angel stoops for my deliverance, I see them grasp eagerly
their lance and sword. The gates are forced, the bolts are
riven, the walls fall beneath their conquering hands, and
Egmont advances joyously, to hail the freedom of the rising
morn! How many well known faces receive me with loud
acclaim! Oh Clara! wert thou a man, I should see thee here
the very first, and thank thee for that which it is galling to
owe even to a king—liberty.

### *Clara's House.*

#### CLARA.

CLARA. (*enters from her chamber with a lamp and a glass of water; she places the glass upon the table and steps to the window*). Brackenburg, is it you? What noise was that? No one yet? No one! I will set the lamp in the window, that he may see that I am still awake, that I still watch for him. He promised me tidings. Tidings? horrible certainty!—Egmont condemned!—What tribunal has the right to summon him?—And they dare to condemn him!—Is it the king who condemns him, or the duke? And the Regent withdraws herself! Orange hesitates, as do all his friends!—Is this the world, of whose fickleness and treachery I have heard so much, and as yet experienced nothing? Is this the world?—Who could be so base as to bear malice against one so dear? Could villainy itself be audacious enough to overwhelm with sudden destruction the object of a nation's homage? Yet so it is—it is—Oh Egmont, I held thee safe before God and man, safe as in my arms! What was I to thee? Thou hast called me thine, my whole being was devoted to thee. What am I now? In vain I stretch out my hand to the toils that environ thee. Thou helpless, and I free!—Here is the key that unlocks my chamber door. My going out and my coming in, depend upon my own caprice; yet, alas, to aid thee I am powerless!—Oh bind me that I may not go mad; hurl me into the deepest dungeon, that I may dash my head against the damp walls, groan for freedom, and dream how I would rescue him if fetters did not hold me bound. —Now I am free, and in freedom lies the anguish of impotence —Conscious of my own existence, yet unable to stir a limb in his behalf, alas! even this insignificant portion of thy being, thy Clara, is, like thee, a captive, and separated from thee, consumes her expiring energies in the agonies of death.—I hear a stealthy step,—a cough—Brackenburg,—'tis he!—Kind, unhappy man, thy destiny remains ever the same; thy love opens to thee the door at night,—alas! to what a doleful meeting.

*Enter* BRACKENBURG.

CLARA. You look so pale, so terrified! Speak, Brackenburg! What is the matter?

BRACKENBURG.  I have sought you through perils and circuitous paths.  The principal streets are occupied with troops;—through lanes and by-ways I have stolen to you!

CLARA.  Tell me what is going on.

BRACKENBURG.  (*seating himself*).  Oh Clara, let me weep, I loved him not.  He was the rich man who lured to better pasture the poor man's solitary lamb.  Yet I cursed him not, God has created me with a true and tender heart.  My life was consumed in anguish, and each day I hoped would end my misery.

CLARA.  Let that be forgotten, Brackenburg!  Forget thyself.  Speak to me of him!  Is it true?  Is he condemned?

BRACKENBURG.  He is!  I know it.

CLARA.  And still lives?

BRACKENBURG.  Yes, he still lives.

CLARA.  How can you be sure of that?  Tyranny murders its victim in the night!  His blood flows concealed from every eye.  The people, stunned and bewildered, lie buried in sleep, dream of deliverance, dream of the fulfilment of their impotent wishes, while, indignant at our supineness, his spirit abandons the world.  He is no more!  Deceive me not; deceive not thyself!

BRACKENBURG.  No,—he lives! and the Spaniards, alas, are preparing for the people, on whom they are about to trample, a terrible spectacle, in order to crush, by a violent blow, each heart that yet pants for freedom.

CLARA.  Proceed!  Calmly pronounce my death-warrant also!  Near and more near I approach that blessed land, and already from those realms of peace, I feel the breath of consolation.  Say on.

BRACKENBURG.  From casual words, dropped here and there by the guards, I learned that secretly in the market-place they were preparing some terrible spectacle.  Through by-ways and familiar lanes I stole to my cousin's house, and from a back window, looked out upon the market place.  Torches waved to and fro, in the hands of a wide circle of Spanish soldiers.  I strained my unaccustomed sight, and out of the darkness there arose before me a scaffold, dark, spacious, and lofty!  The sight filled me with horror.  Several persons were employed in covering with black cloth such portions of the wood-work as yet remain exposed. The steps were covered last, also with black;—I saw it all. They seemed preparing for the celebration of some horrible sacrifice. A white crucifix, that shone like silver through the night, was raised on one side. As I gazed, the terrible conviction strengthened in my mind. Scattered torches still gleamed here and there; gradually they flickered and went out. Suddenly the hideous birth of night returned into its mother's womb.

CLARA. Hush, Brackenburg! Be still! Let this veil rest upon my soul. The spectres are vanished; and thou, gentle night, lend thy mantle to the inwardly fermenting earth, she will no longer endure the loathsome burden, shuddering, she rends open her yawning chasms, and with a crash swallows the murderous scaffold. And that God, whom in their rage they have insulted, sends down his angel from on high; at the hallowed touch of the messenger bolts and bars fly back; he pours around our friend a flood of splendour, and leads him gently through the night to liberty. My path leads also through the darkness to meet him.

BRACKENBURG (*detaining her*). My child, whither would'st thou go? What would'st thou do.

CLARA. Softly, my friend, lest some one should awake! Lest we should awake ourselves! Know'st thou this phial, Brackenburg? I took it from thee once in jest, when thou. as was thy wont, didst threaten, in thy impatience, to end thy days.—And now my friend—

BRACKENBURG. In the name of all the saints!

CLARA. Thou can'st not hinder me. Death is my portion! Grudge me not the quiet and easy death which thou had'st prepared for thyself. Give me thine hand! At the moment when I unclose that dismal portal through which there is no return, I may tell thee, with this pressure of the hand, how sincerely I have loved, how deeply I have pitied thee. My Brother died young; I chose thee to fill his place; thy heart rebelled, thou didst torment thyself and me, demanding with still increasing fervour, that which fate had not destined for thee. Forgive me and farewell! Let me call thee brother! 'Tis a name that embraces many names. Receive, with a true heart, the last fair token of the departing spirit—take this kiss. Death unites all, Brackenburg—us too it will unite!

BRACKENBURG.   Let me then die with thee !  Share it !  oh share it !  There is enough to extinguish two lives.

CLARA.   Hold !  Thou must live, thou can'st live.—Support my mother, who, without thee, would be a prey to want. Be to her what I can no longer be, live together, and weep for me.   Weep for our fatherland, and for him who could alone have upheld it.   The present generation must still endure this bitter woe ; vengeance itself could not obliterate it. Poor souls, live on, through this gap in time.   To-day the world suddenly stands still, its course is arrested, and my pulse will beat but for a few minutes longer.   Farewell !

BRACKENBURG.   Oh, live with us, as we live only for thy sake !  In taking thine own life thou wilt take ours also ; still live and suffer.   We will stand by thee, nothing shall sever us from thy side, and love, with ever-watchful solicitude, shall prepare for thee the sweetest consolation in its loving arms.   Be ours !  Ours !  I dare not say, mine.

CLARA.   Hush, Brackenburg !  You know not what chord you touch.   Where you see hope, I see only despair.

BRACKENBURG.   Share hope with the living !  Pause on the brink of the precipice, cast one glance into the gulf below, and then look back on us.

CLARA.   I have conquered ; call me not back to the struggle.

BRACKENBURG.   Thou art stunned ; enveloped in night thou seekest the abyss.   Every light is not yet extinguished, yet many days !——

CLARA.   Alas !  Alas !  Cruelly thou dost rend the veil from before mine eyes.   Yes, the day will dawn !  Despite its misty shroud it needs must dawn.   The citizen gazes timidly from his window, night leaves behind an ebon speck ; he looks, and the scaffold looms fearfully in the morning light.   With re-awakened anguish the desecrated image of the Saviour lifts to the Father its imploring eyes. The sun veils his beams, he will not mark the hero's death-hour.   Slowly the fingers go their round—one hour strikes after another—hold !  Now is the time .  The thought of the morning scares me into the grave.   [*She goes to the window as if to look out, and drinks secretly.*

BRACKENBURG.   Clara !  Clara !

CLARA.   (*goes to the table, and drinks water.*)   Here is the

remainder. I invite thee not to follow me. Do as thou
wilt; farewell. Extinguish this lamp silently and without
delay; I am going to rest. Steal quietly away, close the
door after thee. Be still! Wake not my mother! Go,
save thyself, if thou wouldst not be taken for my murderer.

[Exit.

BRACKENBURG. She leaves me for the last time as she
has ever done. What human soul could conceive how
cruelly she lacerates the heart that loves her. She leaves
me to myself, leaves me to choose between life and death,
and both are alike hateful to me. To die alone! Weep ye
tender souls! Fate has no sadder doom than mine. She
shares with me the death-potion, yet sends me from her side!
She draws me after her, yet thrusts me back into life! Oh,
Egmont, how glorious is thy lot! She goes before thee!
From her hand thou wilt receive the victor's crown. She
will bring heaven itself to meet thy departing spirit. And
shall I follow? Again to stand aloof? To carry this in-
extinguishable jealousy even to yon distant realms? Earth
is no longer a tarrying place for me, and hell and heaven
offer equal torture. How welcome to the wretched the dread
hand of annihilation! [Exit.

[The scene remains some time unchanged. Music sounds,
indicating CLARA'S death; the lamp which BRACKEN-
BURG had forgotten to extinguish, flares up once or
twice, and then suddenly expires. The scene changes to

A prison.

EGMONT is discovered sleeping on a couch. A rustling of
keys is heard; the door opens; servants enter with torches;
FERDINAND and SILVA follow, accompanied by soldiers.
EGMONT starts from his sleep.

EGMONT. Who are ye that thus rudely banish slumber
from my eyes? What mean these vague and insolent
glances? Why this fearful procession? With what dream
of horror come ye to delude my half awakened soul?

SILVA. The duke sends us to announce your sentence.

EGMONT. Do ye also bring the headsman who is to
execute it?

SILVA.   Listen, and you will know the doom that awaits you.

EGMONT.   It is in keeping with the rest of your infamous proceedings.   Alike conceived and executed in the night, so would this audacious act of injustice shroud itself from observation!   Step boldly forth, thou who dost bear the sword concealed beneath thy mantle; here is my head, the freest ever doomed by tyranny to the block.

SILVA.   You err!   The righteous judges who have condemned you, will not conceal their sentence from the light of day.

EGMONT.   Then does their audacity exceed all imagination and belief.

SILVA.   (*takes the sentence from an attendant, unfolds it, and reads.*)   "In the king's name, and invested by his majesty with authority to judge all his subjects, of whatever rank, not excepting the knights of the Golden Fleece, we declare——"

EGMONT.   Can the king transfer that authority?

SILVA.   "We declare, after a strict and legal investigation. you, Henry, Count Egmont, Prince of Gaure, guilty of high treason, and pronounce your sentence :—That at early dawn you be led from this prison to the market-place, and that there, in sight of the people, and as a warning to traitors, your head be severed from your body.   Given at Brussels." (*date and year so indistinctly read as to be imperfectly heard by the audience.*)   "Ferdinand, Duke of Alva, president of the tribunal of twelve."

You know your doom.   Brief time remains for you to prepare for the impending stroke, to arrange your affairs, and to take leave of your friends.

[*Exit* SILVA, *with followers.*   FERDINAND *remains with two torch-bearers.   The stage is dimly lighted.*

EGMONT.   (*stands for a time, as if buried in thought, and allows* SILVA *to retire without looking round.   He imagines himself alone, and, on raising his eyes, beholds* ALVA's *son.*) Thou tarriest here?   Wouldst thou, by thy presence, augment my amazement, my horror?   Wouldst thou carry to thy father the welcome tidings that thou hast seen me overpowered by womanish despair?   Go, tell him that he deceives neither the world nor me.   At first it will be whispered cautiously behind his back, then spoken more and more loudly, and when, at some future day, the ambitious man descends from his proud eminence, a thousand voices will proclaim—that 'twas not the welfare of the state, nor the honour of the king, nor the tranquillity of the provinces, that brought him hither. For his own selfish ends he, the warrior, has counselled war, that the value of his services might be enhanced. He has excited this monstrous insurrection .that his presence might be deemed necessary in order to quell it. And I fall a victim to his mean hatred, his contemptible envy. Yes, I know it, dying and mortally wounded I may utter it; long has the proud man envied me, long has he meditated and planned my ruin.

Even then, when still young, we played at dice together, and the heaps of gold passed rapidly from his side to mine, he would look on with affected composure, while inwardly consumed with rage, more at my success than at his own loss. Well do I remember the fiery glance, the treacherous pallor that overspread his features, when, at a public festival, we shot for a wager before assembled thousands. He challenged me, and both nations stood by; Spaniards and Netherlanders wagered on either side; I was the victor; his ball missed, mine hit the mark, and the air was rent by acclamations from my friends. His shot now hits me. Tell him that I know this, that I know him, that the world despises every trophy that a paltry spirit erects for itself by base and surreptitious arts. And thou! If it be possible for a son to swerve from the manners of his father, practise shame betimes, while thou art compelled to feel shame for him whom thou wouldst fain revere with thy whole heart.

FERDINAND. I listen without interrupting thee! Thy reproaches fall like blows upon a helm of steel. I feel the shock, but I am armed. They strike, but do not wound me; I am sensible only to the anguish that lacerates my heart. Alas! Alas! Have I lived to witness such a scene? Am I sent hither to behold a spectacle like this?

EGMONT. Dost thou break out into lamentations! What moves, what agitates thee thus? Is it a late remorse at having lent thyself to this infamous conspiracy? Thou art so young, thy exterior is so prepossessing. Thy demeanour towards me was so friendly. so unreserved! So long as I

beheld thee, I was reconciled with thy father; and crafty,
ay, more crafty than he, thou hast lured me into the toils.
Thou art the wretch! The monster! Whoso confides in
him, does so at his own peril; but who could apprehend
danger in trusting thee? Go! Go! Rob me not of the
few moments that are left to me! Go, that I may collect my
thoughts, forget the world, and thee, first of all!

FERDINAND. What can I say! I stand, and gaze on
thee, yet see thee not; I am scarcely conscious of my own
existence. Shall I seek to excuse myself? Shall I aver that
it was not till the last moment that I was made aware of my
father's intentions? That I acted as the constrained, the
passive instrument of his will? What signifies now the
opinion thou mayst entertain of me? Thou art lost; and I,
miserable wretch, stand here but to assure thee of it, and to
lament thy doom.

EGMONT. What strange voice, what unexpected consolation comes thus to cheer my passage to the tomb? Thou,
the son of my first, of almost my only enemy, thou dost pity
me, thou art not associated with my murderers? Speak!
In what light must I regard thee?

FERDINAND. Cruel father! Yes, I recognize thy nature
in this command. Thou didst know my heart, my disposition, which thou hast so often censured as the inheritance of
a tender-hearted mother. To mould me into thine own likeness thou hast sent me hither. Thou dost compel me to
behold this man on the verge of the yawning grave, in the
grasp of an arbitrary doom, that I may experience the pro-
foundest anguish; that thus, rendered callous to every fate,
I may henceforth meet every event with a heart unmoved.

EGMONT. I am amazed! Be calm! Act and speak like
a man.

FERDINAND. Oh, that I were a woman! That they
might say—what moves, what agitates thee? Tell me of a
greater, a more monstrous crime, make me the spectator of a
more direful deed; I will thank thee, I will say this was
nothing.

EGMONT. Thou dost forget thyself. Consider where thou
art?

FERDINAND. Let this passion rage, let me give vent to
my anguish. I will not seem composed when my whole

inner being is convulsed.   Must I behold thee here?   Thee?
It is horrible?   Thou understandest me not!   How shouldst
thou understand me?   Egmont!   Egmont!

*[Falling on his neck.*

EGMONT.   Explain this mystery.

FERDINAND.   It is no mystery.

EGMONT.   How can the fate of a mere stranger thus
deeply move thee?

FERDINAND.   Not a stranger!   Thou art no stranger to
me.   Thy name it was that, even from my boyhood, shone
before me like a star in heaven?   How often have I made
inquiries concerning thee, and listened to the story of thy
deeds.   The youth is the hope of the boy, the man of the
youth.   Thus didst thou walk before me, ever before me;
I saw thee without envy, and followed after, step by step;
at length I hoped to see thee—I saw, and my heart embraced
thee.   I had destined thee for myself, and when I beheld
thee, I made choice of thee anew.   I hoped now to know
thee, to associate with thee, to be thy friend—'tis over, and
I meet thee here!

EGMONT.   My friend, if it can be any comfort to thee, be
assured that the very moment we met, my heart was drawn
towards thee.   Now listen!   Let us exchange a few quiet
words; is it the stern, the settled purpose of thy father to
take my life?

FERDINAND.   It is.

EGMONT.   This sentence is not a mere scarecrow, designed
to terrify me, to punish me through fear and intimidation, to
humiliate me, that he may then raise me again by the royal
favour?

FERDINAND.   Alas, no!   At first I flattered myself with
this delusive hope, and even then my heart was filled with
anguish to behold thee thus.   Thy doom is real!   Is certain!
I cannot command myself.   Who will counsel, who will aid
me to meet the inevitable?

EGMONT.   Listen!   If thy heart is impelled so powerfully
in my favour, if thou dost abhor the tyranny that holds me
fettered, then deliver me!   The moments are precious.   Thou
art the son of the all-powerful, and thou hast power thyself.
Let us fly!   I know the roads; the means of effecting our
escape cannot be unknown to thee.   These walls, a few shor*

miles, alone separate us from my friends. Loose these fetters, conduct me to them; be ours. The king, on some future day, will doubtless thank my deliverer. Now he is taken by surprise, or perchance he is ignorant of the whole proceeding. Thy father ventures on this daring step, and majesty, though horror-struck at the deed, must needs sanction the irrevocable. Thou dost deliberate? Oh, contrive for me the way to freedom! Speak; nourish hope in a living soul.

FERDINAND. Cease! Oh cease! Every word deepens my despair. There is here no outlet, no counsel, no escape.— 'Tis this thought that tortures me, that lays hold of my heart, and rends it as with talons. I have myself spread the net; I know its firm, inextricable knots; I know that every avenue is barred alike to courage and to stratagem. I feel that I too am fettered, like thyself, like all the rest. Think'st thou that I should give way to lamentation if any means of safety remained untried? I have thrown myself at his feet, I have remonstrated, I have implored. He has sent me hither, in order to blast in this fatal moment, every remnant of joy and happiness that yet survived within my heart.

EGMONT. And is there no deliverance?

FERDINAND. None!

EGMONT. (*stamping his foot*) No deliverance!—Sweet life! Sweet, pleasant habitude of being and of activity! Must I part from thee! So calmly part! Not amid the tumult of battle, the din of arms, the excitement of the fray, dost thou send me a hasty farewell; thine is no hurried leave; thou dost not abridge the moment of separation. Once more let me clasp thy hand, gaze once more into thine eyes, feel with keen emotion, thy beauty and thy worth, then resolutely tear myself away, and say;—depart!

FERDINAND. Must I stand by, and look passively on; unable to save thee, or to give thee aid! What voice avails my lamentation! What heart but must break under the pressure of such anguish?

EGMONT. Be calm!

FERDINAND. Thou can'st be calm, thou can'st renounce life: led on by necessity, thou can'st advance to the direful struggle, with the courage of a hero. What can I do? What ought I to do? Thou dost conquer thyself and us; thou art

the victor ; I survive both myself and thee. I have lost my
night at the banquet, my banner on the field. The future
lies before me, dark, desolate, perplexed.

EGMONT. Young friend, whom by a strange fatality, at
the same moment, I both win and lose, who dost feel for me,
who dost suffer for me the agonies of death,—look on me ;—
thou wilt not lose me. If my life was a mirror in which thou
didst love to contemplate thyself, so be also my death. Men
are not together only when in each other's presence ;—the
distant, the departed, still live for us. I shall live for thee,
and for myself I have lived long enough. I have enjoyed
each day ; each day, I have performed, with prompt activity,
the duties enjoined by my conscience. Now my life ends, as
it might have ended, long, long, ago, on the sands of Gravelines. I shall cease to live ; but I have lived. My friend,
follow in my steps, lead a cheerful and a joyous life, and
dread not the approach of death.

FERDINAND. Thou should'st have saved thyself for us,
thou could'st have saved thyself. Thou art the cause of thine
own destruction. Often have I listened when able men dis-
coursed concerning thee ; foes and friends, they would dispute
long as to thy worth ; but on one point they were agreed,
none ventured to deny that thou wert treading a dangerous
path. How often have I longed to warn thee! Hadst thou
no friends ?

EGMONT. I was warned.

FERDINAND. And when I found all these allegations,
point for point, in the indictment, together with thy answers,
containing much that might serve to palliate thy conduct,
but no evidence weighty enough fully to exculpate thee.

EGMONT. No more of this. Man imagines that he directs
his life, that he governs his actions, when in fact his existence
is irresistibly controlled by his destiny. Let us not dwell
upon this subject ; these reflections I can dismiss with ease —
not so my apprehensions for these provinces ; yet they too
will be cared for. Could my blood bring peace to my people,
how freely should it flow. Alas ! This may not be. Yet it
ill becomes a man idly to speculate, when the power to act is
no longer his. If thou canst restrain or guide the fatal
power of thy father ; do so. Alas, who can ?—Farewell !

FERDINAND. I cannot leave thee.

EGMONT.   Let me urgently recommend my followers to thy care! I have worthy men in my service; let them not be dispersed, let them not become destitute! How fares it with Richard, my Secretary?

FERDINAND.   He is gone before thee. They have be-headed him, as thy accomplice in high treason.

EGMONT.   Poor soul!—Yet one word, and then farewell, I can no more.   However powerfully the spirit may be stirred, nature at length irresistibly asserts her rights; and like a child who enjoys refreshing slumber though enveloped in a serpent's folds, so the weary one lays himself down to rest before the gates of death, and sleeps soundly, as though a toilsome journey yet lay before him.—One word more.—I know a maiden; thou wilt not despise her because she was mine.   Since I can commend her to thy care, I shall die in peace.   Thy soul is noble; in such a man, a woman is sure to find a protector.   Lives my old Adolphus? Is he free?

FERDINAND.   The active old man, who always attended thee on horseback?

EGMONT,   The same.

FERDINAND.   He lives, he is free.

EGMONT.   He knows her dwelling; let him guide thy steps thither, and reward him to his dying day, for having shown thee the way to this jewel.—Farewell!

FERDINAND.   I cannot leave thee.

EGMONT. (*urging him towards the door*). Farewell!

FERDINAND.   Oh let me linger yet a moment!

EGMONT.   No leave-taking, my friend.

(*He accompanies Ferdinand to the door, and then tears himself away; Ferdinand overwhelmed with grief, hastily retires.*)

EGMONT (*alone.*)

EGMONT.   Cruel man!   Thou didst not think to render me this service through thy son.   He has been the means of relieving my mind from the pressure of care and sorrow, from fear and every anxious thought.   Gently, yet urgently, nature claims her final tribute. 'Tis past!—'Tis resolved! And the reflections which, in the suspense of last night, kept me wakeful on my couch, now with resistless certainty, lull my senses to repose.

(*He seats himself upon the couch; music.*)

Sweet sleep! Like the purest happiness, thou comest most

willingly, uninvited, unsought.    Thou dost loosen the knots
of earnest thoughts, dost mingle all images of joy and of sorrow, unimpeded the circle of inner harmony flows on, and
wrapped in fond delusion, we sink into oblivion, and cease
to be.

> *[He sleeps; music accompanies his slumber.   The wall*
> *behind his couch appears to open and discovers a bril-*
> *liant apparition.   Freedom, in a celestial garb, sur-*
> *rounded by a glory, reposes in a cloud.   Her features*
> *are those of Clara and she inclines towards the sleeping*
> *hero.   Her countenance betokens compassion, she seems*
> *to lament his fate.   Quickly she recovers herself and*
> *with an encouraging gesture exhibits the symbols of free-*
> *dom, the bundle of arrows, with the staff and cap.   She*
> *encourages him to be of good cheer, and while she sig-*
> *nifies to him, that his death will secure the freedom of*
> *the provinces, she hails him as a conqueror, and extends*
> *to him a laurel crown.   As the wreath approaches his*
> *head, Egmont moves like one asleep, and reclines with*
> *his face towards her.   She holds the wreath suspended*
> *over his head;—martial music is heard in the distance,*
> *at the first sound the vision disappears.   The music*
> *grows louder and louder.   Egmont awakes.   The prison*
> *is dimly illumined by the dawn.—His first impulse is to*
> *lift his hand to his head, he stands up, and gazes round,*
> *his hand still upraised.*

The crown is vanished!   Beautiful vision, the light of day
has frighted thee!   Yes, they revealed themselves to my
sight, uniting in one radiant form the two sweetest joys of
my heart.   Divine Liberty borrowed the mien of my beloved
one; the lovely maiden arrayed herself in the celestial garb
of her friend.   In a solemn moment they appeared united
with aspect more earnest than tender.   With blood-stained
feet the vision approached, the waving folds of her robe also
were tinged with blood.   It was my blood, and the blood of
many brave hearts.   No!   It shall not be shed in vain!
Forward!   Brave people!   The goddess of liberty leads you
on!   And as the sea breaks through and destroys the barriers
that would oppose its fury, so do ye overwhelm the bulwark
of tyranny, and with your impetuous flood sweep it away
from the land which it usurps.                          *[Drums.*

Hark!   Hark!   How often has this sound summoned my joyous steps to the field of battle and of victory!   How bravely did I tread, with my gallant comrades, the dangerous path of fame!   And now, from this dungeon I shall go forth, to meet a glorious death; I die for freedom, for whose cause I have lived and fought, and for whom I now offer myself up a sorrowing sacrifice.

> [*The back-ground is occupied by Spanish soldiers with halberts.*

Yes, lead them on!   Close your ranks, ye terrify me not. I am accustomed to stand amid the serried ranks of war, and environed by the threatening forms of death, to feel, with double zest, the energy of life.                          [*Drums.*

The foe closes round on every side!   Swords are flashing; courage, friends!   Behind are your parents, your wives, your children!                              [*Pointing to the guard.*

And these are impelled by the word of their leader, not by their own free will.   Protect your homes!   And to save those who are most dear to you, be ready to follow my example, and to fall with joy.

> [*Drums.   As he advances through the guards towards the door in the back ground, the curtain falls.   The music joins in, and the scene closes with a symphony of victory.*

# GOETZ VON BERLICHINGEN,

## WITH THE IRON HAND.

## A TRAGEDY.

TRANSLATED BY WALTER SCOTT, Esq., Advocate.

1799.

GOETZ VON BERLICHINGEN, the hero of the following drama, flourish' 1 in the 15th century, during the reign of Maximilian the First, Emperor of Germany. Previous to this period, every German noble holding a fief immediately from the Emperor, exercised on his estate a species of sovereignty subordinate to the imperial authority alone. Thus, from the princes and prelates possessed of extensive territories, down to the free knights and barons, whose domains consisted of a castle and a few acres of mountain and forest ground, each was a petty monarch upon his own property, independent of all control but the remote supremacy of the Emperor

Among the extensive rights conferred by such a constitution, that of waging war against each other by their own private authority, was most precious to a race of proud and military barons. These private wars were called *feuds*, and the privilege of carrying them on was named *Faustrecht* (club-law). As the empire advanced in civilization, the evils attending feuds became dreadfully conspicuous: each petty knight was by law entitled to make war upon his neighbours without any further ceremony than three days previous defiance by a written form called *Fehdbrief*. Even the Golden Bull, which remedied so many evils in the Germanic body, left this dangerous privilege in full vigour. In time the residence of every free baron became a fortress, from which, as his passions or avarice dictated, sallied a band of marauders to back his quarrel, or to collect an extorted revenue from the merchants who presumed to pass through his domain  At length whole bands of these free-booting nobles used to league together for the purpose of mutual defence against their more powerful neighbours, as likewise for that of predatory excursions against the princes, free towns, and ecclesiastic states of the empire, whose wealth tempted the needy barons to exercise against them their privilege of waging private war. These confederacies were

2 D

distinguished by various titles expressive of their object: we find among them the Brotherhood of the Mace, the Knights of the Bloody Sleeve, &c., &c. If one of the brotherhood was attacked, the rest marched without delay to his assistance; and thus, though individually weak, the petty feudatories maintained their ground against the more powerful members of the empire. Their independence and privileges were recognised and secured to them by many edicts; and though hated and occasionally oppressed by the princes and ecclesiastical authorities, to whom in return they were a scourge and a pest, they continued to maintain tenaciously the good old privilege (as they termed it) of *Faustrecht*, which they had inherited from their fathers. Amid the obvious mischiefs attending such a state of society, it must be allowed that it is frequently the means of calling into exercise the highest heroic virtues. Men daily exposed to danger, and living by the constant exertion of their courage, acquired the virtues as well as the vices of a savage state; and among many instances of cruelty and rapine, occur not a few of the most exalted valour and generosity. If the fortress of a German knight was the dread of the wealthy merchant and abbot, it was often the ready and hospitable refuge of the weary pilgrim and oppressed peasant. Although the owner subsisted by the plunder of the rich, yet he was frequently beneficent to the poor, and beloved by his own family dependents and allies. The spirit of chivalry doubtless contributed much to soften the character of these marauding nobles. A respect for themselves taught them generosity towards their prisoners, and certain acknowledged rules prevented many of the atrocities which it might have been expected would have marked these feuds. No German noble, for example, if made captive, was confined in fetters or in a dungeon, but remained a prisoner at large upon his parole (which was called *knightly ward*), either in the castle of his conqueror or in some other place assigned to him. The same species of honourable captivity was often indulged by the Emperor to offenders of a noble rank, of which some instances will be found in the following pages.

Such was the state of the German nobles, when, on the 7th of August, 1495, was published the memorable edict of Maximilian for the establishment of the public peace of the empire. By this ordinance, the right of private war was totally abrogated, under the penalty of the Ban of the empire, to be enforced by the Imperial Chamber then instituted. This was at once a sentence of anathema secular and spiritual, containing the dooms of outlawry and excommunication.— This ordinance was highly acceptable to the princes, bishops, and free towns, who had little to gain and much to lose in these perpetual feuds; and they combined to enforce it with no small severity against the petty feudatories:—these, on the other hand, sensible that the very root of their importance consisted in their privilege of declaring private war, without which they foresaw they would not long be able to maintain their independence, struggled hard against the execution of this edict; by which their confederacies were declared unlawful, and all means taken from them of resisting their richer neighbours.

Upon the jarring interests of the princes and clergy on the one hand, and of the free knights and petty imperial feudatories on the other, arise the incidents of the following drama. The hero, Goetz von Berlichingen, was in reality a zealous champion for the privileges of the free knights, and was repeatedly laid under the Ban of the empire for the feuds in which he was engaged, from which he was only released in consequence of high reputation for gallantry and generosity. His life was published at Nuremberg, 1731; and some account of his exploits, with a declaration of feud (Fehdbrief) issued by him against that city, will be found in Meusel's Inquiry into History, vol. 4th.

While the princes and free knights were thus banded against each other, the peasants and bondsmen remained in the most abject state of ignorance and oppression. This occasioned at different times the most desperate insurrections, resembling in their nature, and in the atrocities committed by the furious insurgents, the rebellions of Tyler and Cade in England, or that of the *Jacquerie* in France. Such an event occurs in the following tragedy. There is also a scene founded upon the noted institution called the Secret or Invisible Tribunal. With this extraordinary judicatory, the members and executioners of which were unknown, and met in secret to doom to death those criminals whom other courts of justice could not reach, the English reader has been made acquainted by several translations from the German, particularly the excellent romances called Herman of Unna, and Alf von Duilman.

The following drama was written by the elegant author of the Sorrows of Werter, in imitation, it is said, of the manner of Shakespeare. This resemblance is not to be looked for in the style or expression, but in the outline of the characters, and mode of conducting the incidents of the piece. In Germany it is the object of enthusiastic admiration; partly owing doubtless to the force of national partiality towards a performance in which the ancient manners of the country are faithfully and forcibly painted. Losing, however, this advantage, and under all the defects of a translation, the translator ventures to hope that in the following pages there will still be found something to excite interest. Some liberties have been taken with the original, in omitting two occasional disquisitions upon the civil law as practised in Germany*. Literal accuracy has been less studied in the translation, than an attempt to convey the spirit and general effect of the piece. Upon the whole, it is hoped the version will be found faithful; of which the translator is less distrustful, owing to the friendship of a gentleman of high literary eminence, who has obligingly taken the trouble of superintending the publication.

WALTER SCOTT.

Edinburgh, *3rd February*, 1799.

---

* In the present revision these omitted portions are restored.

# DRAMATIS PERSONÆ

---

MAXIMILIAN, Emperor of Germany.
GOETZ VON BERLICHINGEN, a free knight of the empire.
ELIZABETH, his wife.
MARIA, his sister.
CHARLES, his son—a boy.
GEORGE, his page.
BISHOP OF BAMBERG.
ADELBERT VON WEISLINGEN, a free German knight of the empire.
ADELAIDE VON WALLDORF, widow of the Count von Walldorf.
LIEBTRAUT, a Courtier of the Bishop's.
ABBOT OF FULDA, residing at the Bishop's court.
OLEARIUS, a doctor of laws.
BROTHER MARTIN, a monk.
HANS VON SELBITZ,
FRANZ VON SICKINGEN, } Free knights, in alliance with Goetz.
LERSE, a trooper.
FRANCIS, esquire to Weislingen.
Female Attendant on Adelaide.
PRESIDENT, Accuser, and Avenger of the Secret Tribunal.
METZLER,
SIEVERS,
LINK, } Leaders of the Insurgent Peasantry.
KOHL,
WILD,
Imperial Commissioners.
Two Merchants of Nuremberg.
Magistrates of Heilbronn.
MAXIMILIAN STUMF, a vassal of the Palsgrave.
An unknown.
Bride's father,
Bride, } Peasants.
Bridegroom,
Gipsy captain.
Gipsy mother and women.
STICKS and WOLF, gipsies.
Imperial captain.
Imperial officers.
Innkeeper.
Sentinel.
Serjeant-at-arms.
Imperial Soldiers—Troopers belonging to Goetz, to Selbitz, to Sickingen, and to Weislingen—Peasants—Gipsies—Judges of the Secret Tribunal —Gaolers—Courtiers, &c. &c. &c.

# GOETZ VON BERLICHINGEN,

## WITH THE IRON HAND.

---

## ACT I.

---

SCENE I.   *An Inn at Schwarzenberg in Franconia.*

METZLER *and* SIEVERS, *two Swabian peasants, are seated at a table—At the fire, at some distance from them, two troopers from Bamberg—The Innkeeper.*

SIEVERS.   Hansel! Another cup of brandy—and Christian measure.

INNKEEPER.   Thou art a Never-enough.

METZLER (*apart to Sievers*).   Repeat that again about Berlichingen—The Bambergers there are so angry they are almost black in the face.

SIEVERS.   Bambergers !—What are they about here ?

METZLER.   Weislingen has been two days up yonder at the Castle with the Earl—they are his attendants—they came with him I know not whence; they are waiting for him—He is going back to Bamberg.

SIEVERS.   Who is that Weislingen ?

METZLER.   The Bishop of Bamberg's right hand! a powerful lord, who is lying in wait to play Goetz some trick.

SIEVERS.   He had better take care of himself.

METZLER (*aside*).   Prithee go on! (*Aloud.*)   How long is it since Goetz had a new dispute with the Bishop? I thought all had been reconciled and squared between them.

SIEVERS.   Aye! Reconciliation with Priests !—When the Bishop saw he could do no good, and always got the worst of it, he pulled in his horns, and made haste to patch up a truce—and honest Berlichingen let him off very easily, as he always does when he has got the advantage.

METZLER.   God bless him! a worthy nobleman.

SIEVERS.   Only think! Was it not shameful?  They fell upon a page of his, to his no small surprise; but they will soon be mauled for that.

METZLER.   How provoking that his last stroke should have missed.   He must have been plaguily annoyed.

SIEVERS.   I don't think anything has vexed him so much for a long time.  Look you, all had been calculated to a nicety; the time the Bishop would come from the bath, with how many attendants, and which road; and, had it not been betrayed by some traitor, Goetz would have blessed his bath for him, and rubbed him dry.

FIRST TROOPER.   What are you prating there about our Bishop; Do you want to pick a quarrel?

SIEVERS.   Mind your own affairs; you have nothing to do with our table.

SECOND TROOPER.   Who taught you to speak disrespectfully of our Bishop?

SIEVERS.   Am I bound to answer *your* questions?—Look at the fool!—(*The first* TROOPER *boxes his ears.*)

METZLER.   Smash the rascal!  (*They attack each other.*)

SECOND TROOPER (*to* METZLER). Come on if you dare—

INNKEEPER (*separating them*).   Will you be quiet? Zounds! Take yourselves off if you have any scores to settle; in my house I will have order and decency.  (*He pushes the* TROOPERS *out of doors.*)—And what are you about, you jackasses?

METZLER.   No bad names, Hansel! or your sconce shall pay for it.   Come, comrade, we'll go and thrash those blackguards.

*Enter two of* BERLICHINGEN'S TROOPERS.

FIRST TROOPER.   What's the matter?

SIEVERS.   Ah!  Good day, Peter!—Good day, Veit!— Whence come you?

SECOND TROOPER.   Mind you don't let out whom we serve.

SIEVERS (*whispering*).   Then your master Goetz isn't far off?

FIRST TROOPER.    Hold your tongue!—Have you had a quarrel?

SIEVERS.    You must have met the fellows without—they are Bambergers.

FIRST TROOPER.    What brings them here?

SIEVERS.    They escort Weislingen, who is up yonder at the Castle with the Earl.

FIRST TROOPER.    Weislingen?

SECOND TROOPER (*aside to his companion*).    Peter, that is grist to our mill—How long has he been here?

METZLER.    Two days—but he is off to-day, as I heard one of his fellows say.

FIRST TROOPER (*aside*).    Did I not tell you he was here?—We might have waited yonder long enough—Come, Veit—

SIEVERS.    Help us first to drub the Bambergers.

SECOND TROOPER.    There are already two of you—We must away—Farewell!        [*Exeunt both* TROOPERS.

SIEVERS.    Scurvy dogs, these troopers!  They won't strike a blow without pay.

METZLER.    I could swear they have something in hand.—Whom do they serve?

SIEVERS.    I am not to tell——They serve Goetz.

METZLER.    So!—Well, now we'll cudgel those fellows outside—While I have a quarter-staff I care not for their spits.

SIEVERS.    If we durst but once serve the princes in the same manner, who drag our skins over our ears!    [*Exeunt.*


SCENE II.    *A cottage in a thick forest.*

GOETZ VON BERLICHINGEN *discovered walking among the trees before the door.*

GOETZ.    Where linger my servants?—I must walk up and down, or sleep will overcome me—Five days and nights already on the watch—It is hardly earned, this bit of life and freedom.  But when I have caught thee, Weislingen, I shall take my ease. (*Fills a glass of wine and drinks; looks at the flask.*)—Again empty.——George!—While this and my courage last, I can laugh at the ambition and chicanery of

princes?—George!—You may send round your obsequious
Weislingen to your uncles and cousins to calumniate my
character—Be it so—I am on the alert.—Thou hast escaped
me, Bishop; then thy dear Weislingen shall pay the score.—
George!—Doesn't the boy hear?—George! George!

GEORGE (*entering in the cuirass of a full-grown man*),
Worshipful sir.

GOETZ.  What kept you?  Were you asleep?—What in
the devil's name means this masquerade?—Come hither;
you don't look amiss.  Be not ashamed, boy; you look
bravely.  Ah! if you could but fill it!—Is it Hans' cuirass?

GEORGE.  He wished to sleep a little, and unbuckled it.

GOETZ.  He takes things easier than his master.

GEORGE.  Do not be angry! I took it quietly away and
put it on, then fetched my father's old sword from the wall,
ran to the meadow, and drew it——

GOETZ.  And laid about you, no doubt?—Rare work
among the brambles and thorns!—Is Hans asleep?

GEORGE.  He started up and cried out to me when you
called—I was trying to unbuckle the cuirass when I heard
you twice or thrice.

GOETZ.  Go take back his cuirass, and tell him to be
ready with the horses.

GEORGE.  I have fed them well and they are ready
bridled; you may mount when you will.

GOETZ.  Bring me a stoup of wine.  Give Hans a glass
too, and tell him to be on the alert——there is good cause;
I expect the return of my scouts every moment.

GEORGE.  Ah! noble Sir!

GOETZ.  What's the matter?

GEORGE.  May I not go with you?

GOETZ.  Another time, George! when we waylay merchants and seize their waggons—

GEORGE.  Another time!—You have said that so often.—
O, this time, this time!  I will only skulk behind; just keep
on the look-out—I will gather up all the spent arrows for you.

GOETZ.  Next time, George!—You must first have a
doublet, a steel cap, and a lance.

GEORGE.  Take me with you now!—Had I been with you
last time, you would not have lost your cross-bow.

GOETZ.  Do you know about that?

GEORGE. You threw it at your antagonist's head; one of his followers picked it up, and off with it he went.—Don't I know about it?

GOETZ. Did my people tell you?

GEORGE. O yes: and for that, I whistle them all sorts of tunes while we dress the horses, and teach them merry songs, too.

GOETZ. Thou art a brave boy.

GEORGE. Take me with you to prove myself so.

GOETZ. The next time, I promise you! You must not go to battle unarmed as you are. There is a time coming which will also require men. I tell thee boy, it will be a dear time. Princes shall offer their treasures for a man whom they now hate. Go, George, give Hans his cuirass again, and bring me wine. (*Exit* GEORGE.) Where can my people be? It is incomprehensible!——A monk! What brings him here so late?

*Enter Brother* MARTIN.

GOETZ. Good evening, reverend father! Whence come you so late? Man of holy rest, thou shamest many knights.

MARTIN. Thanks, noble Sir! I am at present but an unworthy brother, if we come to titles. My cloister name is Augustin, but I like better to be called by my christian name, Martin.

GOETZ. You are tired, brother Martin, and doubtless thirsty.

*Enter* GEORGE *with wine.*

GOETZ. Here, in good time, comes wine!

MARTIN. For me a draught of water. I dare not drink wine.

GOETZ. Is it against your vow?

MARTIN. Noble Sir, to *drink* wine is not against my vow; but because *wine* is against my vow, therefore I drink it not.

GOETZ How am I to understand that?

MARTIN. 'Tis well for thee that thou dost not understand it. Eating and drinking nourish man's life.

GOETZ. Well!

MARTIN. When thou hast eaten and drunken, thou art as it were new born, stronger, bolder, fitter for action. Wine rejoices the heart of man, and joyousness is the mother of every virtue.  When thou hast drunk wine thou art double what thou shouldst be! twice as ingenious, twice as enterprising, and twice as active.

GOETZ.  As I drink it, what you say is true.

MARTIN.  'Tis when thus taken in moderation that I speak of it.  But we——(GEORGE *brings water.*  GOETZ *speaks to him apart.*)

GOETZ (*to* GEORGE).  Go to the road which leads to Daxbach: lay thine ear close to the earth, and listen for the tread of horses.  Return immediately.

MARTIN.  But we, on the other hand, when we have eaten and drunken, are the reverse of what we should be.  Our sluggish digestion depresses our mental powers; and in the indulgence of luxurious ease, desires are generated which grow too strong for our weakness.

GOETZ.  One glass, brother Martin, will not disturb your sleep.  You have travelled far to-day.  (*Helps him to wine.*)  Here's to all fighting men!

MARTIN.  With all my heart!  (*They ring their glasses.*)  I cannot abide idle people—yet will I not say that all monks are idle; they do what they can: I am just come from St. Bede, where I slept last night.  The Prior took me into the garden; that is their hive.  Excellent salad, cabbages in perfection, and such cauliflowers and artichokes as you will hardly find in Europe.

GOETZ.  So that is not the life for you?  (*Goes out and looks anxiously after the boy.  Returns.*)

MARTIN.  Would that God had made me a gardener, or day labourer, I might then have been happy!  My convent is Erfurt in Saxony; my Abbot loves me; he knows I cannot remain idle, and so he sends me round the country, wherever there is business to be done.  I am on my way to the bishop of Constance.

GOETZ.  Another glass.  Good speed to you!

MARTIN.  The same to you.

GOETZ.  Why do you look at me so steadfastly, brother?

MARTIN.  I am in love with your armour.

GOETZ.  Would you like a suit?  It is heavy, and toilsome to the wearer.

MARTIN.  What is not toilsome in this world?—But to me nothing is so much so as to renounce my very nature!

Poverty, chastity, obedience—three vows, each of which taken singly seems the most dreadful to humanity—so insupportable are they all;—and to spend a life-time under this burthen, or to groan despairingly under the still heavier load of an evil conscience—Ah! Sir Knight, what are the toils of your life compared to the sorrows of a state, which, from a mistaken desire of drawing nearer to the Deity, condemns as crimes the best impulses of our nature, impulses by which we live, grow, and prosper!

GOETZ. Were your vow less sacred, I would give you a suit of armour and a steed, and we would ride out together.

MARTIN. Would to heaven my shoulders had strength to bear armour, and my arm to unhorse an enemy!—Poor weak hand, accustomed from infancy to swing censers, to bear crosses and banners of peace, how couldst thou manage the lance and falchion? My voice, tuned only to Aves and Halleluiahs, would be a herald of my weakness to the enemy, while yours would overpower him; otherwise no vows should keep me from entering an order founded by the Creator himself.

GOETZ. To your happy return! (*Drinks,*)

MARTIN. I drink that only in compliment to you! A return to my prison must ever be unhappy. When you, Sir Knight, return to your castle, with the consciousness of your courage and strength, which no fatigue can overcome; when you, for the first time, after a long absence, stretch yourself unarmed upon your bed, secure from the attack of enemies, and resign yourself to a sleep sweeter than the draught after a long thirst—then can you speak of happiness.

GOETZ. And accordingly it comes but seldom!

MARTIN (*with growing ardour*). But when it does come, it is a foretaste of paradise.—When you return home laden with the spoils of your enemies, and, remember, " such a one I struck from his horse ere he could discharge his piece—such another I overthrew, horse and man;" then you ride to your Castle, and—

GOETZ. And what?

MARTIN. And your wife—(*Fills a glass.*) To her health! (*He wipes his eyes.*) You have one?

GOETZ. A virtuous, noble wife!

MARTIN. Happy the man who possesses a virtuous wife,

his life is doubled. This blessing was denied me, yet was woman the glory or crown of creation.

GOETZ (*aside*). I grieve for him. The sense of his condition preys upon his heart.

*Enter* GEORGE, *breathless.*

GEORGE. My Lord, my Lord, I hear horses in full gallop! --two of them--'Tis they for certain.

GOETZ. Bring out my steed; let Hans mount. Farewell, dear brother, God be with you. Be cheerful and patient, He will give you ample scope.

MARTIN. Let me request your name.

GOETZ. Pardon me—Farewell! (*Gives his left hand.*)

MARTIN. Why do you give the left?--Am I unworthy of the knightly right hand?

GOETZ. Were you the Emperor, you must be satisfied with this. My right hand, though not useless in combat, is unresponsive to the grasp of affection. It is one with its mailed gauntlet—You see, it is *iron*!

MARTIN. Then art thou Goetz of Berlichingen. I thank thee, Heaven, who hast shown me the man whom princes hate, but to whom the oppressed throng! (*He takes his right hand.*) Withdraw not this hand, let me kiss it.

GOETZ. You must not!

MARTIN. Let me, let me—Thou hand, more worthy even than the saintly relique through which the most sacred blood has flowed! lifeless instrument, quickened by the noblest spirit's faith in God.

(GOETZ *adjusts his helmet, and takes his lance.*)

MARTIN. There was a monk among us about a year ago. who visited you when your hand was shot off at the siege of Landshut. He used to tell us what you suffered, and your grief at being disabled for your profession of arms; till you remembered having heard of one who had also lost a hand, and yet served long as a gallant knight—I shall never forget it.

*Enter the two* TROOPERS. *They speak apart with* GOETZ.

MARTIN (*continuing*). I shall never forget his words uttered in the noblest, the most childlike trust in God : "If I had twelve hands, what would they avail me without thy grace? then may I with only one——"

GOETZ. In the wood of Haslach then. (*Turns to* MARTIN.) Farewell, worthy brother!        [*Embraces him.*

MARTIN.    Forget me not, as I shall never forget thee!

[*Exeunt* GOETZ *and his* TROOPERS.

MARTIN.    How my heart beat at the sight of him.   He spoke not, yet my spirit recognized his.   What rapture to behold a great man!

GEORGE.    Reverend sir, you will sleep here?

MARTIN.    Can I have a bed?

GEORGE.    No, sir!   I know of beds only by hearsay; in our quarters there is nothing but straw.

MARTIN.    It will serve.   What is thy name?

GEORGE.    George, reverend sir.

MARTIN.    George!   Thou hast a gallant patron saint.

GEORGE.    They say he was a trooper; that is what I intend to be!

MARTIN.    Stop!   (*Takes a picture from his breviary and gives it to him.*)  There behold him—follow his example; be brave, and fear God.                    [*Exit into the cottage.*

GEORGE.    Ah! what a splendid grey horse!   If I had but one like that—and the golden armour.   There is an ugly dragon.   At present I shoot nothing but sparrows.   O, St. George!  make me but tall and strong; give me a lance, armour, and such a horse, and then let the dragons come!

[*Exit.*


SCENE III.    *An Apartment in Jaxthausen, the Castle of Goetz von Berlichingen.*


ELIZABETH, MARIA, *and* CHARLES *discovered.*


CHARLES.    Pray now, dear aunt, tell me again that story about the good child; it is so pretty——

MARIA.    Do you tell it to me, little rogue! that I may see if you have paid attention.

CHARLES.    Wait then till I think.—"There was once upon"—Yes—"There was once upon a time a child, and his mother was sick; so the child went——"

MARIA.    No, no!——"Then his mother said, 'Dear child,' —— ."

CHARLES.    "I am sick——"

MARIA.    "And cannot go out."

CHARLES. "And gave him money and said, 'Go and buy yourself a breakfast.'  There came a poor man——"

MARIA. "The child went.  There met him an old man who was——"  Now. Charles!

CHARLES. "Who was—old——"

MARIA. Of course.  "Who was hardly able to walk, and said, 'Dear child'——"

CHARLES. "'Give me something; I have eaten not a morsel yesterday or to-day.'  Then the child gave him the money——"

MARIA. "That should have bought his breakfast."

CHARLES. "Then the old man said——"

MARIA. "Then the old man took the child by the hand——"

CHARLES. "By the hand, and said—and became a fine beautiful saint—and said—'Dear child'.——"

MARIA. "'The holy Virgin rewards thee for thy benevolence through me: whatever sick person thou touchest——'"

CHARLES. "'With thy hand——'"  It was the right hand, I think.

MARIA. Yes.

CHARLES. "'He will get well directly.'"

MARIA. "Then the child ran home, and could not speak for joy——"

CHARLES. "And fell upon his mother's neck and wept for joy."

MARIA. "Then the mother cried, 'What is this?' and became——"  Now, Charles.

CHARLES. "Became—became——"

MARIA. You do not attend—"and became well.  And the child cured kings and emperors, and became so rich that he built a great abbey."

ELIZABETH. I cannot understand why my husband stays. He has been away five days and nights, and he hoped to have finished his adventure so quickly.

MARIA. I have long felt uneasy.  Were I married to a man who continually incurred such danger, I should die within the first year.

ELIZABETH. I thank God that he has made me of firmer stuff!

CHARLES.  But must my father ride out, if it is so dangerous?

MARIA.  Such is his good pleasure.

ELIZABETH.  He must indeed, dear Charles!

CHARLES.  Why?

ELIZABETH.  Do you not remember the last time he rode out, when he brought you those nice things?

CHARLES.  Will he bring me anything now?

ELIZABETH.  I believe so.  Listen: there was a tailor at Stutgard who was a capital archer, and had gained the prize at Cologne.

CHARLES.  Was it much?

ELIZABETH.  A hundred dollars; and afterwards they would not pay him.

MARIA.  That was naughty, eh, Charles?

CHARLES.  Naughty people!

ELIZABETH.  The tailor came to your father and begged him to get his money for him; then your father rode out and intercepted a party of merchants from Cologne, and kept them prisoners till they paid the money.  Would you not have ridden out too?

CHARLES.  No; for one must go through a dark thick wood, where there are gipsies and witches——

ELIZABETH.  You're a fine fellow; afraid of witches!

MARIA.  Charles, it is far better to live at home in your castle, like a quiet Christian knight.  One may find opportunities enough of doing good on one's own lands.  Even the worthiest knights do more harm than good in their excursions.

ELIZABETH.  Sister, you know not what you are saying.— God grant our boy may become braver as he grows up, and not take after that Weislingen, who has dealt so faithlessly with my husband.

MARIA.  We will not judge, Elizabeth.—My brother is highly incensed, and so are you; I am only a spectator in the matter, and can be more impartial.

ELIZABETH.  Weislingen cannot be defended.

MARIA.  What I have heard of him has interested me.— Even your husband relates many instances of his former goodness and affection.—How happy was their youth when they were both pages of honour to the Margrave!

ELIZABETH.  That may be.  But only tell me, how can

a man ever have been good who lays snares for his best and
truest friend? who has sold his services to the enemies of my
husband; and who strives, by invidious misrepresentations,
to poison the mind of our noble emperor, who is so gracious
to us? (*A horn is heard.*)

CHARLES.  Papa! papa! the warder sounds his horn--
Joy! joy! he opens the gate!

ELIZABETH.  There he comes with booty!

*Enter* PETER.

PETER.  We have fought—we have conquered!—God save
you, noble ladies!

ELIZABETH.  Have you captured Weislingen?

PETER.  Himself, and three followers.

ELIZABETH.  How came you to stay so long?

PETER.  We lay in wait for him between Nuremberg and
Bamberg, but he would not come, though we knew he had set
out.  At length we heard of his whereabouts; he had struck
off sideways, and was staying quietly with the earl at Schwarzenberg.

ELIZABETH.  They would also fain make the earl my husband's enemy.

PETER.  I immediately told my master.—Up and away
we rode into the forest of Haslach.  And it was curious,
that while we were riding along that night, a shepherd was
watching, and five wolves fell upon the flock and attacked
them stoutly.  Then my master laughed, and said "Good
luck to us all, dear comrades, both to you and us!"  And the
good omen overjoyed us.  Just then Weislingen came riding
towards us with four attendants—

MARIA.  How my heart beats!

PETER.  My comrade and I, as our master had commanded,
threw ourselves suddenly on him, and clung to him as if we had
grown together, so that he could not move, while my master
and Hans fell upon the servants, and overpowered them.
They were all taken, except one who escaped.

ELIZABETH.  I am curious to see him.  Will he arrive soon!

PETER.  They are riding through the valley, and will be
here in a quarter of an hour.

MARIA.  He is no doubt cast down and dejected?

PETER.  He looks gloomy enough.

MARIA.  It will grieve me to see his distress!

ELIZABETH. O! I must get food ready. You are no doubt all hungry?

PETER. Hungry enough, in truth.

ELIZABETH (*to Maria*). Take the cellar keys and bring the best wine. They have deserved it.  [*Exit* ELIZABETH.

CHARLES. I'll go too, aunt.

MARIA. Come then, boy.  [*Exeunt* CHARLES *and* MARIA.

PETER. He'll never be his father, else he would have gone with me to the stable.

*Enter* GOETZ, WEISLINGEN, HANS, *and other* TROOPERS.

GOETZ (*laying his helmet and sword on a table*). Unbuckle my armour, and give me my doublet. Ease will refresh me. Brother Martin, thou said'st truly. You have kept us long on the watch, Weislingen!

[WEISLINGEN *paces up and down in silence.*

GOETZ. Be of good cheer! Come, unarm yourself! Where are your clothes? I hope nothing has been lost. (*To the attendants.*) Go, ask his servants; open the baggage, and see that nothing is missing. Or I can lend you some of mine.

WEISLINGEN. Let me remain as I am—it is all one.

GOETZ. I can give you a handsome doublet, but it is only of linen; it has grown too tight for me. I wore it at the marriage of my Lord the Palsgrave, when your bishop was so incensed at me. About a fortnight before I had sunk two of his vessels upon the Maine—I was going up stairs in the Stag at Heidelberg, with Franz von Sickingen. Before you get quite to the top, there is a landing-place with iron rails— there stood the bishop, and gave his hand to Franz as he passed, and to me also as I followed close behind him. I laughed in my sleeve, and went to the Landgrave of Hanau, who was always a kind friend to me, and said, "The bishop has given me his hand, but I'll wager he did not know me." The bishop heard me, for I was speaking loud on purpose. He came to us angrily, and said, "True, I gave thee my hand, because I knew thee not." To which I answered, "I know that, my lord; and so here you have your shake of the hand back again!" The manikin grew red as a Turkey cock with spite, and he ran up into the room and complained to the Palsgrave Lewis and the Prince of Nassau. We have laughed over the scene again and again.

WEISLINGEN. I wish you would leave me to myself.

GOETZ.   Why so?   I entreat you be of good cheer.   You are my prisoner, but I will not abuse my power.

WEISLINGEN.   I have no fear of that.   That is your duty as a knight.

GOETZ.   And you know how sacred it is to me.

WEISLINGEN.   I am your prisoner—the rest matters not.

GOETZ.   You should not say so.   Had you been taken by a prince, fettered and cast into a dungeon, your gaoler directed to drive sleep from your eyes—

*Enter* SERVANTS *with clothes.*   WEISLINGEN *unarms himself.   Enter* CHARLES.

CHARLES.   Good morrow, papa!

GOETZ (*kisses him*).   Good morrow, boy!   How have you been this long time?

CHARLES.   Very well, father!   Aunt says I am a good boy.

GOETZ.   Does she?

CHARLES.   Have you brought me anything?

GOETZ.   Nothing this time.

CHARLES.   I have learned a great deal.

GOETZ.   Aye!

CHARLES.   Shall I tell you about the good child?

GOETZ.   After dinner.

CHARLES.   I know something else, too.

GOETZ.   What may that be?

CHARLES.   "Jaxthausen is a village and castle on the Jaxt, which has appertained in property and heritage for two hundred years to the Lords of Berlichingen——"

GOETZ.   Do you know the Lord of Berlichingen? (CHARLES *stares at him.   Aside*) His learning is so abstruse that he does not know his own father.   To whom does Jaxthausen belong?

CHARLES.   "Jaxthausen is a village and castle upon the Jaxt——"

GOETZ.   I did not ask that.   I knew every path, pass, and ford about the place, before ever I knew the name of the village, castle, or river.—Is your mother in the kitchen?

CHARLES.   Yes, papa!   They are cooking a lamb and turnips.

GOETZ.   Do you know that too, Jack Turnspit?

CHARLES.   And my aunt is roasting an apple for me to eat after dinner—

GOETZ. Can't you eat it raw?

CHARLES. It tastes better roasted.

GOETZ. You must have a tit bit, must you?—Weislingen, I will be with you immediately. I must go and see my wife. —Come, Charles!

CHARLES. Who is that man?

GOETZ. Bid him welcome. Tell him to be merry.

CHARLES. There's my hand for you, man! Be merry—for the dinner will soon be ready.

WEISLINGEN (*Takes up the child and kisses him*). Happy boy! that knowest no worse evil than the delay of dinner. May you live to have much joy in your son, Berlichingen!

GOETZ. Where there is most light the shades are deepest. Yet I thank God for him. We'll see what they are about.

[*Exit with* CHARLES *and* SERVANTS.

WEISLINGEN. O that I could but wake and find this all a dream! In the power of Berlichingen!—from whom I had scarcely detached myself—whose remembrance I shunned like fire—whom I hoped to overpower! and he still the old true-hearted Goetz! Gracious God! what will be the end of it? O Adelbert! Led back to the very hall where we played as children; when thou didst love and prize him as thy soul! Who can know him and hate him? Alas! I am so thoroughly insignificant here. Happy days! ye are gone. There, in his chair by the chimney, sat old Berlichingen, while we played around him, and loved each other like cherubs! How anxious the bishop and all my friends will be. Well, the whole country will sympathize with my misfortune. But what avails it? Can they give me the peace after which I strive?

*Re-enter* GOETZ *with wine and goblets.*

GOETZ. We'll take a glass while dinner is preparing. Come, sit down—think yourself at home! Fancy you've come once more to see Goetz. It is long since we have sat and emptied a flagon together. (*Fills.*) Come: a light heart!

WEISLINGEN. Those times are gone by.

GOETZ. God forbid! To be sure, we shall hardly pass more pleasant days than those we spent together at the Margrave's court, when we were inseparable night and day.   I think with pleasure on my youth.   Do you remember the scuffle I had with the Polander, whose pomaded and frizzled hair I chanced to rub with my sleeve?

WEISLINGEN.   It was at table; and he struck at you with a knife.

GOETZ.   I gave it him, however; and you had a quarrel upon that account with his comrades.   We always stuck together like brave fellows, and were the admiration of every one.   (*Fills, and hands to* WEISLINGEN.)   Castor and Pollux! It used to rejoice my heart when the Margrave so called us.

WEISLINGEN.   The bishop of Wurtzburg first gave us the name.

GOETZ.   That bishop was a learned man, and withal so kind and gentle.   I shall remember as long as I live how he used to caress us, praise our friendship, and say: "Happy is the man who has an adopted brother for a friend."

WEISLINGEN.   No more of that!

GOETZ.   Why not?   I know nothing more delightful after fatigue than to talk over old times.   Indeed, when I recall to mind how we bore good and bad fortune together, and were all in all to each other, and how I thought this was to continue for ever.   Was not that my sole comfort when my hand was shot away at Landshut, and you nursed and tended me like a brother?   I hoped Adelbert would in future be my right hand.   And now——

WEISLINGEN.   Alas!

GOETZ.   Hadst thou but listened to me when I begged thee to go with me to Brabant, all would have been well.   But then that unhappy turn for court-dangling seized thee, and thy coquetting and flirting with the women.   I always told thee, when thou wouldst mix with these lounging, vain court sycophants, and entertain them with gossip about unlucky matches and seduced girls, scandal about absent friends, and all such trash as they take interest in.—I always said, Adelbert, thou wi't become a rogue!

WEISLINGEN.   To what purpose is all this?

GOETZ.   Would to God I could forget it, or that it were otherwise!   Art thou not free and nobly born as any in Germany; independent, subject to the emperor alone; and dost thou crouch among vassals?   What is the bishop to thee?

Granted, he is thy neighbour, and can do thee a shrewd turn; hast thou not power and friends to requite him in kind? Art thou ignorant of the dignity of a free knight, who depends only upon God, the emperor, and himself, that thou degradest thyself to be the courtier of a stubborn, jealous priest?

WEISLINGEN.   Let me speak!

GOETZ.   What hast thou to say?

WEISLINGEN.   You look upon the princes as the wolf upon the shepherd.   And can you blame them for defending their territories and property?   Are they a moment secure from the unruly knights, who plunder their vassals even upon the high-roads, and sack their castles and villages? Upon the other hand, our country's enemies threaten to over-run the lands of our beloved emperor, yet, while he needs the princes' assistance, they can scarce defend their own lives; is it not our good genius which at this moment leads them to devise means of procuring peace for Germany, of securing the administration of justice, and giving to great and small the blessings of quiet?   And can you blame us, Berlichengen, for securing the protection of the powerful princes, our neigh-bours, whose assistance is at hand, rather than relying on that of the emperor, who is so far removed from us, and is hardly able to protect himself?

GOETZ.   Yes, yes, I understand you.   Weislingen, were the princes as you paint them, we should all have what we want.   Peace and quiet!   No doubt!   Every bird of prey natu-rally likes to eat its plunder undisturbed.   The general weal! If they would but take the trouble to study that.   And they trifle with the emperor shamefully.   Every day some new tinker or other comes to give his opinion.   The emperor means well, and would gladly put things to rights; but because he happens to understand a thing readily, and by a single word, can put a thousand hands into motion, he thinks everything will be as speedily and as easily accomplished. Ordinance upon ordinance is promulgated, each nullifying the last, while the princes obey only those which serve their own interest, and prate of peace and security of the empire, while they are treading under foot their weaker neighbours. I will be sworn, many a one thanks God in his heart that the Turk keeps the emperor fully employed!

Weislingen.   You view things your own way.

Goetz.   So does every one.   The question is, which is the right way to view them?   And your plans at least shun the day.

Weislingen.   You may say what you will; I am your prisoner.

Goetz.   If your conscience is free, so are you.   How was it with the general tranquillity?   I remember going as a boy of sixteen with the Margrave to the Imperial Diet.   What harangues the princes made!   And the clergy were the most vociferous of all.   Your bishop thundered into the emperor's ears his regard for justice, till one thought it had become part and parcel of his being.   And now he has imprisoned a page of mine, at a time when our quarrels were all accommodated, and I had buried them in oblivion.   Is not all settled between us?   What does he want with the boy?

Weislingen.   It was done without his knowledge.

Goetz.   Then why does he not release him?

Weislingen.   He did not conduct himself as he ought.

Goetz.   Not conduct himself as he ought?   By my honour, he performed his duty, as surely as he has been imprisoned both with your knowledge and the bishop's!   Do you think I am come into the world this very day, that I cannot see what all this means?

Weislingen.   You are suspicious, and do us wrong.

Goetz.   Weislingen, shall I deal openly with you?   Inconsiderable as I am, I am a thorn in your side, and Selbitz and Sickingen are no less so, because we are firmly resolved to die sooner than to thank any one but God for the air we breathe, or pay homage to any one but the emperor. This is why they worry me in every possible way, blacken my character with the emperor, and among my friends and neighbours, and spy about for advantage over me.   They would have me out of the way at any price; that was your reason for imprisoning the page whom you knew I had dispatched for intelligence: and now you say he did not conduct himself as he should do, because he would not betray my secrets.   And you, Weislingen, are their tool!

Weislingen.   Berlichingen!

Goetz.   Not a word more.   I am an enemy to long

explanations; they deceive either the maker or the hearer, and generally both.

Enter CHARLES.

CHARLES.   Dinner is ready, father!

GOETZ.   Good news!   Come, I hope the company of my women folk will amuse you.   You always liked the girls. Aye, aye, they can tell many pretty stories about you.   Come!

[Exeunt.

SCENE IV.   The Bishop of Bamberg's Palace.

The BISHOP, the ABBOT of Fulda, OLEARIUS, LIEBTRAUT, and COURTIERS at table.   The dessert and wine before them.

BISHOP.   Are there many of the German nobility studying at Bologna?

OLEARIUS.   Both nobles and citizens; and, I do not exaggerate, in saying that they acquire the most brilliant reputation.   It is a proverb in the university :—" As studious as a German noble."   For while the citizens display a laudable diligence, in order to compensate by learning for their want of birth, the nobles strive, with praiseworthy emulation, to enhance their ancestral dignity by superior attainments.

ABBOT.   Indeed!

LIEBTRAUT.   What may one not live to hear.   We live and learn, as the proverb says.   " As studious as a German noble."   I never heard that before.

OLEARIUS.   Yes, they are the admiration of the whole university.   Some of the oldest and most learned will soon be coming back with their doctor's degree.   The emperor will doubtless be happy to entrust to them the highest offices.

BISHOP.   He cannot fail to do so.

ABBOT.   Do you know, for instance, a young man—a Hessian——

OLEARIUS.   There are many Hessians with us.

ABBOT.   His name is——is—— Does nobody remember it?   His mother was a Von—— Oh! his father had but one eye, and was a marshal——

LIEBTRAUT.   Von Wildenholz!

ABBOT.   Right.   Von Wildenholz.

OLEARIUS.   I know him well.   A young man of great

abilities.    He is particularly esteemed for his talent in disputation.

ABBOT.    He has that from his mother.

LIEBTRAUT.    Yes; but his father would never praise her for that quality.

BISHOP.    How call you the emperor who wrote your *Corpus Juris?*

OLEARIUS.    Justinian.

BISHOP.    A worthy prince:—here's to his memory!

OLEARIUS.    To his memory!    (*They drink.*)

ABBOT.    That must be a fine book.

OLEARIUS.    It may be called a book of books; a digest of all laws; there you find the sentence ready for every case, and where the text is antiquated or obscure, the deficiency is supplied by notes, with which the most learned men have enriched this truly admirable work.

ABBOT.    A digest of all laws!—Indeed!—Then the ten commandments must be in it.

OLEARIUS.    Implicitè; not explicitè.

ABBOT.    That's what I mean; plainly set down, without any explication.

BISHOP.    But the best is, you tell us that a state can **be** maintained in the most perfect tranquillity and subordination, by receiving and rightly following that statute-book.

OLEARIUS.    Doubtless.

BISHOP.    All doctors of laws!    (*They drink.*)

OLEARIUS.    I'll tell them of this abroad. (*They drink.*) Would to heaven that men thought thus in my country!

ABBOT.    Whence come you, most learned sir?

OLEARIUS.    From Frankfort, at your eminence's service!

BISHOP.    You gentlemen of the law, then, are not held in high estimation there?—How comes that?

OLEARIUS.    It is strange enough—when I last went there to collect my father's effects, the mob almost stoned me, when they heard I was a lawyer.

ABBOT.    God bless me!

OLEARIUS.    It is because their tribunal, which they hold in great respect, is composed of people totally ignorant of the Roman law.    An intimate acquaintance with the internal condition of the town, and also of its foreign relations, acquired through age and experience, is deemed a sufficient qualification. They decide according to certain established edicts of their own, and some old customs recognised in the city and neighbourhood.

ABBOT. That's very right.

OLEARIUS. But far from sufficient. The life of man is short, and in one generation cases of every description cannot occur; our statute-book is a collection of precedents, furnished by the experience of many centuries. Besides, the wills and opinions of men are variable; one man deems right to-day, what another disapproves to-morrow; and confusion and injustice are the inevitable results. Law determines absolutely, and its decrees are immutable.

ABBOT. That's certainly better.

OLEARIUS. But the common people won't acknowledge that; and, eager as they are after novelty, they hate any innovation in their laws, which leads them out of the beaten track, be it ever so much for the better. They hate a jurist as if he were a cut-purse or a subverter of the state, and become furious, if one attempts to settle among them.

LIEBTRAUT. You come from Frankfort?—I know the place well—we tasted your good cheer at the emperor's coronation. You say your name is Olearius—I know no one in the town of your name.

OLEARIUS. My father's name was Oilman—But after the example, and with the advice of many jurists, I have latinised the name to Olearius for the decoration of the title-page of my legal treatises.

LIEBTRAUT. You did well to translate yourself: a prophet is not honoured in his own country—your books if written in German might have shared the same fate.

OLEARIUS. That was not the reason.

LIEBTRAUT. All things have two reasons.

ABBOT. A prophet is not honoured in his own country.

LIEBTRAUT. But do you know why, most reverend sir?

ABBOT. Because he was born and bred there.

LIEBTRAUT. Well, that may be one reason. The other is, because, upon a nearer acquaintance with these gentlemen, the halo of glory and honour shed around them by the distant haze totally disappears; they are then seen to be nothing more than tiny rushlights!

OLEARIUS.  It seems you are placed here to tell pleasant truths.

LIEBTRAUT.  As I have wit enough to discover them, I do not lack courage to utter them.

OLEARIUS.  Yet you lack the art of applying them well.

LIEBTRAUT.  It is no matter where you place a cupping-glass, provided it draws blood.

OLEARIUS.  Buffoons are known by their dress, and no one takes offence at their scurvy jests.  Let me advise you as a precaution to bear the badge of your order—a cap and bells!

LIEBTRAUT.  Where did you take your degree?  I only ask, so that, should I ever take a fancy to a fool's cap, I could at once go to the right shop.

OLEARIUS. You carry face enough.

LIEBTRAUT.  And you paunch.  (*The* BISHOP *and* ABBOT *laugh.*)

BISHOP.  Not so warm, gentlemen!—Some other subject.  At table all should be fair and quiet. Choose another subject, Liebtraut.

LIEBTRAUT.  Opposite Frankfort lies a village, called Sachsenhausen—

OLEARIUS (*to the* BISHOP).  What news of the Turkish expedition, your excellency?

BISHOP.  The emperor has most at heart, first of all to restore peace to the empire, put an end to feuds, and secure the strict administration of justice : then according to report, he will go in person against the enemies of his country and of Christendom.  At present internal dissensions give him enough to do; and the empire, despite forty years of peace, is one scene of murder.  Franconia, Swabia, the Upper Rhine, and the surrounding countries are laid waste by presumptuous and reckless knights.—And here, at Bamberg, Sickingen, Sel-bitz with one leg, and Goetz with the iron hand, scoff at the imperial authority.

ABBOT.  If his Majesty does not exert himself, these fellows will at last thrust us into sacks.

LIEBTRAUT.  He would be a sturdy fellow indeed who should thrust the wine-butt of Fulda into a sack !

BISHOP.  Goetz especially has been for many years my mortal foe, and annoys me beyond description.  But it will not last long, I hope.  The emperor holds his court at

Augsburg.　We have taken our measures, and cannot fail of success.—Doctor, do you know Adelbert von Weislingen?

OLEARIUS.　No, your eminence.

BISHOP.　If you stay till his arrival, you will have the pleasure of seeing a most noble, accomplished, and gallant knight.

OLEARIUS.　He must be an excellent man indeed to deserve such praises from such a mouth.

LIEBTRAUT.　And yet he was not bred at any university.

BISHOP.　We know that. (*The attendants throng to the window.*) What's the matter?

ATTENDANT.　Farber, Weislingen's servant, is riding in at the Castle-gate.

BISHOP.　See what he brings.　He most likely comes to announce his master.

(*Exit* LIEBTRAUT—*They stand up and drink.*)
LIEBTRAUT *re-enters.*

BISHOP.　What news?

LIEBTRAUT.　I wish another had to tell it—Weislingen is a prisoner!

BISHOP.　What?

LIEBTRAUT.　Berlichingen has seized him and three troopers near Haslach—One is escaped to tell you.

ABBOT.　A Job's messenger!

OLEARIUS.　I grieve from my heart.

BISHOP.　I will see the servant; bring him up—I will speak with him myself.　Conduct him into my cabinet.
[*Exit* BISHOP.

ABBOT (*sitting down*).　Another draught, however.
[*The* SERVANTS *fill round.*

OLEARIUS.　Will not your reverence take a turn in the garden?　"Post cœnam stabis, seu passus mille meabis."

LIEBTRAUT,　In truth, sitting is unhealthy for you.　You might get an apoplexy. (*The* ABBOT *rises. Aside.*)　Let me but once get him out of doors, I will give him exercise enough!
[*Exeunt.*

## SCENE V. *Jaxthausen.*

### MARIA, WEISLINGEN.

MARIA. You love me, you say. I willingly believe it, and hope to be happy with you, and to make you happy also.

WEISLINGEN. I feel nothing but that I am entirely thine. (*Embraces her.*)

MARIA. Softly!—I gave you one kiss for earnest, but you must not take possession of what is only yours conditionally.

WEISLINGEN. You are too strict, Maria! Innocent love is pleasing in the sight of Heaven, instead of giving offence.

MARIA. It may be so. But I think differently; for I have been taught that caresses are, like fetters, strong through their union, and that maidens, when they love, are weaker than Sampson after the loss of his locks.

WEISLINGEN. Who taught you so?

MARIA. The abbess of my convent. Till my sixteenth year I was with her—and it is only with you that I enjoy happiness like that her company afforded me. She had loved, and could tell——She had a most affectionate heart. Oh! she was an excellent woman!

WEISLINGEN. Then you resemble her. (*Takes her hand.*) What will become of me when I am compelled to leave you?

MARIA (*withdrawing her hand.*) You will feel some regret, I hope, for I know what my feelings will be. But you must away!

WEISLINGEN. I know it, dearest! and I will—for well I feel what happiness I shall purchase by this sacrifice! Now, blessed be your brother, and the day on which he rode out to capture me!

MARIA. His heart was full of hope for you and himself. Farewell! he said, at his departure, I go to recover my friend.

WEISLINGEN. That he has done. Would that I had studied the arrangement and security of my property, instead of neglecting it, and dallying at that worthless court!—then couldst thou have been instantly mine.

MARIA. Even delay has its pleasures.

WEISLINGEN. Say not so, Maria, else I shall fear that thy

heart is less warm than mine.  True, I deserve punishment, but what hopes will brighten every step of my journey. To be wholly thine, to live only for thee and thy circle of friends—far removed from the world, in the enjoyment of all the raptures which two hearts can mutually bestow.  What is the favour of princes, what the applause of the universe, to such simple, yet unequalled felicity?  Many have been my hopes and wishes; but this happiness surpasses them all.

*Enter* GOETZ.

GOETZ.  Your page has returned.  He can scarcely utter a word for hunger and fatigue.  My wife has ordered him some refreshment.  Thus much I have gathered: the bishop will not give up my page—imperial commissioners are to be appointed, and a day named, upon which the matter may be adjusted.  Be that as it may, Adelbert, you are free.  Pledge me but your hand that you will for the future give neither open nor secret assistance to my enemies.

WEISLINGEN.  Here I grasp thy hand.  From this moment be our friendship and confidence, firm and unalterable as a primary law of nature!  Let me take this hand also (*takes* MARIA's *hand*), and with it the possession of this most noble lady.

GOETZ.  May I say yes for you?

MARIA (*timidly*).  If—if it is your wish——

GOETZ.  Happily our wishes do not differ on this point. Thou need'st not blush—the glance of thine eye betrays thee. Well then, Weislingen, join hands, and I say *Amen!*  My friend and brother!  I thank thee, sister; thou canst do more than spin flax, for thou hast drawn a thread which can fetter this wandering bird of paradise.  Yet you look not quite at your ease, Adelbert.  What troubles you?  *I* am perfectly happy!  What I but hoped in a dream, I now see with my eyes, and feel as though I were still dreaming.  Now my dream is explained.  I thought last night that, in token of reconciliation, I gave you this iron hand, and that you held it so fast that it broke away from my arm; I started, and awoke.  Had I but dreamed a little longer, I should have seen how you gave me a new living hand.  You must away this instant, to put your castle and property in order. That cursed court has made you neglect both.  I must call my wife.—Elizabeth!

Maria.   How overjoyed my brother is!

Weislingen.   Yet I am still more so.

Goetz (*to* Maria).   You will have a pleasant residence.

Maria.   Franconia is a fine country.

Weislingen.   And I may venture to say that my castle lies in the most fertile and delicious part of it.

Goetz.   That you may, and I can confirm it.   Look you, here flows the Maine, around a hill clothed with corn-fields and vineyards, its top crowned with a Gothic castle; then the river makes a sharp turn, and glides round behind the rock on which the castle is built.   The windows of the great hall look perpendicularly down upon the river, and command a prospect of many miles in extent.

*Enter* Elizabeth.

Elizabeth.   What would'st thou?

Goetz.   You too must give your hand, and say, God bless you!   They are a pair.

Elizabeth.   So soon?

Goetz.   But not unexpectedly.

Elizabeth.   May you ever adore her as ardently as while you sought her hand.   And then, as your love, so be your happiness!

Weislingen.   Amen!   I seek no happiness but under this condition.

Goetz.   The bridegroom, my love, must leave us for awhile; for this great change will involve many smaller ones. He must first withdraw himself from the bishop's court, in order that their friendship may gradually cool.   Then he must rescue his property from the hands of selfish stewards, and—— But come, sister; come, Elizabeth; let us leave him; his page has no doubt private messages for him.

Weislingen.   Nothing but what you may hear.

Goetz.   'Tis needless.   Franconians and Swabians!   Ye are now more closely united than ever.   Now we shall be able to keep the princes in check.

[*Exeunt* Goetz, Elizabeth, Maria.

Weislingen (*alone*).   God in heaven!   And canst thou have reserved such happiness for one so unworthy?   It is too much for my heart.   How meanly I depended upon wretched fools, whom I thought I was governing, upon the smile of princes, upon the homage of those around me!   Goetz, my faithful Goetz, thou hast restored me to myself, and thou, Maria, hast completed my reformation. I feel free, as if brought from a dungeon into the open air. Bamberg will I never see more—will snap all the shameful bonds that have held me beneath myself. My heart expands, and never more will I degrade myself by struggling for a greatness that is denied me. He alone is great and happy who fills his own station of independence, and has neither to command nor to obey.

*Enter* FRANCIS.

FRANCIS. God save you, noble sir! I bring you so many salutations that I know not where to begin. Bamberg, and ten miles round, cry with a thousand voices, God save you.

WEISLINGEN. Welcome, Francis! Bring'st thou aught else?

FRANCIS. You are held in such consideration at court that it cannot be expressed.

WEISLINGEN. That will not last long.

FRANCIS. As long as you live; and after your death it will shine with more lustre than the brazen characters on a monument. How they took your misfortune to heart!

WEISLINGEN. And what said the bishop?

FRANCIS. His eager curiosity poured out question upon question, without giving me time to answer. He knew of your accident already; for Farber, who escaped from Haslach, had brought him the tidings. But he wished to hear every particular. He asked so anxiously whether you were wounded. I told him you were whole, from the hair of your head to the nail of your little toe.

WEISLINGEN. And what said he to the proposals?

FRANCIS. He was ready at first to give up the page and a ransom to boot for your liberty. But when he heard you were to be dismissed without ransom, and merely to give your parole that the boy should be set free, he was for putting off Berlichingen with some pretence. He charged me with a thousand messages to you, more than I can ever utter. O how he harangued! It was a long sermon upon the text, "I cannot live without Weislingen!"

WEISLINGEN. He must learn to do so.

FRANCIS. What mean you? He said "Bid him hasten; all the court waits for him."

WEISLINGEN.　Let them wait on.　I shall not go to court.

FRANCIS.　Not go to court!　My gracious lord, how comes that?　If you knew what I knew; could you but dream what I have seen——

WEISLINGEN.　What ails thee?

FRANCIS.　The bare remembrance takes away my senses. Bamberg is no longer Bamberg.　An angel of heaven, in semblance of woman, has taken up her abode there, and has made it a paradise.

WEISLINGEN.　Is that all?

FRANCIS.　May I become a shaven friar, if the first glimpse of her does not drive you frantic!

WEISLINGEN.　Who is it, then?

FRANCIS.　Adelaide von Walldorf.

WEISLINGEN.　Indeed! I have heard much of her beauty.

FRANCIS.　Heard!　You might as well say I have *seen* music.　So far is the tongue from being able to rehearse the slightest particle of her beauty, that the very eye which beholds her cannot drink it all in.

WEISLINGEN.　You are mad.

FRANCIS.　That may well be.　The last time I was in her company I had no more command over my senses than if I had been drunk, or, I may rather say, I felt like a glorified saint enjoying the angelic vision!　All my senses exalted, more lively and more perfect than ever, yet not one at its owner's command.

WEISLINGEN.　That is strange!

FRANCIS.　As I took leave of the bishop, she sat by him; they were playing at chess.　He was very gracious; gave me his hand to kiss, and said much, of which I heard not a syllable, for I was looking on his fair antagonist.　Her eye was fixed upon the board, as if meditating a bold move.— Traces of attentive intelligence around the mouth and cheek. —I could have wished to be the ivory king.　The mixture of dignity and feeling on her brow—and the dazzling lustre of her face and neck, heightened by her raven tresses——

WEISLINGEN.　The theme has made you quite poetical.

FRANCIS.　I feel at this moment what constitutes poetic inspiration—a heart altogether wrapt in one idea.　As the bishop ended, and I made my obeisance, she looked up

and said, " Offer to your master the best wishes of an unknown.  Tell him he must come soon.  New friends await
him ; he must not despise them, though he is already so rich
in old ones."  I would have answered, but the passage
betwixt my heart and my tongue was closed, and I only
bowed.  I would have given all I had for permission to kiss
but one of her fingers!  As I stood thus, the bishop let
fall a pawn, and in stooping to pick it up, I touched the
hem of her garment.  Transport thrilled through my limbs,
and I scarce know how I left the room.

WEISLINGEN.   Is her husband at court?

FRANCIS.   She has been a widow these four months, and
is residing at the court of Bamberg to divert her melancholy.
You will see her ; and to meet her glance is to bask in the
sunshine of spring.

WEISLINGEN.   She would not make so strong an impression on me.

FRANCIS.   I hear you are as good as married.

WEISLINGEN.   Would I were really so!  My gentle
Maria will be the happiness of my life.  The sweetness of her
soul beams through her mild blue eyes, and, like an angel of
innocence and love, she guides my heart to the paths of
peace and felicity!  Pack up, and then to my castle.  I
will not to Bamberg, though St. Bede came in person to fetch
me.                                        [*Exit* WEISLINGEN.

FRANCIS (*alone*).   Not to Bamberg!  Heavens forbid!  But
let me hope the best.  Maria is beautiful and amiable, and a
prisoner or an invalid might easily fall in love with her.
Her eyes beam with compassion and melancholy sympathy ;
but in thine, Adelaide, is life, fire, spirit.  I would——
I am a fool; one glance from her has made me so.  My
master must to Bamberg, and I also, and either recover my
senses or gaze them quite away.


END OF THE FIRST ACT.

# ACT THE SECOND.

## SCENE I.  BAMBERG.  *A Hall.*

THE BISHOP *and* ADELAIDE *(playing at chess)*, LIEBTRAUT *(with a guitar)*, LADIES *and* COURTIERS *(standing in groups)*.

LIEBTRAUT *(plays and sings)*.
Armed with quiver and bow,
With his torch all a glow,
Young Cupid comes winging his flight.
Courage glows in his eyes,
As adown from the skies,
He rushes, impatient for fight.

Up! Up!
On! On!
Hark! The bright quiver rings!
Hark! The rustle of wings!
All hail to the delicate sprite!

They welcome the urchin;—
Ah maidens, beware!
He finds every bosom
Unguarded and bare.
In the light of his flambeau
He kindles his darts;—
They fondle and hug him
And press to their hearts.

ADELAIDE.  Your thoughts are not in your game.  Check to the king!

BISHOP.  There is still a way of escape.

ADELAIDE.  You will not be able to hold out long. Check to the king!

LIEBTRAUT.  Were I a great prince, I would not play at this game, and would forbid it at court, and throughout the whole land.

ADELAIDE.  'Tis indeed a touchstone of the brain.

LIEBTRAUT.  Not on that account  I would rather hear

a funeral bell, the cry of the ominous bird, the howling of
that snarling watch-dog, conscience; rather would I hear
these through the deepest sleep, than from bishops, knights,
and such beasts, the eternal—Check to the king!

BISHOP. Into whose head could such an idea enter?

LIEBTRAUT. A man's, for example, endowed with a weak
body and a strong conscience, which, for the most part,
indeed, accompany each other. Chess is called a royal game,
and is said to have been invented for a king, who rewarded
the inventor with a mine of wealth. If this be so, I can picture
him to myself. He was a minor, either in understanding
or in years, under the guardianship of his mother or his
wife; had down upon his chin, and flaxen hair around his
temples; was pliant as a willow-shoot, and liked to play
at draughts with women, not from passion, God forbid! only
for pastime. His tutor, too active for a scholar, too intractable for a man of the world, invented the game, *in usum
Delphini*, that was so homogeneous with his majesty—and
so on.

ADELAIDE. Checkmate! You should fill up the chasms
in our histories, Liebtraut. [*They rise.*

LIEBTRAUT. To supply those in our family registers
would be more profitable. The merits of our ancestors being
available for a common object with their portraits, namely, to
cover the naked sides of our chambers and of our characters,
one might turn such an occupation to good account.

BISHOP. He will not come, you say!

ADELAIDE. I beseech you, banish him from your thoughts.

BISHOP. What can it mean?

LIEBTRAUT. What! The reasons may be told over like
the beads of a rosary. He has been seized with a fit of com-
punction, of which I could soon cure him.

BISHOP. Do so; ride to him instantly.

LIEBTRAUT. My commission——

BISHOP. Shall be unlimited. Spare nothing to bring
him back.

LIEBTRAUT. May I venture to use your name, gracious
lady? .

ADELAIDE. With discretion.

LIEBTRAUT. That's a vague commission.

ADELAIDE. Do you know so little of me, or are you so

young as not to understand in what tone you should speak of me to Weislingen?

LIEBTRAUT.  In the tone of a fowler's whistle, I think.

ADELAIDE.  You will never be reasonable.

LIEBTRAUT.  Does one ever become so, gracious lady?

BISHOP.  Go! Go! Take the best horse in my stable; choose your servants, and bring him hither.

LIEBTRAUT.  If I do not conjure him hither, say that an old woman who charms warts and freckles knows more of sympathy than I.

BISHOP.  Yet, what will it avail?  Berlichingen has wholly gained him over.  He will no sooner be here than he will wish to return.

LIEBTRAUT.  He will wish it, doubtless; but can he go? A prince's squeeze of the hand and the smiles of a beauty, from these no Weislingen can tear himself away.  I have the honour to take my leave.

BISHOP.  A prosperous journey!

ADELAIDE.  Adieu!  [*Exit* LIEBTRAUT.

BISHOP.  When he is once here, I must trust to you.

ADELAIDE.  Would you make me your lime-twig?

BISHOP.  By no means.

ADELAIDE.  Your call-bird then?

BISHOP.  No; that is Liebtraut's part.  I beseech you do not refuse to do for me what no other can.

ADELAIDE.  We shall see.  [*Exeunt*


SCENE II.  *Jaxthausen.*  *A Hall in Goetz's Castle.*

*Enter* GOETZ *and* HANS VON SELBITZ.

SELBITZ.  Every one will applaud you for declaring feud against the Nurembergers.

GOETZ.  It would have eaten my very heart away had I remained longer their debtor.  It is clear that they betrayed my page to the Bambergers.  They shall have cause to remember me.

SELBITZ.  They have an old grudge against you.

GOETZ.  And I against them.  I am glad they have begun the fray.

SELBITZ.  These free towns have always taken part with the priests.

GOETZ.  They have good reason.

SELBITZ.  But we will cook their porridge for them!

GOETZ. I reckon upon you.  Would that the Burgomaster of Nürnberg, with his gold chain round his neck, fell in our way, we'd astonish him with all his cleverness.

SELBITZ.  I hear Weislingen is again on your side.  Does he really join in our league?

GOETZ.  Not immediately.  There are reasons which prevent his openly giving us assistance; but for the present it is quite enough that he is not against us.  The priest without him is what the stole would be without the priest!

SELBITZ.  When do we set forward?

GOETZ.  To-morrow or next day.  There are merchants of Bamberg and Nuremberg returning from the fair of Frankfort—We may strike a good blow.

SELBITZ.  Let us hope so!


## SCENE III.  *The Bishop's Palace at Bamberg.*

### ADELAIDE *and her* WAITING-MAID.

ADELAIDE.  He is here, sayest thou?  I can scarce believe it.

MAID.  Had I not seen him myself, I should have doubted it.

ADELAIDE.  The bishop should frame Liebtraut in gold for such a masterpiece of skill.

MAID.  I saw him as he was about to enter the palace. He was mounted on a grey charger.  The horse started when he came on the bridge, and would not move forward.  The populace thronged up the street to see him.  They rejoiced at the delay of the unruly horse.  He was greeted on all sides, and he thanked them gracefully all round.  He sate the curvetting steed with an easy indifference, and by threats and soothing brought him to the gate, followed by Liebtraut and a few servants.

ADELAIDE.  What do you think of him?

MAID.  I never saw a man who pleased me so well.  He is as like that portrait of the emperor, as if he were his son (*pointing to a picture*).   His nose is somewhat smaller, but just such gentle light-brown eyes, just such fine light hair, and such a figure !  A half melancholy expression on his face, I know not how, but he pleased me so well.

ADELAIDE.   I am curious to see him.

MAID.   He would be the husband for you !

ADELAIDE.   Foolish girl!

MAID.   Children and fools——

*Enter* LIEBTRAUT.

Now, gracious lady, what do I deserve?

ADELAIDE.   Horns from your wife!—for, judging from the present sample of your persuasive powers, you have certainly endangered the honour of many a worthy family.

LIEBTRAUT.   Not so, be assured, gracious lady.

ADELAIDE.   How did you contrive to bring him?

LIEBTRAUT.   You know how they catch snipes, and why should I detail my little stratagems to you?—First, I pretended to have heard nothing, did not understand the reason of his behaviour, and put him upon the disadvantage of telling me the whole story at length—then I saw the matter in quite a different light to what he did—could not find—could not see, and so forth—then I gossipped things great and small about Bamberg, and recalled to his memory certain old recollections; and when I had succeeded in occupying his imagination, I knitted together many a broken association of ideas.   He knew not what to say—felt a new attraction towards Bamberg—he would, and he would not.   When I found him begin to waver, and saw him too much occupied with his own feelings to suspect my sincerity, I threw over his head a halter, woven of the three powerful cords, beauty, court-favour, and flattery, and dragged him hither in triumph.

ADELAIDE.   What said you of me ?

LIEBTRAUT.   The simple truth—that you were in perplexity about your estates, and had hoped as he had so much influence with the emperor, all would be satisfactorily settled.

ADELAIDE.   'Tis well.

LIEBTRAUT.   The bishop will introduce him to you.

ADELAIDE.   I expect them.  [*Exit* LIEBTRAUT.]   And with such feelings have I seldom expected a visitor.

## SCENE IV.   *The Spessart.*

*Enter* SELBITZ, GOETZ, *and* GEORGE *in the armour
and dress of a trooper.*

GOETZ.   So, thou didst not find him, George?

GEORGE.   He had ridden to Bamberg the day before, with
Liebtraut and two servants.

GOETZ.   I cannot understand what this means.

SELBITZ.   I see it well—your reconciliation was almost
too speedy to be lasting—Liebtraut is a cunning fellow, and
has no doubt inveigled him over.

GOETZ.   Think'st thou he will become a traitor?

SELBITZ.   The first step is taken.

GOETZ.   I will never believe it.   Who knows what he may
have to do at court—his affairs are still unarranged.   Let us
hope for the best.

SELBITZ.   Would to Heaven he were deserving of your good
opinion, and have acted for the best!

GOETZ.   A thought strikes me!—We will disguise George
in the spoils of the Bamberg trooper, and furnish him with
the password—he may then ride to Bamberg, and see how
matters stand.

GEORGE.   I have long wished to do so.

GOETZ   It is thy first expedition.   Be careful, boy; I
should be sorry if ill befel thee.

GEORGE.   Never fear.   I care not how many of them crawl
about me ; I think no more of them than of rats and mice.

[*Exeunt.*

## SCENE V.   *The Bishop's Palace.   His Cabinet.*

THE BISHOP *and* WEISLINGEN.

BISHOP.   Then thou wilt stay no longer?

WEISLINGEN.   You would not have me break my oath.

BISHOP.   I could have wished thou hadst not sworn it.—
What evil spirit possessed thee?—Could I not have procured
thy release without that?   Is my influence so small in the
imperial court?

WEISLINGEN.   The thing is done!—excuse it as you can.

BISHOP.   I cannot see that there was the least necessity
for taking such a step—To renounce me?—Were there not
a thousand other ways of procuring thy freedom?—Had we

not his page? And would I not have given gold enough to boot? and thus satisfied Berlichingen. Our operations against him and his confederates could have gone on——But, alas! I do not reflect that I am talking to his friend, who has joined him against me, and can easily counterwork the mines he himself has dug.

WEISLINGEN.   My gracious lord .....

BISHOP.   And yet—when I again look on thy face, again hear thy voice—it is impossible—impossible!

WEISLINGEN.   Farewell, good my lord!

BISHOP.   I give thee my blessing—formerly when we parted, I was wont to say "Till we meet again!"—Now Heaven grant we meet no more!

WEISLINGEN.   Things may alter.

BISHOP.   Perhaps I may live to see thee appear as an enemy before my walls, carrying havoc through the fertile plains which now owe their flourishing condition to thee.

WEISLINGEN.   Never, my gracious lord!

BISHOP.   You cannot say so. My tempora. neighbours all have a grudge against me—but while thou wert mine——Go, Weislingen!—I have no more to say—Thou hast undone much —Go—

WEISLINGEN.   I know not what to answer.   [*Exit* BISHOP.
*Enter* FRANCIS.

FRANCIS.   The Lady Adelaide expects you. She is not well—but she will not let you depart without bidding her adieu.

WEISLINGEN.   Come.

FRANCIS.   Do we go then for certain?

WEISLINGEN.   This very night.

FRANCIS.   I feel as if I were about to leave the world—

WEISLINGEN.   I too, and as if besides I knew not whither to go.


SCENE VI.   *Adelaide's Apartment.*

ADELAIDE *and* WAITING-MAID.

MAID.   You are pale, gracious lady!

ADELAIDE.   I love him not, yet I wish him to stay—for I am fond of his company, though I should dislike him for my husband.

MAID.   Does your ladyship think he will go?

ADELAIDE.   He is even now bidding the bishop farewell.

MAID.   He has yet a severe struggle to undergo.

ADELAIDE.   What meanest thou?

MAID.   Why do you ask, gracious lady?  The barb'd hook is in his heart—ere he tear it away he must bleed to death.

*Enter* WEISLINGEN.

WEISLINGEN.   You are not well, gracious lady!

ADELAIDE.   That must be indifferent to you—you leave us, leave us forever: what matters it to you whether we live or die?

WEISLINGEN.   You do me injustice.

ADELAIDE.   I judge you as you appear.

WEISLINGEN.   Appearances are deceitful.

ADELAIDE.   Then you are a cameleon.

WEISLINGEN.   Could you but see my heart—

ADELAIDE.   I should see fine things there.

WEISLINGEN.   Undoubtedly!—You would find your own image—

ADELAIDE.   Thrust into some dark corner, with the pictures of defunct ancestors!  I beseech you, Weislingen, consider with whom you speak—false words are of value only when they serve to veil our actions—a discovered masquerader plays a pitiful part.  You do not disown your deeds, yet your words belie them ; what are we to think of you?

WEISLINGEN.   What you will—I am so agonised at reflecting on what I am, that I little reck for what I am taken.

ADELAIDE.   You came to say farewell.

WEISLINGEN.   Permit me to kiss your hand, and I will say adieu!——You remind me—I did not think—but I am troublesome—

ADELAIDE.   You misinterpret me : Since you will depart, I only wished to assist your resolution.

WEISLINGEN.   O say rather, I must!—were I not compelled by my knightly word—my solemn engagement—

ADELAIDE.   Go to!  Talk of that to maidens who read the tale of Theuerdanck, and wish that they had such a husband.—Knightly word!—Nonsense !

WEISLINGEN.   You do not think so?

ADELAIDE.   On my honour, you are dissembling.  What have you promised? and to whom? You have pledged your alliance to a traitor to the emperor, at the very moment when he incurred the ban of the empire by taking you prisoner

Such an agreement is no more binding than an extorted, unjust
oath.    And do not our laws release you from such oaths?
Go, tell that to children, who believe in Rübezahl.   There
is something behind all this.—To become an enemy of the
empire—a disturber of public happiness and tranquillity, an
enemy of the emperor, the associate of a robber!—Thou,
Weislingen, with thy gentle soul!

WEISLINGEN.   Did but you know him.

ADELAIDE.   I would deal justly with Goetz.   He has a
lofty indomitable spirit, and woe to thee, therefore, Weislingen.
Go, and persuade thyself thou art his companion: Go, and
receive his commands: Thou art courteous, gentle——

WEISLINGEN.   And he too.

ADELAIDE.   But thou art yielding, and he is stubborn.
Imperceptibly will he draw thee on.   Thou wilt become the
slave of a baron; thou that mightest command princes!—
Yet it is cruel to make you discontented with your future
position.

WEISLINGEN.   Did you but know what kindness he
showed me.

ADELAIDE.   Kindness!—Do you make such a merit of
that?   It was his duty.   And what would you have lost had
he acted otherwise.   I would rather he had done so.   An
overbearing man like—

WEISLINGEN.   You speak of your enemy.

ADELAIDE.   I speak for your freedom; yet I know not
why I should take so much interest in it.   Farewell!

WEISLINGEN.   Permit me, but a moment.   (*Takes her
hand.   A pause.*)

ADELAIDE.   Have you aught to say?

WEISLINGEN.   I must hence.

ADELAIDE.   Then go.

WEISLINGEN.   Gracious lady, I cannot.

ADELAIDE.   You must.

WEISLINGEN.   And is this your parting look?

ADELAIDE.   Go, I am unwell, very inopportunely.

WEISLINGEN.   Look not on me thus!

ADELAIDE.   Wilt thou be our enemy, and yet have us
smile upon thee—go!

WEISLINGEN.   Adelaide!

ADELAIDE.   I hate thee!

*Enter Francis.*

FRANCIS.    Noble sir, the bishop inquires for you.
ADELAIDE.    Go! go!
FRANCIS.    He begs you to come instantly.
ADELAIDE.    Go! Go!
WEISLINGEN.    I do not say adieu: I shall see you again.
                              [*Exeunt* WEISLINGEN *and* FRANCIS.
ADELAIDE.    Thou wilt see me again? We must provide for
that.  Margaret, when he comes, refuse him admittance.  Say
I am ill, have a head-ache, am asleep, anything.  If this does
not detain him, nothing will.                    [*Exeunt.*

### SCENE VII.    *An ante-room.*

WEISLINGEN *and* FRANCIS.

WEISLINGEN.    She will not see me!
FRANCIS.    Night draws on; shall we saddle?
WEISLINGEN.    She will not see me!
FRANCIS.    Shall I order the horses?
WEISLINGEN.    It is too late; we stay here.
FRANCIS.    God be praised!                    [*Exit.*
WEISLINGEN (*alone*).    Thou stayest! Be on thy guard—
the temptation is great.  My horse started at the castle
gate.  My good angel stood before him, he knew the danger
that awaited me.  Yet it would be wrong to leave in confusion the various affairs entrusted to me by the bishop,
without at least so arranging them, that my successor may be
able to continue where I left off.  That I can do without breach
of faith to Berlichingen, and when it is done no one shall detain
me.  Yet it would have been better that I had never come.
But I will away—to-morrow—or next day:—'Tis decided!
                              [*Exit.*

### SCENE VIII.    *The Spessart.*

*Enter* GOETZ, SELBITZ, *and* GEORGE.

SELBITZ.    You see it has turned out as I prophesied.
GOETZ.    No, no, no.
GEORGE.    I tell you the truth, believe me.  I did as you
commanded, took the dress and pass-word of the Bamberg
trooper, and escorted some peasants of the Lower Rhine,
who paid my expenses for my convoy.
SELBITZ.    In that disguise?  It might have cost thee dear

GEORGE.  So I begin to think, now that it's over.  A trooper who thinks of danger beforehand, will never do anything great.  I got safely to Bamberg, and in the very first inn I heard them tell how the bishop and Weislingen were reconciled, and how Weislingen was to marry the widow of Von Walldorf.

GOETZ.  Mere gossip!

GEORGE.  I saw him as he led her to table.  She is lovely, by my faith, most lovely!  We all bowed—she thanked us all.  He nodded, and seemed highly pleased.  They passed on, and everybody murmured, "What a handsome pair!"

GOETZ.  That may be.

GEORGE.  Listen further:  The next day as he went to mass, I watched my opportunity ; he was attended only by his squire ; I stood at the steps, and whispered to him as he passed, " A few words from your friend Berlichingen." He started—I marked the confession of guilt in his face. He had scarcely the heart to look at me—me, a poor trooper's boy!

SELBITZ.  His evil conscience degrades him more than thy condition does thee.

GEORGE.  " Art thou of Bamberg ?" said he.  "The Knight of Berlichingen greets you," said I, " and I am to enquire—" " Come to my apartment to-morrow morning," quoth he, " and we will speak further."

GOETZ.  And you went.

GEORGE.  Yes, certainly, I went, and waited in his ante-chamber a long—long time—and his pages, in their silken doublets, stared at me from head to foot.  Stare on, thought I.  At length I was admitted.  He seemed angry.  But what cared I ?  I gave my message.  He began blustering like a coward who wants to look brave.  He wondered that you should take him to task through a trooper's boy.  That angered me.  " There are but two sorts of people," said I. " true men and scoundrels, and I serve Goetz of Berlichingen."  Then he began to talk all manner of nonsense, which all tended to one point, namely, that you had hurried him into an agreement, that he owed you no allegiance, and would have nothing to do with you.

GOETZ.  Hadst thou that from his own mouth ?

GEORGE.  That, and yet more.  He threatened me—

GOETZ.  It is enough.  He is lost for ever.  Faith and

confidence again, have ye deceived me.  Poor Maria! how
am I to break this to you?

SELBITZ.   I would rather lose my other leg than be such
a rascal.


## SCENE IX.   *Hall in the Bishop's Palace at Bamberg.*

### ADELAIDE *and* WEISLINGEN *discovered.*

ADELAIDE.  Time begins to hang insupportably heavy here.
I dare not speak seriously, and I am ashamed to trifle with
you.  Ennui, thou art worse than a slow fever.

WEISLINGEN.   Are you tired of me already!

ADELAIDE.  Not so much of you as of your society.  I
would you had gone when you wished, and that we had not
detained you.

WEISLINGEN.   Such is woman's favour!  At first she
fosters with maternal warmth our dearest hopes; and then, like
an inconstant hen, she forsakes the nest, and abandons the
infant brood to death and decay.

ADELAIDE.  Yes, you may rail at women.  The reckless
gambler tears and curses the harmless cards which have been
the instruments of his loss.  But let me tell you something about
*men.*  What are you that talk about fickleness?  You that
are seldom even what you would wish to be, never what you
should be.  Princes in holiday garb! the envy of the vulgar.
O what would a tailor's wife not give for a necklace of the pearls
on the skirt of your robe, which you kick back contemptu-
ously with your heels.

WEISLINGEN.   You are severe.

ADELAIDE.  It is but the antistrophe to your song.  Ere
I knew you, Weislingen, I felt like the tailor's wife.  Hundred-
tongued rumour, to speak without metaphor, had so extolled
you, in quack-doctor fashion, that I was tempted to wish—
O that I could but see this quintessence of manhood, this
phœnix, Weislingen!  My wish was granted.

WEISLINGEN.  And the phœnix turned out a dunghill cock.

ADELAIDE.  No, Weislingen, I took an interest in you.

WEISLINGEN.  So it appeared.

ADELAIDE.  So it *was*—for you really surpassed your reputation.  The multitude prize only the reflection of worth.  For
my part, I do not care to scrutinize the character of those

whom I esteem; so we lived on for some time. I felt there
was a deficiency in you, but knew not what I missed; at
length my eyes were opened—I saw instead of the energetic
being who gave impulse to the affairs of a kingdom, and was
ever alive to the voice of fame—who was wont to pile princely
project on project. till, like the mountains of the Titans, they
reached the clouds—instead of all this, I saw a man as querulous
as a love-sick poet, as melancholy as a slighted damsel, and
more indolent than an old bachelor.   I first ascribed it to your
misfortune which still lay at your heart, and excused you as
well as I could; but now that it daily becomes worse, you
must really forgive me if I withdraw my favour from you.
You possess it unjustly; I bestowed it for life on a hero
who cannot transfer it to you.

WEISLINGEN.   Dismiss me, then.

ADELAIDE.   Not till all chance of recovery is lost.  Solitude
is fatal in your distemper.  Alas! poor man! you are as
dejected as one whose first love has proved false, and therefore I won't give you up.  Give me your hand, and pardon
what affection has urged me to say.

WEISLINGEN.   Could'st thou but love me, could'st thou
but return the fervour of my passion with the least glow
of sympathy.—Adelaide, thy reproaches are most unjust.
Could'st thou but guess the hundredth part of my sufferings,
thou wouldst not have tortured me so unmercifully with
encouragement, indifference, and contempt.  You smile.  To
be reconciled to myself after the step I have taken must be
the work of more than one day.  How can I plot against the
man who has been so recently and so vividly restored to my
affection.

ADELAIDE.   Strange being!  Can you love him whom you
envy?  It is like sending provisions to an enemy.

WEISLINGEN.   I well know that here there must be no
dallying.  He is aware that I am again Weislingen; and
he will watch his advantage over us.  Besides, Adelaide,
we are not so sluggish as you think.  Our troopers are rein-
forced and watchful, our schemes are proceeding, and the diet
of Augsburg will, I hope, soon bring them to a favourable issue.

ADELAIDE.   You go there?

WEISLINGEN.   If I could carry a glimpse of hope with me.

                                   [*Kisses her hand.*

ADELAIDE. Oh! ye infidels! Always signs and wonders required. Go, Weislingen, and accomplish the work! The interest of the bishop, yours, and mine, are all so linked together, that were it only for policy's sake—

WEISLINGEN. You jest.

ADELAIDE. I do not jest. The haughty duke has seized my property. Goetz will not be slow to ravage yours; and if we do not hold together, as our enemies do, and gain over the emperor to our side, we are lost.

WEISLINGEN. I fear nothing. Most of the princes think with us. The emperor needs assistance against the Turks, and it is therefore just that he should help us in his turn. What rapture for me to rescue your fortune from rapacious enemies; to crush the mutinous chivalry of Swabia; to restore peace to the bishopric, and then—

ADELAIDE. One day brings on another, and fate is mistress of the future.

WEISLINGEN. But we must lend our endeavours.

ADELAIDE. We do so.

WEISLINGEN. But seriously.

ADELAIDE. Well, then, seriously. Do but go—

WEISLINGEN. Enchantress!      [*Exeunt.*


## SCENE X. *An Inn.*

### *The Bridal of a* PEASANT.

*The* BRIDE'S FATHER, BRIDE, BRIDEGROOM, *and other Country-folks,* GOETZ *of Berlichingen, and* HANS *of Selbitz all discovered at table.* TROOPERS *and* PEASANTS *attend.*

GOETZ. It was the best way thus to settle your lawsuit by a merry bridal.

BRIDE'S FATHER. Better than ever I could have dreamed of, noble sir—to spend my days in peace and quiet with my neighbour, and have a daughter provided for to boot.

BRIDEGROOM. And I to get the bone of contention and a pretty wife into the bargain! Aye, the prettiest in the whole village. Would to Heaven you had consented sooner

GOETZ. How long have you been at law?

BRIDE'S FATHER. About eight years. I would rather

have the fever for twice that time, than go through with it again from the beginning. For these periwigged gentry never give a decision till you tear it out of their very hearts; and after all, what do you get for your pains? The Devi! fly away with the assessor Sapupi for a damn'd swarthy Italian!

BRIDEGROOM. Yes, he's a pretty fellow; I was before him twice.

BRIDE'S FATHER. And I thrice; and look ye, gentelmen, we got a judgment at last, which set forth that he was as much in the right as I, and I as much as he; so there we stood like a couple of fools, till a good Providence put it into my head to give him my daughter, and the ground besides.

GOETZ (*drinks*). To your better understanding for the future.

BRIDE'S FATHER. With all my heart! But come what may, I'll never go to law again as long as I live. What a mint of money it costs! For every bow made to you by a procurator, you must come down with your dollars.

SELBITZ. But there are annual imperial visitations.

BRIDE'S FATHER. I have never heard of them. Many an extra dollar have they contrived to squeeze out of me. The expenses are horrible.

GOETZ. How mean you?

BRIDE'S FATHER. Why, look you, these gentlemen of the law are always holding out their hands. The assessor alone, God forgive him, eased me of eighteen golden guilders.

BRIDEGROOM. Who?

BRIDE'S FATHER. Why, who else but Sapupi.

GOETZ. That is infamous.

BRIDE'S FATHER. Yes, he asked twenty: and there I had to pay them in the great hall of his fine country-house. I thought my heart would burst with anguish. For look you, my lord, I am well enough off with my house and little farm, but how could I raise the ready cash? I stood there, God knows how it was with me. I had not a single farthing to carry me on my journey. At last I took courage and told him my case: when he saw I was desperate, he flung me back a couple of guilders, and sent me about my business.

BRIDEGROOM.  Impossible!  Sapupi?

BRIDE'S FATHER.    Aye, he himself!—What do you stare at?

BRIDEGROOM.  Devil take the rascal!  He took fifteen guilders from me too!

BRIDE'S FATHER.   The deuce he did!

SELBITZ.  They call us robbers, Goetz!

BRIDE'S FATHER.   Bribed on both sides!  That's why the judgment fell out so queer.—Oh!  the scoundrel!

GOETZ.   You must not let this pass unnoticed.

BRIDE'S FATHER.   What can we do?

GOETZ.   Why—go to Spire where there is an imperial visitation : make your complaint ; they must enquire into it, and help you to your own again.

BRIDEGROOM.   Does your honour think we shall succeed?

GOETZ.  If I might take him in hand, I could promise it you.

SELBITZ.   The sum is worth an attempt.

GOETZ.  Aye; many a-day have I ridden out for the fourth part of it.

BRIDE'S FATHER (*to* BRIDEGROOM.) What think'st thou?

BRIDEGROOM.   We'll try. come what may.

*Enter* GEORGE.

GEORGE.   The Nurembergers have set out.

GOETZ.   Whereabouts are they?

GEORGE.   If we ride off quietly, we shall just catch them in the wood betwixt Berheim and Mühlbach.

SELBITZ.  Excellent!

GOETZ.  Well, my children, God bless you, and help every man to his own!

BRIDE'S FATHER.   Thanks, gallant sir!  Will you not stay to supper?

GOETZ.  I cannot.  Adieu!

[*Exeunt* GOETZ, SELBITZ, *and* TROOPERS.


END OF THE SECOND ACT

# ACT THE THIRD.

### SCENE I.  *A Garden at Augsburg.*

*Enter two* MERCHANTS *of Nuremberg.*

FIRST MERCHANT.  We'll stand here, for the emperor must pass this way.  He is just coming up the long avenue.

SECOND MERCHANT.  Who is that with him?

FIRST MERCHANT.  Adelbert of Weislingen.

SECOND MERCHANT.  The bishop's friend.  That's lucky!

FIRST MERCHANT.  We'll throw ourselves at his feet.

SECOND MERCHANT.  See! they come.

*Enter the* EMPEROR *and* WEISLINGEN.

FIRST MERCHANT.  He looks displeased.

EMPEROR.  I am disheartened, Weislingen.  When I review my past life, I am ready to despair.  So many half—aye, and wholly ruined undertakings—and all because the pettiest feudatory of the empire thinks more of gratifying his own whims than of seconding my endeavours.

[*The* MERCHANTS *throw themselves at his feet.*

FIRST MERCHANT.  Most mighty!  Most gracious!

EMPEROR.  Who are ye?  What seek ye?

FIRST MERCHANT.  Poor merchants of Nuremberg, your majesty's devoted servants, who implore your aid.  Goetz von Berlichingen and Hans von Selbitz fell upon thirty of us as we journeyed from the fair of Frankfort, under an escort from Bamberg; they overpowered and plundered us.  We implore your imperial assistance to obtain redress, else we are all ruined men, and shall be compelled to beg our bread.

EMPEROR.  Good heavens!  What is this?  The one has but one hand, the other but one leg; if they both had two hands and two legs what would you do then!

FIRST MERCHANT.  We most humbly beseech your majesty to cast a look of compassion upon our unfortunate condition.

EMPEROR.  How is this:—If a merchant loses a bag of pepper, all Germany is to rise in arms; but when business

is to be done, in which the imperial majesty and the empire
are interested, should it concern dukedoms, principalities,
or kingdoms, there is no bringing you together.

WEISLINGEN.   You come at an unseasonable time.   Go,
and stay at Augsburg for a few days.

MERCHANTS.   We make our most humble obeisance.

[*Exeunt* MERCHANTS.

EMPEROR.   Again new disturbances; they multiply like
the hydra's heads!

WEISLINGEN.   And can only be extirpated with fire and
sword.

EMPEROR.   Do you think so?

WEISLINGEN.   Nothing seems to me more advisable, could
your majesty and the princes but accommodate your other
unimportant disputes.   It is not the body of the state that
complains of this malady—Franconia and Swabia alone glow
with the embers of civil discord; and even there many of
the nobles and free barons long for quiet.   Could we but
crush Sickingen, Selbitz—and—and—and Berlichingen, the
others would soon fall asunder; for it is the spirit of these
knights which quickens the turbulent multitude.

EMPEROR.   Fain would I spare them; they are noble and
hardy.   Should I be engaged in war, they would follow me
to the field.

WEISLINGEN.   It is to be wished they had at all times
known their duty; though even in that case it would have
been dangerous to reward their mutinous bravery by offices
of trust.   For it is exactly this imperial mercy and forgiveness
which they have hitherto so grievously abused, and upon which
the hope and confidence of their league rests, and this spirit
cannot be quelled till we have wholly destroyed their power
in the eyes of the world, and taken from them all hope of ever
recovering their lost influence.

EMPEROR.   You advise severe measures then?

WEISLINGEN.   I see no other means of quelling the spirit
of insurrection which has seized upon whole provinces.   Do
we not already hear the bitterest complaints from the nobles,
that their vassals and serfs rebel against them, question their
authority, and threaten to curtail their hereditary prerogo-
tives?   A proceeding which would involve the most fearful
consequences.

EMPEROR. This were a fair occasion for proceeding against Berlichingen and Selbitz; but I will not have them personally injured. Could they be taken prisoners, they should swear to renounce their feuds, and to remain in their own castles and territories upon their knightly parole. At the next session of the Diet we will propose this plan.

WEISLINGEN. A general exclamation of joyful assent will spare your majesty the trouble of particular detail.

*[Exeunt.*

## SCENE II. *Jaxthausen.*

*Enter* GOETZ *and* FRANZ VON SICKINGEN.

SICKINGEN. Yes, my friend, I come to beg the heart and hand of your noble sister.

GOETZ. I would you had come sooner. Weislingen, during his imprisonment, obtained her affections, proposed for her, and I gave my consent. I let the bird loose, and he now despises the benevolent hand that fed him in his distress. He flutters about to seek his food, God knows upon what hedge.

SICKINGEN. Is this so?

GOETZ. Even as I tell you.

SICKINGEN. He has broken a double bond. 'Tis well for you that you were not more closely allied with the traitor.

GOETZ. The poor maiden passes her life in lamentation and prayer.

SICKINGEN. I will comfort her.

GOETZ. What! Could you make up your mind to marry a forsaken——

SICKINGEN. It is to the honour of you both, to have been deceived by him. Should the poor girl be caged in a cloister because the first man who gained her love proved a villain? Not so; I insist on it. She shall be mistress of my castles!

GOETZ. I tell you he was not indifferent to her.

SICKINGEN. Do you think I cannot efface the recollection of such a wretch? Let us go to her.  *[Exeunt*

SCENE III.    *The Camp of the Party sent to execute the Imperial mandate.*

*Imperial* CAPTAIN *and* OFFICERS *discovered.*

CAPTAIN.    We must be cautious, and spare our people as much as possible.    Besides, we have strict orders to overpower and take him alive.    It will be difficult to obey; for who will engage with him hand to hand?

FIRST OFFICER.    'Tis true.    And he will fight like a wild boar.    Besides, he has never in his whole life injured any of us, so each will be glad to leave to the other the honour of risking life and limb to please the emperor.

SECOND OFFICER.    'Twere shame to us should we not take him.    Had I him once by the ears, he should not easily escape.

FIRST OFFICER.    Don't seize him with your teeth, however, he might chance to run away with your jaw-bone. My good young sir, such men are not taken like a runaway thief.

SECOND OFFICER.    We shall see.

CAPTAIN.    By this time he must have had our summons. We must not delay.    I mean to dispatch a troop to watch his motions.

SECOND OFFICER.    Let me lead it.

CAPTAIN.    You are unacquainted with the country.

SECOND OFFICER.    I have a servant who was born and bred here.

CAPTAIN.    That will do.                    [*Exeunt.*


SCENE IV.    *Jaxthausen.*

SICKINGEN (*alone*).

All goes as I wish!    She was somewhat startled at my proposal, and looked at me from head to foot; I'll wager she was comparing me with her gallant.    Thank Heaven I can stand the scrutiny!    She answered little and confusedly.    So much the better!    Let it work for a time

A proposal of marriage does not come amiss after such a cruel disappointment.

*Enter* GOETZ.

SICKINGEN.    What news, brother?

GOETZ.    They have laid me under the ban.

SICKINGEN.    How?

GOETZ.    There, read the edifying epistle. The emperor has issued an edict against me, which gives my body for food to the beasts of the earth and the fowls of the air.

SICKINGEN.    They shall first furnish them with a dinner themselves. I am here in the very nick of time.

GOETZ.    No, Sickingen, you must leave me. Your great undertakings might be ruined, should you become the enemy of the emperor at so unseasonable a time. Besides, you can be of more use to me by remaining neutral. The worst that can happen is my being made prisoner; and then your good word with the emperor, who esteems you, may rescue me from the misfortune into which your untimely assistance would irremediably plunge us both. To what purpose should you do otherwise? These troops are marching against me; and if they knew we were united, their numbers would only be increased, and our position would consequently be no better. The emperor is at the fountain head; and I should be utterly ruined were it as easy to inspire soldiers with courage as to collect them into a body.

SICKINGEN.    But I can privately reinforce you with a score of troopers.

GOETZ.    Good. I have already sent George to Selbitz, and to my people in the neighbourhood. My dear brother, when my forces are collected, they will be such a troop as few princes can bring together.

SICKINGEN.    It will be small against the multitude.

GOETZ.    One wolf is too many for a whole flock of sheep.

SICKINGEN.    But if they have a good shepherd?

GOETZ.    Never fear! They are all hirelings; and then even the best knight can do but little if he cannot act as he pleases. It happened once, that to oblige the Palsgrave, I went to serve against Conrad Schotten; they then presented me with a paper of instructions from the chancery, which set forth—Thus and thus must you proceed. I threw down the paper before the magistrates, and told them

I could not act according to it; that something might happen
unprovided for in my instructions, and that I must use my
own eyes and judge what was best to be done.

SICKINGEN.   Good luck, brother!   I will hence, and
send thee what men I can collect in haste.

GOETZ.   Come first to the women.   I left them together.
would you had her consent before you depart!   Then
send me the troopers, and come back in private to carry
away my Maria; for my castle, I fear, will shortly be no
abode for women.

SICKINGEN.   We will hope for the best.        [*Exeunt.*


### SCENE V.   *Bamberg.   Adelaide's Chamber.*

ADELAIDE *and* FRANCIS.

ADELAIDE.   They have already set out to enforce the ban
against both?

FRANCIS.   Yes; and my master has the happiness of
marching against your enemies.   I would gladly have gone
also, however rejoiced I always am at being dispatched to
you.   But I will away instantly, and soon return with good
news; my master has allowed me to do so.

ADELAIDE.   How is he?

FRANCIS.   He is well, and commanded me to kiss your
hand.

ADELAIDE.   There!—Thy lips glow.

FRANCIS (*aside, pressing his breast*).   Here glows something yet more fiery.   (*Aloud*) Gracious lady, your servants
are the most fortunate of beings!

ADELAIDE.   Who goes against Berlichingen?

FRANCIS.   The Baron von Sirau.   Farewell!   Dearest
most gracious lady, I must away.   Forget me not!

ADELAIDE.   Thou must first take some rest and refresh
ment.

FRANCIS.   I need none, for I have seen you!   I am
neither weary nor hungry.

ADELAIDE.   I know thy fidelity.

FRANCIS.   Ah, gracious lady!

ADELAIDE.   You can never hold out; you *must* repose
and refresh yourself.

FRANCIS.   You are too kind to a poor youth.        [*Exit.*
ADELAIDE.   The tears stood in his eyes.   I love him
from my heart.   Never did man attach himself to me with
such warmth of affection.                          [*Exit.*


## SCENE VI.   *Jaxthausen.*

### GOETZ *and* GEORGE.

GEORGE.   He wants to speak with you in person.   I do not
know him—he is a tall, well-made man, with keen dark eyes.
GOETZ.   Admit him.                         [*Exit* GEORGE.
*Enter* LERSE.
GOETZ.   God save you!   What bring you?
LERSE.   Myself: not much, but such as it is, it is at your
service.
GOETZ.   You are welcome, doubly welcome!   A brave
man, and at a time when, far from expecting new friends,
I was in hourly fear of losing the old.   Your name?
LERSE.   Franz Lerse.
GOETZ.   I thank you, Franz, for making me acquainted
with a brave man!
LERSE.   I made you acquainted with me once before, but
then you did not thank me for my pains.
GOETZ.   I have no recollection of you.
LERSE.   I should be sorry if you had.   Do you recollect
when, to please the Palsgrave, you rode against Conrad
Schotten, and went through Hassfurt on an Allhallows eve?
GOETZ.   I remember it well.
LERSE.   And twenty-five troopers encountered you in a
village by the way?
GOETZ.   Exactly.   I at first took them for only twelve.   I
divided my party, which amounted but to sixteen, and halted
in the village behind the barn, intending to let them ride
by.   Then I thought of falling upon them in the rear, as I
had concerted with the other troop.
LERSE.   We saw you, however, and stationed ourselves
on a height above the village.   You drew up beneath the hill
and halted.   When we perceived that you did not intend to
come up to us we rode down to you.
GOETZ.   And then I saw for the first time that I had

thrust my hand into the fire.   Five-and-twenty against eight
is no jesting business.   Everard Truchsess killed one of my
followers, for which I knocked him off his horse.   Had they
all behaved like him and one other trooper, it would have
been all over with me and my little band.

LERSE.   And that trooper——

GOETZ.   Was as gallant a fellow as I ever saw.   He
attacked me fiercely; and when I thought I had given him
enough and was engaged elsewhere, he was upon me again,
and laid on like a fury: he cut quite through my armour,
and wounded me in the arm.

LERSE.   Have you forgiven him?

GOETZ.   He pleased me only too well.

LERSE.   I hope then you have cause to be contented with
me, since the proof of my valour was on your own person.

GOETZ.   Art thou he?   O welcome! welcome!   Canst
thou boast, Maximilian, that amongst thy followers, thou
hast gained one after this fashion?

LERSE.   I wonder you did not sooner hit upon me.

GOETZ.   How could I think that the man would engage
in my service who did his best to overpower me?

LERSE.   Even so, my lord.   From my youth upwards I
have served as a trooper, and have had a tussle with many
a knight.   I was overjoyed when we met you; for I had
heard of your prowess, and wished to know you.   Yow saw I
gave way, and that it was not from cowardice, for I returned to the charge.   In short, I learnt to know you, and
from that hour I resolved to enter your service.

GOETZ.   How long wilt thou engage with me?

LERSE.   For a year, without pay.

GOETZ.   No; thou shalt have as the others; nay more,
as befits him who gave me so much work at Remlin.

Enter GEORGE.

GEORGE.   Hans of Selbitz greets you.   To-morrow he
will be here with fifty men.

GOETZ.   'Tis well.

GEORGE.   There is a troop of Imperialists riding down
the hill, doubtless to reconnoitre.

GOETZ.   How many?

GEORGE.   About fifty.

GOETZ.   Only fifty!   Come, Lerse, we'll have a slash at

them, so that when Selbitz comes he may find some work done to his hand.

LERSE.    'Twill be capital practice.

GOETZ.    To horse!                                  [*Exeunt.*


SCENE VII.    *A Wood, on the borders of a Morass.*

*Two* IMPERIALIST TROOPERS *meeting.*

FIRST IMPERIALIST.    What dost thou here?

SECOND IMPERIALIST.    I have leave of absence for ten minutes.    Ever since our quarters were beat up last night, I have had such violent attacks that I can't sit on horseback for two minutes together.

FIRST IMPERIALIST.    Is the party far advanced?

SECOND IMPERIALIST.    About three miles into the wood.

FIRST IMPERIALIST.    Then why are you playing truant here?

SECOND IMPERIALIST.    Prithee, betray me not.    I am going to the next village to see if I cannot get some warm bandages, to relieve my complaint.    But whence comest thou?

FIRST IMPERIALIST.    I am bringing our officer some wine and meat from the nearest village.

SECOND IMPERIALIST.    So, so! he stuffs himself under our very noses, and we must starve—A fine example!

FIRST IMPERIALIST.    Come back with me, rascal.

SECOND IMPERIALIST.    Call me a fool, if I do!    There are plenty in our troop who would gladly fast, to be as far away as I am.                       [*Trampling of horses heard.*

FIRST IMPERIALIST.

Hear'st thou?—Horses!

SECOND IMPERIALIST.    Oh dear! Oh dear!

FIRST IMPERIALIST.    I'll get up into this tree.

SECOND IMPERIALIST.    And I'll hide among the rushes.
                                   [*They hide themselves.*

*Enter on horseback,* GOETZ, LERSE, GEORGE, *and* TROOPERS, *all completely armed.*

GOETZ.    Away into the wood, by the ditch on the left— then we have them in the rear.            [*They gallop off.*

FIRST IMPERIALIST (*descending*).    This is a bad business —Michael!—He answers not—Michael, they are gone! (*Goes *towards the marsh.*) Alas, he is sunk!—Michael!—He hears me not: he is suffocated.—Poor coward, art thou done for—We are slain—Enemies! Enemies on all sides!

*Re-enter* GOETZ *and* GEORGE *on horseback.*

GOETZ.   Yield thee, fellow, or thou diest!

IMPERIALIST.   Spare my life!

GOETZ.   Thy sword!—George, lead him to the other prisoners, whom Lerse is guarding yonder in the wood—I must pursue their fugitive leader.                    [*Exit.*

IMPERIALIST.   What has become of the knight, our officer?

GEORGE.   My master struck him head over heels from his horse, so that his plume stuck in the mire. His troopers got him up and ran as if the devil were behind them.

[*Exeunt.*


SCENE VIII.   *Camp of the Imperialists.*

CAPTAIN *and* FIRST OFFICER.

FIRST OFFICER.   They fly from afar towards the camp.

CAPTAIN.   He is most likely hard at their heels—Draw out fifty as far as the mill; if he follows up the pursuit too far, you may perhaps entrap him.          [*Exit* OFFICER.

*The* SECOND OFFICER *is borne in.*

CAPTAIN.   How now, my young sir—have you got a cracked headpiece?

OFFICER.   A plague upon you! The stoutest helmet went to shivers like glass. The demon!—he ran upon me as if he would strike me into the earth!

CAPTAIN.   Thank God that you have escaped with your life.

OFFICER.   There is little left to be thankful for; two of my ribs are broken—where's the surgeon?        [*He is carried off.*


SCENE IX.   *Jaxthausen.*

*Enter* GOETZ *and* SELBITZ.

GOETZ.   And what say you to the ban, Selbitz?

SELBITZ.   'Tis a trick of Weislingen's.

GOETZ.   Do you think so?

SELBITZ.  I do not think—I know it.

GOETZ.  How so?

SELBITZ.  He was at the Diet, I tell thee, and near the emperor's person.

GOETZ.  Well then, we shall frustrate another of his schemes.

SELBITZ.  I hope so.

GOETZ.  We will away! and course these hares.


### SCENE X.  *The Imperial Camp.*

CAPTAIN, OFFICERS *and* FOLLOWERS.

CAPTAIN.  We shall gain nothing at this work, sirs!  He beats one troop after another; and whoever escapes death or captivity, would rather fly to Turkey than return to the camp.  Thus our force diminishes daily.  We must attack him once for all, and in earnest—I will go myself, and he shall find with whom he has to deal.

OFFICER.  We are all content; but he is so well acquainted with the country, and knows every path and ravine so thoroughly, that he will be as difficult to find as a rat in a barn.

CAPTAIN.  I warrant you we'll ferret him out.  On towards Jaxthausen!  Whether he like it or not, he must come to defend his castle.

OFFICER.  Shall our whole force march?

CAPTAIN.  Yes, certainly—do you know that a hundred of us are melted away already?

OFFICER.  Then let us away with speed, before the whole snow-ball dissolves; for this is warm work, and we stand here like butter in the sunshine.  [*Exeunt—A march sounded.*


### SCENE XI.  *Mountains and a Wood.*

GOETZ, SELBITZ and TROOPERS.

GOETZ.  They are coming in full force.  It was high time that Sickingen's troopers joined us.

SELBITZ.  We will divide our party—I will take the left hand by the hill.

GOETZ.  Good—and do thou, Lerse, lead fifty men straight through the wood on the right.  They are coming across the heath—I will draw up opposite to them. George, stay by me—when you see them attack me, then fall upon their flank: we'll beat the knaves into a mummy—they little think we can face them.        [*Exeunt.*

SCENE XII.    *A heath—on one side an eminence, with a ruined tower, on the other the forest.*

*Enter marching,* the CAPTAIN OF THE IMPERIALISTS *with* OFFICERS *and his* SQUADRON—*Drums and standards.*

CAPTAIN.    He halts upon the heath! that's too impudent. He shall smart for it—what! not fear the torrent that threatens to overwhelm him!

OFFICER.    I had rather you did not head the troops; he looks as if he meant to plant the first that comes upon him in the mire with his head downmost. Prithee ride in the rear.

CAPTAIN.    Not so.

OFFICER. I entreat you. You are the knot which unites this bundle of hazel-twigs; loose it, and he will break them separately like so many reeds.

CAPTAIN.    Sound, trumpeter—and let us blow him to hell!
        [*A charge sounded—Exeunt in full career.*
SELBITZ, *with his* TROOPERS, *comes from behind the hill, galloping.*

SELBITZ.    Follow me!  They shall wish that they could multiply their hands.
        [*They gallop across the stage, et exeunt.*
*Loud alarm—*LERSE *and his party sally from the wood.*
LERSE.    Ho! to the rescue!  Goetz is almost surrounded. —Gallant Selbitz, thou hast cut thy way—we will sow the heath with these thistle heads.        [*Gallop off.*
    [*A loud alarm, with shouting and firing for some minutes.* SELBITZ *is borne in wounded by two* TROOPERS.]
SELBITZ.    Leave me here, and hasten to Goetz.

FIRST TROOPER.    Let us stay, sir—you need our aid.

SELBITZ.    Get one of you on the watch-tower, and tell me how it goes.

FIRST TROOPER.    How shall I get up?

SECOND TROOPER.    Mount upon my shoulders—you can then reach the ruined part, and thence scramble up to the opening.        [FIRST TROOPER *gets up into the tower.*

FIRST TROOPER,   Alas! Sir!

SELBITZ.   What seest thou?

FIRST TROOPER.   Your troopers fly towards the hill.

SELBITZ.   Rascally cowards!—I would that they stood their ground, and I had a ball through my head!—Ride one of you full speed—Curse and thunder them back to the field—Seest thou Goetz?                                    [*Exit* SECOND TROOPER.

TROOPER.   I see his three black feathers floating in the midst of the wavy tumult.

SELBITZ.   Swim, brave swimmer—I lie here.

TROOPER.   A white plume—whose is that?

SELBITZ.   The captain's.

TROOPER.   Goetz gallops upon him—crash! Down he goes!

SELBITZ.   The captain?

TROOPER.   Yes, Sir.

SELBITZ.   Hurrah! hurrah!

TROOPER.   Alas! alas! I see Goetz no more.

SELBITZ.   Then die, Selbitz!

TROOPER.   A dreadful tumult where he stood—George's blue plume vanishes too.

SELBITZ.   Come down!   Dost thou not see Lerse?

TROOPER.   No!—Everything is in confusion!

SELBITZ.   No more.   Come down.—How do Sickingen's men bear themselves?

TROOPER.   Well!—One of them flies to the wood—another—another—a whole troop.—Goetz is lost!

SELBITZ.   Come down.

TROOPER.   I cannot—Hurrah! Hurrah! I see Goetz, I see George.

SELBITZ.   On horseback?

TROOPER.   Aye, aye, high on horseback—Victory! victory! —they fly.

SELBITZ.   The Imperialists?

TROOPER.   Yes, standard and all. Goetz behind them. They disperse,—Goetz reaches the ensign—he seizes the standard; he halts.   A handful of men rally round him—My comrade reaches him—They come this way.

*Enter* GOETZ, GEORGE, LERSE, *and* TROOPERS, *on horseback*

SELBITZ.   Joy to thee, Goetz!—Victory! victory!

GOETZ (*dismounting*).  Dearly, dearly bought.  Thou art wounded, Selbitz!

SELBITZ.  But thou dost live and hast conquered!  I have done little; and my dogs of troopers!  How hast thou come off?

GOETZ.  For the present, well!  And here I thank George, and thee Lerse, for my life.  I unhorsed the captain, they stabbed my horse, and pressed me hard.  George cut his way to me, and sprang off his horse.  I threw myself like lightning upon it, and he appeared suddenly like a thunderbolt upon another.  How camest thou by thy steed?

GEORGE.  A fellow struck at you from behind: as he raised his cuirass in the act, I stabbed him with my dagger. Down he came! and so I rid you of an enemy, and helped myself to a horse.

GOETZ.  Then we held together till Francis here came to our help; and thereupon we mowed our way out.

LERSE.  The hounds whom I led were to have mowed their way in, till our scythes met, but they fled like Imperialists.

GOETZ.  Friend and foe all fled, except this little band who protected my rear.  I had enough to do with the fellows in front, but the fall of their captain dismayed them:  they wavered, and fled.  I have their banner, and a few prisoners.

SELBITZ.  The captain has escaped you?

GOETZ.  They rescued him in the scuffle.  Come lads, come Selbitz.—Make a litter of lances and boughs: Thou can'st not mount a horse, come to my castle.  They are scattered but we are very few; and I know not what troops they may have in reserve.  I will be your host, my friends.  Wine will taste well after such an action!

[*Exeunt, carrying Selbitz.*

## SCENE XIII.  *The Camp.*

### *The* CAPTAIN *and* IMPERIALISTS.

CAPTAIN.  I could kill you all with my own hand.—What! to turn tail!  He had not a handful of men left.  To give way before one man!  No one will believe it but those who wish to make a jest of us.  Ride round the country, you, and you, and you: collect our scattered soldiers, or cut them down wherever you find them. We must grind these notches out of our blades, even should we spoil our swords in the operation. [*Exeunt.*

### SCENE XIV. *Jaxthausen.*

#### Goetz, Lerse, *and* George.

GOETZ. We must not lose a moment. My poor fellows, I dare allow you no rest. Gallop round and strive to enlist troopers, appoint them to assemble at Weilern, where they will be most secure. Should we delay a moment, they will be before the castle.—(*Exeunt* LERSE *and* GEORGE)—I must send out a scout. This begins to grow warm.—If we had but brave foemen to deal with! But these fellows are only formidable through their number. [*Exit*

#### *Enter* SICKINGEN *and* MARIA.

MARIA. I beseech thee, dear Sickingen, do not leave my brother! His horsemen, your own, and those of Selbitz, all are scattered; he is alone. Selbitz has been carried home to his castle wounded. I fear the worst.

SICKINGEN. Be comforted, I will not leave him.

#### *Enter* GOETZ.

GOETZ. Come to the chapel, the priest waits; in a few minutes you shall be united.

SICKINGEN. Let me remain with you.

GOETZ. You must come now to the chapel.

SICKINGEN. Willingly!—and then—

GOETZ. Then you go your way.

SICKINGEN. Goetz!

GOETZ. Will you not to the chapel?

SICKINGEN. Come, come! [*Exeunt.*

### SCENE XV. *Camp.*

#### CAPTAIN *and* OFFICERS.

CAPTAIN. How many are we in all?

OFFICER. A hundred and fifty—

CAPTAIN. Out of four hundred.—That is bad. Set out for Jaxthausen at once, before he collects his forces and attacks us on the way.

## SCENE XVI.  *Jaxthausen.*

GOETZ, ELIZABETH, MARIA, *and* SICKINGEN.

GOETZ.   God bless you, give you happy days, and keep those for your children which he denies to you!

ELIZABETH.   And may they be virtuous as you—then let come what will.

SICKINGEN.   I thank you.—And you, my Maria! As I led you to the altar, so shall you lead me to happiness.

MARIA.   Our pilgrimage will be together towards that distant and promised land.

GOETZ.   A prosperous journey!

MARIA.   That was not what I meant—We do not leave you.

GOETZ.   You must, sister.

MARIA.   You are very harsh, brother.

GOETZ.   And you more affectionate than prudent.

*Enter* GEORGE.

GEORGE (*aside to* GOETZ).   I can collect no troopers: One was inclined to come, but he changed his mind and refused.

GOETZ (*to* GEORGE).   'Tis well, George. Fortune begins to look coldly on me.   I foreboded it, however.   [*Aloud.* Sickingen, I entreat you, depart this very evening.   Per · suade Maria—You are her husband—let her feel it.—When women come across our undertakings, our enemies are more secure in the open field, than they would else be in their castles.

*Enter a* TROOPER.

TROOPER (*aside to Goetz*).   The Imperial squadron is in full and rapid march hither.

GOETZ.   I have roused them with stripes of the rod! How many are they?

TROOPER.   About two hundred—They can scarcely be six miles from us.

GOETZ.   Have they passed the river yet?

TROOPER.   No, my lord!

GOETZ.   Had I but fifty men, they should not cross it. Hast thou seen Lerse?

TROOPER.   No, my lord!

GOETZ.   Tell all to hold themselves ready.—We must part,

dear friends.   Weep on, my gentle Maria—Many a moment of
happiness is yet in store for thee—It is better thou shouldst
weep on thy wedding-day, than that present joy should be
the fore-runner of future misery.—Farewell, Maria!—Farewell, brother!

MARIA.   I cannot leave you, sister.   Dear brother, let us
stay.   Dost thou value my husband so little as to refuse his
help in thy extremity?

GOETZ.   Yes—it is gone far with me.   Perhaps my fall
is near.   You are but beginning life, and should separate
your lot from mine.   I have ordered your horses to be
saddled; you must away instantly!

MARIA.   Brother! brother!

ELIZABETH (*to* SICKINGEN).   Yield to his wishes.   Speak
to her.

SICKINGEN.   Dear Maria! we must go.

MARIA.   Thou too?   My heart will break!

GOETZ.   Then stay.   In a few hours my castle will be
surrounded.

MARIA (*weeping bitterly*).   Alas! alas!

GOETZ.   We will defend ourselves as long as we can.

MARIA.   Mother of God, have mercy upon us!

GOETZ.   And at last we must die or surrender.   Thy tears
will then have involved thy noble husband in the same
misfortune with me.

MARIA.   Thou torturest me!

GOETZ.   Remain! Remain!   We shall be taken together!
Sickingen, thou wilt fall into the pit with me, out of which
I had hoped thou should'st have helped me.

MARIA.   We will away—Sister—sister!

GOETZ.   Place her in safety, and then think of me.

SICKINGEN.   Never shall I repose a night till I know
thou art out of danger.

GOETZ.   Sister! dear sister!   (*Kisses her.*)

SICKINGEN.   Away! away!

GOETZ.   Yet one moment!   I shall see you again.   Be
comforted, we shall meet again.   (*Exeunt* SICKINGEN *and*
MARIA.)   I urged her to depart—yet when she leaves me, what
would I not give to detain her.   Elizabeth thou stayest with me.

ELIZABETH.   Till death!                         [*Exit.*

GOETZ.   Whom God loves, to him may He give such a wife.

*Enter* GEORGE.

GEORGE. They are near! I saw them from the tower. The sun is rising, and I perceived their lances glitter. I cared no more for them than a cat would for a whole army of mice. 'Tis true *we* play the mice at present.

GOETZ. Look to the fastenings of the gates; barricade them with beams and stones. (*Exit* GEORGE.) We'll exercise their patience, and they may chew away their valour in biting their nails. (*A trumpet from without.* GOETZ *goes to the window.*) Aha! Here comes a red-coated rascal to ask me whether I will be a scoundrel! What says he? (*The voice of the* HERALD *is heard indistinctly, as from a distance.* GOETZ *mutters to himself.*) A rope for thy throat! (*Voice again.*) "Offended majesty!"—Some priest has drawn up that proclamation. (*Voice concludes, and* GOETZ *answers from the window.*) Surrender—surrender at discretion! With whom speak you? Am I a robber? Tell your captain, that for the emperor I entertain, as I have ever done, all due respect; but as for him, he may——(*Shuts the window with violence.*)


## SCENE XVII. *The Kitchen.*

ELIZABETH *preparing food—Enter* GOETZ.

GOETZ. You have hard work, my poor wife!

ELIZABETH. Would it might last! But you can hardly hold out long.

GOETZ. We have not had time to provide ourselves.

ELIZABETH. And so many people as you have been wont to entertain. The wine is well nigh finished.

GOETZ. If we can but hold out a certain time, they must propose a capitulation. We are doing them some damage I promise you. They shoot the whole day, and only wound our walls and break our windows. Lerse is a gallant fellow. He slips about with his gun: if a rogue comes too nigh— Pop! there he lies! (*Firing.*)

*Enter* TROOPER.

TROOPER. We want live coals, gracious lady!

GOETZ. For what?

TROOPER. Our bullets are spent; we must cast some new ones.

GOETZ.    How goes it with the powder?

TROOPER.    There is as yet no want : we save our fire.
(*Firing at intervals.*)           [*Exeunt* GOETZ *and* ELIZABETH.
*Enter* LERSE *with a bullet-mould.   Servants with coals.*

LERSE.    Set them down, and then go and see for lead
about the house; meanwhile I will make shift with this
(*Goes to the window, and takes out the leaden frames*).   Everything must be turned to account.   So it is in this world—
no one knows what a thing may come to :   the glazier who
made these frames little thought that the lead here was to
give one of his grandsons his last headache; and the father
that begot me, little knew whether the fowls of heaven or the
worms of the earth would pick my bones.
                *Enter* GEORGE *with a leaden spout.*

GEORGE.    Here's lead for thee !   If you hit with only
half of it, not one  will return to tell his Majesty,  "Thy servants have sped ill !"

LERSE (*cutting it down*).   A famous piece !

GEORGE.    The rain must seek some other way.   I'm not
afraid of it—a brave trooper and a smart shower will always
find their road.   (*They cast balls.*)

LERSE.    Hold the ladle.   (*Goes to the window.*)   Yonder
is a fellow creeping about with his rifle; he thinks our fire
is spent.   He shall have a  bullet warm from the pan.   (*He
loads his rifle*).

GEORGE (*puts down the mould*).   Let me see.

LERSE.    (*Fires.*)   There lies the game !

GEORGE.    He fired at me as I stepped out on the roof to
get the lead.   He killed a pigeon that sat near me ; it fell
into the spout.   I thanked him for my dinner, and went back
with the double booty.   (*They cast balls.*)

LERSE.    Now let us load, and go through the castle to
earn our dinner.
                    *Enter* GOETZ.

GOETZ.    Stay, Lerse, I must speak with thee.   I will not
keep thee, George, from the sport.                [*Exit* GEORGE.

GOETZ.    They offer terms.

LERSE.    I will go and hear what they have to say.

GOETZ.    They will require me to enter myself into ward
in some town on my knightly parole.

LERSE.    That won't do.   Suppose they allow us free

.iberty of departure? for we can expect no relief from Sickingen. We will bury all the valuables, where no divining-rod shall find them; leave them the bare walls, and come out with flying colours.

GOETZ. They will not permit us.

LERSE. It is worth the asking. We will demand a safe-conduct, and I will sally out.


## SCENE XVIII. *A Hall.*

GOETZ, ELIZABETH, GEORGE, *and* TROOPERS *at table.*

GOETZ. Danger unites us, my friends! Be of good cheer; don't forget the bottle! The flask is empty. Come, another, dear wife! (ELIZABETH *shakes her head.*) Is there no more?

ELIZABETH (*aside*). Only one, which I have set apart for you.

GOETZ. Not so, my love! Bring it out; they need strengthening, more than I, for it is my quarrel.

ELIZABETH. Fetch it from the cupboard.

GOETZ. It is the last, and I feel as if we need not spare it. It is long since I have been so merry. (*They fill.*) To the health of the emperor!

ALL. Long live the emperor!

GOETZ. Be it our last word when we die! I love him, for our fate is similar; but I am happier than he. To please the princes, he must direct his imperial squadrons against mice, while the rats gnaw his possessions.—I know he often wishes himself dead, rather than to be any longer the soul of such a crippled body. (*They fill.*) It will just go once more round. And when our blood runs low, like this flask; when we pour out its last ebbing drop (*empties the wine drop by drop into his goblet*), what then shall be our cry?

GEORGE. Freedom for ever!

GOETZ. Freedom for ever!

ALL. Freedom for ever!

GOETZ. And if that survive us we can die happy; for our spirits shall see our children's children, and their emperor happy! Did the servants of princes show the same filial attachment to their masters as you to me—did their masters serve the emperor as I would serve him——

GEORGE.    Things would be widely different.

GOETZ.    Not so much so as it would appear.    Have I not known worthy men among the princes?    And can the race be extinct?    Men, happy in their own minds and in their subjects, who could bear a free, noble brother in their neighbourhood without harbouring either fear or envy; whose hearts expanded when they saw their table surrounded by their free equals, and who did not think the knights unfit companions till they had degraded themselves by courtly homage.

GEORGE.    Have you known such princes?

GOETZ.    Ay, truly.    As long as I live I shall recollect how the Landgrave of Hanau made a grand hunting-party, and the princes and free feudatories dined under the open heaven, and the country-people all thronged to see them; it was no selfish masquerade instituted for his own private pleasure or vanity.—To see the great round-headed peasant lads and the pretty brown girls, the sturdy hinds, and the venerable old men, a crowd of happy faces, all as merry as if they rejoiced in the splendour of their master, which he shared with them under God's free sky!

GEORGE.    He must have been as good a master as you.

GOETZ.    And may we not hope that many such will rule together some future day, to whom reverence to the emperor, peace and friendship with their neighbours, and the love of their vassals, shall be the best and dearest family treasure handed down to their children's children?    Every one will then keep and improve his own, instead of reckoning nothing as gain that is not stolen from his neighbours.

GEORGE.    And should we have no more forays?

GOETZ.    Would to God there were no restless spirits in all Germany!—we should still have enough to do!    We would clear the mountains of wolves, and bring our peaceable laborious neighbour a dish of game from the wood, and eat it together.    Were that not full employment, we would join our brethren, and, like cherubims with flaming swords, defend the frontiers of the empire against those wolves the Turks, and those foxes the French, and guard for our beloved emperor both extremities of his extensive empire.    That would be a life, George!    To risk one's head for the safety of all Germany.    (GEORGE *springs up*.)    Whither away?

GEORGE.    Alas!   I forgot we were besieged—besieged by that very emperor; and before we can expose our lives in his defence, we must risk them for our liberty.

GOETZ.    Be of good cheer.

*Enter* LERSE.

LERSE.    Freedom! freedom!   The cowardly poltroons—the hesitating, irresolute asses.   You are to depart with men, weapons, horses, and armour; provisions you are to leave behind.

GOETZ.    They will hardly find enough to exercise their jaws.

LERSE (*aside to* GOETZ).   Have you hidden the plate and money?

GOETZ.    No!   Wife, go with Lerse; he has something to tell thee.                                                                          [*Exeunt.*

### SCENE XIX.    *The Court of the Castle.*

GEORGE (*in the stable.    Sings.*)

An urchin once, as I have heard,
  Ha! ha!
Had caught and caged a little bird
  Sa! sa!
  Ha! ha!
  Sa! sa!
He viewed the prize with heart elate,
  Ha! ha!
Thrust in his hand—ah treacherous fat
  Sa! sa!
  Ha! ha!
  Sa! sa!
Away the titmouse wing'd its flight
  Ha! ha!
And laugh'd to scorn the silly wigh
  Sa! sa!
  Ha! ha!
  Sa! sa!

*Enter* GOETZ.

GOETZ.    How goes it?

GEORGE (*brings out his horse*).    All saddled!

GOETZ.    Thou art quick.

GEORGE.    As the bird escaped from the cage.

*Enter all the besieged.*

GOETZ.  Have you all your rifles?  Not yet!  Go, take the best from the armoury, 'tis all one; we'll ride on in advance.

GEORGE (*sings*).

Ha! ha!
Sa! sa!
Ha! ha!


## SCENE XX.  *The Armoury.*

*Two* TROOPERS *choosing guns.*

FIRST TROOPER.   I'll have this one.
SECOND TROOPER.   And I this—but yonder's a better.
FIRST TROOPER.   Never mind—make haste.
                    [*Tumult and firing without.*
SECOND TROOPER.   Hark!
FIRST TROOPER (*springs to the window*).  Good heavens, they are murdering our master!  He is unhorsed!  George is down!
SECOND TROOPER.  How shall we get off?  Over the wall by the walnut-tree, and into the field.          [*Exit.*
FIRST TROOPER.  Lerse keeps his ground; I will to him. If they die, I will not survive them.          [*Exit.*

END OF THE THIRD ACT.

---

# ACT THE FOURTH.

## SCENE I.   *An Inn in the city of Heilbronn.*

### GOETZ (*solus*).

GOETZ.  I am like the evil spirit whom the capuchin conjured into a sack.  I fret and labour, but all in vain. The perjured villains!  (*Enter* ELIZABETH.)  What news, Elizabeth, of my dear, my trusty followers?

ELIZABETH.    Nothing certain: some are slain, some are prisoners; no one could or would tell me further particulars.

GOETZ.    Is this the reward of fidelity, of filial obedience?——" That it may be well with thee, and that thy days may be long in the land!"

ELIZABETH.    Dear husband, murmur not against our heavenly Father. They have their reward. It was born with them—a noble and generous heart. Even in the dungeon they are free. Think now of appearing before the imperial commissioners; their heavy gold chains become them——

GOETZ.    As a necklace becomes a sow!   I should like to see George and Lerse in fetters!

ELIZABETH.    It were a sight to make angels weep.

GOETZ.    I would not weep—I would clench my teeth, and gnaw my lip in fury.   What! in fetters!   Had ye but loved me less, dear lads!   I could never look at them enough.——What! to break their word pledged in the name of the emperor!

ELIZABETH.    Put away these thoughts.   Reflect; you must appear before the council—you are in no mood to meet them, and I fear the worst.

GOETZ.    What harm can they do me?

ELIZABETH.    Here comes the serjeant.

GOETZ.    What! the ass of justice that carries the sacks to the mill and the dung to the field?   What now?

Enter SERJEANT.

SERJEANT.    The lords commissioners are at the Council-House, and require your presence.

GOETZ.    I come.

SERJEANT.    I am to escort you.

GOETZ.    Too much honour.

ELIZABETH.    Be but cool.

GOETZ.    Fear nothing.                              [*Exeunt.*

SCENE II.    *The Council-House at Heilbronn.*

*The* IMPERIAL COMMISSIONERS *seated at a table.   The* CAPTAIN *and the* MAGISTRATES *of the city attending.*

MAGISTRATE.    In pursuance of your order, we have col-

lected the stoutest and most determined of our citizens.  They
are at hand, in order, at a nod from you, to seize Berlichingen.

COMMISSIONER.  We shall have much pleasure in com-
municating to his imperial majesty the zeal with which you
have obeyed his illustrious commands.—Are they artizans?

MAGISTRATE.  Smiths, coopers, and carpenters, men with
hands hardened by labour; and resolute here.

[*Points to his breast.*

COMMISSIONER.  'Tis well!

*Enter* SERJEANT.

SERJEANT.  Goetz von Berlichingen waits without.

COMMISSIONER.  Admit him.

*Enter* GOETZ.

GOETZ.  God save you, sirs!  What would you with me.

COMMISSIONER.  First, that you consider where you are;
and in whose presence.

GOETZ.  By my faith, I know you right well, sirs.

COMMISSIONER.  You acknowledge allegiance.

GOETZ.  With all my heart.

COMMISSIONER.  Be seated.          [*Points to a stool.*

GOETZ.  What, down there?  I'd rather stand.  That stool
smells so of poor sinners, as indeed does the whole apartment.

COMMISSIONER.  Stand, then.

GOETZ.  To business, if you please.

COMMISSIONER.  We shall proceed in due order.

GOETZ.  I am glad to hear it.  Would you had always
done so.

COMMISSIONER.  You know how you fell into our hands,
and are a prisoner at discretion.

GOETZ.  What will you give me to forget it?

COMMISSIONER.  Could I give you modesty, I should better
your affairs.

GOETZ.  Better my affairs!  could you but do that?  To
repair is more difficult than to destroy.

SECRETARY.  Shall I put all this on record?

COMMISSIONER.  Only what is to the purpose.

GOETZ.  As far as I'm concerned you may print every
word of it.

COMMISSIONER.  You fell into the power of the emperor,
whose paternal goodness got the better of his justice, and, instead

of throwing you into a dungeon, ordered you to repair to his beloved city of Heilbronn. You gave your knightly parole to appear, and await the termination in all humility.

GOETZ. Well; I am here, and await it.

COMMISSIONER. And we are here to intimate to you his Imperial Majesty's mercy and clemency. He is pleased to forgive your rebellion, to release you from the ban and all well-merited punishment; provided you do, with becoming humility, receive his bounty, and subscribe to the articles which shall be read unto you.

GOETZ. I am his majesty's faithful servant, as ever. One word, ere you proceed. My people—where are they? What will be done with them?

COMMISSIONER. That concerns you not.

GOETZ. So may the emperor turn his face from you in the hour of your need. They were my comrades, and are so now. What have you done with them?

COMMISSIONER. We are not bound to account to you.

GOETZ. Ah! I forgot that you are not even pledged to perform what you have promised, much less—

COMMISSIONER. Our business is to lay the articles before you. Submit yourself to the emperor, and you may find a way to petition for the life and freedom of your comrades.

GOETZ. Your paper.

COMMISSIONER. Secretary, read it.

SECRETARY (*reads*). "I, Goetz of Berlichingen, make public acknowledgment, by these presents, that I, having lately risen in rebellion against the emperor and empire—"

GOETZ. 'Tis false! I am no rebel, I have committed no offence against the emperor, and with the empire I have no concern.

COMMISSIONER. Be silent, and hear further.

GOETZ. I will hear no further. Let any one arise and bear witness. Have I ever taken one step against the emperor, or against the house of Austria? Has not the whole tenor of my conduct proved that I feel better than any one else what all Germany owes to its head; and especially what the free knights and feudatories owe to their liege lord the emperor? I should be a villain could I be induced to subscribe that paper.

COMMISSIONER. Yet we have strict orders to try and persuade you by fair means, or, in case of your refusal, to throw you into prison.

GOETZ.    Into prison!—Me?

COMMISSIONER.    Where you may expect your fate from the hands of justice, since you will not take it from those of mercy.

GOETZ.    To prison!   You abuse the imperial power!   To prison!   That was not the emperor's command.   What, ye traitors, to dig a pit for me, and hang out your oath, your knightly honour as the bait!   To promise me permission to ward myself on parole, and then again to break your treaty!

COMMISSIONER.    We owe no faith to robbers.

GOETZ.    Wert thou not the representative of my sovereign, whom I respect even in the vilest counterfeit, thou shouldst swallow that word, or choke upon it.   I was engaged in an honourable feud.   Thou mightest thank God, and magnify thyself before the world, hadst thou ever done as gallant a deed as that with which I now stand charged.   (*The* COMMISSIONER *makes a sign to the* MAGISTRATE *of Heilbronn, who rings a bell*.)   Not for the sake of paltry gain, not to wrest followers or lands from the weak and the defenceless, have I sallied forth.   To rescue my page and defend my own person— see ye any rebellion in that?   The emperor and his magnates, reposing on their pillows, would never have felt our need.   I have, God be praised, one hand left, and I have done well to use it.

*Enter a party of Artizans armed with halberds and swords.*

GOETZ.    What means this?

COMMISSIONER.    You will not listen.—Seize him!

GOETZ.    Let none come near me who is not a very Hungarian ox.   One salutation from my iron fist shall cure him of head-ache, tooth-ache, and every other ache under the wide heaven!   (*They rush upon him. He strikes one down; and snatches a sword from another. They stand aloof.*)   Come on! come on!   I should like to become acquainted with the bravest among you.

COMMISSIONER.    Surrender!

GOETZ.    With a sword in my hand!   Know ye not that it depends but upon myself to make way through all these hares and gain the open field?   But I will teach you how a man should keep his word.   Promise me but free ward, and I will give up my sword, and am again your prisoner.

COMMISSIONER. How! Would you treat with the emperor, sword in hand?

GOETZ. God forbid!—only with you and your worthy fraternity! You may go home, good people; you are only losing your time, and here there is nothing to be got but bruises.

COMMISSIONER. Seize him! What! does not your love for the emperor supply you with courage?

GOETZ. No more than the emperor supplies them with plaister for the wounds their courage would earn them.

*Enter* SERJEANT, *hastily*.

OFFICER. The warder has just discovered from the castle-tower, a troop of more than two hundred horsemen hastening towards the town. Unperceived by us, they have pressed forward from behind the hill, and threaten our walls.

COMMISSIONER. Alas! alas! What can this mean?

A SOLDIER *enters*.

SOLDIER. Francis of Sickingen waits at the drawbridge, and informs you that he has heard, how perfidiously you have broken your word to his brother-in-law, and how the Council of Heilbronn have aided and abetted in the treason. He is now come to insist upon justice, and if refused it, threatens, within an hour, to fire the four quarters of your town, and abandon it to be plundered by his vassals.

GOETZ. My gallant brother!

COMMISSIONER. Withdraw, Goetz. (*Exit* GOETZ.) What is to be done?

MAGISTRATE. Have compassion upon us and our town! Sickingen is inexorable in his wrath; he will keep his word.

COMMISSIONER. Shall we forget what is due to ourselves and the emperor?

CAPTAIN. If we had but men to enforce it; but situated as we are, a show of resistance would only make matters worse. It is better for us to yield.

MAGISTRATE. Let us apply to Goetz to put in a good word for us I feel as though I saw the town already in flames.

COMMISSIONER. Let Goetz approach. (*Enter* GOETZ.)

GOETZ. What now?

COMMISSIONER. Thou wilt do well to dissuade thy brother-in-law from his rebellious interference. Instead of rescuing thee, he will only plunge thee deeper in destruction, and become the companion of thy fall !

GOETZ (*sees Elizabeth at the door, and speaks to her aside*). Go ; tell him instantly to break in and force his way hither, but to spare the town.  As for these rascals, if they offer any resistance, let him use force.  I care not if I lose my life, provided they are all knocked on the head at the same time.


SCENE III.    *A large hall in the Council-House, beset by* SICKINGEN's *Troops.*

*Enter* SICKINGEN *and* GOETZ.

GOETZ.    That was help from heaven.  How camest thou so opportunely and unexpectedly, brother?

SICKINGEN.    Without witchcraft.  I had dispatched two or three messengers to learn how it fared with thee ; when I heard of the perjury of these fellows, I set out instantly, and now we have them safe.

GOETZ.    I ask nothing but knightly ward upon my parole.

SICKINGEN.    You are too noble.  Not even to avail yourself of the advantage which the honest man has over the perjurer!  They are in the wrong, and we will not give them cushions to sit upon.  They have shamefully abused the imperial authority, and, if I know anything of the emperor, you might safely insist upon more favourable terms.  You ask too little.

GOETZ.    I have ever been content with little.

SICKINGEN.    And therefore that little has always been denied thee.  My proposal is, that they shall release your servants, and permit you all to return to your castle on parole—you can promise not to leave it till the emperor's pleasure be known.  You will be safer there than here.

GOETZ.    They will say my property is escheated to the emperor.

SICKINGEN.    Then we will answer thou canst dwell there. and keep it for his service till he restores it to thee again.  Let them wriggle like eels in the net, they shall not escape us!  They may talk of the imperial dignity—of their commission.  We will not mind that.  I know the emperor, and have some influence with him.  He has ever wished to

have thee in his service.   You will not be long in your castle
without being summoned to serve him.

GOETZ.   God grant it ere I forget the use of arms!

SICKINGEN.   Valour can never be forgotten, as it can
never be learnt.  Fear nothing!  When thy affairs are
settled, I will repair to court, where my enterprises begin to
ripen.  Good fortune seems to smile on them.  I want only
to sound the emperor's mind.  The towns of Triers and
Pfalz as soon expect that the sky should fall, as that I shall
come down upon their heads.  But I will come like a hail
storm! and if I am successful, thou shalt soon be brother
to an elector.  I had hoped for thy assistance in this under-
taking.

GOETZ (*looks at his hand*).  O! that explains the dream
I had the night before I promised Maria to Weislingen.  I
thought he vowed eternal fidelity, and held my iron hand
so fast that it loosened from the arm.  Alas!  I am at this
moment more defenceless than when it was shot away.
Weislingen!  Weislingen!

SICKINGEN.   Forget the traitor!  We will thwart his
plans, and undermine his authority, till shame and remorse
shall gnaw him to death.  I see, I see the downfall of our
enemies.—Goetz—only half a year more!

GOETZ.   Thy soul soars high!  I know not why, but for
some time past no fair prospects have dawned upon me.  I
have been ere now in sore distress—I have been a prisoner
before—but never did I experience such a depression.

SICKINGEN.   Fortune gives courage.  Come, let us to
the bigwigs.  They have had time enough to deliberate, let
us take the trouble upon ourselves.                    [*Exeunt.*

SCENE IV.   *The Castle of Adelaide—Augsburg.*

ADELAIDE *and* WEISLINGEN *discovered.*

ADELAIDE.   This is detestable.

WEISLINGEN.   I have gnashed my teeth.  So good a plan
—so well followed out—and after all to leave him in possession of his castle!  That cursed Sickingen!

ADELAIDE.   The council should not have consented.

WEISLINGEN.   They were in the net.  What else could

they do? Sickingen threatened them with fire and sword,—
the haughty, vindictive man! I hate him! His power
waxes like a mountain torrent—let it but gain a few brooks,
and others come pouring to its aid.

ADELAIDE.   Have they no emperor?

WEISLINGEN.   My dear wife, he waxes old and feeble;
he is only the shadow of what he was.   When he heard what
had been done, and I and the other counsellors murmured
indignantly: "Let them alone!" said he; "I can spare my
old Goetz his little fortress, and if he remains quiet there,
what have you to say against him?"   We spoke of the welfare of the state: "Oh," said he, "that I had always had
counsellors who would have urged my restless spirit to consult more the happiness of individuals!"

ADELAIDE.   He has lost the spirit of a prince!

WEISLINGEN.   We inveighed against Sickingen!—"He is
my faithful servant," said he; "and if he has not acted by
my express order, he has performed what I wished better than
my plenipotentiaries, and I can ratify what he has done as
well after as before."

ADELAIDE.   'Tis enough to drive one mad.

WEISLINGEN.   Yet I have not given up all hope.   Goetz
is on parole to remain quiet in his castle.   'Tis impossible
for him to keep his promise, and we shall soon have some
new cause of complaint.

ADELAIDE.   That is the more likely, as we may hope that
the old emperor will soon leave the world, and Charles, his
gallant successor, will display a more princely mind.

WEISLINGEN. Charles! He is neither chosen nor crowned.

ADELAIDE.   Who does not expect and hope for that event?

WEISLINGEN.   You have a great idea of his abilities; one
might almost think you looked on him with partial eyes.

ADELAIDE.   You insult me, Weislingen.   For what do
you take me?

WEISLINGEN.   I do not mean to offend; but I cannot be
silent upon the subject.   Charles's marked attentions to you
disquiet me.

ADELAIDE.   And do I receive them as in

WEISLINGEN.   You are a woman; and no woman hates
those who pay their court to her.

ADELAIDE.   This from you?

WEISLINGEN.  It cuts me to the heart—the dreadful thought—Adelaide.

ADELAIDE.  Can I not cure thee of this folly?

WEISLINGEN.  If thou would'st—Thou canst leave the court.

ADELAIDE.  But upon what pretence?  Art thou not here?  Must I leave you and all my friends, to shut myself up with the owls in your solitary castle?  No, Weislingen, that will never do; be at rest, thou knowest I love thee.

WEISLINGEN.  That is my anchor so long as the cable holds.                                                    [*Exit.*

ADELAIDE.  Ah! Is it come to this?  This was yet wanting.  The projects of my bosom are too great to brook thy interruption.  Charles—the great, the gallant Charles—the future emperor—shall he be the only man unrewarded by my favour?  Think not, Weislingen, to hinder me—else shalt thou to earth; my way lies over thee!

*Enter* FRANCIS (*with a letter*).

FRANCIS.  Here, gracious lady.

ADELAIDE.  Hadst thou it from Charles' own hand?

FRANCIS.  Yes.

ADELAIDE.  What ails thee?  Thou look'st so mournful!

FRANCIS.  It is your pleasure that I should pine away, and waste my fairest years in agonizing despair.

ADELAIDE (*aside*).  I pity him; and how little would it cost me to make him happy.  (*Aloud.*)  Be of good courage, youth!  I know thy love and fidelity, and will not be ungrateful.

FRANCIS (*with stifled breath*).  If thou wert capable of ingratitude, I could not survive it.  There boils not a drop of blood in my veins but what is thine own—I have not a single feeling but to love and to serve thee!

ADELAIDE.  Dear Francis!

FRANCIS.  You flatter me.  (*Bursts into tears.*)  Does my attachment deserve only to be a stepping stool to another—to see all your thoughts fixed upon Charles?

ADELAIDE.  You know not what you wish, and still less what you say.

FRANCIS (*stamping with vexation and rage*).  No more will I be your slave, your go-between!

ADELAIDE.  Francis, you forget yourself.

FRANCIS.  To sacrifice my beloved master and myself——
ADELAIDE.  Out of my sight!
FRANCIS.  Gracious lady!
ADELAIDE.  Go, betray to thy beloved master the secret of my soul!  Fool that I was to take thee for what thou art not.
FRANCIS.  Dear lady! you know how I love you.
ADELAIDE.  And thou, who wast my friend—so near my heart—go, betray me.
FRANCIS.  Rather would I tear my heart from my breast! Forgive me, gentle lady! my heart is too full, my senses desert me.
ADELAIDE.  Thou dear, affectionate boy!  (*She takes him by both hands, draws him towards her and kisses him.  He throws himself weeping upon her neck.*)  Leave me!
FRANCIS (*his voice choked by tears*).  Heavens!
ADELAIDE.  Leave me!  The walls are traitors.  Leave me!  (*Breaks from him.*)  Be but steady in fidelity and love, and the fairest reward is thine.  [*Exit.*
FRANCIS.  The fairest reward!  Let me but live till that moment—I could murder my father, were he an obstacle to my happiness!  [*Exit.*


## SCENE V.  *Jaxthausen.*

GOETZ *seated at a table with writing materials.*  ELIZABETH *beside him with her work.*

GOETZ.  This idle life does not suit me.  My confinement becomes more irksome every day; I would I could sleep, or persuade myself that quiet is agreeable.
ELIZABETH.  Continue writing the account of thy deeds which thou hast commenced.  Give into the hands of thy friends evidence to put thine enemies to shame; make a noble posterity acquainted with thy real character.
GOETZ.  Alas! writing is but busy idleness; it wearies me.  While I am writing what I have done, I lament the misspent time in which I might do more.
ELIZABETH (*takes the writing*).  Be not impatient.  Thou hast come to thy first imprisonment at Heilbronn.

GOETZ.    That was always an unlucky place to me.

ELIZABETH (*reads*).    "There were even some of the confederates who told me that I had acted foolishly in appearing before my bitterest enemies, who, as I might suspect, would not deal justly with me."And what didst thou answer? Write on.

GOETZ.    I said, "Have I not often risked life and limb for the welfare and property of others, and shall I not do so for the honour of my knightly word?"

ELIZABETH.    Thus does fame speak of thee.

GOETZ.    They shall not rob me of my honour.    They have taken all else from me—property—liberty—everything.

ELIZABETH.    I happened once to stand in an inn near the Lords of Miltenberg and Singlingen, who knew me not. Then I was joyful as at the birth of my first-born; for they extolled thee to each other, and said,—He is the mirror of knighthood, noble and merciful in prosperity, dauntless and true in misfortune.

GOETZ.    Let them show me the man to whom I have broken my word.    Heaven knows, my ambition has ever been to labour for my neighbour more than for myself, and to acquire the fame of a gallant and irreproachable knight, rather than principalities or power; and, God be praised! I have gained the meed of my labour.

*Enter* GEORGE *and* LERSE *with game.*

GOETZ.    Good luck to my gallant huntsmen!

GEORGE.    Such have we become from gallant troopers. Boots can easily be cut down into buskins.

LERSE.    The chase is always something—'tis a kind of war

GEORGE.    Yes; if we were not always crossed by these imperial gamekeepers.    Don't you recollect, my lord, how you prophesied we should become huntsmen when the world was turned topsy-turvy?    We are become so now without waiting for that.

GOETZ.    'Tis all the same, we are pushed out of our sphere.

GEORGE.    These are wonderful times!    For eight days a dreadful comet has been seen—all Germany fears that it portends the death of the emperor, who is very ill.

GOETZ.    Very ill!    Then our career draws to a close.

LERSE.    And in the neighbourhood there are terrible commotions; the peasants have made a formidable insurrection.

GOETZ.    Where?

LERSE.    In the heart of Swabia; they are plundering, burning, and slaying.    I fear they will sack the whole country.

GEORGE.    It is a horrible warfare!    They have already risen in a hundred places, and daily increase in number.    A hurricane too has lately torn up whole forests; and in the place where the insurrection began, two fiery swords have been seen in the sky crossing each other.

GOETZ.    Then some of my poor friends and neighbours no doubt suffer innocently.

GEORGE.    Alas!    that we are pent up thus!

END OF THE FOURTH ACT.

---

# ACT THE FIFTH.

SCENE I.    *A Village plundered by the insurgent Peasantry. Shrieks and tumult.    Women, old Men, and Children fly across the Stage.*

OLD MAN.    Away! away! let us fly from the murdering dogs.

WOMAN.    Sacred heaven!    How blood-red is the sky! how blood-red the setting sun!

ANOTHER.    That must be fire.

A THIRD.    My husband! my husband!

OLD MAN.    Away! away!    To the wood!            [*Exeu*

*Enter* LINK *and Insurgents.*

LINK.    Whoever opposes you, down with him!    The village is ours.    Let none of the booty be injured, none be left behind.    Plunder clean and quickly.    We must soon set fire——

*Enter* METZLER, *coming down the hill.*

METZLER.    How do things go with you, Link?

Link.  Merrily enough, as you see; you are just in time for the fun.—Whence come you?

Metzler.  From Weinsberg.  There was a jubilee.

Link.  How so?

Metzler.  We stabbed them all, in such heaps, it was a joy to see it!

Link.  All whom?

Metzler.  Dietrich von Weiler led up the dance.  The fool!  We were all raging round the church steeple.  He looked out and wished to treat with us.—Baf!  A ball through his head!  Up we rushed like a tempest, and the fellow soon made his exit by the window.

Link.  Huzza!

Metzler (*to the peasants*).  Ye dogs, must I find you legs?  How they gape and loiter, the asses!

Link.  Set fire!  Let them roast in the flames!  forward!  Push on, ye dolts.

Metzler.  Then we brought out Helfenstein, Eltershofen, thirteen of the nobility—eighty in all.  They were led out on the plain before Heilbronn.  What a shouting and jubilee among our lads as the long row of miserable sinners passed by; they stared at each other, and, Heaven and earth! we surrounded them before they were aware, and then dispatched them all with our pikes.

Link.  Why was I not there?

Metzler.  Never in all my life did I see such fun.

Link.  On! on!  Bring all out!

Peasant.  All's clear.

Link.  Then fire the village at the four corners.

Metzler.  'Twill make a fine bonfire!  Hadst thou but seen how the fellows tumbled over one another, and croaked like frogs!  It warmed my heart like a cup of brandy.  One Rexinger was there, a fellow, with a white plume, and flaxen locks, who, when he went out hunting, used to drive us before him like dogs, and with dogs.  I had not caught sight of him all the while, when suddenly his fool's visage looked me full in the face.  Push! went the spear between his ribs, and there he lay stretched on all-fours above his companions.  The fellows lay kicking in a heap like the hares that used to be driven together at their grand hunting parties.

LINK.   It smokes finely already!

METZLER.   Yonder it burns!  Come, let us with the booty to the main body.

LINK.   Where do they halt?

METZLER.   Between this and Heilbronn.  They wish to choose a captain whom every one will respect, for we are after all only their equals; they feel this, and turn restive.

LINK.   Whom do they propose?

METZLER.   Maximilian Stumf, or Goetz von Berlichingen.

LINK.   That would be well.  'Twould give the thing credit should Goetz accept it.  He has ever been held a worthy independent knight.  Away, away!  We march towards Heilbronn!  Pass the word.

METZLER.   The fire will light us a good part of the way. Hast thou seen the great comet?

LINK.   Yes.  It is a dreadful ghastly sign!  As we march by night we can see it well.  It rises about one o'clock.

METZLER.   And is visible but for an hour and a quarter, like an arm brandishing a sword, and bloody red!

LINK.   Didst thou mark the three stars at the sword's hilt and point?

METZLER.   And the broad haze-coloured stripe illuminated by a thousand streamers like lances, and between them little swords?

LINK.   I shuddered with horror.  The sky was pale red streaked with ruddy flames, and among them grisly figures with shaggy hair and beards.

METZLER.   Did you see them too?  And how they all swam about as though in a sea of blood, and struggled in confusion, enough to turn one's brain.

LINK.   Away! away!                                    [*Exeunt.*

SCENE II.   *Open country.   In the distance two villages and an abbey are burning.*

KOHL, WILD, MAXIMILIAN STUMF, *Insurgents.*

STUMF.   You cannot ask me to be your leader; it were bad for you and for me: I am a vassal of the Palsgrave, and how shall I make war against my liege lord?  Besides, you would always suspect I did not act from my heart.

KOHL.   We knew well thou wouldst make some excuse.

*Enter* GEORGE, LERSE, *and* GOETZ.

GOETZ.    What would you with me?

KOHL.    You must be our captain.

GOETZ.    How can I break my knightly word to the emperor.    I am under the ban; I cannot quit my territory.

WILD.    That's no excuse.

GOETZ.    And were I free, and you wanted to deal with the lords and nobles as you did at Weinsberg, laying waste the country round with fire and sword, and should wish me to be an abettor of your shameless, barbarous doings, rather than be your captain, you should slay me like a mad dog!

KOHL.    What has been done, cannot be undone.

STUMF.    That was just the misfortune, that they had no leader whom they honoured, and who could bridle their fury. I beseech thee, Goetz, accept the office!    The princes will be grateful; all Germany will thank thee.    It will be for the weal and prosperity of all.    The country and its inhabitants will be preserved.

GOETZ.    Why dost not thou accept it?

STUMF.    I have given them reasons for my refusal.

KOHL.    We have no time to waste in useless speeches. Once for all! Goetz, be our chief, or look to thy castle and thy head!    Take two hours to consider of it.    Guard him!

GOETZ.    To what purpose?    I am as resolved now as I shall ever be.    Why have ye risen up in arms?    If to recover your rights and freedom, why do you plunder and lay waste the land?    Will you abstain from such evil doings, and act as true men who know what they want?    Then will I be your chief for eight days, and help you in your lawful and orderly demands.

WILD.    What has been done was done in the first heat, and thy interference is not needed to prevent it for the future.

KOHL.    Thou must engage with us at least for a quarter of a year.

STUMF.    Say four weeks, that will satisfy both parties.

GOETZ.    Then be it so.

KOHL.    Your hand!

GOETZ.    But you must promise to send the treaty you have made with me in writing to all your troops, and to punish severely those who infringe it.

WILD    Well, it shall be done.

GOETZ.   Then I bind myself to you for four weeks.

STUMF.   Good fortune to you!  In whatever thou doest, spare our noble lord the Palsgrave.

KOHL (*aside*).   See that none speak to him without our knowledge.

GOETZ.   Lerse, go to my wife.  Protect her; you shall soon have news of me.

[*Exeunt* GOETZ, STUMF, GEORGE, LERSE, *and some* PEASANTS.
*Enter* METZLER, LINK, *and their followers.*

METZLER.   Who talks of a treaty?  What's the use of a treaty?

LINK.   It is shameful to make any such bargain.

KOHL.   We know as well what we want as you; and we may do or let alone what we please.

WILD.   This raging, and burning, and murdering must have an end some day or other; and by renouncing it just now, we gain a brave leader.

METZLER.   How?  An end?  Thou traitor! why are we here but to avenge ourselves on our enemies, and enrich ourselves at their expense?  Some prince's slave has been tampering with thee.

KOHL.   Come, Wild, he is like a brute-beast.

[*Exeunt* WILD *and* KOHL.

METZLER.   Aye, go your way, no band will stick by you. The villains!  Link, we'll set on the others to burn Miltenberg yonder; and if they begin a quarrel about the treaty, we'll cut off the heads of those that made it.

LINK.   We have still the greater body of peasants on our side.                        [*Exeunt with Insurgents.*


SCENE III.   *A hill and prospect of the country.   In the flat scene a Mill.   A body of horsemen.*

WEISLINGEN *comes out of the Mill, followed by* FRANCIS *and a* COURIER.

WEISLINGEN.   My horse!  Have you announced it to the other nobles?

COURIER.   At least seven standards will meet you in the wood behind Miltenberg.  The peasants are marching in that direction. Couriers are dispatched on all sides; the entire confederacy will soon be assembled. Our plan cannot fail; and they say there is dissension among them.

WEISLINGEN. So much the better. Francis!

FRANCIS. Gracious sir!

WEISLINGEN. Discharge thine errand punctually. I bind it upon thy soul. Give her the letter. She shall from the court to my castle instantly. Thou must see her depart, and bring me notice of it.

FRANCIS. Your commands shall be obeyed.

WEISLINGEN. Tell her she *shall* go. (*To the* COURIER) Lead us by the nearest and best road.

COURIER. We must go round; all the rivers are swollen with the late heavy rains.


## SCENE IV. *Jaxthausen.*

### ELIZABETH *and* LERSE.

LERSE. Gracious lady, be comforted!

ELIZABETH. Alas! Lerse, the tears stood in his eyes when he took leave of me. It is dreadful, dreadful!

LERSE. He will return.

ELIZABETH. It is not that. When he went forth to gain honourable victories, never did grief sit heavy at my heart. I then rejoiced in the prospect of his return, which I now dread.

LERSE. So noble a man—

ELIZABETH. Call him not so. There lies the new misery. The miscreants! they threatened to murder his family and burn his castle. Should he return, gloomy, most gloomy shall I see his brow. His enemies will forge scandalous accusations against him, which he will be unable to refute.

LERSE. He will and can.

ELIZABETH. He has broken his parole:—Canst thou deny that?

LERSE. No! he was constrained; what reason is there to condemn him?

ELIZABETH. Malice seeks not reasons, but pretexts. He has become an ally of rebels, malefactors, and murderers:— he has become their chief. Say No to that.

Lerse.   Cease to torment yourself and me.   Have they not solemnly sworn to abjure all such doings as those at Weinsberg? Did I not myself hear them say, in remorse, that, had not that been done already, it never should have been done? Must not the princes and nobles return him their best thanks for having undertaken the dangerous office of leading these unruly people, in order to restrain their rage, and to save so many lives and possessions?

Elizabeth.   Thou art an affectionate advocate.   Should they take him prisoner, deal with him as with a rebel, and bring his grey hairs——Lerse, I should go mad!

Lerse.   Send sleep to refresh her body, dear Father of mankind, if thou deniest comfort to her soul!

Elizabeth.   George has promised to bring news, but he will not be allowed to do so.   They are worse than prisoners.   Well I know they are watched like enemies.— The gallant boy! he would not leave his master.

Lerse.   The very heart within me bled as I left him.— Had you not needed my help, all the terrors of grisly death should not have separated us.

Elizabeth.   I know not where Sickingen is.—Could I but send a message to Maria!

Lerse.   Write, then:—I will take care that she receives it.
[*Exit.*

## SCENE V.   *A Village.*

### *Enter* Goetz *and* George.

Goetz.   To horse, George! Quick! I see Miltenberg in flames—Is it thus they keep the treaty?—Ride to them, tell them my purpose.—The murderous incendiaries—I renounce them—Let them make a thieving gipsy their captain, not me! —Quick, George! (*Exit George.*) Would that I were a thousand miles hence, at the bottom of the deepest dungeon in Turkey!—Could I but come off with honour from them! I have thwarted them every day, and told them the bitterest truths, in the hope they might weary of me and let me go.

### *Enter an Unknown.*

Unknown.   God save you, gallant Sir!

Goetz.   I thank you! What is your errand? Your name?

UNKNOWN.  My name does not concern my business.  I come to tell you that your life is in danger.  The insurgent leaders are weary of hearing from you such harsh language, and are resolved to rid themselves of you.  Speak them fair, or endeavour to escape from them ; and God be with you !

*[Exit.*

GOETZ.  To quit life in this fashion, Goetz, to end thus ! But be it so—My death will be the clearest proof to the world that I have had nothing in common with the miscreants.

*Enter Insurgents.*

FIRST INSURGENT.  Captain, they are prisoners, they are slain !

GOETZ.  Who ?

SECOND INSURGENT.  Those who burned Miltenberg; a troop of confederate cavalry suddenly charged upon them from behind the hill.

GOETZ.  They have their reward.  O George ! George ! They have taken him prisoner with the caitiffs—My George ! my George !

*Enter Insurgents in confusion.*

LINK.  Up, sir captain, up !—There is no time to lose —The enemy is at hand, and in force.

GOETZ.  Who burned Miltenberg ?

METZLER.  If you mean to pick a quarrel, we'll soon show you how we'll end it.

KOHL.  Look to your own safety and ours;—Up !

GOETZ (*to Metzler*).  Darest thou threaten me, thou scoundrel——Thinkest thou to awe me, because thy garments are stained with the Count of Helfenstein's blood?

METZLER.  Berlichingen !

GOETZ.  Thou mayest call me by my name, and my children will not be ashamed to hear it.

METZLER.  Out upon thee, coward?—Prince's slave ! (*Goetz strikes him down—The others interpose.*)

KOHL.  Ye are mad !—The enemy are breaking in on all sides, and you quarrel !

LINK.  Away ! Away !—(*Cries and tumult—The Insurgents fly across the Stage.*)

*Enter* WEISLINGEN *and* TROOPERS.

WEISLINGEN.  Pursue ! Pursue ! they fly !—Stop neither for darkness nor rain.—I hear Goetz is among them ; look

that he escape you not.   Our friends say he is sorely wounded.
(*Exeunt Troopers.*)   And when I have caught thee—it will
be merciful secretly to execute the sentence of death in
prison.   Thus he perishes from the memory of man, and then,
foolish heart, thou may'st beat more freely.


SCENE VI.   *The front of a Gipsy-hut in a wild forest—
Night.—A fire before the hut, at which are seated the mother
of the gipsies and a girl.*

MOTHER.   Throw   some   fresh   straw   upon   the   thatch,
daughter: There'll be heavy rain again to night.
                *Enter a* GIPSY-BOY.
BOY.   A dormouse, mother! and look! two field mice!
MOTHER.   I'll skin them and roast them for thee, and thou
shalt have a cap of their skins.   Thou bleedest!
BOY.   Dormouse bit me.
MOTHER.   Fetch some dead wood, that the fire may burn
bright when thy father comes: he will be wet through and
through.
        *Another gipsy-woman with a child at her back.*
FIRST WOMAN.   Hast thou had good luck?
SECOND WOMAN. Ill enough.   The whole country is in an
uproar, one's life is not safe a moment.   Two villages are in
a blaze.
FIRST WOMAN.   Is it fire that glares so yonder?   I have
been watching it long.   One is so accustomed now to fiery
signs in the heavens.
    *The Captain of the Gipsies enters with three of his gang.*
CAPTAIN.   Heard ye the wild huntsman?
FIRST WOMAN.   He is passing over us now.
CAPTAIN.   How the hounds give tongue! Wow! Wow!
SECOND MAN.   How the whips crack!
THIRD MAN.   And the huntsmen cheer them—Hallo—ho!
MOTHER.   'Tis the devil's chase.
CAPTAIN.   We have been fishing in troubled waters. The
peasants rob each other; there's no harm in our helping
them.
SECOND WOMAN.   What hast thou got, Wolf?
WOLF   A hare and a capon, a spit, a bundle of linen, three
spoons, and a bridle.

STICKS.   I have a blanket and a pair of boots, also a flint and tinder-box.

MOTHER.   All wet as mire, I'll dry them, give them here!
(*Trampling without.*)

CAPTAIN.   Hark!—A horse! Go see who it is.

*Enter* GOETZ *on horseback.*

GOETZ.   I thank thee, God! I see fire—they are gipsies. —My wounds bleed sorely—my foes are close behind me!— Great God, this is a fearful end!

CAPTAIN.   Is it in peace thou comest?

GOETZ.   I crave help from you—My wounds exhaust me —assist me to dismount!

CAPTAIN.   Help him!—A gallant warrior in look and speech.

WOLF (*aside*).   'Tis Goetz von Berlichingen!

CAPTAIN.   Welcome! welcome!—All that we have is yours.

GOETZ.   Thanks, thanks!

CAPTAIN.   Come to my hut!         [*Exeunt to the hut.*


## SCENE VII.   *Inside the Hut.*

CAPTAIN, GIPSIES, *and* GOETZ.

CAPTAIN.   Call our mother—tell her to bring blood-wort and bandages. (GOETZ *unarms himself.*)   Here is my holiday doublet.

GOETZ.   God reward you!   [*The mother binds his wounds.*

CAPTAIN.   I rejoice that you are come.

GOETZ.   Do you know me?

CAPTAIN.   Who does not know you, Goetz? Our lives and heart's blood are yours.

*Enter* STICKS.

STICKS.   Horsemen are coming through the wood. They are confederates.

CAPTAIN.   Your pursuers! They shall not harm you. Away, Sticks, call the others: we know the passes better than they. We shall shoot them ere they are aware of us.

[*Exeunt* CAPTAIN *and* MEN-GIPSIES *with their guns.*

GOETZ (*alone*).   O Emperor! Emperor! Robbers pro·

tect thy children [*A sharp firing.*] The wild foresters!
Steady and true!

*Enter* WOMEN.

WOMEN. Flee, flee! The enemy has overpowered us.

GOETZ. Where is my horse?

WOMEN. Here!

GOETZ. (*Girds on his sword and mounts without his armour*).
For the last time shall you feel my arm. I am not so weak
yet. [*Exit.—Tumult.*

WOMEN. He gallops to join our party. [*Firing.*

*Enter* WOLF.

WOLF. Away! Away! All is lost.—The Captain is
shot!—Goetz a prisoner.

[*The* WOMEN *scream and fly into the wood.*

## SCENE VIII. ADELAIDE'S *Bed-chamber.*

*Enter* ADELAIDE *with a letter.*

ADELAIDE. He or I! The tyrant—to threaten me!
We will anticipate him. Who glides through the anti-
chamber? [*A low knock at the door.*] Who is there?

FRANCIS (*in a low voice*). Open, gracious lady!

ADELAIDE. Francis! He well deserves that I should
admit him. [*Opens the door.*

FRANCIS. (*Throws himself on her neck.*) My dear, my
gracious lady!

ADELAIDE. What audacity! If any one should hear you?

FRANCIS. O—all—all are asleep.

ADELAIDE. What wouldst thou?

FRANCIS. I cannot rest. The threats of my master,—
your fate,—my heart.

ADELAIDE. He was incensed against me when you parted
from him?

FRANCIS. He was as I have never seen him.—To my
castle, said he, she must—she *shall* go.

ADELAIDE. And shall we obey?

FRANCIS. I know not, dear lady!

ADELAIDE. Thou foolish, infatuated boy! Thou dost not
see where this will end. Here he knows I am in safety.

He has long had designs on my freedom, and therefore wishes
to get me to his castle—there he will have power to use me
as his hate shall dictate.

FRANCIS.   He shall not!

ADELAIDE.   Wilt thou prevent him?

FRANCIS.   He shall not!

ADELAIDE.   I foresee the whole misery of my fate.   He
will tear me forcibly from his castle to immure me in a
cloister.

FRANCIS.   Hell and damnation!

ADELAIDE.   Wilt thou rescue me?

FRANCIS.   Anything!   Everything!

ADELAIDE.   (*Throws herself weeping upon his neck.*)
Francis!   O save me!

FRANCIS.   He shall fall.   I will plant my foot upon his
neck.

ADELAIDE.   No violence!   You shall carry a submissive
letter to him announcing obedience—Then give him this vial
in his wine.

FRANCIS.   Give it me!   Thou shalt be free!

ADELAIDE.   Free!—And then no more shalt thou need
to come to my chamber trembling and in fear.   No more
shall I need anxiously to say, " Away, Francis! the morning
dawns."


SCENE IX.   *Street before the Prison at Heilbronn.*

ELIZABETH *and* LERSE.

LERSE.   Heaven relieve your distress, gracious lady!
Maria is come.

ELIZABETH.   God be praised!   Lerse, we have sunk into
dreadful misery.   My worst forebodings are realized!   A
prisoner—thrown as an assassin and malefactor into the
deepest dungeon.

LERSE.   I know all.

ELIZABETH.   Thou knowest nothing.   Our distress is too
—too great!   His age, his wounds, a slow fever—and, more
than all, the despondency of his mind, to think that this
should be his end.

LERSE.   Aye, and that Weislingen should be commissioner!

ELIZABETH.   Weislingen?

LERSE.   They have acted with unheard-of severity.
Metzler has been burnt alive—hundreds of his associates
broken upon the wheel, beheaded, quartered, and impaled.
All the country round looks like a slaughter-house, where
human flesh is cheap.

ELIZABETH.   Weislingen commissioner!  O Heaven!  a
ray of hope!  Maria shall go to him: he cannot refuse her.
He had ever a compassionate heart, and when he sees her
whom he once loved so much, whom he has made so miserable
—Where is she?

LERSE.   Still at the inn.

ELIZABETH.   Take me to her.  She must away instantly.
I fear the worst.                                    [*Exeunt.*

SCENE X.   *An Apartment in Weislingen's Castle.*

WEISLINGEN *alone.*

WEISLINGEN.   I am so ill, so weak—all my bones are
hollow—this wretched fever has consumed their very marrow.
No rest, no sleep, by day or night! and when I slumber, such
fearful dreams!  Last night methought I met Goetz in the
forest.  He drew his sword, and defied me to combat.  I
grasped mine, but my hand failed me.  He darted on me a
look of contempt, sheathed his weapon, and passed on.  He
is a prisoner; yet I tremble to think of him.  Miserable
man! Thine own voice has condemned him; yet thou trem-
blest like a malefactor at his very shadow.  And shall he
die?  Goetz!  Goetz! we mortals are not our own masters.
Fiends have empire over us, and shape our actions after their
own hellish will, to goad us to perdition.  (*Sits down.*)
Weak!  Weak!  Why are my nails so blue?  A cold, clammy,
wasting, sweat drenches every limb.  Everything swims
before my eyes.  Could I but sleep!  Alas!

*Enter* MARIA.

WEISLINGEN.  Mother of God!  Leave me in peace—
leave me in peace!  This spectre was yet wanting.  Maria is

dead, and she appears to the traitor.  Leave me, blessed spirit!  I am wretched enough.

MARIA.  Weislingen, I am no spirit.  I am Maria.

WEISLINGEN.  It is her voice!

MARIA.  I come to beg my brother's life of thee.  He is guiltless, however culpable he may appear.

WEISLINGEN.  Hush!  Maria—Angel of heaven as thou art, thou bringest with thee the torments of hell!  Speak no more!

MARIA.  And must my brother die?  Weislingen, it is horrible that I should have to tell thee he is guiltless; that I should be compelled to come as a suppliant to restrain thee from a most fearful murder.  Thy soul to its inmost depths is possessed by evil powers.  Can this be Adelbert?

WEISLINGEN.  Thou seest—the consuming breath of the grave hath swept over me—my strength sinks in death— I die in misery, and thou comest to drive me to despair— Could I but tell thee all, thy bitterest hate would melt to sorrow and compassion.  Oh Maria!  Maria!

MARIA.  Weislingen, my brother is pining in a dungeon— The anguish of his wounds—his age—O hadst thou the heart to bring his grey hairs——Weislingen, we should despair.

WEISLINGEN.  Enough!——— (*Rings a hand-bell.*)
        *Enter* FRANCIS, *in great agitation.*

FRANCIS.  Gracious sir!

WEISLINGEN.  Those papers, Francis.  (*He gives them.* WEISLINGEN *tears open a packet, and shows* MARIA *a paper.*) Here is thy brother's death-warrant signed!

MARIA.  God in heaven!

WEISLINGEN.  And thus I tear it.  He shall live!  But can I restore what I have destroyed?  Weep not so, Francis! Dear youth, my wretchedness lies deeply at thy heart.

        [FRANCIS *throws himself at his feet, and clasps his knees.*

MARIA (*apart*).  He is ill—very ill.  The sight of him rends my heart.  I loved him!  And now that I again approach him, I feel how dearly——

WEISLINGEN.  Francis, arise and cease to weep—I may recover!  While there is life, there is hope.

FRANCIS.  You cannot!  You must die!

WEISLINGEN.  Must?

FRANCIS (*beside himself*).  Poison! poison!—from your wife!  I—I gave it.                                [*Rushes out.*

WEISLINGEN. Follow him, Maria—he is desperate.
*[Exit MARIA.*
Poison from my wife! Alas! alas! I feel it. Torture and death!

MARIA (*within*). Help! help!

WEISLINGEN. (*Attempts in vain to rise.*) God! I cannot.

MARIA. (*Re-entering.*) He is gone! He threw himself desperately from a window of the hall into the river.

WEISLINGEN. It is well with him!—Thy brother is out of danger! The other commissioners, especially Seckendorf, are his friends. They will readily allow him to ward himself upon his knightly word. Farewell, Maria! Now go.

MARIA. I will stay with thee—thou poor forsaken one!

WEISLINGEN. Poor and forsaken indeed! O God, thou art a terrible avenger! My wife!

MARIA. Remove from thee that thought. Turn thy soul to the throne of mercy.

WEISLINGEN. Go, thou gentle spirit! leave me to my misery! Horrible! Even thy presence, Maria, even the attendance of my only comforter, is agony.

MARIA (*aside*). Strengthen me, heaven! My soul droops with his.

WEISLINGEN. Alas! alas! Poison from my wife! My Francis seduced by the wretch! She waits—listens to every horse's hoof for the messenger who brings her the news of my death. And thou too, Maria, wherefore art thou come to awaken every slumbering recollection of my sins? Leave me, leave me that I may die!

MARIA. Let me stay! Thou art alone: think I am thy nurse. Forget all. May God forgive thee as freely as I do!

WEISLINGEN. Thou spirit of love! pray for me! pray for me! My heart is seared.

MARIA. There is forgiveness for thee.—Thou art exhausted.

WEISLINGEN. I die! I die! and yet I cannot die. In the fearful contest between life and death lie the torments of hell.

MARIA. Heavenly Father, have compassion upon him! Grant him but one token of thy love, that his heart may be opened to comfort, and his soul to the hope of eternal life, even in the agony of death!

SCENE XI.  *A narrow vault dimly illuminated.  The Judges of the Secret Tribunal discovered seated, all muffled in black cloaks.*

ELDEST JUDGE.  Judges of the Secret Tribunal, sworn by the cord and the steel to be inflexible in justice, to judge in secret, and to avenge in secret, like the Deity!  Are your hands clean and your hearts pure?  Raise them to heaven, and cry,—Woe upon evil-doers!

ALL.  Woe! woe!

ELDEST JUDGE.  Cryer, begin the diet of judgment.

CRYER.  I cry, I cry for accusation against evil-doers! He whose heart is pure, whose hands are clean to swear by the cord and the steel, let him lift up his voice and call upon the steel and the cord for vengeance! vengeance! vengeance!

ACCUSER (*comes forward*).  My heart is pure from misdeed, and my hands are clean from innocent blood: God pardon my sins of thought, and prevent their execution.  I raise my hand on high, and cry for Vengeance! vengeance! vengeance!

ELDEST JUDGE.  Vengeance upon whom?

ACCUSER.  I call upon the cord and the steel for vengeance against Adelaide of Weislingen.  She has committed adultery and murder.  She has poisoned her husband by the hands of his servant—the servant hath slain himself—the husband is dead.

ELDEST JUDGE.  Dost thou swear by the God of truth, that thy accusation is true?

ACCUSER.  I swear!

ELDEST JUDGE.  Dost thou invoke upon thine own head the punishment of murder and adultery, should thy accusation be found false?

ACCUSER.  On my head be it.

ELDEST JUDGE.  Your voices?

[*They converse a few minutes in whispers.*

ACCUSER.  Judges of the Secret Tribunal, what is your sentence upon Adelaide of Weislingen, accused of murder and adultery?

ELDEST JUDGE.  She shall die!—she shall die a bitter and twofold death!  By the double doom of the steel and the cord shall she expiate the double crime.  Raise your hands

to heaven and cry, Woe, woe upon her! Be she delivered
into the hands of the avenger.

ALL.   Woe! woe!

ELDEST JUDGE.   Woe!  Avenger, come forth.

[*A man advances.*

Here, take thou the cord and the steel! Within eight
days shalt thou blot her out from before the face of heaven:
wheresoever thou findest her, down with her into the dust.
Judges, ye that judge in secret and avenge in secret like the
Deity, keep your hearts from wickedness, and your hands
from innocent blood!                       [*The Scene closes.*


## SCENE XII.   *The Court of an Inn.*

### LERSE *and* MARIA.

MARIA.   The horses have rested long enough; we will
away, Lerse.

LERSE.   Stay till to-morrow; this is a dreadful night.

MARIA.   Lerse, I cannot rest till I have seen my brother.
Let us away: the weather is clearing up—we may expect
a fair morning.

LERSE.   Be it as you will.


## SCENE XIII.   *The Prison at Heilbronn.*

### GOETZ *and* ELIZABETH.

ELIZABETH.   I entreat thee, dear husband, speak to me.
Thy silence alarms me; thy spirit consumes thee, pent up
within thy breast.   Come, let me see thy wounds; they
mend daily.   In this desponding melancholy I know thee no
longer!

GOETZ.   Seekest thou Goetz?  He is long since gone!
Piece by piece have they robbed me of all I held dear—my
hand, my property, my freedom, my good name!  My life!
of what value is it to me?  What news of George?  Is Lerse
gone to seek him?

ELIZABETH.   He is, my love!  Be of good cheer; things
may yet take a favourable turn.

GOETZ. He whom God hath stricken lifts himself up no more! I best know the load I have to bear.—To misfortune I am inured.—But now it is not Weislingen alone, not the peasants alone, not the death of the emperor, nor my wounds—it is the whole united—— My hour is come! I had hoped it should have been like my life. But His will be done!

ELIZABETH. Wilt thou not eat something?

GOETZ. Nothing, my love! See how the sun shines yonder!

ELIZABETH. It is a fine spring day!

GOETZ. My love, wilt thou ask the keeper's permission for me to walk in his little garden for half an hour, that I may look upon the clear face of heaven, the pure air, and the blessed sun?

ELIZABETH. I will—and he will readily grant it.


## SCENE THE LAST. *The Prison Garden.*

### LERSE *and* MARIA.

MARIA. Go in, and see how it stands with them.

[*Exit* LERSE.

*Enter* ELIZABETH *and* KEEPER.

ELIZABETH (*to the* KEEPER). God reward your kindness and attention to my husband! (*Exit* KEEPER.) Maria, how hast thou sped?

·MARIA. My brother is safe! But my heart is torn asunder. Weislingen is dead! poisoned by his wife. My husband is in danger—the princes are becoming too powerful for him: they say he is surrounded and besieged.

ELIZABETH. Believe not the rumour; and let not Goetz hear it.

MARIA. How is it with him?

ELIZABETH. I feared he would not survive till thy return: the hand of the Lord is heavy on him. And George is dead!

MARIA. George ! The gallant boy!

ELIZABETH. When the miscreants were burning Miltenberg, his master sent him to check their villany. A body

of cavalry charged upon them: Had they all behaved as
George, they must all have had as clear a conscience.
Many were killed, and George among them; he died the
death of a warrior.

MARIA.   Does Goetz know it?

ELIZABETH.   We conceal it from him.  He questions me ten
times a-day concerning him, and sends me as often to see what
is become of him.  I fear to give his heart this last wound.

MARIA.   O God! what are the hopes of this would!

*Enter* GOETZ, LERSE, *and* KEEPER.

GOETZ.   Almighty God! how lovely it is beneath thy
heaven!  How free!  The trees put forth their buds, and all
the world awakes to hope.——Farewell, my children! my
roots are cut away, my strength totters to the grave.

ELIZABETH.   Shall I not send Lerse to the convent for
thy son, that thou may'st once more see and bless him?

GOETZ.   Let him be; he needs not my blessing, he is
holier than I.—Upon our wedding-day, Elizabeth, could I
have thought I should die thus!—My old father blessed us,
and prayed for a succession of noble and gallant sons.—God,
thou hast not heard him.  I am the last.——Lerse, thy countenance cheers me in the hour of death, more than in our
most daring fights: then, my spirit encouraged thine; now,
thine supports mine——Oh that I could but once more see
George, and sun myself in his look!  You turn away and
weep.  He is dead?  George is dead?—Then die Goetz!
Thou hast outlived thyself, outlived the noblest of thy servants——How died he?  Alas! they took him among the
incendiaries, and he has been executed?

ELIZABETH.   No! he was slain at Miltenberg! while fighting like a lion for his freedom.

GOETZ.   God be praised! He was the kindest youth under
the sun, and one of the bravest——Now release my soul.  My
poor wife! I leave thee in a wicked world.  Lerse, forsake
her not!  Lock your hearts more carefully than your doors.
The age of fraud is at hand, treachery will reign unchecked.
The worthless will gain the ascendancy by cunning, and the
noble will fall into their net.  Maria, may God restore thy
husband to thee! may he not fall the deeper for having

risen so high!   Selbitz is dead, and the good emperor, and
my George——Give me a draught of water!——Heavenly
air!  Freedom! freedom!                              [*He dies.*

ELIZABETH.   Freedom is above! above—with thee!  The
world is a prison-house.

MARIA.   Noble man! Woe to this age that rejected thee!

LERSE.   And woe to the future, that shall misjudge thee'

THE END.

LONDON : PRINTED BY WILLIAM CLOWES AND SONS, STAMFORD STREET
AND CHARING CROSS.

# LIST OF

# BOHN'S VARIOUS LIBRARIES.

---

A Complete Set, in 637 Volumes, Price £132 8s.

---

## SEPARATE LIBRARIES.

---

| | No. of Volumes. | Price. £ | s. | d. |
|---|---|---|---|---|
| STANDARD LIBRARY (including the Atlas to Coxe's Marlborough) . . . . . . . | 165 | 29 | 15 | 0 |
| HISTORICAL LIBRARY . . . . . . | 21 | 5 | 5 | 0 |
| LIBRARY OF FRENCH MEMOIRS . . . . | 6 | 1 | 1 | 0 |
| UNIFORM WITH THE STANDARD LIBRARY . . . | 46 | 8 | 14 | 0 |
| PHILOLOGICAL LIBRARY . . . . . . | 22 | 4 | 15 | 0 |
| BRITISH CLASSICS . . . . . . . | 29 | 5 | 1 | 6 |
| ECCLESIASTICAL LIBRARY . . . . . | 8 | 2 | 0 | 0 |
| ANTIQUARIAN LIBRARY . . . . . . | 40 | 10 | 0 | 0 |
| ILLUSTRATED LIBRARY . . . . . . | 79 | 20 | 8 | 0 |
| CLASSICAL LIBRARY (including the Atlas) . . . | 91 | 22 | 7 | 0 |
| SCIENTIFIC LIBRARY . . . . . . | 68 | 17 | 17 | 0 |
| REFERENCE LIBRARY . . . . . . | 1 | 0 | 6 | 0 |
| CHEAP SERIES . . . . . . . | 61 | 4 | 18 | 6 |

# A CATALOGUE OF
# BOHN'S VARIOUS LIBRARIES.

PUBLISHED BY

# GEORGE BELL AND SONS,

4, 5, & 6, YORK STREET, COVENT GARDEN,
LONDON.

1875.

1.

## Bohn's Standard Library.

A SERIES OF THE BEST ENGLISH AND FOREIGN AUTHORS, PRINTED IN
POST 8VO., AND PUBLISHED AT 3s. 6d. PER VOLUME
(EXCEPTING THOSE MARKED OTHERWISE).

**Bacon's Essays, Apophthegms, Wisdom of the Ancients, New Atlantis, and Henry VII., with Introduction and Notes.** *Portrait.*

**Beaumont and Fletcher, a popular Selection from.** By LEIGH HUNT.

**Beckmann's History of Inventions, Discoveries, and Origins.** Revised and enlarged. *Portraits.* In 2 vols.

**Bremer's (Miss) Works.** Translated by MARY HOWITT. *Portrait.* In 4 vols
   Vol. 1. The Neighbours and other Tales.
   Vol. 2. The President's Daughter.
   Vol. 3. The Home, and Strife and Peace
   Vol. 4. A Diary, the H—— Family, &c.

**Butler's (Bp.) Analogy of Religion, and Sermons, with Notes.** *Portrait.*

**Carafas (The) of Maddaloni:** and Naples under Spanish Dominion. Translated from the German of Alfred de Reumont.

**Carrel's Counter Revolution in England.** Fox's History and Lonsdale's Memoir of James II. *Portrait.*

**Cellini (Benvenuto), Memoirs of.** Translated by ROSCOE. *Portrait.*

**Coleridge's (S. T.) Friend.** A Series of Essays on Morals, Politics, and Religion.

**Coleridge's (S. T.) Biographia Literaria, and two Lay Sermons.**

**Condé's Dominion of the Arabs in Spain.** Translated by Mrs. FOSTER. In 3 vols

**Cowper's Complete Works.** Edited, with Memoir of the Author, by SOUTHEY. *Illustrated with 50 Engravings.* In 8 vols.
   Vols. 1 to 4: Memoir and Correspondence.
   Vols. 5 and 6. Poetical Works. *Plates.*
   Vol. 7. Homer's Iliad. *Plates.*
   Vol. 8. Homer's Odyssey. *Plates.*

**Coxe's Memoirs of the Duke of Marlborough.** *Portraits.* In 3 vols.
   **** An Atlas of the plans of Marlborough's campaigns, 4to. 10s. 6d.

—————— **History of the House of Austria.** *Portraits.* In 4 vols.

**De Lolme on the Constitution of England.** Edited, with Notes, by JOHN MACGREGOR.

**Emerson's Complete Works.** 2 vols.

**Foster's (John) Life and Correspondence.** Edited by J. E. RYLAND. In 2 vols.

—————— **Lectures at Broadmead Chapel.** Edited by J. E. RYLAND. In 2 vols.

—————— **Critical Essays.** Edited by J. E RYLAND. In 2 vols.

—————— **Essays—On Decision of Character, &c. &c.**

—————— **Essays—On the Evils of Popular Ignorance, &c.**

—————— **Fosteriana: Thoughts, Reflections, and Criticisms of the late JOHN FOSTER,** selected from periodical papers, and Edited by HENRY G. BOHN (nearly 600 pages). 5s.

**Fuller's (Andrew) Principal Works.** With Memoir. *Portrait.*

**Irving's (Washington) Complete Works.** In 11 vols. 3s. 6d. each.
Vol. 1. Salmagundi and Knickerbocker. *Portrait of the Author.*
Vol. 2. Sketch Book and Life of Goldsmith.
Vol. 3. Bracebridge Hall and Abbotsford and Newstead.
Vol. 4. Tales of a Traveller and the Alhambra.
Vol. 5. Conquest of Granada and Conquest of Spain.
Vols. 6 and 7. Life of Columbus and Companions of Columbus, with a new Index. *Fine Portrait.*
Vol. 8. Astoria and Tour in the Prairies.
Vol. 9. Mahomet and his Successors.
Vol. 10. Conquest of Florida and Adventures of Captain Bonneville.
Vol. 11. Biographies and Miscellanies.
*For separate Works, see Cheap Series,* p. 31.

**Joyce's Introduction to the Arts and** Sciences. With Examination Questions. 3s. 6d.

**Lawrence's Lectures on Comparative** Anatomy, Physiology, Zoology, and the Natural History of Man. *Illustrated.* 5s.

**Lilly's Introduction to Astrology.** With numerous Emendations, by ZADKIEL. 6s.

**Miller's (Professor) History Philoso**phically considered. In 4 vols. 3s. 6d. each.

**Political Cyclopædia.** In 4 vols. 3s. 6d. each.

———— Also bound in 2 vols. with leather backs. 15s.

**Uncle Tom's Cabin.** With Introductory Remarks by the Rev. J. SHERMAN. *Printed in a large clear type. Illustrations.* 3s. 6d.

**Wide, Wide World.** By ELIZABETH WETHERALL. *Illustrated with 10 highly-finished Steel Engravings.* 3s. 6d.

III.

# Bohn's Historical Library.

UNIFORM WITH THE STANDARD LIBRARY, AT 5s. PER VOLUME.

**Evelyn's Diary and Correspondence.** *Illustrated with numerous Portraits, &c.* In 4 vols.

**Pepys' Diary and Correspondence.** Edited by Lord Braybrooke. With important Additions, including numerous Letters. *Illustrated with many Portraits.* In 4 vols.

**Jesse's Memoirs of the Reign of the** Stuarts, including the Protectorate. With General Index. *Upwards of 40 Portraits.* In 3 vols.

**Jesse's Memoirs of the Pretenders** and their Adherents. 6 *Portraits.*

**Nugent's (Lord) Memorials of** Hampden, his Party, and Times. 12 *Portraits.*

**Strickland's (Agnes) Lives of the** Queens of England, from the Norman Conquest. From official records and authentic documents, private and public. Revised Edition. In 6 vols.

———— Life of Mary Queen of Scots. 2 vols.

IV.

# Bohn's Library of French Memoirs.

UNIFORM WITH THE STANDARD LIBRARY AT 3s. 6d. PER VOLUME.

**Memoirs of Philip de Commines,** containing the Histories of Louis XI. and Charles VIII., and of Charles the Bold, Duke of Burgundy. To which is added, The Scandalous Chronicle, or Secret

History of Louis XI. *Portraits.* In 2 vols.

**Memoirs of the Duke of Sully, Prime** Minister to Henry the Great. *Portraits.* In 4 vols.

V.

# Bohn's School and College Series.

UNIFORM WITH THE STANDARD LIBRARY.

**Bass's Complete Greek and English** Lexicon to the New Testament. 2s.

**Donaldson's Theatre of the Greeks.** Illustrated with Lithographs and numerous Woodcuts. 5s.

**New Testament (The) in Greek.** Griesbach's Text, with the various readings of Mill and Scholz at foot of page, and Parallel References in the margin; also a Critical Introduction and Chronological Tables. *Two fac-similes of Greek Manuscripts.* (650 pages.) 3s. 6d.; or with the Lexicon, 5s.

## VI.
## Bohn's Philological and Philosophical Library.

UNIFORM WITH THE STANDARD LIBRARY, AT 5s. PER VOLUME
(EXCEPTING THOSE MARKED OTHERWISE).

**Draper (J. W.) A History of the** Intellectual Development of Europe. By JOHN WILLIAM DRAPER, M.D., LL.D. A New Edition, thoroughly Revised by the Author. In 2 vols. [*In the press.* "Social Advancement is as completely under the dominion of Natural Law as is bodily growth. The life of an individual is a miniature of the life of a nation. These propositions it is the special object of this book to demonstrate.

**Hegel's Lectures on the Philosophy** of History. Translated by J. SIBREE, M.A.

**Herodotus, Turner's (Dawson W.)** Notes to. With Map, &c.

—————— **Wheeler's Analysis and** Summary of.

**Kant's Critique of Pure Reason.** Translated by J. M. D. MEIKLEJOHN.

**Logic; or, the Science of Inference.** A Popular Manual. By J. DEVEY.

**Lowndes' Bibliographer's Manual of** English Literature. New Edition, enlarged, by H. G. BOHN. Parts I. to X. (A to Z). 3s. 6d. each. Part XI. (the Appendix Volume). 5s. Or the 11 parts in 4 vols., half morocco, 2l. 2s.

**Smith's (Archdeacon) Complete Col-** lection of Synonyms and Antonyms.

**Tennemann's Manual of the History** of Philosophy. Continued by J. R. MORELL

**Thucydides, Wheeler's Analysis of.**

**Wheeler's (W. A., M.A.) Dictionary** of Names of Fictitious Persons and Places.

**Wright's (T.) Dictionary of Obsolete** and Provincial English. In 2 vols. 5s. each; or half-bound in 1 vol, 10s. 6d.

## VII.
## Bohn's British Classics.

UNIFORM WITH THE STANDARD LIBRARY, AT 3s. 6d. PER VOLUME.

**Addison's Works.** With the Notes of Bishop HURD, much additional matter, and upwards of 100 Unpublished Letters. Edited by H. G. BOHN. *Portrait and 8 Engravings on Steel.* In 6 vols.

**Burke's Works.** In 6 Volumes.
    Vol. 1. Vindication of Natural Society, On the Sublime and Beautiful, and Political Miscellanies.
    Vol. 2. French Revolution, &c.
    Vol. 3. Appeal from the New to the Old Whigs; the Catholic Claims, &c.
    Vol. 4. On the Affairs of India, and Charge against Warren Hastings.
    Vol. 5. Conclusion of Charge against Hastings; on a Regicide Peace, &c.
    Vol. 6. Miscellaneous Speeches, &c With a General Index.

**Burke's Speeches on Warren Hast-** ings; and Letters. With Index. In 2 vols. (forming vols. 7 and 8 of the works).

—————— **Life.** By PRIOR. New and revised Edition. *Portrait.*

**Defoe's Works.** Edited by Sir WALTER SCOTT. In 7 vols.

**Gibbon's Roman Empire.** Complete and Unabridged, with Notes; including, in addition to the Author's own, those of Guizot, Wenck, Niebuhr, Hugo, Neander, and other foreign scholars; and an elaborate Index. Edited by an English Churchman. In 7 vols.

## VIII.
## Bohn's Ecclesiastical Library.

UNIFORM WITH THE STANDARD LIBRARY, AT 5s. PER VOLUME.

**Bleek (J.) An Introduction to the** Old Testament, by FRIEDRICH BLEEK. Edited by JOHANN BLEEK and ADOLF KAMPHAUSEN. Translated from the German by G. H. VENABLES, under the supervision of the Rev. E. VENABLES, Minor Canon of Lincoln. New Edition. In 2 vols. [*In the press.*

**Eusebius' Ecclesiastical History.** With Notes.

**Philo Judæus, Works of;** the con-

temporary of Josephus. Translated by C. D. Yonge. In 4 vols.

**Socrates' Ecclesiastical History, in** continuation of Eusebius. With the Notes of Valesius.

**Sozomen's Ecclesiastical History,** from A.D. 324-440: and the Ecclesiastical History of Philostorgius.

**Theodoret and Evagrius.** Ecclesiastical Histories, from A.D. 332 to A.D. 427, and from A.D. 431 to A.D. 544.

## IX.

## Bohn's Antiquarian Library.

UNIFORM WITH THE STANDARD LIBRARY, AT 5s. PER VOLUME.

**Bede's Ecclesiastical History, and** the Anglo-Saxon Chronicle.

**Boethius's Consolation of Philoso-** phy. In Anglo-Saxon, with the A. S. Metres, and an English Translation, by the Rev. S. Fox.

**Brand's Popular Antiquities of Eng-** land, Scotland, and Ireland. By Sir HENRY ELLIS. In 3 vols.

**Browne's (Sir Thomas) Works.** Edited by SIMON WILKIN. In 3 vols.
  Vol. 1. The Vulgar Errors.
  Vol. 2. Religio Medici, and Garden of Cyrus.
  Vol. 3. Urn-Burial, Tracts, and Correspondence.

**Chronicles of the Crusaders.** Richard of Devizes, Geoffrey de Vinsauf, Lord de Joinville.

**Chronicles of the Tombs.** A Collection of Remarkable Epitaphs. By T. J. PETTIGREW, F.R.S., F.S.A.

**Early Travels in Palestine.** Willibald, Sæwulf, Benjamin of Tudela, Mandeville, Ia Brocquière, and Maundrell; all unabridged. Edited by THOMAS WRIGHT.

**Ellis's Early English Metrical Ro-** mances. Revised by J. O. HALLIWELL.

**Florence of Worcester's Chronicle,** with the Two Continuations: comprising Annals of English History to the Reign of Edward I.

**Giraldus Cambrensis' Historical** Works: Topography of Ireland; History of the Conquest of Ireland; Itinerary through Wales; and Description of Wales. With Index. Edited by THOS. WRIGHT.

**Handbook of Proverbs.** Comprising all Ray's English Proverbs, with additions; his Foreign Proverbs; and an Alphabetical Index.

**Henry of Huntingdon's History of** the English, from the Roman Invasion to Henry II.; with the Acts of King Stephen, &c.

**Ingulph's Chronicle of the Abbey of** Croyland, with the Continuations by Peter of Blois and other Writers. By H. T. RILEY.

**Keightley's Fairy Mythology.** *Frontispiece by Cruikshank.*

**Lamb's Dramatic Poets of the Time** of Elizabeth; including his Selections from the Garrick Plays.

**Lepsius's Letters from Egypt, Ethio-** pia, and the Peninsula of Sinai.

**Mallet's Northern Antiquities.** By Bishop PERCY. With an Abstract of the Eyrbiggia Saga, by Sir WALTER SCOTT. Edited by J. A. BLACKWELL.

**Marco Polo's Travels.** The Translation of Marsden. Edited by THOMAS WRIGHT.

**Matthew Paris's Chronicle.** In 5 vols.
  FIRST SECTION: Roger of Wendover's Flowers of English History, from the Descent of the Saxons to A.D. 1235. Translated by Dr. GILES. In 2 vols.
  SECOND SECTION: From 1235 to 1273. With Index to the entire Work. In 3 vols.

**Matthew of Westminster's Flowers** of History, especially such as relate to the affairs of Britain; to A.D. 1307. Translated by C. D. YONGE. In 2 vols.

**Ordericus Vitalis' Ecclesiastical His-** tory of England and Normandy. Translated with Notes, by T. FORESTER, M.A. In 4 vols.

**Pauli's (Dr. R.) Life of Alfred the** Great. Translated from the German.

**Polyglot of Foreign Proverbs.** With English Translations, and a General Index, bringing the whole into parallels, by H. G. BOHN.

**Roger De Hoveden's Annals of Eng-** lish History; from A.D. 732 to A.D. 1201 Edited by H. T. RILEY. In 2 vols.

**Six Old English Chronicles, viz.:—** Asser's Life of Alfred, and the Chronicles of Ethelwerd, Gildas, Nennius, Geoffrey of Monmouth, and Richard of Cirencester.

**William of Malmesbury's Chronicle** of the Kings of England. Translated by SHARPE.

**Yule-Tide Stories.** A Collection of Scandinavian Tales and Traditions. Edited by B. THORPE.

X.

## Bohn's Illustrated Library.

UNIFORM WITH THE STANDARD LIBRARY, AT 5s. PER VOLUME
(EXCEPTING THOSE MARKED OTHERWISE).

**Allen's Battles of the British Navy.** Revised and enlarged. *Numerous fine Portraits.* In 2 vols.

**Andersen's Danish Legends and** Fairy Tales. With many Tales not in any other edition. Translated by CAROLINE PEACHEY. 120 *Wood Engravings.*

**Ariosto's Orlando Furioso.** In English Verse. By W. S. ROSE. *Twelve fine Engravings.* In 2 vols.

**Bechstein's Cage and Chamber Birds.** Including Sweet's Warblers. Enlarged edition. *Numerous plates.*
*** All other editions are abridged.
*With the plates coloured.* 7s. 6d.

**Bonomi's Nineveh and its Palaces.** New Edition, revised and considerably enlarged, both in matter and Plates, including a Full Account of the Assyrian Sculptures recently added to the National Collection. *Upwards of 300 Engravings.*

**Butler's Hudibras.** With Variorum Notes, a Biography, and a General Index. Edited by HENRY G. BOHN. *Thirty beautiful Illustrations.*
———; or, *further illustrated with* 62 *Outline Portraits.* In 2 vols. 10s.

**Cattermole's Evenings at Haddon** Hall. 24 *exquisite Engravings on Steel, from designs by himself,* the Letterpress by the BARONESS DE CARABELLA.

**China, Pictorial, Descriptive, and** Historical, with some Account of Ava and the Burmese, Siam, and Anam. *Nearly 100 Illustrations.*

**Craik's (G. L.) Pursuit of Knowledge** under Difficulties, illustrated by Anecdotes and Memoirs. Revised Edition. *With numerous Portraits.*

**Cruikshank's Three Courses and a** Dessert. A Series of Tales, *with 50 humorous Illustrations by Cruikshank.*

**Dante.** Translated by I. C. WRIGHT, M.A. New Edition, carefully revised. *Portrait and 34 Illustrations on Steel, after Flaxman.*

**Didron's Christian Iconography.** Characteristics of Christian Art in the Middle Ages. From the French. *Upwards of 150 outline Engravings.*

**Dyer (T. H.) The History of Pompeii;** its Buildings and Antiquities. An account of the City, with a full description of the Remains and the Recent Excavations, and also an Itinerary for Visitors. Edited by

T. H. DYER, LL.D. *Illustrated with nearly 300 Wood Engravings a large Map, and a Plan of the Forum.* A New Edition, revised and brought down to 1874. 7s. 6d.

**Flaxman's Lectures on Sculpture.** *Numerous Illustrations.* 6s.

**Gil Blas, The Adventures of.** 24 *Engravings on Steel, after Smirke, and* 10 *Etchings by George Cruikshank.* 6s.

**Grimm's Gammer Grethel;** or, German Fairy Tales and Popular Stories. Translated by EDGAR TAYLOR. *Numerous Woodcuts by Cruikshank.* 3s. 6d.

**Holbein's Dance of Death, and Bible** Cuts. *Upwards of 150 subjects, beautifully engraved in fac-simile,* with Introduction and Descriptions by the late FRANCIS DOUCE and Dr. T. F. DIBDIN. 2 vols. in 1. 7s. 6d.

**Howitt's (Mary) Pictorial Calendar** of the Seasons. Embodying the whole of Aiken's Calendar of Nature. *Upwards of 100 Engravings.*
——— (Mary and William) Stories of English and Foreign Life. *Twenty beautiful Engravings.*

**India, Pictorial, Descriptive, and** Historical, from the Earliest Times to the Present. *Upwards of 100 fine Engravings on Wood, and a Map.*

**Jesse's Anecdotes of Dogs.** New Edition, with large additions. *Numerous fine Woodcuts after Harvey, Bewick, and others.*
———, or, *with the addition of* 34 *highly-finished Steel Engravings.* 7s. 6d.

**King's Natural History of Precious** Stones, and of the Precious Metals. *With numerous Illustrations.* Price 6s.
——— Natural History of Gems or Decorative Stones. *Finely Illustrated.* 6s.
——— Handbook of Engraved Gems. *Finely Illustrated.* 6s.

**Kitto's Scripture Lands and Biblical** Atlas. 24 *Maps, beautifully engraved on Steel,* with a Consulting Index.
———; *with the maps coloured,* 7s. 6d.

**Krummacher's Parables.** Translated from the German. *Forty Illustrations by Clayton, engraved by Dalziel.*

**Lindsay's (Lord) Letters on Egypt,** Edom, and the Holy Land. New Edition, enlarged. *Thirty-six beautiful Engravings, and 2 Maps.*

**Lodge's Portraits of Illustrious Personages** of Great Britain, with Memoirs. *Two Hundred and Forty Portraits, beautifully engraved on Steel.* 8 vols.

**Longfellow's Poetical Works.** *Twenty-four page Engravings, by Birket Foster and others, and a new Portrait.*

———; or, *without illustrations,* 3s. 6d.

——— **Prose Works, complete.** 16 *page Engravings by Birket Foster, &c.*

**Loudon's (Mrs.) Entertaining Naturalist.** Revised by W. S. DALLAS, F.L.S. *With nearly 500 Woodcuts.*

**Marryat's Masterman Ready; or,** The Wreck of the Pacific. 93 *Woodcuts.* 3s. 6d.

——— **Mission; or, Scenes in Africa.** (Written for Young People.) *Illustrated by Gilbert and Dalziel.* 3s. 6d.

——— **Pirate; and Three Cutters.** New Edition, with a Memoir of the Author. *With 20 Steel Engravings, from Drawings by C. Stanfield, R.A.* 3s. 6d.

——— **Privateer's-Man One Hundred Years Ago.** *Eight Engravings on Steel, after Stothard.* 3s. 6d.

——— **Settlers in Canada.** New Edition. *Ten fine Engravings by Gilbert and Dalziel.* 3s. 6d.

**Maxwell's Victories of Wellington** and the British Armies. *Steel Engravings.*

**Michael Angelo and Raphael, their** Lives and Works. By DUPPA and QUATREMÈRE DE QUINCY. *With 13 highly-finished Engravings on Steel.*

**Miller's History of the Anglo-Saxons.** Written in a popular style, on the basis of Sharon Turner. *Portrait of Alfred, Map of Saxon Britain, and 12 elaborate Engravings on Steel.*

**Milton's Poetical Works.** With a Memoir by JAMES MONTGOMERY, TODD'S Verbal Index to all the Poems, and Explanatory Notes. *With 120 Engravings by Thompson and others, from Drawings by W. Harvey.* 2 vols.
Vol. 1. Paradise Lost, complete, with Memoir, Notes, and Index.
Vol. 2. Paradise Regained, and other Poems, with Verbal Index to all the Poems.

**Mudie's British Birds.** Revised by W. C. L. MARTIN. *Fifty-two Figures and 7 Plates of Eggs.* In 2 vols.

———; or, *with the plates coloured,* 7s. 6d. per vol.

**Naval and Military Heroes of Great** Britain; or, Calendar of Victory. Being a Record of British Valour and Conquest by Sea and Land, on every day in the year, from the time of William the Conqueror to the Battle of Inkermann. By Major JOHNS, R.M., and Lieutenant P. H. NICOLAS, R.M. *Twenty-four Portraits.* 6s.

**Nicolini's History of the Jesuits:** their Origin, Progress, Doctrines, and Designs. *Fine Portraits of Loyola, Lainès, Xavier, Borgia, Acquaviva, Père la Chaise, and Pope Ganganelli.*

**Petrarch's Sonnets, and other Poems.** Translated into English Verse. By various hands. With a Life of the Poet, by THOMAS CAMPBELL. *With 16 Engravings.*

**Pickering's History of the Races of** Man, with an Analytical Synopsis of the Natural History of Man. By Dr. HALL. *Illustrated by numerous Portraits.*

———; or, *with the plates coloured,* 7s. 6d.

*** An excellent Edition of a work originally published at 3l. 3s. by the American Government.

**Pictorial Handbook of Modern Geography,** on a Popular Plan. 3s. 6d. *Illustrated by 150 Engravings and 51 Maps.* 6s.

———; or, *with the maps coloured,* 7s. 6d.

**Planché's History of British Costume.** Third Edition. *With numerous Woodcuts.*

**Pope's Poetical Works.** Edited by ROBERT CARRUTHERS. *Numerous Engravings.* 2 vols.

——— **Homer's Iliad.** With Introduction and Notes by J. S. WATSON, M.A. *Illustrated by the entire Series of Flaxman's Designs, beautifully engraved by Moses (in the full 8vo. size).*

——— **Homer's Odyssey, Hymns,** &c., by other translators, including Chapman, and Introduction and Notes by J. S. WATSON, M.A. *Flaxman's Designs beautifully engraved by Moses.*

**Pope's Life.** Including many of his Letters. By ROBERT CARRUTHERS. New Edition, revised and enlarged. *Illustrations.*

*The preceding 5 vols. make a complete and elegant edition of Pope's Poetical Works and Translations for 25s.*

**Pottery and Porcelain, and other Objects of Vertu** (a Guide to the Knowledge of). To which is added an Engraved List of all the known Marks and Monograms. By HENRY G. BOHN. *Numerous Engravings.*

——; or, *coloured.* 10s. 6d.

**Prout's (Father) Reliques.** New Edition, revised and largely augmented. *Twenty-one spirited Etchings by Maclise.* Two volumes in one. 7s. 6d.

**Recreations in Shooting.** By "CRAVEN." New Edition, revised and enlarged. 62 *Engravings on Wood, after Harvey, and 9 Engravings on Steel, chiefly after A. Cooper, R.A.*

**Redding's History and Descriptions** of Wines, Ancient and Modern. *Twenty beautiful Woodcuts.*

**Rennie's Insect Architecture.** *New Edition.* Revised by the Rev. J. G. WOOD, M.A.

**Robinson Crusoe.** With Illustrations by STOTHARD and HARVEY. *Twelve beautiful Engravings on Steel, and 74 on Wood.*

—— ; or, *without the Steel illustrations,* 3s. 6d.

**Rome in the Nineteenth Century.** New Edition. Revised by the Author. *Illustrated by 34 fine Steel Engravings.* 2 vols.

**Southey's Life of Nelson.** With Additional Notes. *Illustrated with 64 Engravings.*

**Starling's (Miss) Noble Deeds of** Women; or, Examples of Female Courage, Fortitude, and Virtue. *Fourteen beautiful Illustrations.*

**Stuart and Revett's Antiquities of** Athens, and other Monuments of Greece. *Illustrated in 71 Steel Plates, and numerous Woodcuts.*

**Tales of the Genii; or, the Delightful** Lessons of Horam. *Numerous Woodcuts, and 8 Steel Engravings, after Stothard.*

**Tasso's Jerusalem Delivered.** Translated into English Spenserian Verse, with a Life of the Author. By J. H. WIFFEN. *Eight Engravings on Steel, and 24 on Wood, by Thurston.*

**Walker's Manly Exercises** Containing Skating, Riding, Driving, Hunting, Shooting, Sailing, Rowing, Swimming, &c. New Edition, revised by "CRAVEN." *Forty-four Steel Plates, and numerous Woodcuts.*

**Walton's Complete Angler.** Edited by EDWARD JESSE, Esq. To which is added an Account of Fishing Stations, &c., by H. G. BOHN. *Upwards of 203 Engravings.*

—— ; or, *with 26 additional page Illustrations on Steel,* 7s. 6d.

**Wellington, Life of.** By AN OLD SOLDIER, from the materials of Maxwell. *Eighteen Engravings.*

**White's Natural History of Selborne.** With Notes by Sir WILLIAM JARDINE and EDWARD JESSE, Esq. *Illustrated by 40 highly-finished Engravings.*

—— ; or, *with the plates coloured,* 7s. 6d.

**Young, The, Lady's Book.** A Manual of Elegant Recreations, Arts, Sciences, and Accomplishments; including Geology, Mineralogy, Conchology, Botany, Entomology, Ornithology, Costume, Embroidery, the Escritoire, Archery, Riding, Music (instrumental and vocal), Dancing, Exercises, Painting, Photography, &c., &c. Edited by distinguished Professors. *Twelve Hundred Woodcut Illustrations, and several fine Engravings on Steel.* 7s. 6d.

—— ; or, *cloth gilt, gilt edges,* 9s.

## XI.

# Bohn's Classical Library.

*5s. per Volume, excepting those marked otherwise.*

**Æschylus.** Literally Translated into English Prose by an Oxonian. 3s. 6d.

——, **Appendix to.** Containing the New Readings given in Hermann's posthumous Edition of Æschylus. By GEORGE BURGES, M.A. 3s. 6d.

**Ammianus Marcellinus.** History of Rome from Constantius to Valens. Translated by C. D. YONGE, B.A. Dble. vol., 7s. 6d.

**Antoninus. The Thoughts of the** Emperor Marcus Aurelius. Translated by GEO. LONG, M.A. 3s. 6d.

**Apuleius, the Golden Ass; Death of** Socrates; Florida; and Discourse on Magic. To which is added a Metrical Version of Cupid and Psyche; and Mrs. Tighe's Psyche. *Frontispiece.*

**Aristophanes' Comedies.** Literally Translated, with Notes and Extracts from Frere's and other Metrical Versions, by W. J. HICKIE. 2 vols.

> Vol. 1. Acharnians, Knights, Clouds, Wasps, Peace, and Birds.
> Vol. 2. Lysistrata, Thesmophoriazusæ, Frogs, Ecclesiazusæ, and Plutus.

**Aristotle's Ethics.** Literally Translated by Archdeacon BROWNE, late Classical Professor of King's College.

———— **Politics and Economics.** Translated by E. WALFORD, M.A.

———— **Metaphysics.** Literally Translated, with Notes, Analysis, Examination Questions, and Index, by the Rev. JOHN H. M'MAHON, M.A., and Gold Medallist in Metaphysics, T.C.D.

———— **History of Animals.** In Ten Books. Translated, with Notes and Index, by RICHARD CRESSWELL, M.A.

———— **Organon; or, Logical Treatises.** With Notes, &c. By O. F. OWEN, M.A. 2 vols., 3s. 6d. each.

———— **Rhetoric and Poetics.** Literally Translated, with Examination Questions and Notes, by an Oxonian.

**Athenæus.** The Deipnosophists; or, the Banquet of the Learned. Translated by C. D. YONGE, B.A. 3 vols.

**Cæsar.** Complete, with the Alexandrian, African, and Spanish Wars. Literally Translated, with Notes.

**Catullus, Tibullus, and the Vigil of Venus.** A Literal Prose Translation. To which are added Metrical Versions by LAMB, GRAINGER, and others. *Frontispiece.*

**Cicero's Orations.** Literally Translated by C. D. YONGE, B.A. In 4 vols.

> Vol. 1. Contains the Orations against Verres, &c. *Portrait.*
> Vol. 2. Catiline, Archias, Agrarian Law, Rabirius, Murena, Sylla, &c.
> Vol. 3. Orations for his House, Plancius, Sextius, Cœlius, Milo, Ligarius, &c.
> Vol. 4. Miscellaneous Orations, and Rhetorical Works; with General Index to the four volumes.

———— **on the Nature of the Gods,** Divination, Fate, Laws, a Republic, &c. Translated by C. D. YONGE, B.A., and F. BARHAM.

———— **Academics, De Finibus, and** Tusculan Questions. By C. D. YONGE, B.A. With Sketch of the Greek Philosophy.

———— **Offices, Old Age, Friendship,** Scipio's Dream, Paradoxes, &c. Literally Translated, by R. EDMONDS. 3s. 6d.

**Cicero on Oratory and Orators.** By J. S. WATSON, M.A.

**Demosthenes' Orations.** Translated, with Notes, by C. RANN KENNEDY. In 5 volumes.

> Vol. 1. The Olynthiac, Philippic, and other Public Orations. 3s. 6d.
> Vol. 2. On the Crown and on the Embassy.
> Vol. 3. Against Leptines, Midias, Androtion, and Aristocrates.
> Vol. 4. Private and other Orations.
> Vol 5. Miscellaneous Orations.

**Dictionary of Latin Quotations.** Including Proverbs, Maxims, Mottoes, Law Terms, and Phrases; and a Collection of above 500 Greek Quotations. With all the quantities marked, & English Translations.

————, **with Index Verborum.** 6s. Index Verborum only. 1s.

**Diogenes Laertius.** Lives and Opinions of the Ancient Philosophers. Translated, with Notes, by C. D. YONGE.

**Epictetus.** Translated by GEORGE LONG, M.A. [*Preparing.*

**Euripides.** Literally Translated. 2 vols.

> Vol. 1. Hecuba, Orestes, Medea, Hippolytus, Alcestis, Bacchæ, Heraclidæ, Iphigenia in Aulide, and Iphigenia in Tauris.
> Vol. 2. Hercules Furens, Troades, Ion, Andromache, Suppliants, Helen, Electra, Cyclops, Rhesus.

**Greek Anthology.** Literally Translated. With Metrical Versions by various Authors.

**Greek Romances of Heliodorus.** Longus, and Achilles Tatius.

**Herodotus.** A New and Literal Translation, by HENRY CARY, M.A., of Worcester College, Oxford.

**Hesiod, Callimachus, and Theognis.** Literally Translated, with Notes, by J. BANKS, M.A.

**Homer's Iliad.** Literally Translated, by an OXONIAN.

———— **Odyssey, Hymns, &c.** Literally Translated by an OXONIAN.

**Horace.** Literally Translated, by SMART. Carefully revised by an OXONIAN. 3s. 6d.

**Justin, Cornelius Nepos, and Eutropius.** Literally Translated, with Notes and Index, by J. S. WATSON, M.A.

**Juvenal, Persius, Sulpicia, and Lucilius.** By L. EVANS, M.A. With the Metrical Version by Gifford. *Frontispiece.*

**Livy.** A new and Literal Translation. By Dr. SPILLAN and others. In 4 vols.

> Vol 1. Contains Books 1—8.
> Vol. 2. Books 9—26.
> Vol. 3. Books 27—36.
> Vol. 4. Books 37 to the end; and Index.

**Lucan's Pharsalia.** Translated, with Notes, by H. T. RILEY.

**Lucretius.** Literally Translated, with Notes, by the Rev. J. S. WATSON, M.A. And the Metrical Version by J. M. GOOD.

**Martial's Epigrams, complete.** Literally Translated. Each accompanied by one or more Verse Translations selected from the Works of English Poets, and other sources. With a copious Index. Double volume (660 pages). 7s. 6d.

**Ovid's Works, complete.** Literally Translated. 3 vols.
    Vol. 1. Fasti, Tristia, Epistles, &c.
    Vol. 2. Metamorphoses.
    Vol. 3. Heroides, Art of Love, &c.

**Pindar.** Literally Translated, by DAWSON W. TURNER, and the Metrical Version by ABRAHAM MOORE.

**Plato's Works.** Translated by the Rev. H. CARY and others. In 6 vols.
    Vol. 1. The Apology of Socrates, Crito, Phædo, Gorgias, Protagoras, Phædrus, Theætetus, Euthyphron, Lysis.
    Vol. 2. The Republic, Timæus, & Critias.
    Vol. 3. Meno, Euthydemus, The Sophist, Statesman, Cratylus, Parmenides, and the Banquet.
    Vol. 4. Philebus, Charmides, Laches, The Two Alcibiades, and Ten other Dialogues.
    Vol. 5. The Laws.
    Vol. 6. The Doubtful Works. With General Index.

——— **Dialogues,** an Analysis and Index to. With References to the Translation in Bohn's Classical Library. By Dr. DAY.

**Plautus's Comedies.** Literally Translated, with Notes, by H. T. RILEY, B.A. In 2 vols.

**Pliny's Natural History.** Translated, with Copious Notes, by the late JOHN BOSTOCK, M.D., F.R.S., and H. T. RILEY, B.A. In 6 vols.

**Propertius, Petronius, and Johannes** Secundus. Literally Translated, and accompanied by Poetical Versions, from various sources.

**Quintilian's Institutes of Oratory.** Literally Translated with Notes, &c., by J. S. WATSON, M.A. In 2 vols.

**Sallust, Florus, and Velleius Paterculus.** With Copious Notes, Biographical Notices, and Index, by J. S. WATSON.

**Sophocles.** The Oxford Translation revised.

**Standard Library Atlas of Classical** Geography. *Twenty-two large coloured Maps according to the latest authorities.* With a complete Index (accentuated), giving the latitude and longitude of every place named in the Maps. Imp. 8vo. 7s. 6d.

**Strabo's Geography.** Translated, with Copious Notes, by W. FALCONER, M.A., and H. C. HAMILTON, Esq. With Index, giving the Ancient and Modern Names. In 3 vols.

**Suetonius' Lives of the Twelve** Cæsars, and other Works. Thomson's Translation, revised, with Notes, by T. FORESTER.

**Tacitus.** Literally Translated, with Notes. In 2 vols.
    Vol. 1. The Annals.
    Vol. 2. The History, Germania, Agricola, &c. With Index.

**Terence and Phædrus.** By H. T. RILEY, B.A.

**Theocritus, Bion, Moschus, and** Tyrtæus. By J. BANKS, M.A. With the Metrical Versions of Chapman.

**Thucydides.** Literally Translated by Rev. H. DALE. In 2 vols. 3s. 6d. each.

**Virgil.** Literally Translated by DAVIDSON. New Edition, carefully revised. 3s. 6d.

**Xenophon's Works.** In 3 Vols.
    Vol. 1. The Anabasis and Memorabilia. Translated, with Notes, by J. S. WATSON, M.A. And a Geographical Commentary, by W. F. AINSWORTH, F.S.A., F.R.G.S., &c.
    Vol. 2. Cyropædia and Hellenics. By J. S. WATSON, M.A., and the Rev. H. DALE.
    Vol. 3. The Minor Works. By J. S. WATSON, M.A.

**XII.**

# Bohn's Scientific Library.

*5s. per Volume, excepting those marked otherwise.*

**Agassiz and Gould's Comparative** Physiology. Enlarged by Dr. WRIGHT. *Upwards of 400 Engravings.*

**Bacon's Novum Organum and Advancement of Learning.** Complete, with Notes, by J. DEVEY, M.A.

**Blair's Chronological Tables, Revised** and Enlarged. Comprehending the Chronology and History of the World, from the earliest times. By J. WILLOUGHBY ROSSE. Double Volume. 10s.; or, half-bound, 10s. 6d.

**Index of Dates.** Comprehending the principal Facts in the Chronology and History of the World, from the earliest to the present time, alphabetically arranged. By J. W. ROSSE. Double volume, 10*s*; or, half-bound, 10*s*. 6*d*.

**Bolley's Manual of Technical Analysis.** A Guide for the Testing of Natural and Artificial Substances. By B. H. PAUL. 100 *Wood Engravings*.

**BRIDGEWATER TREATISES.** —

———— **Bell on the Hand.** Its Mechanism and Vital Endowments as evincing Design. *Seventh Edition Revised.*

———— **Kirby on the History, Habits,** and Instincts of Animals. Edited, with Notes, by T. RYMER JONES. *Numerous Engravings, many of which are additional.* In 2 vols.

———— **Kidd on the Adaptation of** External Nature to the Physical Condition of Man. 3*s*. 6*d*.

———— **Whewell's Astronomy and** General Physics, considered with reference to Natural Theology. 3*s*. 6*d*.

———— **Chalmers on the Adaptation** of External Nature to the Moral and Intellectual Constitution of Man. 5*s*.

———— **Prout's Treatise on Chemistry,** Meteorology, and Digestion. Edited by Dr. J. W. GRIFFITH.

———— **Buckland's Geology and** Mineralogy. 2 vols. 15*s*.

———— **Roget's Animal and Vegetable** Physiology. *Illustrated.* In 2 vols. 6*s*. each.

**Carpenter's (Dr. W. B.) Zoology.** A Systematic View of the Structure, Habits, Instincts, and Uses, of the principal Families of the Animal Kingdom, and of the chief forms of Fossil Remains. New edition, revised to the present time, under arrangement with the Author, by W. S. DALLAS, F.L.S. *Illustrated with many hundred fine Wood Engravings.* In 2 vols. 6*s*. each.

———— **Mechanical Philosophy, Astronomy,** and Horology. A Popular Exposition. 183 *Illustrations*.

———— **Vegetable Physiology and** Systematic Botany. A complete Introduction to the Knowledge of Plants. New Edition, revised, under arrangement with the Author, by E. LANKESTER, M.D., &c. *Several hundred Illustrations on Wood.* 6*s*.

———— **Animal Physiology.** New Edition, thoroughly revised, and in part re-written by the Author. *Upwards of* 300 *capital Illustrations.* 6*s*.

**Chevreul on Colour.** Containing the rules of Harmony and Contrast of Colours, and their application to the Arts. Translated from the French by CHARLES MARTEL. Only complete Edition. *Several Plates.* Or, with an additional series of 16 Plates in Colours. 7*s*. 6*d*.

**Clark's (Hugh) Introduction to** Heraldry. *With nearly* 1000 *Illustrations.* 18*th Edition.* Revised and enlarged by J. R. PLANCHÉ, Rouge Croix. Or, with all the Illustrations coloured, 15*s*.

**Comte's Philosophy of the Sciences.** By G. H. LEWES.

**Ennemoser's History of Magic.** Translated by WILLIAM HOWITT. With an Appendix of the most remarkable and best authenticated Stories of Apparitions, Dreams, Table-Turning, and Spirit-Rapping, &c. In 2 vols.

**Handbook of Domestic Medicine.** Popularly arranged. By Dr. HENRY DAVIES. 700 pages. With complete Index.

**Handbook of Games.** By various Amateurs and Professors. Comprising treatises on all the principal Games of chance, skill, and manual dexterity. In all, above 40 games (the Whist, Draughts, and Billiards being especially comprehensive). Edited by H. G. BOHN. *Illustrated by numerous Diagrams.*

**Hogg's (Jabez) Elements of Experimental** and Natural Philosophy. Containing Mechanics, Pneumatics, Hydrostatics, Hydraulics, Acoustics, Optics, Caloric, Electricity, Voltaism, and Magnetism. New Edition, enlarged. *Upwards of* 400 *Woodcuts*.

**Hind's Introduction to Astronomy.** With a Vocabulary, containing an Explanation of all the Terms in present use. New Edition, enlarged. *Numerous Engravings.* 3*s*. 6*d*.

**Humboldt's Cosmos; or Sketch of a** Physical Description of the Universe. Translated by E. C. OTTÉ and W. S. DALLAS, F.L.S. *Fine Portrait.* In five vols. 3*s*. 6*d*. each; excepting Vol. V., 5*s*.
*₊* In this edition the notes are placed beneath the text, Humboldt's analytical Summaries and the passages hitherto suppressed are included, and new and comprehensive Indices are added.

———— **Travels in America.** In 3 vols.

———— **Views of Nature; or, Contemplations** of the Sublime Phenomena of Creation. Translated by E. C. OTTÉ and H. G. BOHN. A fac-simile letter from the Author to the Publisher; translations of the quotations, and a complete Index.

**Humphrey's Coin Collector's Manual.** A popular Introduction to the Study of Coins. *Highly finished Engravings.* In 2 vols.

**Hunt's (Robert) Poetry of Science;** or, Studies of the Physical Phenomena of Nature. By Professor HUNT. New Edition, enlarged.

**Index of Dates.** *See* Blair's Tables.

**Joyce's Scientific Dialogues.** Completed to the present state of Knowledge, by Dr. GRIFFITH. *Numerous Woodcuts.*

**Knight's (Chas.) Knowledge is Power.** A Popular Manual of Political Economy.

**Lectures on Painting.** By the Royal Academicians. With Introductory Essay, and Notes by R. WORNUM, Esq. *Portraits.*

**Mantell's (Dr.) Geological Excursions** through the Isle of Wight and Dorsetshire. New Edition, by T. RUPERT JONES, Esq. *Numerous beautifully executed Woodcuts, and a Geological Map.*

—————— **Medals of Creation;** or, First Lessons in Geology and the Study of Organic Remains; including Geological Excursions. New Edition, revised. *Coloured Plates, and several hundred beautiful Woodcuts.* In 2 vols., 7s. 6d. each.

—————— **Petrifactions and their** Teachings. An Illustrated Handbook to the Organic Remains in the British Museum. *Numerous Engravings.* 6s.

—————— **Wonders of Geology;** or, a Familiar Exposition of Geological Phenomena. New Edition, augmented by T. RUPERT JONES, F.G.S. *Coloured Geological Map of England, Plates, and nearly 200 beautiful Woodcuts.* In 2 vols., 7s. 6d. each.

**Morphy's Games of Chess.** Being the Matches and best Games played by the American Champion, with Explanatory and Analytical Notes, by J. LÖWENTHAL. *Portrait* and Memoir.

It contains by far the largest collection of games played by Mr. Morphy extant in any form, and has received his endorsement and co-operation.

**Richardson's Geology, including** Mineralogy and Palæontology. Revised and enlarged, by Dr. T. WRIGHT. *Upwards of 400 Illustrations.*

**Schouw's Earth, Plants, and Man;** and Kobell's Sketches from the Mineral Kingdom. Translated by A. HENFREY, F.R.S. *Coloured Map of the Geography of Plants.*

**Smith's (Pye) Geology and** ture; or, The Relation between the Holy Scriptures and Geological Science.

**Stanley's Classified Synopsis of the** Principal Painters of the Dutch and Flemish Schools.

**Staunton's Chess-player's Handbook** *Numerous Diagrams.*

—————— **Chess Praxis.** A Supplement to the Chess-player's Handbook. Containing all the most important modern improvements in the Openings, illustrated by actual Games; a revised Code of Chess Laws; and a Selection of Mr. Morphy's Games in England and France. 6s.

—————— **Chess-player's Companion.** Comprising a new Treatise on Odds, Collection of Match Games, and a Selection of Original Problems.

—————— **Chess Tournament of 1851.** *Numerous Illustrations.*

**Principles of Chemistry, exemplified** in a series of simple experiments. Based upon the German work of Professor STOCKHARDT, and Edited by C. W. HEATON, Professor of Chemistry at Charing Cross Hospital. *Upwards of 270 Illustrations.*

**Stockhardt's Agricultural Chemistry** or, Chemical Field Lectures. Addressed to Farmers. Translated, with Notes, by Professor HENFREY, F.R.S. To which is added, a Paper on Liquid Manure, by J. J. MECHI, Esq.

**Ure's (Dr. A.) Cotton Manufacture** of Great Britain, systematically investigated; with an introductory view of its comparative state in Foreign Countries. New Edition, revised and completed to the present time, by P. L. SIMMONDS. *One hundred and fifty Illustrations.* In 2 vol

—————— **Philosophy of Manufactures** or, An Exposition of the Factory System of Great Britain. New Ed., continued to the present time, by P. L. SIMMONDS. 7s. 6

## XIII.

## Bohn's Reference Library.

**The Epigrammatists.** Selections from the Epigrammatic Literature of Ancient, Mediæval, and Modern Times. With Notes, Observations, Illustrations, and an Introduction. By the Rev. HENRY PHILIP

DODD, M.A., of Pembroke College, Oxfo Second Edition, revised and considerab enlarged, containing many new Epigram principally of an amusing character